# RISE OF TYRANTS

*WHISPERS OF WAR*

CALLUM M BROOKS

The characters and events portrayed in this book are fictitious. Any similarity to real persons, living or dead, is coincidental and not intended by the author.



Cover design by: Callum M Brooks
Printed in the United Kingdom

First Edition: March, 2025
ISBN: 978-1-0684318-1-4

This book contains mature themes and language not suitable for all audiences. Reader discretion is advised.

*Dedication*

*This is the first dedication I've ever written, so it's only fitting that I start by thanking you—my reader. Among so many books, you chose to pick up or download this one, and that means everything.*

*I was never much of a bookworm. I couldn't quote Shakespeare, nor could I make much sense of his works. In truth, getting lost in a book wasn't even on my radar.*

*That changed when my dad—better known to me as the Old Boy—dumped a pile of books on me. To my surprise, I read through most of them. But when I finally hit one that didn't quite grip me, I thought, I could do better than that. So, I started writing.*

*Turns out, I had a passion for stories—both reading and writing. It had been there all along, just waiting to be unlocked. And it was my Old Boy who handed me the key.*

*Like every good father, my Old Boy is a fountain of wisdom and advice. I've picked his brain on anything and everything, and his unwavering support—whether intentional or not—set me on the path that led to this moment: the completion of my first novel, a milestone I couldn't be prouder of.*

*So, it's only right that this book is dedicated to him—Ben Brown, my Old Boy. Without you, this book wouldn't exist.*

*Thank you.*

# RISE OF TYRANTS

*Whispers of War*

*Tides of an Avalanche*

*Vows and Prophecy*

*Valour in Ruin*

*The Last Rampart*

# CONTENTS

# AUTHOR NOTES

So, here's the thing, I'm not a writer, well I didn't think so. I'm not even a book worm and I certainly wasn't an academic at school. So begs the question why did I write a book, well ever since I can remember I've always had a vivid imagination in all walks of life. The TV goes on, I'm straight in that world, I'm invested, when I'm visiting historical landmarks, I always picture how it could have been, the people that lived there.

One thing with school though I always remember, was I could create a decent story if the task were set, not necessarily the one's when my homework went missing, but certainly a fictional essay. My problem was putting the words in an enjoyable and descriptive way for the reader, and well after leaving school that never improved as of course I left it all behind.

It wasn't until one day, sort of out of the blue, my Dad dumped a whole load of books on me, crates of the things. Going through the various different books, of course by order of best-looking front cover at that stage, I picked one out, a brown book with a doubled sided axe posted on its front. 'Legend' by David Gemmell and to this day is still my favourite. I've read it a bunch of times and love it, even now I'll go back to it.

After finishing it I got back into reading for a couple of years until I picked up one book and as I was reading it, I thought, well the story isn't gripping me, the characters aren't interesting, I could do better than this. Before I knew it, ideas were flying at me.

My first idea was set in a futuristic Earth after an apocalyptic event, which went to the scrap bin pretty fast. And so, the beginnings of 'Rise of a Tyrant' came to me, focused on a young warrior rising through the ranks essentially. I wrote about six chapters of material that I sadly no longer have, the first I ever did was a battle on the ramparts that I certainly could have picked from. But the bug was there, I made a plot with plenty of holes but realised this has some legs, I drafted a whole cluster of material and it was apparent I wanted to focus on more than one character, in fact several and so the Book Title changed to 'Rise of Tyrants'.

Again sadly, real life had other plans for me, and my project got put on the back burner. But every so often I would pick up my phone and notes were made, or the odd text stumbled together. You see there's the other thing, I haven't owned a laptop until recently so most of this book, ideas, art, and texts have all been done on my phone. Thankfully, screen sizes have increased over the years.

So, there I was, probably fifteen years after I first put pen to paper, delayed and stuck at Dubrovnik airport for thirteen hours and needed something to burn the hours. I looked at everything I'd done, put it all together and wrote a plot, a real plot with twists and turns, structured characters that had depth and an arc to believe in. I realised with what I'd already wrote it wouldn't take much to actually put together a finished Book. And I set to task, my first Book of the Book series 'Rise of Tyrants'

This last year my imagination has run wild with ideas, and I have a whole world now with lore and histories I really want to tap into. This is going to be Book One of what is currently a Five Book series, but if I can find my passion and there's interest, I have a whole lot more in the works.

I hope you enjoy the read, lose yourself in the characters and it doesn't take as long to finish it as I did writing it.

# WORLD MAP

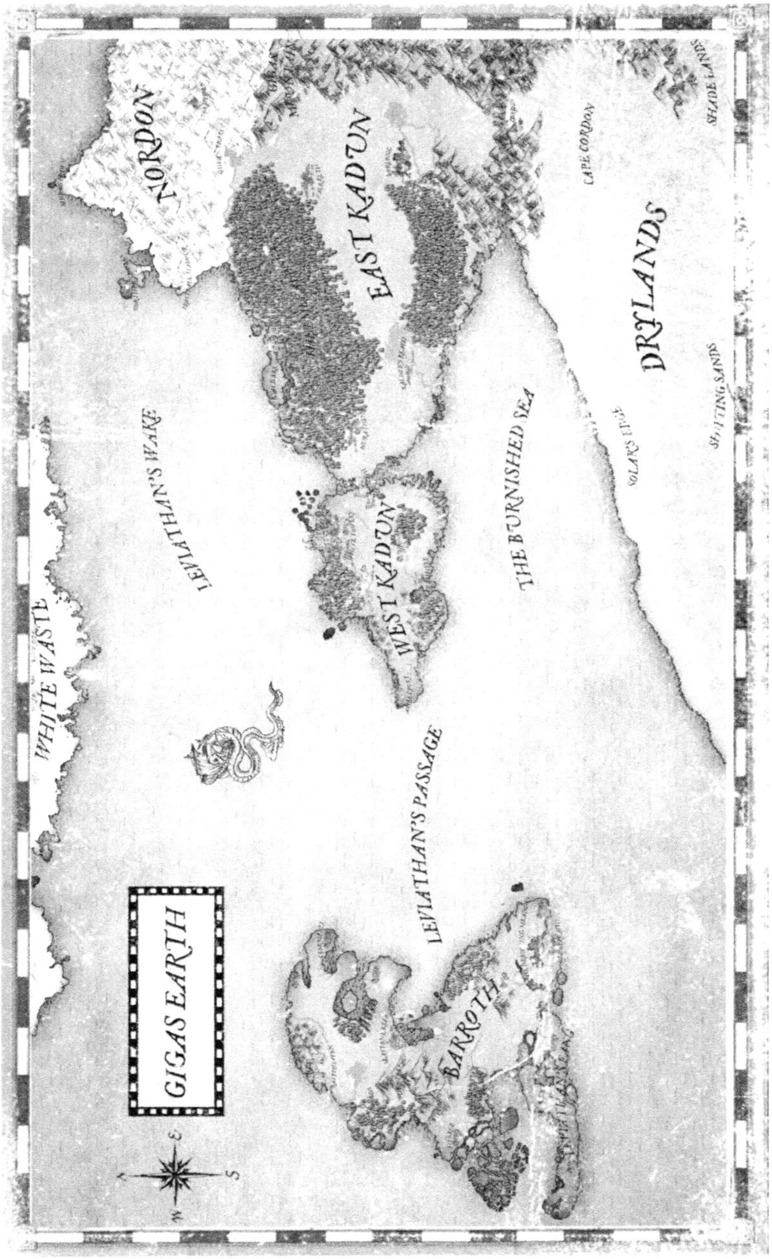
GIGAS EARTH
NORDON
EAST KADUN
WEST KADUN
DRYLANDS
CAPE GORDON
SHADE LANDS
SHIFTING SANDS
SOLAR'S EDGE
THE BURNISHED SEA
LEVIATHAN'S WAKE
LEVIATHAN'S PASSAGE
WHITE WASTE
BARROTH

# WEST KADUN

## *The Power of the Eastern Kingdoms*

West Kadun, often hailed as the heart of the Eastern Kingdoms, stands as a testament to prosperity and resilience. Ruled by a single king, it is a land of vast, fertile plains and orderly pastures that stretch unbroken across its western expanse, forming the backbone of the realm's wealth and influence. This abundance contrasts sharply with the rugged, untamed terrains of the north, reinforcing West Kadun's image as a beacon of stability and order.

In the northern reaches lies The Hundred Isles, a cluster of fourteen tiny, uninhabited islands that hug the coast. Among them, the largest features an imposing lighthouse known as Beacon, a sentinel lit only during the harsh winter months to guide ships through stormy waters. Dominating the coastline, however, is the capital city of White Towers. Renowned for its gleaming stone spires, the city is a hub of commerce and governance, nestled at the mouth of the White Waters River. This wide waterway flows through the city's heart, linking its bustling harbour to the fertile hinterlands beyond. The city's towering walls stretch along the coast, providing both a natural defence and a symbol of its enduring strength.

Just southwest of White Towers, dense forests sprawl across the landscape, their towering canopies forming a natural barrier between the cultivated lands of the north and the fertile farmlands that extend toward the western coast. These forests, thick with pine and oak, are a haven for wildlife and an occasional refuge for hunters and wanderers who brave their shadowy depths.

As the forests give way to open plains, the vast farmlands begin to dominate, stretching endlessly toward the western horizon. Here, the lifeblood of West Kadun flows—crops of wheat, barley, and rye sway in the summer's warmth and herds of cattle and sheep graze on rolling hills. This agricultural heartland is dotted with small villages, where farmers and labourers toil to sustain both the local population and the bustling cities of West Kadun.

At the westernmost edge of the country lies Amberport, a vibrant city perched on the tip of the coast. Known for its amber-coloured stone buildings that catch the sunlight in warm, golden hues, the city thrives as a hub of trade and maritime activity. Fishing boats crowd its bustling harbour, their nets heavy with the bounty of the sea. However, while the waters teem with life, they are also fraught with danger. Fishermen rarely venture far from shore, for beyond the safety of the bay lurk threats both known and unseen.

To the north, Nordon ships prowl, their crews ever watchful for opportunities to raid and plunder. To the west, pirates from the distant and mysterious land of Barroth haunt the waters, their black sails striking fear into the hearts of even the most seasoned sailors. Amberport's harbourmasters maintain a vigilant watch, ensuring the city's defences remain strong, while its people, ever resourceful, find ways to thrive despite these threats.

In the south, the landscape transforms into the dramatic cliffs of Cheddar Gorge, where three majestic waterfalls, known as The Sisters, cascade into the sea. Revered as a symbol of the kingdom's natural beauty, these falls epitomize West Kadun's harmony with its environment.

To the east, the great gorge separating East and West Kadun serves as both a physical and symbolic reminder of the region's turbulent history. Seventy years ago, West Kadun was forever changed by King Stenton, known as the Breaker of Bridges. Faced with rebellion among his sons, he destroyed all crossings over the gorge except one—the great fortress of The Reach.

This act plunged the realm into the Divided Wars, a brutal fifty-year conflict that fractured the kingdom. King Stenton met his end in the gorge, and his legacy of division endured as his sons and nobles waged war for the throne. When the bloodline dwindled, power eventually consolidated under King Ruben Whitehart, whose rise brought peace. His reign formalized the division of East and West Kadun into two nations, though both remained under his authority.

Today, the scars of the Divided Wars linger, with The Reach standing as both a bridge and a barrier between the two nations. Yet, West Kadun thrives, its fertile lands and unified rule enabling it to flourish as a prominent force in the Eastern Kingdoms. Its people, forged by hardship and tempered by time, take pride in the strength and unity their land represents.

# EAST KADUN

## *Beneath the Tree, Hearts of the Free*

East Kadun, a sprawling land three times the size of its western counterpart, boasts a diverse and striking geography. Its western coastline runs unbroken touching Nordon to the north and the Drylands to the south, while the eastern horizon is dominated by the Gigas Mountains, a mighty range stretching from the arid Drylands through East Kadun and into Nordon's frozen reaches. This vast and varied terrain serves as both a natural barrier and a defining feature of the kingdom's identity.

Once unified with West Kadun, the land was torn apart by the Divided Wars—a brutal, fifty-year conflict that left deep scars on the nation. At the heart of this struggle was The Reach, a massive fortress spanning the only crossing of the gorge that separates East and West Kadun. Even now, The Reach stands as a grim monument to the past, its fortifications a constant reminder of the war that ended just two decades ago. Though an alliance was forged to ensure peace, tensions between the two nations simmer beneath the surface, threatening to reignite old hostilities.

The kingdom's borders are as turbulent as its history. To the north, East Kadun shares a tenuous boundary with Nordon, where marauders frequently raid southern settlements, testing the nation's defences. To the south lies a critical valley connecting East Kadun to the Drylands. Guarding this vital passage is the ancient fortress city of Cordon, constructed after the Tribal Wars—a relentless series of battles against the Drylands tribes. Cordon's fortifications are legendary: its walls span the entire valley, flanked by three ramparts. The outermost, named after the war hero Cordon, boasts four towers overlooking the arid plains. The second, Mitsurugi, honours the Drylands leader Mitsurugi Khan, whose near victory in the Tribal Wars still echoes through history. The innermost rampart, smaller and unnamed, awaits a hero worthy of its title, its two watchful towers standing in quiet vigilance.

Amidst these defences lies the heart of East Kadun's civilization: Borlong, the capital city. Once a humble outpost, Borlong has grown into a sprawling, bustling labyrinth. Its narrow alleys and crowded markets hum with life, while grand structures commemorate the peace that followed the Divide Wars. The Pines Forest to the west and the River Kalm to the south provide natural beauty and vital resources, further enriching the capital's prominence as the kingdom's cultural and economic hub.

To the north, the Emerald Sea dominates the landscape—a vast and untamed forest capable of engulfing all West Kadun within its depths. This ancient wilderness shelters countless forest clans who live amidst towering trees and shadowy groves. Yet their existence is fraught with peril: Nordon raiders and border skirmishes with the West leave these clans isolated and vulnerable, with little aid from Borlong to alleviate their struggles. Survival here is a precarious balance between resilience and despair, reflecting the harsh realities faced by those who dwell in the shadows of East Kadun's borders. Yet, just as its landscapes demand fortitude, its culture offers a counterpoint—a diverse and deeply rooted spiritual tradition that shapes the identity of its people.

Unlike Nordon and the Drylands, where devotion centres on a single god, East Kadun embraces a pantheon of deities. Every god finds reverence across its borders, creating a rich spiritual tapestry that unites the kingdom's many traditions. This pluralistic faith underscores East Kadun's heritage of inclusion and resilience, binding its people together in times of both prosperity and hardship.

At its core, East Kadun is a land shaped by conflict yet defined by its endurance. Centuries of war and division have forged a proud and fiercely self-reliant people, unwavering in their commitment to protect their homeland. While peace now binds East and West Kadun, the memories of past struggles linger. And in the South the towering walls of Cordon stand as an enduring symbol of their strength and determination, a testament to their resolve to face whatever challenges lie ahead.

# NORDON

## *Strength to You, The Winter Realm*

Nordon, known as the Winter Realm, lies in the far northern reaches of the continent—a frostbitten expanse where winter's grip never loosens. Towering peaks of the Gigas Mountains rise like an unyielding wall of ice and stone, casting long shadows over snowbound valleys and shielding the realm from the most brutal northern winds that are believed to carry Shiva's voice—a blend of rage and guidance. Even in summer, temperatures rarely rise above freezing, and storms plunge the land into eerie twilight, shrouding its rugged beauty in an air of foreboding.

Despite its harshness, Nordon thrives as a proud and indomitable nation, slightly smaller than its southern neighbour, East Kadun. Jagged peninsulas thrust into the icy northern seas, creating treacherous cliffs and rocky shores that mirror the resilience of its people. This unforgiving land has forged a culture steeped in strength, survival, and pride.

Stormhold, the capital, clings to the southern slopes of the Gigas Mountains. Built into the rock, it serves as both fortress and sanctuary, its ancient halls warmed by fires that have burned for generations. In its heart lies Nordon's throne, once a symbol of unyielding strength and authority. In the past, a king's rule was not guaranteed; their right to lead could be challenged each season by any warrior who deemed them unworthy of upholding Nordon's sacred traditions. These trials, fierce and uncompromising, ensured that only the strongest and most resolute held the mantle of leadership. Yet, in recent times, the throne's power has shifted—no longer contested through combat but passed down through lineage, a legacy carried by blood rather than by blade.

Beyond the city lies Shiva's Tears, a vast frozen lake whose haunting beauty draws both awe and reverence. Nearby, Shiva's Tomb, a sacred cave hidden deep within the mountains, is said to house the spirit of the Winter Goddess herself. These landmarks are revered as symbols of endurance, divine guidance, and ancestral strength, grounding the people of Nordon in their spiritual heritage.

On the western coast stands Frostfall Harbour, Nordon's bustling maritime hub and home to its legendary fleet. Here, the largest assembly of ships in the known world awaits its next voyage, whether for trade, exploration, or raids. The port is alive with the constant energy of sailors and traders, who brave the ice-choked northern seas with unmatched skill. Frostfall's rugged independence reflects the resilience of its people, who take pride in their seafaring heritage and their ability to navigate the most treacherous waters. The fleet, a symbol of Nordon's enduring power, is a living legacy of the nation's ancient raiding traditions.

To the northwest, the desolate Northrend Islands rise from the icy seas, their barren cliffs battered by relentless waves. These remote islands, though sparsely populated, play a vital role in Nordon's legacy. They serve as training grounds for young warriors, where the unforgiving environment tests their strength and resolve, and as staging points for northern expeditions, further cementing Nordon's dominance in the frozen north.

The people of Nordon, forged by their unforgiving environment, hold resilience and strength as their highest virtues. Their lives are a testament to endurance: miners carve precious metals from the icy depths, sailors brave treacherous seas, and raiders carry forward traditions steeped in blood and honour. For the people of Nordon, raiding is not merely a means of survival—it is a rite of passage, a measure of character, and an homage to their storied ancestry.

This spirit was never more evident than during the bloody era known as The Winter Wars. For centuries, Nordon's warriors stormed into Kadun with unmatched ferocity, razing settlements and testing the mettle of Kadun's armies. These relentless incursions left an indelible mark on the southern lands, etching Nordon's reputation as a realm of strength and ambition. Though peace now binds Nordon to its neighbours, the echoes of those wars remain—a haunting legacy of the Winter Realm's unyielding might.

Proud descendants of conquerors and survivors, the Nordon people live by the credo Durak Karesh—"Strength to you." These words, spoken with reverence, embody their connection to a land that demands fortitude at every turn. For Nordon, strength is more than a virtue; it is survival, identity, and an enduring legacy passed from one generation to the next.

# DRYLANDS

## *Solar's Sea*

The Drylands, known to its people as Solar's Sea, is the largest and most populous country in the Realms of Men. With a harsh reputation among northern nations, the people of the Drylands are viewed as wild and unrestrained, living in tribes that remain fiercely independent and often at odds with one another. These tribes are united only by their reverence for the Sun God Solar, whose fierce light they believe gives life to their barren land.

Stretching from the foothills of the Gigas Mountains in the north to the desolate southern reaches, the Drylands is a realm of cracked earth and scarce water. Though hostile, the land sustains countless tribes through scattered oases, providing a rare lifeline across the otherwise arid landscape. The terrain divides naturally into four distinct regions, each with unique traditions and lifestyles shaped by the land's extremes.

Cape Cordon marks the northernmost region, a vast expanse stretching from the borders of East Kadun down into the central Drylands. The tribes here, despite being bitter rivals over scarce resources, sometimes band together in skirmishes against the walls of Cordon, throwing themselves against the fortress that has held them back for centuries. Those who fall often end up as slaves in northern countries, their lives taken as spoils by Cordon's defenders. Though united only briefly under Mitsurugi Khan, who once rallied a hundred thousand warriors in a doomed march north, the tribes still cling to legends of that era. A prophecy foretells that an albino child with blood-red eyes will emerge to unite the tribes once more, rekindling the fierce spirit of Mitsurugi Khan.

To the south lies The Shifting Sands, an endless desert where dunes rise and fall with the winds, leaving the land in constant, restless motion. It is a desolate place, home only to fierce cave dwellers who eke out a living beneath the sands, using ancient caves for shelter. The Shifting Sands stretch far beyond known borders, its full extent a mystery even to those who live within it. Only the most resilient survive here, emerging from the dunes with stories of endless deserts and whispers of strange creatures lurking beneath the sand.

Along the western coast lies a narrow but fertile strip where tribes subsist as fishermen, taking what they can from the sea. Unlike the other regions, the tribes of the western coast are relatively peaceful, even engaging in occasional trade with one another, though their independence remains steadfast. The coast is dotted with small fishing villages, where people live in harmony with the rhythm of the ocean, their lives sheltered from the more violent customs of inland tribes.

To the east, under the shadow of the Gigas Mountains, lie the Shadelands—a region infamous for its violent rites and brutal traditions. Here, strength and survival are honoured above all else. Upon reaching their thirtieth summer, men and women alike must face the Trials: brutal, full-moon battles in which a hundred participants fight until only one remains. For men, victory means the right to pass on their lineage, fathering as many children as possible to ensure the strength of future generations. For women, triumph in the Trials allows them to retire as revered elders, guiding the tribe with wisdom earned in blood. Each year, the twelve champions from the monthly Trials meet in a grand final battle, where the victor earns the right to challenge the tribe's current chieftain. Should they succeed, they become the new leader, securing the tribe's loyalty until they, too, are challenged. This merciless system ensures that only the strongest survive in the Shadelands, and the tribes remain formidable and unyielding.

Despite the Drylands' infighting and harsh customs, their fierce pride and connection to the land run deep. To the outside world, they are seen as feral and untamed, yet within the Drylands, every trial, every tradition, is a testament to their resilience and their loyalty to Solar, the Sun God. It is said that one day, the prophecy will be fulfilled, and the tribes will rise as one under a new leader with blood-red eyes, bringing the Drylands back to their days of glory and power.

# BARROTH

## *The Island of Titans and Curses*

Barroth, an island steeped in mystery and legend, lies far to the west, its shores reachable only by those daring enough to brave the open sea. Sailors speak in hushed tones of the God Leviathan, said to guard the waters surrounding the island, her presence a deterrent to all but the boldest souls who dare to attempt the treacherous passage.

The land itself is forged by relentless earthquakes and the fiery eruptions of Titan's Fist—an ancient volcano at its heart—bears a landscape shaped by the raw, untamed power of the earth. Encircling the volcano is The Steeps, a formidable mountain range that stands like a ring of silent sentinels. Their jagged peaks, shrouded in clouds and veils of ash, dominate the horizon, a perpetual reminder of the island's volatile nature and the primal forces that shaped its rugged beauty.

The island's northern region is as eerie as it is beautiful, defined by a vast lake shaped uncannily like a face, with an island at its centre resembling an eye. This place is sacred to the people of Barroth, who believe it is Gigas himself, the watchful guardian over the land. To the west lies Wailing Woods, a dense, dark forest steeped in myth and haunted by an ancient curse. It is said that men of a bygone era were condemned to live as beasts within these woods, their mournful cries giving the forest its name and a reputation that keeps most travellers at bay.

On the eastern coast, the land juts out like clawed talons into the sea, each 'talon' lined with bustling fishing ports. Along this coast stretches Sapphire Sands, a large bay famed for its clear blue waters and vibrant settlements. Fisherfolk, traders, and travellers gather here, creating a lively hub of activity in an otherwise solitary kingdom.

The southern region of Barroth is divided into three distinct and isolated sections, each with its own character and history. To the southwest lie The Shattered Isles, a fragmented archipelago of thirty small islands scattered across the sea. Legend tells of a comet that struck the land ages past, splintering the coast and leaving behind this maze of jagged rocks and verdant isles. The Shattered Isles are a place of both beauty and peril, where thriving marine life contrasts with treacherous currents and hidden reefs that challenge even the most skilled sailors.

In the south-central region of Barroth lies Leviathan's Fang, a distinct island carved away from the mainland by ancient upheavals. Dominated by a sprawling harbour, it has earned a notorious reputation as a haven for pirates and mercenaries. This lawless port thrives under a brutal code, where strength, cunning, and the sharpness of one's blade determine survival. The harbour bustles with activity—ships laden with stolen treasures dock alongside vessels carrying contraband, while taverns and brothels hum with the chaos of outlaws seeking refuge or their next venture. Governed by an ever-shifting hierarchy of the most ruthless, Leviathan's Fang embodies the untamed spirit of Barroth's southern frontier.

The southeastern region of Barroth, known as The Drowning Meadows, is a vast and perilous marshland, its shape resembling the gaping jaws of a mighty beast. This treacherous expanse is a labyrinth of bogs, reeds, and hidden sinkholes, where the unwary risk being swallowed by deep, muddy waters with every misstep. Mist clings to the ground like a shroud, obscuring the paths and adding an eerie stillness to the air. The Drowning Meadows are as inhospitable as they are hauntingly beautiful, a place where survival depends on keen instincts and an intimate knowledge of the land's ever-shifting terrain.

Nearly four and half thousand years ago, Barroth was embroiled in the infamous War of Three Kingdoms, a conflict so brutal it is said the god Titan intervened, shaking the earth and quelling the bloodshed with a mighty tremor. While the true story has faded into myth, this war left Barroth wary of outside entanglements. Since that time, the island has remained mostly isolated, governed by independent states rather than a single sovereign ruler. Barroth has prospered, its people left to their own devices, adapting to the land's wild landscapes and unpredictable nature.

Barrothians rarely venture eastward, viewing the conflicts of other realms as reason enough to remain secluded. However, the island welcomes the occasional foreign visitor, who typically returns with tales of Barroth's fierce beauty, its volcanic landscapes, and the unyielding spirit of its people—a people who live in harmony with the land's mysteries and powers, and who honour the ancient gods said to dwell among them.

# THE FIRST GOD

*Before the first man, before the first sun, before*
*time was time, there was but one.*

*A God that could see, distance stars throughout the galaxy.*

*A millennia passed and the God could feel, a being*
*with conscience, the emotion surreal.*

*So the God gave its name, Gigas it would be, to*
*watch over the stars for eternity.*

*The millenniums passed and loneliness drew near, so*
*Gigas almighty, created a planet so dear.*

*The planet was Earth, a sphere that would spin and*
*Gigas felt pride, so time could begin.*

# THE ELEMENTAL GODS

*The God Gigas wished for a son, an heir to Earth when time was done.*

*And so it was, a son to see, born to the world—Titan, the deity.*

*For centuries, Titan roamed the land, across the Earth, both sea and sand.*

*But soon his heart could take no more, he slammed the ground with a mighty roar.*

*The Earth beneath him cracked and broke, mountains flew as if they'd spoke.*

*Boulders soared toward the sky, and craters deep were left to lie.*

*Titan tired, and sought his rest, leaving the world in utter distress.*

*Gigas wept, his sorrow deep, tears rained down in oceans steep.*

*An ocean dark, where light was none, a place where Titan's rage had run.*

*To guard the sea from Titan's might, Gigas created a fearsome sight.*

*Leviathan rose from beneath the wave, a serpent fierce, the sea its grave.*

*Gigas, to calm his son's terrible strife, gave him Shiva, an alluring wife.*

*But Shiva, cold as winter's frost, blew a gale that left Earth lost.*

*When her breath had ceased its fight, the land was locked in endless night.*

*Gigas, wise, then birthed the twins, Solar and Lunar, to ease the winds.*

*To bring the day, to calm the night, and give the Earth a peaceful light.*

*And so the Gods, in realms of air, roamed the Earth, their power to share.*

# THE BALLARD HOLY

*Shiva and Titan, a marriage of despair, at night it*
*was Lunar who had Shiva's care.*

*Not as intended, a life was born, Holy its name, the Gods were torn.*

*Gigas so furious, took back what gave, Strength and Power went to the grave.*

*Holy, a child, approached the almighty, 'Gigas, my*
*lord, I have an offer to delight thee'.*

*'Your Earth so empty, nothing to see', 'I can give life, with mortality'.*

*Gigas appeased, and Holy gave life, nature blossomed, animals rife.*

*Giants roamed the land, dwarves mined the cave, until a*
*hybrid was born, a man that could enslave.*

# THE WRATH OF GODS

*Man, a curious creature, never content, drove*
*dwarves to ruin, their end was sent.*

*The giants fell, desolation grew, land consumed for castles, forts anew.*

*Gigas enraged, returned Titan's might, his strength restored, a fearsome sight.*

*Titan obliged, his fists like thunder, the Earth did shake, it split asunder.*

*Yet Holy, life's eternal guide, would stand with man, on their side.*

*Split into Twenty, the Paladins bright, Immortal beings, aglow with light.*

*Beneath the mountains, dry plains in view, Titan*
*met the Twenty, battle ensue.*

*Fierce and colossal, the earth it cried, the Paladins bled, yet still they tried.*

*Victory came not from Titan's fall, but in life's spark, the greatest of all.*

*With a Holy seal, they bound him tight, beneath the plains, forever in night.*

# A PROPHECY

*Whispers abound of a time yet to see, when Lunar will set, and Solar will be.*

*An albino awaken with blood-red eyes, destined to reign, a country will rise.*

*A generation will unite, blood will spill, leading one army, all will kneel.*

# THE PALADINS PROLOGUE

The Paladin known as 'Seven' hung in the skies above the Drylands, a crimson specter against the barren expanse of parched earth and fractured stone. Far below, the fortress of Cordon rose defiantly from the desolation, its towering walls a testament to its unyielding purpose. Tiered battlements climbed in relentless layers, each ascending level casting a foreboding shadow over the one below, a fortress carved as much from resolve as from stone.

Shouts echoed upward, carried by the searing winds. Another skirmish raged at the base—tribesmen hurling themselves against the stronghold with wild abandonment, their crude weapons flashing in the dying sunlight.

The defenders of Kadun answered with arrows and steel, cutting down the wave. Blood spilled once more, dark rivulets pooling beneath the fallen, seeping into the thirsty sands. It had always been this way.

Seven watched in silence, anger simmering within. *What a waste of life. What was the sacrifice for?* For centuries, this cycle had played out—men killing men, tribes against kingdoms, brothers against brothers. The fortress endured, but at what cost? Its stones were steeped in blood, its walls raised upon broken bodies.

*It was not always this way.*

Once, Seven had been part of something greater, bound to a purpose that gave existence meaning. They were one of Holy's chosen twenty—Paladins, forged from divine essence. Together, they had been a shield between humanity and the wrath of the God Titan.

The name *Titan* still resonated, a lingering echo of dread and duty. The God of Earth had unleashed his wrath to cleanse the world of humanity. Seven remembered that day—the Paladins standing defiant as the air trembled with his rage, the ground fracturing beneath his colossal strides.

For three days and nights, the battle raged on the sun-scorched plains where the Fortress now stood. The Paladins fought as one, twenty against the unstoppable. Each strike against Titan was met with overwhelming force. One by one, Seven's brethren fell, their radiant light extinguished.

On the fourth day, the Paladins who remained enacted a final gambit. They forged celestial chains of Holy to bind Titan, trapping him beneath the earth in a prison not even a God could break. For almost four millennia, the Paladins held their vigil, their combined will sustaining the prison.

Then the blood from the world above came. It began as a trickle, then a stream, then a torrent, seeping through the fractured earth. Blood pooled, thick and suffocating. While the other Paladins remained unscathed, Seven was drenched in its venomous corruption. And with it came hatred—a foreign, corrosive emotion—surging through Seven like a plague of infection.

Desperately, Seven tried to suppress it, recalling the faces of those they had fought to protect: families, children, fragile hopes. But the blood did not stop, and with each drop, Seven's light dimmed.

It was not just the blood—it was what it represented. Humanity's cruelty. Their ingratitude. Their insatiable hunger for destruction. Humanity had forgotten the sacrifice of the Paladins, and the realization fractured Seven's purpose. The pure light of Holy within them twisted, turning dark and crimson. An insurmountable rage for humanity took over.

And then, they let go, their chain over Titan relinquished.

The winds of the Drylands dragged Seven back to the present. They refused to dwell on what came next—the screams, the death they unleashed. Centuries had passed since that day, though it might as well have been a blink.

Below, the battlefield was quiet now, littered with the dead. Blood glistened in the fading light, soaking into the sands that concealed Titan's prison. How many times had Seven witnessed this? How many battles, how many lives wasted?

The other Paladin—those who still clung to their purpose within the tomb—believed in humanity's worth. But they had not seen what Seven had. They had not borne witness to humanity's failure.

As night descended, the air grew heavy with the acrid stench of burning flesh as the dead were consigned to the flames, their pyres casting flickering light against the darkened sky. Below, the survivors were herded like cattle, their chains rattling softly as they were passed from hand to hand, faces etched with despair.

Seven's gaze drifted upward, away from the grim scene below. Beyond the jagged walls of the fortress, the horizon stretched endlessly, where distant mountain peaks stood like solemn sentinels, their towering forms reduced to shadowy silhouettes in the dying light. Above, the stars pierced the velvet darkness, their cold brilliance unmarred by the carnage below. The night sky felt vast, timeless, and utterly indifferent, a stark contrast to the human suffering that clung to the earth.

For a moment, Seven lingered in that quiet expanse, their crimson form illuminated faintly by the glow of the fires, as if searching for something beyond the reach of bloodshed and ruin. But the stars offered no solace, only an eternal, unyielding gaze.

Days blurred into weeks, perhaps even months; time lost its rhythm, no longer a steady march but a series of disjointed flashes. It came not in hours or minutes but in vivid, fleeting moments: the clash of steel and anguished cries from battles raging below, the thunderous roar of a mountainside collapsing into chaos, or the brief, silent arc of a streaking star cutting through the night sky. Each fragment of time etched itself into the void, sharp and unrelenting, while the rest dissolved into an endless haze.

Suddenly, one of those fragmented flashes of time erupted in Seven's peripheral vision—a searing beam of holy light tearing through the darkness, piercing the heavens with blinding intensity. Its source lay below, in the depths of Titan's tomb.

Seven's gaze sharpened, their mind racing as recognition struck like a thunderclap. It was Six. The long-dormant sentinel had awakened, its presence undeniable in the sacred radiance. A shiver ran through Seven's form, for the meaning was clear: Titan's chains had weakened once again —or worse, the God had shattered them entirely.

The beam lingered, its unyielding brilliance casting jagged shadows across the barren earth and fortress walls. The air vibrated with an otherworldly hum, a sound that spoke of ancient power stirring from its slumber. Seven hovered motionless, the implications of the moment coiling around them like a vice, the balance of the world teetering on the brink once more.

Their crimson form silhouetted against the fading glow of Six's holy light as it stretched toward the horizon. The radiance diminished gradually, leaving behind an oppressive stillness that hung in the air like a held breath.

Watching in silence, their eyes fixed on the ground below, waiting for the inevitable—the moment Titan would tear through rock and earth, shattering the fragile peace with his wrath. The anticipation coiled tightly within Seven, each second stretching into eternity.

But the ground did not quake, nor did the sky roar in defiance. The moment never came. The earth remained still, unbroken. The silence deepened, not with relief but with unease, as though the world itself was holding its secrets just out of reach. Seven's gaze lingered, searching the shadows for answers that refused to reveal themselves.

Night gave way to day, only to dissolve once more into darkness, the cycle repeating until it lost all meaning. Weeks blurred into months, months into years. Below, wars raged ceaselessly, the din of battles merging into a cacophony of chaos, indistinguishable from one another. Time became a shapeless blur, a tide that ebbed and flowed without rhythm.

And still, Seven hovered above, unmoving, their crimson form a silent sentinel against the endless sky. They waited, their vigilance unbroken—whether for the return of Six's radiant light or for Titan to rise and consume the world. Twelve years of bloodshed and ruin unfolded beneath them, the carnage a constant churn that seemed eternal.

Until the stillness came.

It began with a silence so profound it swallowed the battlefield's usual roar. The plains stretched wide and empty, a strange and unnatural calm settling over the land. Seven's gaze sharpened, drawn to the fortress below, where the stillness seemed to originate.

Then, from its shadowed walls, a solitary figure emerged.

A girl.

She stumbled across the desolate plains, frail and trembling, her every step a struggle against the weight of exhaustion and despair. Her thin frame swayed, and her steps faltered as though the very earth sought to swallow her. Seven watched, unblinking, the crimson glow of their presence casting faint shadows on the barren ground below.

And then, for the first time in centuries, Seven descended.

Their form cut through the air, silent and swift, like an omen breaking through the stillness. As Seven neared the girl, something stirred—a faint, delicate glow emanating from deep within her. It was fragile, barely perceptible, but unmistakable: a flicker of Holy's light, buried beneath layers of weakness and pain.

The girl carried life within her.

A child.

Both were dying.

For the first time in millennia, Seven felt something other than rage: empathy. They hovered closer, their crimson light casting an otherworldly glow over the girl. She seemed to sense them, her glassy eyes following their movements. Her life was fading, and the child's spark within her was dimming.

In that moment, Seven made a choice. Redemption was beyond reach—an illusion for a being whose hands were stained with the blood of countless lives, whose very existence was steeped in destruction. The weight of their sins hung heavy, an unshakable burden carved into the essence of their being.

But this was different, perhaps, the child could yet be saved.

The faint glow within the girl, fragile and fleeting, stirred something long buried within Seven—a flicker of purpose amidst the void.

Seven knelt, the crimson glow of their presence softening as they extended a hand toward the girl. Her trembling form seemed impossibly small, the faint pulse of life within her resonated, a defiance against the inevitability of death.

For the first time in centuries, Seven acted not as an instrument of ruin, but as a guardian of hope.

Summoning the remnants of their power, Seven poured their essence into the girl. Crimson light mingled with her failing spirit, reigniting the child's spark. The girl collapsed, her body unable to endure more. Her breathing slowed, but the child's light flared to life.

Seven felt their existence unravel, their being fading into the void. But for the first time in centuries, they felt peace.

And as they dissolved into nothingness, the faint cry of a newborn echoed across the desolate plains.

# THE ORPHAN
# CHAPTER ONE

The slap of bare feet against cobblestones chased Auron through the labyrinth of alleys, each step louder, closer, hungrier. He wove through every twisting turn, his instincts guiding him as the maze of alleys blurred past, yet the pounding footsteps stayed close, relentless. His chest heaved with the effort, his heart hammering against his ribs as if begging him to surrender, to stop. But the curses and ragged breaths of his pursuers spurred him onward. They were tiring—he could hear it in the faltering rhythm of their chase—but they hadn't slowed enough. Not yet.

Veering around another corner at incredible speed, Auron felt his footing slip on the slick surface. For a fleeting moment, he lost all control, skidding wildly. His momentum carried him straight into a large man draped in a white toga, who stood at the bend balancing a wooden box brimming with assorted materials. The box flew from the man's grasp, shattering into splinters as it crashed onto the cobblestones, its contents scattering.

The man staggered back, cursing loudly, and swung a heavy arm at Auron. The clumsy swipe missed its mark, as the collision had knocked Auron upright. Without pausing, he darted away from the wreckage, his heart pounding as the man's angry shouts faded behind him.

The street widened ahead, a bustling artery teeming with market stalls and haggling traders. Auron plunged into the chaos, weaving between carts and clusters of people with nimble precision. The noise of pounding feet behind him was growing fainter, but when he dared a quick glance over his shoulder, he still caught sight of three boys pushing through the crowd. A fourth had fallen behind, clutching his knees, though Auron's relief was short-lived. His legs burned with exhaustion, each step feeling heavier than the last. He couldn't keep this up. He needed a place to hide—and fast.

Frantically scanning the crowded street ahead, Auron's eyes locked onto an open doorway tucked between two bustling market stalls. A spark of hope flared within him, and with a surge of energy, he darted toward it, slipping inside unnoticed. Pressing himself flat against the far wall, he fought to steady his breathing, his chest heaving as he strained to listen.

He clung to the shadows, willing himself to disappear, but his pounding heart betrayed him, thundering in his ears like a war drum. Every sound outside blurred together—the hum of market chatter, the clatter of cartwheels—but no sign of the pursuing boys. Yet, the fear of discovery gnawed at him, every second stretching into an eternity.

After several minutes, Auron peeled himself away from the wall, his racing heart finally beginning to calm. His senses returned, and he took in his surroundings. The room was small and cloaked in shadow, the only light seeping through the crack in the doorway. The air felt close and heavy, amplifying the silence. He noticed there were no windows or other exits, only the door he had stumbled through, and he guessed it might serve as a storage space. Letting out a weary sigh, he slid back down against the wall, his body aching from the chase. Shrugging the bag from his shoulder, he placed it on the floor in front of him and began rummaging through its contents, eager to see what treasures his flight had secured.

It had been another fruitful day at the markets. Auron had slipped past several unwitting marks, his quick hands relieving them of fifteen copper pieces and even a coveted silver coin. Alongside the coins, he'd pocketed a few scraps of papyrus with scribbled lists and a slightly worn handkerchief. He tossed the papyrus into a shadowy corner of the room, dismissing it as useless, and carefully wrapped the coins in the handkerchief before tucking it securely into his small bag. His stomach growled as he reached for the large apple he'd swiped from a fruit stand earlier. Sinking his teeth into it, he savoured the crisp bite, the sweetness a rare indulgence in his otherwise gritty day.

Pickpocketing had become second nature to Auron, a skill born of necessity rather than choice. His mother, a prostitute, had brought him into the world without knowing—or caring—who his father was. A nameless man lost in the parade of men who paid for a moment of her time. For several years, she had struggled to care for him, but the burden of motherhood eventually became too much, abandoning the boy to the streets of Borlong.

Somehow, he had survived those fragile early years, and now, at eleven, the alleys were his home, the shadows his refuge. He stole to keep himself alive, slipping through the cracks of a world that had no place for him. But survival wasn't without its dangers. Rival children were his greatest threat. While other street kids banded together in gangs, carving the city's poorest neighbourhoods into fiercely guarded territories, Auron remained a loner. He stole wherever he could, unconcerned with invisible boundaries, a habit that earned him the ire of the gangs.

Market traders rarely caught him—his hands were too quick, his escapes too nimble—but the gangs were another story. They often spotted him, and when they did, the hunt began. Most days, he managed to slip away. On others, he wasn't so lucky. The beatings they dealt out left bruises on his body and a searing resentment in his heart, but he endured, because he had no other choice.

Sitting in the cramped, shadowy room, Auron began to plot his next move. Midday was approaching, and with it, the bustling markets would start to wind down. He guessed this space would soon fill with merchants packing up their stalls or unloading stock. He needed to be gone before then—being caught by the traders meant risking a severe whipping. The thought made his shoulders tense. He had felt the sting of the whip before, and the scars etched into his back were reminders of just how unforgiving the world could be.

When the stalls closed, there was often a brief window when unsold food was discarded into the gutters. Auron wanted to be there before the gangs arrived, scavenging scraps before they claimed the streets for themselves. Tossing the gnawed apple core into a dark corner, he stood and began gathering his stolen treasures, carefully tucking them into his shoulder bag. His heart quickened as he approached the door. He needed to risk a glance outside, to see if the way back to his alley was clear.

Steeling himself, Auron pressed flat against the wall and inched toward the doorway, his every nerve bristling with tension. The rough wooden frame scraped against his bony shoulder as he crept closer, his movements painstakingly slow. When he reached the edge, he paused, his breath shallow, and cautiously tilted his head, careful not to reveal too much of himself.

The street he had bolted through earlier stretched out before him, eerily quiet now, but Auron knew better than to trust its calm. He needed a wider view, a clearer picture of the scene beyond. Edging further, he exposed a sliver of his face, the bustling marketplace gradually coming into view. The hum of bartering merchants and the clinking of coins filled the air, the crowd oblivious to the small boy hiding just out of sight.

His head was fully exposed now, and his eyes darted to the left, where a heated argument had erupted between several traders. Arms flailed, fingers jabbed the air, and voices clashed, loud and accusatory. Auron lingered for a moment, watching the drama unfold. Likely a dispute over short change—arguments like these were common in the markets, fuelled by suspicion and desperation. The commotion might serve as his cover, but it also heightened his anxiety; any distraction could draw unwelcome attention his way.

Glancing back toward the first street, Auron's breath caught, his eyes widening in sudden panic. The boys from earlier were charging toward him from the right, their faces alight with grim determination. His stomach dropped, and he instinctively pressed himself deeper into the shadows of the room, praying the darkness would shield him. But it was too late—one of them had already spotted the slight figure lurking in the gloom. A shout went up, and all of them surged toward the doorway like a pack of wolves closing in on their prey.

Auron stumbled back into the centre of the room, his pulse hammering in his ears. He frantically scanned for an escape, but the walls felt like they were closing in, trapping him. The door was no longer an option. His fleeting chance to flee had vanished, and now there was nowhere to run, nowhere to hide. He clenched his fists, his body trembling with a volatile mix of fear and grim acceptance as he braced for what was to come. There was no avoiding it now—he would have to face their punishment, endure it as he had so many times before.

Auron pressed himself against the far wall, his breath shallow and uneven as the four boys prowled into the room. The dim light cast their gaunt, angular faces into shadow, twisting their features into something even more sinister. They were older, taller, and stronger than Auron, their confidence bolstered by the imbalance of power. Fear gripped him, cold and unrelenting, just as it had so many times before.

One boy stepped forward, his voice low and taunting. "You've not learned, little boy. We've caught you before, but it seems our message didn't sink in." His words dripped with malice, each syllable a calculated threat. "This is the last time you'll steal on our patch—or anyone's patch." The boy's voice turned to a venomous hiss as he leaned closer, his shadow looming over Auron.

The group advanced, their movements slow and deliberate, savouring his terror. The boy spoke again, his tone icy and final. "You won't wake up from this one, little boy." From the folds of darkness, he pulled out a jagged wooden post, splintered at one end, likely torn from the leg of a market stall. Without warning, they charged at Auron, their eyes burning with cruel intent. He cowered instinctively, throwing his arms up to shield his face, bracing for the onslaught.

The wooden post slammed into Auron's bare forearms with brutal force, the sharp sting radiating through his bones. Before he could recover, it came down again, harder this time, sending a jolt of agony up his arms. A fist struck his ribs on the left, followed by another blow to his right side. A sudden, vicious kick landed against his leg, buckling his stance. Pain surged through him like fire, but there was no time to react.

The post crashed down once more, tearing into his skin. He cried out, the sound raw and desperate, as he felt warm blood trickling down his arm, pooling at his elbow. The boy raised the post again, his movements cruel and deliberate, and brought it down with a sickening crack. Auron's left arm gave way, the bone snapping under the force. The pain was blinding, his scream piercing the air, but it was drowned out by the din of the bustling marketplace beyond. No one would hear him, no one would come to help.

The blows came relentlessly, fists hammering down from every angle, their impact leaving him dazed and battered. His right leg trembled under the relentless barrage of kicking feet, threatening to give way. He clenched his jaw, willing himself to stay upright, knowing that collapsing would only make things worse. But his strength was fading fast, drained by the unending assault.

A brutal kick to his stomach knocked the wind from his lungs. He doubled over, coughing violently as blood sprayed from his mouth in a crimson mist. Instinctively, he dropped his arms to shield his abdomen, leaving his head exposed. The wooden post crashed down on his skull with a sickening thud. Pain exploded in his mind as the room around him seemed to dim, the edges of his vision blurring. Warm blood streamed down his face, dripping from his chin, its sticky heat a cruel reminder of his vulnerability.

Dizziness overtook him, and his legs wavered, barely holding him upright. Another savage swing of the post struck his unprotected head, the impact sending a deafening thrum through his body. This time, his legs buckled completely, and he crumpled to the floor, his body limp and defenceless.

The world around him was slipping away. Auron's senses dulled as his body went limp, no longer registering the kicks and blows raining down. The dim light in the room seemed to blur and fade, the edges swallowed by creeping darkness. Just before the void consumed him entirely, he thought he saw a new figure enter the room—a shadow darker than the rest—but his vision swirled and collapsed inward before he could be certain.

The pain dissolved, replaced by an eerie weightlessness as he drifted into the black void of his subconscious. Somewhere, distant and faint, a voice broke through the haze. Soft and steady, it whispered, *"You are safe now."*

# THE ORPHAN
# CHAPTER TWO

Lord Malum slammed his tightly clenched fist down on the long oak desk, the sound piercing the silence that followed the heated argument with his son. He had spent the afternoon in the bathhouses east of his stately home, relaxing with a few senior council members after the morning's debate. He had expected to return home to a prepared feast and perhaps enjoy a gentle stroll through his gardens. Instead, he was met by his son, Malament, who had dragged a half-dead street urchin into their home.

Fury coursed through Malum at the news. In his rage, he threatened to finish the child off. This was the second time Malament had brought a small child into the household. The first had stolen a few insignificant trinkets and a loaf of bread before vanishing back into the squalid streets and dirty alleyways. For reasons Malum could not fathom, his son had recently taken to wandering the streets of Borlong in a hooded disguise, seeking out these forlorn orphans and offering them sanctuary. Malum hoped it was just a passing phase, but it was a wretched habit.

Most of the children living in the slums were infested with lice and plagued by unsavoury diseases. Malum could not bear the thought of the shame if any council members found out he was sheltering such a wretch. The senate meetings were fierce battlegrounds; any hint of weakness was ruthlessly exploited, even against the head of state, Lord Malum Thalron of East Kadun.

The argument between father and son stretched from late afternoon into early evening, and Malum's hunger gnawed at his stomach. He turned to face his son, who stood in the centre of the study like a coiled snake, poised but ready to strike.

Malament, now eighteen, wore a plain red tunic that accentuated his slim frame, revealing the subtle muscle definition from his combat training. He shared his mother's features: a youthful face with thin lips and a rounded nose, his blue eyes narrow like a clear summer sky, framed by long lashes. Wavy blonde hair tumbled to his shoulders, with a portion expertly gathered into a tidy bun perched at the crown.

In contrast, Malum bore little resemblance to his son, save for their shared stubbornness. His own hair, once a deep black, was now streaked with grey and thinned with age, cascading to the upper length of his back. He wore a navy tunic embroidered with ivory and gold trimmings. His face was sharp, marked by high cheekbones and a protruding chin concealed by a meticulously groomed beard.

Though he did not want the stray boy to stay, Malum was weary from their prolonged confrontation. Subconsciously, he ran his fingers through his greying beard, allowing his thoughts to crystallise into words. "Let me see the boy," he commanded, his voice calm yet still carrying an unmistakable authority.

Malament's expression softened, and a smile threatened to break through his stoic demeanour. He had remained remarkably calm during his father's tirade, knowing that if he stayed resolute long enough, his father would eventually concede. Growing up as the son of Lord Malum, he had known isolation; children his age often avoided him because of his father's status. This loneliness had shaped him into a young man who sought companionship in the unlikeliest of places.

The first boy he had brought home had been a wild creature, scavenging for scraps in an alleyway, gnawing on a bone like a feral dog. Though the boy had come with him, he had no loyalty to Malament and fled as soon as he found an opportunity, taking with him what little he could steal. Malament soon realised that to succeed, he needed to find a child who would rely on him from the very beginning—a child who would see him as a protector rather than a master.

That morning, clad in his dark cloak and hood, he had wandered through the bustling markets, loose change jingling in his pocket. It was not long before a small boy slipped his hand inside, stealing a few coppers. Malament had observed with fascination as the child moved gracefully among unsuspecting merchants, lifting small treasures with an almost balletic finesse.

He had then noticed a group of older boys lurking nearby, their eyes scanning their own marks with prized possessions ready for lifting. Intrigued, he tipped them off about the child's presence, watching the scene unfold with a mix of excitement and dread. The chase was captivating; he was surprised to see the boy evade capture with such skill. As the child darted into a small storeroom, Malament had taken action, handing the four boys a wooden stick and guiding them on where to strike. The beating continued for a time, the air thick with tension, until he could bear it no longer. He rushed in, rescuing the young boy from fatal harm, determined to nurse him back to health and secure his loyalty.

Now, as he turned his attention back to his father, he nodded low in a show of respect, a customary gesture in the land of Kadun. Rising gracefully, he pivoted and strode toward the double doors of the study, stepping out into the expansive hallway. The landing stretched across the second tier of the house, a balcony overlooking the grand reception area below.

Gripping the ornate gold-trimmed handrail, Malament allowed himself a moment to take in the vast space. The reception area was a remarkable sight, with large white pillars of stone reaching from the polished marble floor to the ceiling above. His fingers glided along the rail, following its elegant curve as it transitioned into the wide royal red-carpeted staircase. As he descended, the soft sound of his father's footsteps followed, muffled by the thick woven carpet, a reminder of the tension that still lingered between them. As Malament reached the bottom of the staircase, he knew he would need to navigate this delicate balance between his father's expectations and his own desires.

The reception area opened up before them, a grand space adorned with rich tapestries and intricate murals depicting the history of East Kadun. Flickering torchlight cast shadows on the walls, dancing like whispers of the past, each tale steeped in triumph and betrayal. Malament's heart quickened as he thought of the boy hidden away in the chambers below. He could not help but feel a sense of responsibility for the child's fate, a feeling that clashed violently with his father's disdain.

He moved across the marble floor, the sound of his footsteps lost amidst the vastness of the room. Every step reminded him of the loneliness that had been his companion for so long. The echo of his father's footsteps was a stark contrast, an assertion of dominance that Malament had grown accustomed to, yet never fully accepted.

"Malament," his father's voice cut through the silence, a deep rumble filled with authority. "You need to understand the implications of your actions. This isn't just about some street urchin; it's about our name, our legacy."

Malament turned to face his father, trying to suppress the irritation that bubbled beneath the surface. "He's just a child, Father. One who needs help. Can't you see that?"

"Help?" Lord Malum scoffed, his brow furrowing in disbelief. "You think sheltering a filthy beggar will earn you respect? The council will see this as a weakness, an invitation for mockery. They will use it against us."

Malament clenched his jaw, resisting the urge to retort. He had long learned that arguing with his father rarely ended well. Instead, he chose to remain silent, allowing the tension to thicken between them. In his mind, he envisioned the boy—the way he had darted through the market, quick and agile, and the look of fear in his eyes as he was chased by the other boys. It was not just about the child; it was about something deeper—a chance to create a bond that he had never had.

"Do you not understand what it's like to be so alone?" Malament's voice came out steadier than he felt, each word imbued with an earnestness he could not conceal. "I've spent my life surrounded by people yet never truly connected to anyone. They see me as your son, not as Malament. This boy... he could be different. He could be a companion, someone who might actually choose to be by my side."

Lord Malum's expression shifted, surprise flickering across his face. "And you think you can find companionship in a street urchin? Someone raised in the filth of the alleys? It's madness!"

"Maybe it is madness," Malament replied, his resolve hardening. "But I can't continue living this way—drowned in expectation, suffocated by the burden of our name. This child represents a chance to forge a new connection, to break free from the isolation that has consumed me for years."

"You are not merely my son, Malament—you are my heir," Malum stated coldly, his tone sharp and unyielding. "The weight of expectation was placed upon you the moment you drew your first breath, and it will remain bound upon your shoulders until your last. Loneliness, companionship... these are distractions, burdens not guides, they have no place in the life of one destined to lead."

Malament wanted to respond, but his father would never understand. Without another glance he turned away, the weight of their conversation heavy on his shoulders. He needed the boy as much as the stricken child needed him. Determination coursed through him and for the first time, Malament felt the flicker of hope—an opportunity to break free from the chains of his upbringing and forge a new path, one that could redefine what it meant to be Malament Thalron. The boy must stay, even if it meant defying his father's wishes.

Hurriedly he crossed the hall and approached a small unadorned wooden door in the far corner, which seemed almost out of place amongst the beautifully decorated grand hall. Arriving first at the plain doorway,

Malament held it open for his father, the creak of the hinges echoing down the narrow stone stairwell that lay beyond. The descent was steep and unwelcoming, the air thick with a stale chill that contrasted sharply with the luxurious warmth of the house above. Each step felt warped beneath his sandals, the well-trodden stones a reminder of countless journeys taken down to this unkempt level, a descent of about thirty feet that felt more like a plunge into another world.

His father followed, descending with an air of disdain that wrapped around him like a cloak. Lord Malum scorned the dim passage, his expression a mask of contempt as he glanced down into the darkness. Malament could sense his father's loathing for this place; it was the slave quarters, a realm of subservience that Lord Malum considered beneath him.

As they reached the bottom, the narrow corridor stretched out before them, lined with doors that stood close together on both sides. The flickering flames of torches mounted on the damp walls offered scant illumination, casting long shadows that seemed to dance in mockery of their presence. The air was heavy with moisture, the humidity palpable, suffocating the space with the stench of mildew and neglect. Each breath brought with it the dampness that clung to the walls. The uneven stone floor pooled with water in the shadows, forming slick puddles that turned their passage treacherous.

Malament walked in careful steps, aware of the deepening frown etched on his father's face. Lord Malum held a stern gaze, his lips pressed into a thin line, radiating an unmistakable displeasure at being seen among the very people he governed. He was their master—nothing more. The very thought of mingling with the slaves in their chambers seemed to ignite a flame of fury within him, as if their very presence could tarnish the bloodline he so desperately sought to uphold.

Fortunately, the corridor was relatively quiet; most of its occupants were still labouring in the household above, and the atmosphere bore an uneasy stillness. As they traversed the narrow passage, the faint sounds of whispered conversations and the clatter of utensils from the wash area echoed softly, blending with the distant hum of activity above.

As they moved, some of the doors swung open, revealing glimpses into the lives of those who dwelled within. The inhabitants, accustomed to the hierarchy of their existence, quickly bowed their heads in respect, their bodies instinctively bending to acknowledge their lord's presence. Others, however, remained engrossed in their own affairs, seemingly oblivious to the powerful figures gliding past their thresholds, lost in the routine of their daily lives.

Malament's gaze flickered over the faces of the slaves. Some were young, their expressions filled with a mix of fear and resignation; others bore the deep lines of hardship, their eyes betraying stories of survival and suffering. In those brief moments, he felt a twinge of empathy, a stark contrast to his father's detached arrogance. The boy he had rescued from the streets was a part of this world—a world that Malament understood far too well, yet one that his father sought to ignore.

As they continued down the corridor, the oppressive atmosphere pressed in around them. Malament's heart raced, torn between his loyalty to his father and his growing commitment to the boy he had saved. Each step deeper into the slave quarters felt like a step further away from the life that had been laid out before him, and closer to the possibility of forging a new path—one defined not by status, but by choice, his choice, and perhaps even the hope of true companionship.

After several more doorways, Malament finally stopped at one on the left. He paused at the wooden door, glancing back at his father as if waiting for a command to enter. Malum's stern face remained impassive, but he nodded, gesturing for his son to continue. Pushing open the door revealed a small room, the only light emanating from an old lantern on a bedside cabinet. Instantly, a nauseating smell of sickness engulfed both men as they stepped inside. Against the left side of the room lay a frail boy on a narrow bed, his eyes closed and breath barely perceptible. Next to him sat Saanvi, the plump nurse, gently dabbing the child's forehead with a bloodstained cloth. At her feet, a bucket overflowed with a mixture of water, blood, and vomit, adding to the cramped room's oppressive atmosphere.

Malum nearly gagged, lifting his tunic over his nose to shield himself from the foul stench. He and Malament looked down at the limp figure, noting the dark purple bruises covering the boy's face and the dried blood matted in his black hair, remnants of a concealed head wound. The child's left arm was in a small cast, resting outside his blanket on his chest, and his feverish skin glistened with sweat.

Malum's thoughts turned cold; the boy seemed on the brink of death. Perhaps this entire affair could be forgotten if he succumbed to the night. "He looks dead, Malament, and he's filling the air with the stench of it. Will he even live?"

Malament remained silent, his gaze fixed on Saanvi. The nurse was a robust woman in her late thirties, her round face emanating warmth and care. Strands of prematurely grey hair escaped the confines of a tightly coiled bun. She wore a long sky-blue garment, its fabric smeared with blood from her work. Having served the household since childhood, she knew both men well and sensed their scrutiny.

"The night will be hard for him, sir," she replied in her usual placid tone. "His left arm is broken, as are several ribs. I believe his jaw is fractured, but I can't be certain through all the swelling. I've stitched a nasty gash on his head, but he has a terrible fever. My main concern isn't what I can see, but what I can't. He continues to vomit blood. It could be internal bleeding or worse. If that is the case, I can't give you a truthful answer. But if he makes it through tonight, I believe he'll survive."

Holding his breath at her words, Malament watched his father's reaction. Malum stood perfectly still, assessing the weak boy with a calculating gaze. He knew if he denied his son this child, Malament would seek another. The older man uncrossed his arms, letting out a sigh that betrayed his dejection, as if acknowledging defeat.

"If the boy survives the night, he can stay. But I want no more of this, Malament. If he dies tonight, that shall be the end of it. I won't have these disgusting bastards under my roof. He lives down here, if he survives, and when able, you'll clean the filth from him. I don't want the others catching his diseases. Nurse, leave him now; it seems you've done all you can. The night shall be his own battle."

Saanvi wiped the boy's brow one last time, leaving the damp cloth resting on his forehead. With a moan of discomfort, she lifted herself from the chair, glancing at Malament with a thin, sympathetic smile. Her caring nature had always been a soothing balm, even during his own childhood. "Thank you, Saanvi," Malament replied quietly, though his gaze remained on the boy. He turned to his father, allowing a smile to break through his earlier concern. "Thank you, Father."

But Malum's eyes hardened, catching both Saanvi's smile and his son's, which ignited his ire. "If I catch him stealing like the last little bastard you brought into my home, I will personally cut off his hand and ram it down his throat." His voice was a bark, each word heavy with authority and menace, echoing in the small room.

A tense silence followed, the weight of Malum's anger thick in the air, before he turned sharply and stormed out, his footsteps crashing against the stone floor, leaving a trail of curses in his wake. Malament and Saanvi exchanged glances, the tension dissipating with the Lord's departure.

Once calm returned, an unspoken understanding passed between them that the tension had dissipated. Malament turned his attention back to the almost lifeless figure on the bed, his heart racing with a mix of hope and anxiety. The boy would survive the night, he was sure of it. Once recovered, he would teach him their ways, treating him as an equal, and in return, he hoped for unwavering loyalty.

Saanvi broke the silence, her voice a soothing balm. "Don't you worry, sir; I have a feeling he will be just fine. Living in those back alleys is no small task, especially for one so young. I'm going to set off to bed now. I'll check on him at first light tomorrow. Can I leave you to lock up his room, sir?" The nurse smiled at him, though her stained yellow teeth contrasted with the warmth in her eyes. Malament nodded in her direction, grateful for her reassuring presence.

After Saanvi departed, her footsteps retreating gently down the corridor, he felt the weight of solitude envelop him. Now alone with the fragile boy, he leaned closer, speaking softly as if the child could hear his every word. "Do not fear, child, for your body shall heal and your spirit mend. You will be looked after here, and once recovered, you will be taught well and trained hard. Together, we will achieve great deeds, you and I. Rest now and recover your strength; you will need it."

He paused, studying the boy's still face, pondering the horrors that had haunted him and when he might awaken. Malament felt again the surge of determination. This time would be different. He would not fail in his attempt to forge a bond, to build a life together.

Collecting the small lantern, he walked backward out of the room, pulling the door tightly shut behind him. Outside, he turned the key with a loud crunch, locking the boy into the darkness. But within him, a flicker of hope ignited; the boy's survival could mean the beginning of something new, a chance at the companionship he had long sought.

# THE ORPHAN
# CHAPTER THREE

Auron's sleep was restless, a fever-induced haze twisting his dreams into a nightmarish landscape. In his mind, he soared over vast forests, their treetops dancing like emerald waves beneath a gusty wind. Towering mountains cloaked in snow loomed ahead, their peaks glistening under a pale moonlight. He wove between these titanic structures, exhilarated by the freedom that seemed so far removed from his waking life.

But as the grandeur of the mountain range began to unfold, it gave way to sprawling plains of cracked, dry earth, the thrill of flight replaced by a suffocating sense of despair. With a graceful dive, he swept down the mountainside, gathering speed as the ground rushed up to meet him, hovering mere inches above the parched soil before ascending again, leaving a swirling cloud of dust in his wake-a fleeting moment of escape from the reality that awaited him.

Suddenly, the scenery shifted violently, and he found himself gliding over a tremendous river winding through a deep gorge. The exhilaration of freedom drained away, replaced by a suffocating sense of unease. The river's dark waters churned below, their surface reflecting fleeting glimpses of the moonlight. Auron hovered above its banks, his movements slower now, as if the very air around him had thickened, resisting his every motion. A wide bridge emerged in the distance, and on its centre stood a solitary figure. Auron's pulse quickened with recognition. The man was tall and muscular, clad in glistening black steel armour trimmed in platinum silver, perfectly moulded to his powerful frame. Each hand gripped a black sabre, their tips dripping with blood, the crimson droplets glinting like rubies in the moonlight.

Floating above the scene, Auron's heart sank as he gazed upon the stranger's face, feeling a jolt of shock: it was his own, but older, fierce, and imbued with a chilling power he had never known. Then, as if the world were unravelling, a darkness descended. Scattered across the bridge lay piles of human skulls, their empty eye sockets glaring up at him with accusing stares. The skulls began to rattle, the sound building into a dreadful cacophony. It scraped at his mind like nails on stone, each clatter an unrelenting assault on his sanity.

The echo of teeth clattering grew deafening, sending a jolt of panic coursing through him. In desperation, Auron shot up into the night sky, but the skulls surged after him, relentless in their pursuit. Higher and higher he climbed until the sky morphed into a fortress, flanked by towering mountains. The skulls lined the walls like sentinels, watching him with an insatiable hunger. Auron found himself standing atop a second battlement, looming high above the sea of skulls, the fortress stretching endlessly around him.

A massive, bare-chested tribal warrior stepped forward, parting the skulls with a menacing presence. His deep black eyes pierced through the distance, locking onto Auron with a predatory intensity. Auron staggered back, but the stone beneath his feet seemed to betray him, cracking open as shackles erupted from the ground, coiling around his wrists and ankles.

Paralyzed, a tidal wave of skulls ascended toward him, crashing upward in a relentless surge. The clatter of bone grew louder, a sound so consuming it seemed to bleed into his very thoughts. Desperation overtook him, and he closed his eyes, bracing for the inevitable.

He awoke violently, gasping for breath, the remnants of the skulls still haunting him. Panic gripped him as he lay in a cold sweat, the bed beneath him soaked from his feverish body. The reality of his new surroundings began to seep into his consciousness. He struggled to orient himself, a dim light filtering through the crack under the door revealing the contours of a small, barren room-a cell, he realised with dread.

A numbing pain radiated throughout his body, a cruel reminder of his injuries. His face felt as if it were on fire, swollen and tender to the touch. Probing gently with trembling fingers, he winced at the grotesque reality of his wounds. Each shift brought a sharp stab of agony, and he tried to cry out, but only a muffled groan escaped his cracked lips. The weight of his injuries settled heavily on his chest, suffocating him as he struggled to take a breath, each inhalation sending shockwaves of pain through him.

The darkness around him felt alive, wrapping around him like a shroud as the pain surged in relentless waves. Desperation clawed at him, and he succumbed to the overwhelming sensation of nausea. Unable to hold it back, he was violently sick, choking and heaving until tears mingled with the remnants of his torment. The stench of vomit filled the room, and shame washed over him-he was reduced to this, a broken boy in a cell, alone and powerless.

After several long minutes, his suffering eased slightly, and he lay still, taking shallow breaths through his nostrils. Each inhale was a conscious effort, as if he were fighting against a tide that threatened to pull him under. A profound weariness settled over him, a heavy blanket that blurred the edges of his reality. He wondered if this was death-a purgatory of perpetual torment.

Yet, as he felt around the bed with his right hand, the hardness of the mattress and the roughness of the thin blanket beneath him offered a strange comfort. This was no alleyway; he was sheltered, at least. The rough fabric felt foreign yet oddly grounding, a stark contrast to the cold, unforgiving streets where he had often sought refuge.

His fingers brushed against the uneven stone wall beside him, and as he explored, a thin glowing amber line caught his attention. A crack of light seeped through the door, illuminating the gloom and revealing the truth-he was trapped in a cell, confined and vulnerable. Fragments of memory returned, rushing back to him like a tide. The boys racing toward him, their fierce expressions and enraged eyes locked onto his, haunted him. Each face was etched in his mind, a painful reminder of his past, and he promised himself he would not forget them.

Auron realised he had been found, left for dead, and carried off to this prison. The thought filled him with dread; he would need help, someone to rescue him from this nightmare. But without light, he could not assess the severity of his injuries or how long it would take to heal. Fear gripped him as he wondered how he would find food or water.

With a heavy sigh, he tried to push his injuries from his mind, but the pain surged anew, an explosive reminder of his suffering. His head swirled, dizziness enveloping him as a wave of nausea overtook him again. He doubled over, violently expelling the remnants of his torment, the bed becoming a foul, soaking mess. The shame of his situation crashed over him like a tidal wave. In that moment, he felt utterly defeated, swallowed by the darkness.

As the pain reached its peak, Auron succumbed once more to oblivion, drifting into unconsciousness, the world around him fading into an abyss where nightmares and reality entwined, leaving him adrift in a sea of despair.

# THE ORPHAN
# CHAPTER FOUR

Saanvi awoke early, as she often did, with the stately home still shrouded in night's last whispers. She savoured the cool quiet, the faint scent of lingering wood smoke drifting down the hallways, and the soft murmurs of the other early-rising servants. It was her favourite time: none of the household's family were yet awake, leaving the servants free from sharp demands or hurried commands. Here, among familiar faces —or occasionally, a new one quietly slipping away after an overnight rendezvous—the house felt like a world of its own. The morning after a party brought a different charm, with half-dressed nobles and servants alike weaving their way through the estate in various states of disarray.

Today, however, was quiet and predictable. She had a particular task and found herself in the sprawling manor kitchen, helping Quinn, the house cook, finish the morning's porridge. The kitchen itself was impressive, lined with towering cupboards and long counters, with a clay oven at its heart, its cast-iron door waiting cool and untouched for the day's grander meals. It sat dormant now—porridge needed no such fire—but later, it would roar with heat for roasting meats or baking the breads essential for Lord Malum's frequent banquets.

When the porridge was ready, other maids prepared the bowls and cutlery for the still-slumbering household. Saanvi spooned a portion into a wooden bowl, filled a small clay mug with water, and set both carefully on a brass tray. She slipped into the wide corridor, the marble floors underfoot glistening even in the faint morning light. Portraits lined the walls—former lords of Kadun, each portrayed with painstaking grandeur. As she passed Lord Malum's likeness, she found herself lingering. Painted only a few years prior, the artist had granted him broader shoulders, softened his sharper features. She imagined how many others in these portraits wore similarly adjusted faces, idealised versions framed for public admiration. Did anyone look past them, she wondered, or were they content with these carefully curated masks?

Further down, she passed the grand dining hall, capable of seating over a hundred guests. Malum hosted senators, diplomats, and, come summer, would welcome the merchants of Nordon to its tables. She imagined the opulence layered into those future banquets, the endless stream of strangers drifting in and out of these walls. Finally, the hallway broadened into the ground-floor reception area, with its towering pillars and sweeping staircase leading to the upper floors. It was a breathtaking space, fitted with every luxury befitting the custodian of East Kadun.

As Saanvi crossed the open floor, dawn began to spill over Borlong, casting the first light into the silent hall. She carried the tray carefully, her footsteps echoing softly as she reached the plain wooden door leading to the slave quarters.

As Saanvi approached, the muffled clamour of activity beyond the door grew louder: the bustling voices of maids, cleaners, gardeners, and other household staff preparing for their daily duties. She waited patiently; hearing footsteps clamber up the narrow staircase. The heavy wooden door swung open to reveal Cora, a young and striking maid with an effortless grace. Still in her teens, Cora had a slim, delicate frame made more noticeable by her slightly snug uniform. Her bronzed skin, inherited from her Drylands-born father, complemented her dark, cascading hair and warm brown eyes.

Cora seemed unaware of the attention she drew, returning Saanvi's smile with innocent enthusiasm as she passed and hurried off across the reception hall, her footsteps trailing up the grand stairwell. Saanvi watched her go, then descended the staircase herself, carefully balancing the brass tray. The corridor below was a hive of early morning activity, and she wove her way through the bustling servants, sidestepping their flurry as they passed. Finally, she reached the narrow door to the small boy's room.

Setting the tray on the floor, she pulled a key from her pocket and slid it into the lock, which turned with a solid clunk. As the door cracked open, a sour smell of stale vomit and other fouler odours wafted out, and she paused, her stomach recoiling. Bracing herself, she took a deep breath, retrieved the tray, and nudged the door fully open, letting it swing inward with a soft groan.

Torchlight seeped into the dim room, casting an eerie glow over the small figure curled in bed. The boy's bruised face was swollen nearly beyond recognition, his once-soft features now a mosaic of cuts and mottled purple bruises. A faint groan escaped his cracked, swollen lips—a sound that twisted her heart with relief and sorrow. He had survived the night, but only just.

Stepping closer, Saanvi took in the extent of his injuries. His eyes were puffy slits, almost like a newborn's barely able to open. His mouth was raw and split, a dark line of dried blood crusting over the wound on his upper lip. The pillow beneath his head was soaked with dried blood, and the bed linens surrounding him were marred with patches of vomit and bile. She noticed, too, that he had soiled himself in his fevered state, adding another layer to the room's suffocating odour.

Her heart ached for the boy. He had endured a brutal night, but if he could hold on, perhaps the worst was behind him.

"Good morning to you, young man," Saanvi greeted gently, studying his bruised and battered form. "You have the look—and smell—of death about you, but I'm pleased to see you still among us. I've brought some porridge and water, and you're going to finish them. It may end up on the bed with the rest, but you'll eat it nonetheless." She set the brass tray on a nearby chair, glancing at the foul contents of the bucket beside his bed. "We can't keep this in here any longer. Dear, oh dear, that would be the end of you. I'll empty it now, and when I'm back, we'll sit you up."

She lifted the bucket, leaving him alone once again. Auron had been awake for some time, listening to the sounds of the household outside his door—the voices and hurried footsteps echoing down the hall, the distant clangs of dishes and clatter of shoes. He could barely open his eyes, each attempt met with a blurred, slanted vision through swollen eyelids. The light from the open door had been blinding, stinging even behind closed eyes, and Saanvi's voice, though kind, had sent sharp pulses of pain through his head. He had retreated beneath the thin blanket, hoping to shield himself from both the light and sound. Everything hurt —his body, his ears, even the faintest of movements. If only he could fall back into sleep, he thought, and slip away from the agony.

In the washroom, Saanvi emptied the bucket, rinsing it out before filling it with fresh water. She grabbed a small cloth, determined to give the boy some comfort with a proper cleaning once he had eaten. Returning to the cramped room, she set the bucket aside, then took up the brass tray and sat down in the chair beside the bed. "Come now, hiding under that blanket won't do," she coaxed. "Sit up."

Auron responded with a muffled groan, and she sighed, setting the tray down. "Alright, then—I'll help." With gentle hands, she lifted him from under his thin arms, pulling him into a sitting position. He cried out in pain, and she steadied him. "There now, you're alive to feel it, and that's something. If it weren't for the young lord of this house, you'd be nothing but gutter scraps." She raised the cup to his lips. "Drink."

Auron tried to swallow, but his throat seized painfully, and water dribbled down his chin, stinging his split lip. Embarrassment flickered in his foggy mind, and he forced himself to try again, swallowing down the fresh, cool liquid. The taste was surprisingly pure, reviving him slightly, and he took another sip.

"That's better," she murmured approvingly. "You've got a bit of spirit yet. Now, some porridge, made by yours truly, so I expect you to eat it all." She scooped up a small spoonful, easing it past his lips. The initial sting subsided, and he managed to swallow, his hunger overriding the pain.

When he had finished, she set the empty bowl and mug aside and turned back to him, her expression softening. "Now, child, let me introduce myself and explain a few things. I am Saanvi, and you're in the house of Lord Malum Thalron. Not just the Lord of Borlong, mind you, but the whole eastern Kadun region. You'll meet him formally when you're better, but until then, I'll care for you. I serve as head maid here and, as it happens, the unofficial nurse. I don't know what future the lord's son, Malament, has in mind for you, but you're lucky he rescued you. You owe him your life, and don't you forget that."

She paused, considering the boy's pitiful state. His body bore signs of brutal abuse—his arm, jaw, and several ribs broken, his face and legs covered in bruises, and a deep gash on his head. "Now," she continued, "about yourself. You've taken some serious injuries that will take months to heal. A cleaning is necessary to keep you from catching a fever, painful though it may be."

Gathering the tray, Saanvi rose and headed back out to the hallway. "I'll return shortly. Once things quiet down, we'll have the washroom to ourselves. Hold tight, young man." And with a final glance, she disappeared into the corridor beyond, leaving him in the muted silence of the dim room.

Auron was once more left alone in the small room, though this time the door remained ajar, allowing him a glimpse of the bustling hall beyond. Through blurred vision, he saw shapes and shadows flitting past, servants rushing through their morning tasks. Saanvi, Lord Malum, Malament—their names echoed faintly in his mind, though most of what she had said was lost to the dull ringing in his ears. She had mentioned something about a cleaning ordeal he would have to endure, yet he could not focus on it. But the food had settled warmly in his stomach, and he felt a touch stronger, even if his body still ached.

He listened to the faint, rhythmic hum of the servants at work, their voices and footsteps weaving together into a gentle lullaby. As he let himself sink into that sound, his mind began to drift, easing him back into a deep, dreamless sleep.

When he awoke, a tall figure stood at his bedside, watching him intently. As Auron's eyes adjusted, he saw a young man with striking blue eyes and shoulder-length blond hair, softly illuminated by torchlight. The man wore an emerald-green robe that draped elegantly to the floor, and his expression was gentle, his mouth lifting in a slight, reassuring smile.

Blinking to clear his vision, Auron slowly took in his surroundings. The dim room was now filled with a soft glow, a lavender-scented candle on the bedside table masking the staleness in the air. The bed beneath him felt unexpectedly soft, the blanket warm and clean. His fingers, brushing against the sheet, felt different somehow—smooth, no longer gritty and sore. Surprised, he looked down at his hands, pulling them into the candlelight. His skin was fair, clean, and soft, his nails free of dirt and broken edges. Tentatively, he brought a hand to his face, feeling where his wounds had been. The swelling had receded, his lips were no longer split, and his face—though still tender—was almost unrecognisable.

The young man beside him, noticing Auron's wonderment, smiled again. "I am Malament. How are you feeling, child?" His voice was gentle, warm with a kindness that soothed Auron's bewildered mind.

"I... I think I'm okay," Auron replied, his voice tentative but tinged with excitement at his newfound health.

Malament's smile deepened. "Think, or know? In this household, certainty is valued, lessons for another time, of course." He seemed to assess Auron, nodding slightly. "You've been asleep for nearly eight days. That rest has been essential to your healing, and Saanvi has tended to you daily. Remarkably, you've recovered at a speed that surprises even us, though you've eaten very little. Now, tell me—what is your name?"

Still dazed, Auron murmured, "Auron."

Malament's eyes lit with amusement. "Auron—well met! That's a fine name, strong. And you've answered me with more conviction already—quick learning will serve you well here, child." His eyes twinkled with a hint of mystery. "Now, Auron, how about a trip to the kitchens to properly fill that stomach?"

Auron nodded, a flicker of eagerness giving him the strength to sit up unaided, though he still felt weak. Malament reached out a hand, and Auron grasped it gratefully, allowing him to help him stand. His bare feet met the cold stone floor, and a shiver ran through him, but it was a welcome sensation—a reminder that he was alive. Malament handed him a light blue tunic, which he slipped over his head, and then a pair of simple sandals that felt strange but comforting on his feet.

Malament looked him over with an approving nod, observing how the grime and tangled hair were gone, his face and skin now clean and refreshed. Auron's once-matted hair was now cropped short, revealing bright turquoise eyes flecked with gold, a detail Malament seemed to note with interest. "Come now, Auron," he said, his voice soft but commanding. "Let me show you your home."

With that, Malament turned toward the doorway, a confident presence that Auron found both reassuring and oddly imposing. As he followed, each step brought a mixture of nerves and excitement—he was no longer the child of the streets, and here, within Lord Malum's house, something new awaited him.

# THE ORPHAN
# CHATPER FIVE

The door groaned as it closed behind the pair, Auron looked about him, a corridor that stretched on, dimly lit by a handful of sputtering oil lamps mounted unevenly along the walls. Shadows clung to the corners, thickening the gloom, and the faint scent of stale air and damp wood hung in the narrow space that lacked the lavender disguise his room embellished. The walls were rough stone, worn down by the years and marked by faint scratches, as if they held stories of their own.

Rough, splintered wooden doors lined both sides of the corridor, spaced tightly, each one leading to small, spartan rooms. Near the end of the corridor was a cramped washroom, the damp air thick with mildew and the scent of stale water. A sunken, stone bath lay in the centre, surrounded by cracked and mouldy tiles. The water inside was murky green, its surface disturbed only by the ripples of water droplets falling from a leaky ceiling above. Dim, wavering light reflected off the water, casting twisted shadows onto the walls. Despite the starkness and disrepair, Auron found himself thankful. Compared to what he had known, this place, bleak as it was, offered warmth and safety—two luxuries he could not take for granted.

Malament led the pair through and just as they prepared to leave, Saanvi, the head serving maid, appeared at the end of the corridor. Her presence was a comfort to Auron against the cold atmosphere, her voice warm and gentle as she approached with a welcoming smile. She placed a light hand on his small shoulder, and he felt the steadiness in her touch, grounding him in a way he had not expected.

"I was worried, you know," Saanvi murmured, her eyes softening as they searched his face. "You were in rough shape when they brought you here, but you're tougher than you look."

Auron looked down, his voice almost a whisper. "Thank you... I don't remember."

A faint smile touched Saanvi's lips as she squeezed his shoulder. "Well, it's my job, after all. But if you need anything, come find me, alright?"

Her sincerity struck him, and an odd warmth rose in his chest—something unfamiliar yet welcome. In her presence, he felt more than just cared for; he felt seen, and it was a feeling he realised he had not known he'd missed.

They soon moved out of the dim quarters and into the grand entrance hall. Auron's breath caught as he stepped into a space unlike anything he had ever imagined. Towering stone columns stretched from the gleaming white marble floor to the high vaulted ceiling, each carved with images of past lords and warriors in relief, their faces captured in expressions of fierce pride and quiet dignity. The marble beneath his feet was polished to a mirror shine, so pristine he could see his own reflection faintly staring back, wide-eyed with awe.

Above, chandeliers hung like luminous constellations, dripping with sparkling crystals that caught and scattered the sunlight streaming in from the high, arched windows. The windows themselves were framed with delicate wrought-iron designs, casting intricate patterns of shadow that danced across the hall as the light shifted. Every detail seemed meticulously crafted, a testament to generations of care and artistry that had shaped this hall into a sanctuary of beauty and power.

Auron whispered, almost to himself, "It's... it's beautiful." His gaze drifted along the walls, lined with vast banners that spoke of East Kadun's history and legacy. Each was a masterpiece, embroidered with the emblems of noble houses and symbols of protection and strength. One, in particular, drew his attention—a crimson banner trimmed in shimmering gold, with the image of a grand tree at its centre, its branches stretching outward as if sheltering all who stood beneath it. Within the emblem, an inscription read:

*'Beneath the tree, hearts of the free.'*

Malament noticed his lingering gaze and nodded with quiet pride. "That's the banner of East Kadun," he said, his voice carrying a solemn weight. "It's flown over Borlong for centuries—a symbol of our pride, our resilience, and the land's strength."

Auron looked up at Malament, his voice a murmur. "It feels... almost like it's watching over us."

Malament's expression softened. "In a way, it is. That banner has witnessed generations. Each thread, each stitch is a reminder of what East Kadun stands for. Our people, our history—all woven into that fabric." He paused, holding Auron's attention. "Remember it well, Auron. This house, this land, it stands for a great deal. And now, you're part of that."

Auron swallowed, feeling the weight of those words. "But..."

Malament placed a steady hand on Auron's shoulder, a rare warmth in his gaze. "You're just a boy from nowhere? Every legacy begins somewhere, with someone who feels small. But if you give yourself to this place, serve it with loyalty, it will shape you as much as you shape it. Remember, the smallest branch is still a part of the tree."

Auron looked back at the banner, the image of the grand tree now resonating within him. A sense of purpose stirred, fragile but growing, rooting itself in the vastness of the hall and the weight of Malament's words.

They continued into the kitchen, and Auron felt as if he had crossed into a different world entirely. The aroma hit him first—a mouthwatering blend of roasting meats, fresh-baked bread, and the earthy spice of herbs. The air was thick with warmth and the sound of crackling fires from the massive stone ovens that lined the far wall. Each oven held rows of meats turning slowly on spits, their juices sizzling as they dripped onto hot coals below, casting a flickering glow across the bustling space.

Dark wooden counters, carved from sturdy timber had worn smooth from years of use, were strewn with a dazzling array of spices, herbs, and jars filled with preserved vegetables. The counters were a kaleidoscope of colours—deep reds of paprika, bright yellows of turmeric, and the earthy greens of basil and rosemary leaves. Above them, brass pots and pans hung from hooks, polished to a dull gleam and clanging lightly as they swung when someone brushed past. The kitchen was alive with movement, as staff members bustled from counter to counter with swift, practised precision, their arms laden with trays, baskets, and steaming pots.

"Ah, so you're the new one!" a booming voice cut through the noise. Auron turned to see a short, round man with a thick cinnamon-coloured beard that framed his face like a mane. He wore a stained apron over his ample belly, which jiggled as he laughed. Quinn wiped his flour-dusted hands on his apron and gave Auron a broad grin. "Hungry, lad?"

Auron's stomach gave a rumble that was answer enough, but he nodded, suddenly feeling a bit self-conscious under Quinn's hearty gaze. "Yes, sir."

"Sir? Ha!" Quinn's laughter filled the kitchen, drawing a few smiles from the other cooks. "I'm no 'sir,' just plain old Quinn." With a flick of his wrist, he cracked a few eggs into a bowl, his movements so swift and practised that Auron barely saw his hands move. He added a pinch of chopped herbs and a sprinkle of ground pepper, whipping the mixture into a golden froth. "One omelette, coming right up. Just a taste of what we do here."

As the eggs sizzled in the pan, Quinn leaned closer, his eyes twinkling. "You see, lad, cooking's more than just food. It's about bringing people together, giving them something to hold onto, something that says 'home.' You understand?"

Auron nodded, feeling a warmth rise in his chest. "I… I think I do."

Moments later, Quinn slid a plate toward him, a fluffy omelette browned to perfection, flecked with green herbs. Auron took a bite, and his eyes widened—the flavours were rich, savoury, with a hint of something warm and spicy that lingered pleasantly on his tongue. "It's incredible!" he said between bites, unable to stop himself from grinning.

Quinn chuckled, clearly pleased. "Good, eh? You've got a good palate, boy. Stick around, and I might just teach you a trick or two. No scullery maid's work for you—you've got promise."

Auron's face lit up with a mixture of pride and surprise. "Really? I'd like that."

Quinn let out a hearty laugh and ruffled Auron's cropped hair with a floury hand. "Good lad! But mind you, no lateness in my kitchen, you'd have to be on time." He gave Auron a mock-serious look, then winked. "Now go on, finish up before the others eat everything in sight."

As Auron savoured the last bite, he realised something—a sense of belonging was settling over him, something he had not felt in as long as he could remember.

After breakfast, Malament led Auron down a narrow stone staircase, and they entered the cool, dim cellar. The air was dense with the scents of aged wood, mingling with a faint, earthy mustiness that seemed to seep from the walls themselves. Rows of shelves lined the long, vaulted room, each filled with dark oak casks marked with careful chalk labels. The names and dates, written in looping script, hinted at histories and vintages older than anything Auron could imagine. In the corners, nestled among the barrels, sat exotic bottles from distant lands, some with dust so thick that their labels were barely legible, while others sparkled faintly in the low, golden light.

Malament nodded toward a particularly large cask resting in the shadows. "Lord Malum has a taste for the finer things," he explained, a hint of reverence in his tone. "Some of these wines were laid down by his father—and some even by his grandfather. They're older than both of us put together, kept safe down here where time moves a little slower."

Auron reached out to brush his fingers along the rough grain of one of the barrels, feeling the history embedded in its wood.

Malament smiled, nodding approvingly. "In a way, every bottle, every barrel tells a story of seasons past, of the land and the people who tend it." He looked at Auron, his eyes serious. "One day, if you prove yourself trustworthy and careful, you might be given the honour of bringing a bottle to the lord's table. But that's a responsibility earned, not given."

Auron nodded, the weight of Malament's words settling on him like a solemn promise. "I'll do my best."

Malament patted his shoulder. "Good lad. Now, let's get you some fresh air."

They exited the cellar, stepping into the sunlight that bathed the estate's garden in a gentle glow. The garden stretched before them—a vast greenery framed by ivy-covered stone walls that rose like a living fortress around them. The grass was thick and a deep, vibrant green, like the sea of emeralds shimmering in the sunlight. The air was heady with the scents of roses, lavender, and lilies, each blossom adding its unique fragrance to the symphony of aromas. Stone paths wound through perfectly trimmed hedges, leading to statues and ornamental fountains that lent the garden a sense of both artistry and quiet grandeur.

Auron's eyes widened as he took in the scene, his voice barely a whisper. "Uh… this, this is yours?"

Malament chuckled softly. "It's one of the finest gardens in all of Kadun. Every corner, every path, each flower—it all has its place. The garden is like the house: orderly, intentional." He pointed to a fountain nearby, where water trickled gently over a carved marble figure of a woman holding a flowering branch. "That fountain was carved by my grandfather's hand. He left it here as a gift to the garden, something to be remembered by. Each generation leaves something behind."

Auron reached out to touch a broad leaf, his fingers grazing the smooth surface as if trying to hold onto the moment. "It's like... it's like a dream."

Malament's face softened as he watched Auron's wonder. "Remember this feeling. The beauty, the peace—it's here to remind us of why we do what we do. Serving this house, protecting it, means we're part of something greater than ourselves."

Auron looked up, meeting Malament's gaze, a glimmer of understanding dawning in his eyes. "I think I'd like to leave something here one day, too."

Malament's smile was approving. "Perhaps you will." He clapped Auron gently on the shoulder. "Now, come on. There's still more to see, and the estate is full of secrets waiting for someone like you to discover."

They finally reached the stable, nestled at the far end of the garden. Auron's pulse quickened as he spotted five black horses grazing within a fenced paddock, their sleek coats shimmering like polished onyx under the afternoon sun. Each horse was a picture of power and grace, muscles rippling beneath their glossy fur with every flick of their tails. The three mares grazed in a loose cluster; their heads low as they nibbled the grass. Close beside one of them stood a young foal, its legs long and spindly, but instinctively alert and curious. Nearby, a powerful stallion kept watch, his posture protective, eyes sharp and almost calculating as they took in his surroundings.

The stable itself was modest in size but immaculate. The wooden walls were weathered but sturdy, lined with neat stacks of hay and an array of well-used tools. Polished leather saddles hung from hooks along one wall, their dark leather gleaming in the light that filtered through the stable door. The air was rich with the scent of hay, leather, and the faint musk of the horses.

"This little one has no name yet," Malament said, nodding toward the foal with a rare softness in his voice. "What do you think, Auron?"

Auron took a moment to study the foal, watching how it stayed close to its mother, its large, dark eyes reflecting an innocent trust and wonder at the world. Finally, he said, "Malaron." He smiled, feeling a faint sense of pride in the name, a blend of both his and Malament's names.

Malament's smile was warm and approving. "Malaron it is, then. Take good care of him. He's gentle now, but he'll grow strong if given the right hand."

Just then, an older man emerged from the stable's dim interior. His face was heavily lined, his skin weathered by years in the sun and wind, and his mouth was set in a thin, bitter line. He had a wiry frame, his movements slow but purposeful. His eyes, small and shrewd, settled on Auron with piercing eyes that held both calculation and a flicker of disdain.

"So, this is the boy, eh?" His voice was rough, a deep rasp that seemed to echo the hardness of his expression. The corners of his mouth twisted as he looked Auron up and down. "We'll see if he's fit for the work."

Malament's tone hardened slightly, a subtle warning in his gaze as he addressed the stable master. "Regal, Auron will be learning under you. I trust you'll give him proper guidance."

Regal nodded, but there was a stiffness to the movement. His gaze never softened, and his eyes lingered on Auron as though already measuring his weaknesses. "If he doesn't mind dirt and hard labour," Regal muttered, his lips barely moving, "then we'll get along fine."

Auron felt the unspoken challenge behind Regal's words, the doubt and scepticism that lingered like a weight in the air. He squared his shoulders, meeting the older man's glare without flinching. "I won't disappoint," he said quietly, his voice steady but resolute.

Regal's thin smile did not reach his eyes, but he gave a curt nod. "We'll see, lad," he replied. "The horses don't care for idle talk—they'll show you quick enough if you're up to the task."

Malament clapped Auron lightly on the back. "Then it's settled. I expect you'll work hard here, Auron. And remember, the horses trust those who earn it."

As Malament walked away, Auron glanced back at the paddock, where Malaron was nudging against his mother's side, curious and unafraid. A sense of determination sparked in him—he would earn the foal's trust and prove himself, not only to Regal but to Malament and, perhaps most of all, to himself.

They spent a little longer in the garden, meandering through the lush paths as Malament pointed out various landmarks and statues. Eventually, they returned to the grand hall and from there the training area. Auron's steps slowed as they entered, his eyes widening as he took in the sheer scope of the room. It was a vast, square chamber, its high ceilings supported by tall stone columns that framed the walls. Each column bore intricate carvings of Kadun's storied past: fierce warriors locked in eternal battle, swords and shields raised high, captured with such detail that even the folds in their armour and the fire in their eyes seemed to breathe with life.

Auron moved closer to one of the pillars, running his fingers lightly over the cold stone. The face of one warrior, etched with expression of courage and resolve, seemed to watch him, silently measuring his worth.

"That man was Malcon, my uncle," Malament interjected with a pause of thought that followed afterwards, how could two brothers be so different, he pondered. "He fought, bled and eventually gave his life at the Reach." He paused again letting Auron and himself take in the craftsmanship, the features of the man. "And so led to my father's reign" snapping both out the trance.

Auron left the figure, till they would next meet taking in the rest of his surroundings. Along the walls, polished armour sets gleamed in the low torchlight—plate vests, leather tunics, and helmets shaped to resemble the heads of wolves, eagles, and bears. They looked both beautiful and menacing, as if waiting for worthy soldiers to don them.

Wooden racks lined the back wall of the hall, holding an assortment of weapons: swords with narrow, gleaming blades; spears tipped with steel points; and daggers, their edges honed to a deadly sharpness. Each weapon caught the flickering torchlight, casting slender shadows across the stone floor and central fight pit.

Malament gestured to a sword resting on a nearby rack. "One day, you'll wield one of these," he said, his tone low but encouraging. "But strength takes patience, Auron. Mastery is a slow journey, one that demands focus and respect for the craft. You'll learn, bit by bit, as all great warriors do."

Auron's eyes lingered on the sword's hilt, his fingers itching to wrap around it. He could almost feel the weight of it in his hands, the balance of the blade and the power that lay within its edge. "I'll do my best," he said, a determined glint in his eyes.

Malament's gaze softened, and he gave a small nod of approval. "I know you will. A strong heart and a keen mind will take you further than any blade."

After their tour of the hall, they made their way back to the kitchen, where a simple meal awaited them. They shared a block of cheese, some bread, and a couple of apples, sitting on wooden stools near the warm glow of the kitchen's hearth. The meal was modest, but to Auron, it felt like a feast after the long morning. Between bites, Malament spoke, his tone gentle yet steady as he laid out the steps of Auron's new life within the lord's house.

"You'll have a few days to rest," he began, watching Auron closely. "Use that time to get to know the estate, to become comfortable in your surroundings. There's no rush yet—you'll find your place here."

Auron nodded, feeling a mixture of excitement and nerves. "I'll make the most of it. I want to know every part, every person."

Malament chuckled softly, his eyes warm. "That's a good start, but don't try to learn it all at once. Focus on the small tasks. Regal, the stable, the horses—they're a part of your world now. Once you're ready, you'll learn more."

Auron took a breath, grounding himself in the reality of his new life. "I'm ready to work, I'll earn my place."

Malament's expression grew thoughtful as he looked at Auron, a trace of pride in his gaze. "I believe you will," he said quietly. "This house stands for something great, and it needs those who will honour it. You have that in you, Auron. Just don't forget—patience and respect are as important as strength. With them, you'll do well here."

# THE ORPHAN
# CHAPTER SIX

It had been a few hours since Malament had left Auron back at his room, yet he lay stretched flat on his back, his small frame sinking into the thin mattress as though he had been pinned there. Every bruise and scrape pulsed faintly, a reminder of the day's intensity. His body yearned for sleep, but his mind spun, replaying fragments of excitement and fear with relentless energy. The thrill lingered in his veins; an insistent rhythm that kept his eyes wide open.

Finally, with a slow exhale, Auron forced himself upright, feeling the cool night air coil around his chest like an icy hand. Goosebumps prickled his skin, a tingling response that stole what little warmth he had. He slid his legs over the side of the bed, stopping just above the cold stone floor, hovering in hesitation. The memory of the chill bit at him, but he lowered his feet anyway. The stone was unyielding, drawing heat from him in an instant, sending a shiver up his legs as he balanced himself on the edge.

He reached across to the worn, pale blue tunic on his bedside table, lifting it carefully over his head. It caught on his left arm, still encased in its cask, and he winced as he adjusted it, his movements careful and slow. Once settled, he took a tentative step onto the floor. The cold climbed up through his soles, bracing and sharp, but it also woke him, snapping his senses into clarity. Despite his aches, he felt invigorated, his pain briefly retreating into the background.

The room was cloaked in shadows, broken only by the last sputtering flickers of a candle on the table. In the dim light, the space seemed smaller, the walls pressing in as though they meant to trap him there. A faint, metallic tang from the candle's wick filled his nostrils as he breathed deeply, grounding himself in the moment.

His room held only the bare essentials. A narrow, straw-filled mattress rested atop a low wooden frame, the blanket threadbare and scratchy. Beside it, a single stool wobbled on uneven legs, and a cracked, cloudy mirror hung lopsided on the wall. Even the dim light seemed reluctant to settle here, casting only a thin glow over the space. He looked toward the door, uncertain why he felt so restless, only that the urge to leave his quarters was a whisper too loud to ignore.

He crept to the door, fingers hovering above the cold iron handle. Would it be locked? Tentatively, he pressed down, feeling the latch resist, then yield with a low groan. Startled, he released it, the lock snapping back into place with a loud crunch that reverberated through the quiet. His heart pounded in response, a quick, desperate thud, as if it feared someone might already be approaching, furious with him for daring to touch the door.

The fear washed over him, swift and unbidden, as he remembered Malament's firm warning: he was not to leave his room, not after being sent to bed. But now, a wild curiosity tugged at him, bolder than his caution. He gripped the handle once more, feeling the faint tremor in his fingers as he applied gentle pressure. The latch groaned as he eased it down, a complaint that echoed through the silence. Pulling the door toward him, he watched the frame shift, each creak amplifying his sense of trespass, like an ancient creature stirring awake.

For a moment, he froze, breath catching, and held himself as still as the stone walls around him. The silence expanded, taut with tension as he waited, expecting the sound of footsteps, a shout, or worse. His body tensed, torn between the urge to run back to his bed and the defiance of staying. But as the echoes faded, the corridor beyond remained still.

He exhaled, his heart rate easing just enough for his senses to return. Through the thin opening, he caught sight of the hallway beyond, cloaked in shadows with faint torchlight casting flickering patches of orange. The empty wash area stood at the far end, dim and unwelcoming, its basin cold and untouched, like a sleeping beast.

Auron inhaled deeply, the scent of wax and smoke grounding him as he listened to the hushed stillness. The quiet reawakened his curiosity. Slowly, he glanced back at his bed, where he had been safe and warm just minutes before. It looked inviting, almost calling him back, but it no longer felt like a refuge. He did not want to return.

With one last controlled breath, he slipped through the narrow opening, easing himself into the corridor. The door creaked in one last protest, but Auron was already gone, swallowed by the shadows, his pulse quickening as he ventured into the unknown.

Outside his room, Auron pressed himself against the doorframe, stretching his lean body along the wood, hoping to disappear into the shadows of the corridor walls. With a cautious grip, he eased the door nearly shut, leaving the latch to rest against the frame, appearing closed but ready to slip back inside if needed. His heart pounded as he scanned the corridor for the first time, a creeping fear stirring inside him. He let the feeling settle, grounding himself in a tentative curiosity that steadied his breath.

The usual warm, stale air hung beyond his door and slivers of light spilled through cracks in nearby doors, revealing amber flames flickering within. Steadying himself, he edged away from his door, pressing against the cool, damp stone of the wall. Moving carefully, he inched along like a shadow, sliding from one doorway's shelter to the next. The glow of torches above danced across the stone floor, his shadow flickering in silent rhythm with each cautious step.

Three doors down, he glimpsed the faint outline of stairs leading up to the grand reception hall above. He quickened his pace, tiptoeing toward the stairs, when a sudden creak shattered the silence behind him. A doorway opened not far down the corridor, and without a second thought, Auron darted into the nearest doorway, squeezing himself into the narrow indentation of the frame. He pressed his thin frame against the cold wall, holding his breath.

Heavy footsteps echoed from behind, growing louder as they shuffled in his direction. Auron watched as a new shadow stretched across the floor, moving toward him. The figure was not stealthy, but each slow, deliberate step suggested caution. He flattened himself further into the doorframe, praying the stranger would pass by without noticing him. The stranger's footsteps drew closer, mere feet away, his shadow stretching long beside Auron's.

To his horror, he heard the faintest rustling sound from the other side of the door he was hiding in front of. An amber glow began seeping through the threshold, and then, as if in dreadful unison, the door handle turned with a grating creak. Panic rooted him in place, and he found himself staring as the door swung open to reveal a slim, naked woman. Her gaze fell on him instantly, sharp and furious. Auron felt the weight of her glare like prey caught by a hawk. His breath caught, his mind froze, and his limbs turned to stone.

As she glared, Auron took an instinctive step backward, but stumbled into the stranger behind him. A rough hand clamped down on his shoulder, the grip painfully tight. He yelped in shock, but the stranger merely threw him to the floor with an annoyed grunt. Auron hit the hard stone with a thud, dazed, but otherwise unhurt. Looking up, he saw the stranger—a tall, broad man—watch him for a brief second, then burst into a quiet chuckle. Without a word, he turned to the woman, embracing her with a fervent kiss, and the two disappeared into the room, the door closing behind them with a dull click.

Silence returned to the corridor, and Auron let out a long, trembling sigh. Moments ago, he had been certain he was about to be caught and punished, but the stranger had barely noticed him. A nervous laugh escaped his lips, a mix of relief and embarrassment. He realised, with some small amusement, that he had been terrified over nothing. He was no one of consequence to them—just a boy sneaking around in the night.

He pushed himself up, dusting off his tunic, now speckled with damp marks from the cold walls and wet stone floor. He glanced down at his left arm, still wrapped tightly with splints and bark, relieved to see it had been spared any damage from his fall. The corridor around him, once filled with ominous shadows, now felt almost peaceful, the flickering flames gentle in their glow.

Emboldened, Auron cast one last look down the dim hall before turning toward the staircase. He felt a renewed sense of freedom, knowing the household did not seem to care about his nighttime wanderings. Taking a steadying breath, he straightened and continued up the stairs, leaving the corridor and his momentary fears behind.

Auron slipped quietly into the grand hall, where the absence of sunlight left the high openings above in shadow. A chill seemed to spill down the towering walls, seeping into the vast space and bringing a fine mist to his breath, which floated briefly before his face. The hall was dimly lit by a handful of flame torches, much like those in the slave quarters, but here they were twice as large and crafted with a refined elegance. The torches cast restless shadows, their flickering light reflecting off polished ornaments and sending glints across the room, adding a sense of mystery to the grand, sombre hall.

He paused beneath a torch fastened high on the wall above the door leading back to the quarters. Its light fell over him, leaving him fully exposed, a lone figure against the shadows. Although the flames did not reach far, anyone glancing in his direction would easily see him beneath this torch's glow. He quickly scanned the hall, his eyes darting over the marble floors and darkened corners. Pockets of the hall lay in complete darkness, leaving him unsure if he was truly alone.

Determined to find cover, he took a final glance at the gleaming ornaments before dashing for a shadowed section of the hall. Despite his attempt to move lightly, each step seemed to echo through the empty space, his sandals slapping against the marble like rain hammering on a tiled roof. He slowed his pace, but the sound continued to rebound off the vast walls until he reached the shelter of a darkened corner, finally able to assess his surroundings.

Now concealed in the shadows, he felt the hall's vastness press down on him, the dim light and pitch-black pockets creating a cavernous emptiness. It was as if he had been plunged into the depths of a dark ocean, with nothing around him but an endless, chilling void. His plan to venture outside his room felt briefly uncertain in the face of the hall's looming silence. Then, just as he steadied himself, a distant banging noise shattered the quiet.

The sound came from the far side of the hall—a rhythmic pounding, each echo startling him anew. It was a familiar sound, reminding him of the clamour of market stalls back near the slums, where traders would slam hammers on tables to attract attention, shouting prices and bargains. Straining to hear, he soon discerned the clash and clamour of what sounded like a struggle in the training area. Intrigued, he crept toward the nearest pillar, pressing himself against its thick, stone surface.

Peeking around the column, he could just make out the training area through a wide archway flanked by two intricately sculpted columns. In the dim glow, he saw two men locked in combat. At first, he could barely believe what he was seeing—two bare-chested figures, their bodies gleaming with sweat, engaged in what appeared to be a sword fight. One of the fighters was a shorter, wiry man who moved with astonishing speed, dodging and parrying every swing with uncanny agility. His opponent, a taller man with wild blonde hair, lashed out repeatedly, his strikes slicing through empty air as his nimble opponent evaded him at every turn.

Auron squinted, his heart catching as he recognized the tall man—it was Malament. A ripple of anxiety surged through him, his gut tightening with helplessness. He could only watch, transfixed, as Malament swung repeatedly, his strikes blocked or sidestepped by the smaller man, who seemed to dance around him with ease. Though he longed to do something, Auron remained frozen, his back pressed against the cold stone, witnessing the battle unfold with a mixture of dread and awe.

Malament sprang backward, shifting his weight onto his right leg as his sandal heel dug deep into the sand, sending a spray of loose grains over his calf as he skidded to a halt. A wooden sword whistled through the air just inches from his exposed midriff, the blade slicing the silence with a sharp hiss. Instinct took over as he steadied his footing, years of gruelling training guiding his movements. He adjusted his stance and launched forward, driving a powerful thrust straight toward his instructor Gordon's midsection, aiming to break through his defence with sheer force.

Gordon, ever the seasoned fighter, anticipated the attack. With a deft sidestep, he evaded the blade and seized Malament's wrist as it passed, using the momentum to pull him slightly off balance. Before Malament could react, Gordon delivered a punishing blow to his exposed ribs. The tip of the wooden blade struck hard, and Malament grimaced as pain shot through his side, knowing the hit would bloom into a vivid bruise by morning.

Gordon released him with a slight shove. "You rush your attacks," he chided, his voice calm but firm. "Patience is as vital in battle as your sword. Without it, you would lie dead."

Malament wiped the sweat from his forehead with the back of his hand, irritation simmering beneath his fatigue. "Not even my father would dare treat me like this."

Gordon allowed himself a wry smile. "Then punish me for my insolence, young lord."

With gritted teeth, Malament swung his sword in a furious arc, the blade cutting through the air toward Gordon's head. But Gordon deftly sidestepped, meeting the strike with a swift parry. "Control, Malament," he instructed, his voice steady even as their weapons clashed. "Harness your anger; let it fuel, not blind you."

Malament's loose hair fell over his eyes, partially obscuring his vision as he struggled to catch his breath. His back was damp with sweat, and a dull ache pulsed in his side where the last blow had landed. His pride was as bruised as his ribs; nearly a decade of intense training, yet he still hadn't managed to land a single solid hit on his tutor. Desperation crept in as he raised his sword overhead, launching a powerful strike aimed squarely at Gordon's head. But once again, Gordon's blade intercepted his, the impact sending a harsh vibration down Malament's arm.

He gritted his teeth against the discomfort and quickly pivoted, attempting a swift, low strike aimed at Gordon's midsection. But Gordon was ready, blocking the attack with ease and pressing him back yet again.

"Again," Gordon urged, his tone both commanding and encouraging. "And this time—think before you strike."

Malament's chest rose and fell with laboured breaths as he steadied his stance, anger and determination smouldering in his eyes. He could feel Gordon watching him intently, waiting, assessing. This was more than just a fight; it was a test, a lesson in restraint and precision. And Malament was determined, bruise or no bruise, to pass it.

The skirmish continued in this relentless rhythm, with Malament delivering heavy, forceful strikes, each one met by a deft block or sidestep from his opponent. The clash of wooden swords echoed through the training area, spilling out into the vastness of the great hall where Auron stood, a lone, slight figure observing the scene with rapt attention.

After a few exchanges, Auron began to understand that this was a training exercise, yet he remained captivated. He could see the difference in their movements—Malament's strikes were powerful but laboured, each thrust and swing seeming to cost him effort. In contrast, Gordon's motions were effortless, fluid, his body shifting with each strike like a dancer evading a partner's advance. Malament appeared almost weighed down by his strength, while Gordon wielded his own skill with lightness and precision.

As the bout paused, the two fighters took a step back, giving Auron a better look. Malament was doubled over, his hands braced on his knees, breath coming in laboured gasps. Gordon, however, stood upright and calm, explaining something with a few brisk gestures, demonstrating subtle techniques in contrast to Malament's forceful style.

As Gordon spoke, his gaze drifted momentarily toward the darkness where Auron hid. His words trailed off, his expression sharpening, and suddenly, he snapped his sword up, pointing it directly toward Auron.

Malament's head jerked up at once, twisting to see what had caught Gordon's attention. Auron felt his breath hitch, his heart pounding as both men stared toward his shadowed hiding spot. Without a second thought, he ducked back behind the pillar, pressing himself against the cold stone, his mind racing. He strained to hear their voices, wondering if they would pursue him or let him be.

But waiting had served him poorly in recent encounters, and instinct took flight. He pushed off from the pillar and bolted, darting back into the darkness of the hall, his footsteps muffled against the cold marble as he fled from sight.

# THE ORPHAN
# CHAPTER SEVEN

Several minutes had passed since Auron had sprinted out of sight, and now he found himself leaning heavily against a wall, his breath coming in hard gasps. He had lost his bearings in his desperate flight and now had no idea where he had ended up. The grand ceilings of the reception hall had vanished, replaced by a narrower, almost claustrophobic corridor. He could not remember crossing into this space, and its confined walls and dim lighting made him feel even more disoriented.

Between the faint glow of two small wall torches, Auron tried to regain his composure. The floor was carpeted in a worn beige material, and both ends of the hall led into shadowed, unfamiliar rooms. He strained to recall his wanderings from earlier in the day, but everything had blurred together in his mind. His own room now seemed impossibly far away, and a creeping sense of regret filled him—why had he left the warmth of his bed for this cold, shadowy maze?

As he took a steadying breath, his injuries began to throb anew, and fatigue started to settle over him like a heavy cloak. The weight of the day's events pressed down, and for a moment, he closed his eyes, trying to will away the ache. When he opened them, he noticed an opening halfway down the corridor in front of him—a possible way back, though he couldn't be certain. With a weary sigh, he pushed himself off the wall and moved toward it, his steps echoing softly in the stillness.

As he crossed through the opening, Auron immediately sensed a shift. Unlike the corridor, this room was lofty, with soaring ceilings and large open windows. Moonlight poured in, illuminating the space in a pale, almost ethereal glow. The walls here were unadorned except near the entrance, where faded tapestries hung in solemn rows. In the centre of the room, a long rectangular pool stretched out, perfectly still, reflecting the night sky above. The silvery light played across the water's surface, casting gentle ripples of shadow across the bare stone floor.

Auron paused, entranced by the quiet beauty of the pool. The stark simplicity of the room felt different from the rest of the estate, almost like a hidden sanctuary. He found himself captivated by the way the water mirrored the stars, the cool serenity contrasting sharply with the tension he'd felt just moments before.

Auron soon realised he had stumbled into a bathhouse—a place far more inviting than the wash area in the servants' quarters, though not quite as luxurious as other rooms he'd glimpsed in the estate. To his left, a tall wall stretched up to the ceiling, acting as a screen for a modest changing area. From behind this partition, a soft glow cast warm light onto the floor, and Auron's curiosity stirred. Could this hidden light lead him back to the halls he knew? Or perhaps he had come from here without realising?

As he walked along the edge of the pool, he could not help but be drawn to its stillness. The water lay perfectly level with the floor, so seamless that it was hard to see where the floor ended, and the pool began. The dark room and faint reflections off the water made the surface appear as smooth as polished glass. Auron paused, gazing at the tranquil pool with a sense of quiet awe; it was a striking contrast to the murky memories he held of filthy, puddle-soaked streets.

He knelt by the edge, leaning over to look at his reflection. A young face stared back at him, bright turquoise eyes wide and curious, framed by a cropped cut of dark hair that replaced the matted locks of his past. He smiled, small but proud, and saw how his pale face held patches of bruised skin—markers of recent hardship—but he hardly cared. Tentatively, he dipped a finger into the water, its coolness spreading across his skin like a gentle whisper. The pool responded with gentle ripples that curved outwards, breaking the stillness he had admired, and Auron felt oddly comforted as he watched the disturbance fade away.

He settled beside the pool, letting his weary body rest. His gaze drifted back to the changing area at the far end, where the light from a concealed flame flickered across the floor, casting long shadows that danced up the wall in time with the soft night breeze filtering through the high windows. The quiet rhythm of the firelight soothed him, and as he watched the playful movement of shadows, he felt a deep, unexpected peace settle over him. His eyelids grew heavy, and for the first time since he had left his room, he felt truly safe.

No more than a few seconds had passed when Auron was jolted from his trance by a large shadow sweeping over the wall near the changing area, casting a brief, unsettling darkness across the room. It was quickly followed by strange, rhythmic groans emanating from behind the illuminated space. Instantly alert, Auron bolted upright, the sudden movement creating a small splash as he whipped his hand clear of the pool. The groaning intensified; a sound he could not believe he had overlooked. His curiosity surged, a primal urge to investigate compelling him forward.

Cautiously, he began to creep toward the changing area, each step deliberate and measured. As he drew closer, he could discern that the groans belonged to a man-perhaps middle-aged-but the heavy, laboured breaths of a woman mingled with them, creating a dissonance that both intrigued and unsettled him.

Auron paused just short of the lit area, rooted in place by a mix of dread and fascination. He listened intently, piecing together the scene unfolding behind the wall. This was not the route he had taken earlier; he had sensed that even before he glimpsed the rectangular pool. Auron was a curious child, having not slept beneath a proper roof since he was a babe, and the luxury of the Lord's house was beyond anything he had ever experienced. The bathhouse, with its serene beauty, was a strange allure he could not resist.

Yet he was no stranger to the act of sex. Memories of his mother flooded back-strange men coming and going, their hushed voices rising through the thin walls, the heavy thud of bodies colliding with the scent of sweat and desperation. He had heard whispers of children like him, snatched from the shadows, subjected to unspeakable horrors. The thought sent a chill through him.

But the sounds emanating from behind the wall were different; they were not filled with the pain and terror he had come to know. Instead, they were infused with groans of pleasure and satisfaction, a stark contrast to his memories. Driven by an insatiable need to understand, he felt an inexplicable pull to uncover the truth.

Clutching the edge of the cold, hard wall, he leaned closer, his heart pounding in his chest. Inch by inch, he edged around the corner, drawn by an unseen force, eager yet terrified to uncover what lay beyond.

Revealed along the back wall was a long wooden bench, upon which a thin naked man, his greying hair clung to the spine of his thin back. Rigorously he thrusted his hips into his female companion. She was much younger than her lover, Auron guessed between fifteen and seventeen. Her thick, dark hair cascaded around her shoulders in graceful waves, moving rhythmically in time with their passionate motions. Each undulation caught the light, enhancing the allure of her bronze skin, which glistened with a sheen of perspiration. The warmth of their intimacy enveloped her as she surrendered to the moment, her eyes shut tight in bliss. Her breasts swayed with an unrestrained vitality, responding instinctively to the fervour of their connection, embodying the essence of youth and desire.

The girl lifted her hands to entwine her fingers behind the man's neck, a gesture of intimacy that drew them closer together. Leaning back, she tilted her head, arching her back to fully expose her breasts, inviting his attention. Her partner responded eagerly, leaning in to kiss her neck, igniting a gasp of excitement that escaped her lips.

As she lifted her head, her large brown eyes fluttered open, locking onto her lover with a gaze that sparkled with delight. A satisfied smile played on her lips as she gently bit her lower lip, surrendering to the moment. Her arms draped languidly over the man's shoulders, drawing him into a warm embrace that seemed to encapsulate their shared bliss.

In that vulnerable position, her head rested over his left shoulder, her beautiful eyes scanning the room before unexpectedly landing on Auron. For a heartbeat, time froze as their gazes met, a silent acknowledgment of his unintentional intrusion into their private world.

She squealed in surprise, her voice cutting through the air as she accidentally discovered the hidden child. Startled, Auron leapt back, his heart racing in his chest. In his panic, his feet became tangled, and he stumbled, the world around him blurring as he lost his balance.

As he fell, a sharp pain jolted through his side, radiating up from where he landed awkwardly on his left arm. The pain was intense and immediate, a cruel reminder of his frailty, and a cry escaped his lips, echoing loudly off the bathhouse walls like a warning bell. It reverberated in the silence, a sound that seemed to linger, amplifying his fear and the reality of being caught in such an intimate moment.

A booming voice pierced the air, matching Auron's cry, "YOU ORPHAN BASTARD!" Auron whipped around, desperate to confront the threat, but it was too late. Long, slender fingers closed around his neck, lifting him effortlessly off the ground. The sharp ends of the man's fingernails pressed cruelly into his skin, and panic surged through Auron as the grip tightened, choking off his breath.

He could not see the man's face clearly, but the twisted features were etched with fury, a mask of rage that sent a wave of terror crashing over him. With a brutal yank, the assailant forced him back into the room where the pool glimmered ominously. "You filthy whore's son," the man spat, his voice a venomous hiss. "This is my home, my house. How dare you intrude?"

The weight of the man's words struck Auron harder than the grip on his throat, igniting a sense of shame and fear that coiled tightly in his chest.

Without warning, Auron's head was thrust violently into the water, a powerful hand pressing down mercilessly. The icy grip held him beneath the surface, submerging even his shoulders as he fought against the weight of his own despair. Panic surged through him; he tried to scream, but only a torrent of bubbles escaped his lips, swirling around him like the darkness that enveloped the pool.

Agony shot through his broken left arm, a reminder of his fragile state, but the primal instinct to survive ignited a fierce determination within him. Auron clawed desperately at the man's wrist, his small hands slipping against the slick skin, the grip unwavering. With each passing moment, his body screamed for air, but as he attempted to cry out again, water surged into his mouth, filling his lungs with a suffocating rush.

He fought against the encroaching darkness, his body instinctively trying to cough, but there was no relief- only the relentless weight of the water pressing down on him. Auron felt the world slipping away, the coldness wrapping around him like a shroud as he began to drown, every instinct urging him to break free, to live.

A piercing cry shattered the tense atmosphere, echoing from the entrance of the room: “Father, NO!” Malament's heart raced as he heard the frantic shouts reverberate through the corridors, spurring him into action. Panic propelled him forward, his feet pounding against the floor as he sprinted toward the source of the commotion.

Bursting into the pool room, he was met with a horrific sight: his father loomed over the shimmering water, the small figure of Auron thrashing beneath the surface, desperately fighting for air. The world around Malament blurred, narrowing to the singular focus of the scene before him.

"Let him go!" Malament shouted, his voice thick with urgency and disbelief. The anger and confusion roared within him, igniting a fierce determination to save the boy he had come to care for.

Malament charged at his father, a surge of adrenaline propelling him forward. He hurled himself into Malum, knocking him off balance and forcing him to release his grip on Auron. Time seemed to stretch as the boy floated motionless in the water, a fragile figure against the darkness of the pool.

Without hesitation, Malament plunged his hand into the cool water, his heart racing as he grasped Auron's limp form and heaved him out. "What were you doing, Father? He's just a boy!"

Auron lay still at the edge of the pool, his drenched tunic clinging to his thin frame like a rag left to soak in the rain. Panic tightened around Malament's chest as he frantically checked for signs of life, but the boy was unresponsive—breathless and pale.

Malum, recovering from the collision, glared at Malament with a mix of fury and contempt. "How dare you stop me? He is not a boy! A boy has a father, a mother, a home—a future! He is filth, filth that would rot in my home!"

His words dripped with venom, each syllable a brutal reminder of Auron's tragic reality. Malament's heart raced, the weight of his father's disdain crashing down around him like the icy water still pooling at his feet. He refused to accept it. Auron deserved a chance—a future—something Malum seemed determined to strip away.

Malament held his father's gaze, a cold stone stare that radiated the resolve of a man who had witnessed too much. The tension crackled in the air between them as he spoke, his voice steady and unwavering. "I shall be his mother, his father, his keeper and carer. His home is where I dwell. You cannot deny me this; he shall have greatness bestowed upon him."

Malum's face twisted in disgust, his contempt palpable. "And who shall grant such greatness? Certainly not you while I reign. You forget your place, son. Filth cannot rise above its position; it is beneath us. We walk over it every day, only to tread it deeper into the dirt."

The calmness in Malament's demeanour only served to infuriate his father further. Yet he remained resolute, refusing to break the connection between their eyes. "No, Father. It is you who forget your position. I am to be the future Lord; your reign will not be a pox on mine. I shall command more than you can dream, and that so-called filth is to be my sword. I will choose where it strikes and who it cuts down."

He leaned in slightly, the fire in his words igniting the atmosphere. "If the boy is the filth, you so claim, I ask myself why my father is naked and firm on a cold night with mother in no sight. Tell me, Father, who is the filth?"

Malum's eyes widened in a mixture of shock and fury, the shame of his own vulnerability now laid bare. The silence that followed felt heavy, suffocating, as the weight of Malament's challenge hung between them. Each man stood on the precipice of a reckoning, the fight for dominance clear in their exchanged glances, the stakes raised higher than ever.

Malum's rage ignited at his son's defiance, and with a furious swing, he struck Malament hard across the face, the force of the blow knocking him back. Blood burst from his split lip, the metallic taste mingling with the fire of anger burning in his chest. "You are no Lord yet! The boy shall have nothing-he is no more than a corpse ready for the dogs!"

As the last words left Malum's lips, a sudden, violent twitch coursed through Auron's lifeless body. With a desperate gasp, he expelled a torrent of water from his throat, swallowing in a large gulp of air. A primal cry erupted from him, shattering the suffocating silence of the room.

Malament, his face stinging from the blow, watched as Auron struggled back to life, a glimmer of hope sparking in the darkness. In a visceral reaction, he spat a mouthful of blood into the dark pool, the crimson droplets swirling in the water, a stark contrast against the chaos that surrounded them.

He locked eyes with his father, a defiant smile spreading across his face. It was a challenge, a promise that Auron's survival would not go unrecognised. "You underestimate him, Father. Perhaps you are the one who should fear the dogs."

# THE ORPHAN
# CHAPTER EIGHT

Malament licked his dry lips, anxiety knotting his stomach as he navigated the damp, musty corridors of the slave quarters. A dull weight hung over his expression, the remnants of yesterday's confrontation with his father lingering like a dark cloud. It had been a long, exhausting day since the incident in the bathhouse, and now he was burdened with the grim task of delivering devastating news to Auron. The argument with his father had escalated, with Malament fighting tooth and nail to defend the child, only to be forced to concede in the end. The boy could stay, but only on the condition that he be whipped for his actions. The thought twisted in Malament's gut like a dagger; it felt like betrayal.

The midday heat seeped into the corridors, thick and suffocating, amplifying the discomfort that already gnawed at him. Servants hurried past, bowing their heads in deference, but Malament felt like an executioner walking toward the gallows, the heavy burden of his father's will weighing down his every step. He knew Auron had acted out of simple curiosity, stumbling into the wrong room at the wrong time, yet in the eyes of the most powerful man in East Kadun, a small boy's innocent misstep would not go unpunished.

As he reached Auron's door, he found it already ajar, swinging slightly on its hinges. The small child sat on the bed, an image of quiet resilience, yet there was an unmistakable sadness in his bright eyes, as if he sensed the storm that was about to break. Malament's heart clenched at the sight. The boy looked so small and vulnerable, waiting patiently, and for a fleeting moment, he wished he could shield Auron from the harsh realities of their world.

Standing in the doorway, Malament fought to keep his emotions in check, to project a calm facade that belied the turmoil within. He did not want Auron to sense his inner conflict, to know how deeply this decision tore at him. He forced a smile, an attempt at comfort that felt hollow even to him. "Hey there, Auron," he said, his voice strained but steady.

Malament moved into the room and settled onto the thin bed beside Auron, the frame creaking under his added weight. He could feel the tension in the air as he turned to the small child. "How have you fared, Auron?"

Auron shuffled on the bed, readjusting his position to face Malament fully. "I have been fine. Saanvi took care of me, though my throat still aches a bit." He paused, his gaze flickering with curiosity and a hint of concern. "Was that your father?"

A slight smile broke across Malament's face at the boy's perceptiveness, but it quickly faded, replaced by a heaviness in his heart. "Yes, Auron. He is the Lord of East Kadun and the head of this house." He hesitated, the weight of his words pressing down on him. "You certainly did not pick the best opponent to tackle with, nor should you make an enemy of him, I'm afraid. Unfortunately, he was against your staying here from the very beginning. He wants you banished."

Auron's eyes widened, the light in them dimming as fear crept in. "Must I leave?" he asked, his voice trembling with apprehension. The prospect of being cast out again, back to the unforgiving streets of Borlong, sent a chill through the boy.

Malament's chest tightened—could he really do this? Could he deliver the news that would shatter the fragile sense of safety they had built? Auron's expression remained, and Malament could see the tension coiling beneath the surface, a silent understanding passing between them. Malament took a deep breath, wishing he could spare Auron the pain of what was to come. But there was no escaping the inevitable.

"Your actions in the bathhouse..." he began, his voice faltering as the truth hung heavy in the air. He swallowed hard, feeling the sting of tears threaten to rise. "They have consequences."

In that moment, he realised the full extent of his helplessness, and it nearly crushed him. Auron deserved a protector, a champion in a world that offered none. Instead, here he was, the bearer of bad news, a reluctant instrument of his father's will.

"Auron, believe me when I say I do not wish for you to leave," Malament replied, his voice thick with emotion. He leaned closer, his heart aching for the boy. "But my father has given us choice. Either accept the banishment, and I am to escort you to the front gates with nothing more than the rags you arrived in or choose to stay and face your punishment in the training area."

The boy's expression shifted, torn between despair and defiance. "What will happen if I stay?" His small hands fidgeted in his lap, the innocence of childhood battling against the harsh realities of their world.

Malament took a deep breath, steeling himself for the truth. "You will be whipped, Auron. It's a punishment for what you did. I wish I could change it—I wish I could protect you from this." The anguish in his voice was palpable, and he could see the flicker of fear in Auron's eyes, the realisation of the decision he had to make.

Auron's gaze dropped to the floor, and for a moment, silence enveloped them, heavy with the weight of their predicament. "I... I don't want to go back to the streets," Auron finally whispered, his voice breaking. "But I don't want to be hurt either."

Malament felt his heart shatter a little at the boy's vulnerability. "I know, Auron. I know," he said softly, reaching out to place a comforting hand on the boy's shoulder. "No matter what happens, you are not alone. I will be with you every step of the way."

He paused, allowing Auron to absorb the gravity of his words, his heart heavy with the weight of the choice laid before the boy. He knew the next words he spoke could sway Auron's decision, so he continued in a calm, measured tone, "Auron, understand this choice must be made, but it is yours alone to make. Take a few moments to consider your path, though heed my words, for you stand at a crossroads. You have two very different paths before you, each fraught with uncertainty and peril, but only one leads to greater deeds."

He leaned closer, his gaze intent on Auron's, wanting to impart the seriousness of what lay ahead. "The path I wish you to take is not an easy one. It will demand your courage and resilience. Challenging times await you, but remember, this choice is not just for today; it is for tomorrow and every day after."

With that, he reached out, brushing a comforting hand against the boy's shoulder. "Whatever you decide, know that you are brave. Facing this punishment doesn't define you; it's how you rise from it that will shape who you become."

Auron met his gaze, determination flickering in his bright eyes, though uncertainty lingered a mix of resolve and fear. Malament nodded, grateful for the boy's courage even in the face of such daunting choices. "Take all the time you need, Auron. I will be right outside when you're ready." With a heavy heart, he left the room, the door closing softly behind him, leaving Auron to wrestle with the weight of his decision.

Outside, the corridor was silent, broken only by the crackling of flames and the occasional drip of water pooling on the damp stone floor. To the far side of the hallway, he spotted a gangly servant pacing toward him, his gait awkward and hurried. Malament recognized the man—a personal servant to his father—no doubt dispatched to deliver a message.

As the servant approached, Malament felt a surge of annoyance. How must his father loathe this place to send a mere messenger in his stead?

"Good day, sir," the tall man began, his voice shaky.

Malament snapped back, his irritation spilling over. "What's good about it?"

The servant stumbled over his words, caught off guard by the sudden outburst. "I—uh, I—"

"Out with it, then, man!" Malament barked, his impatience flaring.

The servant cleared his throat, visibly shaken. "I have been sent by your father. He wishes to know when he will meet you and the boy by the front gates."

A spike of rage threatened to surface, hot and unyielding, but Malament fought to keep it in check. The thought of his father's callousness, expecting him to deliver Auron without a second thought, ignited his anger. "Tell my father," he replied through gritted teeth, "that he shall be waiting a long time. The boy has accepted his punishment, and we shall meet him in the training area. Go now and deliver the message."

The servant, sensing the storm brewing beneath Malament's calm facade, bowed quickly before turning on his heel and hastily retreating down the corridor.

As Malament watched him go, he felt the weight of his father's expectations press down on him, an anchor tethering him to a world he longed to escape. Anger churned in his gut, battling against the fierce desire to protect Auron. He took a deep breath, steadying himself. He would not let his father's cruelty dictate the boy's fate—not now, not ever.

Though for a brief moment, the flicker of satisfaction lightened his expression, his message would infuriate his father. Malament pondered then, he could not pinpoint when he had stopped loving the man, or if he ever truly had. His father had provided him with everything he needed in life—wealth, status, education—but there was no love in their relationship. They shared no bond, no warmth.

Malament remembered the way his father had indulged in the warmth of serving maids behind his mother's back. But that was not what troubled him the most. It was the realisation that the man could not lead. East Kadun had been given a chance at independence, a glimmer of hope, and what had his father done with it? Nothing. Yes, he had helped end the civil war with the West, but at what cost? The terms were unjust, a band-aid over a festering wound, and rumours of raiding parties still echoed through the hamlets and villages, spreading fear among the people.

His father had always bowed to the whims of neighbouring countries, the treaty that cemented their fragile peace came with the unwanted caveat of marrying a girl Malum had no love for. Lady Amelia, his mother, was the daughter of King Ruben Whitehart of West Kadun. His father held the title of Lord over East Kadun, yet their armies and resources were tied to the King's command. The marriage had been arranged to quell an ongoing civil war and maintain the delicate balance between the two realms. Or so the people believed. In reality, Ruben had a spare daughter to marry off, a pawn in his game to ensure compliance from the East.

Now, nineteen years later, here Malament stood, a reluctant pawn ready to toe that line. The East was the larger country, yet it was riddled with deep, impenetrable forests, and its people were divided—those who dwelled in the shadows of the trees and those who lived in the bustling cities like Borlong. Under Malum's reign, instead of bridging the gap, his father had widened it, allowing random skirmishes to erupt and leaving the spectre of civil war haunting the populace.

Malament clenched his fists, his resolve hardening. He vowed to rule differently. He would not be held captive by the ambitions of other nations while his own remained in disarray. He would not bear the weight of his father's failures. He would carve a new path, one that embraced both the forest and the city, and he would not be burdened by the past. The East deserved a leader who fought for unity, who sought to heal the divides rather than deepen them. And that leader, he promised himself, would be him.

Breaking his trail of thought, the door to Auron's room swung open with a loud groan, jolting Malament from his reverie. The child stood there; his worried face transformed into one of unexpected courage. "I have chosen my path," Auron declared, his voice trembling yet resolute. "I am scared, Malament, but the whip does not frighten me as it once did. You shall look after me."

Malament stood frozen in place, his heart racing. He had braced himself for a scene of fear and resistance, anticipating the boy would need to be persuaded, perhaps even dragged, kicking and screaming. But here was Auron, standing tall in the doorway, fear mingled with a burgeoning sense of pride. In that moment, Malament's admiration for the boy swelled, filling him with a profound sense of pride that threatened to overflow.

"Yes, Auron," he replied, his voice thick with emotion. "I shall look after you." The words felt like a vow, a promise not just to the child but to himself. He would protect Auron from the pain ahead, shielding him from the injustices that had plagued his own life. As they stood there, locked in this moment of shared resolve, Malament felt the weight of his own fears lift, replaced by the fierce determination to fight for the boy's future.

Together, they would face whatever challenges lay ahead, and Malament vowed to be the guardian Auron needed, a protector against the harshness of a world that often demanded far too much from those too young to bear its burdens.

# THE ORPHAN
# CHAPTER NINE

Rays of mid-afternoon sunlight poured into the hall from the high openings above, illuminating the vast space in a warm glow. The tall pillars cast long, menacing shadows that loomed across the floor like black spears cutting through the light. Malament and Auron paced through the hall side by side, the sound of their footsteps echoing ominously in the expansive area as they approached the training grounds.

Auron's heart raced as he caught sight of the figures waiting inside. Among them stood the man Malament had fought the previous night, his presence striking fear into Auron's chest. The man was rigid, standing next to a wooden post, clad in dark leathers that seemed to absorb the light. He held a long, looped whip in his hand, its very existence a stark reminder of the punishment that awaited. Yet, as he walked beside Malament, Auron squared his shoulders, determined to show the young man that he could be brave.

As they drew closer to the training area, the atmosphere thickened with tension. The Lord of Borlong stood to one side, flanked by his two personal servants, their expressions a stark contrast to the scene unfolding. One of the servants, the same man Malament had encountered earlier, wore a sheepish expression, as if he had just been scorned by the Lord. His face flushed red; the deep frown etched across it reflecting the anger radiating from his master. Lord Malum's narrowed eyes were fixed on Auron, a silent storm brewing within them.

Auron's pulse quickened under the weight of the stare. Each step felt like a trial, the air heavy with unspoken judgments. It was as if he felt the heat of the Lord's fury washing over him, a stark reminder of the consequences he faced. Despite the fear swirling inside him, Auron stood tall, summoning every ounce of courage he had. With Malament at his side, he silently vowed to face whatever was to come, refusing to be broken by the looming shadow of the whip.

Then he caught sight of it, his eyes locking onto the wooden post at the centre of the training area, fully aware of its purpose. Memories of past punishments flooded his mind, moments when he had been caught stealing in the markets and strapped to similar contraptions. In those instances, he had kicked and screamed, desperately wriggling to free himself as the whip cracked down against his back. Tears had streamed down his face, and he had bellowed out in agony, drowning in the pain and humiliation.

But this time would be different. This time, he would show Malament his courage. He steeled himself, recognizing that he would face the coming pain not as a small boy from the slums but as a young man embarking on a journey. Auron knew what lay ahead, and with that knowledge came a strange sense of empowerment. He took a deep breath, letting the weight of his resolve fill him.

They passed under the archway entrance and Malament led him toward the post, its rough surface standing in stark contrast to Auron's trembling hands. The post was no more than five feet tall, slightly wider than a small barrel, and it loomed like a sentinel of his fate. Auron glanced up at the man beside it—a short, muscular figure named Gordon.

The man had dark charcoal hair cropped close to his scalp, matching dark eyes that seemed to pierce through Auron's bravado. His thin brows furrowed slightly as he regarded the boy, a hint of recognition sparking in his gaze. Auron felt a mix of fear and determination wash over him as Gordon nodded slightly, then turned to Malum, waiting for his Lord's command.

In that moment, the room felt charged with anticipation. Auron's heart pounded in his chest, each beat echoing the conflict within him. He wanted to be brave, to stand tall before the whip and the man who wielded it, yet a tremor of fear rippled through him. He forced himself to focus, drawing strength from the resolve that had brought him this far. He would not allow his past to define him; today, he would carve a new path.

Malum's fury intensified as he had watched the small boy enter the room with an unsettling calmness. He had expected Auron to choose banishment, to flee from the impending punishment. Instead, the child had opted to endure the flogging, which only served to stoke the flames of Malum's rage. Upon receiving Malament's message, he had erupted in a fit of fury, screaming at his servant and even striking the unfortunate man in his wrath.

He barked orders to prepare the training area and ready Gordon for the child's punishment. Still simmering with anger, Malum had envisioned

Auron's tear-streaked face, a boy trembling in fear at the thought of the whip. Instead, the child stood motionless, unfazed, further provoking Malum's ire. His eyes locked onto Gordon's, he spoke through clenched teeth, his fury palpable. "Let us not hesitate or linger idly. Begin the proceedings before I have you all whipped for testing my patience. Son, stand beside me."

Malament placed a reassuring hand on Auron's shoulder, sensing the boy's quiet strength. "Be brave," he whispered, feeling a surge of pride mixed with anguish as he took his place next to his father, the weight of his own conflicted emotions heavy upon him.

Gordon stepped forward, his expression grim as he reached into his pocket, pulling out a small curved blade. With deliberate movements, he gripped Auron's tunic and tore it down its length. The fine cloth fell away like leaves in a gust of wind, leaving Auron standing bare in nothing but his sandals. A gasp escaped one of the servants as Auron's undernourished body was revealed, showcasing long, thin scars that marked him like a map of his past sufferings. Bruises marred his rib cage, remnants of his recent struggles on the streets of Borlong, but still, the boy stood tall and unmoving.

Gordon seized Auron's arms, binding them tightly around the wooden post. The coarse wood pressed painfully against his bare chest, its jagged edges biting into his skin. Auron felt his muscles strain as his arms were pulled taut, a sharp discomfort radiating through his left arm still recovering from the recent break. Normally, he would have cried out, but he clung to that discomfort, letting it anchor him amidst the rising tide of fear and anxiety.

Though his heart raced, a whirlwind of emotions battled within him. Fear coursed through his veins, yet he clung to the courage that had pushed him to this moment. He would not allow Malum to see his trepidation; he would not give the Lord the satisfaction of breaking him. Each scar on his body was a testament to his resilience, a symbol of his determination to rise above his circumstances.

As Gordon stepped behind him, the sound of his leather sandals crunching on the sandy floor faded into the background. Auron dug his own feet into the ground, relishing the cool grains slipping between his toes one last time, a fleeting comfort before the inevitable punishment. A draft swept through the room, and for a brief moment, he savoured the cool air brushing against his exposed skin, a fleeting whisper of freedom before it would be marred.

Then came the sound he dreaded-the whip uncoiling, the ominous rustle that filled the air with tension. This was it. Be brave, he reminded himself, clenching his jaw tightly, steeling himself for the first strike.

Gordon threw his arm back, and in an instant, the whip came to life, snaking through the air with a hiss. Auron braced himself, muscles tightening in anticipation. The whip sliced through the air, a piercing crack echoing in the small room as it crashed down upon his bare back. Pain erupted as the leather lacerated his skin, the sudden shock overwhelming him. Blood spattered, painting the sand a vivid crimson, and a deep gash stretched across his back up to his left shoulder.

Every nerve screamed in protest, the intensity of the pain flooding his senses like wildfire. Auron felt the urge to scream, to collapse under the weight of the agony, but he forced himself to focus, redirecting his attention to the throbbing ache in his arm. It was a pinprick compared to the searing burn radiating across his back. Somehow, he endured the first lash in silence, his body trembling as he fought to remain stoic.

But before he could catch his breath, the whip soared through the air again, snapping down like a viper seeking its prey. Auron steeled himself, knowing he had to be brave, to show Malament-and himself-that he was more than just a boy from the streets. This was his moment of defiance, a testament to his will. He would not let them see him break.

Lord Malum's heart raced as he watched in disbelief, horror etched across his features, as the humiliated child stood bare and defiant. Auron had somehow managed to endure the first two strikes without a sound, his stillness a stark contrast to the fury boiling within Malum. How could this child defy me? The thought ignited a wildfire of rage in him, surging uncontrollably until he could no longer contain it.

"BY TITAN'S COCK! THIS IS AN OUTRAGE!" he roared, his voice cutting through the tense air like a knife. All eyes shifted to him, shock and confusion rippling through the onlookers as he stormed towards Gordon, the man responsible for the punishment. "You fool! You couldn't whip the behind off a Dryland's whore! Give me that whip, you swine!"

Gordon, taken aback but obedient, relinquished the whip without hesitation. Malum seized it, the leather handle burning in his grip, and with a primal scream, he lashed out wildly, the whip slicing through the air with a menacing whistle. It missed Auron by a wide margin, his fury rendering him reckless.

"ARGH!" he bellowed, his face flushed with rage, and he struck again. This time, he swung harder, but his aim was just as errant, the whip spiralling off course, leaving the boy untouched once more. Malum yanked his arm back after the second failed attempt, frustration boiling over as the whip recoiled violently. In a cruel twist it raced back towards its wielder and cracked viciously against his own cheek.

A searing pain shot through Malum, and he stumbled back, shocked to find his own blood spilling from the wound. The pain only fuelled his rage, and he threw the whip to the ground, his palms slick with crimson. "THE BOY MUST DIE!" he screamed, his voice a raw, desperate wail of fury and humiliation.

Malum's eyes blazed with fury as he charged toward the weapon stand, his movements fuelled by a dark, reckless determination. He grasped a short sword, its cold steel glinting ominously in the light. The blade felt heavy in his hand, yet his anger propelled him forward, a primal urge to lash out at the source of his humiliation.

As he raced toward Auron, ready to plunge the sword deep into the boy's already bloody back, the world around him narrowed to a singular focus. In that moment, he was not just a lord; he was a man consumed by his rage, intent on destroying the very defiance that had dared to stand before him.

Just as Malum prepared to strike, a female voice pierced the tension like a bell tolling in the quiet dawn. “MALUM, ENOUGH!”

In an instant, his fury shattered, cascading away like rocks tumbling down a mountainside. The sword slipped from his grasp, sinking into the sand with a soft thud, its hilt protruding awkwardly from the surface. Malum knew that voice all too well, and as he turned, the familiar figure before him ignited a blend of frustration and relief.

Lady Amelia stood there, radiant yet commanding, her beauty undiminished by the years. Golden blonde locks cascaded down her shoulders, framing her face like a halo, and despite the chaos, a part of him still found solace in her presence. Yet, her expression was fierce, a storm of disappointment brewing in her striking blue eyes.

“No husband of mine shall have the blood of a child on his hands,” she declared, her voice steady yet filled with an underlying intensity. “What in all that is holy is happening here? Why do I walk through our halls only to hear such commotion and find my husband wielding a whip, now replaced by a sword? And what of your face? Blood pours freely from a fresh wound."

Malum opened his mouth to respond, but Amelia cut him off, her tone brooking no argument. "No, Malum, I do not wish for your excuses. Have the boy freed and taken to the nurse. Malament, I shall speak with you regarding this matter."

Her command echoed through the training area, the authority in her voice silencing the onlookers. Malum's heart raced with conflicting emotions—shame, anger, and a flicker of gratitude for her intervention. He felt the weight of her gaze upon him, and the storm within him began to quiet, replaced by a gnawing realisation of the madness he had almost succumbed to.

As Malament moved to obey his mother's order, the tension in the air shifted. Auron, still bound but resolute, watched as Lady Amelia stepped closer, her eyes softening. In that moment, he became a child once more, yearning for safety and the assurance that compassion could still exist in a world rife with cruelty.

At that moment the servants and Gordon rushed to Auron's aid, swiftly cutting the bindings that held him to the wooden post. As the ropes fell away, he sagged to the ground, his knees sinking into the bloody sand. The world spun slightly as a chestnut brown blanket enveloped him, and he leaned into the supportive hands of those around him, feeling their strength as his own faltered.

Gordon lifted him gently, cradling Auron against his chest as he carried him back toward the servant quarters. Each movement sent fresh waves of pain coursing through Auron's body, the long lacerations burning like fire against his skin. The stinging discomfort served as a harsh reminder of the ordeal he had just endured, but the warmth of the blanket provided a small comfort against the chill of fear that had gripped him.

When they arrived at his room, Saanvi was already there, her presence a balm amid the turmoil. She moved quickly, gathering bandages and herbs as Gordon placed Auron carefully on the bed. A sharp wince escaped him as Saanvi immediately began treating the open wounds, her touch gentle yet efficient.

Gordon looked down at the stricken boy, with his own sense of astonishment for his bravery, "I shall look forward to our next encounter, Auron," Gordon said, a hint of admiration in his voice. "You have shown great courage today. May your wounds heal with the haste you deserve.

Take good care of this one, nurse. He has earned it." With a respectful bow, he exited the room, closing the door softly behind him.

Auron turned his gaze to Saanvi, his eyes brimming with unshed tears. "Will this place become easier?" he asked, his voice trembling with uncertainty.

Saanvi paused her work, meeting his gaze with warmth and empathy. She handed him a small cup of water, gently bringing it to his lips. "I believe it will now, Auron," she replied softly, her voice steady and reassuring. "I believe it will."

As he sipped the water, he felt a glimmer of hope amidst the pain, a flicker of belief that perhaps this place could offer him something more than just suffering. Saanvi's kindness wrapped around him like the blanket, a promise that he was not alone in his struggle.

# THE ORPHAN
# CHAPTER TEN

The day had faded, and dusk thickened into a pitch-black night that swallowed Borlong. Standing at the edge of a dense forest that loomed like a wall of shadows, Borlong was one of the oldest cities east of the Reach, built generations ago as a bastion against the fierce forest clans. In its early days, Borlong was a cluster of wooden defences and dirt paths, a refuge for wanderers and soldiers alike. But over the years, the city had sprawled outward in layers, like rings of an ancient tree. Tens of thousands now called it home, the original stronghold now lost within a maze of crooked alleys, slums, and sagging tenements.

Though Borlong held the acclaim of the largest city in East Kadun, grandeur was a stranger here. Its buildings were functional, worn, and close-packed, the timber walls bleached grey by the elements. There were no towering walls or imposing forts, just a perimeter fence barely twenty feet high, crudely fashioned from the very trees that encircled it. Guard towers rose at intervals along the perimeter, their wooden beams creaking underfoot as a few weary watchmen paced, scanning the quiet darkness beyond. In daylight, the forest to the west would stretch endlessly, a thick green sea. Now, under night's shroud, it was a black expanse, an immense, impenetrable curtain that devoured the horizon.

To the south, the river stretched wide and dark, its surface a glossy mirror reflecting fragments of moonlight that danced upon the calm currents. The northern banks lay in shadow, but faint glimmers appeared where fishermen's platforms jutted out, their wooden planks worn smooth by years of quiet vigil under the stars. Fishing poles stood propped against the platforms, silhouettes waiting in the silence as if holding their breath alongside the water.

Every few miles, arched stone bridges spanned the river, their mossy pillars softened in the moon's pale glow, casting long shadows that reached across the inky surface. These crossings were hushed in the nighttime stillness, their purpose forgotten in the dark but poised to greet the dawn's first travellers on the road to East Kadun's southern towns.

By the jetties, small fishing boats drifted at the water's edge, rocking gently on invisible currents. The boats, their colours lost in the shadows, looked almost spectral, tethered by thick ropes tied hastily to the posts. Nets hung over the sides, damp and dark, as though they, too, were resting until morning. A distant hoot of an owl echoed along the shore, and the soft murmur of the river seemed to respond, whispering secrets to the night.

From the watchtowers, Borlong stretched like a tapestry of shadows and faint lights. Only a handful of torches still burned, casting amber pools against the darkened streets. The larger buildings jutted from the cityscape like weathered hulks, their forms barely discernible against the night sky. Smaller homes and shops huddled together, their outlines merging in the gloom. Flickering candlelight seeped from stained-glass windows in scattered homes and taverns, illuminating little but hinting at life within. Figures moved beyond the glass—dark, distorted shapes, like shadows of people, drinking, talking, or passing by.

Above it all, the city's lone theatre clung to its last glimmers of pride. Small torches mounted along the rooftop created a beacon of light against the night, their flames licking upward and casting a warm glow. Below, the poorer districts were dense labyrinths of crooked, narrow streets and alleyways. The cobblestone paths there were uneven, cracked, and broken in places, often disappearing beneath layers of mud and refuse. Shadows lurked in these alleys, too dense for moonlight to penetrate, and the silence was broken only by the occasional scrape of a footstep or the distant murmur of voices.

Three dark figures moved like shadows through the deserted streets, hooded and silent. They passed unnoticed beneath the watchful guards in their high towers, the city lying so still that even their footsteps barely broke the silence. In single file, they moved cautiously, the two men, front and rear, tall and broad, with short swords sheathed at their hips. Hidden beneath heavy hoods, their faces remained unseen, the only sign of their presence the faint vapours of warm breath meeting the biting cold.

In the centre, Lord Malum Thalron shivered beneath his cloak, feeling the night air keenly. He was used to the warmth of roaring hearths, the comfort of aged brandy on his tongue—not this stinging cold that pried beneath his cloak and bit into his skin. His teeth nearly chattered, and he clenched his jaw to stop the sound. But it was the fresh wound on his left cheek that throbbed with each icy gust, a long laceration carefully stitched and bound with cloth. The blood had dried in his beard, but the ache pulsed, making his eyes water as the cold seemed to pry deeper into his raw flesh.

Rarely did he find himself walking these streets at night, and for good reason. But tonight, events had left him no choice. Half a moon phase had passed since the arrival of that stray urchin in his home, and with him, a disturbing unravelling of Malum's private life. His son, Malament, had been ungrateful—hostile even—since the boy's arrival, and Malum's patience was wearing thin. Worse yet, his son had discovered his affair with Cora, the young serving maid, and the tension between father and son had only widened.

For all her beauty, Malum's wife offered him little solace. She was a dutiful woman, but affection was a foreign currency between them, a loyalty paper-thin. Malum knew that she viewed their marriage as little more than a gilded prison, and her heart belonged to her homeland in the West. If given the slightest excuse, she would escape back to her father, King Ruben Whitehart, with all the tales of his discretions she could muster. And the consequences could be dire—a foreign king with ill tidings was hardly the kind of enemy Malum wished to rouse. He cursed inwardly, each step heightening his sense of dread and frustration as he weighed the cost of his son's silence, his wife's loyalty, and the dangerous secrets that shadowed him tonight.

King Ruben longed for war—Malum knew it well. Almost twenty years had passed since the treaties were signed, the trade agreements set in place, binding their nations in a tense peace. But the alliance felt as fragile as a spider's web, stretched too thin to hold. Malum understood better than most that East Kadun was ill-prepared for war; they had neither the soldiers nor the coin for such ruinous ambitions. He took comfort in the hope that his son would be wise enough to keep his silence, sparing his mother—and the king in the West—any whisper of scandal.

The marriage had once seemed a perfect solution. It had bound two nations and delivered him the son he had craved, a rightful heir to steady their claim and secure their borders. Yet peace now felt like a strained illusion, threatened by factions within the senate, which was split over the alliance's purpose. Rumours and tales came in waves from the forest clans, who spoke of marauding bands that raided their villages. But Malum had no choice—he had to turn a blind eye, dismissing these warnings as nothing more than wild rumours.

His frustrations only grew when he thought of Amelia. After bearing their son, she had never again carried a child; there would be no further heirs, no strengthening of their line. She remained by his side, dutiful but cold, a fixture rather than a partner. He had loved her once—if only because she had given him an heir. But now, she felt like a stranger, a ghost who haunted their home and, he suspected, nursed dreams of returning westward, back to her father. Their marriage, once the symbol of a strong alliance, had become a thorn, a reminder of how little he could control.

Today had brought a new trial. That wretched orphan boy—the stray who had upended his carefully ordered life—why did he not accept the banishment, leaving him free of this trouble. He had imagined the boy slipping away, being dealt with quietly once outside the estate. But the child had defied him, and they had all endured the ordeal in the training yard, a spectacle that had left him scarred. Malum touched the long gash running down his face, the flesh tender. He was not a vain man, but he knew how important appearances were; his face was a symbol of strength, dignity. Now, he bore a permanent mark, a scar that would forever remind him—and others—of today's failure. He could fabricate a tale to explain the wound, spread some half-truth through his peers, but he would always know its source. This boy, this nuisance, had to be removed—this time, permanently.

The three figures glided between the narrow clefts of buildings, cloaked in shadows that seemed to stretch and deepen with their passing. They had encountered no one, but each of them knew that Borlong's streets harboured unseen dangers after dark, especially for a man of Malum's stature and wealth. He could feel the weight of the coin purse hidden in his cloak—a treasure that might be worth a man's life tonight—or three. The two men accompanying him wore hardened expressions, their eyes scanning every corner and their hands ready to grip the hilts of their blades. Even with their imposing presence, they knew better than to linger on the open streets.

They moved through the twisting back alleys, the cobblestones uneven beneath their feet, until they reached a narrow passage marked by a faint red cross freshly painted on the wall beside its entrance. A shoddy roof of dark fabric stretched overhead, sealing off what little light the moon offered. Here, the darkness was absolute, thick as smoke, swallowing all but the faint glimmers from the street they had left behind. The sight of the red cross reassured them: they were exactly where they needed to be.

Yet Malum could not shake the unease that gnawed at him. In this part of Borlong, loyalty was as fleeting as the shadows, and coin had a way of slipping from one hand to another without a trace. The walls around him felt close, almost stifling, as though the alley itself were watching, waiting. He gave a curt nod to the soldier at the front, who unsheathed his sword with a quiet scrape of metal against leather. The tall man advanced into the pitch-black alley, his blade pointed forward, ready for any sudden strike. From within the depths of the darkness, a cruel voice drifted out, low and mocking. "No further," it said, echoing slightly against the narrow walls. "You did not seek me out to trade blows with an oath. Please, my Lord, step forward. It is only you who requires my... expertise."

The soldier threw a questioning glance over his shoulder, his eyes meeting the faint outline of Malum's face, where only the Lord's eyes gleamed in the moonlight. Malum's gaze was fixed on the darkened alley, his eyes narrowing with suspicion. His voice, cool but cautious, broke the silence. "I wasn't aware you knew my identity. How did you come upon such information?"

A huff of irritation came from the unseen figure. "Please, my Lord. My usual clientele does not send soldiers to arrange secret meetings, only to arrive surrounded by armed guards. Step forward; no harm will come to you here. After all, there is no price on your head... yet."

A slight twitch of anger flared within Malum at the insult. In other circumstances, he might have had the man flogged for such insolence. Yet here, even with his soldiers by his side, he felt exposed, at the mercy of this unseen figure. He forced steel into his voice. "If you know to whom you speak, then I suggest you curb your tongue. Your words inspire little confidence in me, as does your manner."

"This is the manner of my business, my Lord." The voice held a faint note of amusement, unbothered by the veiled threat.

Malum clenched his fists, frustration simmering beneath his cool tone. "Then know this-my men shall remain here within earshot. If they do not hear my voice, they'll cut you down, and I'll see your head mounted on a spike." Yet even as he spoke, his voice lacked the full force he intended, and the response came back quick and unruffled.

"Your threat is folly," the voice replied. "Your men cannot strike what they cannot see. But I understand, time is precious, so let us speak of business, my Lord, before the night grows colder."

The silence lingered, heavy and charged, as Malum steeled himself, sensing he had little choice but to trust, however unwillingly, that this shadowed figure was true to his word.

Against his better judgement, Malum edged into the blackness of the alley, his every nerve taut, eyes straining to catch even the faintest glimpse of the man lurking somewhere within. But the figure was like smoke—unseen, intangible. Not even shadows betrayed his presence. Malum took a few cautious steps, then halted. "I am here now. Let us speak as men, not as rivals."

Silence followed; a stillness so dense it pressed in around him. Seconds stretched into what felt like an eternity, and Malum's pulse quickened as he waited, dread pooling in his stomach.

Then, a voice whispered from just behind his ear, close enough that he could feel the warmth of breath. "Are you with coin, my Lord?"

Malum's eyes widened, his body locking up in startled panic. How had the man slipped behind him undetected? The alleyway felt suddenly narrow, as if invisible walls closed in, and he could almost sense the edge of a blade hovering near his throat, or the point of a dagger poised to pierce his back. Slowly, with a shaky hand, he pulled a small satchel from his cloak, loosening it to reveal a handful of coins, which he then held out, palm open and trembling. Before he could take another breath, a swift hand reached out, snatching the coins away with barely a sound.

"Good," the voice murmured, its edge softened but still unsettling. "Now, what can I aid you with, my Lord?"

Malum shifted uneasily, realising he now held the man's full attention—and uncertain if he had just handed over leverage or gained an ally. His feet shuffled against the cold ground as he swallowed down his unease. He had willingly placed himself in this precarious position, and now he had no choice but to see it through. "I have… a delicate problem," he said, his voice measured, trying to mask the anxiety in his tone. "And I require a man of your particular skill set to assist me with it."

A pause followed, and then the voice responded, calm and cold. "You have my ears, my Lord. Please, continue."

Malum's throat tightened as he prepared to speak, aware that whatever words he chose next could seal his fate as much as his secret dealings.

"My son has taken to a peasant boy who now resides under my roof," Malum said, his voice tight with frustration. "Since his arrival, the boy has been nothing but a thorn in my side. I see no end to it. I need him gone. Can you do this?"

The man's tone turned mocking, a cruel lilt undercutting his words. "A mere boy troubles his lordship? He must be a heavy burden indeed. I can rid you of this child, my Lord, but such an act doesn't come cheap. Ending a child's life is no small thing, even for one of my profession. Do you wish a particular end, my Lord?"

Malum's face tensed, calculating each word. "My son would suspect foul play if the boy simply vanished. He won't leave the residence willingly, nor would he be unaccompanied. You'll need to infiltrate my home undetected. Make it look like an accident... or place blame on one of the servants. I'll leave the finer details to you."

The figure chuckled softly, his voice carrying a dark amusement. "Consider it done, my Lord. But understand this—my price for such a delicate matter is fifty gold pieces. Half shall be left here tomorrow night. The rest, after the deed is completed. My terms are not negotiable."

Relief flooded through Malum, as if a hunter's bow had lowered, sparing him from its deadly aim. With his usual mask of confidence restored, he allowed a faint smile to spread across his face. The price was lower than he had anticipated; he had come prepared with sixty pieces, expecting to pay more if necessary. Without hesitation, he drew the full purse from his cloak, holding it out with both hands.

"There are sixty gold pieces here. Take them all and see it done," he said, his voice firm. "I do not wish to cross paths with you again."

The man's hand extended from the darkness, swift and silent, snatching the purse from Malum's grip. He weighed it in his hand, the faint jingle of gold lost in the night. "As you wish, my Lord. By the next moon's turn, you shall be free of your burden."

Malum inclined his head, a twisted sense of satisfaction settling in as he turned and strode back toward his waiting guards. The deal was struck, and his conscience, as always, could be left for another time.

# THE QUEEN CONSORT
# CHAPTER ELEVEN

The crunch of snow beneath Karak's solitary footsteps was muffled by the howling wind—a sound like the distant calls of a hunting pack, wolves searching the night for their own. Bitter cold sliced through the air, needling at any sliver of exposed skin, even under her thick hooded garment. She fought on, one determined step at a time, the weight of the layered furs both a shield and a burden. Each chilling gust seemed to search out the seams, probing relentlessly for ways to penetrate her defences.

She forced her gaze downward, focusing on her willing legs, trying to ignore the creeping numbness that stole through her body. The cold, however, was a presence she could not ignore, biting and burning even through thick leather and fur. Occasionally, she raised her head to gauge her path. To her left, the landscape stretched out in an endless white expanse, swallowed in a blanket of snow that obliterated the view of the distant mountains. She remembered how, in summer's brief reprieve, their towering shapes punctuated the horizon, but now, they were swallowed by the storm. To her right, the frozen carcasses of once-mighty pine trees loomed like twisted sentinels, jagged and ominous. The wind had shaped them into monstrous forms, their outstretched branches like talons ready to rake the unwary.

Her gaze fixed on these frozen statues, her steps faltering. The way the ice glistened across their smooth surfaces drew her in, an unexpected calm settling over her as she lingered, perhaps only a stolen moment of respite. She took a deep breath through her nostrils, feeling the sudden sting as frost formed in an instant along her nose, sending a shiver down her spine. Just then, the wind shifted abruptly, a fierce gust catching her off guard and pitching her forward. Her right hand plunged into the snow as she struggled to find her balance, and a sharp, icy bite tore through her fur-lined glove. She cursed aloud; her voice instantly swallowed by the relentless wind.

Glaring ahead at the barely visible path, Karak searched for a spark of motivation—but nothing came. She knew well enough that it had been reckless to venture out this early in the season. If the gate guards had glimpsed their Queen prepared for a trek through the fierce winter without companions, they would have raised alarm, refusing to let her pass. But the Queen was too cunning to leave things to chance; she had slipped out by other, less conspicuous routes. They had not seen her—she had made sure of it. The secrecy of this journey was paramount, and none could be trusted with its purpose.

Gritting her teeth against the cold, she rose to her feet, brushing off the snow that clung to her furs. She was Queen of Nordon, ruler of the winter realm, sovereign of Stormhold, the kingdom beneath the mountain's belly. Queen Karak of Clan Thørn, shackled by the name of her loathsome husband, King Ivar Froskgar. No, she would not be defeated by the cold. Straightening her shoulders, she resumed her solitary march, each step a test of will as the wild wind tore at her, unrelenting, almost sentient in its fury, hounding her as though it knew her every defiance.

The journey dragged on, each step a struggle, but Karak could feel her destination drawing closer. After another gruelling stretch, she braved a look upward, more to clear her vision than to measure her progress. The blizzard swirled and danced around her, obscuring all but a few feet ahead, but then—there, faint through the blinding gale, a dark opening appeared no more than twenty paces away. Her heart surged, lifting her weary body. A faint amber glow flickered within, a beacon guiding her forward. Her steps quickened, each one pressing her closer to shelter. Snow crunched more easily underfoot, and then she noticed footprints leading toward the cave—a sign she was not alone.

As she crossed an unseen threshold, the blizzard's wrath softened, its force halting just outside the cave mouth. Though the wind still swept into the cavern, it was but a weakened echo, merely brushing against her tired frame. She reached up, peeling back the hood of her winter furs, allowing the wind to catch in her fiery red hair and toss it wildly. Her expression was grim—a hardened mask of a woman who had wrestled with the elements and still bore their chill in her bones. Here, though, she felt the harshness fade. Tilting her head back into the wind, she savoured the gentler gust, a strange comfort after such unrelenting cold. But the moment passed quickly, her focus sharpening as she approached the raised fire pit at the centre of the cave.

The flames, though low, roared as the wind funnelled through the narrow space, intensifying their glow. She pulled off her fawn fur gloves and extended her hands toward the fire, relishing the tingling warmth that prickled through her numb fingers. Rubbing them together briskly, she coaxed the colour back to her pale skin, feeling the life return slowly, painfully.

The cave mouth was small, its interior simple but deliberate. To her right stood a tall, silent figure—a hooded priest, unmoving, clutching an unlit torch. The priests of Shiva, castrated at birth, had devoted themselves to their ice goddess though to what end only they could know. His stillness was unsettling, a shadow watching her from the periphery, indifferent yet keenly aware. To her left, firewood lay neatly stacked, and beyond that, the mouth of a narrow tunnel stretched into darkness, just high enough for her to pass through without ducking.

Once sufficiently warmed, Karak slipped her gloves back on, her fingers tingling as the heat seeped into them. She tossed a few more pieces of timber onto the fire, watching the flames leap higher before turning toward the shadows of the cave. Yet an impulse halted her—a strange urge to look back at the ferocious storm she had braved. Almost against her will, she spun around, pulling her gaze toward the blinding fury beyond the cave's mouth.

Instantly, she regretted it. The wind lunged forward, taking its final opportunity to lash at her exposed face, searing her cheeks with fresh, biting cold. The chill seemed to cut deeper now that she had tasted warmth, racing down her spine in sharp jolts. The stark brightness of the snow burned her eyes, forcing her to squint painfully. She wrenched her gaze back to the darkness, the scene outside already a fading ghost in her mind's eye. Feeling foolish for giving in to the impulse, Karak let out a low, frustrated snarl.

Without hesitation, she seized the unlit torch from the silent priest's hand, ignoring his expressionless face. There was something unsettling about his presence—his hooded stillness, his indifferent watchfulness, like a statue bound by ancient vows. She jammed the torch into the fire pit, the flames licking up to meet the dry wood. As she waited for it to catch, Karak steadied her breathing, forcing herself to regain control.

Anger had become a constant companion for Karak in these last few years, flaring up whenever she felt wronged, a sharp counterpoint to the hollow ache of depression that consumed her when alone. To be Queen- this had been her life's ambition, the title she had desired more than anything else. Her father, flawed and ruthless as he was, had made it so. But she was bound to King Ivar Froskgar, the 'Fat King,' a man as loathsome as he was powerful, and she felt shackled to him, trapped by the very ambition she had chased. How bitterly ironic that the crown, her symbol of triumph, had become the weight around her neck. She could not endure this much longer.

As she waited for the wax to catch fire, a memory rose, unbidden, to the forefront of her mind. Less than a year ago, she had stood on her balcony, gazing over the subterranean city, the torches below a network of distant stars. And in the cold, still air, a thought had whispered itself to her-a thought she had resisted many times before. I could end it all.

The thought became a pull, drawing her closer, and without realising, she had found herself on the other side of the balcony's edge, fingers barely gripping the stone. Below, the lives of her people continued, unaware of their Queen's peril. She had held on, her heart pounding, eyes fixed on the world below. Her grip weakened, her body tipping forward, the ground below pulling her down like a lover calling her name. For a moment, she let herself fall, a slow, inevitable surrender. As momentum built, a desire for life seized initiative. Her fingers grappled backward, nails clawing desperately at the unforgiving rock surface. But she missed, her grasp failing her, leaving only the fatal plunge.

A strong arm had looped around her waist, pulling her back. She had felt a solid chest against her back, warm breath near her ear, and a familiar voice, quiet but firm. "There is another way."

She turned, and her emerald eyes met her brother's. The despair that had gripped her softened in his presence, his strength a quiet reassurance. She had kissed him, an expression of gratitude and love, and whispered, "Yes. Yes, there is."

The torch finally took to the flame, casting a fragile light as Karak began her trek into the depths of the cave. The path wound sharply, forcing her to press the torch ahead as each corner tightened, the darkness pressing closer around her. Shadows leapt across the cave walls, forming brief, distorted shapes on surfaces. Surfaces etched with ancient hieroglyphics and symbols of a long-lost language. Some of them stirred memories from her studies, vague impressions of meanings and stories—but most were anonymous, faint echoes of an age long dead, painted by hands whose bones had long since turned to dust.

Gradually, the path began a steady descent into the mountain's heart. The ground grew uneven beneath her feet, and Karak strained to keep her balance, one hand brushing the cave wall for support. She noted that the ceiling had crept ever higher, drifting beyond the reach of her torchlight, so that only an endless black void stretched above her. For the first time, a sensation of dread prickled at her, an awareness that something might lurk beyond the shadows, watching, waiting. She knew well enough it was only the effects of the tight confines and the encroaching darkness, yet the thought was unnerving. She forced her attention back to her footing, taking each step deliberately, until finally, the path levelled out, spilling her into a massive cavern where the wind fell silent.

In the stillness, the flame softened, no longer flaring against the gusts, but rising in a gentle, steady rhythm. Her breathing was the only sound, save for the occasional drip of water echoing from somewhere deep within the cavern. She tilted her torch upward, catching glimpses of stalactites stabbing down from the unseen ceiling, mirrored by their counterparts rising from the floor. Here and there, some had formed thick columns, towering sentinels that stood silently as though watching over the cavern's secrets.

Around the edges of the cavern, cloaked priests lingered, their figures half-hidden in the darkness. As Karak's light crossed their faces, they moved with eerie synchronicity, each raising a hand to point toward a distant corner of the cavern. She glanced in the direction they indicated, then cautiously picked her way forward, careful to avoid the patches of slippery stone slicked by centuries of dripping water. The ground was treacherous, several crevices gaping on either side, their depths lost to the shadows.

After several dozen paces, she reached a pile of fallen rocks, large boulders that had been crudely arranged into a staircase. She climbed, her steps careful on the uneven stones, until at the top she found a single priest standing silently, arm outstretched to guide her toward a narrow tunnel beyond. The tunnel's mouth was small, barely wide enough for her to pass, and beyond it lay darkness—a passage leading to an unseen chamber, thick with mystery.

Karak hesitated, feeling the weight of the stone around her. She knew, from the old scholars' tales, that this next chamber was Shiva's tomb. Shiva—the ancient god, a presence whose power had waned but never disappeared. Now a dangerous, immortal being, Shiva had become entombed within the mountain, and those who dared visit her rarely returned. The priests themselves were all eunuchs, a price for surviving the god's presence.

Karak took a deep breath and pressed forward, her steps cautious, torch held tight. The low ceiling sloped toward her, forcing her to duck as the stone walls inched closer. With each pace, she found herself leaning further forward, the walls now shoulder-width, scraping at her cloak. She squeezed through, her breathing growing shallow as the tunnel constricted, forcing her into a crouch. Every step forward dragged at her nerves, the rough stone snagging her furs, pinning her in place and slowing her advance. A flicker of panic stirred as she realised that, here in the narrow passage, there was no way to turn back.

I should have turned back, she thought, gritting her teeth. Better still, my brother should have let me fall. The jest held a bitter truth, and she was painfully aware of her vulnerability. Her slight frame was all that saved her from being wedged within these walls—any larger, and she would have to claw her way through, if she could move at all.

Dropping to all fours, Karak crawled forward, until a low-sloping boulder blocked her path. To continue, she would have to press herself fully flat against the cold, unforgiving stone. The very thought made her heart hammer. She hesitated, gripping the torch tightly, feeling its heat far too close to her face. Steady, she thought, willing herself to calm. Taking a deep breath, she leaned down, the flame dancing inches from her skin, its heat sharp and searing. Instinctively, she jerked back up, her pulse pounding.

The urge to turn back surged again, but she knew there was no turning in this tunnel; the walls forced her onward, trapping her in a single direction. Focus she urged herself, as she started a second attempt at lowering herself down. Bracing against the stone as she finally lay flat, feeling the numbing chill of the cave floor even through the layers of fur. Gritting her teeth, she inched forward, sliding across the rough stone like a slug, her every movement slow and strained. Her furs caught, snagging her with each push forward, as though the mountain itself sought to keep her pinned under its crushing weight.

The thought of the immensity of rock overhead made her breath catch, an oppressive awareness of the earth surrounding her. She pushed forward, focusing only on the narrow patch of tunnel ahead. Her relief was palpable as the slope began to rise, the stone easing its grip.

Sliding out from the narrow passage, Karak felt her shoulders drop as the tension eased. Free of the tunnel's grip, she pressed a weary hand against the cold floor, steadying herself as she rose to one knee. Tentatively, she extended her torch forward, the flame casting shifting shadows across the chamber's walls. Her gaze swept the space, waiting for a sound, a movement—anything that would prove she was not alone. But silence held.

The chamber stretched circular around her, its stark simplicity unnerving. At its centre stood a large, unadorned stone altar. Along the walls, unlit torches were secured, like watchful sentinels, but the room remained empty. Eerily empty.

Holding her torch steady, she took a step inside, then another, each step slow, as if the wrong move might disturb the chamber's strange ambiance. The shadow of the altar stretched and shifted along the wall as she moved, flickering in her torchlight, giving the illusion that something waited, watching. A chill crept through her, winding its way into her bones. Though she knew she was alone, a strange prickling unease crawled up her spine. She could not shake the feeling that eyes were fixed on her from some hidden place within the hollow.

Each step forward was careful, her gaze fixed on the altar, which grew colder with every inch she drew nearer. Her breath began to mist in the air, the temperature dropping so quickly her skin prickled beneath the furs. And then, as if something unseen stirred, a faint vibration rippled across the stone floor. Karak froze, eyes wide, heart pounding as she searched for the source. But the chamber remained still.

Apprehensively, she approached the altar, the dust-covered stone surface dull and unremarkable, seemingly untouched for years. With a gloved hand, she brushed the dust away, revealing the stark, pale stone beneath. Her fingers paused on a small marking, barely visible under layers of grit. She bent closer, curiosity driving her to trace the grooves of the engraving. Slowly, the dust parted, revealing ancient symbols etched in a lost language. She squinted, lowering her torch to decipher the faded characters.

One word emerged, a word she recognized even through the centuries-old text:

ᚺᚷᚦ.

Her breath caught, and in a voice barely above a whisper, she spoke the word's meaning aloud:

"Shiva."

Within a heartbeat, her torch extinguished, plunging the chamber into complete darkness. Karak froze, her breath catching as the darkness pressed in from all sides, the chill seeping deeper into her bones. She was no longer alone. Her skin prickled as an unmistakable presence filled the room, watching her, waiting.

Summoning all the authority she could muster, she called out, her voice steady despite the fear clawing at her chest. "Reveal yourself!"

Silence. Only the sound of her own breathing broke the heavy quiet. She opened her mouth to call out again, but then—swift and close—came the patter of bare feet against the cold stone floor, darting behind her. She spun, her eyes straining to see through the pitch-black. Another scamper of feet cut through the silence, now from the other side of the chamber, then a third, impossibly fast, circling her.

"Who goes there?" Karak's voice wavered despite herself. Her question was met with a low, sinister laugh that seemed to slither around her, wrapping itself in the darkness like an embrace of ice. A shiver ran up her spine. Instinctively, she stepped back, her heel thudding against the stone altar. In an instant, blue flames burst to life along its edges, illuminating the runes carved into its surface. The walls flared with the same eerie, otherworldly light, as torches along the perimeter ignited in an unnatural glow.

A weight filled the air, pressing down on her as an ancient, powerful presence took form. Then, a voice—low and rumbling, dripping with menace—filled the chamber. Its words resonated in runes, etched into the walls as if the stone itself spoke:

ᚦᚨᚱᚠᚺ ᚷᚨᚷᛁᚦ.

Each syllable boomed, foreign and incomprehensible, yet their essence seeped into her very being: "Ice eternal, the god of storms calls to you." The sound pulsed through her, a dark melody laced with dread, reaching beyond her ears and into her soul, shaking her resolve.

She raised her hands to her ears, trying to block out the voice, but it was useless. The sound seemed to come from within the stone walls themselves, reverberating through the chamber, the ground trembling underfoot. Tiny fragments of stone chipped off the ceiling, dust clouds billowing down as the walls shook with each word of the Ice Demon Shiva's incantation.

In desperation, Karak cried out, the terror almost breaking her. And then, as suddenly as it began, the voice stopped. The chamber fell into an unnatural, suffocating silence, broken only by the soft crackle of the ghostly blue flames.

The Queen unwillingly opened her eyes, just a sliver, hiding behind her lids. She squinted into the dim light, which had faded to a comfortable glow, and slowly lowered her hands from her ears. Using the altar for support, she steadied herself, waiting for her enigmatic host.

It was not long before a voice, beautiful and youthful, spoke softly within her mind, like a gentle breeze caressing her thoughts. The words carried the resonance of an ancient tongue, their runic essence shaping the air:

ᚨᛁᛋᚢᚾ ᛜᚢᛚᛜᚨᚾᚺᚷᚦ.

Though the syllables were foreign, they flowed like a soothing melody, wrapping around her consciousness and dissolving her tension. The meaning unfurled within her mind as if whispered by the wind: "Peace within the storm, the eternal ice embraces you."

Karak felt her mood shift, a tranquil calm washing over her, the weight of her journey briefly forgotten in the gentle embrace of the voice.

Before her, the faint image of a woman began to materialise, her hair woven with strands of frost, her skin a shimmering ice blue. As the figure emerged more clearly, Karak saw that the woman was not merely human; she was perfection personified, her skin smooth and unblemished, aglow with an ethereal light. Two alluring eyes, white as freshly fallen snowflakes, sparkled like flawlessly cut diamonds, reflecting the flickering blue flames.

The goddess's body curved with an elegance that mesmerised Karak, and as she raised a willowy blue arm with long, enticing fingers, the soft voice urged her, "Open your eyes."

Unaware that her eyes were still closed, Karak complied. As she opened them fully, the image in her mind solidified into reality. Shiva was even more breathtaking in flesh, her beauty igniting a warmth within Karak that she had not anticipated. The goddess noticed, a subtle smile blooming on her elongated face. "You enjoy my appearance?" she asked, her words echoing in the ancient tongue, yet perfectly understood. Hypnotised by Shiva's allure, Karak nodded in agreement, her breath catching.

With a graceful sway of her hips, Shiva drew nearer, their eyes locked in an intimate dance of recognition. As the goddess stood within a breath's space of Karak, her icy fingers brushed aside Karak's fiery red hair, revealing the delicate skin of her neckline. Leaning in, Shiva exhaled a gentle stream of ice-cold air just above Karak's collarbone. Instantly, the chill sent shivers cascading down Karak's spine, her skin dimpling with delight. A soft whimper escaped her lips, the sensation electrifying every nerve in her body.

"Tell me, Queen," the ice maiden purred seductively as she glided gracefully behind Karak, her cold fingers trailing along the Queen's furs, leaving a tingling sensation in their wake. "I could remove your furs, seduce you, and pleasure you in ways you have yet to imagine. I could ease the anguish in your heart and fulfil your deepest needs. Would you allow me?"

As Shiva spoke, her inquisitive fingers slipped beneath Karak's furs, circling and caressing her skin before drifting down to her breast, where her nipple tightened in response. Karak let out a wanting sigh, caught in the spell of the goddess. "I can sense your desire," Shiva murmured, her hand gliding lower, tracing a line around Karak's flat stomach and descending still further. Each touch ignited a desperate longing within the Queen, and she ached for Shiva's icy fingers to delve deeper.

"I cannot," Karak replied, her voice laced with dejection.

In an instant, Shiva's hand recoiled, the abrupt movement causing Karak's skin to burn against the frost. The tranquil being transformed before her eyes, spinning with a speed that defied human capability. The beauty of her visage twisted into something feral, dread pooling in her once-luminous eyes, now turned a pearlescent black. The frost that had adorned her skin erupted into blue flames, engulfing her form in a terrifying blaze.

Without hesitation, long, dagger-like teeth shot forth from her mouth, a predator poised to strike. Karak fell backward, hitting the cold stone floor hard, instinctively covering her face as fear coursed through her veins, preparing for the worst.

But the moment passed, and after what felt like an eternity, Karak bravely dared to look up. The Ice Maiden had returned, transformed back into the stunning figure she had been before, radiating calmness once more.

"Tell me then, Queen," Shiva intoned, her voice low and inviting. "Why venture to me?"

The Queen rose once more, grimacing as the lingering burn of Shiva's touch radiated through her body. She knew her peril was great, but she summoned every ounce of authority she could muster. "Ice Empress Shiva, Goddess of Blizzards and Bringer of Storms, my cause is such: my husband, the King under the mountain, is unfit for the throne. His bloodline is false, his ways unruly, and his mannerisms vulgar. He leads our fine country into despair, and I seek to remove him."

The demon's voice, tranquil yet icy, responded, "And whose bloodline is true? Was it not your ancestors who forced the dwarves from their dwellings ages past? And what of his mannerisms? Men are vulgar; it is their way. What care is it of mine who sits upon your throne? It matters little to me. You sound as if an impudent child. Do as you choose. The lives of mortals bear little significance to me. I shall even calm my storm this day, so you may return to your precious city unharmed. Put a knife to his neck and let his lifeblood flow. Yet you venture to me, disturb my slumber without offering- why?"

Karak felt a chill of unease wash over her but pressed on, determination bolstering her voice. "I do not ask for your blessing; I ask for a gift.".

Shiva glided closer, each step imbued with a haunting grace, until she stood before the Queen. Her frost-laden fingers caressed the fur of Karak's coat, sending shivers down her spine. "You wish for me to do your bidding?" The moment her fingers brushed the fabric, the individual strands began to freeze, the frost creeping like a living thing across Karak's coat and down her legs.

Within moments, the cold solidified, encasing Karak in a tomb of ice, leaving only her head free. Panic should have set in, yet an unsettling calm washed over her, the demon's presence entrancing. As Shiva moved behind her, out of sight, Karak could feel the icy fingers slowly wrap around her neck, an intimate embrace that both thrilled and terrified her.

"Tell me, Queen," Shiva whispered, her breath a chilling caress against Karak's skin, "what would you sacrifice for power? You come without an offering, asking for a gift I care not to give. Do you wish for your end so dearly? I could grant it to you, leave you to freeze in the depths of despair."

A silent pause enveloped the chamber, the icy fingers unyielding around the Queen's exposed neck. Though Karak was acutely aware of her peril, a strange peace settled over her, as if the demon had woven a spell around her. Time stretched—moments felt like hours—before Shiva's fingers finally slipped away. The goddess reappeared before Karak, a smile gracing her ethereal features as she surveyed her captive.

"Perhaps not, perhaps there is a bargain to be struck. I have lingered in this world for so long, surrounded by priests who claim to serve me. Yet no man can truly serve without the means to offer pleasure. I am presented with goats, prisoners—half-starved and caked in filth. Or children—only the deformed and disfigured. These are not offerings; they are burdens. Once, I was loved. It has been ages since I felt the touch of a strong man."

With a graceful sweep, Shiva raised her hand, palm flat and facing upward. In the centre rested an empty glass vial. "Make me an offering worthy of my favour, and see this vial filled."

As the block of ice encasing Karak began to melt away, she felt the chilling weight lift from her body. Silently, she accepted the small glass vial, its delicate surface cool against her skin. Shiva took several steps back, her form starting to fade along with the vibrant runes and flickering torches that adorned the walls. In that moment, the chamber fell into a haunting stillness, leaving Karak alone, her flame-lit torch casting shadows that danced across the stone.

The trance that held her captive lifted, and she stood in the echoing silence, her expression vacant as if awakening from a dream she struggled to recall. She gazed down at the glass vial in her hand, the implications of her encounter settling into her consciousness. A profound realisation washed over her—she knew what must be done.

# THE QUEEN CONSORT CHAPTER TWELVE

A rapturous cheer bellowed throughout the hall as the laughter of men acclaimed the offensive punch line. Ale spilled as cups were clasped together, further greasing an already hazardous floor. Serving maids navigated between folk as best they could, refilling cups and replenishing cooked meats. Karak watched on as her husband, the King, beat his newly filled cup against the wooden table, its contents spraying all close by. Her disapproval hidden behind a false grin.

Her attention fell to the short blonde serving maid who refilled it, the King snatched her wrist as she did pulling her close. Ale split from the jug drenching her forearm, but she remained calm and able to finish pouring. Ivar leaned into the blonde maid's ear; Karak assumed to mutter something repugnant. Watching as an uncomfortable smile grew on the maid's face, the same smile she was so used to making. Poor girl she thought, having that drunken oath hump her later, his belly slapping into her small frame as his foul stench suffocated her senses.

Karak followed the girl as she filled several more cups before tossing another log to a large central blaze; it did not take long to crackle and spit. Finally, the maid disappeared out of sight and Karak sighed, the little blonde had been a welcome distraction, for the day's events still played heavily on her mind. The trek back to the Stormhold gates had been relatively straightforward, Karak scarcely remembered the journey, it was the audience with Shiva. The contrasting emotions of wonder and fear, how easy it had been to speak openly of treason with this ancestral being. Followed with a dreaded bargain, an offering for a vial filled. An offering of a man, or of livestock more appropriately put.

Sneaking back into the city had not been an issue, but her brother, Konan, was meant to meet her back in her chambers before this evening supper. The longer he took to arrive the more anxious Karak had become, constantly walking her room, back and forth, waiting for his arrival, feeling the full weight of today's decisions. A knock at her door had come but it was not Konan, instead her personal maid, to escort her to this feast. Karak had told the maid Konan was meant to be escorting her but after another hour she could not delay any longer, Konan had never arrived.

The walk to the feast hall was not far, but the whole time she was fidgety, looking over her shoulder. Scratching at the cuticles of her nails, anxiously replying to her maid's innocent smiles in kind. The constant threat every time they passed patrolling guards, waiting for that interruption, waiting to take her away. Karak was sure her venture to Shiva's cave had gone unseen but perhaps not, that nagging doubt wouldn't leave her.

She sank back into her tall chair facing the amassed hall, negative thoughts and scenarios running over in her head, no particular order but each concern starting to weigh heavier. It was one thing to speak of treason, another to put action to it. Even as Queen there was only one outcome, she would be executed without hesitation. The city had many spies, had she been followed, had her own maid notice her leave and speak of it to anyone. Or worse, had her brother been compromised, he was a soldier and would never be taken alive but once dealt with the guard would soon come looking for her.

Karak shuddered at the thought, she was warm but noticed her hands trembling. She gripped the wooden arms and again pushed herself deeper into the chair to counter it, though it made minimal difference. The apparition of Shiva appeared in her mind then. Not the beautiful ice maiden but the feral demon, teeth snarling at her, eyes as black as the night. Ice blue flames flicking off her frost woven skin, Karak had made a deal with this demon.

She shuddered at her mind's image and focused on what she could, taking a sip from her own ale. A bowl of barely touched meat sat in front of Karak, she could not face it, the day had been long, and the evening was late but the feast only in its beginnings. She was desperate to leave or see her brother appear, to give her the reassurance needed, so she knew everything would be ok.

Suddenly her maid interrupted her thoughts "are you cold my Queen, I could fetch furs?"

Karak smiled and shook her head, perhaps she should have requested one. If she were just worrying over nothing it would more than likely be a long laborious night as these feasts normally were. Karak's thoughts drifted back as they always did, how she could escape the proceedings early. These feasts always went the same way, everyone would smile at her, acknowledge her as their Queen, but very few would participate in meaningful conversation. She would suffer the boredom of watching men do as men do, drink ale and lurch over any woman that were unfortunate to cross their paths.

Karak looked upon those men, each living up to her synopsis. It was the same crowd, King Ivar seated at the head of the largest table, several men in close proximity. One being Birger, his first advisor, of course leading the laughter as he normally would. Then Ansgar, the warden of the city, then several other seated men of prominent position. After that were those just outside the inner circle but of equal importance bearing boring titles. They would clamour for attention, constantly trying to breach that inner circle. Then the remaining council members would have jostled for a prime seat prior to the King's arrival, just out of earshot but clinging onto any bits of conversation they could. Finally, the men just happy to be in the feast chamber, they were either young with a point they wanted to prove or elderly whose point had never been relevant. Some did not even have a seat, just stood silently with an ale, backs pressed against the cold wall. Barely included, not even interactive in the conversations, just observers questioning how they could trade places with men of seemingly more worth to their King.

There were no surprises this evening though, every man was where he was supposed to be or at least there or thereabouts. It was very rare for political movement in Stormhold, Karak continued to scan the room once more to pass the time. And then there was a man she did not recognise, surprisingly stood out. He was not the tallest but held a strong posture, stood by the wall but without leaning on it for support. His head was freshly shaved, the shape of his hairline still faintly visible. His bone structure was very pronounced above his temple, ears tightly tucked against his freckled skin. His nose was thin, two piercing pale blue eyes stared ominously forward, occasionally examining the room. A copper red beard was thick on his face but not in length.

Karak noticed he was without a drink, clearly an attempt to keep his mind sharp, possibly his first time at such a prestigious event. His arms unfolded and refolded twice, clearly anxious before he waved away a maid offering him a slice of cooked meat from a silver platter she carried. Karak wondered about his background, clearly not a miner for he was too slender and no soldier for his beard did not have the braids or ironclads.

Men of Nordon by tradition were clean shaven until their sixteenth name day. It was then they were chosen for a profession based on their tutors, fathers and family history. By their eighteenth name day they should have a full beard, a wife could now be chosen, braids and ironclads would be woven into their beards, certain styles representing professions. This man had none, perhaps a highborn who she did not recognise.

Karak again leaned back in her chair, studying the stranger with a mixture of curiosity and concern. There was something about him that stirred an instinctive wariness within her; perhaps it was the way his pale blue eyes scanned the room, sharp and calculating, as if he were assessing every movement, every whisper that danced in the air. She shifted in her seat, trying to shake off the growing tension in her chest.

The laughter of King Ivar boomed once more, drawing her attention back to his table. She noticed his black beard was littered with small unfinished chunks of hams, how his very existence repulsed her increasingly each day. But her thoughts kept wandering back to the stranger. He seemed out of place, an anomaly amidst the boisterous crowd of nobles and soldiers. As she watched, he caught her gaze and held it for a fleeting moment before his lips curled into a subtle, knowing smile. It was disconcerting, yet oddly captivating.

Suddenly, the hall's doors swung open, a gust of cold air swirling through the room, momentarily silencing the laughter. All heads turned as a figure stepped inside, tall and cloaked in dark furs, the heavy fabric trailing behind like a shadow. Karak's breath caught in her throat; it was Konan. Relief washed over her, but the tension remained, for he did not enter with the usual confidence that characterised him.

His eyes scanned the hall quickly, settling on Karak. In an instant, she felt the weight of his unspoken words—something was amiss. She watched as he tried to escape quick pleasantries with some of the men but got stuck for a time with Ivar, who had to share the same awful jest as earlier. At this point Ivar was too intoxicated to make sense of it. Her brother forced a laugh, patted his King on the shoulder and made his exit. As he approached her, weaving through the crowd, the laughter and revelry resuming around them.

“Forgive my tardiness, sister,” he said, his voice low and urgent as he reached her side. “We need to talk. Now.”

Karak’s heart raced, her mind racing with possibilities. She nodded; her lips pressed into a thin line. “Is it about the offering?”

Konan leaned closer, his expression grave. “It’s worse than that. There are whispers a foot. Some suspect you’ve made a pact, and they are looking for proof.”

A chill ran down Karak's spine, colder than any she had felt earlier that day. She glanced around the hall, her eyes flitting over the faces of men she thought she knew, their laughter now feeling like a dangerous mockery. "Who?" she whispered, her voice trembling slightly.

"I know not yet. But we must be careful. I fear the more they drink, the more they talk. I've already heard rumours about you and your visit to the cave. You must act as if nothing is wrong, keep your head high. We'll get through this."

The words hung in the air like a blade, ready to drop. Karak nodded, but inside, doubt began to fester. The weight of the day's events pressed down on her, and she was painfully aware of the stranger still watching from his corner, those piercing eyes never leaving her.

Before she could respond, a loud crash broke through her thoughts. A tankard had slipped from a man's grasp, shattering on the stone floor, ale splattering in all directions. Laughter erupted, but the sound was hollow to Karak's ears. She felt the room shift, a palpable tension settling like a heavy fog.

"Stay close to me," Konan urged quietly, his brow furrowing with concern. "We'll face this together."

As the feast continued around them, Karak felt a strange mix of gratitude and dread. The night was just beginning, but already she could sense that it would not end without bloodshed. The demon she had encountered was not the only entity lurking in the shadows; the realm of men held its own monsters, and they would not be easily ignored. Konan moved round to her side of the table and pulled a bench to be seated next to her. The pair sat in silence as they both shifted their eyes across the scene.

The short blonde maid approached and flashed a flirtatious smile at the broad red maned Konan, passing him a jug and filling it with ale. He nodded in approval, flicking a courteous smile back and took a few large gulps halving his drink. She then placed a plate of meats trying to get his attention once more, but it was ignored, then left the pair in their silence.

Karak watched as her brother grabbed at a chicken leg and sunk his teeth into the meat, always the soldier she thought. He would have the same concerns as her but would know he may need his strength tonight. Karak's plate was still as full as it was half an hour ago, except the food had been pushed from middle to edge and back again as her nervousness stole her appetite. She took a deep breath, summoning the same strength she had found today within Shiva's cave. She would not let fear take hold. If the demon demanded sacrifice, then it would not be her own to give.

As she stole another glance at the stranger, he met her gaze again, his expression unreadable. A flicker of understanding passed between them, a silent acknowledgment of the darkness that loomed ahead. The feast, with all its revelry and camaraderie, felt like a masquerade—a beautiful facade hiding the truth.

Karak placed a hand onto her brother's thigh, her nails dug gently to gain his attention then steered his leg in the stranger's direction as if guiding Konan's eyes. Her brother reacted astutely, pushing his plate aside then moved his hand down onto his thigh, pushing Karak's aside and resting on the hilt of an unseen blade. Karak met her brother's dark brown eyes then; they had a murderous gaze. She greeted him with a smile and ever so subtly shook her head, a smile that said a thousand words without uttering one, his fingers left the hilt and back to his plate.

Her brother was a warrior, a warrior that would fight every man in this hall only to give his sister another few moments of life. It was an unwavering loyalty he had always had for his younger sister. When they were but children an older boy had tried forcing himself upon Karak, she had let out a scream so loud it reached her brother the next home away. Konan had run so fast to his sister's aid the older boy could not even muster up a threat before fists had hit him so hard his jaw was left hanging, mouth full of blood and the floor scattered with broken teeth. But she did not wish to see her brother fight tonight, only to watch him fall before she followed straight after him.

Karak turned her attention back to the feast, her heart racing with the knowledge that danger lurked just beneath the surface of the merriment. She turned forward with a larger smile and raised her cup, joining in the raucous cheers that surrounded her. It was an act of defiance against the anxiety gnawing at her insides, a reminder that she was still the Queen of Stormhold, despite the turmoil that threatened to engulf her.

"More ale!" Ivar bellowed, slapping the table with glee, drawing the attention of the crowd once again. "Let us toast to our prosperity and the strength of our kingdom!"

The hall erupted in cheers, and the sound echoed off the stone walls, drowning out her worries—at least for the moment. As she sipped from her cup, Karak caught sight of the stranger again, standing resolutely against the wall, his blue eyes piercing through the haze of revelry. He did not join in the laughter; instead, he remained an observer, a sentinel amidst the chaos.

With a sudden surge of courage, she excused herself from Konan and approached the stranger. The air felt charged between them as she drew closer, the din of the feast fading into a distant hum.

"Who are you?" she asked, her voice steady despite the flutter of uncertainty in her chest.

He regarded her with a measured calm, his features sharp in the flickering firelight. "I am Thoren, my Queen," he replied, his tone low but clear. "I come from the northern reach of Stormhold but have been in the Capital for some many years now. My trade is in knowing the knowledge others wish to know."

"Why are you here?" Karak pressed, instinctively aware that this man could hold answers to the questions swirling in her mind.

"Not all who arrive at your doors seek glory or wealth," Thoren replied, his gaze unwavering. "Some seek truth, and some seek justice. I have heard the whispers, the echoes of your name, and I believe you may be in need an ally."

Karak's heart raced, both intrigued and wary. "What whispers hold my name Thoren? Your Queen demands your answer."

"I know enough," he said, his voice dropping to a near whisper. "The pact you forged with Shiva—it has not gone unnoticed. There are those who would use it against you."

Her breath caught, the weight of his words settling heavily on her shoulders. "And what do you want in return for this information?"

"A chance to stand beside you," Thoren replied, his eyes intense. "I am no mere soldier seeking to gain favour. I seek a cause worthy of my allegiance, and I believe that is you. But you must tread carefully; the winds of betrayal blow stronger in Stormhold than they do in the blizzards."

Before she could respond, the hall erupted in another round of raucous laughter. Karak turned her gaze back to her husband, who was now regaling the guests with an exaggerated tale of his hunting exploits. The men leaned in, hanging on his every word, oblivious to the darker currents swirling just beneath the surface.

"I cannot promise you anything," Karak said, returning her attention to

Thoren. "Not yet. But if what you say is true, I could be in need of your assistance."

"Then we will speak again," he replied, a hint of a smile breaking through his stoic demeanour. "But for now, blend in. Your enemies are watching."

Karak nodded, the weight of his words settling in her mind. As she walked back toward her table, she felt the fire of resolve igniting within her. If she were to navigate the treacherous waters of her kingdom, she would need allies—both known and unknown.

She returned to Konan's side, her heart steadier than before. "What did he say?" her brother asked, his eyes narrowing with concern.

"Nothing I can share now," she replied, forcing a smile. "But I believe we will have help."

The blonde serving maid made another pass and a thought tickled Karak "Konan, that maid, she likes you."

Konan's eye's left his meal for a moment to take in her features, then darted back down to his plate that seemingly held more interest, "she's too small" he muttered without any interest.

Karak placed gentle fingers on his forearm and leaned into him "next time she feels your cup, make merriment, I would have you copulate with her tonight." His face responded with a puzzled expression, but Karak stroked his arm and nodded reassuringly at him of the task, the seeds of a plot were formulating.

The feast continued, the laughter and music surrounding them, Karak felt a sense of purpose awaken within her. She was no longer merely a pawn in the disguise of a Queen; but in fact, the opposite and she would not let fear dictate her fate.

As the night wore on, she kept a watchful eye on the crowd, her thoughts a tangled web of plans and possibilities. She would prepare for the storm ahead, ready to face whatever darkness awaited her. With each passing moment, the Queen within her grew stronger, ready to embrace the power she had always possessed but had yet to wield.

And as the final toast rang out, a chorus of voices celebrating their shared victories, Karak raised her cup high, her heart a mixture of trepidation and hope. The dance of fate had begun, and she was determined to lead it to a conclusion of her choosing.

# THE QUEEN CONSORT CHAPTER THIRTEEN

Karak stood on the balcony of her chamber; the air cool against her skin as she gazed out over the sprawling city of Stormhold. From her viewpoint the city reached on for miles. Countless columns of enormous size carved straight out the mountain stretched from floor to ceiling. Huge fire pits cast their long shadows across the different dwellings and streets. The distant sounds of laughter and revelry from the feast hall echoed up to her, a stark contrast to the solitude she sought. She felt a flicker of envy for those below, oblivious to the dark designs brewing above their heads.

She took a deep breath, trying to steady her racing heart. This city, her home, held both promise and peril, and she needed to ensure the safety of her plans. With a final glance over the shimmering lights of Stormhold, she turned and stepped back into her chamber, pulling the heavy doors shut behind her. The sound echoed in the silence, sealing her off from the world outside, protecting her secrets from prying eyes.

The interior of her room was dimly lit by the flickering fire in the hearth, casting dancing shadows against the stone walls. Rich tapestries adorned the space, depicting scenes of valour and glory, but tonight, they felt like a facade. She paced the room, her thoughts swirling like the flames, until a soft knock at the door made her heart quicken.

She opened it to reveal Konan, a striking figure with a tall, muscular frame and long red hair tied back in a high bun. His thick red beard, adorned with iron cladding, framed a face that radiated strength and determination. He wore a dark cloak with the hood down, sleeves rolled up revealing his bare forearms—each one scarred from past battles, a testament to his warrior's life. "It's time," he said, glancing over his shoulder as he stepped inside, closing the door firmly behind him.

Thoren arrived moments later, moving quietly, as if the shadows themselves had ushered him in. He took a seat at the small table, a map of Stormhold spread before them, its edges curling slightly from the heat of the fire. Karak felt a rush of urgency coursing through her veins. This was a dangerous game they were playing, but it was one she could no longer avoid.

"Thank you for coming," Karak began, her voice steady despite the turmoil inside her. "We don't have much time. The longer we wait, the more vulnerable we become."

Thoren leaned forward, his eyes glinting in the firelight. "What you propose is not without risks, my Queen. But the reward could be worth the sacrifice."

"Tell us how we can execute this plan," Konan interjected, his expression resolute as he crossed his muscular arms, the scars on his forearms catching the light. "We need to know every detail."

Karak took a deep breath, steadying herself, then let her expression hardened. "Ivar is a vulgar man, a disgrace to the crown and to the people of Stormhold. He treats the common folk as if they mean nought, forgetting what it means to be a citizen of this city, this country. His laughter echoes through the halls while the cries of the oppressed go unheard. Trade agreements he signed with our neighbouring countries squeeze our gold for every last coin, leaving our coffers bare while he lives in excess. He has forgotten that we are all part of this realm, that every citizen deserves dignity and respect. I cannot abide this discontent any longer" She paused for a moment, letting the betrayal of her words flow over the two men really trying to emphasise her points.

"Ivar's death must appear as an accident, a natural outcome of indulgence. Poison from Shiva will be potent; it will mimic the effects of a common ailment, ensuring no one suspects foul play."

Thoren nodded, absorbing the gravitas of her words. "And you believe you can obtain this poison without raising suspicion?"

Karak's mind raced, her thoughts pulling together the threads of her plan. "I did not visit the tomb of Shiva for some folly gain, I met with her." Both men leaned in with anticipation for the untold story. All knew of Shiva's existence but very few would ever witness such encounters. "She is as powerful as she is desiring a male offering, a man unknowing of their fate, a strong man. If we can make such a worthy offering, she will bless us with such a poison."

"Once we have the poison, how do we ensure it reaches the King?" Konan asked, his brow furrowing with concern, his presence both imposing and reassuring.

Thoren leaned back, a calculating expression on his face. “That’s where I come in. I’ll spread rumours, sow distrust among the court. The more chaos we create, the easier it will be to slip the poison into his cup unnoticed.”

“And what of his advisors?” Konan interjected. “They will be watching closely. If we act too soon, they might smell our treachery.”

Thoren turned to him “As skilled as you are with your axe, I am with my flowers, I plant small seeds of distrust among them, watch as they blossom into our will. Ivar is arrogant, perhaps too arrogant to see the danger closing in around him. Let him revel in his ignorance.”

Karak felt a flicker of hope. “If we can create a rift between Ivar and his advisors, he’ll become isolated, easier to target. We’ll need to make him believe he is surrounded by enemies, that even those closest to him are conspiring against him.”

“Good,” Thoren said, his voice low and confident. “I’ll start tonight. Whispers of rebellion, discontent—those will flow like ale through the halls of Stormhold.”

“Be careful, Thoren,” Konan cautioned. “We cannot trust anyone but each other.”

Thoren smirked, a glint of mischief in his eyes. “Trust is a fragile thing, dear warrior. But I assure you, I have no interest in being on the wrong side of your blade.”

Konan nodded, his jaw set. “And I will choose the offering. It must be a man who has lived on the fringes, who is seen as expendable by the court. There are always men who have fallen out of favour, soldiers whose deeds have been overlooked. We must ensure that he is strong and without families who will miss him.”

Karak glanced at Konan, her heart swelling with pride. “You know the city well. Choose wisely, brother. We cannot afford any loose ends that might lead back to us.” She held his gaze “tell me brother, that maid at the feast two nights back, did you bed her?”

Konan shifted his eyes from her, his head followed almost in guilt “I did your bidding my Queen.”

Karak sat back taking in a deep breath through her nostrils and let the air exhale before she spoke again. “Did she enjoy you?”

“What has this to do with our plans?” Konan questioned back, unsure of where his sister’s interrogation was leading.

“Did she enjoy you brother?” she firmly spoke, Konan without a word gestured the answer she wanted. “Good, you shall see her again” Karak responded, her brother carrying a puzzled look. Karak next spoke in a softer tone “you shall see her again, and again, and again, until you have left your mark on her such that when the time comes, you ask her to pour a fine wine, a wine of my choosing, into the King’s cup.” A broad smile rose to Konan then followed with a smirk, the missing pieces in his head beginning to fill with admiration for his sister’s detail. Thoren patted the table gently in a complementary sign of agreement.

As their discussion drew to a close, Karak felt a sense of finality settle over the room. They were bound together in this dark pact, each knowing the stakes involved. “Thank you for your loyalty,” she said softly. “It means more than you know.”

Thoren stood, the shadows enveloping him like a cloak. “I will not betray your trust. But remember, secrets have a way of unravelling.” With that, he slipped out of the chamber, the door closing silently behind him.

Karak turned to Konan, a new weight of concern settling in her chest as she studied him. His tall, muscular form was a stark contrast to the shadows around them, and his fierce red hair seemed to burn even in the dim light. “We must be careful. Thoren’s motives remain unclear. I need you to find out everything you can about him—his past, his connections, and whether he can be trusted.”

Konan’s brow furrowed, and he flexed his bare forearms, revealing the scars that mapped his battles. “I will. But do you truly believe he will help us, or is he merely playing his own game?”

“I know not,” Karak admitted, a tremor of uncertainty creeping into her voice. “But if he can deliver what we need, we must take the chance.”

“And what will you do now I take my leave, these next days we must keep distance” Konan asked, concern etched across his features.

“I’ll remain vigilant,” she replied, crossing her arms. “There’s much to consider, and I’ll need to monitor the court’s reactions closely. I won’t let my guard down.”

As Konan stood and prepared to leave, Karak could not shake the lingering thoughts of Thoren's motivations. The man was an enigma—outwardly calm and collected, yet there was a hunger in his eyes. He was a man with nothing to lose and everything to gain. With King Ivar's assassination, Thoren would find himself elevated from obscurity to a position of power at Karak's side. The thought both intrigued and unsettled her.

Thoren had expressed a desire for change, but it was clear he was not simply a loyalist. His loyalty was contingent upon the success of the plan. He wanted influence, a voice in the ear of the new Queen. What would he demand in return? Karak turned back to the fire, the flames licking at the wood with an insatiable hunger. She needed to proceed with caution, not just against her enemies but also against potential allies like Thoren.

As she watched the flames dance, she resolved to keep her guard up. They were playing a dangerous game, and even the allies who seemed most trustworthy could turn treacherous at the slightest whiff of ambition.

"Be cautious, brother," she called after Konan as he reached the door to leave. "We cannot afford to be blindsided."

"Trust me, I will" he replied before slipping out into the dim corridor.

Alone once more, Karak let the silence envelop her like a heavy shroud. The shadows in the corners of her chamber seemed to grow darker, the flickering fire casting an uncertain light over her features. She moved to the hearth, staring into the flames as if searching for answers within their chaotic dance. Each flicker reminded her of the precariousness of her situation—one misstep, one whispered word, and everything she had worked for could crumble into ash.

A storm of emotions roiled within her. Anger surged at the thought of Ivar, that vulgar man whose laughter echoed through the halls like a cruel taunt. She thought of his gluttony, the way he revelled in feasting like a starved pig. How could he call himself a king when he had the idiosyncrasy so similar to such a beast. He was a disgrace, a betrayal of everything Stormhold stood for. Her heart burned with righteous indignation, fuelling her resolve to rid the throne of him once and for all.

Yet with that anger came a deep-seated fear, gnawing at her insides. What if their plans failed? What if Thoren's ambitions overshadowed her own, or worse, what if he was not to be trusted? She felt the weight of her choices bearing down on her like a physical force, the reality of her actions pressing against her chest until it was hard to breathe. Could she truly bring herself to sacrifice an innocent life, to condemn a man to a fate they did not deserve? The thought churned in her stomach, mixing uneasily with her determination.

Karak felt utterly alone in this endeavour. The walls of her chamber, once a sanctuary, now felt like a prison, confining her within her own thoughts. She longed for the comfort of family, the camaraderie of her brother, but even Konan was caught in the web of their scheme. Their bond, once unbreakable, now seemed tethered to the precarious fate of their plans.

As she turned her back to the fire, strode to the doors of her balcony pushing them open. She gazed out over the scene once more, the city sprawling beneath her like a living beast. The flickering lanterns dotted the streets, each representing a life, a family, unaware of the storm brewing above them. A sense of sorrow washed over her—she was about to plunge Stormhold into chaos for the sake of their freedom. Would the blood on her hands haunt her?

The weight of her crown felt heavier than ever, pressing down on her with the realisation of what it truly meant to be a ruler. She craved power, yet it came with a cost she could scarcely bear to contemplate. Doubts whispered in her mind, calling into question her decisions. Was she strong enough to carry the burden of leadership? Could she handle the consequences of her actions?

Karak wrapped her arms around herself, the warmth of the fire contrasting sharply with the chill in her heart. She felt the flicker of hope within her—a hope that once Ivar was gone, she could bring about the change Stormhold desperately needed. But that hope was fragile, like the flame flickering in front of her, easily snuffed out by the winds of betrayal or failure.

Taking a deep breath, she forced herself to focus on the resolve that had brought her to this moment. The people of Stormhold deserved better than the inadequacy of her husband. She would not let fear paralyse her; she would not let doubt dictate her actions. She had made a choice, and now she had to see it through, no matter the cost.

As she stood there, staring out at her city in waiting, she felt a fierce determination settle within her. Whatever challenges lay ahead, she would confront them head-on. She was Queen Karak, and she would not be defined by the actions of others. With each passing moment, her conviction solidified, forging her into a weapon against tyranny.

Stepping back from the balcony, she turned her back on the view and faced her chamber. The night was over, she would need her sleep for the path ahead was treacherous. But for the sake of Stormhold and the people she loved, she would embrace the darkness and use it to her advantage. Her heart pounded with both fear and exhilaration, knowing that she was on the precipice of a change that would forever alter the course of her life and the fate of her kingdom.

# THE QUEEN CONSORT
# CHAPTER FOURTEEN

The great hall of Stormhold buzzed with the sounds of laughter, raised voices, and the clinking of goblets, the echoes filling the vast chamber. It was a space built to inspire awe, with immense, arching domes that seemed to soar nearly twenty stories high, supported by colossal stone columns that rose like ancient trees. Each column, carved with intricate patterns and symbols of old wars, stretched up to brace the ceiling, giving the hall a powerful yet ominous beauty. The sheer scale of the space could accommodate twenty thousand men with room to spare, a striking testament to the grandeur and ingenuity of its architecture.

Every ten metres along the hall, massive flags of Nordon hung from the towering walls, each draped in rich navy cloth embroidered with the kingdom's white-crowned sigil: a royal crown set above a sturdy anvil. Beneath the anvil, three mountains stood in outline, a symbol of the lands' strength and endurance. The banners swayed gently in the hall's subtle drafts, giving an impression of life, as though the walls themselves breathed with the pride of Stormhold.

At the centre of the grand dome was a sunken, circular gladiator pit, fifty metres across, lined with iron and rough-hewn stone. Feats of strength and skill unfolded before the watchful eyes, it served as the focal point of all festivities. This afternoon, the pit held a grand tug-of-war tournament, drawing nobles and soldiers alike to its edge. The nobles, clustered in small groups, wore fine silks and velvets that shimmered in the firelight from towering iron braziers scattered around the hall, casting a warm glow over their jewelled attire. It was the third turn of the moon, a celebration to the God Lunar, marked by games of skill and endurance—a tradition meant to showcase the strength of the realm's finest and draw together the kingdom's elite.

In the pit below, two teams of fifty men each grunted and heaved, their powerful bodies straining against each other as they fought to drag the thick rope to their side. The crowd cheered, their voices mingling in a roar that filled the cavernous hall, a sound that echoed off the domed ceiling and down the columns like thunder.

Queen Karak watched from her seat on the dais beside the King, her fingers lightly clasping the goblet in her hands. Around her, men pledged allegiance to either team and barked orders to the competitors, their eyes darting between the contest and each other. A few seats away from her sat Birger, a loyal steward to the King, he looked on in near silence, casting quick glances in her direction with eyes sharp and discerning.

Karak forced herself to join in the laughter, nodding when prompted, her gaze shifting to meet those who approached. Her cheeks grew warm under the watchful Birger, she felt as if even the smallest gesture could be misread, sparking suspicion. Each second she spent in this hall only heightened her awareness of the danger surrounding her.

Thoren caught her eye from across the vast hall, lifting his goblet in a discreet salute. Karak allowed herself the faintest of smiles, a signal that went unnoticed by all but him. Thoren knew his place, weaving through the courtiers, his whispers seeming to spread, keeping a careful distance but always within her line of sight. It brought a thin layer of reassurance, though her heart betrayed her, beating quickly beneath her ribs.

A sudden commotion drew her attention to the game as the rope shifted direction, the crowd roaring as one team dragged the other to its knees. One of the soldiers stumbled, his hands slipping along the hemp fibres. The match was lost within seconds, and the victorious team threw their hands up, cheering while their opponents fell back, panting on the stone floor. The King rose, his thick, gauntleted hands clapping together, his booming laughter ringing out across the hall.

"Brutes, all of you!" he bellowed, flashing his teeth in a broad grin. "But fine brutes at that!" He waved a hand, catching the attention of a passing serving maid. "Bring these lads something to wet their tongues, eh?" His laughter boomed; his enjoyment as loud as it was genuine.

The maid curtsied low, moving swiftly to obey, while the King's gaze swept his courtiers before settling on Karak. His tone, warm but boisterous, filled the space between them. "Ah, come, wife! You've yet to smile," he said, giving her a nudge with his elbow. "Is there no joy for you in watching these fine feats? Or have the poets won you over with talk of clever words and fancier spectacles?"

Karak managed a polite smile, her tone restrained. "The feats are indeed admirable, my King. Our realm is fortunate to have such strength among its ranks."

“Aye, that’s true enough,” he replied, nodding vigorously. “Strength and loyalty, those are the pillars of any kingdom worth its name! You could stack all the gold in Stormhold, and it wouldn’t add up to the value of men like these.” He gestured broadly to the soldiers with a proud, possessive gleam in his eye.

He took another hearty gulp from his goblet, grinning as he set it down with a loud clink. His gaze fell upon the amassed crowd, nobles, merchants and common folk alike would have been trading coins over the victors. “Gold and goods... merchants think they hold the world in their hands with a cart full of silks and wine.” He scoffed. “As if all their crates and barrels could give a kingdom its backbone. No, no! They wouldn’t last a day without men like these to keep them safe on their roadways.”

The thought clearly amused him, his laughter bubbling up as he leaned toward Karak, almost conspiratorial. “They call themselves traders, as if hauling trinkets and coin is some grand achievement,” he sneered, waving his goblet dismissively. “Their hands are softer than any courtly ladies, and yet they whine louder than all of them combined.”

He paused, catching a glint in Karak’s eyes, though he did not seem to notice her tension. “And still,” he went on, almost to himself, “they’ll look you dead in the eye and say they’re owed a place of honour, simply for piling up gold in their stalls.” His lip curled slightly; the contempt apparent as he shook his head. “Owed respect, simply for existing. They think they hold the kingdom together, yet they rely on the very strength they’d never understand.”

Karak’s gaze was steady, her smile thin but polite. “Strength and loyalty, yes,” she replied, though her mind turned with thoughts of her own. The merchants and traders who brought life into the kingdom’s markets, who helped the realm’s cities grow and prosper—they were the very ones he so readily dismissed. To him, they were little more than children clamouring for treats, as far from his idea of loyalty as the stars were from the earth.

“Leave it to me to handle these people, wife,” he added, patting her shoulder with a hearty confidence that was both careless and overbearing. “Let them fill the coffers, complain, bow, and scrape. There’s no harm in them as long as they’re kept in their place.”

She managed a nod, her own goblet untouched. "No doubt you’ve always had their measure, my King.”

"Of course," he replied with a grunt, as if the thought were obvious. "Their words mean nothing beside steel and stone." He lifted his goblet once more, turning his gaze back to his soldiers, and raised it high with a cheer for the men.

"Surely, my King, prosperity among the common folk only strengthens your rule," she replied, a touch of insistence in her voice.

"By Shiva's teat, strengthen my rule, you say?" He barked a laugh, clapping a hand on his thigh. "You're as clever as those councillors, always with your ideas on mercy and prosperity. A good heart, my Karak!" He turned back to the hall, motioning grandly. "These people know their place, and they'll follow me because they respect the strength of their King! Leave it to me to keep them in line. You'd sooner see the throne given to one of those merchants!"

Her hand tightened on her goblet, though she forced her smile to remain steady. "I know the throne is in capable hands, my King."

"Aye!" he said, raising his goblet with a hearty cheer. "Long live Stormhold and all who serve her King!"

The guests echoed his cheer, their voices filling the hall as Karak looked away, her complexion hardening as he continued to laugh and toast the soldiers. To him, all was fair, and he held his rule over his kingdom with the same careless weight he placed on his cup. And as long as his people fell in line, he would go on thinking himself their shepherd.

She raised her own goblet to her lips, her face composed, her focus shifting towards the crowd once more, where Thoren watched her with a keen, knowing look. Karak nodded, barely a movement, but enough. She would endure these games, her husband's arrogance, Birger's prying eyes but it would not last. She had made her bargain, and her resolve was set. The next time the King presided over his people, he would be no more than a fading voice, his reign a memory, swept away as quickly as the losers of the tug of war.

Her eyes lingered on the crowd; the King idle banter had drifted from her. She watched the shaved head Thoren as once more he slipped through clusters of nobles and soldiers, his gaze sharp and purposeful. She noticed his path: direct, unwavering, as he made his way to one of the men from the victorious tug-of-war team. The soldier straightened, pulling himself to attention as Thoren reached him, his posture a clear mark of respect.

Thoren leaned in close, his voice a murmur too low for anyone nearby to overhear. Karak watched with practised subtlety, her own expression masked, as the soldier nodded, his brows drawing together in concentration. Thoren's hand clasped the man's shoulder, his fingers tightening in what could only be a show of authority. The soldier gave a quick, almost imperceptible nod before turning and disappearing into the crowd, weaving between clusters of armoured men, his purpose clear.

One by one, the soldier stopped beside others, speaking in hushed tones, passing along instructions, each man he approached slipping from the hall in swift, practised movements. Karak recognized the signs; these were no ordinary soldiers. They were Thoren's men, strategically placed and hidden in plain sight. As one of the soldiers vanished through the great doors at the far end of the hall, a faint satisfaction crept through her. Thoren was thorough, and his influence reached further than most realised. His web of loyal men was woven into the very fabric of the court, unseen yet everywhere.

She cast a quick glance back at the King, who remained oblivious, engrossed in his boasts and laughter. His kingdom was already slipping from his grasp, though he was too blind to see it. Ivar believed he was untouchable, ruling from his seat of power without regard for those he trampled underfoot. But now, with each quiet instruction passed through Thoren's men, her vision of a kingdom free of his ignorance edged closer to reality. Soon, it would no longer be her burden to endure his disdain.

As Karak raised her goblet to her lips, the wine heavy and rich on her tongue, a troubling thought settled in her mind. Thoren—his reach, his hidden web of faces. Just how far did it extend? She knew he had men embedded within Nordon's ranks, but was that all? If their plans succeeded and her ambitions bore fruit, would Thoren remain an ally... or might he evolve into a formidable rival?

Her hand tightened around the goblet as the thought took root, branching out with unsettling clarity. She lowered her cup, her attention drifting across the hall, seeking Konan. He stood a short distance away, absorbed in a small gathering of men. Maintaining a gracious smile, Karak offered polite, hollow responses to the nobles around her, her words well-rehearsed but absent of feeling. Then, with a practised elegance, she excused herself, gliding through the crowd toward her brother. Konan's presence was a rare comfort, his unwavering gaze a steady anchor as he observed the room in his usual stoic silence.

She reached Konan's side, her hand slipping around his to guide him away from the group. “Brother, a word,” she murmured, her tone quiet yet insistent. Konan, ever attuned to her subtleties, fell in step beside her, awaiting her direction.

With a slight tilt of her head, she indicated a soldier engaged in conversation nearby. “That man,” she whispered, her voice just carrying to Konan’s ear. “Who is he?”

Konan's gaze followed her line of sight, his expression hardening as he assessed the man. “Bodvar,” he replied in a low tone. “A seasoned soldier. Has served with distinction.” He paused, sensing there was more to her inquiry. “Why do you ask?”

Karak’s expression grew thoughtful, her eyes lingering on the man. “It’s clear Thoren considers Bodvar his man,” she said softly, a flicker of calculation in her tone. “If Thoren believes he will have command of the armies once the King is gone, he’s mistaken. We cannot allow him such power.”

Konan’s brow lifted slightly, a glint of approval flashing in his eyes. “So, you mean to break his hold?”

“Let him continue his scheming, for now” she replied, a subtle smile curving her lips. “Though Bodvar would make a fine offering, do you not agree?”

Konan’s lips twitched, almost a smile. “Clever,” he murmured.

Karak gave a faint nod, her gaze once more moving to Thoren, who now laughed and jested among a new group. He was useful, to be sure, but he was a man who saw opportunity in every shadow, who would soon fancy himself indispensable. A dangerous ally if left unchecked.

“Thoren will have his time,” she said quietly. “But it will be on our terms.”

As she stood beside her brother, an unspoken resolve settled between them, binding their pact. The King’s end would come soon enough, but Thoren’s ambition, too, would be brought to heel.

# THE QUEEN CONSORT
# CHAPTER FIFTEEN

The council chamber was a marvel, its soaring ceilings vanishing into shadowed heights that defied even the sharpest gaze. It felt as if the stones themselves reached toward the heavens, bound to the mountain yet yearning to break free. Stone arches seemed to grow organically from the rock, as though they had always been part of Nordon's rugged spine. Alongside them, beams of dark wood crossed like a woven tapestry, each carved with intricate, ancient patterns mimicking the jagged peaks of Nordon, lending the room an almost mythic presence. They bore the weight of the mountain itself, daring gravity, while the walls displayed towering reliefs of past kings and queens. Their stony faces, austere and watchful, flickered in the firelight, as if shifting expressions in the shadows, almost alive.

Massive columns flanked the hall, each crowned with raised iron fire pits. Flames burned low within them, casting a hazy, smoky glow. Shadows flickered like restless spirits on the polished stone floors, the scent of smoke mingling with the colder tang of the stone. The atmosphere was thick with expectation, as if every inch of the hall held its breath, the cold eyes of the walls bearing silent witness to the unseen power struggles unfolding below.

Thoren moved through clusters of nobles, each one a target for his carefully curated charm. He knew his role well—a warm smile here, a knowing glance there, laughter precisely measured to resonate just long enough before slipping away like smoke. His words drifted across the room in gentle suggestions, veiled references that would linger in his listeners' minds. Every seed he planted was chosen with care, waiting to sprout into rumours or doubts. He wielded words as if they were weapons, each one leaving an invisible scar or igniting the spark of rivalry.

Finally, his gaze settled on Ansgar, the lone figure leaning against one of the farthest columns. Ansgar's posture was unassuming, his expression contemplative, his eyes fixed on the distant flames as if lost in thought. But Thoren knew better. He saw the opportunity gleaming beneath Ansgar's placid facade. For Thoren, Ansgar was not just an ally—he was a chess piece, one that had been nudged into position over countless, carefully orchestrated conversations.

He drew a breath, feeling the weight of the moment pressing down. To the watching nobles, it might appear as if he was simply gliding across the floor to greet a friend, but in Thoren's mind, he was crossing a battlefield.

"Ansgar," Thoren greeted, inclining his head with a carefully measured respect, a glint in his eye betraying a hint of familiarity. "How do you fare? I hear it was your son's sixteenth name day last moon? My felicitations. Is he to follow in his father's footsteps?"

Ansgar, the Warden of Stormhold, stood as one of the King's most trusted advisors. Together with Birger, he upheld the King's law, protecting the realm from threats both within the mountain and beyond. It was a lofty position, one few achieved, and fewer still held with such steadfast loyalty. But even within his role's power, a shadow of resentment lingered. Birger, that perpetual thorn, sometimes dared to speak for the King himself, a privilege that gnawed at Ansgar whenever it occurred. Still, the mention of his son touched a vein of pride—a flash of memory of the boy, proud and tall, receiving his title among his kin.

"Thoren, well met," Ansgar replied, returning the nod with an equal touch of formality. "Yes, indeed it was. The first whiskers of a beard sprout upon his chin." He let a faint chuckle escape, the usual reserved man briefly softening. "Though politics is not the life he would pursue. In truth, we are a conniving lot, aren't we? I would have him well away, if he's wise."

"A miner has his pickaxe," Thoren replied, a sly smile spreading across his face as he gestured broadly to the vast chamber around them, "and we have but our words." His voice was velvet, rich with both admiration and the faintest hint of irony, as if to imply they wielded far sharper tools than mere picks.

"Have you been out of the keep recently?" Thoren asked, his voice low, as though the very walls might listen. "The storm seems determined to test our endurance. They say the blizzard will not relent until spring."

Ansgar met his gaze, eyes shadowed with the weight of countless sleepless nights. "Aye," he replied, voice tinged with a solemn weariness. "Shiva seem restless, as if she rages battles in the skies above." His tone was dry, but the heaviness of his words spoke of a deeper exhaustion. "Though I suspect the real storm lies here, within these walls—dark and perhaps even less forgiving."

A knowing smile tugged at the corner of Thoren's mouth, his eyes flickering with kindred understanding. "A fitting metaphor. We have enough tempests of our own, do we not? And court is alive with whispers this day, like winds stirring before a storm."

Ansgar's gaze sharpened, suspicion hardening his features as he studied Thoren. The air between them grew taut, and for a brief moment, a flicker of doubt crossed Ansgar's mind. "Whispers?" he murmured; his voice edged with challenge. "You speak as if you know something, Thoren."

Thoren maintained his scrutiny, unflinching, and a slight gleam danced in his eyes, just enough to hint at knowledge withheld. "Only what I've heard," he replied, voice smooth and unreadable. "But then, whispers have a habit of finding the right ears."

"Of course, the usual currents of discontent," Thoren added, his tone almost nonchalant, though a keen edge lurked beneath. "Though I have heard whispers of 'Gunnar Stonkar' in Frostfall Harbour. Some say he might yet march south once again."

Ansgar's expression tightened, a flicker of anger flashing in his eyes. The feuds between Stormhold and its neighbouring cities were ancient, but Gunnar was a particular thorn. The man owned Nordon's largest fleet, his lust for dominance insatiable. It was not enough to command the seas; Gunnar yearned to drive his ships southward, raiding villages and pillaging the forest clans of East Kadun or the settlements scattered between Frostfall Harbour and Stormhold. Ansgar's jaw clenched. "That man is perpetually dissatisfied. May he take another wife to bed and appease his warmongering for another season."

Thoren inclined his head, concealing his satisfaction; this was no mere rumour, after all—his own informants had confirmed as much. Though still only a threat on the distant horizon, information was his blade, and he would use it to wield his narrative. "And how does the King sway on this matter?"

Ansgar's eyes narrowed as he scrutinised Thoren, suspicion sparking behind his gaze. "The King has other matters to attend," he replied cautiously. "He is untroubled, as is his council."

Thoren took a slow, considered breath, resisting the urge to display his disapproval. While he disagreed with the King's apathy, he sensed an opportunity to weave his perspective into the conversation. With a deliberate calm, he clasped his hands and leaned a little closer to Ansgar. "There are those who question the King's resolve. With Frostfall so restless, there are whispers—doubts about whether Ivar still has the strength to keep Nordon united."

Ansgar's brow knit together, his arms crossing in a defensive gesture that shielded his chest, signalling a growing mistrust. The line between warning and threat danced in his gaze. "And who, exactly, are these discontented souls?" he asked, his voice cold, each word weighted. "It's dangerous to entertain such rumours."

"Names are elusive," Thoren replied, shrugging with feigned indifference as he let his attention drift to the fire pits. "Rumours have a way of lurking in shadows, do they not? But discontent has a scent, Ansgar, and even the staunchest loyalists can smell it."

Ansgar's face hardened, his voice lowering to a steely whisper. "Be careful with your insinuations. Our King's rule is firm, and our loyalty unshakeable—or, at least, it should be."

Thoren inclined his head, a flicker of amusement crossing his face. The tension lay thick between them, but he sensed he had sown the seeds he intended. "Of course," he murmured, allowing just the faintest hint of a smile to show. "I merely share what is in the air. It would be remiss of me not to." His voice slipped into a smooth, almost conversational cadence. "Yet as I walk these halls, I hear otherwise. The miners' guild murmurs about their dwindling share of spoils. The alchemists count the days till spring, for their stocks run dangerously low. And the common folk—why, they grow resentful as we feast night after night while they ration what little they have, praying the blizzards will pass." He paused, letting his words linger, watching as each observation took root. Then, sensing the moment was ripe, he leaned in, voice dropping to a near whisper.

"And look who Birger breaks words with." His head tilted subtly, gesturing for Ansgar to glance over his left shoulder.

Ansgar shifted, casting a sidelong glance through the throng of nobles and advisors. True enough, Birger was standing among three familiar figures—Joran, Sigurd, and Ulrik. These men had long been on the fringes of the council, never granted access to the inner circle. Their loyalty was to the old ways of Nordon, and whenever they gathered, the talk inevitably turned to raiding and conquest, whispers of a bygone era that had no place in King Ivar's court.

Confusion etched across Ansgar's face. Birger would never lower himself to entertain these men. And yet, there he was, plain as day, speaking with them as though they were trusted allies. The tension in the hall was suddenly electric, each noble's gaze flickering with barely concealed curiosity. Ansgar's jaw tightened, a shadow of apprehension crossing his eyes as he turned back to Thoren. "And what of it?" he asked, his tone edged with darkness.

Thoren's gaze softened, his posture one of carefully calculated restraint. "I come to you not for answers nor questions, for you owe me none," he murmured, his voice measured, soothing. "Simply as an observer, one who wishes no harm to come of these whispers."

Ansgar's judgement lingered, searching Thoren's face, his own expression guarded. He knew the game Thoren was playing, and yet... something in the man's tone planted a seed of doubt. Thoren waited, watching as the weight of his words settled like an invisible burden across Ansgar's shoulders. There, in the silent pause, he knew his work was done. Ansgar's face paled, anxiety tightening his features as memories flooded his mind. Every recent conversation with Birger replayed with a new, unsettling clarity. Had there been signs, small cracks in Birger's loyalty? Then it struck him like a rude awakening—just four days ago, Birger had spoken brazenly against the Queen, muttering about her recent visit to the tomb of Shiva and whispering of a secret pact. This was not the Birger he knew; he was not one for court gossip. And yet, there he stood, mingling with men known for their disdain for Ivar's rule. What was he plotting?

"His loyalties have been... questionable as of late. Why align himself with those who might wish the throne to falter?" Ansgar's jaw tightened, distrust darkening his eyes. "Do you think he's seeking favour with the enemies of the crown?"

Thoren leaned in, his voice dropping to a murmur that barely reached Ansgar's ears. "I am but a humble tool, my lord. But it's a dangerous game he plays. Perhaps it's nothing, or perhaps..." he let his words trail, watching Ansgar's face intently. "You know him better than most. What could be his motives?"

Ansgar's brow furrowed, his mind working over every recent exchange. "There was something," he said slowly, as though dredging up memories buried by suspicion. "A rumour he mentioned. He spoke of our Queen—she made a pilgrimage to the tomb of Shiva."

Thoren feigned surprise, his brow lifting in puzzled innocence. "And what of it? A Queen has every right to seek blessings. Is that not a custom of our lands?"

Ansgar's gaze shifted left and right, ensuring they were out of earshot before he continued in a hushed tone. "I was told her audience with Shiva was not for blessings—but for something darker."

Thoren allowed a faint frown to cross his face, his voice laced with doubt. "And what would you have me believe, Ansgar? That Karak, of all people, would jeopardise her own reign?" He leaned back, folding his hands as if reluctant to believe. "Let us not forget—court is as unkind to women as the storms are to sea and land..."

The silence between them stretched, thick and charged. Thoren held Ansgar's gaze steadily, waiting, letting the doubt and suspicion take root, sensing Ansgar's resolve beginning to fracture. Finally, he spoke again, voice laden with measured gravity. "Believe what you will. But understand this—if rumours like these persist, they will weaken our Queen's standing, and by extension, Ivar's. We cannot allow this, can we?"

Ansgar leaned in unconsciously, the scepticism in his eyes giving way to an eager desperation. "You speak as if hiding more than you let on, Thoren. What is it?"

Thoren hesitated, letting the moment hang, savouring the tension he had cultivated. Then, with a measured sigh, he leaned closer, his voice barely a whisper. "There is... something I have come to know. A matter that touches on the Queen, a truth I had no intention of sharing. But, given what you have confided, I cannot let these dangerous rumours spread unchecked. You must know, Ansgar, to protect what we hold dear."

Thoren's expression was carefully measured, as if he were balancing on a tightrope of intrigue. "My associations grant me access to information that few others possess. I hear things—know things—that remain hidden from most." He paused, gauging Ansgar's reaction with an intensity that seemed to sharpen the air between them. "It is because of these ties that I'm aware of a significant piece of news that may silence those whispers."

Ansgar's brow furrowed, curiosity igniting in his eyes. "What is it?"

"The Queen is with child."

The words hung in the air, heavy and charged. Ansgar faltered, surprise flashing across his face. "With child?" he echoed; his tone rich with intrigue. "And you're certain of this?"

"I am. I have eyes and ears in the Queen's chambers. Ivar is to have an heir," Thoren replied, allowing a small, satisfied smile to creep onto his lips. "Perhaps that is why she braved the storm—to seek Shiva's blessing for the future heir. A child changes everything. Even the most hardened sceptics will soften in the face of new life."

Ansgar's expression shifted, the pieces in his mind beginning to click into place, though one concern nagged at him. "This is joyful news. No wonder the King has been in such good spirits these past weeks." He paused, narrowing his eyes as he considered Thoren's implications. "But why would Birger embellish such stories?"

"Why indeed?" Thoren leaned back, feigning nonchalance. "I dare not turn around; is he still conversing with Joran, Sigurd, and Ulrik?"

Ansgar nodded, the worry evident in his eyes. "He is."

Thoren inhaled deeply, his expression reflecting Ansgar's concerns. "What does an heir to the throne mean for Birger? Surely this news should be well received. Does he have his own designs?"

Anger flashed in Ansgar's gaze. "Do not speak of such things in the presence of prying ears," he hissed, his voice laced with a suppressed fury. Thoren bowed his head slightly, conceding to Ansgar's authority, but the damage was done; seeds of suspicion had been sown.

"I do not know what this means," Ansgar murmured, his mind racing with possibilities of betrayal. It would not be surprising if Ivar had confided in Birger about the Queen's pregnancy. Perhaps this was not joyful news to Birger, perhaps he did have his own designs and was readying alliances of his own to overthrow the King, spinning false rumours about the Queen's fidelity.

"I must take my leave now. There is much to consider," Ansgar said, his voice low but firm. "Speak of this to no one but me." Thoren gave a noncommittal nod, allowing Ansgar to step away, watching as he disappeared into the depths of the court.

Alone now, Thoren allowed a small smile to cross his lips, savouring the chaos he had begun to orchestrate. The game was afoot, and he had a front-row seat. Leaning up against the stone column Ansgar had occupied, he relished the satisfaction of his day's work. The seeds of discord were sown, and now he only needed to ensure they flourished under the weight of other men's labour. He relished the thought of how easily whispers could spread, how the tension in the air could be stoked with but a few choice words.

His gaze drifted to Birger, still ensnared in conversation with the three men—Joran, Sigurd, and Ulrik—whose eager faces revealed their hunger for chaos. A smirk crept onto Thoren's lips, a sense of triumph swelling within him. The simple breadcrumb he had left, that was now to bear fruit.

As he recalled the earlier conversation, the thrill of manipulation coursed through him. He had orchestrated it masterfully, ensuring the talk of Gunnar reached their ears with precision.

'I hear Gunnar will march south,' one man had pressed, his voice heavy with curiosity.

'I hear Northrend is with him,' another chimed in, eyes gleaming with excitement at the thought of war.

'And the Crowned Islands,' a third added, his tone conspiratorial.

Thoren had leaned into the discussion, his voice low and deliberate, ensuring the right people overheard. 'Do not fret, good men. Just yesterday, I spoke with Ansgar. Birger is seeking men to intercept any charge.'

'Is it true?' the first man had retorted, a spark of alarm flickering in his eyes.

'Of course. Allow me to confirm with Ansgar now,' Thoren had said, feigning nonchalance as he strolled over to the Warden, a calculated move to reinforce his web of deceit.

It was then that he watched as Joran, Sigurd, and Ulrik rushed to Birger, their fervour for war outweighing any shred of judgement. Thoren could see the gears turning in their minds, the intoxicating prospect of conflict pulling them deeper into Birger's orbit.

As he leaned against the cold stone, he allowed himself a moment to revel in the unfolding drama. The court was a stage, and he had taken his place as both puppeteer and audience. All that remained was to listen closely, adjusting the volume of the whispers to suit his purpose, and watch as the tide turned in his favour.

A man in tattered peasant attire approached Thoren, his face pale, betraying the weight of the message he carried. "A word for you, my lord," he murmured, his voice barely audible above the court's chatter. With a furtive glance around, he slipped a folded note into Thoren's hand before vanishing back into the crowd like a spectre retreating into the shadows.

Thoren unfolded the note swiftly, his pulse quickening as the words danced before his eyes: Konan has selected Bodvar as the offering for Shiva.

A surge of anger ignited within him, replacing the triumph that had just bloomed. His grip tightened around the parchment, crumpling it between his fingers. Not Bodvar. Of all his spies, Bodvar was among his most valuable—a trusted operative nestled within the ranks of soldiers and officers. Losing him would create a gaping hole in Thoren's carefully constructed network, an irreplaceable asset sacrificed for the whims of Konan.

With a flash of resentment coursing through him, Thoren thrust the note into the nearby fire. He watched as the flames hungrily consumed the paper, flickering shadows dancing across his face like the turmoil within him. The heat licked at his fingers, but he welcomed it, a reminder of the volatile nature of ambition and the sacrifices it demanded.

His mind raced with questions: Why had Konan chosen Bodvar? It defied everything they had agreed upon. Was this a move to undermine him, a calculated selection that reminded Thoren of his position in the order of things? The thought gnawed at him; Bodvar's loyalty was not easily swayed, but he would be lost to Thoren now—his life cast aside in a misguided bid for favour.

Thoren's gaze lingered on the flames, their bright glow illuminating the depths of his ambition. He felt the full weight of it pressing upon him, an unyielding burden that demanded constant vigilance. Every piece on the board had to remain precisely in place; the stakes were too high for errors.

As the last remnants of the note curled into ash, Thoren resolved to navigate this treacherous terrain with even greater cunning. The power he sought was fraught with peril, but he would not falter. Not now, not when so much was at stake.

# THE QUEEN CONSORT CHAPTER SIXTEEN

The gusty winter winds had eased. It was still cold, but the temperature had risen, and the blizzards subsided. Grey skies lingered over the mountains, and snow continued to carpet the peaks. The recent snowfall had hardened, making the ground easier to traverse. Bjoern, tall and slender, found the walk surprisingly pleasant. He had much to be cheery about; in recent weeks, his fortunes had taken a sharp turn for the better.

First, his elder brother Bodvar—whom he was on his way to meet—welcomed his first son. Afterward, granted a rare leave to stay with his new family, Bodvar returned to a promotion as squadron leader. His pay had increased considerably, and at the evening celebration, Bjoern had met Frida, the innkeeper's daughter. Beautiful and witty, she had quickly captured his heart, and last night, she had all but agreed to marry him. Only her father's consent remained, though Bjoern doubted that would be an obstacle. He was tall and handsome, with a beard bearing two stone clads: one as a soldier, the other his rank. Only craftsmen, soldiers, lords, and the wealthiest could wear these clads in their beards. Her father would have little reason to object—if anything, Bjoern felt certain he would be pleased.

It had only been hours since he had woken beside her, her warm, naked body draped over him like a fine garment. He had slipped from beneath her, kissed her brow, and left her sleeping peacefully under the quilted goose-feather blanket. He would still be there if not for an unusual request from his brother, a request that apparently came directly from Konan of the Royal Guard. Bodvar was to journey to Shiva's cave, enter its depths, find Shiva's chamber, and return with a relic for the foreign king in Kadun. An odd task for a newly promoted squadron leader, Bjoern thought. But his brother would never decline a command from the Royal Guard.

Yet last night, as they sat drinking by the fire, Bodvar had confided his reservations, his voice softened by ale. Bjoern knew the truth: his brother had always feared dark places, especially caves and tombs. They had been trapped in the mines as boys, lost for four days. For Bjoern, it was little more than a distant memory, blurred at the edges, nearly dreamlike.

But Bodvar remembered it all—the endless darkness, Bjoern's frightened howls, the hours crawling blind through black passages, only to reach dead ends or find the lip of unseen pitfalls.

Sometimes, strange sounds—small skitters, faint bickering—had echoed around them. Bodvar believed it was creatures lurking, waiting for them to weaken. For two days, he had followed the faint sounds of a pickaxe on rock, searching for the source. By the time they were found, they looked almost like demons, covered in grime, their limbs skeletal. A wash and some hot food had erased most of Bjoern's memories of those days, but not his brother's. Even now, with a wife beside him, Bodvar needed candlelight to sleep.

Of course, Bjoern had agreed to go with him.

As Bjoern strolled along the tree line, his thoughts drifted back to last night. His brother had left with the other patrons at closing, and once Frida finished clearing tables, she joined him by the fire with a fresh tankard of ale. They talked for hours, though he could not recall about what; her laughter echoed softly as she leaned into his chest, warm and close. When the inn was silent, and all were asleep, they pulled a rug to the hearth and made love. He had never laid with a woman in such a way-each movement was slow and gentle, his kisses tender and hesitant, as though savouring every touch. When she whimpered in release, he stroked her soft red hair, holding her close. And then, without thinking, the words slipped out: "Marry me."

He had meant it, though he was startled to hear himself say it aloud. Frida's response was sweet, her voice a gentle balm. "Why not ask me again come morning, when ale does not steer your actions?"

Then, with a playful twist, he turned her to face him, his lips meeting hers again. When he pulled back, he found her angelic emerald eyes gazing at him, full of warmth. "Say yes," he whispered, feeling his heart race with sudden nerves, a mix of hope and joy building within him.

In that perfect moment, a smile spread across Frida's face, bright and sincere. "Yes," she replied, sealing her answer with another lingering kiss.

The memory filled him with a deep, quiet joy as he marched toward the cave entrance, a warmth against the cold that he would carry with him always.

By the time Bjoern arrived, his brother Bodvar was already waiting outside the cave. Like Bjoern, he was tall and handsome, but broader in build, with a chest like a barrel and shoulders that could intimidate even the bravest soldiers. His auburn hair fell to his shoulders, and his beard, adorned with three stone clads—a mark of his rank, profession, and recent promotion—rested proudly upon his chest. Seated against a fallen boulder near the cave's entrance, Bodvar sharpened the edge of his double-headed axe, a small fire crackling at his feet.

"You're late again," he said sternly, glancing up as Bjoern approached.

Bjoern grinned, unbothered. "Am I not always late, older brother?"

"Yes, yes, you are," Bodvar muttered, his voice still firm. "And don't get comfortable. We need to hurry. We march at midday tomorrow, and I've much to prepare."

"Oh, come now, you always panic," Bjoern replied, stretching out his legs as he sat beside his brother. "Isn't it a fine morning? I could have skipped here whistling."

Bodvar snorted. "Then you're a jolly fool. It's cold, and I've been here half the morning waiting on you."

With a resigned shake of his head, Bodvar rose, sheathed his axe, and strode toward the cave, gathering two torch batons. He dipped each one into the fire, waiting for the flames to catch, then handed one to Bjoern before turning toward the cave's mouth.

"Come on," he urged, his voice echoing with impatience as he stepped into the darkness.

The pair made their way through the narrow, twisting passageways deep within the mountain, their footsteps echoing faintly off the walls. Bjoern often paused, drawn to strange markings on the stone—much to Bodvar's growing annoyance.

"Is it the ale or this cave that sours your mood this morning?" Bjoern teased, glancing over his shoulder with a smirk.

Bodvar's reply was sharp, his voice tense. "Perhaps it was my son, awake and crying all night. Or leaving my wife alone with him for an entire season while we venture off to some shit-stain country where no one speaks our tongue or cares to see us there. Or maybe, just maybe, it was waiting needless hours for you."

"Ah, the ale, then, older brother," Bjoern laughed, the sound bouncing off the stone walls. Bodvar responded with a disapproving shake of his head, but Bjoern's laughter only grew louder, filling the darkened passage. Somewhere ahead, a startled rat scurried away, its tiny claws scraping the rocks, and Bodvar visibly tensed, his torch raised higher as he scanned the shadows.

A heavy silence followed, pressing down on them like the weight of the mountain above. Bodvar pushed his torch into the dark recesses, half hoping to see nothing there, but his grip tightened. His face was pale, eyes ringed with exhaustion. Bjoern could see the fear tainting his strong brother's expression, usually so unyielding, now shadowed by anxieties left long buried.

After a time, they came to the stairs they had been instructed to climb. At the top, they faced a narrow crevasse they would have to crawl through to reach the tomb where the relic supposedly lay. Bjoern and Bodvar paused, staring into the dark, cramped tunnel.

"This cannot be right, Bodvar," Bjoern muttered, eyeing the passage sceptically. "Are you sure of the route? Looks like a dead end."

Bodvar leaned in, studying the tunnel's tight opening, until he caught a glimpse of the tomb beyond. Konan had warned him about this, mentioning he would need to crawl under to reach the chamber. The thought alone sent a shiver through him, stirring memories he had tried to bury—another reason he had asked Bjoern to come.

"There, I see the way," he said, forcing a steadier voice as he pointed toward the awkward path. "Look."

Bjoern gave his brother an encouraging nod. "Very well. Want me to go first?" he offered, sensing Bodvar's unease.

Relief flashed across Bodvar's face, and Bjoern unfastened his belt, setting aside his tomahawks. Without hesitation, he lowered himself to the ground and began the crawl. The cold stone pressed close on either side, and he shuffled forward until he reached a point where he could toss his torch. It spun across the rough floor, casting brief flashes of light along the stone walls as it slid toward the tomb. Suddenly, it came to a dead stop, as though something—or someone—had blocked its path.

A feminine foot. He saw it clearly, just for a moment, halting the torch before slipping back into the darkness.

Startled, Bjoern jolted, banging his head against the low ceiling with a painful thud. "Ow! Damn it," he cursed, rubbing the back of his head where a lump was already forming.

"What is it, you fool?" Bodvar's voice echoed from behind, tinged with impatience.

Bjoern hesitated, his hand still pressed to his scalp. He had seen it—a woman's foot, disappearing into the shadows. But knowing his brother's nerves, he thought better of mentioning it. "It's tight down here," he said instead, his voice steady. "Think I split my head open. Be careful when you follow."

Bodvar watched as his younger brother's legs squirmed forward, vanishing into the dark passage. An unsettling loneliness washed over him, sharp and sudden. Although squeezing through would be uncomfortable, he felt an urge to follow immediately. Why am I such a coward? he cursed inwardly. Steady your breathing. Relax. He forced a sigh, exaggerating it to settle his nerves.

Then, a light female chuckle came from behind him.

Startled, he spun around, expecting to see a priestess. But instead, his torch cast light on an astonishing figure below—a woman, naked and crystal blue, her body curvaceous and ice-white hair woven seamlessly into her skin. Her elongated eyes fixed on him with a piercing gaze, and a slanted smile crept across her lips. Slowly, she raised a willowy hand to her parted lips and blew gently in his direction. A gust of frigid air swept up the rock stairwell, and in an instant, his torch went out.

Darkness swallowed him whole, pressing in on every side. Bodvar's eyes strained to find a hint of light, but there was nothing—not even the glow of embers. It was as though his torch had never been lit. Panic crept in, but he managed to call out to his brother. His voice echoed through the cave, only to be answered by silence. He shouted again, louder this time, but once more, nothing replied but the hollow emptiness of the cave. The only sound was his own panicked breathing, growing quicker with each passing moment.

He stood frozen, unsure how long he had been motionless when he realised his forehead was damp with sweat. It was warmer here than outside, yet still cold enough that the beads of sweat felt unnatural. They rolled down his brow, dripping from his nose into his thick beard.

A footstep echoed on wet stone, shattering the silence. Then another, slow and deliberate, as if some unseen creature crept up the stairs toward him. The temperature plunged further, and an icy chill rippled through him. Fear gripped him tighter, but the soldier in him reacted instinctively. His axe sang out in a release of steel, both hands gripping its leather-bound hilt.

"Come to my axe, pretty. I'll cleave you in two," he growled, his voice rough and steely.

His gloved fingers tightened, shuffling slightly on the hilt. Testing its weight and his own nerve, he swung the axe in a wide arc through the darkness, its edge sharp enough to maim by sheer force alone. He swung again, his movements precise and practised, the blade cutting effortlessly through the black void. Despite his fear, he trusted his ability, and his technique held steady even against the unseen terror before him.

Silence returned, thick and impenetrable. Not even the faint drip of water echoed through the cave. "Come on, you coward," Bodvar growled, his voice steady but seething with anger. "Come to my axe."

At his challenge, the quiet patter of bare feet turned into a frenzied charge up the stairs. Bodvar swung his axe with all his might. A demonic woman, woven from frost and ice, burst into a blinding blue light, the chamber flaring to life as her shrill cry filled the air. But the axe missed its mark-the demon twisted, contorting her body in a way that defied nature to dodge the blow.

She lunged, talons poised, but Bodvar was faster. He swung again, each strike powerful and precise, yet each time she evaded him with impossible speed. For a brief moment, they paused, the demon baring her fangs as her eyes narrowed, recognizing a skilled adversary. She reared back, snarling, her talons swiped through the open space between them. Bodvar gritted his teeth, adjusted his grip, and dug his heels into the cave floor. With a deep, guttural battle cry, he charged forward, swinging his axe in a brutal arc.

The demon ghosted to the side, just out of reach, and swooped in for a counterstrike. But Bodvar twisted his wrist, redirecting his axe at the last instant. The blade nicked her torso, sending shards of ice exploding into the air, scattering across the stone like shattered glass.

The demon recoiled, wailing in pain as she clutched the missing chunk of ice at her side, her fangs snapping toward him in a rage. Confidence surged in Bodvar as he stepped back, granting himself some space. He adjusted his grip but to his surprise the leather had become cold even through his gloves. He stared down at his blade in disbelief. The edge that had struck the demon was now coated in ice, spreading with unnatural speed. The frost crawled over the blade, creeping down to the hilt, and within seconds, both edges were frozen solid.

The chill bit through his gloves, searing his fingers like fire. With a strangled gasp, he released his prized weapon as the pain became unbearable, watching in horror as his beloved axe shattered upon hitting the stone, fragments scattering across the cave floor.

A wicked grin spread across the demon's face, her mouth stretching wide to reveal jagged fangs. But Bodvar did not hesitate. In one swift movement, he dropped to a knee, seizing one of his brother's tomahawks. With a sharp flick of his wrist, he sent it spinning through the air. The blade struck true, embedding itself in the demon's right shoulder, and she shrieked as pain wracked her twisted form.

Bodvar lunged for the remaining tomahawk, gripping it tightly in his right hand. The first tomahawk, buried in the demon's flesh, began to freeze just as his axe had, ice spreading out from the wound until it was encased entirely. The demon snarled and, with a violent swing of her talons, shattered the weapon to shards.

Her fury ignited, she spread her arms wide and let out an ear-splitting scream. Bodvar responded with a roar of his own, but before he could move, she lunged with blinding speed. He tried to spin away, but it was too late. Her talons tore through his furs, ripping deep into his flesh. Blood filled his mouth, spilling out in a torrent as his strength faded.

Desperate, he tried to raise his arm for one last strike, but his fingers went numb, the tomahawk slipping from his grasp. The weapon hit the ground with a hollow clang he barely registered.

In a final, brutal move, the demon's talons speared upward, and Bodvar felt his insides tear. His vision blurred, but in that last moment, he saw her face shift. For a heartbeat, she looked almost human-a beautiful woman with ice-blue skin and soft, haunting eyes. She held his gaze with a strange, fleeting tenderness before her features twisted back into the monstrous form.

Her mouth stretched wide, her fangs gleaming, and with a swift motion, she lunged forward, her jaws snapping shut around his head.

Bjoern rose slowly, collecting his torch and casting its light around the ancient tomb. He searched for any sign of the woman he had glimpsed but found only stale air and a dusty altar. He turned back toward the tight crevasse. "Bodvar, toss me my belt!" he called, unwilling to go further without his weapons. Silence. "Bodvar!" he called again, his voice sharper. Still nothing. Frustration welled up; his brother must have panicked and needed rescuing. He bent down, readying himself to crawl back through the passage when a faint whimper broke the tomb's silence.

He turned at the sound, his eyes scanning the chamber. Another whimper followed, softer this time. Stepping forward, he saw a bare female foot peeking out from behind the altar. His heart raced as he moved closer, first glimpsing a leg, then a slender waist with arms clutching an unseen wound. Rounding the altar, he gasped.

"Frida?"

There she was-his Frida, wounded and naked, leaning against the cold stone for support. Blood stained her skin, seeping from a nasty gash on her shoulder and a deeper wound at her waist. Her hands pressed against the bleeding, but it had already pooled beneath her, spilling between her thighs and onto the floor.

"Frida, you... you're hurt," he stammered, panic rising in his voice. He stripped off his fur cape, draping it over her shoulders to cover her. Her eyes met his, filled with pain, and he could see the brutality of the lacerations. The wounds were deep and vicious; without a healer, he knew she would not last the hour.

"My love," he whispered, his voice trembling. "How did you end up here? Who did this to you?"

She shifted slightly, grimacing, and he placed a comforting hand over hers. Her voice was faint as she muttered, "I followed you... and your brother did this."

"What?" Rage flooded him, hot and consuming. Without a second thought, he stood, ready to charge back through the passage. He would drive an axe into Bodvar's skull, deep enough to struggle pulling it free.

"Wait, my love," Frida's voice called after him, soft yet commanding. He stopped in his tracks, her words like a tether pulling him back. "I will kill him, Frida," he growled, his voice thick with fury. "I'll tear his guts from his belly and take his head clean from his shoulders."

"No, you shall not," she said, her voice firmer than before. In his rage, he had not noticed her rise to her feet, blood now pooling beneath her with each unsteady step. Through the borrowed furs, he could see her shoulder drooping, her life draining with every passing second. A wave of sorrow gripped him, his eyes welling with tears that spilled freely into his beard.

"Frida... you can't... you can't leave me in this world without you," he choked, his voice breaking as he struggled against the grief swelling within him.

Her legs trembled as she fought to stay upright, and Bjoern rushed forward, sweeping her into his arms. She looked up, her hand tenderly stroking his beard. "I love you," she whispered, her voice barely a breath. "I would have been a fine wife to you. Our children... there would have been many." She tried to laugh, but it came out weak, a mere shadow of her usual warmth.

Bjoern managed a smile through the tears, even as her words cut deep, stirring an ache that tore through him. He wanted to be strong, to comfort her, but the agony of her slipping away proved too much, and he sobbed aloud.

"Place me on the table, my love," she murmured, her voice faint, like the last flicker of a candle.

Carefully, Bjoern lifted her, feeling the damp warmth of her blood soaking through the furs. He laid her gently on the altar, cradling her head as he leaned down to kiss her. But her lips were still, lifeless, and when he pulled back, her eyes were closed. Her chest rose one final time, a shallow breath escaping into the tomb's frigid air.

And then, silence.

Bjoern sobbed, dropping to his knees and pressing his head to the cold altar. How had this happened? Only hours before, they had shared her bed, and now she was gone. What had Bodvar done? Why? His fist crashed down on the stone with such force that it seemed to shake. His anguished shout filled the chamber, echoing like a storm, and suddenly, runes along the altar burst into brilliant blue light. In a flash, Frida's back arched, light radiating from her body, and with a sharp gasp, her eyes flew open as she took in a desperate breath.

Bjoern staggered back, watching in awe as Frida sat up, her chest heaving, eyes wide with disbelief. Her shoulder was healed, not a mark remained. She reached down to feel for the wound at her waist, but it, too, had vanished, not a trace of blood in sight. Tears sprang to her eyes as she looked at him, her face alive with colour and joy. She flung herself into his arms, and they embraced, holding each other as though time itself had stopped.

After what felt like an eternity, Bjoern gently pulled back, studying her in awe. She looked radiant, even more beautiful than he remembered. "How... how can this be?" he murmured; his voice thick with emotion.

"Kiss me, my love," she whispered, pulling him close, and Bjoern did not hesitate. Their embrace was tender, deepening with each heartbeat. He tried to part, but Frida's hands slid behind his head, holding him close as if she feared to let go. She pulled away only briefly, her eyes gleaming with joy. "I am alive. I should be dead. Let me cherish this moment-kiss me again, and don't stop."

Bjoern smiled, their lips meeting once more in a kiss that grew fervent and passionate. Removing his gloves, he let his fingers trace her bare skin, revelling in the warmth and softness. Frida slid from the altar, standing close to him, her eyes playful. "You wear too many clothes," she teased, and he laughed, kissing her again as they began to tug at his garments. Piece by piece, they fell away, and soon they stood wrapped in each other, their bodies the only warmth in the cold, ancient tomb.

She pushed him back against the altar, and he flinched as the cool stone touched his skin. Laughing, he gazed up at her. "You're eager. Perhaps death suits you."

Her eyes sparkled, and she bit her lip, a mischievous grin spreading across her face. Frida's hand moved to his chest, her fingers stroking the sporadic hairs that sprouted from his chest, their eyes were locked once more, and she leaned in to kiss her man. As she did so lustfully her fingers traced down his skin which pimpled at the touch, onto the flat of his solid stomach and lower still. She pulled away from their embrace as her fingers encircled him for the first time. She purred in delight as she tightened her grip and flicked a seductive smile at him "perhaps it suits us both."

Bjoern groaned and gripped both edges of the stone altar as she began to pleasure him. Leaning into his chest her soft lips kissed his skin, she moved back up to his lips and their tongues met again.

As their passion grew, Bjoern felt as though the tomb around them had faded away, leaving only the warmth of their embrace. Every moment, every touch felt precious, like a gift granted by some mysterious force. The world seemed to hold its breath as they shared in the miracle of her return, a love rekindled in the heart of the mountain, strong and enduring.

Frida guided Bjoern onto the altar, then in one swift movement, she slid over him, straddling Bjoern with practised ease. She pulled away from his lips, her eyes locking onto his as she guided him inside her, just as she had many times before. Slowly, she sank down, and Bjoern groaned in delight. Frida raised her arms, running her hands through her fiery red hair, which fell in waves around her shoulders as her hips moved effortlessly against him.

His eyes traced her body, drawn to the graceful sway of her hips, the gentle bounce of her breasts, her nipples taut in the cool air. His hands rose from the altar to find his lover's hips, to his surprise she was cold, as cold as the stone beneath them. Curious, he arched his back for a better look, his fingers trailing up her sides. Frida's skin seemed to pale, an unnatural chill radiating from her.

Before he could react, her hands pressed down on his chest, forcing him back against the altar. Her pace quickened, another groan escaping him, his eyes drifting closed in delight. Enjoying every moment he reached for her rhythmic body, his hands slid up her back, the coldness jolted him, like ice against his skin. Startled, he opened his eyes-and the woman before him was no longer Frida.

Wide, icy-blue eyes stared down at him, framed by frost-white hair in place of red. Her skin had turned a chilling blue, woven with patterns of frost, and any trace of Frida's warmth was gone. Horrified, Bjoern tried to pull away, but the altar itself seemed to hold him, ice rising from the stone and freezing him in place.

He went to shove her off, but her hands shot out, clamping his wrists to the altar with inhuman strength. Ice crept down his arms, binding him, his legs frozen in place. When he tried to shout, a freezing palm covered his mouth, silencing him. He stared up, terror-stricken, at this blue-skinned woman who barely resembled a human. She was beautiful, yes-but in an otherworldly, ancient way that struck fear deep in his bones.

With a soft, chilling touch, she stroked his cheek, and something shifted in him. His fear dulled, slipping away as he drifted into a trance under her touch. Pleasure washed over him; his senses overcome by her rhythm. The ice holding him began to melt, loosening just enough for him to move his arms, and he wrapped them around her, his hands exploring her flawless, frost-rimed skin. He leaned forward, pressing his lips to her icy chest, lost in the surreal passion of the moment.

Their bodies moved together in a rising, relentless rhythm, each moment intensifying the strange enchantment she had cast over him. As her hips quickened, he felt himself reaching a peak, unable to hold back. He arched into her, his grip tightening as he surrendered to the ecstasy, feeling her fingers trail across his back and her cold lips press to his neck.

But as his breathing slowed, a sharper chill began to settle over him, piercing the fog of pleasure. He blinked, his vision clearing-and horror gripped him as he took in the creature atop him. Her once-beautiful face had contorted, eyes glowing with a demonic gleam. Her mouth stretched wide, revealing razor-sharp fangs, her fingers now tipped with vicious talons.

"Frida..." he whispered, terror rising within him. "What have I done?"

The demon's jaws opened wide, her mouth descending swiftly, and with a final, chilling scream, she clamped down on his head, the darkness swallowing him whole.

Karak found herself on her balcony once more, the city beaming with the distinct colours only the many fires below could create. The scenery would never get old, the city under the mountain so magnificent, soon it could all be hers. It was then her chest felt a sudden chill, surprised she moved her gown aside, her hand swept into her underlay to find the source. She felt the tips of her fingers surface against cold glass, they grasped round the vial and pulled it free. Between finger and thumb, she presented it in front of her face.

It had been a forgotten instrument, a small glass container, once hollow now glowed as if bright snow on a summer's day. The liquid flowed side to side as she tilted the vial, such a small thing should change the fate of so many she thought. The realisation hit her then, a man had lost his life today to fill its contents, how many others would need to die? Karak stared off into the distance, in the hope it was only one.

# THE QUEEN CONSORT
# CHAPTER SEVENTEEN

The fire roared, casting its glow over the feasting hall just as it always did. Usually, Karak would sit back and watch the flames dance to the ceiling, gaze over the hall at those caught up in the merriment, and silently wish for the night to end. But this past week, much had changed. The hall, normally teeming with bodies and bustling maids bringing food and wine, was now sparsely filled. Only about twenty men, including herself, were gathered tonight. Two large tables had been pushed together, and everyone sat facing inward. Karak was seated among the King and his closest circle, her back to the fire, its warmth brushing against her as the only sign of its presence. The number of guards equalled the guests, and four maids stood off to one side, waiting for any task that arose.

It was peculiar, she thought. In the past week, she had engaged in more conversations than she had during her entire time as Queen. Her recent scheming had somehow brought her precisely where she wished to be, her influence growing. Karak had started forming subtle bonds with some of the men. She learned of their families, how they had earned their place at this table, and where they stood on various matters. Some were still hesitant about a woman joining their circle, even if she was their Queen. Others seemed genuinely pleased, even vying for her attention. And there were a few she herself enjoyed sitting besides, offering them secret smiles or an occasional touch on the hand in response to a story or joke.

Karak had always revelled in attention, especially of a flirtatious nature. Whether light-hearted or more serious, she loved wielding that seductive sway over others. She knew how to use her charm and natural beauty, speaking a language without words—holding a gaze a beat too long, a casual brush of the shoulder, or a hand resting on an upper thigh. It was a language all men, and occasionally women, eagerly conversed in.

The only man she did not enjoy this newfound closeness with, however, was her King. His stories were always crude, even with her there, and his jokes poorly timed. From a distance, she had thought all these men the same. But up close, she saw that most of them shared her feelings. They laughed awkwardly until the ale made it easier to pretend. Once, she noticed Sven, the chief advisor for Stormhold's treasury, fail to hide a look of disgust when a chunk of meat flew from King Ivar's mouth into his meal. She was his only witness; his expression instantly went blank when he realised, she had seen him. But in that moment, she knew she had made an ally. She silently mouthed, "Sorry" to him, apologising on behalf of her husband, and by the next evening, he was seated beside her, where he still sat now.

As they ate, a bard captured the room's attention with jovial songs and lively tales. Karak fought back a scornful glare directed at her grotesque husband, who bellowed at the story, spraying half-chewed bits of food across the table and into his wine-soaked black beard. Without swallowing, he tore into his chicken leg, cramming more into his already full mouth.

Un-kingly behaviour for a king, Karak thought. But tonight, she would not let it vex her as it usually did. The plot was afoot, and the drunken oaf would not trouble her for long. Instead, she hid behind the same false smile she always wore—though tonight, it concealed not her distaste, but her scheming.

The bard's tale was not even amusing. It was the tired, exaggerated story of the King's supposed heroics: slaying a giant to save Karak from its "fearsome clutches" as it ambushed a hunting party. Brave men fell around him, their blood staining the snow, until he alone stood, finally killing the beast with a "heroic" javelin toss. The audience roared as the tale reached its climax, and Karak fluttered her eyes, playing along for the crowd's amusement.

A fickle audience, she mused. She had not even been on that hunting trip —women were not permitted on such outings—and as for the "ferocious giant," it had been old and wounded, its path crossing theirs by pure chance. The men had quickly weakened it, allowing the King to deliver the killing blow. He was no warrior—just a fat man lucky enough to inherit the throne after his uncle's death. She smirked to herself, thinking of his nickname among the common folk: The Fat King.

As the rapturous applause faded, the bard lifted his bowed head, and the King Ivar Froskgar rose from his chair, clapping loudly.

"Well done, my friend! A tale all too accurate, for I still hold those memories close-the sad day we lost dear comrades. But let us drink in their honour and revel until our legs can hold us no more!" He raised his goblet high, then downed its contents, most of the red wine spilling over and soaking into his beard. With a loud slam, he set the empty goblet down on the wooden table and wiped his mouth with his forearm before continuing. “And then, my friends we shall fuck till our cocks turn soft!” A drunken cheer erupted as he waved over a maid. “Bring more wine!” he shouted, his voice hoarse.

Karak struggled to contain a smirk as Konan’s maid hurried away from the inebriated King to fetch more wine. A pretty little thing, she noted, such a shame her life would have to end after this night, for she had thighs to grasp and a face to sit. Her gaze shifted back to Ivar as he tore into his food, his round, weary eyes and blotchy skin speaking of too many years of excess. In such a condition, an animal would be put down out of mercy. Why, she wondered, should a man be allowed to remain and plague others?

She wrapped her fingers around the stem of her goblet, thinking to take a sip, then deciding against it. Perhaps it was best to leave it untouched; no need to risk sharing her husband's wine. Instead, she idly picked at a clump of cheese on her plate, her mind turning over the possibility of others drinking from his cup. What if the bottle were placed on the table for all to pour freely? There were details here she could not control.

Just then, the young maid returned with a fresh goblet for the King and a large glass jug filled with a deep red liquid. Karak hoped it was the poisoned wine. The King’s lecherous grin widened as he watched the maid pour him a large serving, his eyes lingering on her with a drunken, hungry look. Karak could not hide her look of disgust. Even in his final moments, he still managed to offend her. Oddly, she felt a flash of jealousy-an irritation quickly soothed by the knowledge that neither King nor maid would see the morning. She calmed her expression before anyone could catch her scowl.

“Don’t worry, my Queen. Ivar only has eyes for you,” Birger murmured, his voice smooth as silk. “Pretty thighs are an easy target for drunken eyes.”

Karak turned, nearly startled; she hadn’t heard him move beside her. “My dear Birger, you’ve told me this many times—and you’ll tell me many more, I’m sure. I become less desirable to our King with each passing day.”

“My Queen, you are still the most desirable woman in all of Nordon,” he replied with a subtle smile, his gaze lingering just a moment too long.

Karak stroked the slender man’s cheek with feigned affection, aware of the hunger in his eyes. She was certain he sought only to bed her, his ambitions naked behind his charm. But she would never give in to him;

surrendering would mean losing the delicate control she held over him. Birger, for all his posturing, was the one piece she could not fully read—a man of power, standing just close enough to pose a threat. Tonight, there would be a reckoning; accusations would fly in the King's Hall, sharp as daggers. As Ivar's lifeless body lay before them, Birger could easily accuse her. Her reaction to her husband's death would be everything—one false step, and Birger could see her condemned. Commands could change in an instant, orders from the Queen or from the dead King's steward. Tonight, would be a dance on a knife's edge, where the wrong step could end in bloodshed.

An idea took root, sinister and promising. She softened her expression, pressing a gentle kiss to Birger's cheek. "You are a good man, Birger, with kind words. The King is lucky to have such loyalty in his court." She offered an innocent smile. "I believe he's drinking Borlong Red. Go, share a word with him. Bring me a cup as well—I'm weary of this wine I've been nursing—and pour yourself one, too."

"The King is a fortunate man, whether he knows it or not, my Queen." Birger gave a shallow bow, then moved toward the King. She watched with satisfaction as he greeted Ivar, patting the King's broad shoulder before pouring from the fresh jug. Her pulse quickened as they raised their cups, clinking them together with a laugh.

Predictably, Birger forgot her request, lost in his own revelry. Men like Birger, she thought, hear only the words that serve them. But tonight, he and Ivar would fall together, and no one would dare whisper a word against her. Karak let her gaze drift along the table, watching the nobles revel and feast. Not a pair of balls among the lot of them. Those deemed "worthy" were here—the selected nobles, the King's advisors. Soldiers were stationed along the walls, as vigilant as ever. Loyal men, yet curiously deemed unworthy of a seat among such 'distinguished' company.

Her eyes swept across the grand hall beyond their position, noting the long, empty tables stretching out in neat rows. Beyond the tables, small golden torches were mounted along the rugged stone walls, each flame offering a warm yet haunting glow. The torches cast light on thick, luxurious velvet tapestries that adorned the walls, each one unique from the others, depicting scenes of long-past glories. One showed a clash of warriors, their swords mid-swing, locked in an eternal battle; another was woven with the image of a grand banquet, faces laughing and feasting as if frozen in a moment of endless revelry; a third illustrated an ancient fable, the figures in it shrouded in mystery and symbolism, their eyes following her with an unnerving intensity.

As her gaze shifted toward the entrance, she spotted her brother, tall and commanding even in stillness, having quietly slipped into the room. Long, fiery red hair, rich as autumn leaves in their final blaze, cascaded over his broad, muscular shoulders, tied back loosely to keep it from falling over his stern, watchful face. His dark eyes, deep and shadowed like stormy skies, were fixed intently on the two men across the dimly lit room, who were still lost in conversation, blissfully ignorant of the venom snaking through their veins.

Tonight, he was clad in full war attire, a reflection of his formidable presence. The leg guards, made from jet-black metal and etched with fine silver details of the Nordon crest, encased his massive thighs, every inch a testament to his strength. His chest plate, sculpted to follow the broad expanse of his torso, gleamed ominously, shadows casting across the polished metal in sharp angles that only deepened his aura of power. Beneath the armour, leather straps held the pieces together, wrapped tightly over his shoulders, allowing both protection and mobility.

Strapped to his back was his prized weapon—a double-edged battle axe, each blade sharpened to a glinting perfection, one dominant edge extending longer than the other. Its handle was a dark, worn wood, thick and wrapped in black leather, a grip that had felt the fury of countless battles. His gloved fingers twitched slightly, as if impatient for the familiar weight, ready to unsheathe it with deadly precision should the need arise. He was a tempest contained, and in that silent moment, he was already tasting the thrill of blood and steel.

He stood there, half-hidden in the shadows, as if the very spot were clearly chosen, taking great care to orchestrate this moment. Karak likely knew he would have been instructing his maid exactly which wine to serve, ensuring each detail was executed to his silent command. His eyes sparkled with a hint of amusement, an almost imperceptible satisfaction at watching the scene unfold according to his and Karak's design.

A guttural cough tore through the hall, shattering the festivities. Karak turned sharply to see Ivar doubled over, his face contorted in agony as a torrent of blood spilled from his mouth. With a strangled gasp, he staggered to his feet, colliding with the heavy wooden table before crashing onto all fours. Blood oozed from his nose and ears, painting the stone floor beneath him as his arms gave way, sending him sprawling, curled up in torment.

Karak sprang to his side, dropping to her knees as she gathered him into her arms, her voice raw with terror. "Help him-someone, help!" She screamed, barely able to comprehend the horror unfolding before her. The poison was never meant to end this way. It was supposed to be swift, merciful.

Across the table, Birger, wide-eyed, spat out his last mouthful of wine, realisation dawning too late. “It's poison!” His voice wavered as he clawed at his own throat, ramming his fingers deep to expel the liquid. But blood had already begun to leak from his nose, running down his face like a gruesome mask. A wave of agony crashed over him, his expression mirroring the King’s. He toppled over the table beside Karak, his head colliding against the strong wood with a sickening crack. The splatter of blood painted her pale green dress, the dark stain spreading like a curse.

Karak shrieked, her cries filling stunned silence. “Help, you fools!” she shouted at the frozen faces surrounding her.

Konan reached first, his shadow falling over Birger’s lifeless form. Birger’s body lay still, eyes vacant. He was gone. The King, though barely clinging to life, raised his gaze to meet hers, eyes filled with raw agony. Guilt twisted like a knife in her chest. She had planned this death, but not this-never this. The poison was meant to be a release from life's burdens, not a descent into torture. Her mind rebelled against the sight of his blood-soaked face, his silent plea.

As his hands clutched at her arms, his entire body convulsed. Blood seeped from his eyes, staining the whites a furious crimson. She had seen death before, but this-this was carnage. Her heart pounded wildly as her own tears blurred her vision, mixing with his blood on her cheeks as she held him. I did not want this, she thought, trembling. I never wanted this.

The King’s gaze, once filled with contempt and authority, softened in these last moments. His pain etched itself into her soul, lancing through her cold resolve and leaving her bare. They held each other's gaze until his eyes rolled back, his grip on her loosening, and he was still.

Blood continued to spill from his lifeless body, pooling around her as her sobs filled the hall. Her breaths came in ragged gasps, her chest heaving with the weight of grief that mingled with the guilt. She struggled to breathe; her entire body wracked with the full, merciless consequence of what she had done. She barely registered the massive hand that came to rest on her back, firm but calming. Konan’s steady presence seemed to ground her, his composed strength an anchor amidst the storm of her emotions.

A slurred voice shattered the silence, slicing through Karak’s grief like a blade. "What are you crying for, you witch! This was your doing. Witch!"

A fire ignited within her, raw and unstoppable, obliterating every trace of grief. Her tears dried instantly as she straightened, her voice a fierce roar. "YOU SACK OF WORMS! WHICH ONE OF YOU HEARTLESS, WHORE-SONS SPOKE? SHIVA AS MY WITNESS YOU WILL SPEAK NOW!"

Ansgar, drunken and infamous for his brazen tongue, staggered forward with a sneer. "I did. And I speak for all of us. Rumours of your treachery have been spreading for weeks."

Karak's fury flared, and her focus darted around, seeking something sharp-anything to gut this insolent fool. But before she could act, Konan stepped between them, his presence firm and grounding. He wrapped his powerful arms around her, his armour cold against her flushed skin, holding her close as though shielding her from her own rage. For a brief, grounding moment, she was no longer alone in her torment. His hand, gloved and rough, stroked her cheek gently, brushing her hair back from her face as he pressed a protective kiss to her brow. "Be still, sister," he murmured, his deep voice as comforting as it was commanding. His gaze met hers, calm yet unwavering, a reminder of the bond that would carry her through even this.

She pulled back to look at him, his face softening with an affectionate smile-brief, before he released her. His expression grew cold as steel, and his eyes turned deadly. She could almost feel the temperature in the hall drop as he spun on Ansgar.

Without hesitation, Konan strode forward, each step heavy with menace. Ansgar, still emboldened by drink, laughed, oblivious to the shadow of death approaching him. But before he could blink, Konan's axe sliced through the air, a silver flash, and Ansgar's head leaped from his shoulders. Gasps filled the hall as blood sprayed across the floor, spattering the onlookers. The head struck the ground with a sickening thud, rolling several feet before coming to a halt against a table leg, its wide eyes frozen in a final expression of terror.

"Too long have we listened to this weasel's poisoned words. Tell me gathered, for whom else did this man speak?"

As Expected, a lengthy silence followed before Konan questioned "none so bold?" scanning the bleak faces in the room. "Guards seize all here and take them to the cells. Every last man shall be interrogated." The guards were unmoved at first unsure of where their allegiance should lie. "THERE IS A TRAITOR AMONG US MEN AND I WILL BLEED THE TRUTH

OUT OF EVERYONE IF I MUST. NOW SEIZE THEM."

This time the guards set to work swiftly and effectively, the room erupting into chaos. Drunken men hopelessly trying to fight off armed guards pleading their innocence. Konan, hawkeyed, watched the commotion unfold, then casually strolled over to his sister as if it were any other day. A triumphant smile spread widely over his grim expression "and so my sister your reign begins."

Karak felt a wave of relief wash over her, mingled with disbelief. Did that truly just happen? She glanced down, her breath catching as she took in her ruined dress-the once rich green fabric now streaked with dark, drying blood. Crimson splatters traced their way down to the hem, dripping onto the cold stone floor. Around her, guards were rounding up the remaining men, whisking them away one by one, each soldier avoiding her gaze as if the sight of her alone was cursed.

Konan caught her eye and gave a slight nod, his expression unreadable, then made his way toward the fallen King. For a moment, he stood over Ivar's lifeless form, the corpse sprawled awkwardly, almost grotesque in its finality. A flicker of satisfaction passed over Konan's face as he stared down, the gore-splattered figure a testament to a regime toppled. He knelt, wiped his blade deliberately on the fur jacket that still clung to Ivar's chest, and cast a sidelong glance at the remaining guards, daring any of them to question him. But they looked away, silent and compliant, acknowledging the shift in power with their very stillness.

His attention then shifted to Birger, slumped over the heavy table, his head split open in a way that left blood pooling beneath him, thick rivulets cascading from the table's edge to stain the floor. Konan's gaze lingered on the lifeless man for a time, as if paying his last respects to a fallen adversary or a mere casualty of their ambitions. He turned back to Karak, who still stood frozen, visibly shaken by the carnage surrounding her. A slow, knowing smile crept across his face, confident and fierce. It was done. What needed to be done was done. And in that moment, nothing else mattered.

Hours stretched, transforming late evening into early morning, as the Queen stared out over the empty city below her balcony, her vision blurred by more than six satchels of wine. The flickering flames danced off the massive stone columns, illuminating the vast expanse that had once thrived with life. Now, it lay in silence, the city outside gripped in shock from the night's harrowing events. Its usual vibrancy was muted, the populace reeling, perhaps waiting for the funeral games to stir their spirits once more. Karak mused that nothing could liven their mood like a good competition or fight.

She sipped from her glass, the rich liquid swirling in her mind, and recalled the King's ultimate moments. As their eyes locked in that last fleeting connection, did he recognize her betrayal? Was that knowledge the last thought that flitted through his tortured mind? The wine intoxicated her, bringing a bittersweet sadness that hung heavy in her chest. His end had been cruel, laid bare for all to witness, a pain etched into the memory of everyone present.

In the beginning, he could make her laugh, even when his attempts in the bedroom failed miserably, he could always jest at his inability. Those moments felt light and carefree, a distant memory now. As years passed, his jokes turned stale, and boredom crept into her heart, suffocating her spirit. Opportunities to explore foreign lands had been snatched away, leaving her a prisoner in her own life. A Queen cannot simply walk away from her marriage; she was shackled by duty and obligation. Only her secret liaisons had kept her sanity intact, but it was not enough. She had sat idle for too long. The path to freedom lay before her: she could bring death to those who held her captive, or she could die trying.

Now, liberated from the shackles of her former life, Karak was ready to unleash her true power upon the world. She would not merely be a figurehead upon a throne; she would demonstrate the true meaning of authority. Her gaze drifted over the distant city, her mind alive with newfound possibilities. For too long, the treasures of these mountains—the gold extracted from Stormhold's jagged peaks—had flowed outward, only to return in meagre offerings: wheat, barley, timber, and livestock. It was laughable. How could precious gold ever be exchanged for such common resources?

No, her gold should buy strength, not scraps. Why squander it on trade that only enriched others while Stormhold remained bound in dependence? She clenched her fist, knuckles turning white with determination. Karak envisioned Stormhold not as a mere trading hub, but as a formidable fortress with armies capable of seizing what they needed. Wheat and timber should be taken, not bought. The thought ignited a fierce fire within her—a ruthless clarity illuminating her path.

Kadun, the kingdom that had long profited from her land's riches, would soon feel the weight of her power. She understood it would take time—perhaps seasons—to amass an army that could march across their borders. But her patience was as keen as her ambition. The day would come when Stormhold would cast aside its role as a mere trading partner and rise as an empire. And when that moment arrived, her name would be spoken in both fear and reverence across the lands: the Queen who reclaimed the treasures of Stormhold by force, leaving none in doubt of her sovereignty.

A strong hand slid from behind, massaging her naked body just above her right hip, sensuously gliding upward to her bare breast. Soft lips brushed against the back of her neck, and her brother's voice whispered in her ear. "Come back to bed, my Queen. Breda stirs, and I would want nothing more than to share her with you one last time before we throw her from this balcony."

Karak turned, capturing Konan's lips in a passionate kiss. "How do you make something so savage sound so sweet, brother?" she breathed, her heart racing. He did not respond; instead, he smiled, a wicked glint in his eyes, and gently guided her back inside to the bed where the naked blonde maid was just awakening. The silk sheets slipped from the maid's body with a soft rustle, exposing her bare skin, a hardened nipple peeking out in the cool air.

As thoughts of gold and battle faded like the silk slipping through her fingers, Karak positioned herself atop the maid, kissing the soft flesh of her breast. She could feel Konan's presence behind her, his warm body pressing against her, drawing her deeper into this moment of indulgence, away from the weight of her ambitions and the blood yet to be spilled.

# THE APPRENTICE CHAPTER EIGHTEEN

Spring had yielded to the first warm days of summer, and the high sun now bathed Borlong in light, piercing through the dense shadows of the surrounding forest. The city, usually cloaked in the thick canopy of towering pines, came alive under the bright skies, and the extended daylight saw Borlong's foresters hard at work, their rhythmic axe swings echoing through the trees. One by one, the ancient trunks fell, each strike guided by years of practice, each felled tree carefully carved into skinless logs by skilled carpenters. These logs would soon be bundled and prepared for trade, a trade that now surged through every sector of the city.

Borlong was readying itself for the annual arrival of the Nordon merchants. These travellers braved the harsh winter conditions of their homeland, descending from snow-clad mountains and winding down icy trails with wagons laden with gold, the currency that drew Borlong's people into a frenzy of preparation. Alongside the merchants often came men of standing—envoys, advisors, and wealthy senators, their intentions hidden behind careful words in senate meetings. These gatherings, both political and mercantile, brought about the city's peak in trade.

The markets swelled with goods, from vibrant textiles and hand-forged ironworks to the less-than-pristine trinkets and jewellery meant to dazzle Nordon's foreign eyes, at least momentarily. The merchants, often wealthy and discerning, rarely showed interest in the more common wares; they would move through the stalls with faint disdain, their gloved hands bypassing the cheaper offerings, while the craftsmen muttered curses under their breath, watching the gold pass them by. Borlong had little to match Nordon's luxury, yet the merchants stayed just long enough—no more than a moon phase, if fortunate, or two, depending on the year.

At the estate of Lord Malum, however, the merchants' visit would not go unnoticed. Malum, as he did each year, orchestrated a grand banquet to mark their stay. His plans, deliberate and meticulous, hinged upon the arrival of esteemed guests; he would not rush into preparations without first knowing exactly who graced his halls. The Nordon merchants and their esteemed companions would be treated to a spectacle: tables laden with East Kadun's finest meats, fruits, and wines, each dish an attempt to outshine the last. Musicians and bards filled the hall with songs of distant lands and spirited ballads, livening the room until the early hours. Servants discreetly escorted merchants to private chambers, where secrets and schemes unfolded behind closed doors.

By morning, the halls echoed with laughter and murmured tales of the previous night's indulgence. Preparations would not commence, however, until Lord Malum had meticulously catalogued his guest list. He was particular, attuned to the status and preferences of each visitor. For men of importance, certain accommodations would be made, rooms with carefully selected vintages, or perhaps subtle hints of luxury that whispered to their tastes, ensuring Malum's reputation among Nordon's elite endured.

Lord Malum's estate relished the arrival of summer, its grand gardens in full blossom, bursting with vivid colours and lush greenery. Each day, as the sun traced its path across the sky, warm golden light bathed the estate, drifting slowly across the house and filling every room with a glow that seemed almost enchanted. In the reception hall, sunlight poured in through the high-set openings, flooding the space with radiance. The marble floors sparkled underfoot, each polished tile reflecting the light, casting a soft, warm hue that lent the room an air of grandeur. The vast chamber seemed to expand under the brightness, as though the play of light against the high walls and towering pillars gave it new dimensions with every passing hour.

But below the house, the servant quarters remained untouched by the change of season. Hidden in the bowels of the estate like a dungeon, the quarters held none of the warmth or beauty above. Here, the air was perpetually heavy, stale, and damp, the walls cool and slick with moisture no matter how sweltering the world outside became. Light came only from the dim, unsteady flames of torches lining the stone corridors, their reflections dancing across the damp walls, giving the quarters a haunted, almost surreal appearance. The living space was bleak, unyielding—a stark contrast to the lively world above.

Yet, this grim place had become a haven of sorts for its newest resident. The newcomer, Auron, had come to embrace the cold quarters, finding an odd sense of comfort in their shadows. Over the past weeks, he had transformed, shedding the remnants of his former life. His wounds had healed faster than anyone had anticipated; the two long lacerations across his back had faded, now only faint scars tracing patterns alongside the other marks that criss-crossed his pale skin. It had been nearly two months since the brutal beating that had left him broken, and he was finally free of the cast that had once bound his arm. Only the slightest tinge of yellow marked where the bone had fractured, a quiet reminder of the violence he had endured.

But it was not just his wounds that had mended. Auron himself had begun to thrive, filling out with a youthful vigour that was a far cry from the frail figure who had first entered Lord Malum's estate. Regular meals had brought new strength to his thin frame, transforming him from a skeletal shadow into a boy whose once gaunt features had softened and rounded. His cheeks now bore a faint flush of health, and his body had grown lean and solid. His hair, once cut short and left ragged, had thickened and lengthened, a deep shade of black that gleamed in the light as though freshly oiled.

The transformation was nothing short of radical, and Auron had begun to fit seamlessly into this new world, leaving behind the grim alleyways of his past. Even Lord Malum had taken note of his rejuvenated appearance, casting appraising glances at the boy who had, over a few short weeks, become a stranger to the battered, street-worn child he once was.

As the weeks passed, Auron's education had finally begun. His lessons started with the basics—simple mathematics to sharpen his mind and speech exercises to build a vocabulary he had lacked in Borlong's roughest alleys. He took to the lessons well, and soon his rough background seemed like a fading memory. Eventually, he joined Malament, sitting in on his private tutoring sessions with Sidgwick and participating in their rigorous physical training in the estate's exercise yard. What had once seemed impossible for Auron was slowly taking shape: a routine, a life of structure and learning.

Today, however, was different. This was the day he had been waiting for, the day he would finally begin his combat training under Gordon. Since he had first heard the news, Auron had been counting down the days with a mounting eagerness. But before he could get his hands on a practice sword, he had to endure another morning lecture from Malament's tutor, Sidgwick.

Sidgwick was a figure that demanded attention, an old scholar of the world with a mind as sharp as it was wise. Despite his years, Sidgwick retained a youthful vibrance. His sandy blonde hair, just beginning to show traces of grey at the roots, crowned a round, ruddy face with bright, piercing blue eyes. He was solidly built—a broad man with a potbelly concealed beneath his long navy robe, patterned in chalk-white diamonds that swept down to his ankles. Sidgwick's hearty appetite and preference for rich foods were known to all, relics of a life spent in both comfort and indulgence.

Born into wealth, Sidgwick had inherited a substantial estate and fortune early in life, but he had never taken to the sedentary life of a landowner. Instead, he poured his inheritance into years of travel, wandering through ports and settlements across the continent, always in search of fresh experiences. He often joked to his pupils that he had a son in every port, laughing with a glint of nostalgia in his eyes as he recounted wild tales from lands near and far.

Sidgwick's role in the Divided Wars had cemented his reputation. As a military advisor, he knew the rugged terrains of East and West Kadun better than most and had served on the war council, his sharp mind devising tactics that kept West Kadun's forces at bay. Though his battlefield days were over, Sidgwick took pleasure in studying old maps and documents, poring over the tactics and victories of past campaigns and breathing life into the dusty chronicles of history.

His lessons were infused with his vast military knowledge, each session turning into an animated account of old campaigns, failed sieges, and triumphant marches. Malament listened intently, a sponge for every detail, while Auron tried his best to keep up, his mind often drifting as Sidgwick's words became distant sounds. The tutor was aware of this but made an effort to draw Auron back, determined to spark the boy's interest.

Today, the two pupils stood across from him, separated by a wide wooden table with an ancient map unfurled across its surface. Age had stained the map a mottled brown, and wax-dripped candle holders held its edges in place to keep it from rolling up. Sidgwick leaned over it, his broad shoulders casting a shadow as his finger traced the worn paths and river lines of long-ago campaigns.

"So, my young strategists," Sidgwick began, his voice deep and smooth, "imagine you are leading an army from Borlong to the far reaches of the Emerald Sea. Your men are weary, provisions thin. What would you do to ensure your forces survive?"

He looked directly at Auron, his pale blue eyes gleaming with challenge. "Auron," he urged, "consider yourself the captain. What choice would you make?"

Auron blinked, caught off guard, his gaze drifting between Sidgwick and the sprawling map. He scrambled for an answer, his mind flashing with scenes from stories Sidgwick had told. But Sidgwick was not done. His voice softened, patient yet insistent.

"Remember, boy, strategy isn't just the power of numbers; it's understanding terrain, knowing when to advance and when to hold back. Think on your feet. Improvise." His words rolled out slowly, each syllable weighted with purpose, designed to both teach and inspire.

Malament shifted slightly, ready with an answer, but Sidgwick held up a hand. "No, no, Malament. Let Auron speak." There was a hint of a smile on his face as he waited, allowing the silence to settle, the weight of expectation hanging in the air.

Auron hesitated, his eyes darting over the map's faded lines and markings. The question felt massive, and he was not sure where to begin. Finally, he ventured an answer, his voice uncertain.

"Well... I suppose I'd, um, push forward. I'd keep marching the men straight through until we reach somewhere safe. Maybe... maybe if we moved fast enough, the enemy wouldn't catch up?" He looked up at Sidgwick, his face hopeful, clearly feeling he had offered a solid solution.

Sidgwick's eyes softened with a faint smile, and he let out a small, approving hum. "Ah, the courage of the young," he remarked, tapping the map thoughtfully. "Yes, speed is indeed a factor, Auron, and boldness can carry a commander far. But let's consider a few... wrinkles in that plan." He raised his brows, drawing Auron back in.

"What happens if, along this path" tracing a finger down a narrow river crossing on the map, "your men come upon an enemy force camped here? Or perhaps provisions are lower than anticipated, fatigue slows even the bravest soldiers. Marching on, as you suggested, might lead us into an ambush or leave our troops weak."

Auron bit his lip, glancing back at the map, trying to rethink his approach.

"Perhaps," Sidgwick offered, "you could look for a resting point that provides both protection and resources. Somewhere nearby, along a natural barrier—maybe along a riverbank. Not only could it offer a defensive position, making it harder for anyone to approach unnoticed, but it would also provide access to fresh water for drinking, cooking, and cleaning. Allowing your men...?"

He leaned in, nudging Auron to follow his reasoning.

"Erm... to gather strength?" Auron ventured, his voice growing more confident.

"Precisely!" Sidgwick nodded approvingly. "A wise captain not only presses forward but also knows when to regroup and conserve his strength. Sometimes Auron, the initial instinct isn't always the safest." His voice was warm yet instructive, and he gave Auron's shoulder a reassuring squeeze.

With a slight shift in tone, Sidgwick turned his attention to the map before them. "You see, Auron," he continued, pressing his thick index finger firmly onto the marked 'East Kadun.' "We are at the heart of everything." His finger lingered as he spoke, drawing attention to the bold letters beneath it. "The forests cover our nation—they are our lifeblood. Their wood keeps us warm, shelters us from storms." He traced the trade routes upward, his finger gliding along the lines leading toward the northern expanse labelled 'Nordon.'

"To the north," he continued, "lies Nordon, buried in snow and perpetually whipped by blizzards. It is a harsh land, Auron, where only the heartiest of men can endure the open air for long. They live beneath the mountains, deep within halls carved by pickaxe and grit, and they too depend on our forests. Without our timber, their fires would die, leaving them to freeze in the dark." He looked off into the distance, lost in the memory of a place he had visited long ago. "Ah, to see Stormhold, their capital beneath the mountain, one more time—a marvel beyond imagination. Towering halls, walls draped in gold. A city hewn from stone by warriors and miners who have struck wealth beyond our reach." He chuckled to himself, almost as if sharing a private joke. "Imagine that Auron—how Kadun trades wood for gold. Trees for treasure."

He glanced over at Auron, whose usually bright eyes seemed slightly glazed, struggling to keep pace. Sidgwick's smile softened, recognizing the boy's attention wavering. Perhaps a touch of danger would spark him to listen.

"Malament tells me you aspire to be a soldier," Sidgwick said, drawing Auron's focus back. "If so, you may well find yourself here." His finger slid down the map, halting over the southernmost city, 'Cordon.'

"Cordon," he intoned, his voice growing more solemn, "is more than a city. It is a bulwark—our southernmost fortress, nestled between the treacherous peaks of the Gigas Mountains. Beyond it lies the Drylands, a wasteland of cracked earth and endless desert. Millions live there, divided into fierce tribes, each with its own chieftains and rivalries. They are wild, unpredictable, and if they ever united, they would be unstoppable. Cordon stands as our first and only defence."

Sidgwick's gaze turned distant, his eyes narrowing as he recalled his travels into the Drylands. "I've walked those scorched lands twice. They are hostile—unforgiving. I hope you never see them, Auron. Cordon's walls stand to keep the tribes from sweeping over Kadun like a storm." He looked at the boy, his voice dropping to a near whisper, drawing him in. "And yet, once... once, they were united. Seven hundred years ago, a man named Mitsurugi Khan, a warlord the likes of which our world had never seen, brought them together. Under his banner, the tribes surged north, unstoppable. It took all of us—East, West and the Warriors of Nordon—to drive them back. Cordon was built in the wake of that war to stand guard, a constant reminder of what could come again."

He leaned closer, his voice now low, conspiratorial. "In the Drylands some say Mitsurugi Khan was no mere man but a dark paladin, bound by magic. And instead of defeat he merely vanished across the seas after the battle, rumoured to be unkillable. And now the tribes cling to an old prophecy—that a child with eyes like blood will one day rise, a child who will unite them once more, wielding the power of Mitsurugi Khan."

Sidgwick let the silence stretch, watching as Auron's eyes widened, captivated by the tale. "Remember this, Auron," he said softly. "The world is larger and far more dangerous than you might think. If that prophecy were true and should come to pass, it will be men like you standing on the walls of Cordon, defending all that we hold dear."

Sidgwick rubbed his bald chin thoughtfully, his eyes shifting between Malament and Auron, studying their reactions. Seeing little response from either, he moved his finger westward, tracing across the mountainous divide and the sweeping forests beyond. "This is West Kadun," he began again, his voice steady but laced with gravity. "Malament here could tell you, Auron—our past with these neighbours is... prickly. Once upon a time, we weren't neighbours at all; we were one, a single nation called Kadun."

Sidgwick's finger paused over the jagged line of the great gorge, his expression momentarily sombre. "But a fierce civil war tore us apart. We are now split by this gorge, a wound that separated East and West Kadun." His hand moved to a row of leather-bound tomes on the nearby shelf. "These books tell of that brutal age, 'The Divided Wars' the endless battles that bled our people dry. King Ruben Whitehart of West Kadun eventually claimed victory, but the cost was immense. How many lives were lost? Countless, I imagine."

He glanced at Auron, a hint of melancholy in his appearance. "The final stand, twenty years ago, took place at The Reach. After so much bloodshed, Lord Malum had the wisdom to seek peace by marrying a Western princess, a bond that's given us a fragile truce. And with it, we've gained benefits—protected borders, strong trade, and a steadfast ally in Nordon." He paused, then added quietly, "Though I sometimes wonder how long such peace can last."

Auron's face had shifted, a troubled look settling over his features. He studied the map, a world of names and places he had never heard before. Until now, his world had been limited to Borlong's gritty streets and narrow alleys. The realisation that an entire world lay beyond the city's fenced walls filled him with awe and confusion. Sidgwick caught the boy's gaze and offered a reassuring smile, noticing the way Auron's eyes darted uncertainly over the map.

"I know it's a lot to take in," Sidgwick said softly, leaning down to meet Auron's eye level. "But trust me, you'll understand in time. We all started somewhere. Tell me, what is it that troubles you most?"

Auron looked down, his fingers tracing aimlessly over the parchment. His gaze eventually rested on a large, isolated landmass in the far west. He pointed to it, his brow furrowing. "What is this place?"

Sidgwick let out a quiet chuckle, the corners of his eyes crinkling. "Ah, the distant land of Barroth." He straightened, folding his arms across his chest. "You're ambitious, wanting to know it all so soon. But as with most things, best to learn one step at a time." His tone softened as he saw Auron's eagerness. "But in short, Barroth is a land wreathed in mystery. It's said to be populated by beasts of myth and men of ancient sorcery."

He allowed the weight of his words to sink in, then continued, "It's a place encircled by the vast Seas of Leviathan, a kingdom set apart. The Legend goes that Mitsurugi Khan himself fled to Barroth after his defeat, slipping away across the seas. In the days of old Kadun, a fleet was assembled and gave chase, yet Leviathan himself rose from the depths, decimating the ships. Few returned with tales of the horrors they witnessed at sea and strange lands beyond, knowledge so scarce that even our wisest scholars know only fragments."

Sidgwick's gaze returned to Auron, catching a glint of excitement mingling with uncertainty in the boy's eyes. "The real truth? Mitsurugi Khan was slain on the battlefield, nothing more than a mortal end to a mortal man. There's a crypt beneath Cordon where his tomb lies—a sombre reminder of his fall. And as for the Sea God Leviathan? It's far more likely that pirates ravaged the fleet, if there ever was a fleet. Stories grow with time, but behind every legend, there's usually a simpler, harsher truth."

The tutor paused in thought for the briefest moment before continuing. "Though there's more to this world than you'll find in any book, Auron. One day, perhaps, you'll see some of it with your own eyes. But for now…" he gave the boy's shoulder a gentle squeeze, "let's focus on what's before us. There are enough mysteries here in East Kadun to keep even the boldest mind occupied."

Malament had been silent throughout, allowing Auron to absorb Sidgwick's stories, but his interest had been piqued at the mention of Barroth—a land he had always been fascinated with since Sidgwick first mentioned it. "Perhaps we'll venture there one day?" he suggested, a gleam of excitement in his eyes.

Sidgwick raised an eyebrow, his expression briefly puzzled. He could not tell whether Malament was humouring him or truly serious. "Ah, a fine notion, but not likely," Sidgwick replied with a chuckle. "Only the birds cross the deep blue these days. The coastlines of Barroth swarm with pirates, and most ships that venture from the shores of West Kadun are rumoured to vanish without a trace." He paused, his tone shifting to one of quiet gravity. "Besides, to reach Barroth, one would need to sail either from Kaldor's Reach—though navigating the Burnished Sea is no small feat, not with Drylands pirates prowling those waters—or seek passage through West Kadun itself. That would mean traveling either south to Amberport in the far southwest or north to the capital, White Towers. And while we may be officially at peace, I doubt the King would grant us free rein to traverse his lands, let alone his seas."

"Perhaps not," Malament replied, his tone calm but assured, "but is it not my grandfather who sits on their throne?"

Sidgwick nodded. "Indeed, he does, though I understand since your birth, you've yet to meet the man?"

"That may be true," Malament admitted, "but when the day comes that I do meet him, he will open his gates and embrace his grandson."

Sidgwick's gaze softened, a touch of pity in his eyes. "Young Malament, family ties are a fine hope, but politics often cuts deep. Your grandfather may not have the freedom to offer you an open welcome. He is a king, after all, and a king's loyalty is seldom simple."

Malament's expression hardened, his tone growing resolute. "Then he'll have choice. Either he opens his gates willingly, or one day I'll be forced to open them myself."

Sidgwick studied Malament's face, noting the resolve in his young pupil's eyes. Malament was no longer a boy filled with naive dreams but a young man with ambitions that could one day shift the kingdom's course. Though he knew Malament still had much to learn, he found himself wondering what kind of leader this bold youth might one day become. Malum's reign had brought peace, yet that peace felt fragile, as though one wrong move could shatter it. Dangerous times, indeed, Sidgwick mused. Still, with Malum's good health, Sidgwick doubted he would live to see Malament take the mantle of Lord.

"It is easy to speak boldly of opening gates and declaring war, my young lord," Sidgwick replied gently. "But when the time comes, you'll see that such decisions are rarely as simple as they seem. Making enemies of powerful men is a risk, especially men like King Ruben. He is no gentle soul; your father was wise to forge a tie with him through marriage."

Malament met his gaze, unflinching. "I respect my mother, Sidgwick, and I respect the bond of marriage, but my father is no wise man—merely a puppet, dancing to the tune of the senate. I see it every day." He paused; his voice laced with frustration. "Their foresight was as shallow as a rain puddle. The marriage itself is strained, and I have no doubt that if the bond is severed, my mother would return to her father's side. And then the King..." Malament's lips curled with disdain, "he wouldn't hesitate to plunge a sword into our lands, to divide East Kadun further."

Sidgwick hid his agreement behind a thoughtful nod. It did not take a shrewd eye to observe the tensions within Malum's household, nor the subtle power the senate held over their lord. "And tell me, Malament—if the Lordship were yours, what would you do differently?"

Malament's eyes glinted, as if picturing the power of his father's seat. He was eager for the mantle, that much was clear, though he dreaded inheriting it only after age had dulled his edge. He feared that by then, his vision for the realm would be obsolete, his youthful ambition withered under the weight of too many years. Life could change drastically by then

—Borlong could be ruined by civil strife, or perhaps he would kneel before a foreign boot, his own power stripped from him.

"If I ruled today," Malament said, voice steady and clear, "I would seek peace within our borders first. It's no secret that violence ripples through East Kadun—settlements pillaged, innocents brutalised. My father waits, content to sit idle while our people suffer. The forest clans grow restless, tired of watching their trees felled and sent north to warm Nordon while we stand by in our fine robes, idle and blind. I would care for our own, Sidgwick. Our people, united, could shape this world—even Barroth itself." His gaze sharpened. "Yes, I would have peace within our walls first. Then, when we are strong as one nation again, others would tremble before us."

Sidgwick felt a pang of surprise at Malament's response. He had expected bravado, perhaps empty ambition, but there was a spark here—a fierce love of Kadun that stirred something in Sidgwick, something he'd thought long buried. Dangerous ideas, yes, but perhaps truths hidden within them. East Kadun might need a leader with fire, a young 'cockerel,' to ruffle a few feathers.

"My young lord," Sidgwick murmured, a hint of wistfulness in his voice, "you stir an old pride in me—a love for this land that I'd thought buried beneath years of cynicism. But heed my words—such ambitions are best guarded within these walls. The senate holds sharp eyes, and there are those who would see your dreams as threats." He paused, then offered a faint, encouraging smile. "If fate grants me the years to witness your rule, I'd do so with great interest." His gaze softened as he added, "But for now, we've veered far from our lesson, and young Auron looks thoroughly bewildered by our musings. We'll end here for today. Take your leave—I'll see to the tidying up."

Malament inclined his head with respectful grace, and Auron mirrored the gesture, casting a shy smile Sidgwick's way. Sidgwick watched them disappear through the doorway before turning back to his books and maps. Alone, he felt a faint but steady pride warming his chest, mingling with thoughts of a future Kadun shaped by the young man who had just departed. In the quiet, a vision lingered—a hope for the realm that flickered to life, tempered by the knowledge of how fragile dreams could be.

# THE APPRENTICE
# CHAPTER NINETEEN

The two students left the older scholar to his studies, their footsteps echoing softly across the upstairs landing as they made their way to the grand stairwell. Servants lined the walls along their path, standing in quiet readiness, their hands folded, and eyes respectfully lowered. As Malament and Auron passed, each servant dipped into a low bow. Auron felt a thrill of pride swell within him, walking side by side with the young Lord. This was the man who had lifted him from the alleys and given him a life he had never thought possible—a life with meaning. Today, with his first combat lesson ahead, Auron hoped to prove himself worthy of Malament's faith, to show that he could become more than anyone had ever imagined.

Since Malament had told him of the upcoming lesson, the past few days had crawled by, each hour stretching his anticipation to a near-breaking point. Auron was not entirely sure what to expect from Gordon's training, but the thought of wielding a weapon filled him with a feverish excitement. In the quiet of his room each night, he had practised against thin air, swinging an invisible blade, slashing at shadows. His imagination had transformed the small, dim space into a battleground, where he fought off monstrous foes, wielding the strength and skill he hoped to one day master. These silent battles left him breathless, his heart pounding as though he were truly locked in combat.

For Malament, the day held a different kind of anticipation. He would be observing Auron's first steps in the art of combat, the foundation of skills that could one day make him a master. Malament had spoken of Auron as his future blade master, the sword at his side when he ruled, but he knew well enough that words could be as fragile as glass. Auron's promise had to be proven through action, through training. If he struggled to take to it, then his skill would only reach as far as the effort and time put into his lessons.

Malament, however, held a hope that went beyond mere competence. He wanted more than just a skilled fighter; he wanted a warrior feared by others, a swordsman who moved with instinct, whose mastery over his blade would be as natural as drawing breath. And as he considered

Auron's remarkable resilience—his rapid physical recovery, his quiet courage even in the face of Lord Malum's flogging—Malament allowed himself to believe, just for a moment, that Auron might truly be destined for greatness.

As they passed through the hall, the training area came into view, framed by wide, arched columns that led to its entrance. The open space beyond was defined by the coarse sand of the fight pit, which spread across the ground like a blank canvas ready to bear the marks of combat. Waiting at the centre was Gordon, a short, stocky man with a hardened expression and arms folded across his broad chest. Around him, several wooden swords leaned upright against a nearby pillar, their worn surfaces bearing the scars of countless lessons. As Malament and Auron approached, Gordon unfolded his arms, spreading them wide in a gesture of welcome.

"Welcome, my students," he called, his voice carrying a note of rough warmth. "And a special welcome to you, Auron. Today, your training in the art of swordsmanship begins." He paused, his gaze fixed on Auron with a mixture of appraisal and faint amusement. "I am Gordon, a captain of East Kadun, and a long-serving captain under Lord Malum."

With a slight bow of his head, he acknowledged both Auron and Malament, and they returned the gesture in turn. Gordon continued, "I understand Malament has been running you through some basic exercises. We'll see how well you've taken to them today, though I must say, it's clear they've made a difference. Last time I saw you, Auron, you were hardly fit for a crow's feast. You must have put on half your body weight since then." A brief smile crossed his stern face. "It brings me pleasure to see you looking so well."

He turned to Malament, his gaze shifting to a more serious note. "Malament, the boy is ready to begin combat training? His wounds won't hinder him?"

Malament looked down at Auron standing eagerly by his side. The boy's transformation was striking—his once frail frame now filled out, his posture steady, eyes bright with anticipation. Malament felt a surge of pride as he replied, "Auron's recovery has been remarkable. I've never seen someone heal so swiftly from injuries like his. And he's taken to the fitness drills with determination. He's more than ready."

Gordon raised an eyebrow, giving Auron a once-over, as though confirming Malament's words. "Very well," he said with a nod. "Then let's begin."

Gordon strode toward the pillar where a small stockpile of wooden training swords leaned, their handles worn smooth from countless lessons. He picked up three and turned back to Auron, his gaze steely and commanding.

"This sand pit, this training ground—call it what you will—is my realm," he declared, his voice ringing with authority. "Once you step into my realm, my teachings and my commands are all that matter. Do you understand?" He paused, letting his words sink in. "I would have you free your mind of all other thoughts. Leave them at the door; you may return to them once our time is up. Here, they are burdens you cannot afford."

Auron nodded, his eyes wide, a nervous excitement swirling in his chest. Gordon continued, his tone softer but just as firm. "Now, to begin your training, let's see how you hold a sword. Tell me, which arm do you favour?"

Auron blinked, uncertain, the question catching him off guard. He glanced helplessly at Malament, who clarified, "Auron, Gordon wants to know which hand you'll wield your weapon with." But Auron's face remained blank, his brow furrowing as he tried to make sense of the question. "I… I don't know," he answered, his voice small.

Gordon let out a low chuckle, seeming amused by Auron's confusion. "Not to worry, lad. Tell me this, then: which hand do you throw with, or eat an apple with?"

Auron's blank look lingered, followed by a slight shrug. "Whichever hand the apple's in, I suppose."

Malament sucked in a sharp breath, his face twisting with a mix of exasperation and a hint of embarrassment. He realised that Auron's response, though genuine, came off blunt to the point of sarcasm. Gordon's eyes narrowed slightly, but a smirk tugged at the corner of his mouth. "Ah, so we have a jester among us," he said, with a wry glance at Malament. "Very well, boy. If you don't know which hand, then let's start with both."

He passed Auron one of the wooden practice swords, which Auron took in both hands, wrapping his fingers carefully around the hilt. The weight surprised him; it was heavier than he had expected, and the feel of the polished wood under his fingers sent a small thrill through him. Tentatively, he swung it in a wide arc, testing its balance, then bounced it lightly up and down in his grip with a smoothness that caught Gordon's attention.

"How does it feel?" Gordon asked, his eyes narrowing as he observed Auron's movements.

"It's heavier than I thought," Auron replied, a faint smile breaking through his nervousness. "But... it feels good."

"Good," Gordon said, nodding in approval. "These practice swords are crafted from the finest wood in our forests. Polished, varnished, weighted just so—each one is a careful imitation of a true blade. You'll treat this sword not as a piece of wood, but as an extension of your arm."

Gordon's tone turned more instructional. "Now," he said, "hold the hilt with your right hand alone. Extend your arm out to the side and keep both your arm and blade level."

Auron followed the instructions, shifting his grip to his right hand alone. He extended his arm, feeling the weight of the sword dragging downward and the strain building in his shoulder. The stance was awkward, but a flicker of determination hardened his gaze as he resolved to meet Gordon's challenge.

Gordon observed him closely, his expression softening with a hint of approval. "Not bad," he murmured, the warmth in his tone barely perceptible. "We might just make a swordsman of you yet."

Encouraged, Auron extended his arm further to the side, keeping the wooden sword level as instructed. At first, it seemed manageable, but as the seconds wore on, the pull of the weapon grew heavier, his muscles starting to quiver with strain. A subtle smile tugged at the corners of Gordon's mouth, just enough to lift the edges of his neatly trimmed moustache. "Not as easy as it looks, is it?" he remarked, his tone tinged with quiet amusement. "Now, steady yourself. True strength lies in control."

Gordon's gaze sharpened, taking in every detail of Auron's struggle—the tremor in his grip, the subtle adjustments in his stance. Over the years, he had guided countless students through this same exercise. For most, it was a simple test of strength and endurance, a way to reveal their dominant hand. Yet for those with natural instincts, this exercise became something more—a glimpse into how well their instincts matched their favoured side, a subtlety that could shape the path of their training.

Without warning, Gordon raised his hand and brought it down in a controlled strike against Auron's wooden sword. Though the impact was light, it was enough to test him. Auron's arm wobbled under the blow, struggling to hold steady as the weight pulled him off balance. Yet Gordon's practised eye noticed a slight resistance—a reflexive strength in Auron's grip that hinted at raw, untamed potential.

"Well done, Auron," Gordon remarked, nodding in approval. "We've confirmed your favoured hand: your right. And that's a good foundation to start from."

Malament's expression shifted as he took in the news, a subtle shadow of disappointment crossing his face. He had hoped, perhaps irrationally, that Auron would be left-handed—a trait that would have given him a unique edge. Left-handed swordsmen were rare, and their unfamiliar approach gave them an advantage over opponents trained to defend against right-handed strikes. Malament knew that Auron could still become a formidable swordsman, but he had lost a potential advantage before he had even begun.

Yet, as he watched Auron catch his breath, determination still glinting in his eyes, Malament reminded himself that it was only the beginning. There was much to learn, and who knew what other strengths might emerge from this boy whose very presence was a miracle of resilience.

Auron, disappointed by his performance, cast a glance toward Malament, noticing the hint of sadness in his expression. How had he failed to hold his arm steady against such a gentle strike? He felt the need to redeem himself. "Do I not have another chance?" he pleaded; his voice urgent. "I'll keep my arm still this time, I promise. Or maybe... maybe I can try my other hand—it might be stronger."

Gordon's mouth curled in a small smile at the boy's enthusiasm. "Auron, you did not fail. What happened was perfectly normal. The stronger arm offers resistance, which you did, and the weaker arm would struggle to even keep the sword lifted. Testing your other hand would be pointless." His eyes softened slightly. "Besides, with your arm just recently healed, it would be unwise."

But Auron's determination did not falter. "My arm is fine now," he insisted. "Please, let me try."

Gordon exchanged an amused glance with Malament, both of them sensing a fiery spirit in the boy that would make training all the more interesting. "Very well, Auron," Gordon said with a chuckle. "We shall try your other hand." He tossed a second practice sword to Malament, who caught it mid-blade, watching as Auron switched the sword to his left hand.

Before Gordon could give further instructions, Auron had already stretched his left arm out, determination etched across his face. He held the blade steady, though his arm quickly began to tremble from the weight. As with the first test, Gordon waited a beat, then sent a slow, controlled strike down against Auron's outstretched sword. Once again, Auron's arm gave way, though Gordon noted the same faint resistance.

Frustration creased Auron's brow as he lowered his arm. "Why can't I hold it steady?" he asked, more to himself than anyone else.

Gordon's expression shifted, a flicker of surprise mingling with curiosity. "Auron, you resisted the strike just as before. This is unusual but impressive." He paused, studying the boy. "Let's try something different—strike me with each hand, as hard as you can. This may reveal which arm holds the greater strength."

Auron's brow furrowed briefly in confusion, but he did not hesitate. With the sword still in his left hand, he drew his arm back, then slashed down at Gordon in one swift, forceful motion. The strike was strong and quick, and though it lacked polish, there was an unexpected intensity behind it. Gordon deflected the blow with practised ease.

But before he could issue any further instruction, Auron shifted again. With a flash of movement, he switched the sword to his right hand, his grip shifting as he brought it down with newfound speed. The right-handed blow came just as fast as the left, faster than Gordon had anticipated.

Momentarily caught off guard, Gordon reacted instinctively. He dropped to one knee, his own sword sweeping upward in a sharp arc, intercepting Auron's strike just in time. Had Auron been fully grown, his weight and strength behind the attack, the strike might have broken through.

Gordon did not waste a second. In a single fluid motion, he surged upward from his kneeling position, uncoiling like a spring. He launched himself at Auron with calculated force, the impact sending the boy stumbling backward. Auron's sword slipped from his grasp as he fell, his balance faltering under Gordon's relentless advance. Gordon followed through, his movements precise and unyielding, securing both practice swords in his grip. With a quick, controlled motion, he crossed the blades near Auron's neck, holding them poised like the shears of a trap, each blade steady and immovable, a silent warning of his control.

But even as he fell, Auron's instincts kicked in. He twisted in mid-air, using his momentum to roll over his shoulder and land with surprising agility. His feet found the ground near Malament, and in one fluid motion, he snatched Malament's practice sword from his hand, raising it just in time to intercept Gordon's dual-wielded attack.

The three wooden swords met with a resounding crack as Auron blocked Gordon's strike, though the force of the impact was too much. The sword recoiled from his grip, striking Auron squarely on the nose. A sharp sting spread across his face as he felt the skin split, and a slow trickle of blood began to run down the bridge of his nose, dripping onto the sand in small crimson droplets.

Gordon immediately stepped back; a look of shock mixed with admiration crossing his face. With a nod, he drove both practice swords into the ground beside him, leaving them upright in the sand. He reached into his pocket, pulling out a small brown cloth, which he tossed to Auron. The boy caught it, pressing it to his nose to stem the bleeding.

"My apologies, Auron," Gordon said, his voice softer now. "I lost myself there. You fight with the skill of a trained man; only your youth holds you back." He turned to Malament, his eyes wide with newfound respect. "Malament, where did you find this boy?"

Malament had watched the swift exchange in disbelief, his eyes wide as he processed what he had just witnessed. Auron's natural agility and hand speed were nothing short of astonishing. In those brief moments, Gordon—a seasoned captain—had nearly been caught off guard, and even his powerful counterattack had been blocked by the boy. The entire sequence had unfolded with such speed that Malament felt momentarily disoriented, as if he were the one being tested. Gordon's question broke through his daze, and he turned to answer, his voice tinged with lingering awe.

"He was living by the marketplace in the southern quarter. Beyond that, I know little of his past."

Gordon's gaze lingered on Auron, his expression one of intrigue and newfound respect. "There seems to be great mystery to you, Auron, and even greater potential. I have never seen anyone take to a weapon in each hand so effortlessly." With a nod, he reached down, picked up a practice sword jutting out the sand, and offered it to Auron. "Here. Take this. Tell me how it feels."

Auron lowered the cloth from his nose, the bloodied fabric slipping from his fingers and landing in the sand, darkening it in a small blot. He grasped the hilt of the second blade, feeling the added weight settle naturally into his grip. He raised both swords, holding them aloft, his face lighting up as though something had clicked into place.

"That feels... better," he murmured, a quiet confidence in his voice.

Gordon's smile spread, and Malament could not help but mirror it, a contagious pride filling him as he saw Auron take to the dual blades as if born for them. Gordon then pulled the remaining sword from the sand, holding it upright before him. His stance shifted slightly, a warrior preparing for a challenge. "From this day forth, you will train with two blades, Auron," he declared. "Now, strike me again."

Auron needed no further encouragement. With both blades in hand, he dropped instinctively into a stance, his focus narrowing to the target before him. He felt the weight and balance of the two swords, his movements growing surer with each step. Then, with a burst of speed, he lunged, the twin wooden swords sweeping down toward Gordon.

Gordon parried the strike with a practised block, though he felt the power behind Auron's attack reverberate through his arms. He could not deny it: the boy's natural skill was beyond anything he had anticipated. Each clash of their wooden swords echoed through the training yard, a testament to a raw talent that even he had rarely seen.

Malament watched in wonder, his mind racing, he had his sword.

# THE APPRENTICE
# CHAPTER TWENTY

The mid-afternoon sun radiated down onto the cobbled streets, casting a brilliant glare across the paving stones that forced Malament to narrow his eyes as he strode toward the senate house. His lateness today was unusual, and yet he found he could not bring himself to hurry. The morning's training session with Auron had been nothing short of mesmerising. He could still picture the boy's movements, each strike and counter as vivid in his mind as though they were unfolding before him now. Auron's natural instinct and precision had left Malament captivated, bewildered by how swiftly the boy grasped even the most intricate techniques.

There was something uncanny in Auron's fluidity, a sense of innate understanding that Malament rarely saw, even among seasoned fighters. He recalled how Auron had effortlessly mirrored Gordon's every motion, his timing impeccable, his strikes sharp and unwavering. It was as though the boy was tapping into something beyond mere training, some raw, instinctual knowledge that defied his origins. Repetitive blows and blocks, feints and counters—techniques that had taken Malament years to master, and yet Auron had absorbed them within hours, wielding them with a finesse that felt both natural and deeply unsettling.

Malament's thoughts lingered on how far Auron had come. He could still see the image of that scrawny boy he had first spotted, scratching around the streets for scraps, eyes hollow from hunger but brimming with something else—an indomitable spark that Malament had sensed even then, though he had not known what it might mean. Now, to watch him wield a blade was to witness a transformation, a blossoming of untapped potential that made Malament wonder if the boy was destined for something far greater than he had initially imagined.

As Malament approached the looming shadow cast by the senate house, he felt dwarfed by the building's imposing architecture. Tall stone columns rose from the ground like sentries guarding the entrance, each one intricately carved with the symbols of East Kadun's history—a testament to the weight of decisions made within these walls. Large banners of East Kadun's colours, a deep royal red emblazoned with the golden tree and the countries words, draped down from the upper tiers. The flags, vibrant against the grey stone, were a reminder of the nation's might and traditions that these senators claimed to protect.

Beyond the threshold, the forum was alive with movement, a buzzing hive of conversations that blended into a single, overwhelming hum of voices. The air seemed thick with heated debates, the scent of parchment, and the faint tang of ink. Senators in flowing robes moved in clusters, gesturing animatedly as they discussed the matters of the realm. Their movements appeared almost theatrical, each man and woman embodying their rank with exaggerated gestures, as if trying to make their presence more significant amid the crowd.

As he passed beneath the columns and into the dense throng, Malament felt himself swallowed by the sea of bodies. He wove through the crowd, bumping against shoulders and dodging outstretched arms mid-gesture. Just as he began to make some headway, a corpulent man in a richly embroidered robe leaned back unexpectedly, his heel landing squarely on Malament's exposed toe beneath the thin strap of his sandal. A sharp jolt of pain shot up his leg, and he stifled a grimace, fighting the urge to curse aloud. The man, either oblivious or purposely ignoring the incident, continued his conversation, leaving Malament seething in silent frustration.

Brushing off the irritation, he pressed on, manoeuvring through the bustling senate floor with renewed determination. The press of bodies was relentless, each step a struggle against the tides of officials, aides, and advisors who thrived in the noise and spectacle. Finally, after a series of sidesteps and murmured apologies, he reached the towering bleachers at the farthest end of the hall. The seats rose in steep rows, their vantage point distant from the speaker but offering a clear view of the forum below. Malament ascended to the back rows, settling himself among the less prominent observers, where he could watch the proceedings unfold.

The bleachers always had available seats, a peculiar truth that never ceased to amuse Malament. The senators and advisors seemed to clamour for positions on the forum floor, pushing and jostling to secure a spot near the speaker's podium, as if proximity would somehow lend their voices more weight. They believed that by standing in the crowd, their faces would be recognized, their words given significance. Fools, Malament thought with a smirk. From the height of the bleachers, he had a vantage point that captured the entire room, where the ebb and flow of every discussion played out like a grand spectacle. He knew that all it took to command attention was to stand tall, to speak clearly, and to let his voice carry over the half-wits below—a power he had practised many times in private.

Despite his own views on the matters often discussed, Malament held his silence. He had to bide his time, for as much as he felt the pull of debate, he held no official position in the senate; his voice was yet unwelcome in its chambers. Still, there were certain privileges that came from being Lord Malum's son. His father believed it wise that Malament attend as many meetings as possible, to see firsthand how debates twisted and turned, how opinions could sway like leaves in the wind, and how alliances were forged and fractured in a heartbeat. This was his training ground, a place where words were weapons, and Malament was sharpening his ear to each and every one.

And so, he would sit in silence, observing, his gaze steady and discerning. He watched the senator's bicker, squabble, and posture, their heated arguments often dissolving into petty disputes over trivial details. Yet, there was a rhythm to it—a rhythm he was learning to read, where voices rose and fell, alliances shifted, and opinions carried weight based on who spoke rather than what was said. Day by day, he catalogued each figure in the room: who held favour, who made a point worth noting, and who simply sought to be heard for the sake of their own ego.

One day, it would be Malament, not his father, guiding the country. He knew he would need a keen understanding of every man in this chamber—their loyalties, their motives, the force behind their words, and the reach of their influence. This knowledge was his inheritance, a foundation he would need to govern effectively when his time came.

Malament had come to view the senate through a lens of strategy, methodically dividing its members into three distinct factions. The first group consisted of those who unwaveringly supported his family, men like Masum, Modrum, and Malon. These were respected heads of ancient houses, allies who had once stood alongside his father during the hardest decisions, including the controversial end to the war with the West. Their loyalty was steadfast, grounded in shared values and a willingness to see the greater picture—even if it meant heavy sacrifices. Malament regarded them with a measure of respect; they were men with a deep understanding of the weight of governance, the kind who valued stability over personal gain. Their loyalty was not blind, but rooted in their commitment to East Kadun's future, a future they believed Malum's lineage would protect.

The second faction was, by far, the largest and perhaps the most complex. These were men who had, like much of East Kadun, once favoured the war's end and the peace it brought. But their support had waned over time, corroded by bitter memories of the treaty's cost—the loss of noble blood and hard-won riches. For them, the price of peace had been a personal blow, the West's dominance over trade a relentless reminder of the treaty's lopsided terms. They tolerated Malum, perhaps even respected his vision, but they held a lingering resentment, their wounds as much financial as familial. Malament saw them as driven less by principle and more by their ledgers; wealth and status mattered above all else, their loyalty wavering with the weight of their purses. They tolerated his father's presence, but only so long as their fortunes were secure—a fragile allegiance he knew he would have to earn or reshape in time.

And then, there was the third faction, a scattered band of nomads in the political landscape—men of power and influence, yet too mercurial to command consistent sway. These senators flitted between stances, their opinions changing with the prevailing winds, wielding just enough clout to keep their voices from fading entirely but lacking the cohesion or loyalty that bound the other factions. In many ways, Malament found them of course the most unpredictable, each one a potential ally or adversary, depending on the day's discourse. They could be won over by a persuasive word or lost in a single misstep. He regarded them with cautious interest, knowing they could serve as leverage when he needed it but would require vigilance. In the volatile theatre of the senate, they were the wild cards, opportunists with no enduring allegiance but to themselves.

As Malament's gaze travelled over the senators, he felt a quiet resolve harden within him. To lead one day, he would need to know each faction, understand each motivation, and master the art of navigating the forces in this room—the loyal, the resentful, and the unpredictable. Only by doing so could he hope to shape East Kadun into a kingdom of his vision.

His father and tutors often spoke with reverence about the senate, extolling its role as the voice of East Kadun's people, a bastion of democracy where every perspective found a platform. They preached the virtues of collective wisdom, insisting that true strength came from shared counsel and collaboration. Yet, to Malament, this idealism felt hollow. The so-called "democratic voice" of the senate was little more than a cacophony—a mess of competing egos and fragile alliances, voices too diluted to make real impact. While his father saw unity in this assembly, Malament saw weakness.

In his mind, the fate of East Kadun should rest on the judgement of one voice, a voice strong enough to guide and protect without bending to whims and bickering. His voice. It would be his alone that carried the clarity, the vision, and the unwavering will to shape their nation's future. He understood his father's reliance on the senate, saw the prudence in cultivating alliances and fostering loyalty, but to him, it was a necessary step to a greater end. There would come a day when only one voice would need to be heard, when decisions could be made without being shackled by compromise.

As Malament scanned the senators below him, listening to the ebb and flow of their disputes, he felt an unspoken conviction settle within him. One day, he would rise above them all, the single voice that would guide East Kadun—not as one voice among many, but as the voice of authority, a leader who answered only to his own vision.

A familiar figure dropped down beside him with an easy, unassuming grace. Luka, a man who defied typical labels, was difficult to notice at a glance yet impossible to overlook once you knew him. He was not especially tall or short, strikingly handsome or unpleasant to look at, and his build lay somewhere between lean and sturdy. Yet Luka possessed an undeniable presence, a magnetism that made him seem everywhere and nowhere all at once. His black hair flopped carelessly over his forehead, and a matching beard framed a mouth that almost always wore a knowing smile—a smile that hinted he knew more than he let on.

"How goes it, my friend?" Luka greeted; his voice warm as he nudged Malament's shoulder.

Malament turned, returning the smile. "Luka. Keeping yourself busy as always, I'm sure?"

"You know me too well," Luka chuckled, leaning back with a relaxed air. Luka was one of the few in Malament's circle he might truly consider a friend. A nomad by nature and by reputation, Luka's family had inherited an assortment of businesses and substantial wealth from families lost during the war's aftermath and Luka, was the sole custodian. Through his savvy acquisitions—bakeries, brothels, taverns, silk trades—he had built a vast, profitable network that spanned the city and beyond. With fingers in nearly every venture, he moved through the shadows of Borlong's bustling streets with ease, weaving between the city's districts and its secrets.

More than just a businessman, Luka was a broker of information. The taverns brought in stories from all corners, the brothels whispered of liaisons and scandals, and his silk trade exposed him to nobles and merchants alike. Few movements escaped his notice, and fewer motives were hidden from his ever-watchful gaze. If someone had secrets, Luka either already knew them or was well on his way to finding out. Malament had long since recognized the value of Luka's knowledge and insights, making him a friend worth keeping close.

"One of these days, Luka, you'll have the entire city in your pocket," Malament said, his tone half-joking.

Luka shrugged, a mischievous gleam in his eye. "Who needs a whole city? Just knowing its secrets is enough for me." He leaned in, lowering his voice conspiratorially. "And speaking of secrets... you wouldn't believe the news that came in from the West this morning."

Malament's curiosity piqued at Luka's words, his gaze sharpening. "From the West, you say? Go on, then—don't keep me in suspense."

Luka's grin widened, his voice dropping to a near whisper, though there was no real need to be discreet in the noisy forum. "Apparently, our esteemed friends across the gorge have been dealing with a... 'situation' among their noble families. A series of disappearances, strange enough, with no ransom demands, no public outcry. It's as if they were plucked from their estates in the dead of night, leaving only whispers behind."

Malament's brow furrowed, his interest deepening. "And you're sure this isn't just one of your tavern tales? The West has always had a knack for drama."

"Oh, it's more than idle gossip," Luka replied, tapping his chin thoughtfully. "Two different sources confirmed it—one from my silk suppliers, whose shipments have been delayed as a result of increased inspections, and another from a brothel down near the gorge. Seems even the nobles' guards are too distracted by whatever's happening to keep their usual pleasures quiet."

Malament leaned back, letting Luka's words settle, the weight of them hinting at possibilities. Disappearances among Western nobility could mean many things—political purges, retribution, or, perhaps, something more insidious. "And what do you think it all means?"

Luka shrugged, a playful glint in his eyes. "I think it means opportunity. If the nobles in the West are distracted, it could create gaps—moments of weakness that someone with ambition might exploit." He gave Malament a knowing look, his words hovering between suggestion and jest.

"You make it sound so easy," Malament said, smirking. "But you're right. Perhaps it's time we keep an eye on the West. If they're vulnerable, there may be room for influence—though I'd tread carefully. Ruben's reach is long, and he doesn't hesitate to remind us of it."

"Ah, but who better to watch than the cautious?" Luka chuckled, his gaze drifting over the senate floor. "Anyway, you know where to find me if anything interesting comes up on your end." He patted Malament's shoulder with a friendly squeeze before leaning back, his attention once again darting around the bustling forum, ears open, ready to catch the next whisper of intrigue.

As they sat in comfortable silence, Malament felt a renewed sense of reassurance in Luka's presence. Amid so many voices vying for influence, Luka was the rare ally who knew the value of silence—of listening carefully before acting. To Malament, he was not just a friend; he was a vital asset, a key to the hidden currents of East Kadun's politics, and one he intended to keep close as the tides of power continued to shift.

Suddenly, the atmosphere in the senate shifted. Conversations softened, then faded altogether as a lone figure made his way to the centre of the forum. Lord Malum's entrance was a steady, purposeful one, his steps echoing through the hall with a weight that drew every eye. He moved with the kind of presence that demanded attention, his robes sweeping behind him like shadows. His grey hair draped over each shoulder, complementing his freshly trimmed beard that exuded meticulous authority. As he reached the forum's centre, he paused, his gaze sweeping across the gathered senators with a look that seemed to carry the gravity of the news he bore.

Malament straightened instinctively, a quiet tension settling in his chest. He watched his father closely, noting the grave set of his mouth, the dark shadows beneath his eyes—a rare break in his usually composed demeanour. Next to him, Luka, who was so often casual and carefree, leaned forward, his usual smirk replaced by a look of keen interest.

Lord Malum inclined his head in a respectful nod, acknowledging the weight of his audience. "Honoured senators," he began, his voice calm but carrying a hint of solemnity, "I hope this day finds you all well. East Kadun stands as strong as ever, thanks to the diligence and wisdom of this senate—a testament to your tireless dedication to our people."

A few murmurs of approval echoed softly through the hall, senators nodding in response to the customary pleasantries. Lord Malum allowed the brief moment of ease, letting it settle before his expression grew more sombre.

"However," he continued, his tone shifting, "there are times when the stability we hold dear is challenged by forces beyond our borders." He paused, as though choosing his words carefully, his gaze scanning the room. "This morning, I received troubling news from our northern neighbours in Stormhold."

The room grew stiller, senators leaning in slightly, the air thick with anticipation. Malum took a measured breath before delivering the blow.

"King Ivar Froskgar is dead."

A collective gasp swept through the senate like a gust of wind, each senator's response layered over the next. Some men recoiled visibly, eyes widening in alarm, while others leaned forward, gripping the edges of their seats, their knuckles white with tension. A few muttered curses under their breath, their shock giving way to anger, while others cast quick, nervous glances toward their allies, as though seeking silent counsel on what this news might mean for East Kadun.

Among the more stoic senators, brows furrowed deeply, worry lines forming as they processed the impact of King Ivar's death. Here and there, voices rose, a mixture of disbelief and concern, weaving through the chamber in hushed tones that grew louder by the second. For a moment, it was as if a storm had been unleashed, the sound of a hundred voices buzzing with an anxiety that no single word could fully capture.

Malament felt the tension in the room like a taut bowstring, ready to snap. He noted the senators closest to him—a veteran soldier who clenched his fists at the news, his jaw rigid; a young nobleman who looked stunned, eyes darting between his peers as he tried to gauge the mood; and, across the aisle, a weathered merchant who looked downward, his lips pressed into a thin line, perhaps already calculating how Stormhold's uncertain future might affect trade.

Beside him, Luka's usual composure had shifted, his playful demeanour replaced by a rare intensity. His eyes, always sharp, now flickered with rapid calculation, his mind likely already mapping the web of consequences this would have across his many interests. Malament could almost see the gears turning—every trade route affected, every alliance thrown into question. It was a look that reminded Malament why Luka was such a valuable ally; even in the face of chaos, he was thinking several steps ahead.

The gravity of King Ivar's death settled over the room, heavy and unavoidable. It was not merely the loss of a king—it was the fracture of an alliance, a shift in the stability they had come to rely on. Malament could almost feel the ripple of unspoken fears threading through the senate: questions of loyalty, of the power vacuum left behind, of what this would mean with Queen Karak now in command.

Lord Malum raised a steady hand, commanding the room's attention as the murmurs began to swell. His voice, clear and resolute, rang through the forum. "Honoured senators, you know well that King Ivar Froskgar was more than just a neighbouring monarch. He was a staunch ally to East Kadun. Despite the rumours of Forest Clan raids, he remained loyal to our peace and respected our sovereignty. His death—by murder, no less—casts a long and troubling shadow over our alliance and leaves our future with Stormhold precariously balanced."

A ripple of shock and anger surged through the room. Senators leaned into hushed conversations, some voices louder than others, questioning the implications. One senator, an older man known for his bluntness, stood abruptly. "Murder, you say? And we're to believe this is mere misfortune? What's to stop us from assuming Queen Karak herself had a hand in it?"

Lord Malum held up a hand, his expression firm, though there was a hint of caution in his tone. "We cannot assume anything just yet, Senator Raldor. We know only that he has been killed, and to speculate beyond the facts would serve no purpose but to fan the flames of discord. Our next steps must be cautious."

The murmurs grew louder, senators sharing anxious glances, but Malum's voice broke through again. "There is more. Queen Karak has assumed the throne in Stormhold. However," he paused, his eyes sweeping over the room, "in her first decree as sovereign, she signed her letter not as Froskgar, but as Thørn—her maiden name."

The tension in the room spiked immediately, alarm rippling through the senate. Some men's faces flushed with concern, others gripped the arms of their seats, their gazes fixed intently on Lord Malum. To take the name Thørn could mean one thing: a signal of division, an assertion of her own will.

"This could mean anything!" another senator called out, his voice echoing from the bleachers. "She's declaring independence from the legacy of her husband! Surely, she plans to shift alliances."

Malum raised his hand again, though his tone a tempered calm edging his words. "Perhaps, Senator Jonar, perhaps not. Let us not allow conjecture to dictate our actions. Queen Karak may simply be choosing to honour her heritage. She is, after all, a ruler in her own right." He allowed his words to settle, the senators murmuring with uncertainty as they exchanged sceptical glances.

But then Lord Malum's expression softened slightly, and he raised a hand to signal for attention once more. "Yet, amidst the uncertainty, there is a note of promise within Queen Karak's letter," he continued, his voice steady but cautiously optimistic. "The Queen herself has expressed her intention to attend Nordon's annual trade visit here in Borlong. She will bring her council and representatives from Stormhold, offering us the opportunity to meet her directly and gauge her intentions."

The room shifted, the senators exchanging glances, this news sparking a flicker of hope and intrigue amid their earlier apprehension. Some senators leaned forward, curious, while others nodded thoughtfully. An older senator in the front row cleared his throat and spoke up, his voice measured. "A bold move, to come herself. Perhaps she aims to show her loyalty to the alliance?"

Lord Malum acknowledged him with a nod, though his expression remained guarded. "It may very well be that Queen Karak wishes to affirm her ties with us but let us not rush to conclusions. Her visit presents us with a unique opportunity—a chance to observe, to question, and to understand her stance. For now, we shall prepare to welcome her with every courtesy, but we must also remain vigilant."

The senators nodded, some with more enthusiasm, others still with furrowed brows of uncertainty. Malament watched his father's calm handling of the situation with a rare admiration, recognizing the quiet wisdom in balancing caution with diplomacy. The unease in the room eased slightly, though a hum of intrigue lingered. He knew this would only be the beginning of their speculations, but one thing was certain: Queen Karak's visit would reveal more than words could ever convey, and East Kadun would be watching closely.

As the senate session came to an end, senators gathered their things, voices laced with rumour and apprehension. Groups clustered together, exchanging hurried whispers that carried a tone of unease and uncertainty. Malament remained seated, watching as his father lingered in conversation with a few trusted allies, his expression controlled yet shadowed by the weight of this new threat. Lord Malum's posture was tense, his gaze distant, as if already grappling with the implications of Queen Karak's ascent.

Next to him, Luka leaned in, his voice low and serious, an unusual glint of caution in his eyes. "Be careful, Malament. A new ruler is like a blade—sharp and unpredictable. This one might be honed to cut us deeper than we realise."

Malament met Luka's gaze, his own expression steady, though he felt a flicker of unease. He knew his friend's instincts were rarely wrong. For all his ambition and plans, he recognized the truth in Luka's warning: Queen Karak's intentions were still an enigma, and one misstep could turn the tides against them.

"Yes," Malament murmured, eyes shifting back to his father. "We'll need to tread carefully indeed."

The senate hall gradually emptied, its imposing silence settling like a weight. Rising from his seat, Malament cast one final glance over the chamber. Today had shifted something, and he sensed the change would ripple through East Kadun, drawing lines and testing loyalties. His father's caution had kept them secure, but he knew that in time, security alone would not be enough. The moment would come when the path would demand decisiveness and strength—a vision sharp enough to guide the nation through whatever storm lay ahead.

Luka joined him, the two men falling into step as they exited the hall and emerged into the bright afternoon light. The sun hung high, casting sharp shadows across the city's stone streets, its warmth contrasting the cold tension that lingered in Malament's mind. As he looked out over Borlong, the bustling capital alive with merchants, citizens, and the hum of daily life, he felt the weight of his role settle more firmly on his shoulders. The news had already shifted something in him, a silent resolve that, whatever was coming, he would be ready.

The pair exchanged a glance. "Malament, we'd best ensure we're prepared," Luka murmured, his gaze steady as they descended the sunlit steps, the city's steady pulse echoing around them. Malament responded with a firm nod of agreement.

# THE APPRENTICE
# CHAPTER TWENTY ONE

With each hearty bite, chunks of a freshly baked loaf crumbled onto Auron's tunic, the pale blue fabric still marked with damp patches from his recent exertions. Though appearances rarely crossed his mind, the thrill of his lesson with Gordon was enough to block out all else. The morning had stretched well into the afternoon, and even Malament had excused himself before the end. What was meant to be a brief tutorial had evolved into hours of rigorous, one-on-one combat practice.

In his mind's eye, Auron could still picture Gordon, poised and precise, delivering strike after strike. He had been instructed to dodge, parry, even counter—whatever came naturally—and as he relieved each second, every clash and sidestep, it was as though he was still there, wielding the dual blades.

For the first time in his life, he had held a sword—two, in fact. Each had felt like an extension of himself, balanced and attuned to his every movement. His footwork, surprisingly nimble, synchronised with his strikes and defences as if it were all instinct. By the lesson's end, he and Gordon were practically duelling, their movements an almost choreographed exchange of lunges, thrusts, and counterstrike's.

Another bite, nearly the last, and Auron savoured the simple loaf. Usually, he and Malament shared one, but the lesson had left him famished. After changing, he had made straight for the kitchen, where Quinn, his apron stained and hair in disarray, had tossed him the loaf before he even asked. It was as though the cook had sensed he would be ravenous.

Auron found himself tucked into a secluded corner of the estate gardens, unsure how he had wandered there—such was his dazed excitement. This particular nook was a favourite, shaded by tall ivy that cast a delicate pattern of shadows. The sun was high, its warmth muted by the leafy canopy, and, aside from an occasional gardener trimming the bushes, he was alone.

Since his arrival weeks ago, Auron had spent most of his days around the stables, but the gardens were a hidden paradise he had quickly come to love. Despite the beauty of early summer, few ventured into the gardens except for the labourers who tended them, leaving Auron free to roam unnoticed. Regal might grumble if Auron lingered too long near the horses, but in the gardens, no one cared what he did. It had become his domain, and he knew the paths and plantings intimately now, often running the perimeter or navigating the hedge maze by memory.

With the final bite of his loaf, he rose from his shaded spot and began a light jog. For a moment, he closed his eyes, feeling the warm breeze play across his face. Stretching out his arm, he let his fingertips brush against the dense ivy leaves as he passed. This place, with its quiet trails and hidden corners, felt like home. Not a perfect home—he was not loved here, nor doted upon—but that had never been his reality. Malament was kind, but for most of the estate's residents, he was merely another presence. Still, compared to the uncertainty of Borlong's streets, it was enough. Here, there was no dread of the next day, no scramble for food or shelter, no fear of beatings or taunts.

Here, he ate three meals a day, and not scraps either. Breakfast was usually oats, though sometimes Saanvi convinced Quinn to fry eggs or bacon—a luxury he had scarcely imagined before. Midday often brought a fresh loaf with jams or honey, and Quinn, knowing Auron's fondness for bread, kept one ready most days. That first split of the crust, the steam rising and the aroma of garlic and herbs filling his nose, was a ritual he savoured. Supper, though, was his favourite: the dishes varied each day, and he was always given something beyond the usual servants' stew. Just last night, he had roasted pigeon, served with buttery potatoes and honey-glazed vegetables. He found himself hungrier with each passing day, no longer the constant gnaw of want but a gentle reminder of his body's newfound routine.

He drifted from the garden's edge onto a well-trodden path leading north, toward the hedge maze. The path shifted to stone-edged cobble, where he ducked past two gardeners—one grumbling in a foreign tongue, the other unbothered. Ahead loomed the maze, its boxwood walls towering eight feet high, meticulously pruned to keep the edges crisp. From above, it would appear as a perfect square, each side stretching fifty paces, with entrances aligned on each side.

Inside, the maze narrowed to single file, its dense greenery creating a cool, shadowed sanctuary that felt almost otherworldly on overcast days. In the maze's centre lay a small circular clearing, where a timber gazebo with seating for two waited in quiet seclusion. Here, Auron often hid from the world, stretching out on the bench as the sun traced its path across the sky. The chirping of birds flitting between the bushes, the rhythmic snip of shears from distant gardeners—it was all part of a peace he had rarely known, a stolen refuge in the heart of his newfound life.

The maze was no longer a mystery to Auron; he had memorised every twist, every narrow passage, and knew each exit by heart. What had once been a winding labyrinth was now a convenient shortcut, a secretive path he preferred over walking the estate grounds. Entering from the east side, he set into an easy jog, as was his habit—Auron rarely walked unless Malament was with him. His tendency to dash through corridors and gardens was a mild nuisance to the household staff, but he scarcely noticed their exasperation.

He moved through the maze with practised ease, slipping through the openings with a series of swift, instinctive turns: first a quick tuck to the right, then a left, passing through an arch of dense greenery. Above, the sky was a brilliant, cloudless blue, and the sun hung high, casting a blanket of heat over the garden. He felt beads of sweat on his brow, heightening his anticipation for the cool shade of the gazebo, where he planned to rest until supper. After a few more turns, he reached the maze's centre, ducking through the narrow entrance—only to freeze mid-step, surprised by what he found waiting.

Bare feet, slightly sun-kissed, dangled from the gazebo, swinging in the dappled sunlight. They stilled as Auron approached. A head of gently curled blonde hair caught the light, gleaming as it turned toward him, and then a pair of striking cyan eyes met his own, widening with surprise before softening into a smile. Lady Amelia sat inside the gazebo, an elegantly bound leather book resting open on her lap. Her emerald dress was gathered above her knees, allowing her legs to bask in the warmth, and her blouse was loosely draped off each shoulder. Freckles dotted her sun-kissed skin, a touch of the outdoors warming her typically composed appearance.

Auron's pulse quickened; he had not expected to find anyone here, least of all Lady Amelia, looking so unguarded. Her smile was one of familiarity and relief, as though she had been hoping to encounter someone, even him, in this quiet corner of the world.

"It's Auron, isn't it?" Lady Amelia asked in a pleasant tone, gathering her blouse back over her shoulders and gently closing her book. With a graceful movement, her dress fell slowly to her ankles, the fabric brushing along her smooth legs before settling in place. Her toes wiggled in the warm afternoon air, and Auron, eyes wide, noticed the casual elegance of her posture. She tilted her head, her curls slipping to one side as she waited. "Well?"

"Y-yes, milady," he replied, voice catching slightly as he forced himself to look up and meet her gaze. He could not quite believe she was here; in the quiet spot he'd claimed for himself. And more than that, he was stunned by her effortless beauty—the sunlight glinting on her lightly bronzed skin, her collarbone's graceful curve, and the warm smile she gave, a gentle one without parting her lips. He felt rooted in place, watching her every move, held in her gaze.

Amelia's smile softened. "Well, Auron, where were you off to in such haste?" she asked with a tone of genuine curiosity.

Auron hesitated, feeling a sudden tightness in his throat. He was not used to questions from anyone but Malament, and they rarely felt this...personal. It was as though she genuinely cared to know. He must have paled, because Amelia's smile deepened as she spoke gently, "Relax, Auron. You're not in any trouble, I assure you. I'm just making conversation."

He swallowed hard, his throat dry, and shifted his feet, fingers toying nervously with the fabric of his tunic. Amelia rose then, her movements as graceful as they were natural, her gaze steady on his. She extended a hand, palm up, gesturing to the bench. "Come, sit with me a while," she offered. "There's plenty of room for two."

As she stood, Auron noticed her height—taller than expected, nearly half a foot taller than he. Her wavy blonde hair fell into place as she moved. Her emerald dress was fitted closely to her frame, draping over her shoulders and dipping just low enough to catch the warmth of the sun against her chest. The dress hugged her waist, gently accentuating the curves of her body, before falling down her long legs. Her sandals lay off to the side, her bare feet pressing against the stone floor of the gazebo.

Auron had never seen beauty quite like this, and he stood, rooted in awe. It was more than her appearance; it was the effortless way she smiled, her openness and kindness toward him. His heart raced as he approached, half-wondering if she would vanish as soon as he sat down, a dream too perfect to be real.

As Auron timidly approached, the rich scent of rose and jasmine drifted toward him, enveloping him before he even reached her. He settled onto the bench, and Lady Amelia sat beside him, her leg brushing against his in the cosy space. She held his gaze, her voice soft and calming. "How do you fare, Auron?"

"Good," he replied shyly, unsure how to continue. Conversation beyond his lessons was rare, and he struggled to think of what else to say.

"Good, is that all?" Amelia tilted her head, a gentle smile gracing her lips. "Are the resident's kind to you? Are you eating well?"

"Yes," he managed, a one-word answer for all three questions. The residents were fair enough—Saanvi, kind, the others tolerable. And as for food, he still marvelled daily at the abundance laid before him, generous portions that filled him more than he had ever imagined.

Amelia chuckled, her laugh light and genuine. "A man of many words, I see," she teased, watching him closely. She remembered the last time she had seen him—strapped to a post, blood staining his torn clothes. The transformation was striking; now, his hair was longer, a thick, healthy black that shone in the sunlight. His face was round and vibrant with colour, like any well-nourished noble child, though it still held a trace of uncertainty. His eyes—large, turquoise flecked with gold—gazed back at her, bright with youth and a guarded curiosity. She thought to herself, yes, he would grow into a fine young man.

"Do you remember me, Auron?" she asked softly, a note of eagerness creeping into her tone, surprising even herself.

"Yes," Auron said quietly, bowing his head, as though embarrassed by the memory. They both fell silent, Amelia hoping he might elaborate, but Auron seemed unable to speak further.

"I'm sorry, Auron. I'm sorry you had to endure...such an ordeal. I can't imagine how—"

"It's okay," he interjected, his suddenness catching her off guard. She let him continue, holding back the urge to apologise further. His gaze shifted to the ground, fingers fiddling with his tunic as he added, "Sorry."

"For what?" Amelia asked, genuinely puzzled.

Auron hesitated, feeling awkward under her kindness. He could not relax as he did with Malament. Here, he felt self-conscious, as though each word needed careful consideration. "Interrupting you," he murmured, his voice tinged with an old shame.

"Oh, Auron, nonsense." She laughed gently, a warm, inclusive sound. "It's a beautiful summer's midday, and we're merely having a conversation.

No interruption at all—just my curiosity and, perhaps, your...reluctance to indulge it." She caught herself, realising she did not want to sound critical, and quickly softened. He was no courtier or family member—here, she could be more open, more at ease. "Forgive me, let me start again. You have nothing to be sorry for. Let's just sit here, enjoying the sun and this quiet moment, with nothing expected from you. Speak, if you wish, or simply enjoy the silence with me."

She smiled down at him, her gaze warm and reassuring.

Auron was not quite sure what she meant, but the sound of her voice was soothing. He rarely spoke with women—not like this, at least. Saanvi was different. Practical, blunt, always dressed in the same grease-stained attire, she spoke to give instructions, her words straightforward and often curt. But Lady Amelia's voice was soft, her questions gentle, her words patient and unhurried, drawing him into a calm he could not explain.

Auron wanted to speak, to say something clever or ask a question that mattered, but his mind was frustratingly blank. Searching for something, he settled on the last shared memory between them. "Was Lord Malum... alright?" he asked quietly, his voice tinged with uncertainty.

Amelia let out a loud tut, likely louder than she intended. "Why ever would you care for his well-being?" She caught herself, glancing cautiously around as if the maze's hedges held unseen listeners. Lowering her voice, she continued, "Do not repeat what I just said, Auron."

A brief silence followed, lingering as she stared off with an air of weariness. A flicker of despondence clouded her face, her posture tightening as though under a familiar weight. The realisation crept over her once again—this was her home, a place where every word needed guarding, every expression carefully measured, even in the presence of a young boy.

Her gaze drifted to the stillness in front of her, the unchanging scenery that mirrored her life. She thought back to her own childhood, her heart tugged with longing for her homeland in the West. At thirteen, she had been sent away as part of a peace treaty arranged by her father, King Ruben. By fourteen, she was a wife; a year later, she had borne Malament. The years that followed were stained with loss: stillbirths, miscarriages, until eventually, Lord Malum ceased visiting her chambers altogether. Loneliness had settled in, thick and inescapable, her life confined to her chambers or the rare corridors she dared venture.

She sighed, her words spilling softly, almost as if speaking to herself. "This place, Auron... on the surface, it's beautiful. The gardens, the marble halls, the towering pillars—all suggest calm and luxury. But beneath it all..." She hesitated; her voice heavy with a sadness that bordered on bitterness. "Beneath the well-kept lawns and the grandeur, it's nothing but a perfumed prison. A place where none are truly free. Those without titles live in squalor, hidden away from the eyes of guests, and even I, with all my fine possessions and lavish chambers... I am no more than a slave."

She paused, her gaze drifting upward as if seeing her chambers from afar. "My balcony looks out over these gardens, beyond these walls, and yet, I cannot leave. I am locked away, sometimes for days, with only the same books to reread, the same portraits to stare at. Sometimes, I dream of leaping from that balcony—not out of despair, but out of a desire to feel the wind on my face, to know freedom, if only for a moment." Her voice softened, trembling slightly. "In my dreams, I wander beyond these walls without titles or finery. I buy fruit from the market with silver earned by my own hands, speak to people who know nothing of me... But then I wake."

A moment of silence settled between them, and she drew a breath, as if to collect herself. "It's a fine prison, Auron. A prison of status, a marriage of possession and appearances. A husband who does not care for me, a son who scarcely needs me, no friend to call my own." She paused, her voice barely above a whisper. "It is a prison..."

"I would be your friend," Auron interrupted softly.

The words settled gently between them, yet they seemed to pull Amelia from her reverie. She turned to him, her expression shifting from surprise to something softer, something almost tender. In his clear, earnest gaze, she saw a kindness rarely offered to her within these walls. Here was Auron, a young boy who barely knew her, offering her something she had forgotten she wanted—a friendship, free of expectations, simple and honest.

A smile slowly blossomed on her lips, one of the first genuine ones in as long as she could remember. Reaching out, she rested a hand on his shoulder, her touch light but sincere. "Thank you, Auron. That... that means more than you know."

In that moment, the garden felt less like a gilded cage and more like a haven, the quiet connection between them filling the still air with an unspoken understanding.

After a pause, Amelia's eyes brightened with a playful glint. "So, Auron, now that we're friends—what would friends do together?" The question coaxed a smile to the corners of her mouth.

Auron's face lit up with youthful excitement. "I've always wanted to race here!" he exclaimed. "I asked Malament, but... he didn't." His eagerness was infectious, his eyes sparkling with the innocent thrill of a simple game.

Amelia's initial reaction was to dismiss the idea—how absurd, how childish. But as she looked down at Auron, his turquoise eyes wide and hopeful, she felt her resistance melt. This was an innocent request: no hidden agenda, no motive, just the simple wish to play. A smirk crept onto her face as she placed her hands on her knees and then, with a pause, helped herself to her feet. She stretched, arms reaching high above her, toes pressing into the earth below. Glancing at Auron, who waited with baited breath, she reached over, ruffling his hair before giving his head a playful push. And then, with a sudden grin, she darted toward the opening between the hedges.

Auron's eyes lit up, and he leapt to his feet, quickly closing the gap. She made it to the hedge opening first, but a misjudged turn led her straight to a dead end. Behind her, Auron's laughter filled the air. "Wrong way!" he called gleefully.

He spun around, dashing back toward the maze's centre, letting her catch up enough to keep the chase alive. They zigzagged through twists and turns, Amelia reaching for him in vain, her laughter joining his. At one point, Auron took a mischievous route to another dead end, then spun around and tried to overtake her. Amelia laughed, wrapping her arms around his waist and gently spinning him back toward the hedge wall. Auron offered no resistance, thrilled by the game. Now it was Amelia's turn to be pursued; she dashed into an opening, choosing the right path this time, while Auron's delighted laughter echoed close behind.

As they ran, the years seemed to slip away. Amelia was simply a woman enjoying a game, her golden hair flying behind her, sometimes whipping into her face, momentarily blinding her. Her feet pounded the dirt, each step a release from the worries that usually weighed on her. Muscle memory kicked in, her strides strong and steady, her arms moving in rhythm despite the impracticality of her gown. In that moment, her mind was blissfully empty, focused only on the thrill of the chase.

Ahead, she saw a choice—a left turn leading outward, a right back toward the centre. She hesitated, her bare feet skidding against the dusty path, and, unable to choose in time, stumbled forward. Her knee hit the ground first, followed by her outstretched hands as she tumbled into the dirt in a cloud of dust.

For a heartbeat, she lay still, waiting for the sting of pain to settle in. But there was none, just a faint scratch on her knee and dust coating her palms. She looked down at her gown, now torn and smeared with dirt—a sight that, in any other moment, would have horrified her. But instead, a laugh bubbled up, then another, until she was laughing uncontrollably, the kind of laughter that left her gasping for breath.

Auron, seeing her mirth, burst into laughter as well, flinging himself to the ground and rolling around in pure, unrestrained joy. His laughter was contagious, and soon they were both lying in the dirt, their shared amusement echoing through the maze.

For a few blissful moments, they were just two friends, caught up in the simple joy of play. As her laughter subsided, Amelia felt a sense of freedom she had not known in years. This child had drawn her out of herself, out of her fears, and into a moment that was purely, unforgettably hers.

Still catching her breath, Amelia looked at Auron, whose beaming smile and bright eyes were alight with joy. She had not felt this carefree in years. Then, a mischievous glint in her eye, she looked over his shoulder and gasped, "Who's that?"

Auron spun around instinctively, and Amelia took off again, laughing as Auron quickly followed, delighted by the game. They dashed in and out of the hedge maze, tagging each other, weaving around surprised gardeners who dared not utter a word—after all, it was the Lady of East Kadun herself at play. Time seemed to slip by until, panting and flushed, they finally made their way back to the gazebo. Their outfits were smudged with dirt and their faces flushed; Amelia's usually perfect hair tousled yet somehow even more alluring in its wild state.

Auron reached the gazebo first and leaped up onto its perch, spinning to face her with a proud grin. "Beat you!" he declared triumphantly.

Amelia, equally breathless but grinning, walked up and nudged him aside, taking a seat next to him. She glanced down at herself, laughing. "Look at me—a complete mess!"

Auron, still smiling, saw only her radiance. "You still look lovely to me," he replied without a second thought. As the words left his mouth, he blushed, realising what he had said. Amelia's eyes softened, and she looked at him with gentle surprise.

"Thank you, Auron," she said, touched. "You are quite the gentleman." She paused, catching her breath as she gathered her thoughts. "Auron, I can't remember the last time I had this much fun. Thank you for reminding me I'm more than just the Lady of East Kadun—more than someone to be looked at and little else."

In response, Auron bowed his head, a gesture Malament had taught him was respectful in Kadun culture, though his playful smile showed he meant it lightly. Amelia laughed, understanding his intent.

"I think I'm beginning to meet the real Auron," she said warmly. They shared a comfortable silence then, one that filled Auron with a sense of ease he had rarely known.

After a moment, he gathered his courage and spoke up. "Amelia," he began, and she turned to face him, waiting patiently. "You said you wanted to explore the city..." He hesitated, glancing down, a hint of sadness shadowing his expression. "I've lived outside the walls... it's not as nice. There aren't many kind people, just those who take."

Amelia's heart softened as she saw the flicker of pain in his eyes, a glimpse of hardships she could only imagine. She had opened up to him about her struggles, but his burdens seemed far greater, already carried so young. Yet, despite everything, he seemed happy here, content, even grateful.

"Auron," she said, her voice gentle, "you are an inspiration." She leaned over, placing a soft kiss on his forehead, smiling as he looked up at her, wide-eyed and astonished.

Rising gracefully, Amelia dusted off her gown and slipped her feet back into her sandals. Then, with a surprising depth of sincerity, she bowed to him—not in jest, but as a mark of respect. "Thank you for this day, Auron. I shall not forget it, and I look forward to our next adventure."

With that, she turned, her hair settling elegantly across her back as she walked away, slipping through the opening in the hedges without looking back, leaving Auron sitting in awe of the kindness and friendship she had shown him. As he sat motionless, staring at the space where Amelia had just been, half-expecting her to reappear. The urge to chase after her flared within him; he knew he could catch up in no time. She might even have taken a wrong turn on her way out. But why? he thought. What reason did he have to follow her, other than to see her once more? That did not feel right, so he continued to stare at the empty place before the gazebo, his feet dangling off the bench, toes just grazing the dirt as they swung back and forth.

He raised a hand to his forehead, fingers pressing lightly where Amelia had kissed him. It felt no different, yet he willed it too somehow. Closing his eyes, he tried to picture her face, her flowing blonde hair, her warm smile—but the image was incomplete. Her dress, her hair, even her face seemed blurred and fragmented in his mind. Frustrated, he opened his eyes, suddenly aware of the solitude around him. This little haven, usually a comfort in its quiet seclusion, now felt oddly empty, like it would never be the same without her.

Auron had no desire to linger here alone, not now. He looked about himself and then he saw it—her book, still leaning against the gazebo, with a determined jolt, he sprang up, snatching it up. Maybe, just maybe, if he was quick, he could catch her before she disappeared into the house. Without hesitation, he set off, darting through the maze faster than he had ever run, weaving between the hedges, taking the shortest route he knew. At last, he burst free of the maze, scanning the garden.

And there she was—but she was not alone.

Lord Malum stood over her, his expression dark, his frame tense and unyielding. Several household members flanked him, and Auron instantly recognized some of the men from his own quarters. Instinctively, he ducked back into the shadow of the maze, positioning himself just close enough to see without being seen. He watched as Malum threw his arms in angry gestures; his voice harsh though the words were muffled by distance. At one point, Malum grabbed the torn fabric of her gown, jerking her forward before shoving her back. Auron's fists clenched as he saw her stumble, only to right herself and stand still, enduring the onslaught with quiet resilience.

Minutes passed as Malum continued his berating, his face a mask of disdain. Then, with a final shake of his head, he turned sharply and strode back toward the house, leaving Amelia and two household members behind. They moved to assist her, but she dismissed them quickly, brushing off their concern as she prepared to follow.

Auron watched, his heart heavy. Moments before, they had been laughing, free from the constraints of titles and propriety. Now, the weight of her reality bore down on him, and he longed to call out, to break through the silence and reach her somehow. But he held back, knowing that anything he did now would only worsen her situation. So he stayed hidden, his gaze fixed on her as she walked away, trying to memorise the sight of her, unsure when—or if—he'd ever have another chance.

Amelia's pace was measured, her movements graceful even now, her hair swaying gently against her back. She followed the two servants, trailing just behind, and Auron's urge to reach out intensified. His heart felt heavy with words left unspoken, but when he tried to form them in his mind, nothing came. He simply watched.

Then, as if sensing his presence, Amelia glanced back over her shoulder. Her gaze found his, and for a brief moment, they shared a silent connection. She offered him a warm, reassuring smile, one that melted his sadness into quiet joy. Auron's face broke into a grin, and he beamed back at her, his spirits lifted by her silent acknowledgment.

With a final nod, she turned away, slipping out of sight as she entered the house, leaving Auron with a feeling of hope—a fleeting yet precious memory that he would carry with him, a reminder of their shared moment in the maze.

# THE QUEEN REGNANT
# CHAPTER TWENTY TWO

In the warm, muted glow of her private chambers, Queen Karak leaned back into her chair, she felt at ease, the normal weight of tension had dissolved from her shoulders. The room seemed expansive tonight, its dark corners softened by flickering candlelight, and the tall balcony doors stood open. A faint breeze stirred the sheer curtains, allowing the air to drift in. The air felt lighter, freer—like a veil lifted from their ambitions, leaving them unbound, almost fearless.

The table between them was set with a modest spread of wine and cheese, though tonight it held a richness beyond its simplicity. The three of them—Karak, her brother Konan, and Thoren—sat in an atmosphere both heady and unrestrained, the taste of victory mingling with their wine. For once, the shadows around them felt less oppressive, their conversation no longer whispered or guarded. In this rare reprieve from the weight of their plans, the three shared a sense of triumph, a fleeting joy in their hard-won success.

Thoren lifted his goblet, his attention moving from Karak to Konan. "To success, then," he said, his voice subdued yet brimming with satisfaction. But his eyes held a flicker of unease. "Though I must say, I didn't expect the poison to be so... brutal."

A shadow passed over Karak's face, her smile fading slightly as she glanced down, swirling her wine in silence. A faint pang of shame flickered within her. The intention had been clear enough, but the end had been far more savage than she had envisioned. "Brutal, yes," she murmured, her voice thoughtful. "The dose was precise, yet... it was as if the man burned from within. It was too much."

Konan, watching her, only shrugged and tore a piece of cheese with his scarred fingers. "Brutality has its appeal," he said with a faint smirk, casting a sidelong glance at her. "A reminder, if you will. A clear warning to any with ears to listen and eyes to watch—the price of defiance is nothing less than suffering." Karak held his attention for a moment, the flicker of guilt hardening into something resolute.

A comfortable silence settled over them, stretching out like the shadows that pooled in the corners of the room. The crackling of the hearth was soft, an almost gentle rhythm that filled the space between them, mingling with the faint rustle of the curtains stirred by the breeze. They each seemed to savour this pause, this rare moment of quiet camaraderie. It was a luxury to sit without the weight of plotting bearing down upon them, to feel the whisper of success rather than the press of danger.

Karak let the silence linger a moment longer, her gaze distant as if lost in thought. But then, as her eyes refocused, a change came over her—her gaze sharpened, her posture straightened, and her fingers stilled on the stem of her goblet. She leaned forward, the light catching the resolute glint in her eyes.

"With this chapter closed," she said, her voice steady and clear, cutting through the quiet with an edge of determination, "we move to the next."

At her words, both men shifted in their seats, as though the calmness they had just shared was slipping away before they were ready to relinquish it. Thoren gave a slight sigh, his fingers tracing the rim of his goblet before setting it down, his gaze settling on the queen with a look of mild resignation. Konan, meanwhile, leaned back, crossing his arms as his eyes flicked between Karak and the open balcony doors, his expression caught between curiosity and reluctance. The silence that had felt like a rare gift moments before now grew heavier, weighted with the unspoken uncertainty on both their minds.

Karak took in their subtle reactions with an almost imperceptible smile. It was natural that they would savour the quiet after the strain of their recent efforts, but in her mind, the victory they had achieved was only the beginning—a small foothold in the climb to something far greater. She let the tension build, waiting for their attention to return fully to her.

"Our success has granted us certain liberties," she began, letting her words hang just long enough to draw them back into the moment. "We could revel in our newfound sovereignty, indulging season after season in wine and feasts, growing complacent as Ivar did. But that is not why we acted. Why act at all if our efforts yield nothing of worth?"

She let the question settle, her gaze sweeping over them. A faint gust stirred the heavy drapes, carrying the distant sounds of the city below. In the quiet, the weight of her words pressed upon them.

"I have considered patience—waiting as the seasons turn, strengthening our armies and swelling our coffers further. But to what end? Shall we grant our enemies the luxury of preparation, only to march south into a slaughter of our own making? How many lives would we squander in such folly?"

She leaned forward slightly, voice quieter but no less commanding. “Brother, you once told me there is another way—and there is. Stormhold, no, Nordon itself, cries out for change. If we are to rise, to truly advance our position, we must not place our faith in patience, but in resolve, in decisive action."

Then, after a brief pause, she added with finality, "I have taken steps to ensure our next moves are not only strategic but necessary."

She sat back observing as the men’s postures shifted again, shoulders squaring, their relaxation fading as they settled into the familiar readiness of the scheme at hand.

Karak’s eyes remained steady, her voice calm but with a steely undercurrent. “I’ve sent three letters,” she began, letting the weight of her words settle over them. “The first to Borlong.”

Thoren’s brow creased, his attention sharpening. “Borlong?”

“Yes,” Karak replied, a glint of satisfaction flickering in her eyes. “I’ve informed Lord Malum Thalron that I’ll be attending the summer trade trip.” She paused; her stare unwavering as she assessed their reactions. “To him, it will appear as nothing more than a gesture of faith—a reassurance that my ascension changes nothing, that our alliance remains steadfast. But beneath the surface, it’s an opportunity.”

“An opportunity?” Konan echoed, tilting his head in curiosity, his expression intent.

Karak nodded, leaning forward. “The trip allows me to assess his true strength—Borlong’s resources, their defences, and, more crucially, Malum’s standing within his own domain. I need to see firsthand if Borlong has any weaknesses, any signs of unrest, and where his loyalties truly lie. If we are to take action in the future, it must be with full knowledge of their strengths, their vulnerabilities.”

Thoren’s expression shifted, a look of wary understanding dawning on his face. “So… this isn’t an alliance you’re seeking,” he murmured, his voice low with realisation. “It’s reconnaissance. You want him comfortable, unsuspecting.”

Karak's lips curved into a small, knowing smile. "Precisely. We need him content in the illusion that our alliance holds firm. Only then will he let his guard down enough for us to understand what lies beneath the surface. To take Borlong, or even influence it, I must appear as though I am... playing the dutiful queen, honouring past alliances."

Konan's gaze grew thoughtful, his scepticism fading as he saw the logic in her approach. "And once we know his weaknesses?"

Karak looked between them, her expression hardening. "Then we know how and when to act, with no need for haste. Borlong will be lulled into comfort while we gather everything we need. Malum may think he understands me, but his vision of me is a mirage. He'll only see what I allow him to see."

A faint sense of admiration sparked in Konan's eyes, and even Thoren gave a slow, approving nod, as they began to realise the full depth of her strategy.

Karak inclined her head, her fingers drumming rhythmically on the arm of her chair, as if punctuating the gravity of her next move. She continued, her voice steady. "Then, my second letter was sent to White Towers. I intend to visit King Ruben Whitehart."

A beat of stunned silence followed, broken only by the faint crackle of the hearth.

Thoren's eyes widened, and he leaned forward, his voice barely above a whisper. "White Towers?" he repeated, disbelief underscoring each word. "You're reaching out to the West directly? No Nordon man or woman has set foot in West Kadun since the end of the Winter Wars." He shook his head, almost as if trying to make sense of her decision. "Nearly two hundred years of silence, and now... you're proposing to visit him?"

Karak's expression remained impassive, though a glint of resolve shone in her eyes. "Precisely. That silence has endured long enough. We've only ever communicated through East Kadun, through Malum. But our kingdom's future cannot hinge upon the whispered words of an intermediary. Not anymore. My coronation marks a new beginning for Nordon, and that means reaching beyond the confines we've adhered to for centuries."

Konan's face tightened, scepticism mingling with concern. "Sister, this is not just any alliance you're toying with. Nordon's raids on Kadun are still etched into their memory. They see us as conquerors, raiders—savages from the north. King Ruben may view this as a provocation rather than a diplomatic gesture. Do you honestly believe he will receive you?"

Karak met her brother's gaze without wavering, her tone resolute. "That's exactly why I must go myself, Konan. I have to prove that our intentions go beyond what they've come to expect from us. This is an opportunity to forge something new. If King Ruben grants me an audience, he will see the queen herself—the woman who now rules Stormhold, not the ghost of our forebears' conquests. And he will understand that we are here to negotiate on equal terms, not in the shadows or through intermediaries."

Thoren frowned, his fingers tapping against his goblet as he thought. "And if he sees it as a threat? If he refuses you, or worse, considers this a breach of our long-held truce?"

Karak's eyes grew cool and calculating. "Then he will have shown us where he stands—and we will act accordingly. But if I can appeal to his reason, if I can open even a crack in the door to Kadun, we have the chance to bring Nordon into the future. And we'll do it without relying on East Kadun or on Malum's good graces."

Konan's scepticism softened, replaced by a grudging respect. "You're determined, then. This is more than a gesture of goodwill."

"A gesture, yes—but one that shifts the foundations of the old order," Karak replied. "This is our path forward, and it begins with me. Nordon's strength is nothing if it does not grow beyond the past."

The two men exchanged a wary look, the weight of her words heavy upon them, hinting at the enormity of what this alliance—or its failure—could mean. Thoren shifted in his seat, his expression darkening. "Is this truly your reason to seek an audience in White Towers... with King Ruben?" he asked, suspicion edging his voice.

Karak's eyes glinted as she met his gaze. "Ah, Thoren, now you begin to see the greater scheme," she said smoothly. "Think on it: White Towers is a fortress, a city carved out of stone and nearly impenetrable. Even if we marched every soldier south and waged open war with Kadun, their gates would remain sealed against us. We would fall upon The Reach, the bridge would run red with our blood, and, even if we breached it, White Towers itself would remain beyond our grasp. No, I do not wish my reign to end in such needless slaughter."

She leaned forward, first tilting her head to Konan with a smile, her voice echoing his words again but lowering to a determined murmur. "There is another way, another way to take White Towers, Thoren—a quieter way. From within. Once we're inside, their harbour lies at the city's heart. All we would need is a small fleet to dock within White Harbour, our men poised and ready. We could take the city without a single trumpet's call."

Thoren's face darkened further, scepticism etched deep into his features. "We have no ships, my Queen, and even if we did, it would take more than a handful of vessels and men to storm the harbour and city as vast and fortified as White Towers. You speak of a thousand men—at least twenty ships, maybe more. And forgive my bluntness, but they would see us coming long before we reached the harbour walls. How could we possibly bring a force that large into White Towers unseen?"

Karak held their gaze, her calm unshaken, and leaned under the table to produce a rolled parchment. She unfurled it with deliberate care, her finger tracing the jagged coastline until it stopped just north of White Towers. "Here," she said, tapping a small cluster of islands on the map, known as The Hundred Isles. "One of these islands holds The Beacon, a tower that casts its light across the northern waters. If we take The Beacon, we take control of the main passage into White Harbour."

She looked up, a gleam of determination in her eyes. "With The Beacon as our signal, we can hide our ships among The Hundred Isles until the time is right. Our men could lie in wait, sheltered within the islands' coves, ready to move on my command. And when we strike, it will be from within the city itself, from the heart of White Towers. To claim White Towers is to hold the Western Realms in the palm of our hand."

Konan, who had remained silent until now, watched his sister closely, his wary expression giving way to a spark of respect as he absorbed the depth of her vision. He leaned forward, his scarred hands resting on the table. "Twenty ships, a thousand men, hidden among The Hundred Isles..." he murmured, a glint of anticipation in his eyes. "When the time comes, I'll lead the attack myself. Once our forces are inside the harbour, White Towers won't know what hit them. I'll see to it personally."

Karak's gaze held his, her approval clear. "And that is precisely why I need you by my side, Konan. With you here, the signal will be swift, and the men will know you await them on the other side of those walls. We'll be inside the heart of White Towers before they realise they've been infiltrated. Together, we'll take the city by storm."

Thoren raised an eyebrow, his attention flicking between them. "You're prepared to walk straight into the lion's den, Konan? To rely on a fleet you cannot command from the front?"

Konan's mouth twisted into a confident smirk, his gaze steady. "When those ships dock, Thoren, they'll have me waiting for them on the ground, ready to lead. I trust Karak's vision—and when the gates open, it's her name they'll surrender to. If White Towers can fall, I'll make sure it does."

The weight of Konan's words settled among them, lending a forceful finality to Karak's ambitious plan. For a moment, the silence held steady, the three of them bound by the bold certainty of their shared resolve.

A flicker of amazement crossed Thoren's face, but it was swiftly replaced by a look of reluctant concern. "My Queen, there are... too many risks. White Harbour is a mystery to us; you speak of its layout as if you've walked it yourself. And the ships—let alone a thousand men—where would we summon such forces? Moreover, I must remind you, your kingdom will be vulnerable. You've only just claimed the throne, and now you'd leave Stormhold exposed? Who will safeguard your crown in your absence?"

Karak turned to Konan, her eyes sharp, calculating. "Brother, our armies—how strong are we?"

Konan met her gaze, his face solemn. "We've a hundred royal guards, loyal to the last. I would advise keeping them within these walls, for they'll guard you against any treachery. Five hundred axemen, a thousand shield-bearers, and another thousand men-at-arms, all battle-hardened and trained to the teeth, await your command, my Queen," he replied, his voice steady but edged with the weight of responsibility. "If we left half to defend Stormhold, we'd still command an imposing force on the field. We will not be left vulnerable."

Karak studied him, her expression hardening with satisfaction. "And they're prepared for this? They know their Queen's demands?"

Konan's eyes gleamed, fierce and loyal. "Every man is prepared to spill his blood for you, Karak. They know who they fight under—and what they fight for. They'll do whatever you require."

She nodded, a hint of pride flickering in her gaze. "Good. Their strength and loyalty will be what carries this vision forward."

Then, her gaze sharpened further as she turned to Thoren, her tone resolute. "To secure Nordon's future, we'll need a council—a strong one, willing to hold the kingdom together in my absence. I've compiled a list of nobles I trust, but I want your counsel as well. We must choose wisely, selecting those who'll guard our interests without hesitation."

Thoren took a long, contemplative sip of his wine, the creases in his brow deepening. "And you would place your faith in this council to protect the throne? To hold Nordon steady with the memory of Ivar barely gone from their minds?"

Karak's tone sharpened, a glint of steel in her eyes. "Yes, Thoren. I have chosen wisely, and I expect you to stand among them. When I return, I trust you will be here to welcome me back—to welcome us all back to a stronger Stormhold."

The silence that followed was thick with the tension of unspoken doubts, but Thoren knew his place well enough not to press further. He inclined his head, a reluctant acceptance in his posture. "My loyalty remains with you, my Queen. But I must say again, we do not have the ships. This grand vision cannot succeed without them."

Karak lifted her chin, her gaze unyielding, as if daring him to question her judgement further. "And that is why I have sent a third letter," she said, her voice steely. "A letter to Frostfall, inviting Gunnar Stonkar to Stormhold to treat with us."

Thoren's eyes narrowed, a sharp edge of alarm in his expression. "Frostfall?" he repeated, his voice laced with scepticism. "You're inviting the wolf to dine at your table, Karak. Gunnar Stonkar is forever warmongering; he's built his name on it. The man's ambitions are notorious, and he holds one of the greatest fleets in the world. He'll seize this as an opportunity to meddle in our affairs, to sniff out Stormhold's vulnerabilities."

Karak's gaze did not waver. "Gunnar is many things, but he is also a pragmatist. And like all pragmatists, he values what benefits him most. He doesn't need to love Stormhold to recognize an offer worth his while. What I have proposed to him is… enticing." Her voice softened, growing almost contemplative. "To Gunnar, a fleet is a tool, and I intend to give him every reason to place that tool in our hands."

Konan, who had been listening intently, crossed his arms, a dark frown settling over his face. "Enticing or not, remember who you're dealing with. I've killed his brother—and two more of his kin—over the last eight seasons. Gunnar's blood feuds run as deep as the oceans his fleet commands. He won't soon forgive, and he won't forget. You ask him to dine with us, but he's as likely to put a dagger to my throat as he is to accept any terms we offer."

Karak looked at her brother, a faint smile at the corner of her mouth. "And yet, Konan, he's pragmatic. He may loathe us, but he will still come to the table if it suits him. Gunnar is well aware of the riches that Stormhold could bring, and he knows that his ships are his greatest bargaining power. He can look past grudges if it means gold in his coffers and an opportunity to further his own goals."

Thoren gave a bitter chuckle, shaking his head. "And you're willing to wager Nordon's security on that hope? That the wolf will sit peacefully at your table without baring his teeth?"

Karak's voice carried an edge of steel as she met Thoren's steady look. "I trust my instincts, Thoren. This is my vision—one that does not bend to sentiment or fear. We are no strangers to wolves in our midst." She turned her attention to the flickering hearth, her tone softening as she continued. "We will offer him a chance to be part of something far greater than Frostfall's endless skirmishes. And in exchange, we gain the strength of his fleet. If he agrees, we shall have the means to seize our future."

The gravity of her words settled between them, the firelight casting shadows that flickered across Konan's face, drawing his expression tight with tension. But she continued, her voice now lower, measured. "And more than gold," she said, each word deliberate. "I offered him a marriage—a union to solidify our cause."

Thoren's eyes widened, his brow furrowing as he absorbed this revelation. "Marriage?" he repeated, his voice laced with apprehension. "You would... bind yourself to Stonkar?" His eyes narrowed thoughtfully; concern etched into his face. "It's a dangerous bargain, my Queen. But Gunnar is no fool—he'll see the value in such an offer. If anything could lure him, it would be the promise of both gold and a union with the throne itself."

Konan's reaction was more immediate, his posture stiffening, protective instinct flashing across his face. "Sister, this is too much," he said, his voice thick with protest. "Gunnar is not a man you should even consider aligning yourself with, let alone binding yourself to. He's cunning, brutal, and..." Konan's jaw tightened as he struggled for words. "I would sooner see Stormhold fall than see you in his hands."

Karak turned to him, her expression unyielding. "Konan," she said softly, her voice laced with a calm certainty. "A queen without a king is an anomaly—one that Nordon will only tolerate for so long. And Gunnar would not hold the power. That would remain mine. But with him, the throne gains the legitimacy—and the strength—it needs to secure our future."

Thoren gave a reluctant nod, his voice heavy with resignation. "He's right to worry, my Queen. Gunnar is not a man of restraint; his history of conquest shows as much. But... he is a man of ambition. He'll recognize the value in a union with you—perhaps even more than the fleet itself." He paused, casting a wary look at Konan. "Though it is a gamble, it's one Gunnar might well take."

Konan's gaze darkened as he considered her words, his hand curling into a fist. "And what if he uses that power against us, Karak? Gunnar may swear loyalty, but once his ambitions are tied to the throne... he may reach for it himself."

Karak met Konan's steady eyes, her voice unwavering. "Then he would be a fool, for he would find himself opposed by all the forces I've set in place. This is a means to an end, Konan. Gunnar may see his advantage, but the crown rests with one ruler—and that is me."

She allowed a slight pause, her focus shifting back to the fire, the glow casting a steely glint across her features. "The ceremony, however, will not take place until White Towers is ours. Once we've secured West Kadun and claimed its throne, then, perhaps, Gunnar may wear the title of consort. Until then, his loyalty remains provisional."

She turned back to her brother, a trace of a smile on her lips. "And who knows, Konan? Battles have a way of deciding matters of allegiance and family lines. Perhaps your axe will find another brother or cousin of the Stonkar clan before all is said and done."

Konan's mouth twisted into a faint, grim smile, catching the dark humour in her words, while Thoren's expression shifted to one of reluctant understanding. They both saw the cunning in her plan—the depth of her ambition, honed as sharp as any blade.

The silence that followed was laden with weight, the two men exchanging a final look as they resigned themselves to the fierce edges of her ambition, bound now by both loyalty and her vision of conquest.

Facing her allies, the flickering light casting shadows across her face that shifted between soft and severe, as if capturing the duality within her—a queen fierce and calculating, yet touched by something human, something unresolved.

She picked up her goblet, raising it toward Konan and Thoren, her voice low, steely. “To White Towers and to the throne Nordon deserves.”

Konan inclined his head, his loyalty unwavering, though a glint of something more—perhaps a quiet admiration, perhaps a flicker of fear—caught in his eyes. Thoren lifted his goblet, though he hesitated a breath longer, his gaze sharp, scrutinising. Then, silently, he clinked his goblet against hers, the sound echoing faintly in the quiet chamber.

As they drank, a breeze swept in through the balcony doors, extinguishing one of the candles and casting a momentary darkness across the table, a reminder of the delicate balance they were treading.

Karak’s voice dropped to a murmur, almost lost in the rustling of the curtains. “Every kingdom must choose between living in shadow or burning with light.” She glanced at Konan, a fierce pride in her gaze. “We will be the fire, Konan. The kind that consumes.”

The silence that followed was one of unspoken acceptance, bound by purpose and ambition, as they each stared into the embers of the hearth, the glow casting their faces in shades of resolve and recklessness. The faint scent of smoke lingered, a reminder that, soon enough, this fire would spread far beyond these walls.

And with that, they rose, shadows slipping quietly through the flickering light, three figures poised to shape Nordon’s fate, prepared for whatever the flames would demand.

# THE QUEEN REGNANT CHAPTER TWENTY THREE

In the dim light of the backroom, whispers slithered like venomous threads through the stale air, each voice steeped in bitterness. The room lay tucked away in a quiet quarter of the city, far from the grand halls and prying ears of the Queen's Keep. It was a cramped, makeshift space, walls bare and cracked, with the musk of dust and disuse thickening the atmosphere. Flickering candlelight cast elongated shadows across their faces, illuminating the hard lines of their expressions, each noble marked by anger and resentment.

They had chosen this place deliberately—its shabbiness a quiet defiance against the throne they felt had betrayed them. There was no sign of luxury here, no tapestries or finery, only cold stone and creaking wooden benches. It was a stark, unadorned room, fitting for those who had come under a shroud of secrecy, their grievances shared in hushed tones that dared not rise above a murmur. The nobles wore simple cloaks, concealing their identities from anyone who might wander too close, for their cause demanded both caution and the pretence of anonymity.

Thoren sat at the edge of the group, his expression carefully neutral, eyes cast downward as though in quiet contemplation. He seemed detached, a shadow among the others, but his stillness belied the sharpness of his focus. Around him, the nobles muttered and whispered, their voices simmering with frustration that grew sharper and more heated with each passing minute. Words like "betrayal" and "usurper" were hissed under breaths, carrying a bitterness that filled the room like smoke.

Some nobles clenched their hands into fists, their knuckles white with barely restrained fury; others leaned forward, casting dark glances across the room, their faces twisted in anger. Thoren observed it all from beneath hooded eyes, absorbing every flicker of outrage, every pointed whisper, each thread of discontent weaving together into something darker, something dangerous.

"This is her doing," Lord Balgin spat, his voice a venomous hiss as his fist struck the rough table, the impact sending a low thud through the room. "Our king—poisoned in his own hall, his legacy trampled beneath the feet of an ambitious queen. And we sit here, idle, while she seizes the throne, unchecked and unchallenged."

A murmur of agreement rippled through the group, a low, simmering sound like the rumble of distant thunder. Lady Hilda, a slender, severe woman with hawk-like features and eyes that glinted with a dangerous sharpness, inclined her head, her gaze sweeping over the gathered nobles. "It's an affront to us all," she said, her voice soft but laced with steel. "King Ivar ruled for decades—steadfast, unshaken. To die so suddenly, and by poison of all things..." Her eyes narrowed, a glint of cold fury in them as she looked around, as if daring any among them to challenge her assessment. "This reeks of betrayal, and I, for one, will not sit quietly."

Thoren listened, offering an occasional nod, his face a mask of mild agreement, betraying nothing of his inner thoughts. To the others, he was merely another sceptic—a disillusioned councillor, wary of the queen's motives and unsettled by the rapid shift in power. They knew nothing of his true connection to her, his place in her schemes. Had they suspected even a fraction of his loyalty to her, he would not be here among them.

For now, though, he let their assumptions cloak him, allowed them to believe him one of their own. It suited him to listen, to let their bitterness swell around him like a tide—each accusation, each word of dissent, another piece in the growing tension that filled the air.

Lady Hilda's gaze lingered on Thoren, her eyes narrowing as though she were attempting to peel back his mask. Thoren met her stare, his expression a careful blank, giving nothing away. After a moment, she raised a brow, her tone pointed. "And what of you, Thoren? You've served in the court as long as any of us. Surely you see the danger in allowing her ambition to go unchecked."

He paused, letting the silence stretch just enough to appear as though he were carefully weighing his words. Finally, he nodded slowly, projecting an air of cautious agreement. "The situation is... unsettling," he replied, his voice as neutral as he could manage. "If the queen did indeed orchestrate the king's death, as it seems, it would suggest a far-reaching ambition. One that concerns us all."

A glint of dark satisfaction crossed Lord Balgin's face as he leaned forward, his eyes gleaming with the thrill of an ally found. "Then you see the need for action, don't you? She has overreached, and her thirst for power will only grow if we allow her to go unchallenged."

Thoren met Balgin's enthusiasm with a level gaze, his expression carefully measured, refusing to give in to the frenzy around him. "I understand your concern, Balgin," he said, his tone steady and almost cooling. "But if we are to act, it must be with caution. A hasty move would only serve to expose us all, leaving the court divided and vulnerable."

A murmur of frustration passed through the nobles, several of them shifting uncomfortably. Thoren saw their impatience, their hunger for a swift overthrow, yet he maintained his calm. He could feel the dangerous tension building in the room, their desire for action pressing in like a current, but he remained unmoved. For him, caution was more than a virtue; it was a shield, one he knew he must wield carefully if he were to remain close to them without betraying himself.

A flicker of uncertainty passed over Balgin's face, but it was quickly masked by a sneer. "Caution?" he spat; his voice sharp with disdain. "Our king lies cold, poisoned, his memory tarnished by betrayal, and you speak of caution? What we need is resolve, Thoren—not cowardice, not excuses. She must be stopped before her hold on the throne is unbreakable."

Thoren felt a ripple of irritation rise within him but suppressed it, managing only a small, noncommittal nod. Balgin's zeal grated against his patience, but he knew that his own conflict lay beyond anything these nobles could comprehend. The grief they wore like cloaks—their claims of loyalty to Ivar—felt shallow, performative. Thoren's reservations had little to do with the late king, a distant figure he had respected in title alone. His hesitations were rooted elsewhere, in something unspoken, a tension he felt pull tighter with each day under Karak's rule. He knew her ambition was vast, perhaps even perilous, but he could see a purpose in it, a vision that burned with something larger than the petty squabbles in this room.

Lady Hilda's eyes were upon him again, sharp and probing, as though she sensed the fracture in his resolve. Her voice softened, taking on a tone both persuasive and insistent. "Thoren, we don't expect you to lead this cause. But your support... it would change everything. The court listens to you; they trust your judgement." Her gaze held him captive, a silent plea flickering beneath her words. "You could tip the scales, you know. You could be the one to turn the tide."

He felt the weight of her words settle over him, a cloak of expectation that seemed to tighten with every passing moment. Thoren knew what she wanted—a declaration, a sign that he was as outraged as they were, that he too felt the sting of betrayal they wore like a badge. But his loyalty, he knew, lay in murky waters, tangled up with Karak in ways they could never fathom. Lady Hilda's eyes did not leave his face, watching him intently, but beneath her probing stare, he could feel his thoughts drift back to Karak, her ruthless clarity, her relentless ambition. He admired her vision, and even as he sat among these nobles, his mind was half with her, wondering how she would respond if she knew of this meeting.

"I understand the need for… unity in purpose," Thoren said finally, his voice low, each word carefully measured. "But know this—if we move against her, it must be done with precision, with no room for error. A misstep would not only expose us but would plunge Nordon into chaos. We must be certain, or risk losing everything."

A ripple of agreement ran through the room, hushed murmurs rising as some nodded in reluctant approval. But Thoren noticed the flicker of frustration on several faces, a visible bristling at his caution. They wanted swift action, a clean and decisive end to her rule, something bold and forceful. He saw their hunger for immediacy, their impatience simmering just beneath the surface, ready to burst.

He let their restlessness hang in the air, let them feel the weight of his hesitation, a deliberate display to remind them of the peril in hasty decisions. Each word he chose was like a thread in a taut web, binding them to his counsel, yet leaving them uncertain, wary. He wanted them to be uneasy, to feel that the path to action was fraught, to see him as the voice of reason, the careful hand guiding their brash impulses.

Balgin, sensing the tension, leaned forward, his face mere inches from Thoren's, his breath hot with anger. "Chaos?" he sneered, his tone dripping with contempt. "Is there any greater chaos than a throne stolen under the cover of night? She manipulates us like pawns in her twisted game, and we are fools to sit by in silence. Ivar was our king—are you truly suggesting we let his murder go unanswered?"

Thoren held Balgin's gaze, his expression unwavering, a calm defiance that seemed to only fan Balgin's fury. "I am saying," he replied, his voice steady and unyielding, "that if you intend to challenge the queen, you will need far more than anger and wounded pride. You will need allies—reliable ones. Preparation. A plan that does not further shatter Nordon but strengthens it."

Balgin's face contorted, his disdain momentarily faltering under the weight of Thoren's words. Around them, a tense silence settled, each noble watching, waiting for Thoren's words to take hold. He felt the force of their expectations, their anger, pressing in, but he held firm. Thoren knew that anger alone, untethered to reason, would only lead to ruin, and he was not about to let their fury lead them into the abyss.

Lady Hilda's tone softened, the sharpness in her voice giving way to something almost imploring. She reached across the table, her hand settling near his, a gesture of quiet entreaty. "Thoren, we respect your wisdom—that is precisely why we need you with us. We must act, but we need your judgement to guide us."

The air thickened with expectation, an invisible weight pressing down on him as the nobles' eyes remained fixed on his every move, each gaze a silent plea. They were searching for reassurance, for a sign that he would take on this unspoken mantle, that he would stand as their anchor amidst the turbulent shift in power. Yet even as he felt the draw of their desperation, a pull that wrapped around him like tendrils, he knew his loyalties were entangled. His heart was neither wholly with them nor wholly against them, caught in a delicate balance that only he could feel.

He glanced down, his voice barely more than a murmur. "I will do what is best for Nordon," he said, his tone soft but steady, letting the ambiguity hang in the air, unclarified. "I want to see this kingdom stable, secure... whatever that may require."

The nobles exchanged glances, their faces a blend of reluctant respect and thinly veiled frustration. Each one seemed to be weighing Thoren's words, searching for a thread of commitment, yet finding only the carefully placed ambiguity he'd left behind. They had not won his full allegiance; they sensed that much. But in his measured response, he had left them a sliver of hope—a faint, tantalising suggestion that he might yet be swayed. For now, it was enough. They clung to that glimmer, exchanging subtle nods and resigned looks, each silently agreeing to let this quiet promise linger unchallenged, trusting that time and circumstance might yet tilt him fully to their cause.

The silence hung for a moment, but it was quickly broken as Lord Balgin leaned forward, his voice a sharp whisper. "If we are to move against her, it should be done openly. Publicly, with the plunge of each our blades—something the people can see, something that will shake their confidence in her rule. Let her fall in the very throne room she stole."

A few murmurs of agreement passed through the room, but Lady Hilda's eyes narrowed, her voice cutting through the low hum. "Too bold, Balgin. A public spectacle like that risks drawing unwanted attention, and it would only rally her loyalists around her, making her a martyr. No, we must strike more subtly."

Balgin sneered. "Subtlety? The time for subtlety is over, Hilda. Do you think she spared a thought for subtlety when she poisoned the king?"

Lady Hilda held his gaze with steely calm. "That poison worked, didn't it? If poison was enough to end a king, it can end a queen just as efficiently."

Thoren watched as Balgin's face twisted in reluctant consideration, but another noble, a thin, wiry man named Aldric, spoke up, his tone thoughtful. "There is merit in poison. There's an alchemist in the Lower Quarter—a recluse, but skilled in his trade. He has provided... remedies for certain indiscretions in the past. If we approached him carefully, we might acquire a poison that would leave no trace, something delicate yet deadly."

Lady Hilda nodded slowly, intrigued. "And this alchemist... you're certain he could be trusted?"

Aldric shrugged. "For the right price, he would serve anyone. He's discreet, a man of little ambition. He wouldn't ask questions as long as the coin was right. A subtle poison slipped into her wine at the right time, she would see out the feast, then once back in the safety of her chambers it would take hold—no spectacle, no scene, just the quiet end she deserves."

Balgin let out a scoff, though he seemed to be warming to the idea. Lady Hilda's gaze grew colder, "yes, we use a poison that seeps slowly, one that could even strike days later. Something that appears as an illness, an unfortunate end in her sleep." Her eyes flicked around the group, hard and calculating. "Let her death seem natural, a quiet punishment."

A tense silence fell, and all eyes turned to Thoren, who had remained quiet, absorbing each suggestion. He let the weight of the moment stretch, then gave a small, barely perceptible nod. "If this is to be done, it must be without error. I trust you all understand the risks."

The nobles exchanged resolute glances, their expressions settling into grim determination. The beginnings of a plan had been laid, and with each passing moment, the tension around the table solidified into something far more dangerous.

Lady Hilda straightened, her gaze sweeping over the group as if weighing each of them in turn. "It is settled, then," she said, her tone resolute. "Aldric, you understand our needs. Arrange a meeting with this alchemist and ensure he knows what's required. Make it clear that the price we pay will buy not only his skill but his silence."

Aldric nodded, a flicker of nervousness in his eyes quickly masked by a show of confidence. "Consider it done. I'll speak with him discreetly and see to it that he understands his place in this arrangement."

"Good," Lady Hilda replied, her voice steely. "Meet with us here next week with an update. We'll discuss the final details then. And remember —no one must know of this. We cannot afford loose words or lingering suspicions."

The others exchanged solemn nods, a murmur of agreement settling over the group as the meeting drew to a close. One by one, the nobles slipped out, cloaked in silence, their expressions tense and shadowed with intent. Lady Hilda lingered behind, her gaze resting on Thoren, her eyes sharp with a trace of doubt that seemed to pierce through his carefully composed demeanour.

"You will have to choose a side, Thoren," she murmured, her voice barely more than a whisper, yet it seemed to echo in the stillness. "We cannot wait in limbo forever. Soon, the throne will demand your answer."

Without another word, she turned and disappeared into the shadows, leaving him alone with her words pressing heavily upon him. The tension coiled tight within his chest, her warning settling in his mind like a dark, unshakable weight. He lingered in the dim light of the near-empty room, feeling the clash of loyalties within him, a friction as sharp as two blades scraping against each other.

His mind drifted, unbidden, to Karak—to her fierce determination, her unrelenting will. She was ruthless, driven by a vision that few could fathom, let alone share. He knew that if she were to discover this plot, she would deal with it swiftly, mercilessly, without hesitation or remorse. That strength, that conviction, was precisely what drew him to her. And yet here he was, caught in the shadow of doubt, tethered to two paths that both felt inevitable and inescapable.

As he finally left the room, his footsteps echoed through the empty hall, each step weighted by the knowledge of the choice that loomed before him. He felt the tightening grip of the decision he would soon have to make—a decision that would bind him either to the queen's ruthless vision for Nordon or to the fractured loyalties of those who clung to the memory of a king he had barely known.

In the flickering shadows of the corridor, Thoren knew that he would either stand beside Karak in her quest to reshape the kingdom—or against her, a reluctant pawn in the hands of those who would resist her at any cost. And as the candlelight faded behind him, so too did any illusions he held of staying uninvolved. The throne would indeed demand an answer, and he would be forced, soon enough, to give it.

# THE QUEEN REGNANT
# CHAPTER TWENTY FOUR

The narrow stone corridors beneath the great hall reeked of damp rot, a smell that clung to the walls as stubbornly as the moisture that dripped down their rough surfaces. Queen Karak's footsteps cut through the thick silence, each step echoing off the dark stone, punctuated by the distant drip of water somewhere deeper in the dungeon. The wavering torchlight cast jagged shadows across her face, hollowing her eyes and lending a cold edge to her expression as she moved with measured purpose. Six guards flanked her, silent and tense, their hands firm on their weapons. Each was acutely aware of the charged air surrounding their queen, her calm exterior masking the calculated severity of her mission.

Ahead, a row of cramped cells stretched into the dim light, each holding a man who had sat at Ivar's table on the night of his demise. The prisoners occupied their solitary cages in strained silence, each wearing a different expression: shock, indignation, resentment—but all muted, their bravado drained by the cold, unforgiving confinement. Rough-hewn iron bars separated them, thick with rust and grime, a chilling reminder of the finality of their imprisonment. The floor of each cell was slick with mud and straw, half-rotted from the constant seep of water from above, and the low ceiling seemed to press down, compressing the stale air.

Karak moved slowly along the row of cells, her footsteps deliberate, the torchlight casting long, wavering shadows across the damp stones. She passed each prisoner with a casual menace, angling the torch to pierce the gloom, its harsh light cutting into the depths of each cell. The hollow eyes and gaunt faces of the men were revealed in stark relief, their expressions weary and haunted. Her scrutiny lingered on each man in turn, as if she were appraising livestock at auction, weighing worth against weakness. Most averted their eyes, unwilling to endure the steady, penetrating stare of their new queen. It was a quiet display of dominance—a predator's measured prowl, a reminder of their utter helplessness.

She lingered briefly at Sven's cell, the last in the row, where he stood with his back against the stone wall, his arms crossed. Though a faint hint of defiance lingered in his stance, she could see the shadow of unease in his eyes. Before Ivar's death, Sven had managed the kingdom's coffers with surprising skill, balancing the lavish spending of the court against the more pressing needs of the realm. A skilful treasurer, yes—but whether his loyalty ran as deep as his accounting was the question she aimed to answer tonight.

Sven shuffled forward, his steps tentative but deliberate. His voice was low, almost a whisper, yet it carried an edge of desperation. "My queen," he called out, his hand gripping the iron bars tightly, "might I borrow your ear?"

She had ignored the others, but Sven's approach pleased her—he was breaking the silence first. Let him think he was choosing this. She stopped, her gaze drifting over him without warmth. His once-fine tunic was marred with grime and fresh tears, his face shadowed with a hasty, unkempt beard, and his eyes—now rimmed with exhaustion—held a flicker of anxiety. His hair, once meticulously groomed, hung limp and greasy against his cheeks.

“Sven,” she said with cold amusement, “can it not wait? I am deep in thought.”

"I shall speak swiftly, my queen," he replied, almost stumbling over his words.

“Then do not make me wait.” She stepped closer, stopping just outside his reach, her torchlight casting his cell in harsh relief. The acrid smell of urine mingled with the thick dampness, and a dark stain spread across the far corner of his cell—a silent testament to his discomfort.

Sven took a steadying breath. “Ansgar did speak some truths at the feast,” he began.

Karak's eyes narrowed, and she instinctively drew back, her expression shifting from curiosity to suspicion. But before she could pull further away, Sven raised a pleading hand. "Please, my queen, hear me out."

She hesitated, assessing him with a glint of intrigue, then edged forward, her gaze unrelenting. “Speak carefully, Sven. You test my patience.”

He swallowed, nodding. “Most of us... suspect it was you who plotted against the king,” he said, his tone carefully measured. “But we do not mourn him. We are loyal, my queen. To you, who now holds the throne and the power to keep it.”

Karak's expression remained inscrutable, though a flicker of satisfaction passed through her. He continued, his voice gaining a hint of confidence. "I served under King Ivar because he ruled Nordon. Now, the ruler is you. My loyalty is to the one who commands, the one with the strength to secure the throne. We wish only to share in your ambitions—if you would confide in us."

His words hung in the air, and for a long moment, Karak simply watched him, her face unreadable, the torchlight flickering in her eyes. She mulled over his words. These men had spent long, silent nights confined to these damp cells, left with nothing but each other's company. Though she held little respect for them, she knew each possessed a keen mind. They had once been the king's advisors—clever, cunning men. With time on their hands and only whispers to fill the darkness, it was no surprise that plans and schemes might have brewed among them.

"You said 'most of us,'" she repeated, her voice laced with curiosity. "Are there some who do not see my claim to the throne as rightful?" She watched his reaction carefully, testing her theory directly.

"There are some, my queen," Sven replied, a note of reluctance in his voice. That was all she needed to confirm it: conversations had been had, and treacherous alliances may well have formed. How far their plans had advanced, she could not be sure, but trust was no longer an option.

For the first time, she allowed herself a rare admission. The truth hung heavily in the frigid air as she spoke, though it mattered little to her now. "It took but three of us to kill the king—only three," she said calmly, her tone almost matter of fact. "I do not fear the armies I can see, but I would be a fool not to fear the lone man with a dagger. Tell me their names, Sven. Who here would see me undone? Give me this, and I shall gather the loyal and speak of Nordon's future beyond this mountain."

Sven's face fell, his confidence visibly shaken by her sudden admission. He shifted his weight, eyes darting downward, a sign of the inner battle waging within him. Sensing his unease, Karak pressed him further. "Names, Sven," she demanded, her voice hardening.

Sven glanced up, his voice faltering. "Is this not a discussion to be held in private, my queen?" he asked, uncertain.

"No, Sven." Her voice was edged with steel. "You should feel free to speak to your queen, were we not but friends a week past? And are these not your peers?" She turned sharply to one of the guards. "Guard, release this man. He has something to say."

The broad-shouldered guard searched through his ring of keys, the clinking echoing in the silence. He found the correct key, inserted it into the lock, and twisted, the heavy clank of metal-on-metal resonating through the chamber. A hush fell over the prisoners as the cell door creaked open.

But Sven hesitated, lingering within his cell, his face a mix of defiance and trepidation. Karak raised an eyebrow, her expression daring him to step forward. "Come now, Sven. Share their names with all," she urged, her voice taunting, an unmistakable command.

At last, he shuffled forward, his every movement slow and reluctant. He came to a stop in clear view of the others, the weight of his decision bearing down upon him.

"So, Sven," Karak's voice was soft, almost playful, as if she were merely indulging in idle gossip. "You mentioned there are men among us who would wish my death. Name these conspirators."

Silence fell, thick and oppressive, broken only by the crackle of the torchlight. Every eye in the chamber fixed on Sven, the flickering flames casting jagged shadows that seemed to mock his hesitation. The man swallowed, his gaze darting between the queen and his fellow prisoners, each second stretching painfully.

Karak watched him closely, relishing the way he squirmed under the weight of the silence. It was cruel, she knew, but cruelty was a necessary test—a probe to see just how deep his loyalty ran, if it ran at all. She held her gaze on him, unblinking, her patience slipping with each beat of his indecision.

Still, Sven remained mute, his lips pressed into a thin line, the faint glimmer of sweat gathering at his brow. The silence swelled, feeding her growing impatience. Perhaps his tale had been a fabrication, a desperate ploy to gain favour. Or perhaps he lacked the courage to betray his supposed allies. Either way, she began to reconsider her approach, calculating her next move with a cold deliberation. Should she wait, let him stew a little longer, or push him, break him open with a well-placed taunt? The possibilities danced in her mind, each one a carefully weighed weapon in her arsenal.

Suddenly, a sharp voice cut through the deadly silence. "I am no conspirator, Queen, but I would see you dead."

Karak spun her torch toward the source of the voice, the flame illuminating a short, stern man standing defiantly in his cell. It was Grolin—one of the few councillors who had resisted her presence at their King's feasting table. His face was worn, dark circles under his eyes revealing the toll of his days in confinement, yet he stood straight, arms crossed, his gaze unflinching. He had barely acknowledged her in the past, avoiding conversation altogether, but now his eyes held nothing but contempt.

She approached him slowly, her steps measured, her feet crossing with each graceful stride. Her long, red hair shifted with each step, cascading like silk down her back. Reaching his cell, she extended her torch closer to his face, the flame's glow illuminating his tired, defiant expression. His pupils contracted sharply in the sudden light, and though he blinked, he held her gaze, unmoving.

"You have courage, Grolin," she said softly, her voice laced with a dangerous admiration. "To speak so boldly of crimes against your queen, to whom you owe your loyalty."

“I served the king, not his murderer.” His voice was steady, almost casual, and for the first time, Karak felt a ripple of unease. This short, defiant man seemed to carry a quiet power in his words, a conviction that could prove infectious. Was this outburst his attempt to disrupt her plans from behind bars? Or worse—had she just stumbled into the centre of a plot more elaborate than she had imagined?

"Now, now, Grolin," she replied, her tone veiled with mock chastisement. "There is courage, and then there is foolhardiness."

"Foolhardy?" He laughed, a bitter, hollow sound. "You, who slay our king and lock up his allies, so you may sit unopposed on his throne—do you truly expect no reaction? No retribution from his people? You, my queen, are the foolhardy one."

His words landed like blows, each one chipping away at her confidence, splintering the veneer of control she had so carefully cultivated. As she glanced around, she caught a glimmer in the eyes of the other prisoners—a faint, dangerous spark of hope. The sight unnerved her, igniting a brief flicker of doubt. This was the power of words, she realised, these clever men with their clever tongues, each one a threat in his own right.

But as quickly as her confidence waned, it surged back, anchored by the solid presence of the six-armed guards at her side, each ready to follow her command without question. She was their queen, and no scheming councillor would unsettle her rule. A dark rage began to burn within her, hotter and fiercer with each passing second. These men—these would-be conspirators, these twisted minds who dared to challenge her—had no place in her court.

They would learn the weight of her wrath; she would make certain of it.

"Guards," she ordered, her voice cold and steely, "release all except our bold friend Grolin here." Her tone brooked no argument, and the guards immediately set to work, unlocking the cells one by one. The prisoners blinked, dazed by their sudden shift in fortune, and a few murmured thanks in her direction. She ignored them, focusing instead on the fierce rage building within her—a storm she would unleash without mercy.

As the last of the prisoners stumbled into the corridor, Karak's gaze remained fixed on Grolin. Her voice, now sharp and dripping with malice, rang through the stone chamber. "Now, cut them down."

Like lightning, swords flashed upward, then sliced down with ruthless precision onto the unarmed men. Screams ripped through the darkness, their echoes reverberating through the stone corridors and out into the cold night beyond the city hall. Arms flew up in desperate attempts to shield, but flesh and bone were no match for steel—forearms were slashed deep, some hacked clean off, blood spraying in arcs across the cell walls. A few of the prisoners stumbled backward, trying to flee into their cells, only to be chased down, guards' blades cutting into their exposed torsos without mercy. Others attempted to fight back, but the effort was as futile as it was fleeting.

Chaos erupted as prisoners shoved and trampled over one another, desperate to escape the storm of blades. In the frenzy, bodies tangled and fell, each movement only fuelling the turmoil as swords hacked through weary flesh, and screams rose and fell, mingling in a cacophony of death.

Finally, the carnage came to an end. The cell floor was strewn with butchered bodies, severed limbs lying limp and motionless, while crimson-stained clothing clung to lifeless forms, indistinguishable in their once-fine fabrics now soaked in blood. Even a couple of the guards bore wounds, unintended casualties of the savage melee, their blood mingling with that of the fallen.

The walls dripped with blood, thick streaks trailing down to form dark red puddles below. Droplets clung to the ceiling, falling in a slow, macabre rhythm, as a small rivulet of blood traced its way down the slope of the stone floor.

For yet another night in recent memory, Karak's blouse was ruined. She glanced down at the dark navy fabric, now spoiled with splatters of scarlet. It would need to be discarded.

"My queen," a guard's voice came from just over her shoulder. She turned, her gaze settling on him—his armour was streaked with blood, his face a mask of grim satisfaction as he gestured toward a trembling figure huddled in the corner. It was Sven, cowering, his body pressed against the wall. In the chaos, he had somehow slipped back, avoiding the worst of the massacre, but his eyes were wide, terror etched deep into his face.

Karak moved toward him, her steps measured, her fingers still slick with blood. She seized his face with both hands, turning his head so he faced the pile of butchered bodies. "Look at them, Sven," she hissed, her voice a cold blade. "Look where their loyalty has taken them."

Sven shuddered, tears forming in his eyes, his lips trembling as he fought to suppress a sob. Karak's gaze bore into him, her grip unyielding. "But you, Sven... you and I were friends, once," she murmured, a hint of mocking softness in her tone. "So, I offer you a choice. Speak now, or I will have your tongue for testing my patience. I am in need of a treasurer—what say you?"

He stared at her, his face pale, torn between the horror of the scene and the promise of his own survival. His mouth opened, but no sound came. Instead, he gave a quick, desperate nod, the shock still freezing him in place.

Satisfied, Karak released him, a thin smile curling her lips as she wiped her bloody hands on the navy fabric of her ruined blouse. Then with a cold and calculated expression she gave Sven instruction, "good. We have our first council meeting tomorrow at noon. Go clean yourself up—I expect a full report on the financials."

Sven remained motionless, stunned, struggling to process the reality of his survival. He could hardly believe this was not some cruel ruse, that at any moment a sword would not pierce him from behind, sending him to join his fallen comrades.

Noting his hesitation, the Queen spoke again, her tone light but undercut with unmistakable menace. "And when you're home, Sven, do give my best wishes to your wife, Ingrid. And to your daughter, Tora, and of course your son, Digan." She paused, watching the colour drain from his face. “I hear your brother Stenn is faring well, too. Be sure to pass along my regards to them all.”

The implications of her words were as deadly as any blade. Sven swallowed hard, his mind reeling from the threat concealed in her well-wishes. He forced himself to bow his head, managing only two words through his dry throat. “My Queen.”

Karak watched him, satisfied, knowing she had secured him in her grasp. Perhaps his loyalty would stem from fear, at least at first. But soon enough, he would come to appreciate the advantages of his position—and the rewards that loyalty to her could bring.

One remained. Karak turned sharply, her gaze locking onto Grolin, still imprisoned. He had collapsed to his knees, his head bowed forward, staring blankly at the pile of corpses before him. She strode to his cell, her steps unhurried but unyielding, coming to a stop just outside the bars. He did not even flinch, his features drawn and ashen, his skin nearly green as though he were on the verge of retching.

“That courage of yours,” she sneered, her voice low and mocking, “we shall test it, Grolin. Guard—see that this one is fed and readied. He’ll need his strength when I address the people, for he is to be sent to the giant pit. Treason demands no less.”

"Very well, and the bodies, my queen?” the guard inquired, his tone cautious.

Karak’s gaze swept over the bloody scene, her expression momentarily vacant, as though contemplating a darker thought. To slay so many required justification, one that would leave no doubt in her people’s minds. She turned back to the guard, her voice cold and resolute. “Remove their heads. Set them on spikes, then burn the remains. Let all see that treason has a cost.”

Without another word, she spun on her heel, storming down the darkened corridor, her bloody footprints trailing behind like ghostly reminders of what she had wrought. As she moved further from the blood-soaked chamber, the adrenaline that had propelled her began to drain, leaving a hollow ache in its place. The silence of the corridor pressed in, thick and unyielding, amplifying the faint rustle of her footsteps and the low, distant echoes of screams that seemed to linger in her mind. Her breaths grew shallower, her heart beating a heavy, uneven rhythm.

What was she becoming?

A month ago, she had been untested by bloodshed, her hands as clean as her conscience. But now... she could almost feel the blood upon them, sticky and persistent, a stain no washing could remove. The faces of the men she had known flickered before her, faces that once held familiarity, trust, even respect. An image of Sven, his laughter at a feast, his face flushed from wine, rose unbidden in her mind. She remembered his words of loyalty whispered in the dim light, promises made under the weight of the king's rule. Those same words had echoed hollowly tonight, a desperate plea for survival.

Her pulse quickened, nausea creeping in as other memories surfaced, sharper, more visceral: Lord Ivar's council seated around the grand table, their voices rising and falling with the force of their ideas, their loyalty unquestionable—until she had tested it. Now, they were gone, replaced by twisted, bloodied forms scattered on the cold dungeon floor. The sight of them came back to her, vivid and searing, filling her mind with their lifeless stares, each one a silent accusation.

Her vision blurred, the corridor spinning as if the stones themselves recoiled from her presence. Her legs weakened, and she dropped to her knees, the cold floor biting through her clothing, grounding her in a reality she wished she could escape. She pressed her palms to the unforgiving stone, but nothing could steady the vertigo twisting within her.

In the silence, a voice echoed from her past—her own voice, the woman she had been before the crown's weight had reshaped her. *'I will rule justly, with wisdom,'* she had once said to herself, her ambition noble, untainted. But that woman felt like a stranger now, a figure who had slipped away, leaving only this version of herself—calculating, ruthless, hollow.

Her stomach heaved, and she retched, her body rejecting the darkness she had embraced, her breath coming in gasps, raw and strained. For a fleeting moment, she felt a pang of longing—a wish that things had been different, that she had not crossed this line that now seemed impossible to retreat from.

A guard appeared beside her; his hands steady as he lifted her to her feet. "My queen," he said gently, his voice laced with concern. "Are you well?"

She managed a weak nod, swallowing down the bitterness that clung to her throat. "Please... take me to my room."

He nodded, guiding her down the shadowed corridors. As they moved, she tried to compose herself, her expression hardening, but each step felt like an anchor pulling her deeper into darkness. The faces, the memories, lingered, haunting her, a grim reminder of the cost of her power and the ghosts she had created along the way.

# THE QUEEN REGNANT CHAPTER TWENTY FIVE

The feasting chamber buzzed with eager anticipation, a current of excitement rippling through the crowd. Tonight, the hall had returned to its former splendour, alive with voices, clinking goblets, and the rustle of fine attire—a stark contrast to the hollow silence that had settled here since King Ivar's death. Nobles and servants alike were intrigued by the scene, stealing glances at the newly appointed council members who now occupied seats once reserved only for the former king's most trusted. Few among them had ever graced such feasts, let alone claimed a place within the inner circle, and the novelty of their presence sparked murmurs throughout the hall.

Adding to the imposing atmosphere, much of the Royal Guard was in attendance, lining the walls in polished armour, their presence a silent but unmistakable show of strength. Under the watchful eyes of Konan and his commanders, they held their positions with disciplined poise, adding a reminder of order and power to the celebration. The gleam of their armour caught the torchlight, casting reflections that flickered across the hall, a visual echo of Queen Karak's authority. Their presence was as symbolic as it was practical—a clear declaration that tonight's feast was protected, and that Karak's reign was safeguarded by Nordon's finest.

At the head of the table, Queen Karak sat in quiet command, her gaze steady, a glint of satisfaction barely concealed. She felt the anticipation swell around her, not only for the feast but for what lay ahead—the table's far end, long empty, was set for invited guests from Frostfall, drawing curious glances and hushed speculations. The crowd sensed that tonight was more than a mere celebration; it was the beginning of something new, a promise that the halls of Stormhold would not remain silent but would ring with the steps and voices of allies to come. The excitement was almost palpable, each smile and whisper brimming with expectation, as if the kingdom itself held its breath, waiting to see the vision of their new queen unfold.

At the Queen's table, a splendid array awaited, carefully laid out for her council and closest allies. Cups of rich, dark wine glistened beside polished goblets, each filled generously, the fragrance of ripe grapes mingling with the warmth of the room. Platters of roasted meats—succulent cuts of lamb, venison, and pheasant—were piled high, their juices glistening beneath the flickering torchlight, enticing even the most reserved of appetites. Cheeses in shades of creamy white, golden yellow, and deep orange lay arranged beside fruits and honeyed nuts, their pungent aromas mingling with the savour of the meats.

A large barrel of ale sat at one end of the table, its spout well within reach of eager hands. Mugs foamed with freshly drawn drink, laughter and cheer bubbling up around the council as each clink of a cup brought with it the taste of revelry. Karak's closest allies shared in the feast, partaking in the abundance, their smiles wide and their voices louder as wine warmed their spirits. This table was more than a meal; it was a declaration—a celebration of new power, unity, and the promise of dominance to come.

At her right sat Konan, her loyal brother and Commander of the Royal Guard. His imposing presence was marked by his muscular build, his loyalty to his sister was absolute, and his protective gaze swept the hall with the alertness of a man prepared to quash any sign of dissent. His presence served as both a reminder of her lineage and a warning to those who might consider challenging her authority.

Beside him was Thoren, now the Lord of Court and her trusted advisor. In this new role, he managed the daily affairs of court with precision, making him both the gatekeeper of royal decisions and the liaison between Karak and the nobility. Thoren's presence exuded quiet authority, and he wore the weight of his power like a second skin, his eyes watchful, taking note of every whisper and gesture around him. His loyalty, while unquestionable in Karak's eyes, was nuanced with ambition—a trait she both relied upon and kept a cautious eye on.

Across from Thoren sat Sven, the newly appointed treasurer. Though his face bore signs of recent hardship, a shadow that lingered around his eyes, he had managed to regain his composure under Karak's command. His experiences had tempered him, leaving a man acutely aware of the costs of betrayal and the privilege of survival. Now, he handled the treasury with vigilance, ensuring every coin spent served Karak's ambitions. His gaze rarely met anyone's directly, as if constantly calculating the risks around him.

Ulric, the Guild Master, was a seasoned statesman with sharp eyes and an even sharper wit, long kept at a distance from the previous king's inner circle. Known for opposing the late king's more passive approach, Ulric had consistently pushed for Nordon to assert itself through raiding parties, advocating strikes south into Kadun and even raids upon Nordon's neighbouring settlements, such as Frostfall. Now, with Queen Karak in power, he found himself not only welcomed but elevated within her council, his ambitions finally aligning with the ruling vision.

Making Ulric Guild Master brought an instant ally to Karak's side—one both ambitious and experienced in rallying the guilds to his cause. Tasked with overseeing all guild operations save the mining guild, Ulric now wielded influence over nearly every trade in Nordon, his authority solidified by Karak's trust. Under his command, the guilds would be steered toward a future of expansion and strength, one aligned with both his and the Queen's shared vision for Nordon. Ulric's voice, a low, steady cadence, held an assurance that belied his years of defiance, yet it now carried a fervour that promised loyalty, not through submission, but through a shared ambition that would reshape the kingdom's destiny.

The mining guild, vast in its members and critical to the kingdom's economy, was represented by Rogren, a man as stoic as the stone he oversaw. His presence on the council was a calculated move by Karak to consolidate control over Nordon's most lucrative resource. Rogren was a man of few words, preferring the predictability of the mines to the whispers of court. However, his loyalty was unmistakable, forged in the same fires that shaped the kingdom's wealth.

Druse, Konan's man and now Lord of Arms, had a reputation for loyalty and ruthlessness on the battlefield. Already a Commander within Stormhold's armies, Druse commanded respect among soldiers and inspired fear among the kingdom's enemies. His position ensured that Nordon's military strength remained firmly aligned with Karak's rule, and his unyielding gaze held a readiness to silence any dissent. His allegiance to Konan and, by extension, to Karak, made him an invaluable asset in their plans.

Thoren had introduced two more figures to the council, both calculated additions. Heidi, the First Advisor, was a shrewd strategist and one of the few who could speak to Karak with unreserved honesty. Her role required her to bring perspectives others might overlook, and she often offered advice that balanced Karak's bold visions with a level-headed realism. Heidi's eyes were sharp, her demeanour calm yet brimming with insight, a steady voice amid the ambitions surrounding her.

Finally, Durin, the Warden of the City, controlled the pulse of Stormhold itself. He was responsible for the city's defences, its law enforcement, and the order of its streets. Durin, a practical man with a keen sense for trouble, was known for his unbreakable dedication to the people of

Nordon. His presence on the council symbolised Karak's commitment to not only ruling from above but maintaining control over the streets themselves. Durin's respect among the city's watchmen made him a critical link between the council's decrees and the people's daily lives.

As the Queen's council, they spoke in low murmurs, their voices intertwining in a careful tapestry of ambition, rivalry, and newfound power. The air was thick with a sense of purpose, each word carrying an edge, as if every syllable forged a new link in the chain binding them to Karak's will. They were not merely advisers but instruments of her ambition, the sharp tools with which she would carve a new path for Nordon. Fully committed to her plans, they each bore the weight of their role with solemn intensity—knowing that the responsibility to realise her vision did not simply rest upon them but demanded their every allegiance, every whisper, and every calculated step until her will reigned supreme.

The feast carried on in full swing, the air thick with laughter, song, and the clink of goblets. Lively tunes filled the hall, played by a small band in the corner, their melodies carrying the revellers through tales of victory, of ancient heroes, and of Nordon's triumphs against its enemies. Servants moved with practised ease, refilling goblets, clearing emptied platters, and replacing them with fresh ones. Every few moments, someone raised a toast to Queen Karak, to Nordon's future, to this gathering of powerful allies. Voices rose and fell in good-natured banter, the kind that only fermented wine and newfound camaraderie could bring.

The warmth of the feast was infectious, spreading through the hall, and even those who had begun the evening with hesitation now joined in with hearty laughs and cheers. A few guests broke out into song, their voices boisterous and half out of tune, drawing cheers and clapping from the crowd. It was a rare, almost surreal scene of joy, as if the burdens of war and conflict could be momentarily set aside. The hall had come alive once more, buzzing with a liveliness that seemed a distant memory in recent months.

But then, as a sharp trumpet sounded, the jubilant hum came to an abrupt halt. The announcer's horn sliced through the revelry, snapping heads toward the great doors. Every goblet was stilled, every voice paused mid-sentence. "Announcing," called the herald in a loud, clear voice that resonated through the hall, "Gunnar Stonkar of Frostfall Harbour." His voice echoed, lingering for a moment as the gathered nobles exchanged looks, a flicker of tension shadowing their faces. Gunnar's name was a reminder of Stormhold's storied past with Frostfall, a history marked by clashes, uneasy truces, and bloody skirmishes in the hills and along the frozen rivers.

The grand doors swung open, creaking slightly as they revealed the figures beyond. Two rows of guards, six men on each side, stood in polished armour, furs draped over their shoulder, each bearing the Frostfall insignia on their breastplates. They moved with disciplined precision, forming a formidable line as they marched into the hall. The silence grew heavier as they took their positions, their presence an unmistakable reminder of the strength Frostfall held—and the many lives lost in battles waged between their cities.

Then, as the guards parted, Gunnar Stonkar entered. He walked with the calm confidence of a man accustomed to holding power, his eyes sweeping over the crowd with a keen, assessing gaze. Gunnar's armour gleamed beneath the torchlight, crafted from dark iron and steel, rough-hewn yet perfectly fitted to his form. His face, lined and weathered, spoke of the countless campaigns he had endured. A thick cloak, trimmed with fur, fell across his shoulders, the dark folds contrasting against the steel of his armour. His steps were unhurried, almost deliberately measured, as if reminding every soul in the room that he entered as both guest and rival.

A heavy silence hung over the hall, the warmth of the feast now tempered by the undeniable tension in the air. Many among Stormhold's nobles had witnessed or lost loved ones to Frostfall's relentless raids, and now the man who had commanded those very forces stood before them. Karak's council members held their expressions steady, though a flicker of mistrust lurked in some eyes, mingling with the residual energy of the feast. All awaited her response, knowing that her command alone could set the tone for this encounter.

Gunnar halted at the centre of the hall; his gaze fixed on Queen Karak at the head of the table. He inclined his head, a slight, formal nod, acknowledging her authority within these walls but nothing more. It was the barest gesture of respect—no bow, no show of reverence, only a subtle acknowledgment. A murmur rippled through the crowd, as those who remembered his reputation as a relentless fighter, a ruthless commander, noted the brevity of his gesture.

As Queen Karak's eyes met his, the hall itself seemed to hold its breath. This was no mere guest; Gunnar Stonkar represented a city that had been both foe and, for now, an uneasy ally. The halls of Stormhold, which had moments before been filled with mirth, now bore the weight of decades of rivalry, a swift shift from revelry to quiet, guarded expectation. The room waited, tension thick in the silence, all watching the exchange between queen and guest, each aware that, beneath this alliance, the embers of old conflicts still smouldered, waiting for the slightest spark.

Queen Karak rose from her seat at the head of the table, her presence commanding every eye in the hall. She wore a gown of deep, rich crimson that seemed to shift with each movement, the fabric catching the golden light as if woven from embers. Intricate black embroidery curled along the sleeves and hem, like vines, accentuating her tall, imposing figure. Her fiery red hair cascaded freely over her shoulders, forming a vivid, almost ethereal halo that framed her face, each strand catching the torchlight and shimmering like molten fire. A black wolf pelt lay draped across her shoulders, adding a fierce, primal elegance to her presence.

Atop her head, she wore a crown more defiant than any she had worn before. Crafted of dark iron with delicate silver filigree, it was adorned with crimson gemstones that gleamed like blood-red stars. The crown's peaks arched in sharp, elegant points, a symbol of her strength and resolve, glistening under the flames that danced in the sconces. It was a crown that left no question as to her authority—a regal reminder that this was no mere feast, and she was no mere queen.

She held herself with unshakable poise, the faintest smile on her lips as her gaze rested on Gunnar Stonkar. "Gunnar Stonkar," she began, her voice clear and unwavering, carrying across the hall with practised ease. "Strength to you, we welcome you to Stormhold." There was warmth in her tone, a cordiality that acknowledged his place as an ally, yet beneath it lay a firmness, a reminder that here, she was sovereign. "It has been too long since our halls have welcomed friends from Frostfall Harbour."

A ripple passed through the hall at the word "friends," a term some knew Karak chose with purpose. Despite the many battles fought between their cities, she extended this title, if only to set the tone for what would follow. Her expression remained pleasant, but her eyes held a guarded, calculating glint, a look that reminded all present that this invitation, this alliance, was one born of necessity and not sentiment.

"Our kingdoms have long shared a… spirited history," she continued, her words carefully chosen, "and I trust that, together, we can find a future that strengthens both Stormhold and Frostfall." She paused, letting the weight of her words settle, a delicate balance of invitation and challenge. "Tonight, let us share in Stormhold's hospitality. Let us raise our cups not only to the alliances we forge but to the promise of peace and prosperity for our people."

Her words hung in the air, resonant and unshakable. With a graceful motion, she extended her hand, gesturing to the seat prepared for Gunnar. "Please, join us at the table," she invited, her voice still warm yet firm, leaving no room for hesitation or refusal. "There is much to discuss, and I look forward to hearing your thoughts on how our kingdoms might walk this path together."

As she resumed her seat, her eyes never left him, watching with unwavering composure as he moved to join her table. In that moment, she had not only greeted him but established the ground on which they would stand—and she, the queen, had made it clear that here, it was her ground.

Gunnar paused before taking his seat, his gaze sweeping over the hall, meeting the vigilant eyes of the Royal Guard and the curious, sometimes wary glances of the gathered nobles. His eyes settled on Konan, seated just beside the Queen. Both men held fierce expressions, a silent reminder of their last encounter and the grim reality of the alliance now binding them.

He inclined his head toward the Queen once more, his expression transformed to a mask of composure, though his eyes held a glint of steel.

"Queen Karak," he began, his voice deep and resonant, carrying through the silence of the hall, "strength to you, it is an honour to be welcomed so openly into your halls." His tone was respectful, yet laced with an edge that reminded all present that he was no mere guest. "Stormhold has long stood as a formidable ally—and rival. But I look forward to a future where our shared strength can forge something... unbreakable." He let the last word linger, a subtle nod to the potential of their alliance and a faint reminder of the power Frostfall still wielded.

He paused, the weight of his words settling over the room, then gave a slight, respectful nod before adding, "May this feast mark the beginning of prosperity for both our lands." With that, he turned, motioning for his men to take their seats, the disciplined line of soldiers breaking apart as they moved to join the tables.

Gunnar's presence filled the space as he sat, his armour creaking slightly, yet every motion exuding confidence. The nobles exchanged glances, the significance of his words and the restrained strength behind them adding a new layer of tension to the hall. Queen Karak, however, remained composed, meeting his gaze with unwavering calm. The lines had been drawn, words exchanged, and now, the feast would begin in earnest.

As Gunnar took his seat, the hall remained silent for a heartbeat longer, the weight of his words lingering in the air. Then, as if on cue, the musicians struck up their lively tune once more, filling the hall with a renewed energy. The tension that had settled over the room loosened just slightly, though an undercurrent of anticipation remained, woven into every note and beat.

Serving maids hurried forward, weaving between tables with practised grace, bearing fresh platters of roasted meats, steaming vegetables, and barrels of dark ale. They moved swiftly, their faces a study in concentration as they placed the offerings before the newcomers, each dish rich with the savoury scents of Nordon's finest fare. Goblets were refilled, and mugs of ale set down with a satisfying clink. The flickering torchlight caught on polished silver platters and golden goblets, casting the scene in a warm, inviting glow.

Gunnar's men accepted the offerings with quiet nods, their eyes still watchful despite the abundance before them. They ate with the disciplined restraint of soldiers accustomed to scarcity and hard campaigns, though they did not hesitate to take their fill. Gunnar himself lifted a goblet to his lips, his gaze drifting momentarily to the Queen as if acknowledging her hospitality even as he savoured its richness.

Around them, the hall began to hum again with conversation and laughter, though the nobles' glances often flickered toward the Frostfall contingent. The feast resumed, but with an undeniable edge, each clink of a goblet and scrape of a knife underscored by the delicate balance between alliance and rivalry that hung in the air.

Karak lifted her goblet, taking a measured sip as she turned to Gunnar, her expression composed and assessing. Gunnar was a formidable man, tall and broad-shouldered, with a gaze sharpened by years of command. He surveyed the hall with a trace of amusement, as though savouring the irony of dining among nobles who had once viewed him as an enemy, while their queen extended an offer that held far more than mere fealty.

He raised his goblet in a casual toast, his eyes glinting with a mix of challenge and curiosity. "Quite the gathering you've assembled, Queen Karak," he remarked, his voice low but effortlessly carrying across the hall's din. "I imagine a shift in power requires a show of strength... or, perhaps, a reminder."

Karak matched his stare, her faint smile revealing nothing. "A reminder, indeed, Lord Gunnar. The strength of Stormhold's army stands ready to defend the crown—and to advance it. My commanders and soldiers are loyal, and their allegiance is as firm as the walls of this fortress." Her tone held the quiet authority of a ruler who knew her power and had no need to flaunt it.

Gunnar's chuckle was deep and resonant, a sound that held both appreciation and a faint hint of mockery. "An army as steadfast as its queen, I'm sure. Yet even armies are only as powerful as the ships that supply them. A queen needs not just soldiers but the reach to command distant shores." He took a leisurely sip from his goblet, his eyes steady. "And I, as you know, command the mightiest fleet in these lands. Storms may rage, and tides may shift, but my ships remain, ready to sail or to strike."

Karak's smile did not falter, her eyes gleaming with steely resolve. "An army and a fleet, then," she replied, her voice carrying a subtle edge. "One does not rule without both. Power, Lord Gunnar, is not a single blade but many, forged together to make an unbreakable force. Which is why I propose a bond that goes beyond mere alliance." She paused, her focus holding his. "A union."

Gunnar's smirk widened as realisation flickered in his expression. He leaned forward, his tone a murmur of intrigue and power. "A union, indeed. A throne fortified by an army and a fleet. But tell me, queen, is this simply politics—or is there something more to your ambition?"

Karak inclined her head, her expression unyielding, her eyes fixed on his. "A marriage, yes. Not merely a political arrangement, but a merging of strength and vision. Together, we could forge a future for Nordon that neither of us could achieve alone. Imagine a Nordon that stretches beyond these borders—a kingdom secured by land and sea alike."

The hall grew noticeably quieter, nobles leaning in, riveted by the unfolding exchange. Karak's council watched with subtle approval, knowing what Gunnar represented—a force that could solidify their queen's rule and extend her reach. To them, Gunnar was not just a partner, but a weapon sharpened by her hand, and his marriage to Karak would only strengthen their positions in the kingdom.

Gunnar took a slow drink, his eyes narrowing thoughtfully as he studied her. "A queen and a warlord," he mused, his voice thick with contemplation. "Nordon has seen alliances, truces, and treaties... but never a marriage of such power." He set his goblet down, his fingers tapping the table, each tap echoing with a quiet, restrained intensity. "What would you ask of me, beyond loyalty? I suspect this union would demand more than simple vows."

Karak leaned forward, her voice softened to a near-whisper, though its edge remained unmistakable. “I ask for commitment—a true partnership. I need a man who can stand beside me when the time comes to defend Nordon, to expand it. My vision for this kingdom is one of conquest, of a legacy that cannot be rivalled. And you, Gunnar, are a man who knows how to seize what he desires. This marriage would bind us, yes, but it would also empower us both.”

For a moment, a flicker of admiration crossed Gunnar’s face, as if recognizing in her the same ambition that drove him. He was not a man easily swayed, but he was one who respected power—and Karak radiated it, her every word a promise of shared strength and dominance.

Raising his goblet once more, he held her gaze, a newfound respect glittering in his eyes. “To the queen’s vision,” he declared, his voice rich with a rough, undeniable promise. “And to a future forged in conquest and iron.”

The council raised their goblets in unison, echoing the toast with enthusiasm, their loyalty to Karak unshaken. Each of them knew that their power, their newfound place at her side, would only grow stronger with this union. They drank deeply, their confidence in her leadership only bolstered by her decision to align with a man as formidable as Gunnar.

As the feasting continued, Gunnar leaned closer, his voice low enough that only she could hear. “You know, there’s danger in sharing power.”

Karak’s gaze hardened. “Make no mistake, Gunnar—I do not intend to surrender my rule. You may be at my side, but the crown remains mine.”

He gave her an appraising look, the faintest trace of admiration in his eyes. “Remember, a wolf does not become a lapdog,” he replied, his voice carrying a note of challenge.

“Nor do I intend to tame you,” she replied smoothly. “Only satisfy your hunger for battle and ensure our interests align.”

He leaned in, his presence pressing against the space between them. “And if my hunger is greater than you can satisfy?” His grin was all teeth, daring her to falter.

Karak held his focus, unshaken. A slow, suggestive smile curved her lips, "then I shall have to find other means to satisfy my betrothed."

The feast stretched into the night, the hall alive with conversation and laughter. Yet, beneath the surface, Karak could feel the tension that lingered, a reminder of the precarious balance she had struck with this new alliance. Her council remained loyal, unwavering, but Gunnar was a different force altogether—one that required both caution and strength.

As the final dishes were cleared and the hall began to empty, Karak lingered, watching as Gunnar exchanged brief words with his men before he approached her once more. His eyes held the same intensity, the same challenge, yet now there was a flicker of understanding beneath it.

"So, queen," he said, his voice softer but no less firm. "When does this union take place? I prefer to know the terms of my obligations before I'm bound by them."

Karak met his gaze, her expression calm. "Soon, Gunnar. Very soon. And when it does, our goals will be aligned in every way. Until then, I expect you to ready your fleet. Nordon's future is not a passive one."

He inclined his head, a faint smirk on his lips. "My fleet is always ready. But know this—I intend to be more than just a sword at your command."

She gave a slight nod, her own smile mirroring his. "Then let us both prove our worth, Gunnar. Together, we will shape Nordon's future. But remember—it is a future I intend to rule."

Their eyes met, an unspoken understanding passing between them. They were allies, yes, but each was fully aware of the other's strength—the sharp edges that made them both dangerous and valuable.

The feast wore on, tension slowly melting into merriment. Even the men of Frostfall, guarded at first, joined in the revelry, their laughter gradually blending into the rising din. As the hours stretched into the depths of the night, Gunnar finally took his leave. Karak watched him disappear into the shadows beyond the hall, her gaze lingering as her mind drifted, already turning to the next step in her plan. She knew that binding herself to a man like Gunnar was as much a risk as it was an asset, yet it was a risk she was prepared to take. For Nordon's future to be secure, she would need the strength of his fleet, his ruthlessness, and the respect his name commanded.

The hall now emptied, and Karak remained seated, her fingers tracing the rim of her goblet as she contemplated the alliance she had forged. Her council would support her decision, for they knew her vision was their own. And as for Gunnar... he may become her partner, her husband, but never her equal. In this alliance of power and ambition, there was only room for one ruler.

And she would ensure that, no matter the cost, that ruler would be her.

# THE QUEEN REGNANT CHAPTER TWENTY SIX

The Great Hall of Stormhold throbbed with anticipation, a living heartbeat under the mountain. Word had spread like wildfire through the city—Queen Karak would address her people today, speaking of Nordon's future, one shaped by her iron will and secured by her might. Every inch of space was claimed, with thousands pressing shoulder to shoulder, spilling into the balconies, and crowding the stone steps that framed the arena below. Overhead, banners of Nordon rippled, casting shadows that flickered like restless spirits across the faces of the gathered crowd.

The arena, a vast pit at the hall's centre, lay bare, its sanded floor pristine—for now. Iron railings encircled the pit, looming ominously, a reminder of the violence that would soon stain the ground below. Around the edge of the platform stood Queen Karak's new council, each figure radiating a silent resolve. Their faces bore pride and steel, each member elevated by the queen herself, bound to her by a fierce loyalty and shared ambition. They held their positions with straight shoulders and unwavering gazes, aware that this spectacle was as much for them as it was for the throngs below.

Queen Karak herself stood at the centre of the elevated dais, a vision of fierce authority, flanked by her royal guard, whose stoic faces and glinting armour formed an impenetrable wall. Just below the platform, her army waited in perfect ranks, a sea of steel and leather that spoke of unwavering discipline and unity. Each soldier, fully armoured and standing at attention, exuded readiness—a silent promise of the force that lay under her command.

To her side stood Gunnar Stonkar, arms crossed, his usual confidence wavering as he took in the immense gathering before him. His own retinue—a band of hardened men who bore the marks of countless battles—stood slightly apart, their presence imposing yet dwarfed by the sheer scale of Stormhold's force. Though his union with Queen Karak had yet to be formalised, Gunnar's presence here was a visible pledge to their alliance, though he now felt the weight of it with an unexpected gravity. The hall, packed with Karak's army and citizens united under her banner, revealed the full might of Stormhold—a power vast and unyielding.

As he looked over the sea of armour-clad soldiers, each one perfectly aligned and ready, Gunnar felt a flicker of awe that unsettled him. Why had he thought to challenge this? The queen held a force at her fingertips that eclipsed anything he could marshal. Even for a man as seasoned as he, the sheer dominance of Stormhold's military left him humbled, a stark reminder of the empire Karak commanded and the unwavering loyalty it inspired.

As the voices of the crowd rose and fell, a chorus of cheers and whispers echoing off the stone walls, a ripple of silence spread outward from the dais. Queen Karak lifted a single hand, and the vast hall fell still, as if the very air obeyed her command. An expectant hush blanketed the chamber, thick with anticipation and the silent awe of twenty thousand souls drawn together under her gaze. In this moment, Stormhold itself seemed to hold its breath, united by the presence of its queen and the unspoken promise of what lay ahead.

Draped in dark robes edged with silver, Queen Karak stood tall and immovable, her figure framed by the torchlight that cast sharp shadows over her face, accentuating the fierce angles of her jaw and brow. Her hair, pulled back to reveal her striking features, lent her an austere beauty that was as daunting as it was mesmerising. Her gaze swept over the crowd, catching every eye, absorbing their mingled emotions—curiosity, unease, reverence. She let the silence stretch, letting each person feel the weight of her presence, the unyielding authority she wielded with effortless command. In that pause, she was more than their queen; she was the embodiment of Stormhold itself, a power as enduring and formidable as the mountain under which they stood.

Karak waited, letting the silence stretch until it was almost a living thing between herself and the thousands before her. She could scarcely comprehend the sight—a sea of faces, more people than she had ever imagined, all waiting for her, ready to hang on her every breath. She felt the weight of their anticipation pressing upon her, and as she steadied herself, memories flooded her mind, drawn up from the dark depths of the past.

She thought of Ivar's penultimate moments—the shock and agony etched into his face as he realised his life was slipping from his grasp, the betrayal that had turned his gaze to stone. She remembered the massacre that followed in the prison cells, their heads now staring down at her from spikes. Alone after she returned to her chambers, the grim silence rang in her ears. Her dress, once pristine, was saturated with blood, the fabric weighed down, clinging to her as if demanding that she feel the burden of what she had done.

In the tall oval mirror, she had stared, transfixed, at her own reflection—a creature more beast than queen. The dress was no longer regal but monstrous, dripping and sodden. For the first time, the weight of her choices had crashed upon her, and the tears had come, unbidden, cutting streaks down her blood-stained face, her beauty marred by brutality. She had looked like one of the savages from the Drylands, her hair thick and matted, the crimson staining her pale skin like a grotesque mask. Shaking, she had torn the dress from her body, standing bare before the mirror, her skin goose-pimpled in the chilled air, feeling exposed and raw beneath the heavy judgement of her own gaze.

Her emerald eyes had met her reflection's, a stark contrast to the blood clinging to her body, and for a moment, she had glimpsed a monstrous version of herself—a warning of what she might become, a woman consumed by power, inescapably darkened by it. Had it merely been her own reflection, or a prophecy of what she would turn into? That image had haunted her, echoing in her mind with each step toward her throne.

Now, standing before her people, the silence of thousands washed over her like an icy wave, grounding her once again in the present. She straightened, lifting her chin, and let the enormity of the moment fill her. She had transformed herself for this, had sacrificed everything—and as she looked out upon her people, she knew, with unflinching certainty, that it had all been worth it.

Her arm fell to her side, and her voice rang out, clear and resolute, slicing through the silence. "People of Nordon, strength to you" she began, her tone firm yet steeped in reverence. "Today, we stand at the dawn of a new era. Ours is a kingdom that has endured the ravages of time, forged in battle, and strengthened by the unbreakable spirit of our people. Yet it is in the shadow of great trials and unthinkable losses that we are truly bound together, stronger than ever."

She swept her gaze over the crowd, her eyes alight with a fervent, almost fierce admiration. "I look upon you all and feel a wonder that no treasure could equal. Not the gold buried deep within our mountains nor the spoils of a hundred victories could compare to the sight of you—united, unyielding, unmatched." She paused, letting the silence deepen as her words settled over them. "If I could, I would lend you my very eyes, that you might glimpse the vision I see before me. You are the heart and strength of Nordon, a force that no enemy can diminish."

She paused, letting the weight of her words sink in, her gaze sweeping across the assembly. A sea of nodding faces stretched out before her, thousands signalling their approval, their expressions resolute and eager. The crowd's murmurs wove together into a low, unified hum, a pulse of agreement and anticipation that filled the hall. Her words had stirred something within them—a shared sense of pride and purpose—and as they waited, eyes fixed upon their queen, an electric anticipation hovered in the air, ready to erupt with whatever proclamation might follow.

“Yet it is with the deepest grievance I stand before you today.” Her voice softened, carrying a weight that stilled the murmurs and drew the crowd into a breathless pause. “You have all heard the news—our beloved king, my husband, was cruelly taken from us.” She paused, her eyes hardening as her voice dropped, thick with sorrow and anger. “What makes it unbearable, what cuts to the heart, is that his death was not one of natural passing. Not the peace of age, nor the honour of a battlefield that would have been worthy of him. No, his life was stolen—stolen by those he trusted most. His so-called loyal men.” Her voice rose, breaking on the final words, which she shouted, raw with fury. “Loyal, trusted men!”

The final words reverberated through the hall, igniting a visceral reaction from the crowd. Her arm extended, and with an accusing finger, she pointed at the grisly display—the heads of the traitors mounted on spikes, their pale, battered faces frozen in agony. The sight struck a nerve, unleashing a fierce wave of anger that spread like fire through the gathered thousands. A roar of outrage swelled, boos and shouts echoing off the stone walls, each voice brimming with betrayal and righteous fury. The noise intensified as those in the back strained forward, eyes narrowing, fists clenched in shared resentment toward the treachery.

As the crowd seethed, Karak felt her nerves ease, replaced by a new, intoxicating sense of power. They were with her, bound to her by shared pain and vengeance, fastened to her every word. She straightened, letting their energy flow into her, and for the first time, she truly felt the exhilaration of holding them all in the palm of her hand.

Raising a commanding hand high into the air, she waited as the crowd’s furious roar ebbed into tense silence. “Good people,” she called, her voice clear and resolute, “it was not only your king who suffered at the hands of this cruel betrayal. Birger—beloved friend to many of you, and loyal steward of this city—was also taken from us.” A fresh wave of boos erupted, louder and more impassioned, at the mention of the well-loved figure.

Before the noise could crest, she raised her voice, cutting through the clamour with a strength that instantly commanded their attention. “And our cherished Warden, Ansgar, fell to their treachery as well. Even I..." She paused, her voice tightening, a spark of fierce vulnerability flashing in her eyes. "Even I was meant to drink their poison." She tried to continue, but her words were swallowed by the crowd's response—a furious, raw sound that surged forth, filling the hall with a fury that was almost palpable.

This time, she did not silence them. Instead, she allowed the noise to swell, a sea of boos and outraged shouts that washed over her, lingering as a display of their loyalty and relief that she had survived the traitors' deadly plot. She stood, letting herself absorb the intensity of their fervour, feeling their affection wrap around her like armour. She indulged in the moment, savouring the power in their devotion and the realisation that they, too, were bound to her by loss—and by vengeance.

Finally, the noise ebbed, and a hush fell over the crowd, each face turned toward their queen, anticipation gleaming in their eyes. Queen Karak's voice rang out, steady and powerful, commanding every ear. "Good people, the heads you see before you are those of men who have paid for their betrayal. But let me tell you this," she continued, her voice dropping to a fierce, ominous tone, "every snake has a head, every dagger a wielder. This brutal plot was not born in isolation. It was the design of one man, a serpent hidden among us, supported by his loyal traitors."

The crowd's murmurs quieted into a tense, almost uneasy silence as their curiosity reached a fevered pitch. She allowed the pause to linger, fuelling the suspense until every eye in the hall was locked on her, waiting for her next words. "We have spared this man," she declared, her voice taking on a chilling edge, "so that you may see with your own eyes the one responsible for this treachery."

A ripple of shock moved through the crowd, the quiet deepening as thousands of breaths were held in anticipation. She let the silence draw out, savouring the moment before delivering her final words, each one echoing with measured finality. "Good people, I give you Grolin, the Killer of Kings."

A collective gasp swept through the hall, the name reverberating like a shockwave as eyes widened, faces twisted in anger and disbelief, and every gaze turned, searching for the one who had dared to betray their realm so completely.

Several guards hauled a wooden cart into view, the wheels creaking under its weight as it rolled forward. Shackled in the stocks atop it was a small, hunched man—Grolin, the traitor. His face was a mask of fear and defeat, a pitiful sight against the seething fury that greeted him. The crowd erupted at once, a pulse of rage sweeping through them, surging them forward in a violent wave that strained against the soldiers holding the line. Deep, guttural boos echoed through the hall, filling every corner as the cart passed, the front rows spitting in disgust and loathing.

A lone, furious voice bellowed from the throng, "Kill him!" The cry struck like a spark, and within moments, a relentless chant swept through the crowd, thousands of voices rising in a pounding rhythm: "Kill him! Kill him!"

Karak watched, feeling a heady satisfaction bloom within her. Any lingering nerves were gone, dissolved in the fiery devotion of her people. The fear of accusation, of blame, seemed a distant, conquered obstacle. She let the scene stretch before her, soaking in the heated atmosphere, savouring the power that filled the hall like thick smoke. This was her moment, a memory she would carry forever—a crowning affirmation of her rule, hard-won and absolute. Her patience, the sacrifices made, and the lives lost along the way, all coalesced into this instant of triumph.

This is my time, she thought, her eyes gleaming as she gazed upon her people. My kingdom. My people.

At last, she lifted her hand, a silent command that rippled through the crowd like a wave. The chants subsided, voices falling away as all eyes turned back to her, the silence thick with anticipation. The cart rolled onward toward the sunken arena pit, Grolin's figure small and helpless beneath the weight of the crowd's collective rage.

"Good people," she called, her voice resonating through the hall, steady and unyielding, "what sort of queen would I be if I did not heed the voices of my people?" Her words hung in the air, each one a promise forged in steel. "Let me put command to your cries and grant you the justice you demand."

A fierce light shone in her eyes as she spoke, her hand still raised in authority, her presence both queen and executioner. In this moment, her power was absolute, bound to her people by the vengeance they craved. The crowd erupted once more, their voices a thunderous roar that shook the very walls of the hall. Their cheers and cries swelled into a deafening crescendo, raw with the anticipation of vengeance. The cart continued its slow, rattling journey until it reached the arena's centre, where it finally came to a halt, surrounded by the gaze of thousands. The people of Nordon looked on, their queen standing tall above them, poised to deliver the justice they had demanded.

Karak let her voice harden, a steely edge cutting through the hall. “Disloyalty, cowardice, treachery—these will have no place in my kingdom.”

With a subtle motion, Karak signalled to the guards surrounding the cart. One guard stepped forward, drawing a spear—a gleaming iron lance that he thrust firmly into the sand. He followed with a short sword, which he placed beside the spear, the blade glinting in the fires that surrounded the hall. Lastly, he untethered a shield from his back, letting it fall to the ground with a dull thud, a final offering of arms. The second guard moved to Grolin, his hands deftly unbinding the condemned man’s shackles. The crowd stilled, their voices fading into a tense, expectant silence, each breath held as they watched Grolin, now free for a fleeting moment.

His figure was pitiful—a broken man clothed in tattered rags, his skin bruised and scraped, bearing the marks of his harsh confinement. Every scrape, every tear in his clothing spoke of the merciless justice he had already faced, and yet, a more profound reckoning awaited him.

Karak’s voice cut through the silence, cold and sharp as steel. “Here stands one who dared defy the throne,” she proclaimed, each word precise and unyielding. “A man who chose rebellion over loyalty, who sought to dismantle the strength and stability of Nordon.” Her gaze travelled over the sea of faces, lingering on those who seemed caught between awe and apprehension. “Let this sight be burned into your memory—a reminder to all who might think to betray their queen. Disloyalty will be met with consequences.” The crowd were ready, waiting with baited breath, "good people, I have spoken at length and now is the time our good king has his justice.”

The guards exited the pit, leaving Grolin a solitary figure, dwarfed by the arena’s vastness, alone with his meagre arsenal. Across the expanse, a massive iron gate creaked open, each inch dragging up slowly, as if savouring the moment. Grolin, desperate yet defiant, lifted his gaze to the Queen, a glare of pure hatred crossing his bruised face. His expression—a final act of rebellion—was met with a deafening chorus of boos, countless accusing faces staring down at him from above, casting judgement he could no longer escape. Ignoring their jeers, he snatched up the sword and shield, his movements quick but trembling.

He turned toward the black maw of the gate, gazing into its depths. The entrance gaped open, silent and impenetrable, showing nothing of what lay beyond. For a fleeting moment, relief washed over him—a fragile, almost hopeful pause. But then, from deep within the shadows, a subtle shift, a barely perceptible cloud of dust, drifted into the open arena. Something moved inside the darkness, watching him, calculating.

The crowd stilled; their attention riveted to Grolin's every movement. Fear seized him, and in his desperation, he ran to the wall, fingers clawing at its rough surface, trying futilely to climb. His efforts only scratched the stone. Realising the futility, he bolted to the gate he had entered through, pounding on it with both fists, pleading with the guards who merely looked on, smirking at his anguish. Laughter rippled through the crowd, cold and merciless, a grim reminder that mercy was long past.

Suddenly, a massive, guttural roar tore through the hall, reverberating from the pit to the high arches above. Grolin froze, his face drained of colour as he turned slowly, terror dawning in his eyes. From the shadows of the gate thundered long, heavy strides, and then, emerging into the light, came a giant—a monstrous figure towering nearly twenty feet tall, hurtling toward him with terrifying speed.

Paralyzed by terror, Grolin barely had time to react before a colossal, three-fingered hand slammed into him. The force sent him flying across the arena, his body colliding with the stone wall in a sickening thud. A scream tore from his throat, raw with pain, as he crumpled to the ground, his ribs and pelvis shattered. Gasping, he looked up, his vision blurred by agony, only to see the giant looming over him.

A grotesque mockery of humanity. Its massive, square head loomed, completely bald and blotched with patches of sickly pale skin, a face marred by thin slits for nostrils where a nose should have been. Two fierce, predatory eyes glared from beneath a thick, overhanging brow—more beast than man, glinting with a savage intelligence. Its enormous shoulders gave way to long, stocky arms that hung low, ending in brutish hands capable of crushing a man with ease. Long, thick legs supported its hulking frame, making its torso seem almost secondary to its towering height.

The creature let out another ferocious roar, flecks of saliva spraying in Grolin's direction, its rage palpable. The pit had become his tomb, and he was left broken and defenceless before the beast that now claimed him as prey.

Its deafening roar came to an abrupt, chilling end, leaving the air heavy with menace. Grolin spotted his fallen sword to his right, his fingers clawing toward it in desperation just as the giant's immense hand swept him up, its grip crushing his body. Air was forced from his lungs, his attempted scream silenced as the giant's hold tightened, squeezing the life from him. With the last of his strength, he raised the sword, gripping it with both hands and driving the blade down into the giant's thick skin. The tip pierced through, and a dark rivulet of blood ran down its massive hand.

With a growl of pain, the giant released him, letting Grolin's battered body hit the ground in a painful jolt. His ribs screamed in agony, but the will to survive pushed him forward. Crawling, he managed to rise, bent and half-collapsed to his right side, his fingers locked tightly around the sword hilt, his gaze fixed on the creature looming above.

The giant snorted, thick mucus spraying from its nostrils as it snarled, then unleashed a roar so powerful that Grolin and much of the crowd clapped hands over their ears, their faces twisted in pain. The beast lunged, leaping a full fifteen feet through the air and landing with a ground-shaking thud, towering over Grolin as it prepared to strike again. Its grotesque face loomed mere feet from the man, mouth open in a feral snarl that showed jagged, yellowed teeth.

Summoning the last remnants of his strength, Grolin raised the sword, thrusting it upward with every ounce of his fury and desperation. The blade drove into the giant's eye, and black liquid sprayed out like ink, splattering onto the arena floor. A howl of agony erupted from the creature, staggering it backward as it clutched at its wound. Grolin, battered but somehow rose slowly, the sword now slick in his hands, his grip unwavering.

A sudden cheer rose from the crowd, their bloodthirsty excitement reaching a fever pitch. Even here, even facing the condemned, they could not help but root for the man's tenacity. It was always the way—no matter the crime, no matter the sentence, the crowd craved a fight, cheering on the defiance and resilience of the one doomed to die.

Grolin staggered, his face drawn with exhaustion, and dropped heavily to one knee. His battered body, broken and bloodied, was finally betraying him. He gasped for air, each breath a ragged, desperate struggle as his crushed lungs strained to pull in the stale arena air. Summoning courage was no longer an option; every ounce of his strength was spent, leaving him drained and defenceless.

The giant watched him with a cold, unfeeling gaze, its one good eye gleaming with cruel satisfaction. In a swift, silent motion, the beast's massive arm shot forward, seizing Grolin in a grip that left him no chance to resist. This time, his limbs hung limp, his body too weakened to fight back as the giant's fingers tightened around him once more, squeezing until his vision blurred.

A low, menacing snarl rumbled from the giant's throat as it bent its enormous head down. In a brutal, animalistic gesture, it opened its mouth wide and clamped its jagged teeth around Grolin's exposed head. With a sickening crunch, the giant tore it free, blood cascading down its chin in thick, dark rivulets as it lifted its gaze to the crowd, the lifeless body still dangling from its fist.

A cheer rose briefly, instinctive and horrified, but quickly died as the reality of the scene settled over the crowd. The sight was more than they had anticipated—a gruesome spectacle that left many turning away, discomfort twisting in their stomachs. Karak, too, felt a wave of revulsion wash over her, a churning unease she could not ignore as she watched the giant descend into a savage, unrestrained feast. The thrill of power she had felt moments before faded, replaced by a bitter taste that lingered as the beast devoured the remains of the man who had dared defy her.

After a few moments, Karak's expression hardened, and with a subtle nod to a distant guard, she signalled for the display to end. Her voice rang out, steady and authoritative. "A valiant effort, good people, from a coward—a so-called slayer of kings. But now, let us close the arena and spare ourselves the sight of the giant's feast."

At her command, unseen mechanisms stirred to life, and the massive stone roof above the pit began to grind forward, casting shadows over the blood-stained sand as it slowly closed off the grisly scene below. The sound of stone on stone filled the hall, muffling the faint, sickening noises that drifted up from the arena floor, until finally, the chamber was sealed from view.

The crowd let out a collective sigh, tension melting into a release as bodies pressed forward, filling the newly opened space. The brutal display had left its mark, and many exchanged uneasy glances, their excitement tempered by the savagery they had witnessed. Karak stood tall above them, her face composed, though a flicker of something unreadable lingered in her gaze as she looked down at her people, reclaiming their attention and their loyalty.

"Now," she continued, her voice calm yet unyielding, "I would have us look upon brighter horizons. Let us look forward." She paused, a hint of warmth in her expression. "Tonight, keep your coin in your pocket, for the crown has filled the alehouses with drink. Feast, celebrate the dawn of a new age—an age free from corruption and deceit. And know this," her voice rose, steady and resolute, "this is an age where we shall no longer sit idle beneath our mountain."

The crowd began to murmur, a low rumble of approval and anticipation sweeping through them as they leaned in, eager for her every word.

"Nordon is strong," she declared, her voice resounding through the hall like the echo of steel, "but our strength must grow. I have forged alliances, binding Nordon's future to those who share our vision—who honour strength and loyalty, just as we do." Her gaze swept over her newly assembled council, lingering on Gunnar, her words carrying the weight of a vow.

"Together," she continued, her tone thick with resolve, "we will secure a future worthy of Nordon's legacy. A future our children will be proud to inherit." She let the moment linger, then lifted her chin, her eyes blazing as she spoke. "This is Nordon's future," she declared, her words crackling with conviction. "A kingdom where strength and loyalty are rewarded. A kingdom that will no longer cower under the mountain, nodding politely to lesser nations."

Her voice rose, each word striking like a hammer upon an anvil. "We are Nordon, forged in the image of our ancestors—unbreakable, undaunted. Let others remember. Let them tremble before our might."

The murmur rippled louder through the crowd, a collective intake of breath as Queen Karak's words took root, sparking something fierce and unyielding in each listener. Faces once shadowed with doubt softened, eyes wide and shining with pride that swelled and intensified under her gaze. For a heartbeat, no one moved, held in place by the raw conviction in her voice, as if entranced by the vision she had ignited. Then, a lone voice broke the silence, rising into a fierce cheer that cut through the hall, and like fire catching dry wood, others joined in until the space erupted into thunderous applause and roaring acclamation.

Some chanted her name, voices hoarse with emotion, while others thrust their fists into the air, faces fierce and alive with loyalty and newfound purpose. They straightened, shoulders back, eyes bright with the fiery vision she had shared—a vision that now burned within them, too. In that moment, any remaining doubt dissolved in the face of an unbreakable unity, the people of Stormhold transformed into a single, unstoppable force, bound to their queen and ready to march into whatever future she had prepared for them.

They looked up at Karak, not merely as a woman who had claimed the throne, but as a force of nature—a leader forged in the fire of their shared ambition and steeled by an iron will. Her authority radiated from her in waves, unquestionable and absolute, casting its spell over the hall. Karak's council exchanged approving glances, each one visibly pleased by the raw power and loyalty her words had summoned. Even Gunnar inclined his head slightly, a rare flicker of respect crossing his features as he observed her command over the crowd.

As she stepped back, signalling the close of her address, a deep, settling satisfaction filled her. Today, she had not only solidified her rule and secured the loyalty of her council, but she had reminded the people of Stormhold where true power lay—beneath her unwavering rule, a vision that would reshape the kingdom and etch her name into the legacy of its history.

Beside her, Gunnar leaned in, his voice a low, conspiratorial murmur. "You know," he remarked, his tone edged with reluctant admiration, "I didn't think I'd enjoy this display as much as I did. But I see now why they follow you. You rule with more than words, Karak. You rule with fear—and they respect that."

She turned to meet his gaze, her expression unwavering, eyes hard and resolute. "Fear has its place," she replied, her voice equally low but firm. "But true loyalty is built on understanding. They understand what I offer them—and what I demand in return." Her words held a quiet strength, a reminder that her rule was forged not just from fear, but from a bond deeper and more enduring.

A faint smile touched Gunnar's lips, a glimmer of interest sparking in his eyes as he regarded her. "Then perhaps this union of ours will prove more... engaging than I expected."

Karak allowed herself the smallest of smiles, barely a shift in her steely expression. "I have no intention of disappointing you, Gunnar. Nor will I disappoint Nordon."

With that, she turned from him and descended the steps of the platform, her stride steady and commanding, her council and Gunnar falling into step behind her. As they moved through the hall, the crowd's whispers grew, echoing in her wake—voices filled with awe, admiration, and a respect newly cemented. She had given them a glimpse of what it meant to rule with strength and purpose, leaving no room for doubt that Nordon's future lay, unshakably, in her hands.

# THE QUEEN REGNANT CHAPTER TWENTY SEVEN

Thoren walked briskly through the quieted court, a thick leather-bound tome tucked under his arm. He glanced at the empty hall, normally bustling with activity, and could not help but smirk, imagining how many sore heads were nursing themselves in darkened rooms across the city. The Queen's gesture of free ale for the people had been a brilliant move, though he knew it would take a bite out of the coffers. He adjusted his grip on the tome and strode forward, his footsteps echoing softly as he approached the council chamber at the far end of the hall.

Two royal guards stood flanking the heavy iron doors, their eyes trained forward. As he neared, their gazes shifted to him, and with practised precision, they moved in unison, their powerful arms pressing against the iron handles. The doors swung open, the hinges whispering rather than groaning, a testament to the care taken in Stormhold's maintenance even after years of use.

The council chamber opened before him, a room of grand yet unpretentious design. At the centre sat a large oak table, its edges smoothed but left uncarved, following the natural contours of the wood. The surface gleamed with fresh oil, the grain catching the light from the fire pits positioned at either end of the room. Warmth radiated from the pits, casting dancing shadows across the walls and providing a welcoming glow that softened the otherwise austere atmosphere.

Twelve high-backed chairs stood around the table, their oiled wood matching the table in richness. Each chair had been crafted from the same oak; its sturdy design intended as much for comfort as for the weight of responsibility that came with each seat. Thoren's fingers brushed along the wood of the chair nearest him as he moved toward his designated spot, noting its solid craftsmanship. These were new additions—another touch Karak had brought to the chamber since assuming her role, along with the flags of Nordon and the sigils of her house.

He glanced upward, taking in the banners draped from the arched ceiling. Every other flag bore the sigil of House Thørn: a deep crimson field emblazoned with a black hammer suspended above an array of ancient black runes, symbols that hinted at both legacy and strength. The flickering light cast shadows on the fabric, making the hammer appear almost as if it were poised to strike. A powerful reminder of their queen's rule, he thought, and a calculated one. She was not simply a monarch seated by inheritance; she was a ruler who held her authority with a relentless grip, unafraid to stamp her identity on every corner of her domain.

As Thoren moved along the table, his gaze fell upon a series of stone figurines positioned in front of each chair, each carved to represent the individuals of the council. He noticed his own immediately, taller than many of the others, a smooth stone figure mounted atop a flat platform, a symbol of his high-standing position in Karak's court. It was meticulously crafted, the stone polished to a sheen that reflected the firelight, adding a quiet dignity to the piece. It was placed close to the top of the table, a position of significance he did not fail to appreciate.

Next to his figurine sat the Queen's symbol: a small stone crown positioned at the head of the table. Its design was simple yet undeniably commanding, much like Karak herself. The placement reminded him of the unspoken hierarchy—she at the head, they at her command. He felt a certain satisfaction, mixed with a caution he had grown accustomed to since being in her service. Karak's council chamber was now fully hers, dressed in the symbols and reminders of her authority.

Thoren settled into his chair, setting the heavy tome before him, its leather cover worn yet well-kept. His fingers drummed idly on its surface as he surveyed the chamber, his eyes tracing over the changes Karak had imposed since her ascension. She had certainly made her mark; the banners, the furnishings, the symbolic figurines—each an unmistakable statement of her authority and vision for Nordon. This was no longer merely a place of governance but a throne room of power and ambition.

About the room stood four royal guards, each stationed silently in a corner, their faces shadowed but alert, their posture rigid and watchful. They wore polished armour, and their hands rested lightly on their weapons, a subtle reminder of the queen's iron resolve. Their presence made it clear—Karak was taking no chances, even here within her inner circle. These men were not ordinary soldiers; they were chosen for their loyalty and ruthlessness, handpicked to ensure no threat could touch her, even from within these walls.

Thoren leaned back, his gaze lingering on the nearest guard, noting the intensity of his stare as he surveyed the room. The guards were more than protection; they were symbols of Karak's vigilance, silent enforcers of her rule, and a warning to those seated at the table. Every council member knew what they meant, loyalty was demanded, betrayal unthinkable. But as he watched, a familiar unease settled over him, tugging at the conflicted loyalties he tried to keep buried.

The night before, amidst the city's celebration, Lady Hilda had sidled up to him, her lips curled in a subtle, knowing smile, her eyes alight with the spark of conspiracy. She had leaned in close, her voice barely a whisper above the revelry. "We have the vial," she had murmured, her tone calculated and soft. "What say you?"

Caught off guard, he had felt the jubilant atmosphere of Stormhold momentarily slip away, replaced by the heavy weight of her words. He remembered the feeling—the city united, a rare cohesion as all eyes turned toward their Queen and her vision for Nordon. Yet here was Lady Hilda, plotting a betrayal that could dismantle the very unity they had achieved, her ambition threatening to plunge the kingdom into chaos.

It had been a question that demanded an answer on the spot, but in those few heartbeats, his mind had raced, contemplating the possibilities. With Karak, his position in court had never been higher; she had granted him respect, status, even influence within the ranks of her closest advisors. But with her out of the way, how far could he reach? The Crown? The thought lingered, tantalising, though it came with the knowledge that failure was unforgivable. Just yesterday, he had witnessed the brutal spectacle of Grolin's execution, an innocent man fed to a beast at Karak's whim. What horrors would she reserve for those who dared openly conspire against her?

In the moment, he had felt the weight of a thousand possibilities, each more dangerous than the last. His ambitions warred with his instincts, leaving him with only a thin veil of a response. "When?" he had asked quietly, masking his uncertainty with a veneer of indifference.

"Tomorrow night, at the feast," she had replied, her gaze fixed upon him, waiting for the slightest nod, a signal of his complicity. He had given it, a subtle, measured tilt of his head, hoping it would buy him time—a nod to satisfy Hilda's impatience without fully committing himself.

Now, sitting in the council chamber under Karak's watchful guard, Thoren felt that small gesture bear down on him like a weight he could not shake. He had manoeuvred his way to power before, but this was no mere political game. The stakes had changed, and each path forward seemed to close around him, carrying a potential for glory or ruin. Betrayal of the Queen was a leap into darkness, a risk that could see him rise—or fall farther than he dared imagine.

At that moment, the heavy iron doors swung open, and the laughter of Ulric and Durin spilled into the chamber, their voices echoing in the otherwise quiet room. They strode in with an easy confidence, Ulric's booming laugh mingling with Durin's sharp chuckle as they teased Rogren, who looked worse for wear, a hand pressed to his temple as he blinked against the firelight, clearly suffering from the excesses of the night before.

Thoren snapped out of his dark thoughts, pulling his mind away from the knot of intrigue that Lady Hilda had tied around him. Standing, he opened his arms with a welcoming grin, the veneer of calm slipping easily over his conflicted thoughts. "Ah, here come the brave survivors of last night's revelry!" he greeted, his tone light, drawing a chuckle from Durin.

Ulric clapped him on the shoulder, his broad frame radiating a warmth that contrasted with the tense formality of the chamber. "The Queen's generosity was a fine excuse to drain half the city's barrels!" he boomed; his eyes gleaming. "And Rogren here did his best to empty them single-handedly."

Rogren groaned, waving them off with a tired grin. "Easy for you to say, Ulric," he muttered, settling heavily into his seat. "You didn't have the brewmaster insisting on that final round."

Durin chuckled, slapping Rogren on the back as he dropped into his own chair. "The last round's what did you in? I'd wager it was the ten before that."

They all shared a laugh, the easy camaraderie filling the room with a warmth that briefly dispelled the underlying tension. Thoren let the moment stretch, savouring the ease among his fellow council members—a fleeting respite from the weight of the choices he faced. Each man took his place at the table, chairs scraping against the floor as they settled in, laughter fading as they adjusted to the gravity of the day's purpose.

Druse and Konan entered next, their solid frames filling the doorway as they paused to greet the two royal guards stationed at their post. The guards exchanged nods, a brief flicker of relaxation breaking their otherwise rigid stances. It was rare for them to acknowledge anyone during duty, but Druse and Konan, with their warrior's bearing and history of loyalty, had earned a respect few others could command.

As Druse and Konan stepped further into the chamber, their presence radiated through the room, drawing the attention of the council members. Their deep voices resonated as they exchanged a few words, rich with camaraderie and mutual respect. Just before parting to take their seats, they clasped arms, a warrior's gesture that spoke volumes without words—a reminder of the strength and unity that lay at the heart of Nordon's inner circle.

Heidi entered last, Sven trailing just behind her, his eyes lowered, shoulders slightly hunched as he followed her lead. Heidi's stride was purposeful, her attention sweeping over the room with a subtle but unmistakable signal. "The Queen is close behind," she announced, her tone low yet carrying easily to each corner of the chamber. "And Gunnar with her."

At her words, the murmurs ceased, the earlier humour dissipating as the council members straightened in their seats, adjusting themselves for the formality Karak's presence required. Thoren felt the shift in the air—the relaxed camaraderie was replaced by a weighty silence that seemed to deepen with each passing second, as if the room itself held its breath in anticipation.

Thoren's familiar unease stirred, the unresolved conflict from his encounter with Lady Hilda clawing back into focus. His gaze flicked over to Sven, who hovered close to Heidi, his sheepish demeanour painfully evident as he fidgeted, casting quick, uncertain glances at the other council members. Sven's presence only heightened the tension, his timid movements a reminder that not all within the council were as confident or secure as they appeared.

Thoren stole a glance around the table, noting the calm, composed faces of his fellow council members, each cloaked in neutrality, yet each harbouring motives and loyalties that were far more complex than what they presented.

The duality of the moment struck him—the lightness of shared humour that had bound them moments ago felt like a distant memory, eclipsed by the knowledge that here, in this chamber, every gesture, every exchange, held the potential to influence or distance. He leaned back into his seat, his fingers resting over the cover of the tome as if to anchor himself. His faint smile faded into an expression of calm, but inwardly, he steeled himself for the discussions that awaited, knowing that with each word spoken, Karak's gaze would assess, measure, and, perhaps, judge them all.

The doors opened for a final time, and a hushed tension fell over the room as Queen Karak entered, her presence commanding and assured. She moved with the measured calm of one entirely aware of the power she held, her eyes scanning the council members, who each straightened instinctively under her watchful regard. Behind her, Gunnar followed, his steps solid and deliberate, his expression as guarded as ever. He broke from her side only to take his seat, settling in with an air of readiness that set the tone for the meeting to come.

Karak paused at the head of the table, her eyes lingering briefly on each council member, her calm demeanour belying the intensity in her gaze. "Good morning, strength to you" she greeted, her voice low but resonant, carrying easily through the chamber. A faint, almost playful glint appeared in her eye as she glanced at Rogren and a few others, adding, "I trust there are a few sore heads this morning?"

A ripple of subdued chuckles moved through the council, the tension lifting slightly as her jest landed. Rogren managed a sheepish grin, and even Thoren found himself smirking, reminded of the shared celebration that had swept the city the night before.

Satisfied, Karak took her seat at the head of the table, her posture poised and controlled, the flicker of warmth already fading as her expression settled back into one of steady authority. She allowed a moment's silence to settle over the room, her presence alone enough to hold their attention. The council members sat with an attentive stillness, awaiting her words. Karak's gaze swept the table one final time before she spoke, her voice clear and unyielding as she began the discussions that would shape the future of Nordon.

"We move south in a fortnight," she began, her voice steady, carrying the weight of certainty that left no room for doubt. "First to Borlong with the merchants, then onward to White Towers. Our preparations must be precise, and there will be no room for missteps." Her eyes swept the table, pausing briefly on each council member in turn, her look sharp and unyielding, a silent demand for their focus.

"We have an opportunity before us that cannot be squandered," she continued, her tone resolute. "This is a journey not just of trade, but of conquest—a move that will secure Nordon's place beyond the mountain." Her words were laden with the gravity of their purpose, casting a subtle tension across the room as her vision unfolded before them.

"You are my eyes, my ears, my very command in my absence," she said, her expression hardening as her attention landed on each of them. "I brought you together for that very purpose."

A brief silence followed, the weight of her words settling over the council, each member straightening slightly, aware of the responsibility placed upon them. Then, her focus shifted to Sven, who appeared to shrink slightly under her watchful stare.

"Sven," she prompted, her voice firm but not unkind, "an estimate of what was spent last night?"

Sven cleared his throat, his eyes darting nervously around the table before he managed to answer. "Well, Your Majesty... based on the reports from the taverns and alehouses, I'd estimate around forty to fifty thousand gold pieces were spent last night to keep the celebrations going."

A faint smile tugged at the corner of Karak's mouth. "Generous indeed," she replied, her tone laced with a hint of amusement. "Consider it an investment in loyalty. Our people will remember this gesture." She paused, her look steady as it returned to Sven. "And how much do we have remaining in the coffers?"

Sven shifted, clearing his throat before responding. "As of the latest audit, Your Majesty, we have approximately six hundred thousand gold pieces at our disposal. A significant amount has already been allocated toward preparations for the journey south and to cover the recent reinforcements."

"How much for the merchants?" Karak continued to quiz.

Sven swallowed, gathering his thoughts before replying. "For the merchants, Your Majesty, we've allocated fifty thousand gold pieces to cover initial investments—provisions, trade goods, and protection fees along the route. Additional funds have been set aside to secure favourable terms in Borlong, should the need arise."

Karak nodded thoughtfully; her gaze fixed intently on Sven. "Fifty thousand for the merchants, we'll need to more than double that," she replied, her tone resolute. "Our storages of timber must be swelled. Every coin must work to strengthen our position, and Borlong will work with us given the new... circumstances. I will ensure it."

A glint of determination flashed in her eyes, her voice hardening. "We'll need enough to endure several winters, and when this venture is done, not another gold piece will go through their greasy hands. This alliance is temporary, one of convenience, nothing more. When we leave Borlong, I will need another hundred thousand gold pieces delivered by boat to White Harbour. It must be ready by the sixth moon, for I intend to arrive at White Towers shortly after. Can that be done?"

Sven hesitated, his brow furrowing as he calculated the logistics. The entire council felt the weight of her words, the tight timeline and precise demands filling the room with a renewed intensity. He cleared his throat, careful to mask any sign of doubt. "Your Majesty, it's... ambitious," he began, glancing down at the table for a moment before meeting her gaze again. "But with the resources we have allocated and additional oversight, I believe we can make it happen. We'll need to prioritise the miners' guild and the smelting guild," Sven replied, his voice steady though a faint line of worry creased his brow.

Karak's attention shifted to Rogren, whose hand had been resting on his temple as he quietly nursed the remnants of last night's excess. Straightening under her scrutiny, he cleared his throat, the weight of her question drawing him fully to attention. "What will you need to meet this demand, Rogren?"

Rogren blinked, his focus sharpening as he considered her question. "Your Majesty, with the scale you're asking, I'll need more hands in the mines and additional forges running at full tilt. And that means diverting labour from other projects—likely doubling shifts for the season, at the very least."

Karak's expression remained steady, though a spark of approval glinted in her eyes. "The miners and forges will have what they need. I want this prioritised above all else," she replied firmly. "With increased production and reserves, we're laying the foundation for our expansion—and ensuring Nordon has what it needs for the future."

Her gaze shifted to Ulric, his posture straightening as her words settled over him. "Ulric," she commanded, "make sure that is your focus. Rogren will need his labour and the forges burning at all hours."

Ulric gave a resolute nod, his mouth setting into a determined line. "Understood, Your Majesty. I'll pull labour from the northern quarters and reassign the idle hands from the watch posts around the halls. They'll be put to work in the mines and at the forges—wherever Rogren needs them."

Karak's eyes gleamed with satisfaction. "Good. I expect this done, there's no margin for error; every piece of metal refined, every beam of timber cut, is essential."

Ulric glanced at Rogren, then back to Karak, his voice steady. "The forges will burn night and day, and the mines will run deeper than ever before. Nordon will have its reserves."

A faint smile touched her lips. "I trust you to make it happen," she replied.

"Durin, what of the arrests last night?" Karak asked, her gaze shifting to the wiry councillor, his usual sharp wit tempered by the weight of his report.

Durin gave a brisk nod, clearing his throat before responding. "Your Majesty, we made several arrests during the celebrations. Thirteen individuals in total—most were locals involved in drunken brawls that got out of hand. Of those, ten were simply caught up in fights around the alehouses. They'll likely sober up with little memory of their offences."

He hesitated, his expression hardening. "The remaining three, however, are former soldiers. They've been voicing complaints for weeks now about the state of their pensions and the Queen's recent focus on new alliances. Last night, with the drink flowing, their grievances turned more… animated."

Karak's gaze narrowed, a flicker of irritation crossing her face. "I see. And do they understand why they've been detained?"

Durin nodded. "Yes, Your Majesty. They're aware they overstepped, and I believe a brief sentence—or perhaps a reminder of who they serve—will quiet their complaints, at least publicly."

Karak leaned back; her expression thoughtful. "Keep them in the cells until morning, then see them released with a warning. I want it clear that loyalty is valued, but disorder will not be tolerated—especially from those who have worn Nordon's colours." She turned her focus to Druse, who sat with his arms folded, listening intently. "Do you agree, Druse? I assume you may know these men?"

Druse's brow furrowed as he considered her words, his gaze shifting slightly as if he could already see the faces of the detained soldiers. "Aye, Your Majesty," he replied, his voice low and steady. "I know them. They served well once, but a few years off the battlefield can dull a man's sense of purpose. A drink or two and some misguided pride can lead them astray."

He leaned forward, his expression resolute. "But they're good men, deep down. A reminder of discipline will set them straight. I'll speak to them myself—let them know that Nordon's honour demands more of them than a tavern brawl."

Karak nodded, satisfied. "Then see to it, Druse. Remind them of the pride they once held and make it clear that we expect no less from them now."

Druse gave a slight nod, his gaze steady. "It'll be done, Your Majesty. They'll understand what's expected—and what they risk should they fail again."

Karak turned her attention to Thoren, a subtle gesture accompanying her words. "Thoren, how did the other lords and nobles take to the display last night?" she asked, a slight flick of her hand gesturing to the brutal execution that had unfolded before them all.

Thoren shifted in his seat, a measured look crossing his face as he recalled the scene. "Your Majesty," he began, his tone respectful yet edged with intrigue, "for most of the lords and nobles, it was exactly what they expected—perhaps even what they needed. Grolin's punishment served as a stark reminder of your authority and the consequences of betrayal. I sensed a mix of awe and... satisfaction from many."

He paused, choosing his next words carefully. "However, a few expressed a measure of discomfort. They are cautious, perhaps, and questioned—privately—if the severity was entirely warranted." He cast a glance around the room, his gaze lingering on Durin and Ulric, who both listened intently. "But none spoke openly against it. If anything, they were reminded of where the true power in Nordon lies."

Karak's lips curved into a faint, knowing smile. "Good. Let them be uncomfortable," she replied, her tone unyielding. "Discomfort breeds vigilance. The purpose of such a display was not just to punish but to show that treachery will not be tolerated. If they have doubts, let them keep them private."

Thoren inclined his head in agreement. "Of course, Your Majesty. And for the majority, it has only strengthened their loyalty. Many would rather be on your side than risk sharing Grolin's fate."

Karak's gaze hardened slightly. "Loyalty won by fear has its place, but I will not rule on fear alone. If they understand that I value loyalty as much as I despise betrayal, we may yet achieve something lasting. I trust you will keep close watch on those with doubts."

Thoren nodded. "Consider it done. I'll keep a careful eye on those who may need... additional reminders of their loyalty."

"And Heidi," Karak said, her eyes shifting to the shrewd councilwoman, "you are to be my voice of reason. Are there any concerns you have heard or wish to add?"

Heidi straightened slightly, a thoughtful look passing over her face as she considered the question. "Your Majesty," she began carefully, "the display last night has, as Thoren mentioned, solidified loyalty in many, but it has also stoked some whispers among the more... prudent lords. They fear the implications of such decisive actions—wondering if, perhaps, the realm could tip into too much aggression. These are voices that value stability above all else, and the execution left them uneasy."

Karak's gaze remained steady, absorbing Heidi's words. Heidi continued; her tone respectful but firm. "While I have no doubt your message reached those who needed to hear it, some may require reassurance. They need to understand that while justice in Nordon is swift and unyielding, you also value the unity of the realm. If we balance these shows of strength with moments of reason, they'll come to see you not just as a queen of force, but one who guides her people with wisdom."

Karak's expression softened slightly; a flicker of appreciation evident in her eyes. "Wise words, Heidi," she replied. "I have no desire to rule through fear alone, nor to foster an atmosphere of constant unease. Strength will command respect, but stability will foster loyalty. These lords and nobles must understand that the path we tread is not one of recklessness, but of intention."

Heidi inclined her head, her eyes calm yet sharp. "Then I will see to it that those with doubts hear this message, Your Majesty. They will come to know that your rule is one of both justice and balance."

Karak gave a faint nod of approval. "Good. Remind them that loyalty to Nordon is not a matter of comfort, but of conviction. This is good; I am pleased with what I hear." She paused, her gaze shifting to Druse. "Now, onto pressing matters. Druse, I will need fifty of your best men to protect our journey south. Konan, of course, will be accompanying me and will lead them in your absence. I need them ready to march in two weeks."

Druse straightened, a glint of pride sparking in his eyes at the Queen's trust in his warriors. "Consider it done, Your Majesty," he replied, his voice solid as iron. "I'll choose only the most seasoned fighters—the ones who know discipline and can handle the journey. They'll be fully equipped and prepared to follow Konan's lead."

Karak's expression held a trace of approval as she regarded Druse. "Good. I'll expect a report from you on their readiness before we depart. The roads south are long, and our progress must be swift and without delay. We cannot afford weakness in this endeavour."

Druse inclined his head, resolute. "I'll see that they're battle-ready and unwavering in their loyalty. These will be men you can depend on, Your Majesty."

A faint smile played at the corners of Karak's lips. "I trust your judgement, Druse. Ensure they know the honour it is to protect their Queen. We'll need strength and vigilance as we travel."

"Once in Borlong, I will play the good Queen," Karak continued, a hint of calculated amusement in her voice. "They'll think me a willing ally, perhaps even submissive, when I come bearing double the gold they expect. With luck, by the time I'm done, I hope to be in White Towers by the eighth moon's pass. All being well, King Ruben will have heard of our torrents of gold flowing in the East and want his share. The gates will open to us—of that, I'm certain." She turned to Gunnar; her eyes sharp. "Gunnar, on the eighth moon, I want your ships ready. How many will we need?"

Gunnar leaned forward; his face thoughtful as he weighed her request. "To be fully prepared, Your Majesty, thirty ships should suffice. But fifty ships—kept out of Ruben's sight—would provide us a stronger assurance. We could hold them in the inlet to the north of the Hundred Isles, just beyond the Beacon's view. It will be a half-day voyage to White Towers from there with a good wind."

Karak's eyes gleamed with satisfaction, a faint smile gracing her lips. "Fifty ships it is, then. Keep them hidden. This will be a joint venture, and I expect precision. How many men do you need to see this through?"

Gunnar inclined his head, calculating quickly. "For this venture, fifty ships, I'd require three thousand fighters, equipped for both sea and land. I have the ships, but I can only commit five hundred men—the rest must remain at our borders to keep them secure."

Karak's eyes narrowed thoughtfully, shifting to Druse. "Druse, what can we spare while ensuring Stormhold's defences remain intact?"

Druse leaned forward, his voice steady and measured. "I can contribute three hundred axemen, seasoned fighters, each of them eager for a chance to join this campaign. We also have a thousand shield-bearers—seven hundred of whom I'd be comfortable deploying to this mission, the remaining three hundred needed here to fortify Stormhold. As for our thousand men-at-arms, I'd suggest leaving them stationed here to maintain our defences. But with some coin from the coffers, I can have three hundred fresh recruits trained and ready in three moons' time."

Karak nodded, absorbing the numbers with a calculating gaze. Her attention shifted to Sven, her tone firm. "Sven, can you find the gold for these recruits?"

Sven's brow furrowed, his fingers tapping lightly on the table. "You ask much, Your Majesty. We'll do what we can to reallocate funds."

Karak's eyes sharpened, her tone leaving no room for hesitation. "You can or you will, Sven?"

Sven's eyes lifted to meet hers, and he nodded, swallowing as he spoke. "It will be done, Your Majesty."

Satisfied, Karak's focus returned to Druse. "Take two hundred from our thousand swords here in Stormhold; that will leave the Royal Guard and more than a thousand soldiers to secure our home. Even with these contributions, we are short a thousand men," she noted, her attention shifting back to Gunnar. "Can it be done?"

Gunnar leaned back, his eyes calculating as he spoke. "That's two thousand fighting men, which means we'll need roughly thirty-five ships to carry the force effectively. It will be my command," he added, a hint of a smirk tugging at the corner of his mouth. "I know the seas better than you mountain dwellers, and if we're to succeed, your men will respect that."

A brief silence settled over the council as Gunnar's words hung in the air, his confidence undeniable. Karak's gaze remained steady, a glint of approval in her eyes as she assessed his self-assured demeanour. "Very well, Gunnar," she replied, her tone laced with quiet authority. "The command at sea is yours—but remember, this is a coordinated effort.

Once we reach land, my orders will be final."

Gunnar inclined his head slightly, his expression respectful but resolute. "Understood, Your Majesty. I'll see the fleet through any waters and deliver our men to White Towers, prepared and ready. Your soldiers will know they have a captain who commands the seas as well as any."

"I will need an extra boat," Karak continued, her voice calm yet charged with purpose. "One that will crew few but hold much. It will carry a hundred thousand gold pieces—enough to give King Ruben the illusion of control. Our safe passage into his keep, a distraction of his choosing. But once that boat passes The Beacon..." She paused, her gaze intent on Gunnar, "...have your men seize it. They must be swift and unseen, for if we control The Beacon, your ships can pass into White Harbour undetected, right under his nose."

A ripple of intrigue crossed the council, each member envisioning the potential of such a bold move. Gunnar's eyes gleamed with approval, and he leaned forward, nodding. "A subtle but powerful play, Your Majesty. The Beacon is the pride of White Towers' defences. If we control it, Ruben won't have time to raise a single alarm. Our fleet would sail straight into White Harbour before he even knew we were there."

Karak's lips curved into a faint, calculating smile. "Precisely. By the time he realises, it will be too late. When the moment comes, we will make sure the gates to White Harbour are open, and Nordon's arrival will be unstoppable."

Gunnar inclined his head, a glint of excitement in his eyes. "The men will be ready, silent and unseen as shadows. The Beacon will be ours, and White Towers will be open for our forces."

Around the table, the council members exchanged tense, approving glances, each grasping the daring simplicity of Karak's plan. This was no mere alliance but a carefully crafted deception, one that would place them at the heart of White Towers without a single battle fought.

"Good, it is settled," Karak said, her voice resonating with finality. She glanced around the table, her gaze sweeping over her advisors. "Is there anything to add?"

Druse shifted slightly; his expression thoughtful. "Only a reminder, Your Majesty—our men must be made fully aware of their roles. They must understand the importance of silence and discipline. One loose word could unravel everything."

Karak nodded, a flicker of appreciation in her eyes. "Agreed, Druse. Select captains who can instil that discipline. Any man who cannot keep silent has no place in this venture."

Ulric leaned forward; his tone cautious but firm. "And once we reach White Towers, should we encounter resistance beyond our expectations... do we have a plan in place to secure our withdrawal?"

Karak's eyes remained unwavering. "The priority will be to hold The Beacon. If we succeed, retreat will not be necessary. But should the situation require it, every man will have orders for fallback points, and Gunnar's ships will be positioned for swift retreat." She let her attention linger on each council member. "Failure is not an option, but preparation is our strength."

Sven gave a slow nod, a hint of unease in his expression. "Then I'll ensure that the resources and provisions for fallback are arranged as well. We'll have what we need, no matter the outcome."

Satisfied, Karak leaned back, allowing a brief moment of silence to settle over the room. She could feel the weight of the decision solidify, each council member's commitment steeling the plan.

"Very well," Karak declared, her voice firm and resonant, filling the chamber with a sense of finality. "We know our course. Take your leave and set action to your path. Each of you knows what must be done—ensure there are no missteps."

Her gaze swept over each council member, holding their attention for a beat longer, the intensity of her command settling into each of them. The weight of her words lingered in the air, an unspoken reminder of the significance of their roles and the precision required to see their plans to fruition.

The council members rose, chairs scraping softly against the stone floor as each took a moment to incline their heads in respect. One by one, they filed out in a solemn line, their expressions resolute, shoulders squared with the weight of what lay ahead. Some exchanged brief, knowing glances, silently acknowledging the gravity of the decisions made here. As they departed, the echoes of their footsteps gradually faded down the stone corridor, until only the stillness of the chamber remained.

Karak sat unmoving, her gaze fixed on the polished wood of the table, her fingers tracing its grain in thoughtful silence. The faint, smoky scent of the fire pits lingered in the air, mingling with the cold stone of the chamber, a sharp contrast to the fierce warmth of the council's earlier deliberations. Alone now, the full weight of her plan settled upon her—no longer spoken of in confident tones or analysed with cool logic, but present, heavy, and absolute. This was a path she had forged with precise ambition, and it would shape the very future of Nordon.

She allowed herself a rare moment of stillness, her breathing steady as she considered each piece of the strategy they had laid, each calculated risk. The banners of Nordon, draped from the high arches above, cast long shadows across the chamber, their deep crimson and black blending into the dimness, symbols of her authority. Here, in the solitude of the council room, it was only her resolve that echoed back to her, reminding her of the burden she bore.

The silence lingered, thick and reflective, when suddenly, a soft, measured knock broke through the quiet. The sound echoed across the chamber, deliberate and calm, like the prelude to a storm. Karak's fingers stilled against the polished wood of the table, her eyes rising toward the heavy iron doors.

"Enter," she called, her voice steady yet edged with curiosity.

The doors creaked open, their weight groaning slightly as a figure stepped inside, cloaked in shadow. For a moment, the dim light from the corridor concealed their features, leaving only the suggestion of broad shoulders and a deliberate gait. The figure moved with quiet confidence, boots striking the stone floor with a steady rhythm.

Karak's expression remained unreadable; her gaze sharp as it followed the figure's approach. "I trust you have something important to say," she said, her voice cool and commanding, though her eyes betrayed a flicker of intrigue.

The figure paused just inside the chamber, their stance purposeful, yet revealing nothing of their intent. The faint, flickering firelight cast fleeting shadows across the room, obscuring more than it revealed.

"Important enough to disturb your solitude, Your Majesty," the visitor replied, their tone even, calm, and impossible to place.

# THE QUEEN REGNANT CHAPTER TWENTY EIGHT

The feasting hall glowed with revelry, laughter rising like a steady tide above the clinking of goblets. Gunnar's men mingled with the soldiers of Stormhold, voices blending as they shared tales and raised their cups. Long tables were laden with rich platters of meats and bread, roasted pheasant and thick cuts of ham, all glistening under the warm light of the torches. Dark wine flowed freely, filling goblets faster than they could be emptied, while mugs of ale were clashed together in raucous cheers.

At the far end of the hall, a bard took up his lute, striking a bold, ringing note that cut through the noise. His fingers danced along the strings as he began a lively tune, the melody echoing from wall to wall, commanding attention. His voice lifted, clear and bright:

*"Raise your cups to Stormhold's might,*
*To the winds that carry and seas that fight,*
*To blades that cut and hammers that pound,*
*And hearts as fierce as battlegrounds!"*

The men took up the chorus, roaring along, their voices merging with the bards in a raw, thundering sound that seemed to shake the very walls:

*"Stormhold stands, proud and tall,*
*In every hearth, in every hall,*
*A pledge to keep, come blood or flame,*
*For Stormhold's honour, for its name!"*

Laughter rang out as Gunnar's men leaned into the song, slinging arms over Stormhold shoulders, their shared allegiance—or the wine—blurring any past grudges. They beat their fists on the table in rhythm, tankards raised high, creating a thunderous percussion that filled the hall. The Queen watched from her place at the high table, her goblet untouched as her gaze swept over the revelry with a slight, satisfied smile. She sat as a pillar of composure amid the wild cheer, her eyes as sharp and steady as a blade, taking in each face and every word with careful attention.

A soldier caught her eye, lifting his goblet in her direction with a reverent nod, and she inclined her head with an approving smile. Queen Karak leaned toward Thoren, who sat beside her, sharing a quiet word. Her voice, though soft, was filled with a warmth that complemented the intensity of her watchful gaze. For tonight, Stormhold was unified, a rare moment of peace and celebration in their midst.

But as the song swelled again, and the men's voices thundered with pride, there was an undeniable edge in the Queen's eyes—a look that suggested she was as much a hunter as a ruler, always listening, always waiting.

Thoren leaned in closer, lowering his voice to be heard above the chorus of men singing, "Do you need anything, my Queen? I must relieve myself."

Karak glanced at him; her eyes bright with the subtle glint of amusement. "Go on, Thoren," she replied, a faint smile gracing her lips.

With a nod and a bow, Thoren rose, weaving through the laughter and swaying figures with skilful ease. The soldiers and sailors sang with increasing fervour, some breaking off into their own rounds of cheering and toasting. He moved carefully past Gunnar's men, who leaned heavily on one another, clinking tankards and exchanging tales of sea battles and narrow escapes, oblivious to his passing.

As he neared the edge of the hall, the voices behind him blended into a deep, rolling chorus, each note reverberating against the high stone walls. He slipped out of the main hall and down a quieter corridor, the lively sounds growing muffled as he put distance between himself and the revelry.

In the shadows beyond the hall's warmth, Thoren felt his heartbeat steady, his mind shifting from the ease of the celebration to a colder, more calculated purpose. He made his way to the small alcove near the far end of the corridor, a well-kept door marking the entrance to the lavatory. Passing through, he paused to take a deep breath, letting the solitude calm him before he relieved himself, momentarily free from the clamour of song and cheer.

But as he stood there, footsteps approached, soft yet unmistakable against the stone floor. A faint rustling, barely audible above the echoes of revelry, pricked at his senses, and he turned slightly, catching sight of a shadow stretching across the wall. Balgin.

Thoren gritted his teeth, straightening as Balgin entered, his figure partially obscured by the dim light. Without a word of greeting, Balgin stepped closer, his face set in an expression of grim purpose.

“Tonight is the night,” Balgin whispered, his voice low, sharp. “You’re on the Queen’s table, Thoren. The moment’s come to slip her the poison.” His gaze was piercing, leaving no room for hesitation. “It’ll be easy—one quick movement, and you’re done.”

Thoren looked away, feigning indifference as he adjusted his cloak. “And if it isn’t so simple?” he replied, his voice tight. “The Queen isn’t one to let her guard slip.”

Balgin’s mouth curled into a faint, humourless smile. “Don’t make it harder than it has to be,” he said, producing a small vial from his cloak, the glass dark and cold. “She won’t notice a thing, not in the middle of all this celebration.”

Thoren’s eyes fell on the vial, the contents swirling within as if alive. His hand wavered, but then, with a look of resignation, he extended his palm and took it. The glass felt cool, unsettlingly solid in his grasp. For a moment, he simply held it, weighing the full weight of what it meant.

Balgin gave a curt nod, his voice dropping to a menacing whisper. “Make no mistake, Thoren. This chance won’t come again—and if you falter...” He left the sentence hanging, its unspoken threat clear.

Thoren clenched his jaw and slipped the vial into the inside pocket of his cloak, feeling it press against his chest like a cold, accusatory stone. He forced a nod, not trusting himself to meet Balgin’s eyes. With a final look, Balgin turned and slipped away, leaving Thoren alone with the small vial and a heart that pounded louder than the revelry beyond the stone walls.

Thoren tightened his belt, steeling himself as he prepared to rejoin the hall. The distant sounds of laughter and song seemed to swell, pulling him reluctantly back to his purpose. As he turned down the corridor, he caught sight of Balgin once more, lingering by the edge of the hall's entryway. Balgin’s eyes met his with a glint of approval, a brief nod acknowledging the weight of the task now set upon Thoren’s shoulders.

But Balgin’s expression quickly shifted, his eyes drifting past Thoren with an almost practised subtlety. Thoren followed his gaze, and his heart gave a sharp twist as he found Hilda and Aldric standing together near the entrance. They were deep in conversation, but as though on cue, their eyes lifted, glancing in Thoren's direction, a spark of silent understanding passing between them. The look they exchanged seemed almost choreographed, as if each of them had been waiting for this precise moment.

Thoren felt a chill run down his spine. This was not just a suggestion or an opportunity; this was a conspiracy intricately woven, each player fulfilling a carefully assigned role. And now, he realised with a sinking clarity, he was the one carrying the final piece.

Pushing down the unease clawing at him, Thoren gave a stiff nod to Hilda and Aldric, slipping past them without a word as he re-entered the hall. The warmth and noise enveloped him again, but he could no longer hear the cheer of celebration without feeling its underlying tension. His eyes drifted to the Queen's table, her goblet shimmering in the glow of torchlight, waiting for his next move.

As Thoren wove through the crowd, the laughter and cheer felt muted, distant, like sounds heard through water. Each step seemed slower, heavier, as though the air itself had thickened around him. He could feel the eyes of his co-conspirators on him, sharp and unrelenting, tracking his every movement across the hall.

Balgin's gaze lingered from the shadows near the entrance, his expression unreadable but his intent unmistakable. Thoren dared a glance back toward Hilda and Aldric, their expressions equally masked, yet their stares burned with expectation, urging him onward. It was as if invisible strings pulled him forward, each conspirator tightening the tension until there would be no escape.

Every familiar face he passed seemed to carry a hidden knowledge, every laugh tinged with a hint of suspicion. Even the soldiers, locked arm-in-arm and swaying with song, seemed to watch him, their eyes glancing up as he passed, adding to the suffocating sense of scrutiny.

Ahead, the Queen's table loomed closer, the goblet gleaming on the table like an invitation—no, an order. It waited, a silent promise and a threat. And in that moment, Thoren realised that he was no longer a man among friends and allies. He was a pawn, a tool, the one piece that could set the whole plan in motion... or bring it all crashing down.

Thoren forced himself to wear an easy smile, nodding and offering quick glances to his fellow councillors as he approached. Each exchanged look felt like a performance, a mask he wore to keep suspicion at bay. He noted how relaxed they seemed, lost in their conversations and unaware of the tension simmering beneath the surface.

Ulric leaned back, laughing heartily at something Durin had said, his booming voice filling the hall. Even Sven, typically so tightly wound, seemed more at ease, his shoulders relaxed, a rare smile playing at his lips as he listened to Rogren recount some tale from the mines. For a fleeting moment, Thoren wondered if any of them had caught wind of the plot—or if the peace they felt was genuine, an oblivious calm before the storm.

He forced his eyes to linger only briefly on each of them, careful to appear casual, not wanting his expression to betray him. But as he neared his seat beside the Queen, he felt the coiled tension within him winding tighter. His conspirators' glances weighed heavily on him, but the ease of his fellow councillors was almost worse.

As Thoren took his seat beside her, Queen Karak turned to him with a faint smile. "Better now?" she asked, her tone light but her attention keen, studying him with a touch more interest than usual.

Thoren gave a polite chuckle, hoping it sounded natural. "Much better, my Queen," he replied, settling into his chair and reaching for his goblet as a way to steady himself. The Queen's eyes lingered on him for a heartbeat longer, her expression unreadable, before she turned her attention back to the table.

He felt a prickle of unease at her question, at the way she had seemed to take note of his brief absence. He forced himself to relax, to take a measured sip of wine, hoping the warmth of it would quell the cold knot forming in his chest. With every passing moment, the vial in his pocket seemed to press more insistently against him, a reminder of the task that lay ahead.

As Thoren set his goblet down, his gaze shifted across the room. The three conspirators—Balgin, Hilda, and Aldric—had slipped into the hall, weaving among the guests like shadows. They moved with a careful ease, each feigning casual interest, but their eyes occasionally darted to the high table, monitoring Thoren's every move. Their proximity tonight was unusual, closer than normal, as if they were positioning themselves to witness the outcome firsthand.

Balgin lingered near a group of soldiers, nodding along to their tales but occasionally casting a sidelong glance in Thoren's direction. Hilda leaned gracefully against a pillar, her face a perfect mask of charm as she laughed softly with a nobleman. Yet Thoren could see the subtle shift in her stance, her focus honed on the high table, on him. Aldric, for his part, positioned himself within earshot of the councillors, a faint smile on his lips as if he were merely enjoying the evening's conversations.

A chill ran down Thoren's spine. They were waiting, each poised like vultures circling prey, ready to swoop in should he falter. At that moment, he noticed the Queen's attention had shifted, her gaze fixed on Konan as they spoke in low, familiar tones. She took a sip from her goblet, leaving it unguarded as her hand returned it to the table. Her focus remained on her brother, her laughter quiet but genuine, the kind of warmth she reserved for only a few.

Thoren's eyes fell on her goblet, still half-full, sitting innocently on the table, an opening waiting to be taken. The conspirators' stares seemed to press in on him, the pressure mounting. He knew the moment had come —the opportunity lay before him, unguarded and fleeting.

Thoren took a steadying breath, letting it exhale through his nose, and felt the weight of tension slip from his shoulders, like rock tumbling down a mountainside. Without the faintest disguise, he pulled the vial from his cloak, holding it openly before him. "My Queen," he said, his voice steady. Karak turned to him, her eyes flashing with interest as he held out the vial, plainly visible to all. "Would you like to do the honours, or should I?"

A knowing smile spread across her face. "Please, Thoren—be my guest."

With a nod, Thoren uncorked the vial, tilting it above her goblet, the viscous poison slipping into the rich red wine. He tapped the vial gently, ensuring the last of the liquid merged with the wine. Karak watched, her gaze cool and unwavering, and then, with a graceful motion, she clasped the goblet and rose to her feet.

She began to swirl the glass, watching the liquid blend as she raised her voice to the hall. "Good folk," she called, her tone clear and commanding.

The hall fell into a tense silence as the bard's song ceased, and all eyes turned toward her. She gave a subtle nod to the royal guards stationed around the room, and in an instant, they shifted their positions. Several moved to each exit, closing the doors and barring them, forming an impenetrable wall of watchful guards.

Gunnar rose, his face taut with suspicion, his eyes darting between the guards and the Queen. For a moment, he appeared ready to react, but Karak met his gaze with a calm, almost tender expression. "Be calm, Gunnar," she said, her voice warm but firm. "You are my future kin. Come, give up your seat and sit beside me, if only for a moment."

Reluctantly, Gunnar nodded, pulling a chair from the neighbouring table and settling himself beside her. He cast her a wary glance, his hand never straying far from his blade, but he made no move to interrupt her.

Karak looked down at the goblet in her hand, swirling the wine once more. "This wine, my betrothed, is now a drink of death," she started, her voice steady as if she were talking directly to Gunnar and not the halls audience. "Were I to drink this, in the days that followed, I would fall ill. By week's end, I would succumb, drawing my last breath—and with me, all our dreams and designs would collapse into dust, brought low by a single, poisonous sip."

Her attention lingered on the goblet, the warmth in her expression fading, replaced by an intensity that silenced the hall. She lifted her eyes, her voice cutting through the tense air.

"Balgin, Hilda, Aldric," she commanded, her tone cold and unyielding. "Take a seat at my table."

The three conspirators froze, their faces blanching as Karak's words rang out, each syllable pressing down on them like an iron weight. Balgin's eyes flickered with a fleeting, desperate calculation, as if already seeking a path of escape, but he found none. Hilda's hands trembled, her carefully crafted composure splintering as her gaze darted between Karak and the soldiers blocking each exit. Aldric looked down, swallowing hard, his lips pressed into a thin line as if fearing even his breath might betray him.

The hall held its breath, the charged silence amplifying the slow, reluctant steps they took toward the Queen's table. The room itself seemed to close in around them with every inch they covered, as though the walls, the guards, and the crowd bore witness to their unmasking. Each footfall echoed like the toll of a bell, a grim procession drawing them nearer to the woman they had conspired to dethrone.

Karak watched them approach, her expression unwavering, her fingers wrapped firmly around the poisoned goblet. The deadly liquid within caught the torchlight, shimmering as she tilted it ever so slightly, a silent reminder of the consequence awaiting those who dared betray her.

As the conspirators reached the table, they could not meet her gaze. Their shame and fear radiated like a palpable force, and the Queen allowed the tension to stretch, her unblinking eyes cold, dissecting each of them. Her stillness was more terrifying than any raised voice could have been —a calm before the storm, promising retribution wrapped in the most exquisite restraint.

The three conspirators exchanged glances, their faces pale and drawn as they took their seats at the Queen's table, forced to sit in silence. The hall around them held its breath, and even the flickering torches seemed to burn with a colder light. They could feel the weight of the room's gaze upon them, the watchful eyes of the soldiers and nobles bearing down, waiting for the Queen's judgement.

Karak's eyes glinted with a fierce blend of authority and amusement as she surveyed the three conspirators before her, each pale and tense under her scrutiny. She allowed the silence to stretch, savouring the weight of their fear before she finally spoke.

"I believe we have a game to play," she announced, her voice unwavering, cutting through the thick tension that clung to the hall. Her eyes shifted to Gunnar, who sat just a few paces away, watchful but silent. "Gunnar," she said, her tone softening ever so slightly, "may I borrow your blade?"

Gunnar hesitated, his brow furrowing. The hall seemed to hold its breath, all eyes on him, but after a moment, he gave her a respectful nod, his expression caught somewhere between admiration and apprehension. With a single, fluid motion, he unbuckled the blade from his side, handing it to her with a low, measured bow.

Karak received the dagger, her fingers brushing over the hilt as she examined its weight and balance. The steel gleamed in the torchlight, cold and unyielding, mirroring the resolve in her eyes. "We shall use Gunnar's blade as our instrument of fate," she declared, her voice carrying through the room, each word thick with purpose.

She placed the dagger in the centre of the table, positioning it with care, as though it were a sacred relic. The conspirators flinched; their eyes fixed on the blade as though it might spring to life at any moment. The weapon lay there, silent yet powerful, embodying both judgement and reprisal.

Karak let her hand linger on the hilt for a moment, her attention shifting from one conspirator to the next. "This blade will determine who among you faces the wrath of your own design," she continued, a hint of sardonic pleasure creeping into her tone. "And I shall be the one to set it spinning."

A thin, twisted smile graced her lips as she met each conspirator's stare, the finality of her decision unmistakable. This was no mere punishment; it was a display of control, of ruthless precision. With the blade before them, each conspirator felt the crushing weight of their fate—now in the hands of the very Queen they had sought to betray.

Balgin exchanged nervous glances with Hilda and Aldric, their bravado slipping away as the reality of the situation set in. They could not hide the tremor in their hands nor the sheen of sweat breaking out on their brows.

Karak's expression turned serious. "But there's a catch. Before you drink, you will confess your sins. Speak the truth of your betrayal, and perhaps I will show mercy." Her gaze piercing, as if daring them to defy her.

With a flick of her wrist, Karak set the blade spinning. It whirled, glinting under the light as the conspirators watched it dance, their breaths held in collective suspense. Time seemed to stretch, and the air thickened with tension as the blade slowed, wobbling on its axis before finally coming to a halt.

The blade pointed directly at Balgin.

His face drained of colour as he met Karak's unyielding gaze, his mouth opening and closing as he struggled to find his words. "I—I was only following orders," he stammered, the bravado in his voice cracking beneath her steely scrutiny.

"Is that so?" Karak replied, her tone as cold as winter frost. "Then speak clearly, Balgin. What were these orders? Who else was involved?"

Balgin swallowed hard, the words caught in his throat. "I did it for the realm! To save us from chaos," he blurted out, desperation clawing at his voice. "I thought... I thought you were leading us to ruin!"

Karak leaned forward, her eyes narrowing to slits, the firelight casting a chilling gleam in their depths. "And now, Balgin, you will pay the price for your treachery. Drink."

His hands trembling uncontrollably, Balgin grasped the goblet, his fingers slipping on its stem as he brought it to his lips. The hall fell into a taut silence, every soul watching as he tipped the glass back, the rich liquid sliding down his throat. He gasped, his eyes widening in horror as realisation struck—his fate sealed by his own hand. The poison coursed through him like icy tendrils, wrapping around his senses and draining him of all warmth.

"Please, my Queen!" he croaked, falling to his knees. "Forgive me!"

Karak's gaze held steady, her expression as cold and unyielding as the blade before her. "There is no forgiveness for betrayal," she said quietly, her voice carrying the weight of finality. "Only consequences."

As Balgin writhed on the floor, Hilda's face twisted in terror. "No! This isn't how it was supposed to happen!" she cried, clinging to the table's edge in desperation. But Karak silenced her with a single, piercing glare.

A dark, twisted smile crossed the Queen's face. "Yes, Hilda, I see the plan isn't quite as you imagined," she said, letting her words drip with cold amusement. "You see, Thoren still has the slow poison in his pocket." She cast a sidelong glance at Thoren, who remained motionless, his hand unconsciously brushing the vial within his cloak.

"When I discovered your treachery, I thought I'd make a simple substitution," she continued, lifting the goblet with a casual elegance. "A swifter poison—something that would bring immediate consequences." She tilted the goblet, watching the last dregs of the wine swirl within. "Now then, where were we?"

With a flick of her wrist, she spun Gunnar's blade once more, the weapon's edge catching the torchlight as it whirled across the table. Hilda and Aldric flinched, terror etched into their faces as they locked eyes, each knowing that their turn was coming.

The blade seemed to spin for an eternity, each rotation drawing the conspirators tighter into its grip. Hilda and Aldric sat rigid, every pass of the blade sending ripples of tension through their bodies. When it finally began to slow, it completed one final loop, then crawled past the pair, pointing straight at Sven.

Hilda and Aldric exhaled, relief flashing across their faces—though they knew it would be short-lived.

Queen Karak's eyes gleamed with amusement as she looked at Sven, whose face had gone white, his gaze locked on the blade as if it might come alive and strike him down. She leaned forward, her smile as unsettling as the game she was playing. "Well, Sven," she drawled, her voice laced with dark humour, "don't suppose you'd care to take a turn?"

Sven swallowed hard, terror twisting his features, his knuckles white as he gripped the edge of the table. For a fleeting moment, it seemed as if he expected this was his end—that she would make him pay now, before them all.

But Karak let out a soft, chilling laugh, shaking her head. "No, I didn't think so," she said, her tone mocking yet dismissive, as if his life were worth nothing more than the flick of her wrist. "Let us spin again."

She reached out and set the blade into motion once more. It spun with a haunting rhythm, drawing every eye in the room, its slow revolutions each a reminder of the deadly game they were trapped in. The conspirators held their breath, knowing that their fleeting relief might soon turn to despair once more.

Glinting ominously the blade began to slow, its speed waning, until finally it shuddered to a halt, pointing directly at Aldric.

Aldric's face went ashen, his mouth opening in a silent gasp as he stared at the blade, unable to tear his gaze away. The hall seemed to grow colder, the weight of judgement settling over him like a heavy shroud.

Karak's expression remained calm, but there was a cruel satisfaction in her eyes. She leaned forward, tapping the edge of the goblet with her finger, the poison-laced wine still swirling within. "Well, Aldric," she said, her voice soft but merciless, "it seems fate has spoken."

Aldric looked up, desperation swimming in his eyes. "My Queen... please, I..." His voice trailed off, words failing him as he searched for some sliver of mercy.

But Karak's eyes hardened. "Speak now, Aldric," she commanded, her tone icy. "Confess your crimes. Explain to me—and to those who once called you an ally—why you chose betrayal."

Aldric's voice trembled as he began to speak, every word dripping with fear. "I only wanted... I thought if I joined them, I could prevent... to stop the madness," he stammered, his eyes darting helplessly around the room. "I was wrong, my Queen. I was foolish—"

"Drink," Karak interrupted, her tone final, cutting off his pleas as sharply as a blade.

With shaking hands, Aldric lifted the goblet, his fingers barely able to keep a steady grip. He closed his eyes, muttering a final, futile prayer under his breath, then tipped the glass, the poisoned wine slipping past his lips. The hall remained silent, each person watching, captivated and horrified, as Aldric swallowed his fate.

The effect was swift, the poison taking hold as his face contorted in pain. His breath turned shallow, his eyes wide with terror, before he crumpled forward, the life draining from him even as the silence stretched on.

Karak's fingers brushed the hilt of the blade with deliberate elegance, her eyes locking onto Hilda's with a look that froze the room. Without breaking that gaze, Karak gave the dagger a slight flick of her wrist, setting it spinning one last time. The hall held its collective breath, every eye fixed on the whirling blade, the anticipation nearly unbearable.

The dagger began to slow, its point drifting, passing by Hilda. A flicker of hope crossed her face. But Karak, with a subtle twist of her hand, adjusted the tilt, letting the blade roll back until it pointed unerringly at Hilda.

Hilda's scream shattered the silence, her voice piercing through the hall in a desperate, raw cry. "No! You can't!" she shrieked, panic seizing her as she leaned forward, hands outstretched as though pleading would reverse her fate. "I did it for you, Karak! I wanted to help you!"

Karak's expression remained unyielding; her gaze sharp as a honed edge. "Your intentions mean nothing to me, Hilda," she replied, her voice as cold and cutting as the steel in her grip. "You conspired against me, betrayed the trust of this court, and for that, you shall join your companions."

Hilda's pleas dissolved into sobs, each desperate breath betraying the realisation that there was no mercy left to beg for. The guards flanking her closed in, their hands firm on her shoulders as they forced her trembling frame back into her seat.

The goblet was placed before her, its dark liquid a grim reminder of the fate that awaited those who dared cross the Queen. Hilda's hands shook uncontrollably as she grasped the stem, her fingers slipping on the glass, her face a mask of horror. She cast one last, pleading glance toward Karak, her eyes wide with terror, but the Queen's expression remained stone, devoid of pity.

With a final, shuddering breath, Hilda lifted the goblet to her lips. The hall watched in absolute silence as she took a hesitant sip, the bitter taste of betrayal sealing her doom. The poison worked swiftly, her face contorting in agony as she choked, her body trembling before she collapsed to the floor, her final, desperate gasp echoing through the hall.

Karak looked down at the three lifeless bodies sprawled on the stone floor, the silence around her thick and heavy. She released a steady breath, the weight of her authority filled the hall, the lingering tension a reminder of her unchallenged power.

Without a word, she lifted her eyes to the crowd gathered before her, meeting each stare that dared to look her way. Her expression softened only slightly, her look sharp but satisfied. She had made her point, and there was no mistaking the message she'd carved into the very air of the hall.

After a moment, she turned to her council, her voice calm and measured. "See that the bodies are removed," she commanded. "And let this hall be restored to its former state. The stains of treason shall not linger here."

The guards stepped forward, moving with practised efficiency, lifting each body with a reverent silence that suited the room's solemnity. The councillors, still pale with the residue of shock, kept their heads bowed, all too aware of the reminder etched into their memories.

As the bodies were carried away and the doors reopened, Karak turned back to the table, she lifted a fresh goblet and filled its contents, then raised it high.

"To loyalty," she declared, her voice clear and unwavering. "To strength." She drank deeply, the wine rich and dark, her poise a symbol of the unyielding rule she had just affirmed.

# THE ASSASSIN CHAPTER TWENTY NINE

Dakeard had been observing the stable for months now, carefully tracking the rhythms of the old stable master and his clumsy young apprentice. Every detail was scrutinised: the times they rose, the way they moved through the morning routine, even the subtle exchanges between them that betrayed familiarity and habit. Dakeard, a patient hunter, allowed himself no indulgence of haste; each day spent watching was another piece in his mental puzzle, fitting together an understanding of their lives and the stable's vulnerabilities.

On his first infiltration, he had carried a long, cumbersome ladder—an unfortunate tool that grated against his instincts. Its weight and bulk slowed him, and the clattering rungs felt like blaring horns in the quiet night. But once he had scaled the high stone wall and dropped onto the other side, his irritation dissipated. He found himself standing in a shadowed stretch of the garden, thick with ivy that sprawled over the walls like nature's own camouflage. For Dakeard, it was an unexpected gift.

The ivy, so dense and tangled, provided him with the ideal cover. He could slip through its leaves with barely a sound, hidden from sight and nearly imperceptible. Within days, he had refined his method: a simple coil of rope tied firmly to one of the ivy's thicker roots at the base. Now he could scale the wall swiftly, quietly, leaving no trace behind. The ladder, awkward and too visible for his liking, was left discarded in a nearby thicket. The rope—silent and efficient—was a professional's choice, blending utility with subtlety.

From his concealed vantage point, Dakeard almost marvelled at the oversight. Did the lord genuinely believe his estate so secure, so impervious, that he allowed this wild ivy to flourish unchecked? He nearly pitied the lord's ignorance. To leave such a glaring weakness exposed was foolish, bordering on arrogance. But perhaps, he thought with a smirk, the lord had simply never encountered someone like him—a seasoned shadow who saw opportunity where others saw only foliage.

The ivy's depth proved invaluable. Its thick leaves and twisted branches created a natural shroud, a shield that allowed Dakeard to observe without fear of detection. Hidden within its verdant depths, he could remain still as stone, his outline vanishing into the greenery, with only the faintest slivers of light slipping through to reach him. Though his view of the stables was partially obscured, it was enough; he could glimpse the stable doors, the flicker of movement within, and the figures of his two unwitting subjects going about their routine.

The garden's keepers rarely ventured to this neglected section. Their work focused on the more presentable parts of the estate, where the manicured lawns and sculpted hedges lined the paths visible from the manor's windows. When they did approach, their steps were careless, eyes fixed on the flowers and shrubs they tended, paying no mind to the overgrown ivy. More than once, Dakeard watched as they wandered within mere feet of his hiding place, blissfully ignorant of the shadowed figure concealed inches away. He listened to their idle chatter, their complaints about the morning chill or the afternoon's endless tasks, and noted the irony: these men, employed to maintain the lord's sanctuary, were oblivious to the hunter lying within their midst.

To them, the ivy was simply overgrowth, an inconvenience in need of pruning. To Dakeard, it was a fortress of shadows, a vantage point from which he could strike when the moment was right.

With the ivy's thick cover concealing him, Dakeard moved through the estate like a ghost, slipping in and out of the grounds at will. His routine visits allowed him to study his prey from every angle, each watchful observation adding to his mental dossier on the stable master and his young apprentice. The old man was a model of habit, his every action bound to a strict schedule. Without fail, he took his lunch at the same time each day, stepping away from the stables and leaving the boy alone. This rigid predictability pleased Dakeard; it was like watching the inner workings of a finely tuned clock, each tick bringing him closer to the perfect moment to strike.

The boy, however, was less predictable. His behaviour was erratic, his movements unmeasured and impulsive. Some days, he would disappear for long stretches, reappearing only after dusk. But one thing was constant: the boy never lunched with the old man. Always, he was left behind, solitary in the stable's shadowed quiet, tending to his tasks in a way that spoke of both diligence and inexperience. It was a vulnerability —a delicate fracture in the stable's daily rhythm—that Dakeard intended to exploit.

This job was different from his usual assignments. His regular clientele were lesser men with simpler requests, tasks that required neither finesse nor patience. But this—this was work for the Lord of Kadun himself, the most influential figure in the land. Such commissions came rarely, if at all, and Dakeard felt the thrill of it. The lord had paid handsomely for the boy's silent removal, and for Dakeard, this was no mere task; it was an opportunity. If he handled it with precision, with the professionalism that set him apart, it would be the first of many lucrative favours. His profile would rise; his reputation would echo through the circles of the powerful.

The prospect tasted sweet on his tongue, the promise of future business waiting just beyond this job. It was more than a kill—it was a carefully laid step up the ladder, and he would climb it without hesitation.

The plan was straightforward, but brilliantly layered. If the boy were to disappear under suspicious circumstances, the first assumption would be a random accident or worse, a targeted act that might link back to the Lord himself. That was unacceptable. No, Dakeard needed a scapegoat—a convenient suspect with motive and means, someone close enough to the boy to make the scenario plausible.

His gaze had quickly landed on the old stable master, a bitter man whose disdain for the boy was palpable even from Dakeard's distant vantage point. Over the weeks, he had watched as the old man's ire flared, his sharp words biting into the boy with the force of a blade. Every snapped order, every raised hand clutching that heavy, sharpened pitchfork, served as evidence that could be twisted to suit Dakeard's purpose. The man had made a habit of brandishing the pitchfork, thrusting it threateningly in the boy's direction when his temper frayed, though never with real intent to harm—at least, not yet.

But if the boy were to be found dead, his body marred with puncture wounds in a way that unmistakably suggested the pitchfork, the blame would practically place itself. Dakeard could already envision the murmurs that would spread through the estate, the quick glances shared among workers who had witnessed the stable master's ill-tempered outbursts. Suspicion would mount like a fire catching dry timber, fuelled by whispers of the old man's long-simmering frustration.

The beauty of it lay in the simplicity. Dakeard would not need to manufacture a motive; the stable master's treatment of the boy had already done that. All he had to do was leave the right trail—a few well-placed wounds, the pitchfork subtly smeared with blood or left discarded nearby, as if in haste. The old man would be the perfect fall, a fool whose blind temper had painted him guilty long before Dakeard set his plan in motion.

Satisfied, Dakeard allowed himself a thin smile. The Lord would have his request fulfilled, and Dakeard would leave no trace of his hand in the deed. His work would be clean, seamless, the mark of a professional who understood that an invisible kill was far more valuable than a simple death. And in the end, the Lord of Kadun would be blameless, shielded by a scapegoat who would never see the trap until it was too late.

It was an hour before dawn, the world lay shrouded in the murky darkness just before the sun breached the tall forests of Kadun. The garden was still, a hushed sanctuary broken only by the soft warble of early birds and the gentle whisper of a breeze stirring the leaves. Dakeard crouched low, his breath slow and measured, blending seamlessly with the earth around him. Beneath him, the damp soil shifted, and he noticed a thin worm pushing through the surface, wriggling free from its underground refuge.

He reached down and pinched it between his fingers, raising it to eye level. The tiny creature twisted and squirmed, desperate to escape, its movements instinctive but futile. Dakeard observed it with the detached curiosity of a man accustomed to watching life cling to its last, fleeting moments. Above, a nest of chicks chirped impatiently, hungry for the meal they expected with each dawn.

With a cold smile, he let the worm fall into their nest, watching as the chicks erupted in frenzied excitement, tiny beaks snapping and tearing. The worm barely touched the bottom before it was claimed, devoured in moments by creatures too young to understand the violence of survival. The sight pleased him, a reminder of nature's indifference—a truth he understood well. The weak fell prey to the strong, a lesson the old stable master and the boy would soon learn in their own way.

Turning his gaze back to the stables, Dakeard felt the anticipation settle over him like a second skin. The building stood alone, wrapped in shadows that would soon surrender to the first light of dawn. But for now, it was his domain—a silent stage waiting for him to set his plan in motion. Today was a day he dealt death, and he felt a certain satisfaction in that knowledge. The world was quiet, awaiting the change he would bring, unaware that death had already begun its approach from the shadows.

He calculated he had forty minutes before the old stable master would begin his morning routine, hauling fresh hay and replenishing the water troughs. The timing was precise, and Dakeard thrived on precision.

Easing out from the tangled ivy, he stepped into the open air, the cool dawn breeze brushing his face. For a moment, he allowed himself to savour the peace of the early morning, the faint glimmer of light beginning to touch the sky, casting the garden in a quiet glow. But as always, just before he moved toward his next kill, his mind drifted back to his first.

The memory was sharp, untouched by time. His father -a brute of a man, perpetually soaked in the stench of cheap ale-would stumble home night after night, fists and rage ready to lash out at anyone in reach. The violence was routine, but that night had been different. He remembered the sound of his mother's scream, her attempt to shield the young Dakeard with her own frail body. He remembered the silence that followed, his mother lying still in a pool of her own blood, her eyes vacant, her final act a sacrifice that gained nothing.

And there, slumped in the corner, was his father, oblivious, too far gone in his drunken stupor to notice the wreckage he had left in his wake. Dakeard could still feel the weight of the knife in his hand as he approached, his fingers steady, his heart cold. Without a shred of hesitation, he had pressed the blade to his father's throat and drawn it slowly, savouring the resistance as steel met flesh. His father had stirred, his eyes flickering open just long enough to grasp his own doom. The man who had lorded over him, who had inflicted terror night after night, had died helpless, his last moments watching up at his son's thin, satisfied smile.

He had felt nothing afterward-no sadness, no guilt. His mother, he decided, had been weak, too dependent on a life that should have been abandoned. His father's end, however, had been a gift, an awakening. The thrill of that first kill was something he would always carry with him, a dark, exquisite pleasure that had set his course. He had thanked his father, in a way, for being the vile man he was, for giving him the freedom to embrace his true self.

The sound of a distant bird brought him back to the present and the memory faded as quickly as it had come, leaving Dakeard with the familiar, sharpened focus he needed. Silently, he began his approach toward the stable, his movements as fluid and soundless as a shadow slipping across the morning landscape. The damp grass underfoot gave the faintest crunch, a nearly imperceptible sound in the soft hush of dawn. Above, the wind whispered through the trees, carrying with it the faint scent of hay and earth. The stable was close now—a well-worn path he had walked many times in preparation, each step rehearsed until he could have made it blind.

His hiding spot was simple but effective, concealed behind a large stack of hay in a shadowed corner where the stable walls met. On previous mornings, he had lain there, still and silent, his eyes fixed on the old man and his apprentice as they worked, neither of them the slightest bit aware of his presence. Today would be no different—except that when the old man slipped away for his lunch, leaving the boy alone, Dakeard would finally make his move.

Approaching the fence that encircled the stable yard, he paused, his gaze sweeping across the garden and the distant estate grounds. Satisfied, he vaulted over the fence in one smooth motion, his landing soft and soundless. The breeze masked any trace of his presence, though he would not have relied on it; in his line of work, caution was as instinctive as breathing. One wrong sound, one misstep, and his own life could be forfeit.

Reaching the stable doors, he halted again, listening. The horses were quiet, their presence barely more than a rustle in the shadows as they shifted in their sleep or stood in a half-dazed stupor. The estate grounds remained still; even the occasional house guard patrolling the perimeter was absent this morning. It struck Dakeard how easily he could slip into the lord's quarters and cut his throat in the dead of night—a suggestion he would keep in mind, perhaps, to hint at the estate's vulnerabilities to secure the lord's favour. But for now, he reminded himself, one job at a time.

He turned back to the stable doors and, with a slow, practised motion, slid them open just enough to slip inside. Shadows wrapped around him as he moved, his figure dissolving into the darkness, his breathing barely a whisper against the still air. Now, he would wait once more, patient as death itself, until the opportune moment arrived.

# THE ASSASSIN
# CHAPTER THIRTY

The knock at the door cut through the stillness, jolting Lord Malum from his quiet thoughts. His breakfast tray lay mostly untouched, a faint wisp of steam rising from his bowl, a silent reprimand to his distracted mind. Annoyance flared at the unexpected intrusion, and he scowled, letting out a rough sigh. The servants knew better than to disturb him without cause. He cleared his throat, pitching his voice with unmistakable dismissal. “I am not finished. Leave me now.”

A familiar female voice replied, soft but resolute, "My Lord, it is me. I’m sorry to disturb you so early, but I beg a moment of your time."

Cora. Malum tensed, his gaze shifting to the door with a flicker of apprehension. He had taken great pains to avoid her since that ill-fated night in the pool house, when Auron’s unexpected arrival had shattered their secrecy. The memory had become both tantalising and troublesome—a reckless indulgence that now threatened to unravel him. He could still recall the warmth of her skin, the way her breath had quickened under his touch, her dark eyes daring him with their forbidden allure. Since that discovery, he had forced himself to keep his distance, but his mind betrayed him, drifting back to their frequent encounters far more often than he would care to admit.

But why had she come to his door? This was not their usual arrangement—he summoned her, not the other way around. A frown pulled at his brow, laced with frustration and something else he dared not name. The sensible choice would be to send her away, yet he hesitated, caught by the promise of her presence, the thought of her pressing close to him, her exotic beauty only a few paces beyond that door.

“Cora, what do you want?” Malum snapped, his voice sharpened by the flicker of irritation that her silence kindled. “I am not yet dressed, or is that the purpose of your visit?” A pause followed, stretching the air taut. His patience thinned, each second feeding his frustration. “Don’t just linger in the hallway,” he called, his voice dropping to a murmur that hinted at more than invitation. “Enter and share more than just your words.”

The door opened with a soft creak, and she slipped inside, graceful as a shadow cast by dawn. His pulse quickened as he watched her approach, a slow heat unfurling beneath his skin. She was a sight to behold—summer had darkened her skin to a deeper shade, a sunlit bronze that only accentuated her allure. Her black, wavy hair bounced softly with each step, framing her face as she made her way across the expanse of his chambers, her every movement a calculated grace.

Malum's gaze traced her as she moved, drawn to the sway of her hips, the effortless rhythm of her stride. When their eyes finally met, an unspoken promise passed between them, igniting a familiar spark deep within him. For a brief, dangerous moment, the anticipation swept away all reason, and he knew—he would have her again. What better way to enliven what might have been a dull, routine morning?

"You are a welcome sight, Cora," Malum murmured, his voice low and inviting. "It has regrettably been too long. Come, share my bed once more."

But she did not move. Standing rooted in place, Cora's expression had shifted, a flicker of something uncertain crossing her face. Her fingers fidgeted with the hem of her uniform, twisting the fabric in a gesture that betrayed her unease. Malum noted the tension in her posture, her shoulders slightly hunched, her gaze lowered. He wondered if the time apart had left her feeling uneasy—though he could hardly fault her. Despite the intimacy they'd shared, he was still Lord of Kadun, a title that often instilled discomfort.

"Come now, my beauty," he coaxed, softening his tone. "My bed is longing for your warmth again, as am I." His eyes traced the line of her collar, the modest drape of her uniform. "Let me watch you slip out of those clothes and join me here."

Yet, despite his words, she held back, her silence filling the room with an unexpected tension. An instinct, something unspoken, began to tug at him, but he brushed it aside, focusing instead on the enticing vision he hoped would come to fruition.

A fleeting smile danced on her lips, gone as quickly as it appeared. "My Lord, I cannot deny that I have longed for your gentle touch," she murmured, her voice soft but resolute. "But I must apologise, for it is not your bed I have come to share."

The words struck him like a blow. Malum's yearning for her was swiftly overshadowed by the sting to his pride, an indignation that simmered beneath his skin. Though his gaze lingered on her youthful form, the taste of rejection soured any lingering desire. "Then you remain of little interest to me," he replied coldly. "My bowl shall be ready to clear in a while; you may return then."

He turned away from her, swivelling his hips to face the untouched breakfast tray. Snatching up his spoon, he dug into the bowl, his movements sharper than usual as he forced himself to ignore her. But even as he raised a spoonful to his mouth, he could feel her presence lingering, an unspoken defiance filling the space between them.

The frustration mounted, boiling over before he could stop himself. His hand paused, and with a sharp intake of breath, he turned back to her, voice laced with a barely restrained edge. "Do you forget yourself, girl? If you are not to be my lover, then you are to be my maid. Leave this instant, or you'll find my 'gentle touch' turn to something far less forgiving."

Her silence, her stillness—each felt like a challenge, and the words he spoke hung heavily in the room, tainted with a frustration he could not quite place. She remained unmoved, her eyes unreadable, and for the first time, he felt the uneasy sense that she had come with a purpose he had yet to grasp.

Cora then wavered, a slight flinch betraying her inner turmoil. For a brief moment, it seemed she might retreat, but she steadied herself, her gaze briefly flickering with a resolve that unsettled him. Malum's irritation flared; he could sense her hesitation, her divided loyalty between caution and courage. His earlier threat was hollow—he had no real desire to strike her—but he had little tolerance for this lingering uncertainty.

"What is the matter with you, girl?" he barked, his voice clipped and cutting. "You are clearly not deaf, yet you persist. You asked for a moment of my time, and I have granted more than enough." He fixed her with a hard stare, his frustration boiling over. "If there is something to be said, then say it quickly. You've already soured my breakfast, and I will not issue further warnings. Try my patience any longer, and you will find my anger turned to action."

Cora's gaze wavered but did not lower, a mixture of fear, perhaps, but also a strange determination. It lingered in the silence between them, an unspoken defiance that gnawed at his composure, leaving him with a disquiet he struggled to shake.

Cora swallowed hard, gathering herself, her fingers still trembling as she fought to control her nerves. She had never seen Malum's temper in full, though the warnings from other maids had cautioned her against testing it. What she had to say would either bring him immense joy or unleash his fury—there would be no middle ground.

"My Lord," she began carefully, her voice soft yet steady, "I would not disturb you unless my news was of the utmost importance, and it is. We spent many nights in each other's company, though it has been a while since I last entered your door. You once told me that your wife could no longer..."

His anger surged abruptly, cutting her off mid-sentence. "Do not speak of my wife. Ever." His voice was a harsh whisper, laced with an edge that made her flinch. "I have heard enough of your 'news,' girl. Get out. Now."

The force of his words left her breathless, the confidence she had barely held onto slipping away. She half-turned, instinct urging her to flee, yet something stronger rooted her to the spot. She could not leave, not without delivering the words that hung in the air between them.

"My Lord, I mean no offence," she whispered, voice wavering.

"Well, it has been caused," he spat, his eyes narrowing with fury.

Her resolve nearly crumbled, but she forced the words out, hurried and trembling. "My Lord... you once asked me for a son. I am to provide you that gift."

Malum's rage evaporated, his face shifting from anger to something closer to horror. His skin paled, and he felt a cold knot forming in his stomach as her meaning settled upon him, heavy and inescapable. He stared at her, his voice a strained, icy whisper. "Choose your next words very carefully. What are you telling me?"

The change in Malum's expression was unmistakable, but Cora could not tell if it meant relief or something far darker. Gathering her remaining courage, she spoke again, her voice steady but laced with the same apprehension. "My Lord, not long ago, you spoke of your desire for a son. Those were your words to me. I carry him within me now."

A flicker of something unreadable crossed Malum's face before anger began to resurface, slowly creeping back like a shadow reclaiming its space. His breathing grew heavier, each intake jagged, and he felt his hands begin to tremble despite himself. "You're certain?" he demanded, his voice low and rough, barely containing his swirling emotions.

"Three new moons have passed since I last bled, my Lord," Cora answered, her tone quiet but firm, her gaze never leaving his. "I feel the life growing within me."

Malum's anger roiled beneath the surface, a storm that turned his thoughts dark even as he forced himself to breathe, steadying his pulse. His skin flushed with heat as he wrestled against the rage that normally consumed him, holding it at bay with an effort that left him taut and strained. But somehow, he managed—if only just—to keep control. He nodded, his expression softening, a mask of acceptance settling over his features. "Yes, Cora, you are correct. I did speak of wanting a son, and though it was in a moment of passion, the words were true. Come," he said, his voice smoother than he felt, "let us embrace this news, rejoice together. We shall make love on this fine morning and plan our future."

A brilliant smile spread across her face, joy lighting her eyes, and in an impulsive burst of happiness, she half-ran, half-skipped toward him. She flung herself onto the bed, her arms encircling his neck as she kissed his cheek, a cascade of warmth in her touch. Malum's hand moved to the back of her head, his fingers sinking gently into her hair, massaging her scalp with a tenderness that belied his conflicted thoughts. He pressed her against his chest, feeling her tears dampen his collar as she wept with joy, clutching him close as if he were her only anchor.

He held her, his grip firm, the embrace warm and reassuring. Yet beneath that warmth lay a thin veneer, concealing the tempest inside. For now, he allowed the embrace to linger, his thoughts shifting between a promise and a threat, all hidden behind the gentle facade he wore for her.

For Cora, the world had transformed. Walking up the stairs to his room, she had dreaded this meeting, unsure of how her news would be received. But he had spoken of planning their future together. The sweetness of those words filled her with hope. In her mind, she saw herself as his wife, bearing him sons and daughters, with maids of her own tending to her every need, just as she would tend to his. She went to tilt her head up, longing to kiss him-but the soothing hand on the back of her head pressed down harder, unexpectedly holding her in place. The pressure increased, and suddenly, she could not pull away.

A surge of panic overtook her. His other hand came up, tightening his grip, pressing her face firmly into his chest, blocking her air. Her spectacular joy twisted into horror, and she began to thrash, her body wild with terror. She struggled, her limbs flailing, kicking out in frantic attempts to break free, but his grip was iron. She gasped, desperate, her hands clawing for anything that might save her, fingers grazing the bed, then the breakfast tray.

Her last ounce of strength surged, and she grabbed the wooden bowl, swinging blindly. It struck his temple with a solid crack, and Malum let out a yelp, releasing her momentarily as he clutched his head. Cora jerked back, gasping as air flooded her lungs, her chest heaving. But her relief was brief; his enraged gaze met hers, and he lunged again, his hand snaking to her throat, squeezing with relentless force. This time, she was ready. Summoning her remaining strength, she slapped him hard, and his grip weakened just enough for her to wrench free and tumble to the floor.

She hit the ground painfully, the shock of it jolting her, but she pushed aside the ache. Malum was already diving after her, tearing quilts and pillows from the bed as he went. They cascaded around him, creating a tangled barrier that slowed his advance. Cora scrambled back, the soft pile of bedding buying her precious seconds. She rose, just as Malum's foot slipped on a trailing bed sheet that slid across the marble, sending him sprawling.

In that brief moment, she saw her chance and bolted for the door. Behind her, Malum's roar echoed, filled with unrestrained fury. "YOU SHALL NOT BRING A SON OF MINE INTO THIS WORLD! I own this house, and you will not escape me! The next time we meet, I'll glare upon your lifeless corpse and curse the day we met!"

She stumbled through the door, his voice chasing her down, but she forced herself to keep moving, heart pounding, clinging to the last threads of her hope and the life within her.

The doorway of Malum's bedroom opened into a small, sparsely furnished waiting area—an unassuming space where guests typically waited in quiet deference for an audience with their lord. But at this early hour, the room stood empty, a silent witness to her flight. Not that it mattered; even if the room had been filled with people, she would have barrelled straight through, her need to escape overpowering any sense of decorum. Malum's enraged voice still echoed behind her, each bellow driving her forward, a fresh wave of terror tearing at her nerves. She dared not look back, too afraid of what she might see.

Tears streaked her face, no longer born of joy but of raw, unyielding panic, blurring her vision as she charged onward. Beyond the waiting room, an archway led to the upstairs landing, a place she had crossed hundreds of times without a second thought. Now it felt vast and foreign, an endless stretch between her and any hope of safety. Below, in the grand hall, she caught sight of other servants, scurrying about their morning tasks, oblivious to her plight. Yet even with their presence, she felt no safer; Malum's fury was all-consuming, and she knew his wrath would follow her wherever she went.

Reaching the stairs, she gripped the rail, nearly losing her footing in her haste. Her ankle twisted slightly, and she cried out, a sharp, panicked shrill that echoed through the hall. Heads turned, startled eyes lifting to the sight of her, but she did not notice. She could not afford to. All that mattered was getting to her room in the servant quarters, grabbing whatever belongings she could carry, and escaping before Malum caught her. Her heart hammered in her chest, a frantic rhythm urging her on, as the realisation settled heavily within her—he would kill her, of that she was certain.

Driven purely by instinct, Cora's legs wavered as she reached the threshold of the servant quarters. Her strength finally gave out, and she collapsed just before the doorway, her body sinking to the floor in a defeated heap. Tears streamed down her cheeks, her breaths coming in sharp, ragged gasps that barely filled her lungs. She tried to rise, to push herself to her feet, but her legs trembled and refused to obey. How could this be happening? How could the man she had once adored now wish for her death, when she carried his child—his son?

She had dreamt of a future with him, of raising their child together, of stepping into a life beyond mere servitude as his new lady, cherished and needed. Yet that vision had shattered, replaced by a terror so profound it left her paralyzed. The realisation gripped her: she had to escape, to leave the only home she had ever known. But where would she go? How could she survive beyond these walls?

She was born into this household, her mother a serving maid before her, and her father—a slave from the Drylands—had been put to death in the arena for daring to love her mother. She had been raised within the confines of these walls, her world limited to the halls and chambers she knew by heart, barely setting foot in the gardens, let alone beyond the gates. The lands outside were a mystery, a vast unknown that offered no safety, only uncertainty.

But she had no choice. She could not stay. The man she had loved now hunted her, and the life she carried within her was all that mattered.

The door creaked open, and Saanvi stood in the space created, her eyes widening in alarm as she took in the sight of Cora, crumpled on the floor, her body wracked with silent tremors. Without hesitation, Saanvi knelt down, wrapping an arm around the younger woman's shoulders, her voice soft and comforting. "What's happened, dear?" she murmured, her tone filled with gentle concern.

But Cora could only sob, words choked by the flood of emotions consuming her. Fits of tears spilled out in jagged breaths, her face twisted in despair, unable to make sense of her own broken thoughts. Each attempt to speak collapsed into more gasps, her sobs uncontrollable.

Saanvi's gaze softened, recognizing that whatever had happened had shaken Cora to her very core. "This is no place for a scene, dear," she whispered soothingly. "Come, let me take you to your room."

With careful patience, Saanvi lifted her to her feet, looping her arm around Cora's shoulders to support her, nearly carrying the girl as they made their way down the dim stairwell to her quarters. Cora leaned into her, her legs barely steady, each step a struggle. Saanvi's presence, warm and steady, became the anchor she needed in that moment, the only source of stability in a world that had turned dark and unforgiving.

Several minutes had passed, and the two women sat in silence on either side of Cora's narrow bed. Saanvi had waited patiently, letting Cora's breathing steady, watching as the waves of panic slowly subsided. Finally, she spoke, her tone gentle but laced with curiosity. "Now then, the next time I go upstairs, I'll have a dozen questions to answer about that little scene. Care to explain what that was about? They'll need an answer, and soon."

Cora sniffed, dabbing at her tear-streaked cheeks, a fresh wave of torment flooding over her. She had never expected to see anyone—just to grab her belongings and disappear. Saanvi was someone she trusted with daily matters, with confidences and quiet companionship, but to trust her with her life? That was something else entirely.

Seeing Cora's struggle, Saanvi softened, perhaps sensing that the girl's story was darker than she could have imagined. She placed a comforting hand on Cora's shoulder. "I see you're troubled—that much is clear. But this is your room, and you're safe here. Trust me, Cora. Let me help."

Cora's body quivered, torn between the impulse to flee and the desperate need for support. She knew she could not escape this place alone. Even if Saanvi refused her or sent word to Lord Malum, her fate was likely sealed either way. With a trembling voice, she spoke, her words laced with a quiet desperation. "You ask me to trust you, though you do not know my plight. All I ask is to live beyond this day—can you help me do that?"

Saanvi's brow furrowed, a flicker of confusion crossing her face. She could see the terror etched in Cora's features, but such a plea seemed incomprehensible. "My dear, who could possibly wish you such harm? Are you certain there hasn't been a mistake?"

Cora's gaze dropped, a fresh tear slipping down her cheek. She struggled to find the words, to make Saanvi understand the danger she faced—a danger that was far more real than any misunderstanding. In that quiet room, she felt herself standing on the edge, the weight of her secret pressing down, waiting to be revealed.

"His Lordship wishes me dead," Cora whispered, her voice breaking under the weight of the words. "He tried to end my life just before you found me. I... I carry his unborn child." Her voice dissolved into sobs, and the tears came again, rushing forth like a broken dam.

Saanvi's breath caught in her throat, her hand flying to her mouth in shock. For a moment, she could not move, uncertain whether to believe what she had just heard—yet knowing, somehow, that it had to be true. The horror of it filled the small room, and she took a step back, her gaze fixed on the trembling figure before her, huddled in distress on the edge of the bed.

Torn between her instinct to comfort the girl and the brutal reality of what this meant, Saanvi's heart ached. She longed to reach out, to hug Cora and tell her that it would all be alright. But she knew, with a sinking dread, that it would not. Lord Malum would indeed want Cora dead, and the reasons were painfully clear. Saanvi may not have understood the finer politics of the nobility, but she knew that a lord could not risk an illegitimate child with a serving girl. The scandal would tear him apart—his standing in the senate, his alliances, even his marriage would be shattered. His wife would surely abandon him, severing any ties with the powerful Western kingdom that bound their union.

The harsh reality crashed over Saanvi like a wave, chilling her to the core. If she were found here, knowing this secret and failing to report it to Lord Malum, she would be implicated—a willing accessory in the eyes of the household, if not the law. The consequences would likely be as dire for her as for Cora. The choice seemed simple: she owed Cora nothing, certainly not her life. Her loyalty was to the estate, to the lord who held her position and safety in his hands. She went to turn, preparing to leave, but at that moment, Cora looked up, her tear-streaked face a portrait of raw desperation, her eyes wide and pleading.

In that instant, a memory stirred—a vivid echo from years ago, when Saanvi had stood at this very bedside, assisting the midwife at Cora's birth. The memory washed over her: Cora's mother, frail and fading, had succumbed moments after the girl entered the world, leaving the newborn orphaned in a matter of breaths. The midwife had gently placed the tiny infant into Saanvi's arms, and as she cradled the newborn close, Cora's cries had ceased, her eyes flickering open to meet Saanvi's own. It had been the briefest of moments, yet profound, the quiet bond of that first gaze settling in her heart.

Why had that memory returned now, of all times? Was it a sign? She had brought this girl into the world, cradled her when she had no one else. Could she now bring herself to walk away, knowing it would seal her fate? Or could she, just once, grant her the freedom her mother and father had never known?

The silence stretched, and Saanvi's eyes locked firmly on Cora's, as if searching for the answer. Finally, without warning, words sprang from her lips, surprising even herself.

"Come, girl," she murmured, her voice a mixture of urgency and resolve. "Compose yourself—we do not have long."

# THE ASSASSIN CHAPTER THIRTY ONE

Regal bent over slowly, feeling each vertebra protest as he reached down to pluck a stray piece of hay. With a weathered hand, he held it out, and the horse accepted the offering gratefully, its large, warm muzzle brushing against his fingers as it chewed. The rhythmic sound of teeth grinding filled the stable, oddly soothing in the quiet morning. Regal pressed his hand to the small of his back, rubbing at the ever-present ache that pulsed there. Old age had taken its toll, creeping in slowly until every movement was met with a stiff resistance and each joint ached as though his bones had turned to rusty metal. Yet his stubbornness kept him working, refusing to yield to his body's demands for rest.

His once-strong frame had withered over the years, leaving his limbs gaunt, his hands skeletal. Even his appetite had waned, meals becoming a chore rather than a pleasure, each bite feeling like a challenge to swallow. Forcing down food he barely wanted had become a daily struggle, leaving him feeling hollow and brittle.

From across the stable, he watched the young lad, Auron, tending to the foal. Tall for his age, the boy was filling out with a vigour Regal could only remember in faint memories. Despite himself, Regal's lip curled with a hint of resentment. Auron was always darting about, brimming with the energy that Regal had long since lost, pestering him with the endless details of his training. The boy's mind buzzed with tales of imaginary battles, of strategies and skirmishes he and Malament had devised in their studies. Each time, he spoke with a fervour that Regal found intolerable, the enthusiasm ringing too loud in the quiet stable.

Even the lashings had not quelled that spirit, his resilience another reminder of the unbridgeable chasm between youth and age. Regal sighed, his fingers tracing along his spine as if searching for some remnant of the strength that had once filled his own bones, yet finding only hollow ache.

The sight of the boy was a constant, silent taunt, a reminder of all that had slipped beyond Regal's reach. Each ache in his bones from even a gentle morning's work seemed to mock him, and he could scarcely stand to look at Auron, so full of life and vigour. He turned back to the horse, patting its long neck, letting his hand rest there for a moment, a grounding touch in the midst of his thoughts. He placed another piece of hay to the horse's mouth, watching as it chewed contentedly, lost in the simplicity of its purpose.

Regal's gaze drifted, and he found himself wondering, not for the first time, why he remained here, working in the stables of a lord he held little regard for. Home was an hour's walk away, a small, solitary shack where no wife waited, no sons tended to land. He felt no particular loneliness; companionship had never been a need of his. Yet there was an empty ache, a silent truth he carried: the stables were all he had ever known.

When the Lord had granted him his freedom, it should have marked the beginning of a new life. But freedom had come with the stark reality of lost stability—his meals, his shelter, his sense of purpose. Continuing his work in the stables had seemed the only option, allowing him a warm meal and a small sense of routine. Still, every morning, the weariness returned, creeping over him as he faced the same stalls, the same hay-strewn aisles, the same echo of hooves. His existence felt paper-thin, and the realisation settled heavily on his shoulders, as it did each day.

The air in the stables was thick, the scent of hay and dust mingling and settling in his lungs, pressing down on him. Regal rubbed his temple, the familiar stuffiness making him yearn for a breath of clean air. He shuffled to the wide doorway and stepped outside, filling his lungs with the warm, open air, letting the freshness revive him. For a brief moment, he felt the weariness lift, the cool touch of freedom brushing against his skin, though he knew it would fade as soon as he stepped back inside.

Stretching his stiff, aching back, Regal tilted his face to the cloudless sky, letting the brightness wash over him as he tried to clear his mind. He squinted against the sun, its harsh light bearing down with a relentless heat, and guessed it must be mid-morning. Summer had settled in fully now, and beads of sweat ran down his balding head, soaking the thin strands of grey hair and darkening them against his scalp. He reached for the small leather water sack at his waist, gripping it with both hands before pouring a splash over his head. The coolness offered only a brief reprieve, but he savoured it, following with a long, deep gulp.

The air hung thick and heavy, the lack of breeze amplifying the heat. Even the simple tasks in the stable had become more arduous, each movement tugging on his tired muscles, his joints protesting under the weight of the morning's work. Turning reluctantly, he cast a glance back at the stables. Through the haze of dust and heat, he could see the pile of hay that still needed shifting and, beside it, the boy, still fussing over the foal. Auron's cheerful voice drifted through the stable, some nonsense about a "brave new warrior in training," no doubt part of his endless fantasies.

Regal's lips twisted into a grimace. He could not be bothered with either of them, not now. His back throbbed, his limbs ached, and even summoning a curse to tell the boy off seemed like too much effort. A low grunt escaped his lips, a sound of resignation more than irritation, and he turned away, plodding slowly toward the house, each step heavy and reluctant.

Back in the stables, Auron glanced up, hearing the steady, fading shuffle of Regal's footsteps. Rising quickly, he stepped outside to catch a glimpse of the old man, now about thirty paces away, hunched slightly as he trudged toward the house. For a moment, Auron considered calling out, but the words lingered, unspoken. Regal often wandered off without a word, leaving Auron to his own devices. It was routine by now, and though Auron was used to it, a pang of sympathy stirred as he watched the old man's slow, limping gait toward the hedgerows lining the path back to the house.

The figure of Regal, bent and weary, tugged at him. While the old man was hardly friendly, his struggle still touched Auron in a quiet way. Regal seemed weighed down by more than just the years, moving like a man whose body and spirit had both grown tired. Auron's gaze lingered, following the stooped figure as he disappeared behind the hedge, swallowed by the greenery.

Turning back, Auron's eyes swept across the garden, lush and radiant under the morning sun, the air warm and fragrant. Suddenly, a flicker of movement along the ivy-covered wall caught his attention, drawing his focus left. For a moment, he squinted, trying to make out the source. The sound of hurried footsteps and the rustling of bushes followed, breaking the peaceful quiet of the garden.

Auron held his breath, curiosity building as he waited for the mystery to reveal itself. Then, two women burst from behind the ivy, their clothes dusted with leaves as they rummaged through the dense foliage. They moved quickly, scanning the wall's leafy interior as though searching for something hidden. At first, he could not make out who they were, but the urgency in their movements told him they were intent on finding something—or someone.

As the women drew closer, Auron recognized them—Saanvi, her face flushed from exertion, and Cora, whose ghostly pallor made her seem almost out of place in the bright morning light. Auron felt a flicker of amusement at the unusual sight and jogged toward them, intrigued. "What are you looking for?" he called, his voice light.

Saanvi whipped around, her eyes wide with surprise, her usually calm demeanour replaced by a look of urgency. "Back to your business, Auron," she commanded, her voice strained but firm. "You cannot help here." The tone startled him—Saanvi had never spoken to him with such severity. The message was clear, though, and he halted his approach, disappointment mingling with curiosity as he began to back away, glancing between them.

But as he turned, he noticed Cora watching him too. Instead of dismissing him as Saanvi had, she moved toward him, her steps light and quiet, her dark hair trailing behind her like a shadow. Her movements were fluid, yet her face was etched with something raw and sorrowful, a look that froze Auron in place. She stopped just before him, her gaze meeting his, and in her expression was a heaviness he could not quite name, something that made his chest tighten.

The feeling stirred in him like the sadness he had felt moments before, watching Regal walk away, a sense of loss and helplessness. He held her gaze, sensing that whatever troubled her ran deep, even if he could not fully understand it.

Before Auron could muster a greeting, Cora spoke, her voice soft and distant, as if each word carried a weight of its own. "I am sorry for the pain I have caused you, Auron. It was never my... intention." Her words drifted toward him, almost like a whisper on the wind, carrying a sadness only she knew.

Auron blinked, taken aback. He hardly understood what she was apologising for, yet her tone filled him with an unexpected comfort. "It's okay... I'm fine," he replied, giving her a reassuring smile. For a fleeting moment, a faint smile softened her grim expression, but it faded as quickly as it had appeared.

"You seem sad," he ventured gently. "Can I not help you?"

She glanced around, her gaze finding Saanvi, who remained preoccupied, still combing through the ivy in a desperate search. It was as if Cora sought guidance, a moment's permission, but none came. Auron's curiosity flared. "What are you looking for?" he asked again, a hint of urgency in his voice.

Cora hesitated, an uneasy silence stretching between them. She seemed to wrestle with her answer before finally speaking, her voice barely above a whisper. "I am looking for a way out. Saanvi thinks there may be a break in the wall, some hidden place where I might slip through. But we've searched and found nothing."

The words hung between them, heavy with an undeniable finality, as if even the walls were complicit in trapping her within. Auron stared at her, shocked. "Why would you leave?"

Cora's expression tightened, a shadow flickering across her face. "I have neither the time to explain nor the belief that you would understand," she replied, her voice edged with impatience. "Do you know of any way out?"

Auron's mind raced, sifting through memories of the grounds, but he came up empty. He had nearly ventured to every corner of the garden, and no hidden paths or doorways came to mind. "I… I don't think so," he stammered, feeling helpless under the weight of her urgency. "But can you not just… climb over?"

Her eyes flashed with something close to frustration as she glanced at the wall, then back at him. "How would you have me climb a wall of such height, child?" Her tone was sharp, as though even the suggestion grated on her. She took a step back, her expression hardening. "I must go. This was a waste, speaking to you. Do not follow us, and forget this encounter, Auron."

As Cora turned back toward Saanvi, her words hung in the air like a fragile thread—a dismissal and a plea intertwined. Suddenly, Auron reached out, catching her trailing hand. Startled, she turned, her eyes meeting his once more, a mix of disbelief and curiosity in her gaze. "I can show you," he whispered, his voice filled with a newfound resolve. Without waiting for her response, he tightened his grip and pulled her forward, leading her toward the thick ivy wall at the far edge of the garden.

Saanvi, now fully aware of the boy's interference, hurried forward, blocking his path as they reached the wall's base. "Auron, what are you doing?" she hissed, her voice tense. "I told you to go away, did I not?"

But Auron paid her no mind, his focus unwavering. Stepping forward, he plunged into the ivy, letting the dense vines envelop him as he began to climb. The thick branches and vines held firm, supporting his weight without a single creak or shift. His limbs moved with the confidence of someone who knew the wall's secrets, his small body manoeuvring nimbly through the twisting green. Soon, his head broke through the upper layers, high above, and he looked down, his face triumphant.

"Come, Cora—climb!" he called, his voice carrying down with a mixture of excitement and encouragement, inviting her to follow.

The two women stared up at Auron, astonished by his valiant, almost effortless ascent. He had all but disappeared into the thick ivy, his small frame navigating the wall's dense foliage with the ease of a young fox climbing rocks. Saanvi's eyes narrowed as she watched him, her tone cutting through the silence. "And how do you intend to climb down the other side, then, Auron?"

Peering over the top, Auron's confidence wavered as he took in the exterior of the wall. Unlike the garden side, this face was bare, offering no footholds save for the layers of brick that jutted out in uneven ridges—nowhere near secure enough for a safe descent. The drop was lower on this side, daunting, some twenty feet down to the rough, uneven stone of the road below. A fall from that height without injury would be nothing short of a miracle.

Auron's brow furrowed, the thrill of his climb fading as the challenge of descent settled in. He looked along the top of the wall—it was about a foot wide, tangled with thinning ivy that offered some stability. Deciding to test his footing, he hoisted himself up, standing carefully on the narrow ledge. From this vantage point, the entire garden sprawled beneath him like a map, each corner and path laid out in detail.

He felt a flicker of exhilaration, his initial uncertainty melting into wonder. From here, he could see everything: Regal's stooped figure still slowly making his way toward the house, his pace unhurried. Several others moved about the garden, tending to plants or carrying bundles. Beyond the walls, hidden parts of the estate sprang into view, and in the distance, the familiar streets of his old home came alive, bustling with activity he could only just make out. Familiar corners, narrow alleys he had once roamed—all were spread before him, captivating him with the sense of boundless possibility.

For a moment, he was completely absorbed, his fading excitement replaced by awe as he took in the view, feeling, if only briefly, as though he were on the edge of a new world.

Though he had found a vantage point with a view like no other, Auron quickly realised how exposed he was, teetering high above the ground. His eyes darted around, searching for a way down that would keep him hidden. Below, Saanvi's voice rang out, her tone sharp with urgency. "Get down from there this instant! You have no idea what danger you place us in, so open like this. This is not the way, Auron—climb down at once!"

Obeying her command, Auron crouched, his hand instinctively reaching for a thick strand of ivy to steady himself. But instead of the familiar tangle of vines, his fingers brushed against something coarse and unexpected—a sturdy, coiled rope hidden within the ivy. Surprised, he tightened his grip, examining the rope's thick, reliable weave, looped round and round in a secure circle, one end trailing down, partially obscured by the ivy. He glanced down at it with growing excitement; the rope was long enough to reach the street below. How long had it been here, waiting, unnoticed?

Saanvi's voice called out again, her words a warning, but Auron barely heard her. A grin spread across his face, his discovery flooding him with exhilaration. He lifted the rope to show it, holding it aloft as his eyes met Cora's below. Her face softened, a matching smile breaking through her earlier tension as she understood the significance of his find.

For the first time, he felt as though he had uncovered something that could make a real difference, his small moment of rebellion lighting a spark of hope in the two women below.

Saanvi's face remained stern, unimpressed by the sudden appearance of a rope that offered a clear path out of the Lord's estate. Her eyes narrowed as she looked up at Auron, her voice laced with suspicion and urgency. "I don't know why you've placed a rope here, Auron, but I don't care to hear it right now. You've given Cora a chance—that is enough. Come down, for you've done all you can."

Auron opened his mouth to protest, ready to insist the rope was not his. But Saanvi's sharp glare silenced him before he could speak, her authority leaving no room for argument. Swallowing his words, he gripped the ivy carefully and began his descent, each movement deliberate as he felt the thrill of discovery wane under the weight of her watchful gaze.

As he climbed down, he could not shake the questions tumbling through his mind—if the rope were not his, who had left it there, and for what purpose? Yet, under Saanvi's scrutinising eyes, he kept silent, his curiosity tempered by a growing awareness that there were secrets at play far beyond his understanding.

"Now Cora this is your only chance, climb these vines as Auron did then help yourself down using the rope. I will meet you at the stables in a few hours when I go into town on my usual errands. They are situated on the edge of Borlong, and I shall not wait longer than thirty minutes or suspicions shall arise where I am, so make sure you are there. You remember the route there I told you?"

Cora had mixed emotions, the Lord's estate was all she knew and how she wished he had taken the news differently. Life would be tough alone especially with a child but at least it would be a life. Almost reluctantly she approached the ivy "I remember the route you told me Saanvi and I shall be waiting there do not worry." Auron jumped the last few feet landing softly just in front of her, smiling she placed a gentle hand on his shoulder. "Auron, I thank you for your kindness this day, you are a sweet boy who should not have endured so much. It is sad we did not become friends, but I will think of you often. Do not let this place turn you from the kind boy you are."

The comforting smile faded from Cora's face, replaced by a flicker of apprehension as the reality of her escape settled upon her. After a quick embrace with Saanvi she steeled herself, slipping her hand into the thick ivy until her fingers closed around a sturdy branch above her head. Testing her grip, she found it strong enough, and with a steady pull, she lifted herself upward, her movements firm yet cautious.

As she neared the top, Cora glanced back. Saanvi's gaze met hers, a blend of encouragement and warning. "Very good, Cora. Remember what I told you—speak with no one, and certainly do not reveal who you are. I'll see you at the stables later, where we can talk more. And toss the rope back once you're over."

Though she needed no extra encouragement, Saanvi's words settled her, and Cora managed a small, slanted smile in acknowledgment. She turned back to the task, her hands pressing against the cool stone as she climbed through the last tangle of ivy, emerging at last to stand atop the high wall. The ledge was wide enough to stand, but from this height, the drop on the other side was dizzying. The uneven street below seemed to tilt and shift, making her feel unsteady.

With a deep breath, she focused, turning her attention to the rope lying neatly to her left. She knelt, grasping the end that trailed into the ivy, tugging it to ensure it was firmly secured to the hidden branch within. Satisfied, she threw the length over the wall, watching it unravel in the air before it settled just above the jagged stone path below.

Her heart thudded, a blend of fear and anticipation coursing through her as she prepared to make her descent, the path to freedom stretching below. Pausing for a final look back, a soft sadness filled her—she had never truly taken the time to appreciate this garden, with its greenery sprawling under the sun. It was a beautiful sight to carry with her, a memory she could cherish, and for a brief moment, she felt grateful for this parting view.

From her vantage, she caught movement near the stables and spotted Auron below. A gentle smile tugged at her lips. "You'd best get back to your chores, mister," she called down lightly. "I believe Regal has returned."

Auron spun around, his face a mixture of surprise and embarrassment as he glanced toward the stables, catching just a glimpse of a figure before it disappeared. Just as he readied himself to run back, Saanvi laid a firm hand on his shoulder, holding him in place. "Wait a moment, young man," she instructed. "When the rope comes back over, I need you to remove it from this wall."

He looked up, expecting to see Cora's figure still poised above, but she was already gone, leaving only the faint trace of her presence as the ivy swayed under her weight.

After a short pause, the rope flung back over the wall, landing with a thud near their feet. Together, Saanvi and Auron managed to tug it free from the thick root that had held it, Saanvi's expression increasingly grim. She brushed her hands off, looking at the boy with a wary frown. "Take this back to the stables," she instructed, her tone laced with displeasure. "Perhaps Regal can make better use of it." She paused, her gaze narrowing on Auron, who stood with the rope looped over his shoulder, his face a blank mask of innocence. "I will echo Cora's thanks, Auron, but understand this: what you did today was dangerous. Do you understand that?"

He nodded, though his expression was still one of mild confusion.

Saanvi's voice dropped, firm and insistent. "And listen to me carefully—you must not discuss today's events with anyone. Not a word, not even to me. Do you understand?"

"Yes, ma'am," he mumbled, a little more serious now.

She sighed, studying his face, uncertain if he truly grasped the gravity of the situation. "I know Malament is your friend, but if he were to find out... well, I fear for both of us. And you don't want another whipping, do you?" She watched as a flicker of panic crossed his face; her words having struck their mark. “Now go. Not another word of this to anyone.”

Auron nodded hastily and scurried off toward the stables, glancing back only once before disappearing into the shadows of the barn. Saanvi watched him go, a knot of tension loosening in her chest, though uncertainty lingered. She had not meant to frighten the boy, but she knew the consequences she would face if today’s events were ever discovered. Her fate would be grim indeed—either strung from a tree or tossed into the arena to face justice. She had seen enough of the Lord’s punishments to know how ruthless he could be.

As Auron vanished from view, Saanvi turned and began her slow journey back to the house, veering through the rosemary bushes. She gathered a handful of herbs, their sharp, earthy scent filling her nose, a familiar comfort amid her worry. She would need these for the evening’s meal, and they would also provide a tidy alibi for her time spent in the garden. If she kept a low profile for the next few hours before heading to town, she might be able to escape further scrutiny.

It had been an eventful morning—one she would rather forget sooner than later. She still could not fully understand why she had helped the girl, and now that it was done, she was not sure if she regretted her choice or found relief in it.

# THE ASSASSIN CHAPTER THIRTY TWO

The scent of rosemary clung to Saanvi's fingertips as she straightened, her thoughts as tangled as the stems in her grasp. She stepped onto the stone path that wound through the heart of the garden, the warmth of the sun pressing against her back as dappled light flickered over the worn stones. Overhead, the sun had climbed higher, deepening the golden glow that filtered through the canopy, stirring the air into a fragrant blend of herbs and late-blooming flowers. She walked slowly, as though by keeping a measured pace, she might find some sense of calm. The events of the morning sat heavily on her mind, a mixture of anxiety and disbelief swirling as she replayed each choice she had made, each word she had spoken.

Along the path, she paused to pluck a few sprigs of thyme, the soft, earthy aroma wafting up as she added them to her bundle. The thyme grew in dense patches beside clumps of lavender, the purple blooms contrasting against the deep green foliage and lending a faint, floral sweetness to the air. She continued on, her fingers brushing over a row of sage leaves, their soft texture grounding her in the familiarity of the garden's tasks. These small, routine acts were her attempt to focus, to find some semblance of normalcy.

As she moved deeper into the garden, passing a bed of golden marigolds and the bright reds and pinks of geraniums, her thoughts drifted to Cora. Saanvi could not shake the image of the girl's fearful, determined face as she had climbed the wall, or the defiant resolve in Auron's innocent eyes as he had offered his help. The decision to aid Cora, to risk so much, still left her unsettled. She had seen the consequences of disobedience many times in this household—the whippings, the harsh dismissals, the silent, crushing reminders of what defiance could bring. And yet, she had acted on impulse, moved by something she could not fully name.

The path curved around a small fountain where water trickled softly, a quiet, steady sound against the backdrop of birdsong. Here, she gathered a few sprigs of mint, tucking them alongside the rosemary and thyme, her mind drifting to the plan she would need to carry out carefully. Cora would expect her at the stables later, where they could talk in private, away from curious ears and watchful eyes. The girl would have questions, and Saanvi hoped she might find answers by then, some guidance to offer. But even she did not know what the future would hold. They would need a careful plan if Cora were to remain hidden or perhaps find a way out of Borlong altogether.

The path widened as it neared the large patio area just outside the house. A soft breeze stirred, and Saanvi felt the warmth on her face as she stepped into the open. She knew she would need to be cautious, blending her daily routine with subtlety to avoid suspicion. With the herbs gathered, she had her alibi, and as she looked back toward the garden, she took a steadying breath, the earthy scent of mint and thyme grounding her as she prepared herself for the hours to come.

Just as Saanvi crossed the patio, she froze. Footsteps broke the garden's quiet, and Lord Malum and his son, Malament, rounded the corner ahead, deep in conversation. Her heartbeat quickened, a wave of anxiety washing over her. Had they somehow discovered her role in Cora's escape attempt? Surely, it was too soon. She considered turning back, but before she could make a decision, Malament's gaze lifted, catching sight of her. He offered a brief, almost absent smile before his attention shifted back to his father, seemingly uninterested in her presence.

Swallowing, Saanvi forced herself to keep moving, hoping she could pass them with little more than a polite bow of her head. Her pulse drummed in her ears as they drew closer, and she kept her gaze respectfully lowered, her fingers tightening around the bundle of herbs in her hands, willing herself to appear calm and neutral.

As they approached, she caught sight of Lord Malum's face, his jaw clenched, the lines around his mouth deep with barely contained anger. Even through his thick beard, his fury was evident, and his face was flushed, his expression rigid and uncomfortable. He wore a smart, mint-green robe with a deep navy trim, the rich fabric suited to his station but seemingly adding to his discomfort as he stood, shifting stiffly, his movements tense and restless. There was a sharp, metallic scent to the air, as if the tension itself had a bite.

In contrast, Malament appeared calm, his expression composed as he listened to his father. Dressed in white linen trousers and a matching tunic, topped with an olive-green waistcoat, he cut a striking figure beside the lord, his ease a stark contrast to Malum's barely concealed rage. Saanvi glanced up briefly, noting Malament's relaxed posture, his hands clasped loosely behind his back as he walked, his demeanour confident but not overbearing. The murmurs of their voices held an intensity, low but firm, each word heavy as though carrying the weight of things unsaid.

They were mere paces apart now, and Saanvi dipped her head in a shallow bow, praying her face betrayed nothing more than the respect expected of her. She felt Malum's gaze flick over her, cold and unreadable, as they passed, and her stomach tightened. But neither man paused, their voices continuing in low, intense murmurs as they moved on. Relief washed over her, though her hands still trembled slightly around the herbs, and she kept her pace measured, her expression neutral, knowing that any display of nerves might raise questions she could not afford to answer.

As Malum and Malament moved away, Saanvi felt the tightness in her chest ease, the tension melting as she prepared to fade back into her usual routines. But just as she rounded the corner, she nearly collided with Regal, who appeared right in front of her. She let out a startled shriek, the old man took a step back, equally surprised.

Before she could recover, a familiar voice came from behind her. "Jumpy, Saanvi?" Malament teased, his tone amused.

Thinking quickly, Saanvi hid her nerves behind a playful jest. "So might you be, if this face popped out at you!" she replied, glancing at Regal with a mock shudder.

Regal's face creased into a grin, his weathered features pulling into a look of wry amusement. "Been a while since I gave anyone a scare, my lady," he said with a chuckle. "But I'll take it."

Malament smiled, glancing between them. "Back to it, then, is it, Regal?" he asked, his tone light but carrying a hint of genuine interest. It was rare for Malament to speak with the old stable master, though he'd taken a bit more interest since Regal had begun schooling Auron.

Regal nodded, baring a grin through his gapped teeth. "No rest for the wicked, sir," he replied, a glint of humour in his eyes. He straightened a bit, savouring the rare acknowledgment, however brief.

Malament studied the old man thoughtfully, a hint of irony in his gaze. There's truth in that, he mused, noting Regal's worn, almost haunted appearance. Though he could not be much older than Malum, Regal looked ancient, his frame gaunt and weary. Thin strands of grey hair clung to his balding scalp like damp cobwebs after a drizzle, and his eyes, ringed with shadows, were set deep into his lined face. There was a certain rough resilience about him, as if every wrinkle and scar were markers of a lifetime of hard labour.

"Come now, Regal," Malament replied with a faint smile. "That's far too kind." The two shared a brief, companionable laugh, while Malum stood silently beside them, his expression unreadable.

Malament shifted the conversation, his tone light but curious. "How is Auron getting on, then?"

Regal scratched his chin, a flicker of fondness crossing his features. "Aye, he's not doing too bad," he replied. "Quick to pick things up, that boy, though his attention does tend to wander." He gave a slight shrug, as though the behaviour were something he tolerated more than approved of. "I'm headed back up there now, if you'd care to join me. Left him alone for a bit while I grabbed an early lunch."

Malament smirked, a flicker of amusement passing over his face. The boy's the same in our sessions, he thought, recalling Auron's wandering focus—except when it came to combat training, the one subject that seemed to ignite his full attention. "No, I'll leave him in your capable hands, Regal," he replied, his tone light but knowing. "I'll catch up with him later."

He cast a sidelong glance at his father, aware of the tension simmering beneath Malum's stern exterior. This was a father struggling to maintain his own sense of control in an environment where even the smallest missteps could undermine his authority. Malament's smirk softened slightly; he understood the predicament well, though he would never speak of it.

Saanvi's curiosity got the better of her, though she knew well the risks of interrupting the Lord and his son. Perhaps it was the lingering tension from the morning, or a sense that something wasn't quite right. "Begging your pardon, my lords," she ventured, her tone carefully respectful, "but Regal, were you not just with Auron? I passed the stables not long ago, and I could have sworn I saw you there with him."

Regal blinked, taken aback by her bold interruption. He did not mind her curiosity, but he knew well enough that both Malum and Malament were known for their sharp tempers. His gaze flickered to Malament, who raised an eyebrow, not seeming perturbed—if anything, he looked intrigued, as though waiting to see what Regal would say.

Clearing his throat, Regal looked back at Saanvi, a hint of amusement in his tired eyes. "No, my lady, I've been here for a good while now," he replied, his voice calm but curious. "How long did you say it's been since you passed the stables?"

Saanvi opened her mouth to respond, but before she could speak, Malum, who had remained silent until now, suddenly surged into life. His face contorted with fury, and with a savage roar, he turned toward the stables, his voice echoing through the garden. "IT'S CORA. I'LL GUT THE BITCH MYSELF."

Malament's eyes widened as he watched his father storm off, momentarily stunned by the outburst. He could not know it's Cora, Malament thought bitterly. His father's emotions had spilled out in a reckless wave, shattering any semblance of control he had tried to maintain. Now, two of his most loyal servants had witnessed his fury, and questions were bound to follow.

Malament sighed inwardly, remembering his father's confession from earlier—a reluctant admission of Cora's visit to his chambers that morning and the news she had brought. Malum's pride had been wounded, and he had shared it begrudgingly, leaving Malament with no illusions about the plan that had to follow. The girl could not be allowed to live. But now his father's foolish outburst had only made matters more complicated; they would have to act swiftly and, above all, discreetly.

He turned to Saanvi and Regal; his expression dark but composed. He could not let them leave now, not when whispers could so easily turn into dangerous gossip. "Come, both of you," he ordered, his tone low but sharp. "You are needed at the stables."

Without waiting for their reply, he strode after his father, hoping against hope that it wasn't Cora they would find—or that, if it was, the two witnesses beside him would have the sense to keep silent, lest they share her fate.

# THE ASSASSIN CHAPTER THIRTY THREE

Auron skidded to a stop on the hay-laden floor, his sprint coming to an abrupt halt. The stables were empty save for their usual four-legged residents, and one of the horses lifted its head, snorting in his direction at the sound of his hasty arrival. He glanced around, his heart still pounding. He could have sworn he had seen Regal lingering here earlier, but maybe the old man had doubled back to the house, forgotten something along the way.

Regardless, Auron felt his nerves ease as he stood in the quiet sanctuary of the stables, Saanvi's warning about another whipping fading into the background. The place always had this effect on him, steadying his heart and calming his thoughts. Perhaps it was the horses—their steady breathing, the soft, comforting rustle of hay as they shifted in their stalls. The rich, earthy smell of the hay mingled with the sharper tang of leather and the musk of the animals themselves, familiar and grounding. Certainly, it was not Regal or the ever-present stench of manure that brought him comfort.

Breathing deeply, Auron moved further inside, his fingers brushing along the rough wooden stall doors as he walked. The sounds of hooves shifting, the occasional snort, and the gentle swish of tails surrounded him, a quiet rhythm that soothed his lingering tension. Here, in this simple, familiar world, the worries of the day seemed a little more distant.

Tossing the rope over one of the gate rails, Auron paused, surveying the stable around him. The floor was scattered with clumps of hay, bits of straw, and a thin layer of dust that coated everything in a dull film. If Regal returned to see the mess, he would surely have words for him. Determined to avoid another scolding, Auron grabbed the old broom, its remaining bristles splayed out like the ragged tail of a worn-out fox.

He began sweeping, the broom scraping over the uneven floor as he pushed the hay into a rough pile. Dust rose in soft clouds with each stroke, catching the slivers of light that filtered through the stable windows. Auron wrinkled his nose but kept at it, moving the broom back and forth in steady motions. The task was familiar and calming, each sweep of the broom grounding him as he tidied up.

The horses watched him with mild curiosity, their large eyes following his movements as he worked. He paused to wipe his forehead, then resumed, pushing the stray bits of straw and debris into a neater pile. The stables seemed to settle into their usual quiet rhythm, the gentle rustling of the horses and the steady scrape of the broom the only sounds breaking the stillness.

The foal in the corner pen snorted in his direction, bobbing its head up and down, eager to catch his attention. Auron chuckled at the young foal's antics, its restlessness mirroring his own, and strolled over, crouching down beside the gate. Malaron, his glossy black coat shining in the filtered sunlight, immediately pushed his small head between the gate posts, nudging Auron's hand with a playful insistence.

"You're a good boy, Malaron," Auron murmured, his voice soft as he stroked the foal's neck, feeling the warmth of the animal's skin beneath the velvety coat. "But I've got work to do."

The foal snorted softly, undeterred, and pressed its head against Auron's chest, its ears flicking with what seemed like pure joy. Auron could not help but smile, his fingers tracing gentle circles along Malaron's neck, the young horse's energy contagious. He could feel the steady rhythm of the foal's breath, a quiet comfort that made him forget his duties, if only for a moment.

With a reluctant sigh, Auron straightened, patting Malaron's neck one last time. The foal's large, trusting eyes followed him, a soft neigh escaping its muzzle as if to plead for more company. Auron grinned, looking down at the bright-eyed creature. "I know, but I've got to get back to it," he said, his tone playful yet regretful. "I'll come back later, alright?"

Malaron watched him step away, his gaze unwavering, and Auron's heart felt lighter, the foal's affection a quiet promise of friendship. But then, suddenly, the young foal's eyes flared wide with fear. Malaron reared up, kicking his hooves against the gate, the loud bangs shattering the stable's silence. Startled, Auron instinctively jumped back, his mind barely processing the foal's panic before something sharp flashed past him, slicing the air where he had just been standing.

An old pitchfork hurtled past, its rusted prongs glinting in the dim light as it narrowly missed him. The shock barely registered before it swung back in a vicious arc, cutting sideways toward him. Auron flung himself back, diving out of reach and landing hard on the hay-strewn floor, his breath escaping in a gasp as he hit the ground.

The fork rose high again, whistling through the air as it came down with deadly intent. Auron rolled just in time, the impact of the prongs striking the floor where he had been lying moments before, sending bits of straw flying. His body moved on instinct now, scrambling to his feet and stumbling toward the nearest pen. Another violent blow crashed against the stable floor, the noise echoing like thunder.

Without a second thought, Auron crawled under the pen's low gate, barely evading another strike as it clattered down, splintering the wooden slats behind him. His heart pounded wildly as he crouched in the shadow of the pen, his mind reeling as he processed the attack. The stables, once a place of peace, had turned into a battleground in a matter of seconds.

The pen was narrow, enclosed by a five-foot fence that divided it from the next stall, and Auron found himself pressed against the wooden slats, his heart pounding as he watched his assailant close in. Moving with lightning speed, he scrambled to his feet just as the gate was kicked open, the heavy wood swinging toward him with a deafening crash as it struck the wall behind.

In the next instant, the five-pronged pitchfork jabbed forward, inches from piercing his side. With a burst of adrenaline, Auron leapt over the dividing fence, landing in the larger pen beyond. His breath came in gasps, his muscles tense as he steadied himself, the fenced barrier now a brief respite between him and his attacker.

He took a precious second to assess the situation, his eyes darting between the pen's limited exits and his advancing foe. Whoever was behind this attack, they moved with ruthless intent, leaving him no doubt that this was no accident. The horses in the surrounding pens stirred, some neighing in alarm, their hooves clattering against the ground, amplifying the tension in the confined space.

The figure was cloaked in heavy black hunting wear, his hood casting shadows over his face, though Auron could still make out the man's features—a calm, eerily composed expression beneath the dark fabric, with cold, steely black eyes fixed on him from across the pen. The man's gaze was like that of a predator, unblinking, focused, as if assessing every move Auron might make. Moving with a deadly calm, the intruder strolled out of the pen and into the wide walkway of the stables, his footsteps quiet yet deliberate, his eyes never leaving Auron, tracking him like a hawk locked onto its prey.

But instead of heading directly for Auron's pen, the man in black turned toward the stable doors. Reaching them, he slid them shut with a slow, menacing ease, cutting off the bright beam of sunlight and leaving the stable drenched in shadow. Auron felt a chill run through him as the last trace of light disappeared, the darkness amplifying the man's looming presence. When the intruder turned back, his gaze was darker, his eyes narrowed with an intent that left no room for doubt—he meant to kill.

Auron felt the realisation settle over him, heavy and unmistakable. Yet, to his surprise, he found he was not afraid. The stables had been a place of comfort, a training ground of sorts, and now his instincts kicked in, treating this as if it were just another exercise. Calmly, he scanned the pen around him, noting each object he could use as a makeshift weapon. A pile of hay, a stack of iron horseshoes, and a metal bucket filled with water lay within reach—none were ideal, but they were all he had.

The intruder began his slow, deliberate approach, moving like a shadow across the stable floor, each step closer increasing the tension. Auron seized the metal bucket, tipping it over and letting the water spill out onto the hay-strewn floor, then snatched up a handful of iron horseshoes. They were cold and heavy in his grip, but he held onto them tightly, feeling the rough metal edges press into his skin. He had no clear plan, only the awareness that he would have to act fast and strike with precision.

There was no more time to think; the man in black had reached his pen. Auron's heart thudded in his chest as he braced himself, his grip tightening around the horseshoes. His eyes locked onto the intruder's, his body tense and ready, every sense heightened. This was no longer a place of sanctuary—this was survival.

Gloved fingers pushed against the wooden gate, easing it open with a slow creak as its old hinges protested. The man stepped inside, moving with a predator's patience, his grip firm on the pitchfork. As he advanced Auron felt a surge of memories flood his mind-flashes of the crowded markets, the cramped, dark room that still haunted his dreams, the merciless boys who had beaten him to within an inch of his life. The scene felt all too familiar, the fear dangerously close. He had promised himself vengeance and though this was not it, he would not let fate be so cruel again, this time, he vowed, he would not be the victim.

His focus snapped back to the present as the pitchfork swung toward him with deadly intent. Auron leapt backward, his back slamming into the wooden wall, barely missing the sharp prongs as they sliced through the air. His attacker was relentless, lunging forward, each move calculated and ruthless. Auron rolled to the side just in time, feeling the prongs tear into the wall behind him, the wood splintering as the weapon punched through to the other side.

For a brief moment, the man hesitated, struggling to yank the pitchfork free, and Auron saw his chance. His heart pounding, he sprang forward, raising the metal bucket high. With every ounce of strength, he slammed it down onto the wooden shaft of the pitchfork, feeling the satisfying snap as the weapon broke in two. The force jolted up his arms, but he held steady, watching as the intruder's prized weapon clattered to the floor in two useless halves.

Auron's breathing was ragged, his hands trembling with adrenaline, but he felt a fierce surge of satisfaction. For once, he was not just reacting, not the victim, he was fighting back, determined not to let fate repeat itself.

The man paused, for half a second stunned as the young boy disarmed him in a blink of an eye. It was half a second too long. In that heartbeat, Auron seized one of the heavy horseshoes, gripping it with all his might, and swung his arm upward like a wrecking ball. The metal connected with the man's jaw, a sickening crack reverberating through the air as blood and shattered teeth sprayed from his mouth, his chin exploding with the impact.

Fuelled by a fierce determination, Auron pressed forward as his attacker staggered back, dazed. Without hesitation, he grabbed a second horseshoe, clenching it in his other hand. Leaping forward, he swung again, this time with a brutal strike to the man's left cheek. The force crumpled the lower part of the man's face inward, a mess of broken bone and flesh, rendering it a useless ruin. Auron's gaze narrowed, his rage unyielding as he swung a third time, the blow landing just under the man's nose with a sickening crunch that shattered any teeth left intact.

Dakeard felt his back slam against what he first thought was a wall, only to realise he was sprawled out on the dirt floor, his limbs refusing to obey him. He could not remember falling; one moment he was fighting, and now he lay paralyzed by pain, his face shattered. Desperately, he willed himself to stand, but there was no strength left. He watched in dazed horror as the broken shard of the wooden pitchfork hurtled down, the jagged end aimed directly at his exposed neck.

The sharp point plunged deep, piercing his throat, and a spray of blood gushed into the air, a crimson mist that hung in the dim light before splattering back onto the hay-strewn floor. After all his years in the shadows, after all the lives he had ended, a child had brought him to his own brutal demise. The irony twisted within him as his vision began to blur, each second stretching into an eternity.

Time seemed to slow, and he looked up at the boy who stood over him. The assault had been relentless, calculated, with a cold precision he recognized instantly-this boy was a born killer, fierce and fearless. Unlike himself, who had spent years lurking in shadows, waiting in haystacks for his chance to strike, this child was different. A cruel twist of fate, he thought, as he felt a sadness settle over him-not because he was dying, but because his legacy would end here, unmarked and unknown. There would be no raised profile, no whispered fear of his name in the streets, no more throats cut in the dark.

His life's blood poured from him, staining the golden hay a deep crimson, his strength seeping into the earth with each fading heartbeat. In these last, helpless moments, he tried to turn his thoughts away from his father-the cruel man who had forged him into what he was. Yet what a horrid twist of fate he had suffered, to die in the same manner of his father, slumped below a child.

Desperately he did not want his last thoughts to be of his cruel father. Through his fading vision staring up at the boy he saw his face, and a slow, slanted smile crept across the youngster's lips-a cruel, knowing smile that mirrored the darkness within him. In his last breath, a flicker of happiness touched Dakeard, strange and hollow. Perhaps he had given this boy the same gift his father had given him: the gift of ruthless survival, a legacy written in blood.

Auron stood over the dying man, his gaze steady, unblinking as he took in every detail of the broken figure before him. The man's face, once so composed and predatory, was now twisted in agony, each feature contorted, the once-cold eyes glazed with pain. Blood gushed from his shattered mouth, each laboured breath sending another wave of crimson across his torn lips. Auron waited, searching within himself for any flicker of pity, regret, or guilt, some feeling that might ground him in the gravity of what he had done.

But there was nothing. No guilt, no pity-only an eerie calm, as if a weight had lifted from his shoulders. As he stared into the man's fading eyes, he felt a strange sense of relief, even a hint of joy, as if he'd cast off a burden he hadn't known he carried. He was unburdened, resolute, the thrill of survival thrumming beneath his skin as he watched the man struggle to cling to his final moments.

The stranger's chest rose in a shallow breath, his dark eyes widening as the last pulses of pain contorted his face. His fingers clawed weakly at the dirt, his mouth opening in a silent gasp as he spluttered blood, his body's final defiance slipping away. Slowly, his eyes began to roll back, the light within them fading like a dying ember. Then, with one last shudder, he went still, his grimace frozen as death finally claimed him.

Auron took a breath, feeling nothing but a steady, cold satisfaction as he looked down at his fallen foe. There was no sorrow in him, no fear-only the knowledge that he had survived, and he felt, perhaps for the first time, that he was stronger for it.

Only the whites of the man's eyes stared back now, vacant and unseeing, his grimace frozen in death. For a moment, it felt as if time itself had paused, the air thick with a silence that held the world still. Then, without warning, a powerful sensation surged through Auron—a rush so intense it seemed to flood every inch of him. It was unlike any surge of adrenaline he had ever felt, unlike anything Gordon had taught him.

His blood roared through his veins, his heart pounding with a fierce rhythm that reverberated in his chest, fighting to keep up with the current of energy coursing through him. Every muscle in his body felt charged, taut and powerful, as if he had been filled with raw strength. His vision sharpened, his senses heightened, and for a brief, exhilarating moment, he felt unstoppable, alive in a way he never had before.

But just as suddenly as it had come, the sensation slipped away, leaving him standing there, yearning for it to return, craving that surge of power again. The loss felt almost hollow, as though he had been given a glimpse of something extraordinary, only to have it snatched away. Yet, in the lingering silence, a part of him remained changed, aware of the potential that had awakened within him, however fleeting.

Auron remained rooted in place, his eyes fixed on the lifeless body sprawled before him. He was not sure how much time had passed, only that he felt strangely calm, detached from the scene. The silence of the stables enveloped him, broken only by the faint rustle of hay beneath his feet. Then, suddenly, the stable doors slid open with a loud creak, and sunlight poured into the dim space, casting sharp beams onto the bloody scene.

Still, Auron did not shift his gaze from the corpse. Malum entered first, his face twisted in anger, his strides swift as he stormed toward Auron. But as he neared the pen, his fury wavered, replaced by an expression of shock.

He stopped short, his eyes widening as he took in the sight before him-the assassin he had hired months prior lay sprawled on the dirt floor, his face mangled, a shard of wood jutting from his neck, dark blood staining the ground around him.

Malum's mouth opened, but no words came. He struggled to process what he was seeing-a mere child standing over the body of the man he had once feared, a ruthless killer he had hired to carry out his dark work. In that moment, disbelief overtook him, mixed with a reluctant sense of awe.

Slowly, the others gathered in the stable, drawn by the disturbance, each one pausing as they stepped inside, their eyes widening at the sight. Regal, Saanvi, and even Malament, who had seen his father's wrath more times than he could count, stood frozen, their expressions mirroring the Lord's shock. The silence stretched, the weight of what had happened sinking in, leaving each of them to wonder how a child could have triumphed over death itself.

Eventually, Auron turned to face them, his expression cold and merciless, a hardened look that belied his youth. His unflinching gaze sent a shudder through those gathered, an unsettling reminder of what he had just done. Breaking the silence, Malum finally spoke, his voice low but steady. “I may not know this man’s name, but I can tell his trade well enough. I doubt he was sent for you, Auron, but for me, as I have no shortage of enemies, both foreign and familiar.”

Malum paused, his eyes narrowing as he regarded the boy before him. “Yet, what I see here,” he continued, “is a boy I may have misjudged. My son sees in you a potential I have overlooked. Malament speaks of you as a son, and though I cannot extend such a bond, you have certainly earned more than the life of a slave.” He looked around, ensuring his words carried to all present. “You saved a life today, in exchange for that of this vile man. For that, I will grant you a place beyond what I’d ever considered.”

Malum straightened, his voice firm with authority. “From this day on, you shall no longer live as one of my slaves. There are guest rooms in this household—I will allow you to choose one to be yours.” He glanced at Malament, his tone softening slightly. “I would have you continue your training, Auron, and I will watch from afar with renewed interest. But let this day be forgotten by all who witnessed it. Speak of it to no one.”

Malum’s eyes swept over each of them in turn, solidifying his orders. “Malament, see to your boy and ensure he rests. Perhaps a week away from stable chores will do him well.” He shifted his focus to Regal. “Regal, you are to remain here until I return. This body cannot stay, especially in such a state. Do not let anyone enter. I must consult certain contacts to deal with such a matter discreetly, as you understand."

Finally, his attention settled on Saanvi. "Saanvi, go with my son and attend to Auron. Do not leave his side until he is ready. This experience may bring many demons, and he will need guidance and care. Make it known to all in the household that Auron is no longer a slave but a branch of my family."

He paused, his words carrying weight and finality. "These are your orders from your Lord. See them followed to the letter."

None of the gathered dared to question the Lord's instructions, each setting quickly to their assigned tasks. Malament moved toward Auron, his hand firm on the boy's shoulder as he guided him away from the bloody scene. His eyes flickered over the remnants of the fight—the shattered pitchfork, the splintered wood, the blood-streaked horseshoes lying amidst scattered hay. He tried to make sense of it, but he was accustomed to the clean cuts of swords and the clash of shields, not improvised weapons and brutal desperation. He would have to wait for Auron's account, though he knew now was not the time.

As they stepped out into the sunlight, Malament glanced down at the boy, catching his eye. He nodded, a silent gesture of approval, one that conveyed both pride and understanding. Auron looked back at him with a faint frown, his dark eyebrows knitted together, though a subtle, almost unconscious smile lingered on his lips—a flicker of satisfaction, perhaps even pride.

Yes, Malament thought, watching the boy's expression shift in that brief, unguarded moment. This boy has the spirit of a fighter, a survivor. He felt a sense of certainty settle over him, stronger than before. He will be my champion.

# THE ASSASSIN CHAPTER THIRTY FOUR

The night air was warm, yet Cora felt a bitter chill deep within, a gnawing reminder of her empty stomach. She had not eaten since the day before, and the hours since her flight from the house had stretched long and taxing. Saanvi's directions had become muddled in her mind as she wandered Borlong's maze of streets and narrow alleyways, each corner unfamiliar, every turn seeming to lead her in circles. At last, after what felt like endless wandering—and perhaps more luck than sense—she stumbled upon the stables, a humble cluster of low, dark buildings nestled in a quiet corner of the city.

Now that she had found them, she was not sure if Saanvi had already come and gone, or if she had even arrived at the right place. Still, she lingered, hidden behind an old dust cart missing its wheels, her form huddled in the shadows as the night deepened. She watched, waiting, every sound sharpening her focus, her empty stomach twisting each time a faint footstep approached.

The day's bustling noise had faded to a stillness broken only by the distant murmur of the city's night life. From within the stable grounds, she saw only one lone figure—a tired-looking man on the night shift, his silhouette occasionally passing by a lantern hung near the stable door. The dim light cast long shadows across the cobblestone, and the silence felt heavy, stretching between her and the sanctuary she sought.

For hours, Cora had wrestled with herself, torn between the need for help and the instinct to remain hidden. She studied the lone stableman, wondering if he was trustworthy or if her approach might invite more danger. But unbeknownst to her, he had already noticed her, his keen eyes catching her subtle movements and wary glances. He had waited, patient, biding his time until the streets fell into deeper silence, the city slipping into its slumber.

Finally, he rose from the short wooden bench where he had been perched, stretching his back with a groan. Though not yet old, his face bore the hard lines of a man weathered beyond his years, deep-set wrinkles clawing into his eczema-ridden skin. His ginger beard, matted and tangled, clung to his chin like dried brambles, and his leather clothes hung from his wiry frame, worn thin and torn in places, more like ragged layers than garments.

Scratching at his beard, he let out a loud belch that broke the quiet, then turned his gaze toward the broken dust cart where she hid. "A'right, girl," he called out suddenly, his voice rough but not unkind. "Come out. I know ya be hidin' there—been hours ain't it." He paused, waiting, his eyes narrowed. "What ya want?"

Cora bit her lower lip, feeling a wave of nervous tension tightening around her. The man's voice came again, rough and insistent. "Come out, girl. Y'after summik, ain't ya? Food? Water? A horse?" The word food tugged at her resolve, and before she could stop herself, she stepped out from behind the broken dust cart, her stomach tightening with anticipation and nerves.

Now, standing in front of the stable master, she felt his gaze sweep over her, lingering a little too long on the outline of her chest, his eyes narrowing as he took in every detail. His scent hit her like a wall—stale sweat mingled with the pungent odours of leather and animal—making her suppress a grimace. He barely moved his gaze from her as he spoke again, a smirk twisting at the corners of his mouth. "So, what ya want?"

Cora fought to steady herself, to mask her desperation with a calmness she did not feel, but the hollow ache of hunger gnawed at her focus. The words stumbled out, her voice wavering. "Please, kind sir," she started, her tone careful, pleading. "A bite to eat, or a drink of water, would be welcome... but I need more than that. I need a horse." She swallowed, willing herself to speak more clearly. "I mean to ride from Borlong."

The stableman hawked up a thick glob of phlegm, spitting it on the ground beside him with a wet splat. "Kind sir?" he sneered; his voice laced with mockery. "You ain't find one of those ere." He paused, his tongue darting out to wet his chapped lips, catching on the bristly edges of his beard. His gaze dropped again, lingering on her chest with a slow, unsettling intensity.

"Got any coin, girl?" he asked, his tone casual but his eyes glinting with something far less innocent. "I got what ya askin, but ain't nothin' come free."

A flicker of disappointment crossed Cora's face, and he noticed it immediately, his amusement deepening. He savoured the sight of her vulnerability, feeling a sick thrill at the power it offered him. It would be cruel to force himself on her, even if she did manage to pay, he thought, his arousal heightening at the notion.

"No coin then, me pretty?" he taunted, though he knew her silence was answer enough. He took a step closer, his voice softening into something almost coaxing, though his words dripped with suggestion. "Well, girl like ya got other ways to pay, ain't ya?"

Cora had known this could happen. The thought of running flickered in her mind, but to where? She needed to leave Borlong, and without Saanvi, there was no other way. A pit of dread opened within her as she considered the possibility that Saanvi had been caught, that she might reveal Cora's plan to flee. And now, here she was, cornered by a man whose foul stench clung to the air, nearly tangible, coating her throat as she tried to breathe.

The man was horrid. His skin, where it was not hidden beneath tangled hair, was covered in peeling patches and rough eczema, his unwashed clothes clinging to him like a second, grimy skin. She felt bile rise at the thought of his touch. No, she told herself, I cannot do this.

As if sensing her hesitation, his hand extended, fingers outstretched, lingering in the air between them—a silent demand. His nails were thick with blackened dirt, his palms rough and grubby. "I got an old mare, your's if ya want," he murmured, a twisted smile pulling at his lips. "Not up to much good, but she'll get ya gone." He leaned closer, his voice dropping to a grating whisper. "Ain't gonna cost ya coin, nah, just ya company, warm me bed." His other hand drifted to the growing bulge in his trousers, squeezing it with a sickening delight as he spoke, making his meaning unmistakably clear.

As she stood before the stableman, his gaze crawling over her, Cora's mind drifted, searching for some anchor, some memory that might lend her strength. Instead, her thoughts fell on Malum, the man who had both captivated and ruined her. The stolen hours they had shared, the whispered promises, the soft press of his lips against her skin—all of it now felt like a cruel echo, distant and hollow. She had trusted him once, allowed herself to be drawn in by his words, his charm. He had promised her things, whispered that she was more than a servant, that she was someone he would keep close, protected. How foolish she had been to believe him.

Even now, she could recall his touch, the way his rough hands had softened in the quiet of those late nights, as though he could mask the power he wielded over her with a gentle caress. In those moments, she had felt cherished, wanted—something she had never felt. And yet, beneath that warmth, a current of danger had always thrummed, something dark and unspoken, like a shadow lurking at the edge of a candle's glow. It had thrilled her and terrified her in equal measure.

And then he had turned on her. The same man who had whispered of shared secrets, of something special between them, had become a threat, a danger she could not escape. She had seen the truth in his eyes, when she told him of the child—his child—and had glimpsed a darkness far colder than she had ever imagined. The promises had shattered, his warmth turned to scorn, and the shelter she thought she had found in his arms became the reason she had had to run, to leave everything she knew behind.

Now, in the dim shadows of the stable yard, with hunger twisting her stomach and nowhere left to turn, she felt the weight of that broken promise like a stone pressing on her chest. She was alone, truly alone, with no one to protect her. The stableman's hand reached out, rough and expectant, the filthy nails curled in silent demand. The warm night air felt stifling, each breath a struggle as his fingers beckoned her forward.

In the pale glow of the distant lantern, she could almost imagine Malum's face, his eyes fixed on her with that same possessive gleam, a reminder of the power he had held over her, a power that had bound her and then left her stranded. She took a shuddering breath, feeling the hollow ache of loss twist within her, as though every illusion she had clung to had been stripped away. She was far from those shadowy chambers, from the warmth of his embrace, and as she looked at the stableman's hand, waiting, her only thought was the bitter truth that she was truly, utterly alone.

Cora's stomach twisted, a wave of nausea rising as the full weight of her predicament settled over her. Tears pricked at the corners of her eyes, but she fought them back, swallowing hard. She had no other options; the streets held no promise, and escape from Borlong without a horse was impossible.

She took a final, lingering look at the darkened streets around her, as if hoping, against all reason, to spot a shadow moving toward her, to catch a glimpse of Saanvi stepping from the darkness with her familiar, comforting presence. But the streets were empty, silent save for the steady thump of her own heartbeat. She drew a sharp breath, steadying herself, trying to quell the nausea rising within her.

With a heavy reluctance, she raised her hand, her fingers trembling as she offered it to him. A crooked smile spread across his face as he took it, his grip rough and possessive. Without another word, he turned, leading her away from the open streets and into the shadows, her heart pounding as she braced herself for what lay ahead.

# THE QUEEN'S PROCESSION CHAPTER THIRTY FIVE

The stables loomed closer, shrouded in shadows as Saanvi's pace quickened, her breath shallow. She tried to run, yet her legs felt leaden, as if bound by unseen chains. The lush gardens around her began to fade, dissolving into a blinding white light that scorched her eyes. Only the stable doors remained, cutting through the brightness, drawing her in with a quiet, insistent pull. Her gaze was trapped, unable to look away.

They creaked open without her touch, revealing an unnatural emptiness within-a hollow expanse devoid of pens, hay, or life. At the centre stood Auron, unmoving, his eyes fixed upon a crippled man sprawled at his feet, cloaked in black. As if sensing her presence, the dead man turned his head, his stare hollow, his eyes a soulless, searing crimson against his pale skin. She struggled to tear her attention away, yet his presence consumed her, dragging her nearer.

"No!" she cried, finding herself hovering over the blood-soaked body. Its disfigured face twisted, the fractured jaw gaping open, its voice a rasping mockery of her name. "Saanvi..."

"No!" she choked again, the word a strangled plea.

"Saanvi. Saanvi." The sound grew softer, yet somehow more urgent, echoing through her mind.

With a shuddering breath, she wrenched herself awake, the terrible vision shattering. Blinking in the morning light, Saanvi's eyes widened, meeting the gentle, concerned gaze of a young maid leaning over her.

"Saanvi," the girl repeated softly, her voice a balm against the remnants of the nightmare.

"Yes, I am awake. Thank you," Saanvi replied, her voice softened by lingering sleep. As her eyes adjusted, she realised with a start that she was not in the familiar servant chambers but propped against a mound of plush pillows on a grand bed. Auron lay nestled in her lap, his small hand clutching her skirt, his face serene in slumber. She remembered, then, the gentle way she had cradled him until sleep had claimed her as well.

With a tender smile, she brushed a strand of hair from his forehead, watching his chest rise and fall with each peaceful breath. The room, Auron's new quarters, was bright and beautifully appointed, with polished wood furniture and sunlight streaming through an open balcony across the room. Its warmth touched everything with a golden glow, creating a cocoon of quiet comfort.

Sudden panic snapped her back to reality. "What is the time?" she asked, her voice sharp with worry as she looked to the young maid by the doorway.

"Mid-morning," the maid replied. "I'm here to make the room and—"

"Yes, yes, get to it," Saanvi interrupted gently, though her tone held authority. "But leave the boy be. He had a distressing day yesterday, and he's now a part of the Lord's family. Any request he makes, you are to obey. Understood?"

The maid's eyes widened slightly before she dipped her head in acknowledgment. "Understood, Mistress Saanvi."

Saanvi nodded, a quiet satisfaction settling over her as she glanced down at Auron again. Today would be the beginning of something new for him—she could feel it. And though the dream still lingered in the back of her mind, its shadow was no match for the bright day awaiting them.

Saanvi carefully eased her rotund frame away from Auron, moving with slow staggered movements to avoid stirring the child. Casting one last glance at his peaceful form, she nodded to the maid and left her to her tasks.

Stepping onto the upper floor balcony overlooking the grand hall, she paused, gripping the rail as a chill crept over her. The dream returned, unbidden, and with it, the memory of yesterday's events. It was not the first time she had witnessed death, but this... this was different. The brutality of it lingered, filling her with an unease that would not be easily dispelled. She shivered, banishing the thought, yet Cora's words surfaced, bringing a fresh tangle of worry. The young girl's admission of her affair with Lord Malum—and her fear of being with child. Foolish, she thought. Cora was caught in a storm she could scarcely imagine.

Then, with a start, Saanvi remembered. "Oh no," she muttered, her hands flying to her mouth. She had agreed to meet the young serving girl at the town stables.

Abandoning all thoughts, she hurried down the stairs, her skirts brushing the banister as she descended. She passed several servants in the grand hall, her swift steps and focused expression warding off any greetings or questions. Thankfully, no members of the household were in sight—her absence was late enough as it was.

Saanvi swept into the kitchen, where Quinn was tidying up after breakfast, his sleeves rolled back as he scrubbed the last of the pots. He looked up, his mouth forming a greeting, but his words drifted past her; her mind was elsewhere. Without slowing, she reached for a small basket near the counter, her movements efficient and brisk.

With her prize in hand, she darted back into the main hall and sped along a wide corridor toward the front entrance. Every step echoed her urgency, and as she reached the doorway, she exhaled in relief. The doorman on duty recognised her immediately; he had known her since her first days in service. He opened the door without question, accustomed to her comings and goings. She barely registered his polite greeting as she slipped past him, her focus already on her destination.

Stepping from the entrance onto the open cobbled street, Saanvi was immediately enveloped by the swirl of city life. Groups of townsfolk lingered in conversation or hurried along in all directions, weaving through the bustling morning. The stables lay a fair distance away, but the route was etched in her memory.

She moved swiftly, her focus narrowing as she pushed through the crowded streets and thrumming markets. Her urgency earned her more than a few curses as she nudged past, but she paid them no mind; it was no different from any other day she ventured into Borlong's streets. Around her, merchants bellowed, hawking their wares in fierce voices that cut through the clamour, while traders squabbled over prices and farmers wrestled with unruly livestock. At the street corners, beggars extended their hands in quiet pleas, and thieves lurked in the shadows, their eyes ever watchful.

The people around her wore a kaleidoscope of colours, some clad in fine, dazzling fabrics, others draped in worn, familiar clothing she half-recognised from previous visits. It struck her, then—she had not changed or even washed since yesterday morning. She had no idea what state she looked to be in, and for a brief second, the thought flickered. But she dismissed it just as quickly. Her mind was set on her goal.

She forged ahead, past the bustling centre, through quieter, poorer streets dotted with faded signs for inns, until the noise softened, and the edge of town came into view. Her lack of fitness caught up with her then and it occurred to her how out of breath she was. Stopping for a moment she bent over resting her hands on her knees and panted while she recovered. What a fool she had been, the poor girl must have been so frightened. Her only hope was Cora had found shelter before dusk fully set in. Very few people ventured the streets after nightfall, even the quieter parts were full of brothels or foul people.

She rose again after feeling rested and set off down the dirt track road to the stables. It seemed quiet, there were two stable boys tending to horses another man leaning against a wooden beam and a further two men in discussion. She expected perhaps more people coming in and out but as she approached the single man noticed her. Possibly in his younger thirties sporting a pop belly with a thinning crown, he addressed her in a gruffly tone. "A'right lass, what a pretty like you doin' out this way."

“Spare me the compliments; I'm looking for a girl,” Saanvi replied, her voice firm, the weight of authority unmistakable.

The man snorted, a leering smirk spreading across his face as he gave a crude gesture. “Aye, ain't we all.” He chuckled, oblivious to her simmering patience.

Saanvi gritted her teeth but pressed on. “Perhaps, though this one was under my care. Younger than me, in a similar uniform.”

The man's eyes darted away, his hand moving to scratch his arm, a telltale shift that spoke volumes. “Nah, not round here, pet,” he muttered, feigning disinterest.

Saanvi tilted her head, focus narrowing as she studied him. He would not meet her gaze—confirmation enough of his lie. She stepped forward until they were nearly toe-to-toe. Though taller, he seemed to shrink under her scrutiny, his bravado fading.

“Oh no,” she said, her tone dangerously low. “I think you know exactly who I mean. A pretty face, long dark hair, and an arse you'd want to slap. Tits you'd want to grab.” Her voice rose with each word until she was nearly shouting, her last words slicing through the air.

The man took an awkward step back, stumbling as he tried to escape her advance, and toppled onto his back. He scrambled, his hands and worn boots sliding against the dirt, until his back thudded against a stable door. Saanvi stalked forward, towering over him, her shadow casting him in darkness. He cursed under his breath, his gaze skittering anywhere but at her.

“Ain’t seen her, ya fat bitch. What ya want?” he spat, his words barely concealing his fear.

Saanvi’s hand shot out, slapping him hard across his bristled, sweaty cheek. He let out a whimper, curling into himself, hands flying up to shield his face as he tried to press himself further into the locked stable door.

“Listen to me, you runt of a whore,” she snarled, each word sharp and unforgiving. “I know you’re lying. When I say she was under my care, I mean she worked for me—at Lord Malum Thalron's estate. She shouldn’t be out here, and I was summoned to fetch her. Perhaps this is a job for Lord Malum himself. Would you like me to pass on how helpful you were?”

The man’s defiance melted, his hands falling slowly as he looked up at her, a glimmer of fear in his eyes. He swallowed hard, clearly torn between pride and survival. He stammered, his voice low and ingratiating. "No, no, milady. I think me memory coming back. Too much ale last night, ya see." He gave a weak, nervous chuckle, avoiding her gaze. "She came by here-the night keeper took her in. Looked after her, he did. Then I turned up, ya see, and... well, we sent her on her way this morning, with a fine horse, even gave her some bread for the road."

Saanvi's eyes narrowed; her stare ice-cold as she watched him squirm. He shifted, glancing anywhere but at her, the truth written plainly on his face.

"Unspoilt?" she demanded, her voice cutting through the silence.

The man's eyes darted further away, his guilty expression enough to confirm her worst fears.

"Pig," she spat, fury igniting. She struck him hard across the face, and when he tried to shield himself, she slapped him again, and again, each blow a release of her rage and sorrow. He whimpered, cowering on the ground as she backed away, her chest heaving.

Her heart twisted as she looked at the man-this loathsome excuse for a human-and an ache of regret washed over her. They were pigs, all of them, playing their roles as they always did. But Cora had no money, no means to protect herself. Cora had trusted her, counted on her, and what had she done? She should have been there to shield her, to help her find a way out. The helplessness in Saanvi's chest tightened, a single tear slipping down her cheek. She should have been there. She had let Cora down.

Drying her eyes with the back of her hand, she took a deep, shuddering breath. At least Cora was gone from this place now, spared the cruelties of the estate. Whatever awaited her would be difficult, but perhaps she had a better chance out there-far from the reach of men like these.

“Good show, young lady. Good show,” a voice chimed in. Saanvi turned to see a slender, bearded man dismounting his horse with honed ease. She did not respond, merely nodded, acknowledging his words.

“Sadly, society keeps such men in its ranks,” he continued, his tone laced with disdain as he glanced at the stable master, who was still rubbing his bruised cheek. “Men like him serve no purpose, save for the pull of coin.” With a casual flick of his thumb, he sent a gold piece spinning through the air, landing in the lap of the astonished stable master.

“See my horse fed and watered. I’ve travelled far, and my company shall arrive soon. Prepare space for twenty stallions, three carriages, and know we bring a further thirty more horses and as many supply wagons. We’ll need all the room you can manage,” he ordered, his voice commanding.

The stable master scrambled to his feet, clutching the gold as if it were his lifeline. “Aye, sir,” he muttered, his tone deferential as he ignored Saanvi entirely and hastily set about his tasks.

The stranger watched him go, a faint smirk on his face. “Point proven, unfortunately.” Turning back to Saanvi, he continued, “Now, if I heard correctly, you mentioned you work at the Lord’s estate?”

Saanvi regarded him with a mix of caution and curiosity. “You did, but… my apologies, sir. Who might you be?”

“Forgive my lack of manners,” he replied with a slight bow. “Durak Karesh, I am Galil Askrson of Nordon, head of Stormhold’s timber guild.”

The words hung in the air for a moment, foreign yet resonant, their meaning clear in the strength of his tone. *'Durak Karesh,'* a formal greeting between warriors and those of respect in Nordon, was not merely a pleasantry—it was a declaration of mutual acknowledgment, an offering of strength to strength. For Galil, it was a way of honouring the customs of his homeland, even here in Borlong, far from the frostbitten lands of the Winter Realm. "I left our travelling party at dawn on the order of Queen Karak Thørn herself. My task is to reach Borlong ahead of the procession and inform Lord Malum Thalron of our imminent arrival."

Saanvi's heart quickened. So, the Queen's presence would soon stir these grounds. Her gaze shifted to Galil, her mind racing. This was no ordinary guest; his title carried weight, and his mission underscored the importance of the meeting to come.

"Well then, Master Askrson, welcome to Borlong," she said, gathering herself with a polite nod. "I'm Saanvi, head maid at the estate. If you need assistance arranging accommodations, I'd be pleased to help."

Galil offered a gentle smile through his greying beard, noting the sudden shift in Saanvi's manner. Her tone had become noticeably more formal—a natural reaction, given the company he represented.

"Queen Karak is accompanied by her Royal Guard Commander, a Stormhold treasury representative, and merchants from the blacksmith, leatherwork, weaver, alchemist, and culinary guilds," he explained. "In addition, she travels with fifty men-at-arms, four handmaids, and twenty horsemen. Altogether, there are thirteen primary guests, though the handmaids will remain with their respective patrons, and the men can be accommodated in nearby taverns. Does the Lord have the accommodations to cater to such a group?"

Saanvi met his gaze with a steady nod. "Yes, we can accommodate them, but arrangements will need to be made. Let us travel to the estate, and I'll see that everything is prepared."

Galil inclined his head, satisfaction evident. "Lead on, then, Mistress Saanvi. But before we do, I must admit I'm parched. Your weather is far warmer than what I'm accustomed to—riding in such heat takes its toll." He gave her a warm smile, his question light but clearly expectant.

Saanvi knew the area well; while there were plenty of inns nearby, none were places she would recommend to even the most unpleasant family member, let alone a foreign diplomat. She thought quickly, choosing her words carefully.

"How thirsty are you, sir? Only because the inns here might be... unbefitting of a man of your stature," she replied, letting the compliment sink in. Years in service had taught her that the powerful never minded hearing of their importance.

Galil paused, clearly pleased. He had intended to delay informing Lord Malum of the approaching party, simply to create a bit of difficulty. Yet her words seemed to sway him. "How far is it to the estate?" he inquired, looking her over with interest.

"Not to worry, sir," Saanvi assured him, her tone reassuring. "I'll have you back sooner than you think, and I'll see that the chef prepares chilled soup with fresh bread—and any drink you'd prefer."

"Very well, lead on," he relented. "My company should arrive just after midday."

With a nod, Saanvi turned back toward the estate, Galil at her side. His stride, however, was leisurely, and he stopped at several market stalls along the way, bartering with locals over trinkets. He purchased a fine linen toga in pristine white and a silver chain, examining each item with an eye for quality.

Saanvi masked her impatience as best she could, watching the sun climb higher with each pause. The diplomats would arrive soon, and there was much to prepare. Still, she knew better than to hurry him, keeping her expression calm as she waited for each exchange to conclude.

# THE QUEEN'S PROCESSION CHAPTER THIRTY SIX

After a laboured journey, the estate finally came into view, its familiar silhouette a welcome sight against the early noon sky. Saanvi's steps slowed as they crossed the final stretch; she could feel the weight of the morning's rush pressing down on her, and her stomach growled, a reminder that she had yet to eat. But there was no time to think of herself now; their guest required immediate attention.

She led the Nordon merchant through the grand entrance, his gaze sweeping over the estate's high arches and polished floors with an approving nod. In the large dining hall, she paused, gesturing toward a carved oak chair at the head of the long table. "Please, Master Askrson," she said, her tone courteous but firm. "The maids will see to your needs."

With a subtle bow, she turned, addressing a nearby maid with quiet authority. "See to the guest's comfort. Have the chef prepare a proper brunch for Master Askrson—he's had a long journey." Her words carried to the kitchen maids bustling nearby, who nodded and disappeared through the side doors in search of Quinn.

After giving her instructions to the maids, Saanvi hurried through the grand hall, her footsteps echoing off the high ceilings and polished marble. She ascended the wide staircase, each step feeling steeper as her fatigue set in, but she pressed on, determination fuelling her. Finally, she reached the small reception area outside Lord Malum's chambers, where a handful of familiar faces had already gathered.

Inside the room, Saanvi could see Amudi, the Lord's trusted servant, tall and imposing with his deep umber skin and deliberate gaze, a mark of his origins in the Drylands. Beside him stood a young maid, her prettiness marked by the quick, shy glances she cast at the nobles nearby—likely just another day attending to their endless inquiries. Two minor nobles were speaking in low voices, their expressions laced with impatience and self-importance, no doubt seeking answers to matters of small significance.

Saanvi barely hesitated. She could not afford to wait for decorum or for her turn to be seen. With purpose, she strode straight for Amudi, her gaze fixed and unwavering. Amudi noticed her approach and met her eyes with a respectful nod, though a hint of curiosity flickered across his face —she seldom appeared with such haste unless the news was urgent.

"Amudi," she said in a low, steady tone as she reached him, aware of the nobles' sudden attention, "I bring important news for the Lord."

Amudi's grasp of Kadun's tongue was limited, but he understood well enough. Saanvi kept her voice low but urgent. "I need an immediate meeting with the Lord, or you must convey my message."

Amudi straightened, his stern expression immediately signalling caution. Bursting into Lord Malum's chambers without invitation—especially as a servant—was nearly unthinkable. Yet, seeing the intensity in her eyes, he leaned closer, willing to listen.

"Queen Karak of Nordon is arriving this afternoon," she whispered, each word deliberate. "She seeks council with the Lord and expects to be accommodated. Her ambassador is already in the dining hall, taking his meal."

Amudi's eyes widened, and he studied her for a moment before nodding. Without a word, he turned, moving toward the others waiting in the reception area. His imposing presence and stern expression were enough; he barely needed to speak.

"You must go," Amudi intoned, his deep accent thick with authority. The two nobles exchanged surprised looks, momentarily defiant as they lingered, their pride clearly bruised by the abrupt dismissal.

The maid, on the other hand, seemed almost relieved, her shoulders softening as she gathered her things and turned to leave. Saanvi's eyes lingered on the girl, noting her features—pleasant, though lacking the delicate charm Cora possessed. She could guess easily enough the reason for the young maid's presence here, her visits perhaps spurred by reasons beyond simple duties.

But the nobles were not so willing to relent. They muttered between themselves, voices thick with discontent, each casting dark glances at Amudi.

"Must go now," Amudi interrupted firmly, cutting off their grumblings with a finality that left no room for dispute. His unyielding stare silenced the nobles, who begrudgingly turned to leave, their discontent still simmering but their courage no match for the servant's imposing presence. As the last of them exited, Amudi turned back to Saanvi, giving her a nod that was both an invitation and a warning.

Amudi turned to the heavy door, rapping his knuckles against the dark wood in a series of measured knocks. He stepped back, hands folded as he waited, his posture a picture of patient deference. The seconds stretched, and when no response came, he glanced at Saanvi before knocking again, this time a shade louder.

A muffled voice sounded from within, too faint for Saanvi to catch the words, but it was enough. Amudi reached for the handle, pushing open the door with a quiet, steady motion. The hinges groaned slightly as the large door swung inward, revealing the luxurious chamber within.

Beyond the threshold lay a room of exquisite luxury, bathed in warm creams and shimmering golds, its elegance divided into two distinct sections. The first was a spacious living area, dominated by a long cream sofa trimmed with golden embroidery, its gleaming surface softened by a matching coffee table and two opposing armchairs, each upholstered in fine fabrics. Against the right-hand wall, a massive gilded fireplace stood, its ornate details catching the light, though it had clearly sat unused for some time, the faint scent of polished metal lingering in the air.

Toward the rear of the room, an imposing bed, elevated four feet above the gleaming marble floor, commanded attention, draped in rich linens and surrounded by opulent curtains that hinted at privacy and indulgence. Three grand pillars ran through the centre, their polished surfaces subtly dividing the living and sleeping spaces.

The second section of the room featured an expansive dressing area, framed by floor-to-ceiling mirrors on two of the walls, each mirror reflecting the grandeur of the surroundings. Beyond this, an open balcony stretched outward, its wide arches revealing the estate's gardens below, a lush and vibrant contrast to the restrained opulence within.

Saanvi paused just within the doorway, the weight of the room's grandeur pressing down on her. It was as if every detail had been carefully chosen to remind anyone entering just who Lord Malum was—a man of power, a man used to the finer things, and a man who rarely welcomed uninvited guests. She steadied herself, preparing to deliver her news.

"What is this?" Malum's voice rang out, his brow furrowing as he caught sight of Saanvi, clearly expecting a different visitor. His gaze lingered, a flash of disappointment betraying his assumption that the guest would be someone of finer proportions.

Amudi bowed low, bending nearly to his waist, before straightening with deliberate grace. "I sorry, forgive. Woman have large news."

Malum's expression shifted as he processed this, realising that Amudi would not have allowed a servant in uninvited without just cause. Trusting Amudi's judgement implicitly, he recalled that it was Saanvi who had witnessed the incident at the stables the day prior—perhaps there had been a complication with the arrangements.

“Thank you, Amudi. You may take your leave.”

“Sir.” Amudi inclined his head in a final bow, then exited, the door closing softly behind him.

Malum turned back to Saanvi, his gaze appraising as he extended a hand toward one of the chairs near the sofa. “Sit,” he instructed, his voice tempered now with curiosity.

Saanvi complied, taking her seat with careful composure as Malum strode to the bedside table. He lifted a silver jug and poured rich red wine into a goblet, filling it halfway before bringing it to his lips for a thoughtful sip. Satisfied, he crossed the room, settling onto the sofa across from her, his eyes keen and watchful.

The slim Lord took another measured sip of wine, setting the goblet down on the coffee table before reclining into the plush cushions of the sofa. He gave a slight nod, signalling her to proceed.

“My Lord,” Saanvi began, her tone steady and respectful. “During my visit to the markets this morning to gather supplies for the kitchens, I encountered a merchant who seemed... distinct. His manner and speech caught my attention, and upon listening closer, I realised he was a man from Nordon. I questioned him further, and as it turns out, he is an ambassador for Queen Karak.”

A smile crept onto Malum's face, slow and satisfied. At last. It was about time they graced Borlong with their presence for the annual visit.

“Very good. Well done, Saanvi,” he praised, his tone tinged with approval. “I'm pleased you brought this to me so swiftly. Tell me, when was his arrival?”

"He arrived only this morning, my Lord, and has requested lodgings here. I brought him directly, and he is currently in the dining hall, taking brunch," Saanvi reported, her tone efficient yet respectful.

Lord Malum nodded; satisfaction clear in his expression as he opened his mouth to speak. But Saanvi, sensing his eagerness, quickly pressed on.

"He is not alone, however. Queen Karak herself, along with eight of her advisors, are also en route to Borlong and will arrive at any moment. I am told they too will require accommodation," Saanvi informed him, her tone steady as she conveyed the urgency.

Malum's eyes brightened, his smile widening like that of a delighted child handed a prized gift. "This is excellent news," he proclaimed, his voice brimming with anticipation. With barely a pause, he reached for his goblet, tipping it back and draining it in a single, triumphant motion.

Setting the goblet down with a firm clink, he straightened, his expression sharpening as he outlined his orders. "Have all nobles and guests ushered out of their chambers. We shall need every available room. If they question you, inform them of the reason, but otherwise, say nothing. We'll prepare a grand feast tonight, with music and dancing. Tell Chef to craft his finest cuisine—any ingredients he requires, have someone fetch them from the market. Spare no expense."

Saanvi listened intently; her focus unwavering as he continued.

"Inform everyone in the household of the Queen's arrival. I expect the highest standards from each of them. If anyone offends our guests, they will be punished severely." His tone softened slightly yet held a certain knowing glint. "And tell the young maids to look their best. If our guests desire... companionship, so be it. Understood?"

Saanvi lowered her head in acknowledgment. "All shall be put in place, my Lord," she replied.

"Also, let's arrange a proper welcome committee to greet our guests at the stables this afternoon," Lord Malum continued, his tone brisk with excitement. "I want Malament to lead this procession, accompanied by enough strong men to carry all their belongings. And have three bottles of Borlong Red sent ahead, along with ample barrels of water for all the travellers."

Saanvi gave a sharp nod, her mind already calculating the logistics.

"Oh, and one last thing," Malum added, leaning back thoughtfully. "Inform our current guest that I shall join him shortly. What was his name?"

"Galil Askrson, my lord," Saanvi replied smoothly.

Malum nodded, pleased. "Yes, Galil Askrson. He has visited the last few seasons I believe, see to it he's comfortable and entertained until I arrive."

Once more, she bowed her head. It seemed that each time Lord Malum spoke, another idea emerged, followed by yet another instruction. The list was growing, and she was beginning to lose track. Recognising that time was slipping away and much needed to be done, Saanvi decided it was best to depart before any more directives were added.

"I shall take my leave, my Lord," she said respectfully. "There is much to prepare."

Lord Malum gave a dismissive nod, already turning his thoughts elsewhere. Seizing the moment, Saanvi turned and exited the chamber, her mind already organising the multitude of tasks ahead. The weight of responsibility settled on her shoulders, but she moved with purpose—there was no room for delay when hosting royalty.

Left alone, Malum felt a surge of exhilaration rise within him. His fingers trembled faintly with the thrill of what lay ahead, and he wasted no time in pouring another goblet of wine, draining the last drops from the jug as he filled it to the brim. The deep red liquid gleamed richly in the goblet, and he savoured the taste, letting the warmth spread through him.

Goblet in hand, he strolled to the open balcony, where the gardens stretched out in a meticulously kept display, each path and bed a testament to his wealth and status. The air carried a slight chill, just enough to make him aware of the breeze brushing through the gardens, stirring the leaves and sending faint ripples through the fountain below. A thin layer of clouds dulled the midday sun, casting the estate in a soft, muted light.

He breathed in deeply, feeling the coolness expand in his chest. The sky hinted at clearing, the way it often would as morning turned into afternoon, with clouds shifting to reveal patches of gentle blue. The thought of Queen Karak, with her entourage and advisors, arriving at his doorstep brought a triumphant smile to his face. To host such esteemed guests and be the centre of attention filled him with a heady sense of power. Today, Borlong would be at its finest, and he, Lord Malum, would preside over it all.

In a single afternoon, his status would be elevated, his influence secured. The prospect sent a thrill coursing through him as he imagined the admiration his estate would inspire in the visiting nobles. He took a long sip from the goblet, savouring every drop, his gaze fixed on the gardens below, already envisioning the grand evening that awaited.

Raising the goblet to his lips, Malum downed the wine in a single, eager gulp, his excitement overtaking any sense of restraint. The rush of warmth hit him immediately, spreading through his limbs and filling his head with a pleasant, dizzying buzz. "It shall be a fine day!" he called out to the empty room, his voice carrying with it a childlike thrill. He staggered slightly, chuckling at his own clumsiness before regaining his balance, a wide grin stretching across his face.

The anticipation coursing through him was intoxicating. He felt invincible, buoyed by the prospect of Queen Karak's arrival and the glory his estate would soon embody. Fuelled by his excitement, he strode to the door and flung it open, finding Amudi standing just outside, ever patient and vigilant. The tall servant turned to face him, his expression stoic, awaiting his lord's next command.

"Bring me a bottle of Borlong Red, Amudi, and a fine maid you find along the way," Malum declared with a broad smile, his voice rich with enthusiasm. "I want to celebrate this morning in style."

Amudi gave a slight bow, his face impassive as he nodded. Malum could see the glimmer of acknowledgment in his servant's eye, and it only amplified his own satisfaction. Today, he would indulge in everything his title afforded him—wine, luxury, and the promise of power.

# THE QUEEN'S PROCESSION CHAPTER THIRTY SEVEN

Malament stood at the front of a grand courtyard, just beyond the city gates and adjacent to the stables where Saanvi had first met the Nordon diplomat. The flagstones gleamed under the late morning light, freshly scrubbed to a fine sheen, each stone a testament to Borlong's meticulous attention to detail for such an occasion. Towering timber walls framed the courtyard, each bearing banners of East Kadun—deep red cloth emblazoned with the golden crest of their nation, fluttering in the gentle breeze. The courtyard had been meticulously prepared for this welcome, a place now designed to convey both East Kadun's hospitality and unyielding resilience.

However, before the arrangements could be set, Malament had first dealt with the locals, who had gathered with curiosity as word of the royal visitors spread. Townsfolk had been lingering around the courtyard, their presence creating a cluttered, chaotic atmosphere that clashed with the poised elegance Malament intended. He had sent a few soldiers to disperse them, mindful that the Queen's first impression of Borlong should not be a crowd of gawking commoners. Now, with the courtyard cleared of all but the most polished of East Kadun's representatives, the scene was set to receive their honoured guests.

His gaze swept over the assembled welcome party, an impressive display of Borlong's elite. At the forefront stood five senators, each draped in the formal sashes of Borlong's council, their expressions dignified and proud, embodying the authority of East Kadun's ruling body. Beside them, twenty soldiers stood in tight formation, their armour polished to a mirror-like gleam, casting flashes of sunlight as they stood at attention. Their presence alone spoke of East Kadun's readiness, each soldier a silent testament to the country's endurance.

Behind them, ten maids moved swiftly and efficiently, attending to the final touches. They straightened sashes, adjusted bridles, and double-checked provisions with focused precision, each task completed with careful grace. Clad in clean, simple gowns, the maids worked with expressions of quiet determination, aware that their presence today was more than routine. Five horse-drawn carts stood ready nearby, sturdy and polished, each with space reserved for the visitors' belongings. One cart bore a large keg of Borlong Red, the estate's renowned and finest vintage, at Lord Malum's insistence—a welcoming gesture symbolising the richness of East Kadun. Alongside it sat several barrels of water, a practical yet thoughtful provision for the journey-weary travellers.

At the edge of the group, Malament's own council, Luka, checked his gear with a relaxed, casual confidence. His steady presence was a source of reassurance for Malament, a reminder of their shared loyalty and understanding. Malament felt a sense of readiness, he would lead this welcome party with the grace and strength that befitted East Kadun. It was an honour to represent his father's estate in such a way, and he intended to make every detail flawless.

Yet even amid the spectacle of the courtyard, Malament's thoughts drifted back to the stables—the air thick with the scent of blood, dark splatters staining the hay, jagged breaks along the wooden boards of a pen, and, above all, Auron, standing there amidst the chaos, alive against all odds. The scene had unsettled him in a way few things could. He was no stranger to bloodshed; violence was a fact of life, and he had once seen brutality firsthand at Cordon, where a rogue group of tribesmen met a savage end against the fort's walls. But there was something different about the stables. The attack on Auron did not fit, and the more he considered it, the more questions it raised.

How had Auron survived?

Malament had seen ambushes before; it was rare for anyone to escape with their life, let alone without a single scratch—especially someone as young and untrained as Auron. The boy was brave; Malament knew that much. There was a resilience to Auron that he had come to admire, but bravery and resilience alone would not have been enough to fend off a deadly ambush, especially unarmed. Auron had walked away unharmed, an impossibility that gnawed at Malament.

The image of Auron standing amidst the bloodstains flashed through Malament's mind. His clothes were spattered with the attacker's blood, not his own, an improbable testament to his survival. Most men, even seasoned fighters, would have been killed instantly. And yet, Auron —unarmed, defenceless—had endured. It was as though he had been protected by some hidden instinct or an unseen force, something that had guided him through the encounter with uncanny precision. How had he known to dodge each blow? How had he sensed the threat at all?

Was it mere luck? Or was there something about Auron that Malament had yet to understand?

Then there was the attacker—the man who had attempted to kill Auron. Why would anyone hide in a busy stable? Malament's mind replayed the scene again, retracing every possible angle. The stables were not quiet, often filled with attendants, sometimes even guards. Hiding there would almost guarantee discovery. Unless… the assailant had been waiting for someone specific. Had Auron accidentally stumbled into a trap meant for another? Or, more chillingly, had Auron himself been the intended target?

The idea twisted uncomfortably in Malament's mind. If Auron was the target, what reason could anyone have to harm him? And if not Auron, then who? Who else would enter the stables alone, becoming an easy mark in such an ambush? A dozen theories swirled in his mind, each more convoluted than the last, yet he could not dismiss any of them.

Later, after everyone had left the stables, Malament had returned to the scene, inspecting every inch, every splintered board and bloodstain, as if the wood and hay held the answers he sought. He could almost see the struggle play out—a brief but violent clash, with Auron somehow fending off his attacker against all odds. The signs were there: a scuff mark here, a splintered board there, all evidence of a fierce, hasty scuffle. But one detail stood out more than any other—the broken pike fork, discarded in two pieces.

The pike fork—an old farm tool, barely good for shifting hay—had been used as a weapon. Malament had picked it up, running his fingers over the snapped handle and twisted prongs, trying to imagine it as anything but an act of desperation. Why use a pike fork? If the attacker had intended to kill, surely he would have brought something purposeful—a blade, a weapon he was adept with.

The choice made no sense. An experienced assailant would have come prepared, with something sharp, deadly, familiar. Instead, the attacker had grabbed a pike fork, a clumsy tool, requiring far more strength than skill. It spoke of haste, perhaps even panic. Was it an improvised weapon chosen in the moment? Or had the attacker entered the stables unarmed, perhaps with no intention to kill?

Malament's brow furrowed as he considered this possibility. If the assailant had not planned to kill Auron, what had been his intent? Was this an act of intimidation gone awry, or something more calculated?

Every piece of evidence pointed to something complex, something staged, almost. As though the killer had not set out with clear intentions.

And the motive... What plausible reason could anyone have to harm Auron? The boy had no enemies, as far as Malament knew; he was merely a child under his father's protection. But maybe that was the key. Perhaps this attack was part of a larger scheme, a strike aimed at Malament's family itself. Could there be threats brewing beneath the surface, dangers connected to his father's political alliances and rivalries?

The stables, the choice of weapon, Auron's improbable survival—it was all a puzzle, pieces scattered in shadow, just beyond reach. Malament's mind churned, each question twisting into another layer of mystery, each detail refusing to settle. He needed answers. And if there were hidden intentions, dark motives behind the attack, he needed to know who was pulling the strings.

Malament's gaze flicked to his friend, Luka, who was standing nearby, seemingly absorbed in his own thoughts. Luka had a way of uncovering things others could not. He knew people, he knew places, he had connections, quiet ones, across Borlong. And if anyone could find the answers Malament sought, it was him.

With a sense of resolve, Malament approached Luka, lowering his voice so that only his friend could hear. "Luka, there's something I need you to look into," he said, his tone measured but intense. "You've got connections around Borlong—more than I, in certain circles. I want to know who that man was in the stables. And more importantly, why he was there."

Luka glanced up, his brow furrowing as he studied Malament's expression. "You suspect something more than a chance encounter?" He asked, his voice quiet, yet his gaze sharp, assessing.

Malament nodded, jaw clenched. "Think about it. The stables are often busy throughout the day—hardly a place for someone to hide unnoticed. Either the man was waiting specifically for Auron, or he was there with a purpose I haven't yet understood." His fingers flexed against the hilt of his sword, a gesture he had not even noticed until Luka's eyes flicked to it. "I examined the scene myself afterward. The broken boards, the blood... it didn't look like an act of desperation. I need answers, Luka. For Auron's sake."

Luka's eyes narrowed slightly, as though weighing the risk, but he nodded. "You've seen something others missed, then," he replied, voice low. “I’ll dig quietly. No one will know I was looking.”

A flicker of relief crossed Malament’s face, yet his mind remained tense, turning over each detail he had observed. He grasped Luka’s shoulder briefly. “I owe you,” he murmured.

“You owe me nothing, Malament.” Luka’s tone softened, the slightest hint of a smile tugging at his lips. “But I’d start watching your back, just in case. Sometimes, answers bring questions we wish we hadn’t asked.”

As Luka turned, Malament exhaled, forcing his mind back to the task at hand. But Luka’s last words lingered, leaving a faint chill in the air, as though a shadow had slipped between them. He resumed his place at the head of the welcome party, yet the thoughts from earlier still hovered, refusing to settle. He sighed, forcing his mind to quiet. Now was not the time for unanswered questions.

His eyes scanned the scene around him, the familiar landscape of Borlong grounding him. To his left, the forests stretched in an endless dark green expanse, their thick branches swaying gently in the light breeze, concealing countless mysteries within their shadows. To his right, the timber wall of Borlong stood tall and steadfast, each log weathered and interlocked, a testament to the city’s enduring strength and resilience against time and turmoil.

Beneath its shadow, just outside the city gates, a pack of stray dogs sniffed around stacks of timber, marking their territory and scavenging for scraps. The ordinary, earthy scent of wood and soil mingled with the air, momentarily distracting him from the tension simmering inside.

Ahead of him, the road stretched north, straight and narrow, its dusty path veering off slightly before disappearing over a distant hill. The sky was a brilliant blue, the air clear and crisp, with only a few sparse clouds drifting lazily above. It was a beautiful day—a deceptive calm that seemed to mock the storm of questions within him.

And then he saw it.

At first, it was just a small black dot, barely discernible atop the distant hill. He narrowed his gaze, squinting as the shape grew, coming slowly into sharper focus. Soon, a faint cloud of dust rose above it, trailing like a shadow in the wind. The shapes solidified, and he could make out the details: banners held high, their colours catching the sun, the figures of marching men, carriages, and horses, all moving in unison. They were drawing closer by the second.

A shiver of anticipation ran through him as he watched the large convoy approach. There they were—the men of Stormhold, the envoy from Nordon. The Queen's retinue moved with the steady, rhythmic march of soldiers accustomed to both pageantry and war. There was an aura of command about them, something dark and powerful. What would they bring with them, he wondered? A blessing? Or perhaps... the storm, as their name suggested?

His heart quickened, his mind racing to anticipate what lay ahead.

# THE QUEEN'S PROCESSION CHAPTER THIRTY EIGHT

Queen Karak leaned forward, peering through the narrow carriage window as Borlong's walls rose in the distance, framed by East Kadun's banners snapping sharply in the breeze. Among them flew her own standard—crimson red with a black hammer—and beside it, Nordon's blue and silver anvil. The sight stirred a ripple of satisfaction within her. This was the first step, the opening act of the performance she had crafted with meticulous care. She would be the gracious monarch they all wanted—dignified, composed, diplomatic. She would give Lord Malum no reason to question her motives.

Yet beneath that polished facade, tension coiled like a drawn bowstring. The journey had tested her in ways she hadn't anticipated. Every mile from Nordon was a reminder of her sacrifices, a relentless erosion of patience. Nights spent in her cramped carriage, cold even beneath heavy furs, had left her shoulders aching and her endurance frayed. The inns they passed—fine by most standards—offered little relief. Thin mattresses, rough stone floors, and food that lacked flavour and underwhelmed her palate. It was a stark contrast to Stormhold's comforts, where tapestries trapped warmth and the faint scent of pine lingered from the timber stores. Here, every jolt of the carriage was a reminder of the luxuries she had left behind.

Karak brushed a lock of hair from her face, her fingers pausing at her temple, as if to push back the headache that had shadowed her since dawn. Her discomfort, however, soon gave way to a sharper focus as Borlong's gates came into view. Her eyes narrowed at the welcome party assembled ahead. Polished armour caught the sunlight, and senators in ceremonial sashes stood rigid, their faces solemn beneath the weight of expectation. At the forefront, a tall figure with blonde hair stood apart—Malament. She had heard much of Lord Malum's son, of his intelligence and potential, though tempered by inexperience. A glance would reveal whether he was as clever as the rumours suggested.

Allowing herself a faint smile, she leaned back, her breath fogging the glass. This was a game, and she was its master player. The long nights, the chill of the road, the aches of travel—mere inconveniences. She had weathered greater trials and would endure this one for her kingdom's sake and the success of her plan.

Drawing the velvet curtain aside, she glanced at her retinue. Her soldiers moved in disciplined formation, their solemnity a reflection of her command. Every step, every gesture, was deliberate—an extension of her authority. Today, they were not conquerors but representatives of Nordon, their behaviour measured to project dignity and restraint. She had impressed upon them the stakes of this journey, but only she understood the full scope of the plan and the precision with which each piece must fall into place.

"Best behaviour," she murmured to herself, the words a cold reminder of the weight she bore. She straightened in her seat, letting the thin cushion take her weight. Her fingers tightened on the edge of her cloak, arranging her features into a mask of calm composure. Whatever discomfort lingered, she allowed it to simmer, feeding the iron resolve within her.

As Borlong drew closer, the hum of anticipation thickened in the air. She could feel the watchful eyes of her entourage, awaiting her signal. With a deliberate breath, Karak straightened once more. She would play her role to perfection. But this time, the stakes were higher, the risks greater—and the rewards beyond measure.

A sharp knock jolted Queen Karak from her thoughts. She pulled the curtain closed and straightened, smoothing her cloak as the door opened. Konan ducked his head as he stepped into the cramped carriage, his tall frame filling the space. He glanced around with a slight frown before settling himself across from her, his broad shoulders brushing against the interior walls.

"Is everything all right, Sister?" he asked, his voice low yet edged with concern. "You've been cooped up in here for hours."

Karak managed a small smile, though her fingers still gripped the edge of her cloak. "Enduring, as ever. Another ten minutes of rough travel will hardly break me."

Konan's gaze softened, and he gave a slow nod. "It's been a hard journey," he admitted, settling back against the seat, though his body remained tense, every inch of him bracing against the constant jostling. "These roads are no match for the stone streets of Stormhold. And the inns we've stayed in..." He trailed off with a shake of his head.

Karak allowed herself a brief chuckle. “I’ve grown fond of thin bedding and questionable food,” she replied dryly. “They keep me grounded.” Her eyes flicked to the curtain again, watching as Borlong’s walls loomed ever closer. “But we’re nearly there. The discomfort will be behind us soon.”

Konan nodded, his eyes creasing as he shifted his vision out the window. For a moment, they sat in silence, the rhythmic rumble of the wheels filling the space between them. Then, as Borlong’s gates drew nearer, Karak caught sight of the young man at the front again, the one who stood a little taller than the others, his stance less rigid, yet every bit as composed.

She tilted her head toward the window. “Look there,” she murmured, just loud enough for Konan to hear. “The Lord’s son. That’s him—Malament. Tell me, what do you make of him?”

Konan leaned forward, his piercing gaze following hers. He studied Malament with a critical eye, silent as he took in the young man’s stance, the way he held himself with an air of self-assuredness yet still betrayed the faintest hint of nerves, his hand resting near the hilt of his sword, as though ready for anything.

After a long pause, Konan gave a slow nod. “Young, but not naive. He’s trying hard to look composed—good posture, eyes forward. Not much different from how I was at his age.” He scratched his beard, his fingers brushing over the iron clasps woven through it. “Still… he looks alert, maybe a touch wary. Seems like he’s been taught well, but he’s not hardened yet. He’s green.”

Karak let out a soft hum, her eyes lingering on Malament. “Green, yes… but that can be to our advantage. Young enough to be guided, still forming loyalties. And yet, Lord Malum’s heir, with all the responsibilities that entails.”

Konan’s mouth twisted slightly. “You think he’ll be a useful tool?”

“Perhaps,” she replied, her voice thoughtful, her attention shifting back to Malament, observing every detail—the way he held himself, the barely concealed tension in his stance, the way his eyes scanned the road ahead, eager yet cautious.

“But I wonder…” She trailed off, as if in thought, then turned back to her brother, her voice lowered, deliberate. “How would you feel about testing him? Try his patience on occasion, challenge him. Make sure he feels uncomfortable around you."

Konan raised an eyebrow, a faint smirk tugging at his lips. "You want me to make the lad sweat a little, do you?"

"Just enough to keep him off-balance," she replied, her tone deceptively light. "I want to see how far we can push him—find out what kind of control he truly has. Wind him up, Konan. Let's see if we can expose a fault line between him and his father. Our presence is merely for show but what damage we can cause in the meantime."

Konan's smirk turned into a dark grin, a glint of mischief and anticipation in his eyes. "Consider it done. I'll measure every inch of his temper, see how much he can take before he cracks. By the end of it, he won't know whether to blame his father or curse himself."

They shared a silent look, an unspoken understanding passing between them. This was only the beginning, a calculated game they intended to play out with subtlety and precision. Malament was but one pawn on the board, but if handled right, he could become a lever against his father, a weakness to be exploited.

Konan reached over and gave his sister's knee a firm, reassuring pat. His eyes met hers with a gleam of excitement and mischief. "Ready?" he murmured, his tone carrying both the weight of the plan they had concocted and a hint of amusement at the game they were about to play.

Karak returned his look with a steady nod, a slight smile curving at her lips. "As ever," she replied, her voice calm and controlled. She straightened, letting her expression shift into the gracious, composed mask of Queen Karak. Every detail of her bearing was deliberate, the queen who would disarm them with warmth and charm.

With a final nod, Konan ducked out of the carriage, his boots landing solidly on the ground. She watched him move with purpose, each step exuding the confidence and strength that would bolster her own presence.

Moments later, the carriage lurched slightly before coming to a full stop. A hush seemed to fall over the convoy, the air tense and expectant. Karak took a steadying breath, smoothing the folds of her cloak as she prepared to make her entrance.

The door swung open, and the heat of the afternoon air rushed in. Karak waited only a heartbeat, then stepped forward, letting her gaze sweep over the gathered welcome party before her.

Stepping down from the carriage with graceful precision, her cloak trailing behind her as she moved toward the waiting welcome party. Once more she scanned the assembly, taking in every detail—the polished armour of East Kadun's soldiers, the senators with their formal sashes, each one bowing with practised respect. Even the soldiers, disciplined and stoic, seemed subtly captivated, their eyes following her every movement, unable to resist the quiet authority she exuded.

At the forefront stood Malament, Lord Malum's son. Karak slowed as she approached him, letting her focus rest on him for a fraction longer than the others. She noted his sharp features, the way his light hair fell slightly over his brow, and the depth in his eyes that spoke of both confidence and uncertainty. There was a youthful handsomeness about him, a certain strength in his stance. Though he tried to present a composed front, she could see a flicker of apprehension beneath his steady demeanour. He was aware he was being scrutinised—and that knowledge seemed to make him all the more intriguing.

As she came to a stop, Karak allowed herself a brief, subtle smile, appreciating the way he held himself under her attention. She saw the tension in his shoulders, the way he met her eyes with a quiet defiance tempered by respect. Yes, she thought, a handsome young man, and likely accustomed to being observed—but perhaps not by someone like her.

A maid approached then, carrying a bottle of Borlong Red, and the moment shifted. The maid poured the wine into a small silver cup and offered it first to Karak. She took it with a nod of acknowledgment, raising it in a subtle toast to Malament, her gaze lingering on his face.

"Borlong's finest," she said, her voice smooth as silk, her eyes glinting with just a touch of interest. "A fitting welcome."

Malament's expression remained carefully controlled, though he could not quite hide the flicker of curiosity in his eyes. He accepted the cup from her, his fingers brushing hers briefly as he lifted it to his lips. "I hope it meets your expectations, Your Majesty," he replied, his voice steady, though she sensed an underlying energy there—a blend of nerves and confidence.

She watched him as he took a sip, admiring the way he moved, his composure despite the scrutiny of his peers. There was strength in him, she noted, a steadiness that belied his youth. She allowed a faint, approving nod as he returned the cup, her smile holding just the slightest hint of warmth.

"More than meets them," she replied, taking another sip herself, letting the silence stretch for a moment. Her attention remained on him, assessing, curious, Malament held it, his expression unreadable but not unaffected. She could sense a growing awareness between them, subtle yet undeniable.

The others watched the exchange, the quiet tension in the air apparent. Karak returned the cup to the maid with a small, graceful gesture, her eyes lingering on Malament for a heartbeat longer before she looked to the assembled party.

Malament stepped forward, inclining his head respectfully as he addressed her. "Your Majesty," he began, his voice carrying formality of one well-versed in diplomatic courtesy, yet with a slight tremor of earnestness. "I am Malament, son of Lord Malum Thalron, and I speak on behalf of Borlong and East Kadun. We are honoured to welcome you to our city and to host you as our esteemed guest."

He gestured to the group assembled behind him. "These are members of Borlong's senate," he continued, his hand sweeping toward the dignified senators in their sashes, each nodding respectfully at his introduction, "and our finest soldiers, here to serve and ensure your safe passage."

Malament paused briefly, his gaze steady on Karak, his features softened with sympathy. "I would also like to extend my deepest condolences for the loss of King Ivar. His strength and leadership have been felt even here in East Kadun, and his memory is honoured among us. We share in your grief, Your Majesty."

Karak inclined her head gracefully in acknowledgment, a touch of solemnity in her expression. "Thank you, Durak Karesh, Malament. Your words honour both his memory and my heart." She held his eyes, letting the weight of her gratitude settle between them, before her lips curved into a faint smile, softening the solemn moment.

Malament nodded, seemingly reassured by her response, he could remember the words *'Durak Karesh'* from his studies, though never heard them aloud. He took a step back, signalling to the others with a subtle hand gesture. "We have prepared everything for your comfort, Your Majesty. If there is anything you require, it will be seen to at once."

He gestured toward the waiting carts. "Please, allow your men to refresh themselves with water, and let your party enjoy our finest wine." He motioned to a group of servants who moved forward promptly. "Let us take your belongings and see them brought to your quarters without delay, so you may begin to rest from your journey."

There was a genuine warmth in his tone, a graciousness that conveyed not only respect but a desire to ensure her ease. Karak inclined her head with a slight smile, allowing a touch of appreciation to show.

"Your hospitality is noted, Malament," she replied, her dark green eyes lingering on him for a moment. "It seems Borlong has indeed made every effort to make us feel at home."

Malament returned her smile with a polite nod, his posture relaxed yet attentive as he oversaw the arrangements, ensuring each member of her party was cared for.

The men of Nordon moved to the water barrels, eagerly helping themselves to cool ladles of water after the long, dusty journey. Servants from Borlong bustled around, unloading Queen Karak's belongings from the carriages with adept efficiency, each item handled with care. The Borlong soldiers kept a respectful distance, watching their foreign counterparts as they refreshed themselves, a quiet curiosity in their eyes.

Malament's gaze swept over the scene, taking note of every detail—the demeanour of the soldiers, the count of her attendants, the items being unloaded. After a moment, his brow furrowed slightly. He took a small step toward Karak, inclining his head politely before speaking.

"Your Majesty," he began, his tone respectful yet observant, "we were told by Galil that your party would include fifty men-at-arms. We've arranged quarters accordingly, but..." He paused, glancing again at the group. "I only see forty men. Were we mistaken?"

Karak took a moment, a faint smile playing on her lips as she regarded Malament with interest. She noted his keen observation, impressed by the young man's attention to detail. He had been correct in his count, and the careful way he phrased his question showed both confidence and tact. She appreciated the astute mind behind his composed exterior.

"No, Malament," she replied smoothly, her voice calm. "You were not mistaken. There are indeed forty men. It seems Galil may have relayed the wrong number to you. The nuances of your language can be challenging, even for a seasoned diplomat."

Malament nodded, accepting her explanation without further question, though his eyes lingered on her for a moment longer, as if considering her words. "Of course, Your Majesty," he said, a faint smile of understanding crossing his face. "I'll ensure the accommodations are adjusted accordingly."

She inclined her head with quiet approval, then let her gaze sweep over him thoughtfully, admiring his ability to notice even the smallest details. Here was a young man with potential, one with a clear and observant mind. It would be interesting, she thought, to see how far she could push that mind in the days to come.

As Malament finished his brief exchange with Queen Karak, Konan approached, his imposing figure drawing a few lingering glances from both Nordon and Borlong's men. His stride was purposeful, each step carrying the weight of a seasoned warrior. His tall, muscular frame and the iron-clad beard marked him as someone who had seen countless battles and emerged stronger from each.

Karak turned slightly; her gaze warm as she looked between the two men. "Malament, allow me to introduce my brother, Konan," she said smoothly. "He has travelled with me from Nordon to assist in our journey." She paused; her expression composed yet slightly amused. "Konan speaks very little of Kadun's language but understands enough of what is said."

Malament inclined his head respectfully, his expression polite, though he could feel the weight of Konan's judging glare upon him, unblinking and unrelenting. The young man forced himself to meet Konan's eyes, and the effect was immediate—a faint tension prickled under his skin. Konan's stare was both assessing and disconcertingly direct, the eyes of a man who had seen enough conflict to recognize strength or weakness with a single look.

"It's an honour to meet you, Sir Konan," Malament said, his voice steady though he could feel a bead of sweat forming under his collar. "We are glad to have you in Borlong and are prepared to assist you in any way."

Konan's mouth barely lifted in a faint smile, his piercing eyes still fixed on Malament, as though silently appraising every word, every movement. He gave a small nod, his silence as heavy as his presence. There was a subtle message in his stare—a quiet but unmistakable reminder of his authority and experience, a force beneath the surface.

Karak, catching the tension, allowed a faint smile to play on her lips. "I trust Konan's presence is... reassuring," she said, her tone light. "He is quite protective, as any brother should be."

Malament nodded, forcing himself to hold Konan's challenge a moment longer before looking back to Karak. "Of course, Your Majesty. Borlong will provide for all your needs—and yours, Sir Konan," he added, a subtle emphasis that acknowledged the elder warrior's unspoken authority.

Konan's eyes glinted with an unreadable expression as he gave another slow nod, then finally shifted his focus away, turning to Karak with an almost imperceptible smile.

Karak allowed herself a moment of satisfaction. Konan's silent scrutiny had done its work, adding just the right amount of pressure. She could already sense Malament's careful composure under strain, a flicker of uncertainty lingering after the exchange. And she could tell that her brother was more than prepared to keep that pressure up, ensuring young Malament would be kept on his toes.

Malament, after a brief pause to steady himself, offered Queen Karak a courteous smile. "Shall we, Your Majesty?" he asked, gesturing toward the gate. Malament offered his arm to Queen Karak as they walked through Borlong's gates, and she took it with a graceful smile, letting her hand rest lightly against his sleeve. As they walked up the main road, passing the stables, she leaned in ever so slightly, her voice warm and casual.

"Your city has a certain charm, Malament," she said, letting her gaze drift over him as much as over the cobbled streets and sturdy buildings. "Resilient, yet welcoming—like its people."

He glanced at her, momentarily caught off guard by the softness in her tone, then nodded, struggling to keep his own voice steady. "Thank you, Your Majesty. We strive to make Borlong a place that reflects East Kadun's values."

She smiled, a little more intimately than he was accustomed to, her interest lingering on his face. "And does that strength of character extend to its sons as well?" she asked, her tone playful, an edge of admiration slipping into her voice.

Malament cleared his throat, uncertain of how to respond. "I suppose so, Your Majesty," he replied, his voice slightly stiff as he attempted to keep his tone formal. "My father expects us all to uphold East Kadun's values, to lead with duty and loyalty."

Karak's smile widened, her eyes sparkling with a hint of mischief as she let her fingers linger on his arm a moment longer than necessary. "Duty and loyalty… admirable qualities, indeed," she murmured, her voice low and smooth. "And yet, I wonder, do you find time for yourself amidst all that duty?"

Malament felt a slight heat rising to his face, and he glanced away, focusing on the road ahead as he searched for a proper response. "I suppose duty doesn't often allow for much personal time," he said, attempting a polite smile but feeling the awkwardness creeping in. Flirting was unfamiliar territory, and the Queen's attention felt both flattering and unnerving.

"Oh, how dedicated," Karak said, her voice laced with amusement as she observed his discomfort with a faint, knowing smile. "A man so focused on duty, without any distractions… it's rare, don't you think?"

Malament managed a tight-lipped smile, his eyes fixed forward. "I suppose so, Your Majesty," he replied, feeling slightly out of his depth. He had never particularly thought about relationships or attractions—his interests always lay in matters of state and his duties and potential future. Now, under the Queen's intent gaze, he felt painfully aware of his inexperience in such interactions.

Karak leaned just a bit closer, her voice dropping to a near whisper. "There's nothing wrong with a little distraction now and then, Malament. Sometimes, a moment away from duty can reveal… unexpected joys." Her eyes drifted from his own to his lips, her expression warm with interest.

He swallowed, willing himself to remain composed, but he could not fully mask his unease. "Of course, Your Majesty," he said, keeping his tone as formal as possible. "But I find my duties… fulfilling enough."

Karak chuckled softly, her laughter light and silken, her head briefly resting on his shoulder before lifting again. "Well, it seems East Kadun has found itself quite the dedicated son," she replied, her eyes resting on him with open admiration. "I must say, it's refreshing."

They walked on in silence for a moment, Malament's cheeks faintly flushed, his focus fixed determinedly on the road ahead. He could feel her attention lingering on him, warm and steady, and the weight of it filled him with an odd mixture of pride and discomfort.

Karak finally broke the silence, her voice casual yet unmistakably playful. "I do look forward to learning more about Borlong, its customs… and its people," she said, her eyes catching his with a spark of mischief.

Malament inclined his head politely, but he could not quite manage to meet her gaze. "We're honoured by your interest, Your Majesty," he replied, his voice steady but his expression carefully blank. He could feel the eyes of Borlong's assembly on them, yet he sensed a game here that was deeper than he could fully grasp.

As they continued, Karak's light touches and playful words kept him off-balance, leaving him uncertain but unwilling to break the dance of words. And she, it seemed, was more than content to watch him squirm, her laughter soft and knowing, as if the discomfort she inspired was precisely what she intended.

# THE QUEEN'S PROCESSION CHAPTER THIRTY NINE

The grand entrance hall of the estate was a portrait of restrained elegance, its marble floors polished to a mirror shine and its high arches casting sweeping shadows across the walls. Lady Amelia stood at the upper gallery, her hands lightly resting on the intricately carved banister. From her vantage point, she could see the gathering below: Lord Malum, composed and resolute as ever, flanked by Borlong's most esteemed senators. Galil, the timber merchant from Nordon also stood to one side, his posture formal and imposing, while a cluster of guards and serving maids lingered unobtrusively at the edges of the scene.

The anticipation in the hall was evident, a quiet hum that seemed to ripple through the gathered, charged with unspoken expectations. Sunlight streamed through the towering windows, bathing the assembly in a golden glow that softened the sharp edges of their ceremonial attire. It was an impressive display, calculated to make the right impression on Queen Karak and her retinue. And yet, despite the grandeur, Amelia's thoughts were elsewhere, drifting back to the curious scene she had witnessed yesterday.

She had been on her balcony, as she often was in the warm summer mornings, watching the gardens below. The hedges were lush and vibrant, their neatly trimmed paths winding like green veins through the estate. Roses swaying in the breeze, the fountain glistening in the centre. The tranquillity of the moment had soothed her, the faint hum of bees and the soft rustle of leaves creating a melody of nature that calmed her mind.

But her peace had been interrupted. She had caught sight of two figures moving swiftly through the garden paths, their hurried pace a stark contrast to the stillness around them. The first she recognized immediately—Saanvi, the head maid, who's bearing always conveyed purpose and control. Yet in that moment, her steps had been uncharacteristically frantic, her head turning as though checking for something—or someone.

Beside her had been another woman, younger, with long dark hair that seemed almost wild as it streamed behind her. Amelia recognized her as one of the estate's many maids, though her name escaped her. The girl had always seemed quiet, the type who moved through the halls unnoticed, blending into the background. But yesterday, there had been nothing quiet about her. Her expression, though distant at Amelia's height, had struck her as tense, almost fearful.

What could have caused such a scene? Amelia wondered now, her brow furrowing slightly as her gaze swept over the entrance hall. She had seen Saanvi handle crises before—she was adept at resolving them before they became visible to the household. But this had felt different, charged with an urgency that Amelia could not quite place.

Her thoughts shifted, unbidden, to the figure she had seen moments later. Near the far edge of the garden, close to the stables and almost out of view, a boy had appeared. Auron. Even from a distance, she had recognized him. His posture had been calm, deliberate, as though he were simply observing the world around him. He had lingered there, one hand resting lightly on the stable gate, his face turned toward the horizon.

A soft smile touched Amelia's lips as she thought of him. She had come to know him over the past couple of months, their paths crossing more often than she could have anticipated. The garden hedge maze had become their unofficial meeting place, a sanctuary for both of them. She often found him there, exploring the winding paths with a curiosity that seemed boundless.

She recalled their last meeting vividly. He had been waiting by an old stone bench, his hands tracing the patterns of the vines that crept along its surface. When he had seen her, his face had lit up with a smile so genuine it had warmed her heart. They had talked for what felt like hours, discussing the garden's hidden nooks, the history of the estate, even the peculiar habits of its crows.

There was something about Auron that drew her in. Despite the hardships he had endured—rumours of which had reached even her ears—he carried a lightness, a resilience that belied his young age. He was a bright spot in a world often shrouded in shadows, and she found herself looking forward to their chance encounters more than she cared to admit.

Below her, the scene shifted. The guards adjusted their stances, and Galil exchanged a quiet word with Lord Malum. The Nordon party would be arriving any moment now. Amelia took a steadying breath, her gaze lingering on the grand doorway for a heartbeat longer. Whatever mysteries the garden held; they would have to wait.

She released the banister and stepped back, smoothing the folds of her gown with deliberate care. As Lady of the estate, it was her duty to stand beside Lord Malum when the doors opened. He had made it clear that no excuse, no delay, would be tolerated.

Amelia allowed herself one last glance toward the windows, where the sunlight painted streaks of gold across the marble floor. The image of the garden lingered in her mind—the hurried figures of Saanvi and the maid, the quiet stillness of Auron at the stables. She could not shake the sense that something significant had passed just out of her reach. But this was neither the time nor the place to dwell on it.

With a final deep breath, she descended the sweeping staircase, her steps measured and graceful. The rustle of her gown whispered softly against the thick carpet, her heels cushioned with each step, a steady rhythm as she approached the assembly below.

Lord Malum glanced up at her, his expression a mask of pride and formality. His vision flicked toward the high arches of the hall, where the sun's rays slanted sharply through the windows, marking the late hour. Though he said nothing, the faint arch of his brow and the cool set of his mouth delivered his reprimand with unmistakable clarity. You are late.

Amelia returned his gaze with serene composure, letting her hand rest lightly on her skirts as she fell into place at his side without hesitation. She offered a small nod, her expression calm, but the slight tension in her shoulders betrayed her frustration.

The room settled as the assembled senators and guards straightened their postures. All eyes were now on the doors, their anticipation almost tangible. Amelia kept her own expression calm, though she could feel the faint stirrings of unease beneath her deft facade.

She would do as duty demanded—stand tall, smile when necessary, and offer gracious words to their esteemed guests. But even as the heavy doors began to creak open, signalling the Nordon party's arrival, her mind lingered on the garden, the strange events she had witnessed, and the boy who had unknowingly brightened her thoughts. The time for answers would come, for now, she set her shoulders, lifted her chin, Lady Amelia was ready.

The heavy doors swung wide, flooding the grand hall with the golden light of late afternoon. The sunlight poured in like liquid gold, casting long, shifting shadows that danced across the polished marble floor, transforming it into a shimmering canvas of light and shadow. The atmosphere shifted instantly, the quiet hum of anticipation evaporating in the glow of the sun, replaced by a weighty silence that seemed to press against every surface. All eyes turned to the threshold as the first figures stepped inside, their presence breaking the stillness and sending a ripple of expectation through the assembled crowd. The air grew heavy, charged with the promise of something monumental, as if the very walls of the estate held their breath.

It was the Nordon soldiers, entering in formation, two at a time. Their appearance striking and unlike anything Borlong had seen. They moved with precision, each step echoing through the hall, their presence radiating strength and menace. Their attire, though uniform, bore a distinct ruggedness that spoke of the unforgiving winters of their homeland. Broad shoulders were adorned with thick fur-lined pauldrons, the coarse pelts exaggerating their already imposing frames. Heavy shields were strapped to their backs, polished but worn with the marks of countless battles, while small hatchets hung from their belts like talons.

Each carried a unique weapon slung across their back—some bore great axes with notched blades, others broad swords or massive hammers, the weight of which seemed to challenge even the strongest of men. Their helmets, crowned with subtle horns or reinforced with iron ridges, added to their menacing appearance, while their braided beards, bound with iron clasps, gave the impression of larger, more formidable faces.

As the Nordon guards took their positions, they raised their weapons in unison, forming a guard of honour that lined the hall, a living corridor of steel and shadow. The polished sheen of their armour caught the sunlight, casting fleeting glints of silver and bronze as they stood in attention.

First through the lined ranks of Nordon's warriors into the reception hall were the Borlong soldiers. They passed through with discipline, though there was a visible unease in their posture, as if they were being swallowed by the shadows cast by the Nordon guards. Their polished armour and short swords were a stark contrast to the raw power of their counterparts. Once through the corridor, they fell back to join the other Borlong men-at-arms already gathered in the hall, forming a unified line of defence near the walls.

Then came Malament, followed by the other senators of Borlong.

Amelia's breath caught as her son entered the hall. Tall and composed, he moved with the measured confidence of someone accustomed to bearing the weight of scrutiny. The late sunlight streamed through the high windows, catching the golden strands of his light hair and lending him an almost ethereal quality. His features, so like her own, were set in a mask of calm resolve, and though his expression was serious, there was a quiet grace to the way he carried himself.

He wore a finely tailored doublet of deep red and gold, the colours of Borlong, that fit him impeccably, accentuating his broad shoulders and athletic frame. His sword hung at his side, and though his hand brushed its hilt as he walked, it was not with unease but with readiness.

A surge of pride swelled in Amelia's chest as she watched him. There had been times—too many, she thought—when their relationship had felt strained, the distance between them more than physical. But in this moment, Malament stood as a reflection of everything she had once hoped he would become: a figure of quiet strength and dignity, someone who could hold his own on the stage of lords and kings.

And yet, as she studied him, a flicker of memory surfaced: a younger Malament, no more than ten, standing in the same hall with his shoulders slouched, his hair tousled from an afternoon of play. He had been fidgeting with the strap of his sword belt, his nervous energy spilling out in every gesture. She had chided her son then gently, straightening his posture and smoothing his hair, murmuring words of encouragement as he prepared to meet visiting dignitaries for the first time.

That boy was gone now, replaced by the composed young man before her, but she could still see traces of the young child he once was—the faint furrow of his brow when he was deep in thought, the way his hands brushed the hilt of his sword when he sought reassurance. He is grown, she thought, a bittersweet pang tightening her chest, but not gone completely.

As he emerged from the corridor of foreign soldiers, Malament paused briefly, his gaze sweeping over the gathered assembly with the careful poise of one who knew the importance of appearances. Then, with deliberate steps, he crossed the remaining distance and came to stand beside his father. His posture straight, his expression calm, he presented an image of unity and purpose.

Amelia's eyes lingered on him; the resemblance between father and son might not have been obvious in their features. Yet in moments like this, it was unmistakable in the way they carried themselves: resolute and unyielding.

The hall settled for a moment, the tension palpable as the Nordon guards stood like statues, their presence a reminder of the power they represented. Then the next wave of arrivals began to file in.

A group of merchants came first, their attire a patchwork of fine furs and embroidered wool that spoke of both wealth and practicality. They walked with purpose but kept their heads respectfully bowed, their arms laden with small chests and cases, no doubt bearing gifts for Borlong's lords and nobles. Behind them came Konan.

Amelia's attention was drawn to him immediately. He moved with a commanding presence, his black armour gleaming dully in the sunlight, each plate etched with intricate, storm-like designs. A double-edged axe was sheathed across his broad back, its handle worn from use but polished to an almost ceremonial sheen. Unlike the guards, who exuded raw menace, Konan's presence carried a deliberate weight—a calculated blend of authority and danger that made it impossible to look away.

His red hair, tied back in a high ponytail, swayed lightly as he walked, and his thick beard, braided with iron clasps, gleamed faintly in the light. He scanned the room as he entered, his eyes sharp and assessing, seeming to take the measure of everyone present.

Even Lord Malum, unyielding in his usual composure, shifted slightly under Konan's gaze. Amelia felt it too—a subtle tension, like the heavy stillness before a downpour.

Konan came to a stop a few paces from the Borlong reception, his head held high, his hands resting lightly on the straps of his armour. He said nothing, allowing the weight of his presence to speak for itself. He stepped back to the edge of his men, crossing his arms, the leather strained against his bulking forearms, waiting with the same quiet patience as the others for his sister, the Queen, to make her entrance.

A moment settled then, from the line of Borlong dignitaries, Galil stepped forward, his every movement precise and measured. He turned to face the reception party, his voice ringing out clearly in the stillness of the hall.

"Honoured guests of Nordon and esteemed hosts of Borlong," he began, his tone carrying the renowned authority of a diplomat, "it is my privilege to present Her Majesty, Queen Karak Thørn of Stormhold, City Under the Mountain, Monarch of Nordon, the Winter Realm."

The hall fell silent, all eyes drawn to the grand doors as Queen Karak stepped inside.

Amelia froze for a moment, struck by the sight of her. The Queen was every bit as commanding as the merchants had described—an elegant storm wrapped in crimson and black. Her fur-lined cloak swept behind her, the silver embroidery catching the light with each deliberate step. The crown atop her head, dark iron studded with blood-red gems, gave her the appearance of a warrior queen from legend, while her piercing eyes swept over the room with the precision of someone accustomed to wielding power.

There was no denying her beauty, but it was not a delicate thing. It was sharp, honed, and deliberate—a beauty that demanded respect rather than admiration. Yet as Amelia's gaze flicked to Lord Malum, she saw none of that respect in his expression.

He could not hide his delight.

His watchful eyes followed the Queen like a moth to flame, the faintest curve of his lips betraying his awe. Even in this moment, surrounded by senators and dignitaries, and with his wife at his side, he made no attempt to conceal it. His attention lingered too long on the pale curve of the Queen's neck, the way her hair, as red as flame, fell in waves over her shoulders.

Amelia felt a bitter pang in her chest, though it was not jealousy. Whatever love she had once held for Malum had long since withered, the roots strangled by his indifference and betrayals. But the lack of respect still stung. Here he was, openly admiring another woman before a room full of their peers—before her. It was not the Queen's fault; she could hardly be blamed for Malum's wandering eye. No, this was entirely his doing, and Amelia's nails bit into her palms as she forced herself to remain composed.

You have had years to grow used to this, Amelia, she thought bitterly. And yet it still manages to sting, doesn't it?

The Queen's gaze swept over the gathered assembly, lingering briefly on each face as if memorising their features. When her eyes landed on Amelia, there was a flicker of something—curiosity, perhaps, or the faintest acknowledgment of her position. Then the moment passed, and Karak's attention moved on to Malum, who bowed deeply, his hand resting over his chest in a gesture of respect.

"Your Majesty," he said, his voice rich with formality, "welcome to Borlong. We are honoured by your presence."

The Queen inclined her head slightly, her lips curving into a faint smile. "Lord Malum," she replied, her voice smooth and melodic, yet edged with a subtle authority. "The honour is mine. Borlong is every bit as grand as I was told to expect."

Her smile deepened as she added, "Fennas dorå vorr, i shol vardem norr." Then, in a gracious yet instructive tone, she explained, "In your tongue, the words translate to: 'May your walls stand strong, and your halls be filled with peace.'"

Amelia watched the exchange closely, noting the slight flush that crept into Malum's cheeks as the Queen's words brushed his ego.

Karak's attention shifted, settling on Malament. Her smile lingered, but there was a glint of something sharper in her eyes—an almost playful edge, as though she were testing the waters.

"And you must be Malament," she teased, addressing him directly.

Malament stiffened slightly, clearly caught off guard by the Queen's attention and jest. He bowed low, his hand brushing the hilt of his sword. "Your Majesty," he said, his voice matching her jovial tone. "It is an honour to stand before you. On behalf of Borlong, I welcome you to our home."

The Queen's smile deepened, and she tilted her head slightly, enjoying his demeanour. "Such composure," she murmured, her tone still teasing. "Your father must be proud."

Amelia's sharp eyes caught the faintest twitch in Malum's jaw at the remark, though he masked it quickly.

"Indeed, I am," Malum interjected, his voice steady but carrying just enough force to reassert his presence.

But the Queen was not finished. Her gaze swept the room again before settling back on Malament. “Perhaps you would be so kind as to introduce everyone to me,” she said smoothly, her tone light but deliberate. “It seems fitting for the future of Borlong to take such a role.”

Amelia felt the shift immediately. The request was unusual—no, it was calculated. Traditionally, it would be Malum’s role as Lord of Borlong to make such introductions. By placing the responsibility on Malament, the Queen was subtly undermining his authority, testing the dynamic between father and son before the entire hall.

Malament hesitated for only a fraction of a second, but it was enough for Amelia to see the tension ripple through him. His eyes flicked briefly to his father, whose expression remained neutral, though his clenched hands betrayed his displeasure.

“Of course, Your Majesty,” Malament said finally, his voice even, though there was a tightness to it now. He turned to face the gathered assembly, his focus sweeping over the room as he began the introductions with careful precision.

Amelia watched the exchange with a mixture of pride and unease. Malament handled himself well, his voice steady as he named each senator, each dignitary, he stumbled only once, hesitating over one of the lesser-known senators, but he recovered quickly.

The Queen listened with polite interest, her gaze flicking occasionally to Lord Malum, as though gauging his reaction. And though Malum maintained his composure, Amelia could see the faint strain at the corners of his mouth, the way his eyes lingered too long on his son as he spoke.

It was a small moment, but the Queen had planted the seed—a subtle wedge between father and son, a reminder that power could shift in unexpected ways.

Malament turned slightly, gesturing toward his father with an opulent poise. “And of course, my father, Lord Malum Thalron,” he said, his voice steady, though Amelia caught the faint hesitation in his tone. “Lord of Borlong and steward of East Kadun. It is through his leadership that our city thrives.”

Lord Malum inclined his head with measured grace, a faint, composed smile playing at his lips as his eyes met the Queen's. “Your Majesty,” he said with effortless authority, his voice deep and resonant, honed by years of governance. “May your visit herald the start of a lasting alliance between our realms. My home, and all within it, are at your disposal."

The Queen's gaze lingered, her smile growing just enough to suggest a mixture of warmth and calculated intent. "You flatter, Lord Malum," she replied, her voice smooth yet tinged with a subtle edge. "Your reputation is not only vast but richly earned. I eagerly await the chance to explore the rest of your home and uncover the hidden treasures Borlong keeps concealed."

Amelia's breath tightened as she watched the exchange. Malum's chest seemed to swell under the Queen's words, his expression bordering on smugness. The lack of subtlety in his delight was galling—more than galling, it was disrespectful. But she let none of it show, standing tall and serene beside him.

"And this," Malament continued, his voice softening slightly as he turned to her, "is Lady Amelia, my mother and Lady of the estate."

Amelia inclined her head with quiet dignity, her eyes meeting the Queen's directly. "Your Majesty," she said, her voice calm and composed. "It is our privilege to host you. May your stay in Borlong be as comfortable as it is memorable."

Queen Karak regarded her with a subtle tilt of her head, her gaze lingering as though appraising Amelia. "Lady Amelia," she said, her tone polite but faintly curious. "It is clear that Borlong is well cared for under your watch. Your son owes you greater credit." A fleeting smile touched her lips as she glanced toward Malament, a hint of amusement in her expression. Amelia observed the exchange with quiet discernment; it was evident that her son's encounter with the Queen at Borlong's gates had left a favourable impression.

She met the Queen's eyes, the faintest smile curving her lips. "You are most kind, Your Majesty," she replied evenly, though she felt the weight of the Queen's scrutiny like a cold wind against her skin.

Karak's expression softened, her lips curving just enough to suggest warmth, yet a glint of something unyielding lingered in her eyes—a predator's curiosity masked by civility. "I understand you are also a princess of West Kadun," she began, her tone as smooth as polished steel. "How is your father these days?"

The air shifted like the hush before a storm, an almost imperceptible tightening among those present. Amelia felt it instantly—a thread of tension weaving through the room with the Queen's calculated words.

Though her posture remained poised, the question struck with the precision of an archer's arrow, and her chest tightened in response.

"He is well, Your Majesty," Amelia replied, each word carefully weighed. Her voice held steady, carrying the grace of royal upbringing, though the faintest flicker of guardedness underpinned her tone. "King Ruben remains devoted to the prosperity of West Kadun."

She met Karak's gaze directly, her serene expression a flawless mask. But beneath the surface, her mind raced, considering the Queen's motives—was this a casual inquiry or a subtle probe, a test of loyalty cloaked in harmless conversation?

"Good to hear," Karak said with a faint smile, her voice carrying an almost disarming warmth. Her gaze swept over the gathered dignitaries, pausing just long enough on each face to remind them of her scrutiny, before returning to Amelia. "I look forward to meeting him after my time here concludes."

The hall seemed to exhale collectively, only to hold its breath again as the Queen's words settled over the room like the silence before the crack of lightning. There was no mistaking their significance. Silence followed—pregnant, taut, and alive with the realisation of what had just been said.

Amelia's composure faltered for the briefest moment, her eyes widening with a flicker of surprise before she quickly masked it. Her mind raced, the implications cascading in every direction. A glance at Lord Malum revealed that even he, with all his refined confidence, had not anticipated this. His features, so often composed, betrayed a fleeting crack of uncertainty.

The senators exchanged hushed murmurs; their unease unmistakable. This was not merely a diplomatic courtesy—it was a move that upended a century of carefully maintained distance. No one from Nordon had crossed into West Kadun since the days when blood had soaked the lands between them, when old grudges had hardened into tradition. Queen Karak's declaration was not just bold; it was seismic.

Amelia inclined her head, regaining her poise with delicate grace. "I am sure my father will be honoured by your visit, Your Majesty," she said, her voice steady though her thoughts churned like storm-tossed seas.

The Queen's smile deepened; an expression as unreadable as the depths of the Emerald Sea. "I hope so," she replied, her tone light yet laden with subtle undertones. "There is much to gain when old wounds are tended, don't you agree?"

Her attention shifted to Malament, her gaze softening just slightly. "You have done well, Malament," she said, her voice carrying a note of genuine approval. "Please, continue."

Malament, visibly bolstered by the compliment, resumed the introductions, his voice steady despite the tension that pressed down on the room like an invisible weight.

But as Amelia watched the Queen, she could not shake the feeling that every word, every glance, was part of a larger design. The sharp edge to Karak's smile lingered as she turned her attention back to Lord Malum, her gaze cutting through the room like a blade.

And though the formalities carried on, the air remained heavy with unspoken questions and looming uncertainties. Amelia felt it like a shadow creeping over the threshold—a quiet but undeniable reminder that, in Queen Karak's presence, nothing was ever as simple as it seemed.

# THE LORD'S MANSE
# CHAPTER FORTY

The late afternoon sun streamed through the grand openings of the dining hall, casting long golden beams across polished marble floors. The light caught on the edges of goblets and armour, refracting into brief flashes of brilliance that danced over the high stone walls. The scent of roasted venison mingled with the faint perfume of roses drifting in from the garden, where a soft breeze carried the gentle rustle of leaves into the otherwise tense atmosphere.

The room was alive with noise, but not harmony. On the western side, the Borlong soldiers sat with a practised rigidity, their polished armour catching the light like molten gold. Their words were clipped and formal, their voices low as though restrained by the weight of decorum. Across from them, the Nordon warriors dominated the eastern tables, a stark contrast with their fur-lined cloaks, untamed hair, and booming laughter. They seemed impervious to the tension, their guttural voices filling the hall like rolling thunder.

Malament stood near one of the arches, his gaze sweeping across the room. The sun warmed his back, but the weight of the air pressed against him like an approaching storm. It was not just the cultural differences—it was the silence between the groups, a silence born of more than language. The Borlong soldiers spoke in their measured, articulate tongue; the Nordon warriors replied with loud, guttural phrases. Neither side could understand the other, their exchanges reduced to wary glances and gestures, the cracks in their uneasy alliance exposed by every moment of miscommunication.

The buffet tables stood like a border, an unspoken no-man's-land. The food—roasted meats, honey-glazed bread, spiced potatoes, and thick stews—lay untouched at first, as though crossing the invisible divide might shatter the fragile balance. But Nordon's warriors knew no such hesitation. A burly man with a braided beard rose first, his boots scraping loudly against the stone as he approached the table. Without a glance at the Borlong soldiers, he grabbed a leg of roasted boar and tore into it with a laugh that echoed through the hall.

His companions roared their approval, their rough voices clashing against the muted murmurs of the Borlong men.

Malament watched the Borlong soldiers stiffen, their fingers twitching toward the hilts of their swords or the goblets in their hands. He knew the Nordon warriors were unaware—or uncaring—of the breach. In Borlong tradition, the host's side of the table was sacred, and no guest took from it without invitation. But in Nordon, survival came before ceremony. To wait for permission was to admit weakness, and weakness had no place in *Froskvel Tan Mirral*, the Winter Realm.

Luka approached silently, his expression grim, his eyes scanning the hall. "They have no sense of manners," he muttered, keeping his voice low but filled with sharp irritation. His hand rested lightly on the hilt of his sword, more from habit than necessity.

"They have their own sense," Malament replied, though his tone was clipped. His gaze remained fixed on the Nordon warriors. "To them, it's not about manners. It's survival—taking what you can, when you can."

Luka snorted softly, crossing his arms. "Survival? I see arrogance, not desperation. Look at them. Laughing, drinking, as if they own the place." His voice dropped lower, tinged with bitterness. "They don't respect us. How could they, when they don't even understand us?"

Malament's jaw tightened, his eyes narrowing as he watched one Nordon man swipe an entire loaf of bread, tearing into it without a second glance toward the Borlong side of the room. "Respect isn't in their nature. Not the way we know it. To them, respect is earned in blood and hardship—not offered freely." He hesitated, then added, "It's something they see as weakness, I think."

"Then maybe they should learn what weakness really looks like," Luka said darkly, his fingers twitching toward his blade.

"Stand down, Luka," Malament said quietly, but there was steel in his tone. "They're guests, not invaders."

Luka's mouth twisted into a scowl. "They act like they're both."

Before Malament could respond, the tension in the hall erupted.

A Borlong soldier, Braddos, rose abruptly to his feet, the sharp scrape of his chair silencing the murmurs at his table. Young and untested, his armour gleamed as though fresh from the smith's forge, and his face was flushed with indignation.

"That's Borlong meat," Braddos said in his native tongue, pointing an accusatory finger toward the roasted boar the Nordon warrior held. "It's not yours."

The Nordon man turned slowly, his grin broadening as he tore another bite from the meat, the juices dripping down his beard. His companions chuckled, their laughter low and guttural.

The warrior said something in Nordon—a rough, mocking phrase that none of the Borlong men understood.

"Mílen gorrik," he repeated louder, his voice dripping with deliberate provocation.

Malament saw the young Borlong soldier stiffen, his shoulders squaring as his hand moved instinctively to the hilt of his sword. The air in the hall grew heavier, the conversations around the room fading into uneasy silence.

Luka leaned closer to Malament, his voice a harsh whisper. "Do something. He's going to draw."

"I see it," Malament murmured, his eyes locked on the scene. "And so do they." He flicked his attention briefly toward the Nordon side of the room, noting how several of the warriors shifted in their seats, their hands resting casually—but purposefully—on the handles of their axes and swords.

"If this turns into a fight, it won't be a scuffle," Luka warned, his voice tight. "It'll be a bloodbath."

Malament did not answer immediately. Instead, he stepped forward, his posture calm but deliberate, positioning himself between the Borlong soldier and the Nordon warrior. "Stay where you are," he said firmly, his words directed at the younger soldier.

But the Braddos barely seemed to hear him. His hand was already tightening on his sword's hilt, his anger outweighing his better judgement.

"Enough!" A sharp voice rang out, cutting through the tension like a blade before the situation could escalate. The merchant Galil, stood near the centre table, his goblet raised as he switched fluidly to Nordon.

"Tól karesh. Istan durr!" he said, his tone brooking no argument. "That's enough. Sit down."

The Nordon warrior hesitated, his grin faltering as he glanced toward Galil. After a moment, he shrugged, stepping back to his seat, though not without one last deliberate bite of the boar. The Borlong soldier, his hand still hovering near his sword, remained frozen until Malament approached and placed a firm hand on his shoulder.

"Stand down," Malament said softly. "It's over."

The younger soldier sat, his face still flushed with frustration, his knuckles white as he gripped the edge of the table. His eyes stayed fixed on the Nordon warriors, simmering with resentment, but he made no further move.

Malament turned to Galil, offering a slight nod of gratitude. The merchant returned it with a faint, knowing smile, his eyes betraying a keen awareness of how precarious the balance had become. As Galil's sharp gaze flicked briefly to the Nordon table, Malament followed it, noting the subtle shifts among the warriors—how they straightened slightly in their seats, how their hands lingered near the hilts of their weapons.

At the far end of the hall, Konan leaned back in his chair, his massive arms crossed over his chest in a posture of effortless command. The late afternoon sunlight caught in his red hair, igniting it like flame against the polished steel of his pauldrons. His smirk deepened as he surveyed the room, his sharp eyes moving between the two groups with an unsettling air of detachment. He looked more like a predator gauging his prey than a leader bridging an alliance.

"Malament, as clear as day turns into night, they have no respect us," Luka muttered beside Malament, his voice low and edged with frustration. Once more his hand hovered near his sword, as though the act of gripping it might offer him some measure of control over the situation.

Malament's lips pressed into a thin line. "They don't need to," he replied, though the words sat bitterly on his tongue. He glanced toward the Nordon table, watching as one warrior whispered something to another, their rough laughter cutting through the uneasy silence like the scrape of steel. "They only need to follow orders."

Luka frowned, his brow furrowing deeply. “Orders? Is that enough?” His voice dropped further, almost a growl. “They come here, mock us in our own hall, and expect us to trust them when the time comes? You think they’ll follow orders when it matters?”

Malament’s eyes flicked toward Konan, who was now watching him. The faint smirk on the man’s face sent a chill down Malament’s spine, though he kept his expression neutral. “If they don’t,” he said quietly, “it won’t be for lack of trying on our part. But they don’t think like we do, Luka. They don’t see respect as we see it. To them, it’s strength or nothing.”

Luka’s scowl deepened as he followed Malament’s gaze. “And what do you see in him?” He gestured subtly toward Konan.

“Someone who’s calculating every move,” Malament replied, his voice barely above a whisper. “He’s not here to make friends. He’s here to remind us how easily this balance can tip.”

Luka let out a slow breath, his shoulders tense. “Then maybe it’s time we reminded them of our own strength.”

“Be Calm,” Malament said firmly. His gaze swept the room again, lingering on the younger Borlong soldier, whose frustration still simmered beneath his rigid posture. “Our strength is in holding the line, Luka. Not crossing it first.”

Luka did not respond immediately, but the tension in his jaw spoke volumes. As the Nordon warriors broke into another round of laughter, the sound grating against the strained silence of the Borlong side, he leaned in closer to Malament.

“They’re testing us Malament,” Luka murmured. “Every move they make, every word they speak—it’s a test.”

Malament nodded, his eyes narrowing as he studied the Nordon warriors, their laughter rising like a tempest. “And we’ll pass it,” he said, his voice low and deliberate. “But not by playing their game.”

From across the room, Konan’s piercing stare met his own, the Nordon leader’s smirk unwavering. It was not a mere show of confidence; it was a quiet declaration of dominance, the kind of expression that spoke of unshakable certainty. It grated against Malament’s composure, like a blade testing the edge of his resolve. His jaw tightened as the weight of the moment pressed down, the sting of helplessness biting deeper than he wanted to admit. This was his home, his hall—yet the Nordon presence loomed, an unspoken challenge to his authority.

The din of conversation and clinking goblets seemed distant now, muffled by the growing unease in his chest. Luka's earlier words echoed in his mind, sharp and undeniable. He had been right—it was not a question of if the next fight would break out but when. Each stolen glance between the Nordon men, every slight posture of defiance, spoke of tensions coiled tight, ready to snap.

Malament's hand clenched around his goblet, the cool metal grounding him. He could not let this imbalance fester. It was not just his pride at stake, nor even the dignity of the hall; it was the safety of everyone within these walls. Yet the thought of acting—of truly stepping into the role demanded of him—unsettled him. What if he failed? What if the threads of control he held so tenuously slipped entirely through his fingers?

He exhaled, steadying himself. The alternative was far worse. If he did nothing, the Nordon's would see it as weakness, and weakness was an invitation for chaos. He forced himself to meet Konan's gaze again, the smirk still cutting across the man's face like a challenge. A cold resolve began to build in Malament's chest, the familiar weight of duty shifting into something sharper, more focused.

For too long, he had hesitated, waiting for the answers to reveal themselves or for someone else to take the reins. But now the path was clear. If he wanted to preserve what was his, he had no choice but to act. The balance of power needed to be restored—and it had to start with him.

An idea sparked in Malament's mind, sharp and sudden, cutting through the haze of frustration clouding his thoughts. If the men of Nordon respected strength, then strength would meet them head-on—not with weapons or anger, but with something they understood and could not dismiss. A test. A challenge.

"I have an idea," Malament said abruptly, his voice barely above a whisper, yet laced with a quiet conviction that made Luka straighten beside him.

Luka turned, his brow furrowing as he searched Malament's face. "What kind of idea?" he asked, his tone cautious, uncertain of what his young lord intended.

Malament did not answer immediately. Instead, he straightened his posture, his shoulders squaring as a newfound resolve took hold. His gaze swept the hall, lingering briefly on Konan's smirk before he took his first step forward. Each movement was deliberate, purposeful, as if the very act of walking was a declaration.

The sharp echo of his boots against the polished marble floor cut through the din of conversation like the ringing of a blade. Heads turned, first among the nearest tables, then further out, as whispers rippled through the hall. Conversations faltered, laughter quieted, and the weight of his presence began to press against the charged atmosphere.

The Nordon warriors turned their attention to him, their voices dropping into curious murmurs. A few leaned back in their chairs, their expressions shifting from amusement to interest as they watched the young lord cross the room with the air of a man who had made a decision.

Even the Borlong soldiers, who had moments ago sat rigid with unease, found their gazes drawn to Malament. Their stiff postures softened into something more attentive, their expressions tinged with curiosity—and perhaps a flicker of hope.

Malament's footsteps seemed louder now, each one reverberating in the hushed hall, carrying the weight of unspoken authority. The flickering sunlight streaming through the open arches caught the edges of his figure, casting a faint glow over his polished boots and the hem of his tunic. It was a simple gesture—walking—but in that moment, it held the power to reshape the room.

When he reached the Nordon table, every eye in the hall was on him. Malament stopped before Konan, who remained seated, his smirk widening ever so slightly. For a moment, the two men stared at each other, the tension between them palpable. Malament's sharp focus met Konan's fiery intensity without flinching.

"Do you understand me?" Malament asked, his tone calm but carrying an edge of authority that cut through the charged air.

Konan's smirk did not waver, but his eyes sharpened as he studied Malament with renewed interest. After a moment's pause, he gave a single, deliberate nod, the gesture weighted with unspoken approval.

"Good," Malament said, his voice steady and controlled, though every word was deliberate, calculated to carry across the hall. He clasped his hands behind his back, his posture deceptively relaxed, exuding an air of command.

"Pick five of your men. I'll pick five of mine." His gaze swept briefly over the Nordon warriors seated behind Konan, their interest now fully captured. He let the weight of his words settle, pausing just long enough for the murmurs to begin.

"We'll finish here and meet in the training area," Malament continued, his tone measured yet firm. "Man-on-man. You choose two challenges, I'll choose two. And if we draw, the final challenge will be settled by a duel—a single victor to determine the winner."

Konan's smirk grew into something sharper, his head tilting slightly as he studied Malament. He did not speak immediately, but the gleam in his eyes spoke volumes. Leaning forward, he rested his forearms on the table, his imposing frame radiating a quiet intensity as though appraising his adversary.

Finally, Konan spoke, his voice low but commanding, the Nordon tongue rolling off his tongue like the growl of an approaching storm.

"Vel torak vésh. Tól karesh—durak tan ashka."

*'Five warriors will stand. Prepare yourselves—strength in the storm.'*

The effect was immediate. A ripple of reaction passed through the Nordon warriors, their eyes brightening with interest as the meaning settled over them. They exchanged eager glances, the corners of their mouths lifting in subtle, predatory smiles. A few leaned forward, their hands tapping the hilts of their weapons, as though itching for the chance to prove themselves.

Low murmurs of approval rose among them, the tone one of anticipation and respect. Even some of the Borlong men straightened in their seats, their expressions a mix of surprise and curiosity, as though sensing the shifting tide.

"You like this idea," Malament said, his tone more observation than question.

Konan's response was a simple word, spoken in Nordon tongue, its meaning unmistakable even to those who did not understand the language. "Vel."

Yes.

Malament inclined his head. "Then it's settled."

Without waiting for further confirmation, he turned and strode back toward Luka, leaving the hall in a buzzing hum of conversation. The Nordon warriors were speaking eagerly now, their rough laughter replaced with nods of approval and a sense of focused energy. Even the Borlong soldiers, who had moments ago sat stiff with unease, exchanged glances of determination. The atmosphere shifted entirely, like the first breath of clean air after a storm.

Malament's steps were measured, deliberate, every inch of his bearing exuding control.

"What in the gods' name are you doing?" Luka hissed as Malament returned to his side, his tone half-curious, half-accusatory.

"Gaining ground," Malament replied simply, his tone cool but his eyes sharp with determination. He glanced back toward Konan, whose smirk had softened into something closer to approval—or perhaps anticipation.

Luka followed Malament's gaze, his brow furrowed. "You've certainly done something. The whole room feels different."

And it was true. The tension that had hung in the air like a drawn blade was gone, replaced by something almost tangible—excitement. Both sides now sat forward with anticipation, their expressions focused not on each other as adversaries, but on the promise of a contest. The warriors of Nordon and Borlong seemed energised, their hands flexing and their voices growing louder, more animated.

The sound of boots approached, and Malament turned to see Galil striding toward him, a rare grin tugging at the corners of the merchant's usually guarded expression.

"Well done," Galil said, his voice low but sincere. "I didn't think it was possible to turn this feast around. Nordon respect strength—and you've just shown them you understand their ways. That will go a long way."

Malament inclined his head slightly, acknowledging the compliment but keeping his expression reserved.

"You did more than earn their attention," Galil continued, his voice softening as his sharp eyes flicked toward the Nordon warriors. "You've started speaking their language—not just in words, but in what they value. To them, challenges like this aren't just sport. They're a test of worth, a way to know the measure of a man. This could be the first step toward something stronger than uneasy silence."

"And the first step is the easiest to misstep," Malament replied, though his tone held no doubt.

"True," Galil agreed with a faint smile, "but you didn't. You've planted the seed. Just be sure the Borlong men are ready to grow it."

Malament's lips curved slightly, the closest he came to a smile. "They'll be ready."

Galil's grin widened. "Spoken like a man who plans to win. And if you do, you won't just win their respect—you might win something more valuable. Trust."

Malament did not deny it. He turned back toward the hall, his eyes sweeping over the gathered men. The Nordon warriors were laughing again, but this time the sound was not grating. It was eager, filled with camaraderie rather than disdain. The Borlong soldiers, emboldened by the shift in tone, were speaking among themselves, their confidence returning.

He felt it too—the shift. The tension that had hung like a blade over the hall was gone, replaced by an electric energy that rippled through both sides. For the first time since Nordon's arrival, he had control of the room, not through force or fear but through purpose. The warriors were no longer divided by suspicion but united by anticipation—a contest, a test of strength that spoke to both nations' deepest traditions.

But Malament knew this fragile balance would shatter if the Borlong soldiers faltered. Their pride and skill would be on trial as much as their strength, and the Nordon warriors would judge every move, every stumble, with the weight of centuries-old grudges.

He let his gaze linger on the Borlong men, noting the flicker of determination in their eyes, the subtle straightening of their shoulders. They were eager, but eagerness alone would not win. This was his house, his ground, and his soldiers would need to prove it.

A part of him welcomed the challenge, the thrill of meeting Nordon on their terms and bending their respect toward Borlong. He would win—not just for himself, but for his men, his people, and the authority that Nordon's presence had threatened to undermine.

As the hall buzzed with rising anticipation, Malament straightened, his thoughts coiling into a singular purpose. This was not just about impressing the Nordon warriors. It was about sending a message—to Konan, to his soldiers, and to himself. Borlong would not bow.

# THE LORD'S MANSE
# CHAPTER FORTY ONE

Lord Malum's study was a space of calculated modesty, meticulously curated to project diligence and authority overindulgence. The walls were panelled in dark walnut, their rich grain polished to a muted sheen that absorbed the late afternoon sunlight spilling through the narrow windows. Heavy velvet curtains, drawn back with tasselled cords, framed the glass panes and allowed the amber hues of a summer's sky to filter in, casting soft patterns on the patterned carpet below. The air smelled faintly of parchment and the lingering tang of sealing wax.

Shelves lined two walls, crammed with neatly arranged tomes and ledgers, their leather spines varying in hue but uniform in their organisation. The oak desk stood at the centre of the room, its surface a battlefield of maps, correspondence, and a brass inkwell whose lid was half-ajar, as though abandoned mid-thought. To the side, an open ledger rested, its page filled with a sprawl of careful figures. Behind the desk, a tapestry bearing the crest of East Kadun hung like a silent sentinel, its deep red and gold threads slightly faded by time.

The hearth was unlit, its iron grate empty and clean, but the scent of a past fire lingered faintly. In its place, the warm glow of an oil lamp on the desk softened the room's hard lines, creating shadows that faintly crossed the polished wood. The atmosphere felt heavy, not with comfort but with purpose—like the quiet tension before an unsheathed blade.

Queen Karak stood near the hearth; her crimson cloak draped over the back of an armchair that she had deliberately avoided sitting in. The chair itself was upholstered in dark green velvet; its wooden arms carved with motifs of coiling vines. Instead of taking the offered seat, she remained upright, letting the angled light catch on her silver-threaded gown. The fabric shimmered faintly with each subtle movement as she turned to face Lord Malum, her posture composed yet quietly commanding. Her hands were clasped loosely before her, but her eyes—sharp and keen as a predator's—betrayed the storm beneath her polished exterior.

"Seventy thousand gold is a remarkable offer," Malum began, his voice low and deliberate as he uncorked a crystal decanter. The faint clink of glass against glass accompanied the rich amber liquid as he poured, its scent—a blend of oak and spice—wafting faintly into the room. His movements were unhurried, measured, as if the weight of her offer demanded gravity. Stepping around the desk, he extended one of the glasses toward her, his expression a careful mask of civility. "But forgive me if I suspect it comes with strings attached."

Karak accepted the glass with an elegance that matched her composed demeanour. Her fingers brushed his briefly—a subtle touch that lingered just long enough to be noticed but not questioned. She offered a smile, warm but undeniably calculated, the kind of smile that invited trust while guarding her true intentions. "Strings, Lord Malum, are for puppets," she said, her voice as smooth as the liquor in her hand. "I prefer to think of this as a partnership. An exchange of strength for strength.

She held the glass lightly, tilting it so the liquor caught the light, swirling the liquid with an absent air that belied the precision of her gaze. Her eyes flicked to the maps spread across the desk, lingering just long enough to make her awareness clear. "The only question, of course," she continued, her tone soft yet pointed, "is whether Borlong values this partnership as highly as Nordon does."

Malum's chuckle was quiet, the sound more akin to a man testing the sharpness of a blade than expressing humour. His grip tightened subtly on his own glass as he leaned against the edge of the desk, his posture deceptively relaxed. "Borlong values many things, Your Majesty—stability, prosperity, independence." His gaze met hers, sharp and unyielding despite the softness of his tone. "Seventy thousand gold is generous, but it won't buy all three."

Karak tilted her head, her smile deepening as she stepped closer to the desk. "Independence," she mused, her voice soft yet carrying a delicate lilt that lingered in the air like the final note of a melody. "A noble aspiration. Though I wonder..." With deliberate grace, she set the untouched glass down on the desk, its quiet clink punctuating her words. Leaning slightly forward, she let the golden light from the oil lamp dance along the faint curve of her collarbone, a subtle but undeniable shift in presence. "How independent can any nation truly be when winter closes in and the fires begin to fade?"

Malum's focus wavered, lingering for a heartbeat too long before he caught himself. His fingers tightened imperceptibly around the frame of his glass, the faint tension betraying his otherwise composed demeanour. "Borlong's fires burn brightly, Your Majesty," he said, his tone steady though his words felt like an assertion as much as a fact. "And our larders are well-stocked, thanks to careful planning and prudent alliances."

Her eyes gleamed as she straightened, her movements deliberate, as if she were withdrawing from a chessboard after a decisive move. The corner of her lips curved upward in a smile that danced on the edge of mockery. "How reassuring," she murmured, her voice light but with a teasing edge sharp enough to cut. "I'd hate to think Borlong might be left cold while Nordon grows warm with its gold."

The space between them thickened, a silence laden with tension and the unspoken weight of power shifting in subtle degrees. The amber liquid in their glasses shimmered, untouched yet charged with meaning, as the room seemed to hold its breath.

The insinuation hung in the air like the lingering smoke of a snuffed-out candle, faint but unmistakable. Malum's expression stiffened, the faintest twitch of his jaw betraying the effort it took not to rise to the bait. Instead, he shifted his weight subtly and gestured toward the chair opposite him, his movements measured and deliberate. "Please, sit," he said, his voice tight with an edge of forced civility. "I'm sure we can find common ground."

Karak's gaze remained fixed on him; her eyes gleaming with the spark of unspoken challenge. She let the silence stretch, her expression shifting to one of playful appraisal, as though weighing his words and his resolve. "I'm quite comfortable as I am, Lord Malum," she replied smoothly, her tone a careful blend of warmth and subtle defiance. The faintest curve of her lips hinted at amusement. "But I appreciate the offer."

She remained standing, the faint shimmer of her gown catching the light as she turned her head slightly, her gaze drifting momentarily to the desk as if dismissing the gesture altogether. The tension between them coiled tighter, unspoken words and power plays settling into the air like a second presence in the room.

Malum exhaled slowly through his nose, the sound low and deliberate as he set his glass down with precision. The faint clink against the desk seemed louder in the charged silence. "Your Majesty, Nordon's needs are clear—timber for your hearths, grain for your tables, produce for your markets. These are staples, not luxuries." His voice was steady, but the faint furrow of his brow betrayed his unease. "If Nordon intends to purchase them in such quantities, it will strain Borlong's resources."

"Perhaps," Karak conceded, her tone light, as though the matter were a mere trifle. She began pacing slowly, her movements languid yet purposeful, her fingertips brushing the edge of the desk with a casual intimacy that seemed to claim the space as her own. "But isn't strain the price of progress?" Her gaze flicked toward him briefly, the faintest glimmer of challenge in her eyes. "Seventy thousand gold is more than fair compensation for such strain. In fact, it is an opportunity—one that Borlong would be wise not to squander."

Malum's lips pressed into a thin line, his attention fixed on her movements with quiet vigilance. "And what opportunity would that be?" he asked, his tone cautious, as though wary of the trap she might be laying.

Karak paused, turning to face him fully. Her hands came to rest lightly on the desk, her posture leaning forward just enough to command his full attention without breaking the illusion of cordiality. The light caught the silver threads of her gown, emphasising the sharpness of her presence. "The opportunity to secure a deeper alliance with Nordon," she said, her voice softening, dipping into a tone that was both intimate and unyielding. Her words carried the weight of unspoken promises. "To become the gateway through which Nordon and East Kadun thrive together." She tilted her head slightly, her smile cool but deliberate. "Gold, Lord Malum, is only the beginning."

The words hung in the air, heavy with implication, as her stare held his, daring him to see the future she was offering—or the threat that lay beneath it.

She is playing a dangerous game, Malum thought, his jaw tightening as he held her gaze. Every movement she made was deliberate—the slow, measured pacing, the feather-light brush of her fingertips along the desk, the way her voice softened at precisely the right moment. It was a performance, calculated and precise, like a blade gliding just above his skin. But charm, no matter how expertly wielded, could not conceal the cold, unyielding realities Borlong faced. Their trade routes were already stretched thin, vulnerable to disruption at the first sign of unrest. Their alliances with West Kadun, tenuous at best, offered little reassurance. If Nordon's demands grew too large, Borlong would not merely strain —it would buckle under the weight. And Malum, for all his measured composure, refused to let his city become a pawn in someone else's ambitions.

The tightening of Malum's jaw, his eyes steady but shadowed by unspoken concerns. She saw it—the faint crease in his brow, the subtle shift of his fingers against the desk. A man weighing the scales, measuring the risks, but still tethered to the notion of control. Foolish, Karak thought, her unwavering focus fixed on him. He thinks he can resist. He thinks his measured words and stoic demeanour are enough to stand against me. But resistance only delays the inevitable.

She allowed her expression to soften, her lips curving in a faint, almost indulgent smile. Men like him were predictable—proud, pragmatic, and utterly convinced of their own invulnerability. But she knew the type too well to be deceived. Strength, when rooted in wealth, was strength built on sand. Borlong's prosperity was its armour, but it was also its weakness. Wealth could shield, but it could not endure. A single misstep, a single bad harvest, and Borlong's golden veneer would crumble like a tower brought low by its own weight.

Karak's fingers brushed the edge of the desk once more as she straightened, her eyes narrowing slightly, though her tone remained smooth. "I don't believe we need to dwell on strain or resistance, Lord Malum," she said, as though the word itself was distasteful. "What I offer is stability—a future where Borlong isn't scrambling to hold its place, but leading the way. That's not a threat," her lips curved further, "it's a gift."

Karak's words hung in the air, the subtle lilt of her voice a reminder that she controlled this conversation as deftly as a conductor led an orchestra. Yet Malum did not yield so easily. He leaned back in his chair, his movements slow and deliberate, as if creating space to regain some semblance of control. Steepling his fingers, he fixed her with a measured gaze, his expression unreadable save for the faint furrow of his brow.

"Of course," he began, his tone light but edged with something sharper, "there is also the matter of your... visit to West Kadun. An intriguing choice, given the history between your kingdom and theirs."

For a fraction of a second, Karak's smile froze, the warmth in it cooling like embers left too long untended. Her gaze sharpened, cutting through the veneer of pleasantries like a blade testing its edge. But when she spoke, her voice remained steady, smooth as silk. "History is a burden for those who cannot see the future, Lord Malum," she said, her tone carrying the faintest hint of admonition, as though scolding a child for clinging to old grudges. Her smile returned, deliberate now, but no less poised. "My visit to King Ruben is a gesture of goodwill—nothing more."

The subtle tension between them tightened, the weight of the conversation pressing down like the humid air before a storm. Karak tilted her head slightly, her eyes glinting with an unspoken challenge. She knew Malum was testing her, probing for cracks, but she had no intention of giving him any.

"Goodwill?" Malum echoed, his tone laced with scepticism. "King Ruben is not known for his generosity, and his lords will not look kindly on a queen of Nordon stepping onto their soil." He leaned forward slightly, his voice steady but weighted with warning. "If your visit sparks conflict, it will not be Nordon that pays the price—it will be Borlong. We are the shield, Your Majesty, not the sword."

Karak stepped closer, the faint rustle of her gown breaking the silence. Her movements were deliberate, her eyes locking onto his like a predator pinning its prey. "Do you fear for Borlong," she asked, her voice low and velvet-smooth, "or for your position within it?" Her tone was soft, almost tender, but the edge beneath it was unmistakable. "King Ruben may cling to his grudges, but I am not a Queen weighed down by the past. I see only opportunity—a chance to mend what others have broken."

Her words wove through the room like threads in an invisible web, precise and unrelenting. Malum held her gaze, but the air between them seemed heavier with each passing moment. He could feel her presence pressing down on him, the sheer force of her conviction like a storm gathering just beyond the horizon. His throat tightened, but he forced his reply, his tone cautious. "And if that opportunity fails?"

Karak's smile deepened, her lips curving into something that was equal parts reassurance and menace. She leaned in slightly, her voice dropping to a near whisper that seemed to wrap around him like smoke. "Then I will ensure it does not. Nordon does not fail, Lord Malum. And neither do I."

The silence that followed was deafening, tension crackling in the air like a spark waiting to ignite. Malum's jaw tightened as he studied her, his mind torn between the flicker of doubt and the practicality that governed his every decision. She had given no room for compromise—only a vision of the future she demanded he share.

Still, the silence stretched on, growing heavier with each passing second, the unspoken words between them bearing an almost physical weight. Karak remained motionless; her sharp features locked onto Malum. He held her stare, refusing to look away despite the unease crawling up his spine, a silent battle of wills unfolding in the charged stillness of the room.

Finally, she reached for her glass, lifting it with deliberate precision. Tilting it slightly, she let the amber liquid catch the light before taking a slow, measured sip. The liquor burned warmly down her throat, and she allowed a faint hum of approval to escape her lips, just loud enough for Malum to hear. She considered the taste, her expression unreadable, before taking another sip, this one slower, more thoughtful.

Setting the glass down on the desk with a soft clink, she lingered for a moment, her fingers brushing the rim as if sealing the moment in place. Her eyes found his again, sharp and unwavering, and her lips moved with deliberate care as she spoke in the Nordon tongue.

"Frostskarn fara verst fyrir óviðbúna."

Her tone was low, almost melodic, the unfamiliar syllables hanging in the air like an incantation. She let the words linger before offering him the translation, her voice smooth and deliberate. "The frost always chills worse for the ill-prepared," she said, her lips curving into a faint, enigmatic smile.

With a practised grace, she turned and collected her crimson cloak, draping it over her shoulders with a flourish. She adjusted the fabric briefly, her movements unhurried, as though time itself waited on her command. At the door, she paused, glancing over her shoulder one final time.

"Consider the offer, Malum," she said, her tone soft but edged with unspoken steel. "It would be most wise."

Then she was gone, the door closing behind her with a quiet finality. Malum remained where he sat, his gaze falling to his untouched glass of liquor on the desk. The faint scent of spice and oak lingered in the air, mingling with the echoes of her parting words. For a long moment, he did not move, the weight of her presence still pressing down on him even in her absence.

Finally, with a slow exhale, he reached for his glass and stared at the shimmering liquid within. He turned it once, watching the ripples settle—steady, controlled. Unlike him. He lifted it slightly, hesitated—then set it back down. The taste, like day, had soured.

# THE LORD'S MANSE
# CHAPTER FORTY TWO

The training hall was a vast, cavernous space branching off from the grand reception hall. The polished marble of the entrance transitioned into rougher stone surrounding the central sand pit, its natural slate worn smooth in places by years of footfall.

The pit itself was bordered by sturdy wooden beams, with thick stone pillars anchoring each corner and framing the space. Wall-mounted sconces flickered along the perimeter, their flames casting shifting shadows that danced across the stone walls and faintly illuminated the grains of sand below. The light spilled unevenly into the area, dimmer here than in the bright, sunlit reception hall, giving the space a hushed, almost reverent atmosphere.

At the centre of the sand pit, Auron stood with his hands loose at his sides, his feet shifting lightly against the unstable ground as he kept his focus on Gordon. The sand beneath him bore the marks of prior movement—scattered footprints and shallow trenches left from skidding to a halt. Gordon paced in a wide circle around him, the polished shaft of his long wooden lance catching occasional glints of firelight as it twirled in his hands.

"Keep moving," Gordon barked, his voice cutting sharply through the quiet murmur of the flames. "The sand's your first enemy—it shifts, steals your footing, and drags you down. Don't let it."

Auron darted to the side as the lance swept toward him, narrowly avoiding the blow. His steps were light, his balance instinctive despite the uneven surface. He was not merely reacting to Gordon's movements; he was anticipating them, his sharp focus reading each feint and strike.

"You're quicker than most," Gordon muttered, stepping forward and aiming low. The tip of the lance brushed just past Auron's boots as he hopped back, scattering sand in his wake.

"But quick won't save you if you don't keep your wits," Gordon added, spinning the lance in a wide arc toward Auron's shoulder.

Auron ducked smoothly, his body folding with youthful ease before springing upright again. His breath came steady, his movements fluid, and for a brief moment, Gordon's grizzled face softened with approval.

"Good," the weapons master said, his tone carrying a rare note of satisfaction. "But stay balanced. Lean too far back, and you'll land on your arse."

"Yes, sir," Auron replied, shifting his stance to distribute his weight more evenly.

As they continued in the distance, a rhythmic clatter of boots against the marble floor of the grand reception hall echoed faintly through the training hall's open archway. Auron's head turned slightly toward the sound, his ears pricking as the noise transitioned from sharp strikes on marble to dull thuds on stone as the soldiers entered.

"Eyes on me, boy!" Gordon snapped, jabbing the lance toward Auron's side.

Auron twisted sharply, dodging the strike, but his attention flickered back toward the newcomers gathering along the stone perimeter that surrounded the sand pit.

The first to appear were the Borlong soldiers. Their polished armour gleamed even under the dim firelight, and their boots struck the stone with steady, measured precision. They moved as one, their postures rigid, their expressions calm and disciplined.

Then came a second group, they were nothing like the Borlong men. These warriors wore fur-lined cloaks and rough leather armour that looked well-worn, almost battered. Their strides were loose, their movements unhurried, but there was a weight to their presence that made Auron's pulse quicken. Their hands rested casually on the hilts of axes or swords, and their laughter, low and rasp, filled the space like rolling thunder. Their voices, harsh and foreign, carried a cadence unfamiliar to Auron, the rough syllables weaving through the air like a storm front approaching.

The contrast was striking. The Borlong soldiers seemed carved from the same mould, their discipline radiating with every precise step. The others were rugged, untamed, their confidence bordering on arrogance as they surveyed the sand pit and the men around them.

"Focus!" Gordon barked again, yanking Auron's attention back to the exercise. The lance came down hard, and Auron twisted sharply, sending a spray of sand scattering as he dodged the blow.

By now, the soldiers had lined the stone perimeter of the pit, their numbers growing with each passing moment. The Borlong men stood in neat, orderly ranks, their hands clasped behind their backs, their eyes fixed forward. The men in furs lounged casually, some leaning against the walls, others crouching low, their sharp expressions betraying their interest in the exercise.

Auron caught fragments of their voices, harsh and rasping. One of the warriors nudged the man beside him and muttered something in their native tongue. "Varinn skell throk," the words rough yet almost amused. His companion chuckled, leaning forward with a sharp grin as he gestured toward Gordon's lance.

Though Auron could not understand the words, their meaning seemed clear—a mix of challenge and derision. It sent a shiver down his spine, the weight of their attention pressing heavier against him.

Then, two figures entered together.

Auron's breath hitched as his attention shifted to the man who strode in beside Malament. The stranger was a towering figure, his broad shoulders draped with a fur-lined cloak that swayed slightly as he walked. His red hair, vivid as flame in the flickering firelight, framed a face marked by battle. Scars glinted faintly along his forearms, their jagged edges catching the light like runes carved in flesh. He moved with an unsettling ease; each step measured yet brimming with a quiet, predatory energy that made Auron's stomach twist.

Malament, by contrast, was a study in precision. His polished boots left crisp marks on the stone, and his posture exuded calm control. His expression was composed, but there was an edge to it, as though his thoughts churned behind his steady exterior.

The two men stopped at the edge of the sand pit, their presence shifting the weight of the room. Malament's attention lingered briefly on Auron, his expression calculating. The red-haired man's smirk deepened slightly as he glanced between Auron and Gordon, a flicker of interest—or amusement—in his eyes.

"Don't let them distract you," Gordon growled, stepping back and driving the lance firmly into the sand. "You're good, boy, but good can turn to dead if you let your mind wander."

"Yes, sir," Auron replied, though his chest tightened under the weight of so many watching eyes.

The sand pit, once a place of focus and routine, now felt stifling. Auron swallowed hard as Gordon stepped back from the lance, giving a slight nod to signal the end of their session. Straightening, Auron wiped his damp palms on his tunic, though the weight of the moment still pressed heavily on him, unrelenting.

The tension in the training hall thickened, the laughter and murmurs from the gathered soldiers dying into a heavy, expectant silence. All eyes shifted to the two leaders standing at the edge of the sand pit. Even Gordon's habitual bark was stilled, his weathered face drawn into a subtle frown.

Then came a slow clap.

Konan's hands collided with deliberate force, the sound reverberating through the cavernous space. The measured rhythm of his applause carried a weight of approval, but there was an unmistakable undertone of mockery. His lips twisted into a smirk as he turned to his warriors, speaking in Nordon with a low, gravelly voice.

"Varinn thal storr."

The phrase rolled off his tongue, harsh and guttural, accompanied by a chuckle that rumbled deep in his chest.

His men erupted in laughter, their voices rough and unrestrained, the echoes bouncing off the stone walls like a storm breaking. One of them slapped another on the shoulder, repeating part of the phrase *"thal storr!"* with an exaggerated grin, sparking another round of laughter.

Auron's cheeks burned hot, though he did not understand a single word. The unfamiliar syllables hung heavy in the air, the weight of them stirring something sharp and uncomfortable in his chest. Was it mockery? Contempt? He glanced toward Gordon, whose stern face betrayed no reaction.

Whatever Konan had said, it was for his men alone, and the laughter that followed felt like a wall separating Auron and the Borlong soldiers from understanding.

Malament stepped forward, his composed demeanour steady against the hum of tension. His sharp gaze swept over the crowd, ignoring the Nordon warriors' smirks and the uneasy silence of the Borlong soldiers.

"This is my nephew, Auron," Malament began, his voice calm but carrying an unmistakable edge. "He is staying with us, learning our values, our traditions...our manners." The pointed emphasis on the final word landed like a blade, an intentional dig directed squarely at Konan.

The Nordon warlord's expression darkened, his piercing eyes narrowing as his shoulders stiffened beneath the thick fur of his cloak. For a moment, he seemed poised to respond, but Malament pressed on, his composed demeanour unflinching under Konan's smouldering glare.

"His tutor, Gordon, trains him in the art of combat. We are very pleased with Auron's progress. He shows much promise." Malament's tone was smooth, but the words carried an undercurrent of challenge as his gaze flicked briefly toward Konan. He added with studied politeness, "This is Konan, and his men of Nordon."

Konan let out a low grunt, dismissive and rough, as though the introduction itself was beneath him. His lips curled into a faint sneer as he muttered something in Nordon, his voice deliberate, thick with disdain.

"Thorin vel an varr ni vethar."

The words were coarse and unfamiliar to Auron, but the meaning did not require translation, the low, rumbling laughter of Konan's men made that much clear.

Malament tilted his head slightly, the tension in his jaw tightening just enough to reveal his irritation. "Care to translate?" he asked, his tone cutting but measured.

Konan did not bother to look at him, his smirk widening as his gaze lingered on Auron instead, his silence more provocative than any response.

Malament's lip twitched, his composure fraying at the edges. Though the words had been foreign, their intent was not. The jest—no, the insult—was aimed squarely at Auron and Gordon, a deliberate provocation Malament could not let stand.

"Perhaps a demonstration before we begin?" Malament suggested, gesturing toward the sand pit. His voice was calm, but his choice of words carried an unmistakable challenge. The offer was indirectly aimed at Konan, though Malament's gaze shifted purposefully to Gordon and Auron.

Konan's smirk did not falter, though his expression grew colder, more calculating. The faintest glimmer of interest flickered in his eyes as the Nordon warriors exchanged low murmurs, their guttural voices filling the charged silence.

Konan's posture did not change, but the flicker of interest in his eyes was unmistakable. He said nothing for a long moment, letting the silence stretch.

Malament turned toward Gordon. "Would you spar with the boy?" he asked, his voice cool and authoritative, though there was a faint undercurrent of unease.

Gordon gave a curt nod, his expression as impassive as ever, and gestured for Auron to follow. Together, they moved toward the wooden rack where the practice weapons were neatly arranged. The faint creak of the weapon rack filled the silence as Auron's hands hovered briefly over the options before he of course selected the two wooden swords. His fingers curled around the hilts, testing their weight and balance with an unconscious precision that didn't escape Konan's notice.

The Nordon commander's gaze sharpened, his posture subtly shifting as he observed the boy's movements with newfound interest. His eyes followed every small adjustment Auron made—the way his wrists rotated, the slight shift in his stance, the quiet focus in his expression.

Auron glanced at Gordon, who gave him a quick nod of approval. With the weapons chosen, the two began to make their way back toward the sand pit. Their steps were deliberate, their focus clear—until a single word cut through the air like a blade.

"Skahr."

Konan's voice was low but carried the weight of command, its meaning unmistakable, No. The sound echoed in the stillness, freezing both Gordon and Auron in their tracks. The tension in the room spiked, palpable and unrelenting, as the Nordon leader's gaze bore into them, daring any protest.

Konan stepped forward, the weight of his presence commanding the attention of the entire hall. A hush fell over the gathered soldiers and warriors, each waiting for him to speak. But instead, he stepped into the sand pit, his boots sinking slightly into the loose ground as he strode toward Auron and Gordon with deliberate purpose.

Gordon shifted subtly, his stance tightening as though readying himself for whatever might come next. Konan stopped before them, his piercing gaze locking onto Gordon, and after a brief, tense pause, he repeated the word, calmer this time, "Skahr."

The single syllable lingered, rippling through the hall, carrying an air of finality.

All eyes followed Konan as he turned away without another glance at Auron or Gordon and made his way to the weapon rack with the swagger of a man utterly in command. His stocky fingers trailed along the polished wooden handles, testing the weight and balance of each as if sizing up his prey. He stopped at a wooden battle axe; a weapon uncannily similar to the one strapped across his back.

The room remained silent as he pulled the weapon from its place, replacing it with his own. He spun the axe in his hands with skilled ease, the motion fluid and confident. The axe shifted quickly between his hands before he gave a single nod of approval, a faint glimmer of respect in his expression—a silent acknowledgment of the craftsmanship.

Malament broke the silence, his tone measured but sharp. "Our weapons are crafted from the finest wood of the forest, varnished for durability. They are near-perfect replicas of the true weapons—balanced in weight and size." His eyes narrowed. "You intend to spar?"

Konan did not answer at first. Instead, he tested the heft of the axe one last time before turning to face Gordon. The Nordon warlord's expression was unreadable, but the flicker of a smirk tugged at the corner of his mouth as his attention shifted to Auron.

Gordon glanced toward Malament; his silent question clear. Malament gave a slight nod, granting his approval, and Gordon stepped into position opposite Konan, gesturing for Auron to step aside.

Konan, however, raised a hand, halting Gordon's movement. His deep voice carried across the room, the single word "Skahr" stopping them all in their tracks. Then, in broken Kadun, he added, "Let see...promise," his focus fixed on Auron.

The words were thick with his accent, but their meaning was unmistakable.

A heavy silence fell over the hall, the air thick with tension. Malament's jaw tightened as he fought to keep his anger in check. Konan had spoken enough Kadun to be understood, proof that his earlier silence had been nothing more than a ploy. And now, he had thrown down a challenge no one wanted: a duel between an elite Nordon warrior and a boy still in training.

Malament saw through it immediately. This was not about the boy; it was a performance. A calculated move to showcase Nordon strength against Kadun vulnerability, to crush the spirit of the room with a symbolic defeat, no matter how "harmless" the duel seemed on the surface. To deny the challenge would only add fuel to Konan's mockery, a public show of Borlong's unwillingness to compete.

Underhanded. Cruel. Typical of Konan's brutal tactics.

But then Malament's gaze shifted to Auron. The boy showed no fear—no hesitation. His turquoise eyes gleamed with determination, and there was even a faint trace of eagerness in his expression. It was enough to give Malament pause. Perhaps...perhaps there was something to gain here.

Malament's voice was steady, though his chest burned with resentment. "Very well," he said finally. "Let us have the duel."

Konan spun the axe in his hand with casual ease once more, the show almost a mocking act of his ability. The polished wood glinting faintly in the dim firelight, before flicking Malament a jesting smile. The gesture was deliberate, a taunt wrapped in the guise of camaraderie. Malament's jaw tightened, his discontent barely concealed as his steely eyes locked onto the Nordon warrior.

Gordon stepped aside, his movements measured, clearing the way for Konan, who now turned to face Auron across the sand. Auron stood firm, his youthful frame composed despite the towering presence of his opponent. Bowing low in the customary Kadun gesture of respect, the boy kept his gaze steady.

Konan returned the gesture with a brief, almost dismissive nod, his smirk never fading. As Auron straightened, the red-haired warrior struck without warning, flashing his axe forward in a swift arc. Auron jumped lightly out of the way, his reflexes sharp and unhesitating. The strike had been calculated—not meant to land but to test the boy's reaction. The duel had begun.

Konan's focus shifted entirely to Auron, his stance shifting as he began circling counterclockwise, the broad muscles in his shoulders rolling with each deliberate step. Auron mirrored his movements, his body light and poised, his eyes locked on his opponent. With a sudden change of direction, Konan closed the distance, but Auron adjusted flawlessly, moving with an ease that surprised even the Nordon warrior.

Konan's sharp gaze assessed the boy's every step, watching his stance, his balance, the subtle grace of his footwork. He was impressed, though his expression betrayed nothing.

For Auron, the world shrank to the sand pit and the towering figure before him. The murmurs of the crowd, the flickering firelight, even the shifting grains of sand beneath his feet—all of it faded into irrelevance. His focus sharpened into a razor's edge, fixed solely on Konan. Every step, every shift of weight, every subtle movement of his opponent became a puzzle to decode.

His gaze darted between Konan's hands and shoulders, watching for the faintest hint of an attack. The warrior's grip on the axe hilt drew his attention, his knuckles shifting between relaxed and tense. Auron waited for the tell—the moment those fingers tightened, the knuckles whitening as the weapon prepared to swing.

He tracked the broader motion of Konan's shoulders, waiting for them to coil like a spring before his eventual strike. The swirl of muscle and the shift of the hips always preceded the weapon's deadly arc, a chain reaction Gordon had taught him to read like a second language.

"Watch their pivot points," Gordon's voice echoed in his mind, steady and sure, the mantra ingrained through hours of relentless training. "It is impossible to swing a weapon without first moving your shoulders and hips."

Each word replayed with precision, guiding Auron's focus as he matched Konan's steps and watched for the moment to act. Every movement of the Nordon warrior told a story, and Auron was determined to read it before the next chapter struck.

Then came the tell. Konan's shoulders pulled back, his grip tightening around the axe's hilt. The weapon arced high above his head before crashing down with brutal force, carving a deep gouge into the sand where Auron had just stood. Moving pre-emptively, Auron had sidestepped the blow, but Konan recovered quickly. With a fluid motion, the axe rose again and swung horizontally, spraying sand in a wide arc as it cut through the air.

Auron retreated a step, the axe whistling past his chest, its force stirring the air. His focus sharpened as he noticed the faint tension rippling through Konan's forearms, the scars across the man's skin catching the dim light. The red-haired warrior had overextended, his attempt to catch Auron with the reverse swing leaving him briefly exposed.

Auron acted on instinct. In the span of a heartbeat, he propelled himself forward, his weight shifting effortlessly off his back foot. Both wooden swords slashed in unison across Konan's bare forearms, the sharp crack of wood meeting flesh reverberating through the hall.

Konan recoiled, his expression flashing with a mix of shock and pride. His hands tightened around the axe, his grip fierce, and with a roar of effort, he swung the weapon in a vicious arc, reversing its momentum toward Auron's now exposed frame.

But Auron had already seen the tells. The tightening of Konan's shoulders, the subtle shift in his hips—it all played out before the swing even began. With fluid precision, Auron dropped into a forward roll, the axe missing him by centimetres as it tore through the space where he had stood. He came out of the roll smoothly, springing to his feet and spinning to face Konan once more, his movements effortless and precise.

A ripple of awe coursed through the gathered spectators, even the Nordon warriors exchanging impressed murmurs. They all knew the truth: had this been a battlefield, the duel would have been over.

Auron barely registered the crowd's reaction. His focus remained fixed, his breathing steady as his twin wooden swords extended before him. Testing their balance, he spun each blade simultaneously, the movements instinctive and fluid. His turquoise eyes locked on Konan once more, ready for whatever came next.

The Nordon warrior paused, his smirk deepening, but there was no mistaking the glint of respect in his stormy gaze. The boy was not the weakling he had expected. The duel was far from over, but it was clear to all that Auron had already made his mark.

Konan could hear the surprised murmurs and excited exclamations of his men, their admiration for the boy's skill cutting through the tense air. He did not let it sting, nor did he allow it to distract him. Instead, he let it fuel a quiet resolve, his focus narrowing on the boy before him. This was no longer a demonstration; it was a test, and Auron was proving himself in ways few could.

Each missed strike was not a failure but an observation. Konan's movements remained controlled, his strikes calculated, his demeanour unwavering. The axe spun in his hands with effective ease, its weight balanced perfectly in his grip. Each arc, each flick of the weapon was deliberate, designed to probe, to read the boy's reactions as much as to strike.

Auron continued to evade with a grace that impressed even Konan, his movements fluid, his instincts sharp. But Konan was no mere warrior swinging blindly. He studied the boy with each pass, noting the lightness of his stance, the precision of his footwork, the confidence in his timing.

Gradually, Konan shifted his approach, adjusting his pace and angle. Each swing pushed Auron back another step, closing the space between them. The boy dodged left—Konan followed. Auron shifted back—Konan pressed forward. There was no frustration in his actions, only strategy.

Slowly, methodically, Konan began herding Auron toward the corner of the pit, his strikes no longer seeking to land but to guide. Each movement was a step in a larger plan, a lesson being written in the sand. For every ounce of respect Konan had gained for Auron, there was still a need to show the boy—and the gathered crowd—the undeniable difference between them.

Konan's mind was sharp, his body poised, his intent clear: to push Auron to his limits, not out of malice, but out of the belief that no warrior is forged without the fire of adversity.

The size difference between them became glaringly apparent as Auron found himself cornered, the once-open space of the sand pit now a narrowing trap.

His agile movements grew restricted, his options diminishing with every carefully placed step Konan had forced him to take.

When the Nordon warrior finally unleashed a crushing downward strike, it came like a thunderclap. Auron's instincts flared, and with no room left to evade, he raised his twin wooden blades to parry. The impact was immense. The axe collided with his weapons in a deafening crack, the force rattling through his arms and nearly sending him to his knees.

Konan saw the opening. Without hesitation, he surged forward, not with a roar of anger but with the focused precision of a predator closing in on its prey. The axe moved in a relentless flurry; each swing controlled yet unyielding. Auron narrowly avoided the first strike, his reflexes saving him by the breadth of a hair.

The second strike came faster than he could adjust.

This time, it was not the sharp edge of the wooden axe but the flat head that crashed into him, slamming into his side beneath his armpit with devastating force. The impact lifted Auron clean off the ground, driving the air from his lungs in an instant.

Before he could even register the blow, Konan's massive hand reached out, gripping him midair with an almost effortless strength. It was not a brutal act but a display of sheer control, a calculated assertion of dominance. With a fluid motion, Konan flung the boy aside, sending him skidding across the sand in a spray of grit.

Auron hit the ground hard, his body rolling with the momentum until he came to a stop. Pain surged through him, his vision spinning, but even as his chest heaved for breath, his spirit remained unbroken. Gritting his teeth, he scrambled to his feet, his movements sharp despite the ache radiating through his body.

His twin swords rose instinctively, crossing in front of his face to guard against the next attack. Auron's turquoise eyes blazed with determination, his focus undimmed. He braced himself, expecting the next strike to come swiftly.

But it did not.

The silence that followed was heavy, thick with expectation. Auron's ears rang with the echoes of the clash, but no new blow came. Slowly, cautiously, he lowered his guard, his gaze locking onto Konan.

The Nordon warrior stood motionless, the axe lowered at his side. His towering frame loomed above Auron like a shadow, but there was no malice in his expression-only something far more complex: respect. Then, without a word, the towering Nordon warrior extended a massive hand toward the boy.

Auron froze, unsure of the gesture. But the offer was genuine, the nod Konan gave him full of approval. Tentatively, Auron took the hand, and Konan pulled him upright with ease. As soon as Auron regained his footing, the Nordon warrior clapped a heavy hand on his shoulder, his nodding approval continuing.

The crowd, stunned into silence, seemed to hold its collective breath. Then, a single voice rose from the Nordon warriors, cutting through the quiet with a tone of deep respect.

"Durak karesh."

The phrase echoed in the hall, its weight and meaning resonating even to those unfamiliar with the words. Strength to you.

Konan nodded in agreement, the faintest flicker of pride softening his stern features. He turned back to Auron, his gaze steady, and bowed deeply—gracefully, with all the dignity the boy had shown at the duel's start. When he straightened, his voice carried through the hall, rich and deliberate.

"Durak karesh."

The words radiated sincerity; a warrior's respect earned. Konan's nod continued, and though he stepped back, the gravity of the moment lingered. The crowd remained silent, reverent, as the Nordon warrior acknowledged the boy not as an opponent, but as an equal in spirit.

The silence lingered for a heartbeat longer, the weight of the duel settling over the gathered crowd like a thick mist. Then came a sound that broke through—a deliberate, steady clap.

Malament.

His hands came together not in jest or mockery but in genuine respect, the measured applause ringing out across the hall. The sound carried with it a sense of finality, an acknowledgment of the skill and spirit both combatants had shown.

The crowd, caught in the moment, joined him. The Borlong soldiers clapped in unison, their disciplined rhythm echoing off the stone walls, while the Nordon warriors followed suit with their own gruff exclamations of approval. The mix of voices, Kadun and Nordon alike, created a rare harmony that filled the hall with a sense of unity.

Malament continued to clap, his gaze locked on Auron. For the first time in his life, he felt real pride swell in his chest, pure and untainted. Like a father had for his son, it was not the hollow satisfaction of achieving political gain or earning fleeting favour—it was something far deeper.

Auron had surpassed every expectation, not just surviving but thriving in the presence of a warrior as formidable as Konan. He had earned the respect of men who had arrived in Borlong as adversaries, and in doing so, he had accomplished something Malament had struggled with. Forging a bridge between Borlong and Nordon, between two cultures that had stood at odds not an hour passed.

As the applause faded, Malament stepped forward, his voice clear and strong. "A duel well fought," he said, his words carrying across the hall. He glanced toward Konan, giving the Nordon warlord a respectful nod. "Our thanks to you, Konan, for showing us the strength of Nordon."

Konan returned the nod, his expression neutral but his eyes betraying a glimmer of approval.

Malament turned back to Auron, who stood with his twin swords at his sides, his chest rising and falling steadily. The boy's face was a mix of exhaustion and determination, but his turquoise eyes still shone with the spark of battle.

"Auron," Malament said, his voice softening slightly, "you've done more today than prove your skill. You've earned respect—ours and theirs. That is a rare thing."

Auron straightened, a faint smile flickering across his face as he lowered himself into a deep bow toward both Malament and Konan. The gesture, though simple, carried the weight of a warrior's respect, and its quiet dignity resonated through the hall.

Konan returned the bow with a subtle nod, his expression unreadable save for the faint flicker of approval in his eyes. The Nordon warlord turned and strode back to the weapon rack, his movements unhurried yet purposeful. Reaching for his steel axe, he replaced the wooden one with respectful care, his fingers lingering for a moment as though acknowledging the craftsmanship that had served him in the duel.

Malament remained rooted where he stood, his gaze trailing Auron as the boy made his way toward Gordon. The seasoned tutor, ever reserved, gave Auron a rare pat on the shoulder—a gesture that, from Gordon, spoke volumes. Auron's smile widened briefly before his face fell back into quiet composure, the weight of the moment settling on his young shoulders.

The hall was quieter now, the tension of the duel dissipating, replaced by a muted buzz of conversation. Nordon warriors spoke in low, gravelly tones, their words carrying a newfound respect, while the Borlong soldiers exchanged impressed glances. The atmosphere had shifted, the duel forging an unspoken bridge between the two groups.

Malament took a step forward, his polished boots crunching softly against the sand, and raised his hand. The subtle motion silenced the murmurs, drawing all attention back to him. His voice, when it came, was clear and commanding, carrying the weight of authority and the pride that still burned in his chest.

"This duel was but the first of many trials today," Malament announced, his words resonating through the cavernous space. "You have seen the skill of our young, now we shall show you the strength of our seasoned. Let this be the spirit that carries us forward."

His eyes swept across the crowd, lingering briefly on Konan, who stood at the edge of the sand pit with his steel axe resting against his shoulder. The Nordon leader gave a faint nod, a silent acknowledgment of Malament's words.

Malament turned back to the crowd. "Let the challenges begin," he declared, his voice firm and resolute.

The hall erupted into motion as the different warriors began to shift, their focus now on the series of contests ahead. Auron glanced back toward Malament, his turquoise eyes meeting his new uncles for a fleeting moment. Malament gave the boy a small, almost imperceptible nod—one that spoke of approval, pride, and something unspoken yet understood.

# THE LORD'S MANSE
# CHAPTER FORTY THREE

The training hall buzzed with the sounds of cheering and jeering, a stark contrast to the solemn silence that had accompanied the earlier duel. At the centre of the sand pit, two men sat across from each other, locked in a fierce contest of strength over a large oak panelled barrel.

On one side was a broad-shouldered man of Borlong, his face a mask of strain. Veins bulged along his neck and temples, his skin reddening as he poured every ounce of his strength into the match. Sweat glistened on his brow, dripping onto the wooden barrel beneath him.

Opposite him sat a Nordon warrior, his expression tight with focus but calmer in comparison. His jaw clenched as his muscles corded beneath his fur-lined tunic. He grimaced, but it was the grimace of a man in control, his strength steady and unyielding like iron.

The two men's hands locked together, knuckles white as their muscles strained against each other's weight. The barrel beneath them creaked under the pressure, its sturdy frame bearing the exertion of their clash.

The Borlong man surged forward, his face twisting with effort as he began to edge his opponent's wrist closer to the surface of the barrel. Cheers erupted from the Borlong soldiers gathered around, their voices rising in support of their man.

"Push! Push, Jareth!" one shouted.

"Break him, man!"

The Nordon warrior's wrist trembled, the strain evident even in his iron-like composure. For a moment, it seemed as though the Borlong man would claim the victory.

But then, like a tide turning with sudden force, the Nordon warrior shifted. His wrist steadied, his grip tightening. His free hand slammed against the barrel's edge as he drew upon some deep reserve of strength. Slowly, inexorably, the Borlong man's hand began to reverse its course.

The crowd roared as the Nordon warrior pressed his opponent's hand down in one swift, final motion. The sound of their clasped hands slamming against the barrel echoed through the hall, followed by a thunderous cheer from the men of Nordon.

Their guttural voices filled the space, jeering and exclaiming in triumph as their champion stood and raised his arms. The Borlong man slumped back, gasping for breath, his face flushed with exhaustion and defeat.

Auron, standing near the edge of the pit, watched the scene unfold with wide eyes. He turned to Gordon, who stood beside him, his arms crossed and his face impassive.

"How does this work?" Auron asked, his voice low but eager, his eyes fixed on the competitors.

Gordon's studied expression did not waver from the competitors as another pair of men began to step forward for the next challenge. "Because it's more than strength, boy," he said gruffly. "Watch closely. Every detail. Every movement. This isn't just about who's stronger. It's about understanding your opponent, knowing when to hold and when to strike."

"But it's an arm wrestle," Auron replied, frowning. "Not a fight."

Gordon's lips curled into a faint smirk. "Every test of strength is a fight, lad, whether it's with fists, steel, or a locked grip over a barrel. Look at the Nordon warrior just now. He didn't win because he was stronger—not entirely. He won because he knew how to conserve his strength. He let Jareth tire himself out and waited for the right moment to push back."

Auron tilted his head, watching as the Nordon victor patted Jareth on the shoulder in a rare gesture of respect before stepping back into the crowd. "So, it's about timing," he said thoughtfully.

"Timing," Gordon agreed. "And patience. You don't always need to overpower your opponent. Sometimes, you just need to outlast them." He glanced down at Auron, his demeanour softening slightly. "That's why you're here. Not just to swing a sword or dodge an axe, but to learn. Every contest, every clash, every moment like this is a lesson. You'd do well to remember that."

Auron nodded, his turquoise eyes narrowing with intent as the next two challengers stepped forward to the barrel. He stayed silent, tracking every movement, every subtle shift, absorbing the lesson Gordon impressed upon him.

Around him, the energy in the hall remained electric, though there was a faint undercurrent of anticipation. Two of the previous matches had gone to the Nordon men, their victories greeted with roars of approval from their comrades. Only one Borlong soldier had managed to overcome his opponent, earning a brief but spirited cheer from his side.

This final match was a dead rubber—the result of the arm-wrestling contest already decided. Nordon had claimed victory in this round, but the pride of both sides remained at stake. For the Borlong men, this was a chance to recover some dignity; for the Nordon warriors, it was about dominance and sealing their triumph.

Auron's attention sharpened as the two final competitors locked hands over the barrel. The Nordon warrior was a younger man, his frame lean but packed with wiry strength, while the Borlong soldier was broader, his muscles coiled with raw power.

Gordon leaned slightly closer to Auron, his voice a low murmur. "This might be decided, but don't think it's meaningless. For them, every contest counts. Pay attention to how they carry themselves—the Nordon man will test his opponent, even in victory. The Borlong soldier? He'll fight like he still has everything to prove."

Auron nodded again, his gaze flicking between the men. Around the pit, the atmosphere remained charged, but quieter now as the crowd braced for Borlong's chosen challenge next. Push-ups—a test of endurance and discipline. And though Nordon had the advantage for now, Borlong's soldiers were eager to prove their mettle.

The signal came, and their hands pressed into motion.

The Borlong soldier surged first, his brute strength driving his opponent's hand toward the barrel in an immediate show of dominance. Cheers erupted from the Borlong side, their voices urging their man onward.

"Push, Avin! Push him down!"

But the Nordon warrior's composure never faltered. His wrist steadied just short of the barrel, his expression tightening as his muscles strained, the veins on his forearm standing out like cords. He gritted his teeth, his grip unyielding. Slowly, he began to resist, his hand inching back toward the centre with a deliberate, measured power.

Auron's breath caught as he watched the struggle, the two men locked in a clash of raw strength and sheer will. Around the pit, the cheers shifted, the Nordon warriors' wild shouts rising to meet the chants of the Borlong soldiers.

For a moment, it seemed as though the match could go either way. The Borlong man roared with effort, his entire frame trembling with exertion as he leaned into his opponent with all his weight.

But the Nordon warrior's smirk deepened, his eyes locking onto his opponents with a sharp, predatory glint. With a final surge of strength, his grip tightened like a vice. His lean frame twisted slightly, the motion channelling the full force of his momentum into one decisive move.

The Borlong soldier's hand slammed against the barrel.

A cheer erupted from the Nordon side, their voices thundering through the hall as their champion rose from his seat, his smirk widening into a triumphant grin. The Borlong man sagged back slightly, panting, his face red and his shoulders slumping in defeat.

The Nordon warrior extended a hand toward his opponent, who hesitated for a moment before taking it. The handshake was brief but firm, and though the Borlong man's pride remained bruised, the gesture carried a quiet acknowledgment of respect.

Auron exhaled, glancing toward Gordon, who nodded subtly.

"That," Gordon said, his voice low but firm, "is what it looks like when strength meets control. Remember it."

Auron's eyes lingered on the two men as they stepped away from the barrel, their contest concluded. He could already feel the next challenge looming, the promise of new lessons to be learned.

After a time, the energy in the hall shifted as the press-up contest was prepared. Five men of Borlong and five men of Nordon stepped forward, each moving with purpose to the sand pit's centre. Their broad frames cast long shadows under the flickering firelight as they formed a line, their hands pressing into the grainy surface of the pit as they lowered.

A caller stood off to the side, his voice ready to set the pace. Around the pit, the crowd buzzed with excitement, both sides shouting encouragement and jeers in equal measure.

"Watch closely," Gordon murmured to Auron, his sharp eyes scanning the competitors. "This isn't just strength or stamina—it's discipline. They'll follow the call, up and down, no faster, no slower. That's harder than it looks. Let the sand shift wrong under your palms, let your shoulders tire just a fraction, and you're done."

Auron nodded, his sight fixed on the warriors. He could already see subtle differences—the steadiness of the Nordon men, their hands pressed firm into the sand, their faces unreadable. The Borlong men, by contrast, looked eager, their expressions sharp and focused, as though their earlier losses had ignited something fierce within them.

The caller raised his hand, his voice cutting through the din. "Ready!"

The warriors braced themselves, muscles tensing, breaths steadying.

"Down!"

All ten men lowered themselves in unison, their chests hovering just above the sand.

"Up!"

They pushed themselves back up, their movements sharp and controlled. The rhythm began to build as the calls came every couple of seconds, steady and relentless.

"Down!"

"Up!"

The first few presses passed easily, each warrior moving with precision. The crowd watched intently, their cheers muted now, replaced by murmurs of speculation.

By the twelfth press, a Nordon warrior—the largest of the group—began to falter. His broad shoulders trembled as his hands pressed into the sand, his face reddening.

"Down!"

"Up!"

He managed one last push before his arms gave out entirely. With a grunt, he collapsed onto the sand, rolling onto his side with a sheepish grin. Laughter erupted from the Nordon warriors, their booming voices filling the hall.

"Hvar mik mead fyrra nótt, Torvald?" one called out, drawing more laughter.

The large warrior chuckled, raising a hand in mock surrender as he stepped back from the pit.

Auron tilted his head. “Why are they laughing? He lost.”

Gordon smirked faintly. “They know their own limits, and they don’t mind admitting it. That’s the thing about Nordon—they’ll laugh at themselves, but that doesn’t mean they’ll quit the contest. It’s part of their pride.”

The calls continued. “Down!”

“Up!”

The strain began to show on the remaining competitors. One of the Nordon men grimaced, his arms shaking violently. By the twenty-fourth press, he collapsed into the sand with a groan.

The crowd roared, but the Borlong men did not flinch. Their faces were set, their movements steady, their pride driving them onward.

“Down!”

“Up!”

The rhythm did not falter, but two more Nordon warriors fell in quick succession, their bodies giving out under the relentless pace. One managed to stand with a grin, clapping the last Nordon competitor on the back before retreating to the crowd.

Now it was five men of Borlong against one lone Nordon warrior.

Auron glanced at Gordon. “He’s outnumbered. How can he win this?”

“He doesn’t have to win,” Gordon said, his tone even. “He just has to last. Sometimes, lasting longer than anyone expects is enough.”

The crowd leaned in closer, their cheers growing louder as the contest reached its peak. Around the pit, warriors from both sides shouted encouragement to their champions. The Borlong men moved like a single unit, their strength holding firm as the Nordon warrior matched their pace, his face a mask of grim determination.

"Down!"

"Up!"

Sweat dripped from every competitor, forming dark patches in the sand beneath them. The crowd grew louder, their cheers and jeers blending into a chaotic roar of support.

One by one, the Borlong men began to falter. The first stumbled on the thirty-fifth press, his arms trembling before he collapsed into the sand. He was followed soon after by another, then a third, each stepping back with gasps of exertion as they patted their comrades on the back.

By the fortieth press, only two men remained for Borlong and one for Nordon.

The Nordon warrior, his wiry frame drenched in sweat, dug deep. His breaths came ragged but steady, his movements precise as he matched the caller's pace. Across from him, the final Borlong men moved with equal determination, their faces set like stone.

"Down!"

"Up!"

The Borlong men glanced at each other briefly, a flicker of unspoken camaraderie passing between them. Together, they bore down on the Nordon man, pushing themselves harder.

At the forty-fifth press, the Nordon warrior's arms buckled. His chest hovered just above the sand; his teeth clenched in defiance as he forced himself up one final time. But his strength gave out, and with a heavy exhale, he collapsed onto the sand, rolling to his side.

A cheer erupted from the Borlong soldiers, their voices rising above the din. The last two Borlong men pressed on, completing an additional push-up in unison to seal their victory before collapsing with triumphant grins.

Auron turned to Gordon, who watched the scene with a calm, knowing expression.

"What did you see?" Gordon asked.

Auron hesitated. "He lasted longer than anyone thought he would," he said, glancing back at the Nordon warrior as he was helped to his feet by his comrades.

"Exactly," Gordon said. "The Borlong men won, but that Nordon warrior—they'll talk about him too. Sometimes, losing with strength and dignity is just as memorable as winning."

The competition was tied, one score apiece. The energy in the hall was electric, with both sides eager to claim the upper hand.

The next event was announced—a stone lift. A massive boulder, its surface rough and uneven, was hauled into the centre of the sand pit. The crowd pressed closer, their voices rising as five men from each side stepped forward, their muscles already tense in anticipation.

Auron leaned toward Gordon, his curiosity uncontainable. "What's the strategy here? Just strength?"

Gordon shook his head, his expression thoughtful as he scanned the competitors. "Not just strength. Lifting a stone like that takes precision. If you grab it wrong, you waste energy. If you don't position your body just so, it can shift and pull you off balance. Watch closely, boy. You'll see why Nordon is favoured for this one."

One by one, the warriors crouched beside the stone, their hands gripping its jagged edges. The Nordon men were methodical, their movements deliberate as they used their knees and hips to lift the stone, hoisting it to their shoulders with practiced ease. The Borlong men, though powerful, were less accustomed to the technique, their brute strength faltering against the awkward weight.

By the end of the event, Nordon had claimed victory, their warriors roaring in celebration as the Borlong men stepped back, their expressions a mix of frustration and begrudging respect.

The caller wasted no time announcing the next challenge: shuttle runs.

The sand pit was quickly transformed, markers placed at either end to create a course for the competitors. Ten men—five from each side—lined up, their feet digging into the loose sand as they prepared to sprint back and forth.

“This one’s Borlong’s to lose,” Gordon murmured, his arms crossed. “They’re lighter on their feet, quicker in the turns. Nordon’s got power, but power doesn’t win a sprint.”

Auron nodded, his eyes fixed on the racers. The signal came, and they were off, their bodies moving in sharp, explosive bursts. The Borlong men excelled, their agility and speed carving out an early lead. Though the Nordon warriors pushed hard, their heavier frames and less practiced technique cost them crucial seconds with each turn.

By the final lap, the Borlong men were ahead by a clear margin. They crossed the finish line to thunderous applause from their comrades, their victory cementing the score at two apiece.

Auron turned to Gordon, who gave a faint nod of approval. “They’ll be pleased with that,” Gordon said. “But the balance won’t last. The remaining duels are inevitable.”

“Inevitable?” Auron asked, tilting his head.

Gordon’s expression hardened slightly, his gaze shifting to the Nordon warriors. “Look at them. Their best is yet to come. Hand-to-hand, weapons, endurance—this is where Nordon thrives. Borlong’s strength lies in unity, but against sheer ferocity and skill, unity only goes so far.”

The tension in the hall grew as the crowd anticipated the next challenge. The matches had been close so far, each side showcasing their strengths. But as Gordon had warned, the tide was about to turn. Auron could feel it too—a shift in the air, the unrelenting certainty of the battles to come.

The hall grew quiet as the caller stepped forward, his presence commanding the draw of every warrior. He raised his hand for silence, and the gathered crowd stilled, the anticipation thick in the air. “And so, to the duelling!” the caller announced, his voice resonating through the cavernous space. “A test of skill, speed, and strength. The rules are simple: each strike is worth one point. The first to three points will claim victory. A knockdown, however, will end the match immediately.”

The crowd murmured in approval, the straightforward nature of the rules adding to the intensity of the event. Around the pit, warriors exchanged glances, some nodding with grim determination while others grinned with eager confidence.

The caller continued, his tone sharp and deliberate. "Weapons are limited to wooden practice blades. Strikes must be clear and clean to count—glancing blows will not be scored. The referee's decision is final." He paused, scanning the crowd before stepping back to make room for the competitors. "Now, step forward, champions!"

Two men approached the centre of the sand pit, their strides measured, their postures exuding confidence. On the Borlong side, a tall, wiry man with sharp features and quick, darting eyes rolled his shoulders, his wooden sword resting easily in his hand. Opposite him, the Nordon champion—a broad-shouldered warrior with a scar running across his cheek—gripped his weapon tightly, his stance low and steady.

The crowd leaned in, their collective focus honing in on the pair as they squared off. The tension was palpable, the stakes clear. Auron felt his chest tighten, his bright eyes locked on the two men.

Beside him, Gordon leaned closer, his voice a low murmur. "This is where you see what they're made of, boy. Not just strength or speed—it's about control, precision, and knowing when to strike."

Auron nodded, his attention unwavering. The caller stepped back, raising his hand to signal the start of the match.

"Begin!"

The duel was underway, and the hall erupted into cheers as the two warriors clashed in a flurry of movement, their wooden blades striking against one another with sharp cracks. Every strike, every parry, every step carried the weight of their pride and the expectations of their comrades.

The two warriors circled each other, their stances as distinct as their origins. The Borlong fighter, tall and wiry, kept his blade low and his movements measured. His eyes darted constantly, assessing, waiting for an opening. His body language radiated patience—a coiled spring ready to snap the moment his opponent overreached.

The Nordon warrior, in stark contrast, was all power and presence. His scarred face twisted into a faint smirk as he shifted his grip on the wooden sword, his posture wide and commanding. Every step he took pushed forward, forcing the Borlong man to retreat or reposition. His aggressive style was relentless, his strikes aimed to overwhelm rather than outmanoeuvre.

"Watch the difference," Gordon murmured beside Auron. "The Nordon man fights like a storm—unrelenting, aiming to break his opponent before they have a chance to react. But the Borlong fighter... look at his stance. He's baiting the attack. Waiting for the right moment to turn the tide."

Auron's bright eyes flicked between the two combatants, tracking their movements with growing fascination. The Nordon warrior made another move, lunging forward with a sharp diagonal slash. The Borlong fighter shifted back smoothly, letting the blade whistle harmlessly past him before snapping his sword upward to parry the follow-through.

The crack of wood meeting wood echoed through the hall.

The Nordon man pressed his advantage, launching a flurry of heavy strikes that forced the Borlong fighter onto the defensive. The crowd roared as the Nordon warrior advanced, his sheer aggression seeming unstoppable.

But the Borlong man did not falter. His sword moved like an extension of his body, deflecting each blow with precise efficiency. He took small, deliberate steps, circling to keep his opponent in view, his posture never breaking.

Then, with the faintest shift in balance, the Borlong fighter struck.

The Nordon warrior overreached on a downward swing, his blade striking nothing but air as the Borlong man twisted to the side. In the same motion, the Borlong fighter's wooden blade lashed out, landing a clean hit on his opponent's exposed side.

"Point, Borlong!" the referee called, raising his hand.

Auron grinned, his excitement bubbling over. "He's waiting for mistakes," he said, glancing at Gordon.

Gordon nodded, his expression approving. "Let the opponent tire themselves out. Every attack leaves a gap—if you're patient enough to find it."

The Nordon warrior stepped back, shaking off the hit with a grunt. His smirk faded, replaced by a grim focus as he adjusted his stance.

The next exchange was even fiercer. The Nordon fighter doubled down on his aggression, his strikes coming faster and heavier, each blow aimed to overwhelm. The Borlong man, however, met the onslaught with calm precision, his movements almost dance-like as he turned aside each strike with proficient ease.

Then came the familiar opening. The Nordon warrior swung overhead—a repeat of the move that had cost him a point earlier in the match. The Borlong soldier saw the opportunity, stepped aside with a parry, and went for the counterstrike.

But this time, it was a trap.

The Nordon warrior's sword snapped back with ferocious speed, sweeping in a low arc. The sudden strike caught the Borlong man's leg, causing him to stumble.

The crowd erupted as the Nordon warrior seized the moment. With a roar of effort, he closed the distance and delivered a crushing blow to the Borlong man's shoulder, sending him sprawling into the sand.

"Down!" the referee declared, raising his hand. "Victory to Nordon!"

The Nordon side of the crowd exploded in cheers, their warrior raising his sword in triumph. The Borlong supporters clapped politely, their respect for the match evident despite the loss.

Auron leaned closer to Gordon, his brow furrowed. "The defensive style doesn't always work?"

"Not always," Gordon replied, his tone thoughtful. He nodded toward the Nordon warrior, who was helping his opponent to his feet. "It works when you're patient and precise, but this wasn't just about defence versus aggression. The Nordon man baited him. Made him think he saw the same opening as before."

Auron's eyes widened slightly. "So, it was a trap?"

Gordon smirked faintly. "Exactly. The Borlong man relied on the same counter, and the Nordon fighter knew it. That's the lesson here, boy—never assume what worked once will work again. The best warriors adapt, and the ones who can't. They fall."

Auron nodded slowly, his turquoise eyes flicking back to the sand pit. The scene replayed in his mind, the precise timing of the Nordon warrior's trap sinking in. Gordon's words lingered: The best warriors adapt.

The tension in the training hall thickened as the matches progressed. The second bout once again highlighted the contrasting styles of the two sides. A shorter, stockier Borlong fighter relied on his low stance and quick footwork to evade the Nordon warrior's relentless attacks. His defensive strategy proved effective, and with a precise counterstrike to his opponent's shoulder, followed by a swift leg sweep, he sent the unbalanced Nordon warrior sprawling onto his back.

The Borlong fighter secured a knockdown, drawing the scores level to the crowd's roaring approval.

Then Nordon struck back in the third bout, where a towering Nordon warrior overwhelmed his Borlong opponent with sheer strength and precision. Every strike of his blade seemed to force his opponent further back, and when the Borlong fighter faltered for a moment, the Nordon man delivered a clean knockdown, drawing thunderous cheers from his comrades.

The fourth duel was a nail-biter. The Borlong fighter, lean and quick, danced just outside the reach of the Nordon warrior's blade, waiting for the perfect opening. His patience paid off when he landed a swift strike to the Nordon warrior's ribs, followed by a second and third point in quick succession. The crowd erupted as Borlong pulled level once more, the overall score at two victories apiece.

The caller stepped forward, raising his hands to quiet the roaring crowd. "Two victories for Borlong! Two victories for Nordon! The final duel will decide it all!"

The hall fell into an expectant hush as two figures stepped forward from opposite sides of the sand pit.

On the Borlong side was the young soldier who had shouted in the dining hall, Braddos, his sharp features set with a mixture of determination and pride. His wooden sword rested lightly in his grip, but his stance was solid, his every step purposeful.

From the Nordon side came Egil, the warrior who had first claimed the roast boar in the dining hall. His fur-lined cloak had been cast aside, revealing his muscular frame. His piercing eyes locked onto his opponent, and his expression held a faint smirk, as if the outcome of this duel were already decided in his mind.

A murmur rippled through the crowd as the two men approached the centre of the pit, their rivalry palpable. Auron leaned forward instinctively, his heart pounding in his chest.

"These two," he whispered to Gordon, "they're the ones who started everything in the dining hall apparently."

Gordon nodded; his gaze fixed on the pair. "Fitting, isn't it?" he said. "They caused the rift. Let's see if they can settle it."

The caller stepped between the two men, his voice cutting through the murmurs. "This is the final duel! The rules remain the same—first to three points wins, or a knockdown decides it all!" He stepped back, his arm raised. "Prepare yourselves!"

The two men took their stances. Braddos crouched slightly, his weight evenly distributed, his eyes darting to track the slightest movement. Egil stood taller, his blade held high and ready, his posture exuding confidence.

"Begin!"

The clash was immediate.

The Nordon warrior lunged forward with a powerful opening strike, his blade slicing through the air with precision. The Borlong soldier ducked low, sidestepping the attack with barely an inch to spare. He responded with a quick jab aimed at his opponent's side, but Egil twisted his body, deflecting the blow with ease.

Their wooden blades collided in a rapid exchange of strikes and parries, the sharp cracks echoing through the hall. The crowd roared; their cheers divided as the two men fought with everything they had.

"Watch him," Gordon muttered to Auron, his voice low. "The Nordon man—he's not just attacking. He's testing. Waiting to see how the boy reacts."

Auron nodded, his eyes darting between the fighters. The Borlong soldier moved with precision, his blade quick and his footwork calculated. But the Nordon warrior's strikes were relentless, each one pushing his opponent closer to the edge of the sand pit.

Then, with a sudden burst of speed, the Nordon warrior feinted a high strike before sweeping low. The Borlong soldier barely managed to block, but the force of the blow knocked him off balance, allowing the Nordon man to land a clean strike to his shoulder.

"Point, Nordon!" the referee called.

Braddos did not falter. He adjusted his stance, his jaw tightening as he squared up once more. The next exchange was fierce, both men moving with blinding speed. Braddos began to find his rhythm, weaving around the Nordon warrior's attacks and landing a sharp counterstrike to his opponent's ribs.

"Point, Borlong!"

The crowd erupted again, their cheers shaking the hall as the score evened out.

Auron watched, his heart pounding. He leaned closer to Gordon. "What happens if it's too close?"

Gordon smirked. "Then you find out who wants it more."

The duel raged on, the fighters giving no quarter. Each strike, each parry, each movement carried the weight of their respective sides. As the score climbed to two points apiece, the hall grew quieter, the tension suffocating.

This was it—the final clash. All eyes were locked on the fighters as they squared off for the decisive exchange. Both men knew what was at stake, and neither seemed willing to concede an inch.

Auron gripped the edge of his tunic, his breath held as he waited for the outcome of the rivalry that had started it all.

The two fighters circled each other, their wooden swords raised, their breaths steady despite the strain. The younger Borlong soldier, sharp-eyed and quick, kept his movements measured, his body light on his feet. The taller Nordon warrior, a pillar of raw power, pressed forward, seeking the decisive blow.

Braddos ducked beneath a heavy swing, his blade flashing upward in a quick counterstrike that narrowing missed its target. Egil shifted backwards knowing how close he came to losing the bout, but he used it to fuel his purpose.

The next exchange was lightning-fast, the Nordon man launching a flurry of powerful strikes. The Borlong fighter twisted and turned, his blade intercepting each blow with precision. With a deft sidestep, he caught Egil overreaching again, and this time landed a clean strike across his shoulder.

"Point, Borlong! Match over!"

The hall erupted into applause as Braddos stepped back, raising his wooden sword in victory. Egil nodded grimly, then extended his hand. The two clasped forearms in a brief moment of mutual respect. Then Egil gave a small nod of approval and said firmly, "Durak karesh."

The younger Braddos bowed low, a smile breaking through his stern expression as he attempted to repeat the phrase. His clumsy pronunciation drew hearty laughter from the Nordon warrior, who clapped him on the shoulder and pulled him into a firm embrace.

The crowd roared with approval, the tension of the duel melting into shared camaraderie. Warriors from both sides began clasping wrists and laughing, the line between rival and ally blurred in the aftermath of the contest. The hall, once filled with the sound of clashing blades, now resonated with unity and respect.

# THE LORD'S MANSE
# CHAPTER FORTY FOUR

The walk back to the estate was quiet, save for the soft crunch of gravel beneath their boots and the occasional burst of laughter from the two men trailing behind Konan. The low, golden light of the setting sun stretched their shadows across the path, merging them momentarily in uneven flickers as they moved.

Egil, the Nordon warrior, reached out to clap a hand on Braddos's shoulder. The Borlong soldier did not flinch or shrug him off as he might have three weeks ago. Instead, he let out a short chuckle, muttering a response in halting Nordon. Egil corrected him, the words rolling off his tongue with exaggerated precision, earning a wry grin from Braddos. Their language was a strange mix now—a rough patchwork of Nordon, Borlong, and a series of gestures that would seem nonsensical to any onlooker. But somehow, it worked. They understood one another now in a way that transcended words, forged by shared exertion and growing respect.

Konan's jaw tightened as he glanced over his shoulder at the two men. Their camaraderie was too easy, too familiar. He could not shake the discomfort it brought him. These were warriors from lands that had drawn blood from one another—a bond like this was unthinkable only weeks prior. The purpose of this arrangement was not friendship. Respect, perhaps. Cooperation, certainly. But not this.

The estate came into view, its high stone walls illuminated by the soft amber glow of the sinking sun. The outer gate stood open, and beyond it, the sprawling grounds teemed with a quiet elegance that betrayed the feasts, performances, and spectacles of the past fortnight. Laughter rose behind him again, louder this time, as Egil and Braddos fell into another shared joke. Their bond had been cemented in the most physical of ways—sparring matches that had left them bruised and bloodied but oddly triumphant. Egil had taken to aiding Braddos in strength conditioning drills, while Braddos had shared tips for endurance running, leading them both on pre-dawn circuits of the estate's sprawling perimeter. They trained, they ate, they bled together. And now, they drank together.

Konan stopped abruptly at the gate, his expression hardening as he turned to face them. The two men slowed their steps, grins faltering slightly, awaiting his signal. He inclined his head—a dismissal.

Egil offered a respectful nod in return, though the easy air about him grated on Konan. Braddos bowed slightly, glancing back at his newfound comrade. Egil smirked and said in accented Borlong, "Ale?" Braddos's response came swift and light-hearted, "Vel." The Nordon word for yes sounded strange from Braddos's lips, but it was enough to spark another burst of laughter between them. Without waiting for further approval, the pair turned and headed toward the town, their voices blending into the hum of the streets.

Konan watched them until they disappeared, their forms swallowed by the bustle of Borlong's evening crowd. His thoughts churned with unease. Three weeks of feasting, parading, and entertainment had dulled the sharpness of their swords and minds. Malum had spared no expense—lavish banquets beneath the great chandeliers, tours of Borlong's bustling markets, bathhouse indulgences, and even a private showing at the city's grand theatre. To the soldiers, this was unity—a blending of cultures and ideals. But to Konan, it was a veneer. A fragile illusion. Unity was not forged in wine and song but in fire and blood. And beneath the laughter and the camaraderie, he wondered: had they forgotten that?

With a sharp exhale, he turned and stepped into the estate, his boots striking the smooth stone path with deliberate force. The air inside was cool, a sharp contrast to the fading warmth of the evening outside. The grand reception hall stretched ahead, an expanse of polished marble and towering columns shrouded in the soft glow of wall-mounted lanterns. Shadows pooled in the high arches, giving the space an almost cathedral-like stillness.

A pair of maids crossed his path, their eyes darting downward as they hurried past with quick, tapping steps. Another lingered near the edge of the hall, adjusting a vase of freshly cut flowers. At the sound of his approach, she stiffened, avoiding his gaze entirely before slipping away down a side corridor. Konan's steps slowed briefly as he observed the deliberate avoidance, his expression unreadable.

This was not something he was used to. Back in Stormhold, servants and warriors alike acknowledged him openly—some with reverence, others with bold admiration. He was a warrior there, a figure of strength and bard's tales, drawing attention wherever he went. Here, he was a stranger. The maids' skittishness was not personal, he understood that much.

They avoided his gaze not out of disrespect, but out of deference to the tension he carried. Still, the unfamiliar quiet pressed against him, a stark reminder of the distance between this place and the life he had left behind.

His boots echoed faintly in the expansive space as he made his way across the hall. Most of the soldiers had already gone to the barracks or the town alehouses, the lingering energy of the day retreating into the shadows along with the dwindling light. Yet, despite the quiet, Konan felt the weight of unseen eyes, a subtle unease that heightened the tension simmering in his chest.

As he approached the grand stairwell, its sweeping bannisters gleaming in the low light, he quickened his pace. The Queen's quarters awaited above, and with them, the answers to the restlessness that churned within him.

The heavy carpet muffled his steps, but his thoughts roared in his mind. The Queen's door stood slightly ajar when he reached it, the flicker of firelight spilling into the dim corridor. He hesitated, his hand hovering above the carved wood. This was not the first time he had lingered here, wrestling with his thoughts before stepping into her domain. How long would they remain in this city, bound to its illusions of peace and unity? How much longer could he hold his tongue?

Konan inhaled deeply, squaring his shoulders, and stepped through the door.

Queen Karak sat by the hearth, her red hair gleaming like molten copper in the firelight. A scroll lay unfurled across her lap, its parchment edges curling faintly under the warmth. Her expression was serene, but Konan recognized the calculating glint in her eyes. The fur-lined mantle draped over the back of her chair softened her silhouette, but it did nothing to diminish her commanding presence. Beside her, a goblet of dark wine sat untouched on the polished table.

She did not look up as the door clicked shut behind him, yet Konan felt her attention shift. She always heard him, always knew.

"You're back," she said at last, her voice smooth but threaded with expectation. Her gaze remained on the scroll for a moment longer before lifting to meet his. "How are your men?"

Konan stepped further into the room; his boots muted against the thick carpet. "They're becoming soft," he replied bluntly. "Too many feasts. Too much wine. They laugh like boys, not warriors."

Her lips curved into a faint smile, though there was no amusement in her eyes. "And that troubles you?"

"It should trouble you," he said, his tone clipped. "Familiarity breeds complacency. This... mingling—it's a distraction."

Finally, she set the scroll aside, rising with deliberate grace. The firelight seemed to ripple across her dark gown, the silver embroidery catching like threads of lightning in a storm. She turned to face him fully, her presence growing larger with the motion, commanding the space between them.

"You think I don't see it?" she asked, her tone sharper now, each word a dagger poised to strike. "That I don't know what you're thinking? I've allowed this mingling because it serves a purpose. Their laughter, their camaraderie—it's a performance, Konan. One for Lord Malum's benefit."

Her eyes burned into his, unyielding. "He must see trust. Not just between you and your men but between Nordon and Borlong. He needs to believe in the strength of this alliance. He is yet to agree to my terms. He is more cautious than I expected, more stubborn. He will only bend when he sees the long-term benefits of unity."

Konan's fists clenched at his sides, his posture rigid. "Trust is earned in battle," he said, his voice a low rumble. "Not at the bottom of a wine goblet."

"You're wrong," she said coolly, turning back toward the hearth. The crackle of the flames punctuated her words. "Trust is earned wherever men are weak enough to hope for it. And Lord Malum needs to hope. He needs to see unity among our men, to believe it can exist, even if only for a moment. This is how we sway him. If we must use laughter and wine to do it, so be it."

Konan remained silent; his jaw tight. Karak knew she would not change his mind. He was a warrior, forged in the fires of conflict. He saw alliances through the lens of strength and survival, and she did not want to strip him of that edge. It was why she relied on him.

After a moment, she glanced over her shoulder. "And what of your other men?"

His tension eased, ever so slightly, a faint smile tugging at his lips. At her command ten men had stayed behind from the initial procession, slipping into the city separately after the others. They kept their distance from the estate, blending seamlessly into the grim corners of Borlong. "They're doing what you bid of them," he said.

"And?" Her tone was calm, but her focus on him sharpened with interest.

Konan's voice was steady, every word deliberate. "They've been listening, watching, and blending into the city's underbelly. They've evaluated the people, their whispers, their grievances. The mood is fractured. Some praise Lord Malum's rule, content with his governance, but others... others speak in hushed tones of dissatisfaction. Quiet dissent simmers in the taverns and markets, the kind that festers if left unchecked."

Konan's voice turned cold, precise. "The defences... they're comfortable. Built for appearance, not for endurance. The city garrison's roughly eight hundred men, but at any given time, no more than half are actively stationed. There are thirty watchtowers spread across the city's perimeter, but the posting is thin—two, maybe three guards per tower during shifts. Most of the focus is concentrated near the estate and main thoroughfares, leaving the outskirts vulnerable."

He shifted slightly, his jaw tightening. "There are three barracks—one near the western gate, another in the northern district, and the last by the southern docks. The eastern district, however, has none, leaving it exposed. Patrols weave through the city, but their paths are predictable, their timing lax. The gates are particularly troubling. They remain open far too long during the day for merchants and travellers, and inspections are cursory at best. At night, they close—but with so few men on duty, it wouldn't take much to breach them."

He paused, letting the weight of his report settle. "It's a system built for peacetime, not for a real threat. If someone wanted to exploit these weaknesses, they'd find ample opportunity."

Karak's lips curved into a smile as sharp as any blade, her vivid green eyes catching the faint gleam of light reflecting off the rim of her wine goblet. She leaned forward slightly, her presence pressing against the room like an unseen force. "Comfort breeds weakness," she murmured, her tone carrying a quiet, dangerous satisfaction.

For a moment, her attention swept over the room, noting the subtle indulgences: the rich tapestries that softened the stone walls, the low hum of voices beyond the door, the faint scent of spiced wine lingering in the air. These trappings of hospitality had a way of lulling even the most disciplined into complacency. The thought coiled around her pride like a snake, tightening with every breath. Had she, too, allowed herself to soften here?

The notion struck like an arrow against her resolve. She straightened in her chair, brushing the thought aside, though a flicker of irritation burned beneath her composed exterior. Comfort was a temptation she could not afford. She drew her fur-lined cloak tighter around her shoulders, the coarse edge of the fabric brushing her neck, a grounding sensation that reminded her of the harsher truths she lived by.

Konan's voice came unbidden, fragments of their past conversations cutting through her thoughts. He had warned her of this—the danger of staying too long, of letting her men grow idle. *'They'll forget why they're here,'* he had said more than once, his tone carrying the weight of experience. *'Soft hands wield dull blades, and dull blades break when it matters most.'* She had dismissed him then, confident in her ability to keep the edge sharp. But now, she could not ignore the truth lurking in his words. Had they lingered too long? Was he right?

Her gaze settled on Konan, standing a few paces away. The tension in his posture betrayed his restlessness, his hand resting lightly on the hilt of his axe as if the weapon's weight tethered him to patience. She saw the tight set of his jaw, the flicker of frustration in his eyes. He was eager for what was to come—for the fight that would strip away all pretence and comfort. As much as his words had grated on her before, they now felt like a lifeline—a reminder of the steel they could not afford to lose.

"Perhaps you are right, Konan," she said at last, her voice measured, each word carrying the weight of reluctant deliberation. It was an acknowledgment she was loath to make, even to him. The idea of conceding to her brother's warnings grated against her pride, but the nagging doubt lingered, coiling in the recesses of her mind. "We may have lingered longer than necessary. What more intelligence is there to gain?"

The question hovered in the air, directed more at herself than him. She turned away from her brother once more, her attention drawn to the fire, its restless flames seeming to hold answers just out of reach. Had they wrung this place dry of value? Or had they merely fooled themselves into believing they had? She could not ignore the way the edges of her confidence seemed to fray under the weight of Konan's earlier warnings. But admitting he might have been right would mean admitting a vulnerability she was not ready to face—not yet.

Her voice turned sharp, a shield against the creeping unease. "The ten men—did you meet with them today?" The question came with a biting edge, a deliberate change in tone, designed to regain control of the conversation and redirect it toward action.

Konan's smile deepened, faint but unmistakable, a flicker of satisfaction glinting in his piercing eyes. He tilted his head slightly in acknowledgement, watching her with the quiet intensity of a predator sensing its prey falter. She was beginning to speak sense, finally aligning with the clarity he had seen all along. It was not often that Karak bent, even fractionally, to another's perspective, and the subtle victory brought a rare sense of vindication.

Karak's silence stretched, the flickering firelight reflecting in her narrowed emerald eyes. Inwardly, she pushed past the irritation that came with entertaining Konan's earlier warnings, letting her thoughts turn inward, sharper, more focused. As the weight of his words settled, a new thread began to weave itself into her mind—a plan, raw but growing in its shape.

Her head tilted slightly, her gaze cutting through the air like a blade seeking its mark. When she finally spoke, her voice was deliberate, every word honed with precision. "And how is your relationship with Malament?" The question hung in the air, loaded and purposeful, the tone as measured and deadly as the edge of a sharpened sword.

Konan hesitated, the question slicing through his thoughts. He could not deny the truth, though it grated against the plans they had so carefully crafted. Manipulating Malament had proven far more difficult than expected. The young lord was not naive or easily swayed. And, against his better judgment, Konan found himself respecting him. That respect complicated everything.

"It's... complicated," Konan admitted at last, his voice low. "Malament isn't like the others. He listens, but he doesn't trust. There's a strength in him—not the kind that bends to flattery or veiled threats. I tried to antagonise him, as we discussed, but..." He paused, his jaw tightening "he has earned my respect."

Karak's smile did not falter, but the flicker in her eyes betrayed that she had anticipated this answer. She leaned back slightly, her demeanour still poised, yet her mind raced. The implications of Konan's words were both limiting and full of potential. Respect could be a double-edged sword, and she intended to wield it.

"Respect can be useful, Konan," she said, her tone softening, though the edge was still there, ready. "If wielded correctly, it can be more effective than loyalty or fear. But it must be precise, unyielding." She paused, her thoughts turning over the pieces of the puzzle. How could this man—Malament—become the trigger?

Her expression sharpened, her eyes like emeralds catching the firelight. "You say he doesn't trust, but does he trust you? Does he believe Konan is the man he claims to be? That the strength you show is genuine, that the words you speak are your own truth?" Her voice, though measured, carried a sharpness that cut through the low crackle of the hearth. It was a question laden with precision, aimed not at friendship or camaraderie but at something deeper—perception and belief.

Konan's brow furrowed, the faintest flicker of uncertainty crossing his features. He knew the weight of her question, "not as a friend," he admitted, his voice quieter, measured. "But I believe he trusts my judgment. He sees the truth in the strength I present, in the conviction of my words."

Karak's lips pressed into a thin line, her mind seizing on his response. Judgment, truth, strength—these could be tools. Weapons, even. If Malament trusted Konan's conviction, then perhaps that was enough. It was not loyalty she needed, nor admiration. It was belief. A fragile thread, but one she could weave into something stronger.

She straightened slightly, the flicker of a plan beginning to take root. "Good," she said at last, her tone cold and deliberate. "Because whether he knows it or not, that belief may be all we need to ensure he does exactly what is required. Tonight, have your men dine with us."

Konan's scepticism was immediate, his eyes narrowing as he studied her. "Extra mouths will be noticed," he said, his voice low but firm. "Malament isn't a fool. He'll see the numbers don't add up. He'll question it."

There was a tension in his tone that hinted at unease—not fear, but wariness. Karak was moving toward something, a destination he could not yet see, and the unknown made him restless. His instincts warned him to tread carefully; she had a way of pulling strings he did not always understand until it was too late.

"Perhaps," Karak replied, her smile deepening, a glint of intrigue flashing in her emerald eyes. "Perhaps not. Malament is no fool, that much is true. And yes, at some point, he will notice." She leaned forward slightly, the firelight casting sharp shadows across her face. "In fact, Konan, I rely on it."

Konan's jaw tightened, his expression hardening as the weight of her words sank in. She was toying with something dangerous—something that required precision and control. He hated being in the dark, and yet here she was, holding the pieces of the game while offering him only fragments of the picture. "And when he notices?" he asked, his voice edged with suspicion. "What then? What's the end to this?"

Konan leaned forward slightly, the tension between them thick as he waited for her to elaborate.

"When he notices, you must act," she continued, her words precise, each syllable cutting through the air with quiet authority. Her gaze remained locked on his, unyielding. "Isolate him from the room. Draw him out, but stay close enough to remain in earshot of us feasting. He will be cautious for sure, but will still bring up the extra men—he cannot let such details lie. It's in his nature to prod at the loose threads." Her voice softened, taking on a tone of almost conspiratorial intrigue, though her eyes gleamed with intent. "Tell me, brother, how is your Kadun? Truly, from our lessons as children."

Konan's brow furrowed slightly, the faintest flicker of suspicion crossing his face. He did not fully grasp her endgame yet, but he knew better than to press too soon. Karak's plans always unravelled in layers, and to push for answers now would only draw her ire. Instead, he offered her what she wanted—a glimpse of his competence, though his own reservations remained unspoken.

His smile returned, faint but steady, as he responded in their hosts language, his deep voice lending weight to their familiar words. "Beneath the Tree, Hearts of the Free." The phrase rolled off his tongue with studied ease, though he watched her carefully, searching for any flicker of reaction that might reveal the direction of her thoughts.

Karak's eyes lit with approval, a flicker of satisfaction gleaming in their depths. "Good, brother. Very good. You shall put it to use tonight. When you have him alone and he questions the extra men, reveal our plan to him. Tell him everything—the watchtowers, the posted men, the gaps in their defences. Tell him we head to White Towers not for peace, but for blood. When I claim their throne, we will hold both the Capital and The Reach. And once that is secured, our focus will turn back to Borlong." Her tone was smooth and deliberate, each word a calculated step toward her ultimate goal.

Konan's expression darkened, the faintest shadow of doubt crossing his face. He held her gaze, his composure steady but laced with curiosity. "And the benefit?" he asked, his voice low, probing. "What am I missing?"

Karak's smile sharpened, the curve of her lips predatory, her voice dropping to a near whisper, as though the weight of her words commanded silence. "If he believes you—if he trusts that you are not lying—that will be when he shows his true colours. You will go from ally to foe in an instant. Duty will demand him to act. He will either draw his sword..." Her eyes gleamed, catching the firelight like a blade poised to strike. "...or you will make him draw."

She let the words hang in the air, her eyes unwavering, watching the faint flicker of excitement ignite in her brother's expression. It was subtle at first, a smouldering ember, but it spread quickly, transforming into a grin he could no longer suppress.

"When the clash of steel echoes through to the feast," Karak continued, her voice rising with quiet intensity, each word measured and deliberate, "and Lord Malum sees his son locked in battle, he will have no choice but to act. He will either cast us out as enemies, fracturing his already crumbling alliances, or yield to our terms and bend to our will." She paused, her emerald eyes gleaming, the firelight dancing in their depths. "I wager he will choose the latter."

Her words lingered, hanging in the charged air like an unspoken challenge. Karak could feel the edges of her plan knitting together, each piece falling into place. This was the way forward, the only path that ensured they emerged victorious. Yet beneath her composed exterior, a flicker of tension stirred—a quiet, unrelenting hum of anticipation. She had walked this line before, threading plans through the narrowest of spaces. But success demanded control, and failure was unthinkable.

Her smile deepened, the curve of her lips carrying a glint of triumph and a trace of something darker—certainty, ruthless and cold. "But in truth," she added, her tone softening, as if speaking a secret only she and Konan could share, "his decision is irrelevant. The outcome will serve our plans regardless. Malament will be an unwitting pawn, a wedge driven deep between father and son. Borlong's hold on Nordon will shatter, whether through a new enemy forged or a reluctant alliance dragged from desperation."

Konan's grin widened, the corners of his mouth pulling back like a predator scenting blood. His understanding clicked into place, each piece of her plan feeding the anticipation simmering within him. The chaos she promised—the clash of steel, the shattering of alliances—was a storm he longed to unleash. His voice, low and edged with excitement, cut through the tension. "And when Malament draws?"

Karak tilted her head slightly, her calculating gaze fixed on her brother's barely contained eagerness. She understood exactly what he was asking, and she shaped her answer with meticulous precision. "Do not kill him—not at first," she said, her tone deliberate, every word measured. "Lord Malum must see it for himself. He must witness his son attacking the Queen's brother, unprovoked and unrelenting." She stepped closer, her presence commanding, her voice dropping to a near-whisper that carried more weight than any shout. "Once the Lord arrives, it matters little. Do what you will, Konan."

Her words lingered in the air like a blade held aloft, and she watched as Konan's expression shifted. The raw excitement in his eyes sharpened into a focused readiness, his anticipation transforming into a quiet resolve. The battle ahead was no longer a distant idea, a vague possibility—it loomed now, inevitable, just hours away. He nodded once, his grin fading into something colder, more dangerous.

Karak turned back to the fire, her smile lingering, faint but unwavering, as she stared into the restless flames. They flickered and danced, their heat mirroring the simmering tension within her. The game was in motion, every piece meticulously placed on the board. Tonight, one decisive move would alter the course of Nordon's future forever.

# BORLONG'S BANQUET CHAPTER FORTY FIVE

'Ching, ching, ching.' The clear ring of Lord Malum's spoon against his goblet silenced the room. A few droplets of wine slid down the polished metal surface, catching the glow of the chandelier's light before pooling on the white linen cloth.

Slowly, the assembled guests turned their attention toward him. Chairs scraped against the marble floor as twenty nobles, clad in silks and velvets of jewel-toned greens, blues, and purples, shifted to face him. Among them sat Nordon merchants in fur-lined coats, their rugged faces and pale, wind-weathered complexions distinct from the fair but sun-touched East Kadun men, whose hair and attire reflected the lighter hues of their southern homeland. Nordon soldiers, stoic and broad-shouldered, their armour dull with the sheen of northern craftsmanship, mingled at the edges of the hall with the elegantly uniformed soldiers of East Kadun, who carried themselves with a more relaxed, almost courtly bearing.

A delicate hush fell over the room, save for the soft clinking of jewellery and the faint rustle of robes. Malum stood at the head of the grand dining table, his slim frame draped in a navy toga edged with white trim—a deliberate nod to the Nordon delegation's colours. His watchful brown eyes swept the room, calculating yet warm, as a faint smile curled the edges of his lips.

"Good evening, once again," Malum began, his voice clear and commanding, drawing a ripple of cheers from the soldiers who raised their tankards in acknowledgment. He inclined his head slightly. "Friends from afar, and friends closer to home. It fills my heart to see such unity gathered beneath this roof. I trust the evening's entertainment has been to your liking?"

He gestured gracefully to the performance area, where the remnants of an elaborate display still lingered—thirty performers had earlier enchanted the crowd, tossing hoops into the air and leaping through them with flawless precision. The memory of their synchronized movements still lingered in the minds of the audience, drawing murmurs of approval.

"It has been a rare blessing, these past three weeks, to welcome such noble allies and to see them become such gracious friends," he said, his gaze briefly resting on Queen Karak, who sat resplendent beside him in a black gown intricately embroidered with silver patterns. He dipped into a courtly bow, the fabric of his toga brushing the floor as he rose again. "As hosts, my family and I have strived to make your stay as pleasant as possible. May you feel not only the warmth of our hearths but also the warmth of our hearts."

A low murmur of agreement passed through the crowd as Malum allowed himself a small, knowing smile. "And perhaps," he added with a faintly teasing lilt, "you might consider staying another moon to enjoy the luxuries of a summer less cruel than the snows of the north."

Gentle laughter rippled through the room, from the stern Nordon merchants to the East Kadun senators. Even a few soldiers chuckled into their cups.

He raised his goblet high, the red wine within catching the light like liquid fire. "Tonight, let us dine together, drink together, and share stories that will carry us into the dawn. Let us not speak only of treaties and alliances but of fellowship and shared dreams. For as we feast, we build not only the bonds of politics but the bonds of kinship."

Several cheers erupted from the more boisterous tables, and Malum waited until they quieted before continuing, his tone turning solemn. "We should take pride in this alliance. It is a rare thing, born not of conquest, but of compromise. Our past is a bloody chronicle of wars waged over what could have been shared, yet here we stand tonight, proof of what is possible when wisdom prevails over wrath."

The audience responded with respectful nods and murmurs of agreement, some raising their goblets in silent toasts. Malum smiled, satisfied.

"Now then, I will not steal your attention any longer, for I see thirsts that must be quenched and appetites that must be sated. Let the wine flow, the music rise, and the feast begin! May we celebrate until the first rays of dawn greet us."

A thunder of applause erupted as Lord Malum reseated himself, his expression composed but tinged with satisfaction. A group of musicians in the corner struck up a lively yet unobtrusive tune, the soft notes of strings and flutes weaving through the air. From the grand double doors, a procession of serving maids glided into the hall, their crisp linen aprons pristine, their movements practiced and fluid. They carried jugs of deep red Borlong wine, tilting them expertly to fill goblets and tankards as they wove among the tables, smiles gracing their lips as they exchanged light pleasantries with the guests.

Two strapping serving men followed close behind, their crisp tunics stretched taut over muscular frames as they carried a rectangular silver serving tray between them. Resting atop it was a magnificent roast stag, its golden-brown skin glistening with a glaze of spiced honey. The aroma of rich, roasted meat infused with thyme and rosemary wafted through the hall, drawing appreciative murmurs and a few audible sighs from the guests. The stag's antlers, polished to a high sheen, had been preserved and mounted above the roast as a decorative flourish, a symbol of the evening's grandeur.

Trailing behind, more maids carried heaping bowls of roasted vegetables—carrots glazed in butter, parsnips with a hint of nutmeg, and perfectly browned potatoes dusted with herbs. The final arrival was Quinn, the estate's head chef, striding into the hall with an air of authority. His apron, freshly donned and spotless, no longer bore the evidence of his labour, and his usually unruly beard and hair had been trimmed back for the occasion. In his right hand, he wielded an impressive carving knife, its blade gleaming wickedly under the chandeliers, while his left hand gripped a steel rod, which he used to periodically sharpen the blade with swift, skilful strokes.

The serving procession paused at the far end of the dining hall, where a wide, sturdy oak table had been cleared to accommodate the spectacle. Quinn took centre stage, holding the knife aloft for a moment as though to consecrate the ceremony before expertly carving into the stag. Each slice came away in generous, succulent portions, which he piled onto ceramic plates lined with sprigs of fresh parsley. His movements were rhythmic, almost hypnotic, the scrape of the blade against the sharpening rod a counterpoint to the music and conversation filling the hall.

Guests leaned forward eagerly, their anticipation palpable, as the first plates, laden with food, were prepared for service. The serving maids stood with poised patience, their movements deliberate and graceful. Their first destination was the head table, where the evening's most notable figures were seated. A cloud of fragrant steam rose from the plates, carrying the tantalizing aroma of roasted venison and spiced vegetables through the air.

The dining hall filled with the harmonious clinking of cutlery, the rich scent of the meal, and the hum of contented conversation. The atmosphere was alive with warmth and indulgence, setting the stage for a night of celebration.

"A mighty fine speech, Lord Malum. You humble us with your words," Queen Karak said, her tone rich and commanding, softened by a smile. Her striking green eyes sparkled in the candlelight, their intensity making even a simple compliment feel like an act of power.

"If only I could have found more to truly honour you," Malum replied, his voice steady but faintly tinged with unease as he inclined his head in respect.

Karak tilted her head slightly, the faintest curve of amusement touching her lips. "You look most distinguished in our colours, Lord Malum." Her tone was laced with playful intrigue, the kind that commanded attention without effort.

Her subtle flirtation unsettled Malum, who struggled to conceal the flush rising to his cheeks. Though he maintained his composure, his fingers gripped his goblet a touch too tightly. Karak, with an air of effortless control, seemed to relish her ability to disarm him.

At their table of six, the dynamics were as intricate as the embroidery adorning their garments. To Malum's left sat Lady Amelia, her delicate features framed by soft waves of blonde hair. She wore a stunning gown of red velvet embroidered with gold, the colours of East Kadun, its cut tailored to perfection. Yet her beauty was marred by a visible tension —her lips pressed into a thin line, her hands resting too stiffly on the tablecloth. Amelia's turquoise eyes flickered toward Queen Karak with a fleeting look of discontent, betraying her discomfort at the Queen's teasing tone.

To Malum's right stood his son, Malament, his posture straight and composed. Dressed in a navy-blue tunic edged with white, his blonde hair was pulled into a tight topknot, exposing features that still held traces of youthful softness beneath their emerging sharpness. His studied expression glanced between his father and Queen Karak, neutral but quietly observant. Malament's hands rested lightly on the edge of the table, his stillness almost too perfect, as though he were weighing every word spoken.

Opposite Malum, seated between Queen Karak and Lady Amelia, was

Galil, his weathered face bore the marks of a man who had braved countless winters, yet his eyes held a spark of sharp wit and ambition. Despite Amelia's obvious disinterest, Galil's focus lingered on her, his attempts at charm thinly veiled beneath polite conversation. He adjusted his fur-lined cloak with an air of confidence, though his glance occasionally darted toward Karak as if assessing the power she exuded.

In the centre, directly opposite Lord Malum, sat the Queen herself, a figure of undeniable presence. Her vivid red hair, cascaded over her shoulder, the strands catching the flickering candlelight. Intricately braided and adorned with silver clasps shaped of runes of Nordon and nods to the God Shiva. The black gown she wore, intricately embroidered with flowing silver patterns resembling waves and storms, hugged her figure with regal precision. Over her chest, where her heart would be, the sigil of Nordon and her house, Thørn, was stitched in fine silver thread, a subtle yet compelling emblem of her lineage. A fur-lined mantle draped across her shoulders, lending her an air of wild elegance and commanding authority.

Her astute, emerald eyes scanned the room with a mix of poise and sharp calculation, framed by an assertive gaze that seemed to hold the weight of command. In her hands, she held a silver goblet with a casual elegance, her fingers adorned with delicate rings that hinted at her authority and refined taste. Atop her head rested the crimson studded crown, the striking symbol of her sovereignty.

Beside her, at the far right of the table, was her brother, Konan. In stark contrast to the evening's opulence, Konan had chosen to wear his full black armour, the fur-lined shoulders adding a savage touch to his already formidable presence. His thick red beard was freshly braided, and his scarred forearms rested on the table as though he were prepared for war even in the midst of revelry. His dark eyes scanned the room, missing little, and his presence seemed to radiate both strength and unease.

Six serving maids appeared around the table, moving in perfect unison to place plates laden with roasted venison, golden potatoes, and buttered vegetables before the diners. With a graceful bow, they stepped back, their departure immediately followed by another maid—a young woman with a delicate frame and a cascade of dark hair. She carried a jug of Borlong Red, pouring the wine carefully into each goblet with a polite smile before retreating as silently as she had come.

Lord Malum leaned back in his chair, the polished wood creaking faintly under his weight. He swirled the wine in his goblet before addressing the table, his tone measured yet warm. "Queen Karak, I trust our efforts in Borlong have met your expectations thus far? My son Malament has taken great care in ensuring your delegation's comfort." His attention flicked briefly to Malament, who sat at his right, his expression composed yet attentive.

Karak tilted her head slightly, her eyes lingered on Malament with quiet intensity before she spoke. "Indeed, Malament has proven himself quite capable. Perhaps even beyond his father's ambitions for him." A subtle smile played on her lips, a knowing glimmer in her eyes as she waited for a response.

Malament met her gaze, his voice steady and deliberate. "It is my duty to serve East Kadun and its alliances. To do otherwise would dishonour both my house and our guests."

"Well spoken," Malum interjected, nodding approvingly. "You have learned that duty binds a man to his purpose. A lesson we all must remember in these times."

Lady Amelia shifted slightly in her chair, her fingers brushing the edge of her goblet as she glanced between Malum and Karak. Her alluring turquoise eyes lingered on the Queen just a moment longer than necessary, catching the faint curve of amusement at the edges of Karak's lips. Why does she always have to toy with him? she considered, her irritation bubbling just beneath the surface. Turning her attention to Malament, his composed demeanour unshaken, a mirror of his father's restraint. So perfect, so calculated... but even steel bends if struck hard enough.

Her tone was light, but there was a deliberate sharpness to her words as she finally spoke. "You've inherited your father's precision, no doubt, Malament. Yet I wonder... can such diligence withstand unexpected pressures?" As the words left her lips, she caught the faintest flicker of a frown on Malum's face, a subtle reaction most would miss. Her gaze flitted back to Karak, who seemed almost amused, her eyes gleaming with an unreadable expression. Amelia straightened her posture, willing herself to maintain her composure.

Malament's brow also furrowed slightly, but before he could respond, Konan's voice rumbled in the tongue of Nordon, low and guttural like distant thunder. "Vinteren tester en manns styrke, men bare en ekte kriger kan overleve Nordon's kulde."

Karak, her lips curving in amusement, translated smoothly. "My brother says, *'Winter tests a man's strength, but only a true warrior can survive the cold of Nordon'*." Her tone softened as she added, "It is, of course, meant as a compliment. Albeit delivered in the bluntest Nordon fashion."

Malament nodded politely. "A Nordon winter would be a worthy test. Though I suspect my resolve, like any man's, could be strengthened by a good cup of Borlong Red."

A soft chuckle escaped Galil, seated next to Amelia. The Nordon merchant, dressed in fur-lined finery, raised his goblet with an easy smile. "True words, young lord. In the north, we say the frost tempers steel as hardship tempers men. But even the sharpest blade dulls without the warmth of wine and good company."

His gaze lingered on Amelia for a moment longer than decorum might dictate, a flicker of warmth in his otherwise shrewd eyes. "And, of course, in your company Lady Amelia, even the harshest Nordon winter would seem mild."

Amelia caught his glance and offered a polite but measured smile, her fingers tracing the rim of her goblet. Enjoying the merchant's charm, though she refrained from commenting, allowing the conversation to continue.

Karak arched her brow with faint amusement. "Spoken like a man who values company over comfort, Galil."

Galil leaned back slightly, his smile easy. "Yet good coin can purchase both."

Karak tilted her head with curiosity. "Ah, but of course. Tell me, Galil, what truly warms a merchant's heart more—gold or the glow of a good fire?"

Galil leaned back slightly, his fur-lined cloak shifting as he took a measured sip of wine, clearly unruffled by the Queen's question. "Ah, Your Grace, that depends on the fire. A hearth's glow is a blessing on cold nights, but gold... gold ensures there's always wood to burn."

His tone was light, almost playful, and his quick reply drew a quiet laugh from a few at the table. Galil turned his attention back to Amelia, tilting his goblet slightly toward her as if offering a private toast. "Though I suspect even the wealthiest merchants would trade their riches for the right company."

Amelia inclined her head slightly, acknowledging his gesture but keeping her expression neutral, even as a faint blush threatened to rise to her cheeks. From the next seat at the table, Lord Malum's gaze flicked briefly between the two, his expression carefully guarded. His fingers tightened ever so slightly around the stem of his goblet before he raised it to his lips, masking his reaction with a long, deliberate sip of wine. Foolish flirtations, he thought, though his face betrayed none of the irritation stirring beneath his composed exterior.

Malum set his goblet down as he reached for his knife and fork cutting a small piece of the roasted venison. The rich aroma wafting upward as he brought it to his lips. The tender meat melted on his tongue; its flavours perfectly balanced—a hint of smokiness complemented by the subtle sweetness of the glaze. He nodded appreciatively, savouring the bite before dabbing the corners of his mouth with a linen napkin.

Turning to Karak, he gestured lightly toward her plate. "Queen Karak, you've not yet sampled the venison. I assure you; our chef's skill rivals that of any Nordon feast." His tone was warm, his smile faint but genuine, though his sharp eyes remained attentive to her reaction.

Karak took a measured bite, cutting into the steak with deliberate precision. She chewed slowly; her expression distant as if she were weighing the flavours on her palate like a strategist assessing a battlefield. The richness of the meat was balanced by the subtle tang of the glaze, and a faint smile tugged at her lips. "A bold claim, Lord Malum," she said at last, her voice smooth and measured. "Though I must admit, the flavour does you credit. Perhaps I should send for your chef when I return to Nordon." Her focus lingered on Malum, her words both a compliment and a subtle test of his reaction.

Malament seized the moment to interject, his lips curving into a faint smile. "As much as we'd love to part with our chef, perhaps we could send the recipe instead. That way, Nordon can enjoy the warmth of East Kadun without the poor man risking frostbite." His tone was light and playful, carrying just the right mix of humour and diplomacy. Internally, he noted the ripple of amusement that followed, his movements flicking briefly to Karak to gauge her reaction. Her faint smile suggested approval, and he leaned back slightly, satisfied with his well-timed remark.

Amelia leaned forward slightly, her turquoise eyes glinting as she caught the interplay between Malament and the Queen. A faint smirk crossed her lips as she added, her tone carrying a teasing edge, "And if the recipe fails, perhaps Malament himself could deliver it to Nordon. A fine envoy, wouldn't you agree?"

Konan let out a low, rumbling laugh, the sound deep and unyielding, like the echo of distant thunder. His words followed in the harsh, guttural tongue of Nordon, each syllable sharp and clipped. "Han ville fryse før han passerte det første tårnet." His tone carried a mix of amusement and faint derision, his deep brown eyes glinting as they flicked toward Malament as if challenging.

Karak leaned back slightly in her chair, her lips curving into an amused smile as she translated smoothly. "He says *'Malament would freeze before reaching the first outpost'*." Her voice was warm, but her eyes, keen and calculating, flicked briefly to Malament as if to gauge his reaction to the playful barb. She tilted her goblet slightly, swirling the deep red liquid within as she added, "A fair warning, no doubt."

Malament's jaw tightened ever so slightly, though he quickly masked the reaction with a faint, polite smile. "I will take that as a test," he replied evenly, his tone calm but carrying a subtle undertone of pride. "Perhaps one day I'll prove to pass it."

Before the tension could escalate, Galil, ever the diplomat and peacemaker, raised his goblet with an easy grin. "Perhaps," he interjected, his voice light and good-humoured, "but I've seen East Kadun's charm warm even the frostiest Nordon hearts."

His eyes sparkled with amusement as he glanced between Malament and Konan, though his gaze lingered briefly on Amelia, a hint of warmth betraying his deeper interest. Laughter rippled softly across the table, the earlier tension dissolving into the ease of shared humour.

As the meal continued, the formalities gave way to a lighter, more convivial atmosphere. Conversation flowed more freely; the weight of ceremony replaced by the warmth of camaraderie.

# BORLONG'S BANQUET
# CHAPTER FORTY SIX

The banquet hall buzzed with the warmth of satisfaction and the low hum of jovial conversation. Nobles and soldiers alike lingered over the last bites of venison, their goblets brimming with the continuous flow of Borlong Red.

As empty plates were cleared and the remnants of the main course whisked away, servers returned in an elegant procession, bearing trays of poached pears glistening in a rich red wine glaze. Their delicate flesh, infused with cinnamon, cloves, and a hint of citrus, released an intoxicating aroma that curled through the air, mingling with the lingering scents of roasted venison and spiced vegetables. Murmurs of approval rippled through the room as the desserts were placed before the diners—a feast for the eyes as much as the palate.

Each bite of the tender pears offered a perfect balance of sweetness and spice, their warmth cutting through the cool evening air. The dessert was met with unanimous praise, a fitting conclusion to the lavish meal. Galil, seated beside Amelia, eagerly polished off his portion and raised his goblet in delight before requesting a second plate, drawing laughter and teasing from those nearby.

Even Amelia, who had maintained a reserved demeanour throughout the evening, found herself relaxing in the convivial atmosphere. Galil's growing interest in her became harder to ignore, his subtle glances and increasingly effusive compliments softening with the effects of wine. Though his words began to slur slightly, his intelligence and charm remained intact, keeping their exchanges lively. Despite her initial caution, she found herself appreciating his wit and the effort he made to hold her attention, though she was careful to deflect his advances with light, measured responses.

Lord Malum, ever the attentive host, devoted himself almost exclusively to Queen Karak throughout the meal. His every comment was directed her way, and he laughed a touch too heartily at her jests, his deep chuckles occasionally lingering just a moment too long. He leaned toward her slightly whenever he spoke, his hands animated in polite gestures that betrayed a nervous energy. He watched carefully as her wine was poured and her plate refilled, nodding discreetly to the maids to ensure her every need was met before she could even voice it. Yet, despite his efforts to exude confidence, his fingers tightened subtly around his goblet when her green eyes lingered on him, sharp and appraising.

Karak, for her part, appeared to indulge his attentiveness with gracious amusement, her lips curling into faint smiles that danced on the edge of mockery. She matched his energy with a measured warmth, her voice low and melodious as she replied to his comments with just enough praise to keep him leaning forward for more. Occasionally, she cast a glance toward her brother, Konan, who sat in quiet detachment at the end of the table. At times, her hand rested lightly on the stem of her goblet, her fingers toying with the engraved silver as she swirled the wine. Each sip she took seemed deliberate, almost ceremonial; her demeanour cool yet undeniably magnetic.

Konan, however, remained a stark contrast to the revelry. Though his hulking frame was present, his mind seemed elsewhere, his dark eyes often fixed on the middle distance or scanning the room with a slow, predatory precision. He spoke only when directly addressed, and even then, his words in the guttural Nordon tongue were clipped and deliberate, devoid of embellishment. While the others drank freely, he let his goblet sit mostly untouched, a silent testament to his vigilance. Yet, the occasional flicker of his gaze toward Malum and his son carried a weight that did not go unnoticed by the host, a shadow of unspoken judgment that added a simmering tension to the evening's otherwise jovial tone.

Malament, as always, moved with quiet precision, navigating the intricate web of social dynamics with practiced ease. He offered measured contributions to conversations, his tone pleasant but never overly familiar, keeping his presence felt without overstepping his station. Unlike the others, he rationed his wine carefully, his goblet always appearing freshly poured but seldom drained, a subtle display of restraint. His sharp eyes flitted between his father and the Queen, noting with quiet amusement the slight crack in Malum's otherwise polished demeanour whenever Karak pressed her advantage with a pointed remark. Though the Queen's words were couched in playfulness, Malament sensed their undercurrent of power—a reminder, perhaps, of the precarious balance Malum was striving to maintain.

Despite the transition into merrier festivities, the remnants of earlier tension still lingered, like the faint bitterness of wine on the tongue. Karak's presence remained a commanding force at the table, her every glance, gesture, and remark rippling outward to shape the mood. Malum worked tirelessly to ease that tension, filling the space with his carefully chosen words and warm hospitality. Yet, for all his efforts, the Queen's cool poise seemed impervious to his charm, her laughter tinged with just enough detachment to remind him—and everyone else—of her sovereignty.

As the evening progressed, the rigid formality of the banquet began to soften, its structured elegance giving way to a more vibrant and unrestrained atmosphere. Guests from the surrounding tables drifted to their feet, weaving between clusters of nobles and merchants as the hum of conversation swelled into a lively chorus. Groups formed and dissolved like ripples on a pond, their movements fluid and organic, while laughter bubbled up in bursts, carried on the warm air alongside the lingering scent of spiced wine.

Servants moved with practiced ease, their steps light and deliberate as they wove through the shifting crowd, refilling goblets and clearing empty plates with unobtrusive precision. The occasional clink of silverware punctuated the rising chatter, mingling with the faint strains of music drifting from the corner of the hall. At intervals, a burst of song erupted from one group of diners, their voices unpolished but spirited, drawing scattered applause and cheers from nearby tables.

The room itself seemed to shift in response to the revelry, its grand chandeliers casting a warmer, softer glow as shadows danced playfully across the marble floors and richly adorned walls. What had begun as a display of formal unity now carried the vibrant energy of celebration, the rigid boundaries of decorum dissolving into the heady intoxication of wine, music, and camaraderie.

Galil to was growing bolder with each sip of Borlong Red. "The south does make for much prettier women," he slurred, his eyes fixed on Amelia with more than interest. "The women of Nordon generally prefer a good fight to a good conversation." His voice carried a mixture of bravado and drunken charm as he leaned against the table, attempting to hold Amelia's gaze.

But in his inebriated state, he misjudged, his elbow slipping off the edge. He just barely managed to catch himself before banging his chin, but the motion sent his shoulder crashing into the table. Plates clattered, cutlery jumped, and an empty cup tumbled to the floor. Worst of all, his goblet tipped, splashing the rich, red wine across his jerkin, the dark stain spreading instantly over the light fabric.

The wine pooled on the table, forming a small puddle that began to stream down the unseen slope of the surface, inching dangerously close to Queen Karak's place. Galil, oblivious, fumbled at his jerkin, smearing the stain further as he muttered under his breath. Karak, meanwhile, had noticed none of the approaching spill, too busy laughing at the merchant's misfortune.

Lord Malum, however, sprang into action, rising with a napkin in hand. "Excuse me, Your Grace," he said, hastily mopping up the spill before it could drip onto Karak's elegant black gown.

Karak glanced down in surprise, only now noticing the near calamity. She let out a theatrical gasp. "Oh, Lord Malum, my saviour!"

"Nonsense," Malum replied smoothly, straightening. "I was merely looking out for your beautiful dress. A gown such as yours must remain pristine."

Karak smiled, her voice dropping to a soft, teasing tone. "A lady's gown is particularly important to her, Lord Malum. It must never be stained... unless she intends it that way."

Malum felt heat rise to his cheeks, a familiar tingling sensation stirring within him. "I have no doubt, my Queen. Though I feel the wine would have spared you far more than our friend Galil. Are you quite alright, sir?" He turned to the merchant.

Galil, his face flushed and his words clumsy, snapped back. "Do I look alright? I'm drunk, and my outfit is ruined!" There was a faint hint of anger in his voice, though it faltered under the amused glances from the others at the table.

Malum remained calm, his tone soothing. "Do not fret, Galil. I'll have a maid fetch another gown for you tonight."

The merchant snorted, clearly dissatisfied, but Malum pressed on. "And tomorrow, I shall take you to the markets myself. I'll purchase a garment of your choosing with my own coin. I know a tailor who will see you dressed better than ever."

Karak, watching with faint amusement, turned to Galil. "That is most generous of Lord Malum, wouldn't you agree, Galil?" Her tone innocent but seeking his compliance, and even in his drunken state, the Nordon merchant found himself nodding.

Malum snapped his fingers, summoning the brunette maid who had been pouring wine to their table all night. She hurried over, her eyes darting nervously toward the stained table. "My good man here has spilled his drink," Malum explained. "Take him to my chambers and allow him to select a robe of his choice for the evening."

The maid nodded and moved around the table to Galil, standing beside him expectantly. The merchant looked at her, then hesitated. "Thank you, though... will there be somewhere to change? I fear I've little beneath."

Malum let out a hearty laugh. "It's a maid, for holy's sake! Have her turn around or fuck her while you change for all I care!" His laughter rang out across the table, and even Karak chuckled lightly at the remark. Galil, emboldened by the laughter, grabbed the maid's hand, a sloppy grin spreading across his face. The maid, however, flinched slightly, her expression betraying a flicker of anguish.

Amelia, who had been quietly observing, suddenly rose, her tone firm but calm. "Let me take Galil." Her turquoise eyes swept over the maid, who froze in place. "She would be better served here in the dining hall, wouldn't you agree? There are many thirsty mouths in need of attention tonight."

Relief washed over the maid's face, her shoulders relaxing as she stepped back. Amelia turned to Galil, a hint of steel in her gaze. "Come, Galil. Let us find you something suitable." She took the merchant's arm with a practiced air of authority, gently but firmly leading him away. As they left, Amelia cast a final glance back at the maid, silently assuring her she was safe—for now.

Malum and Karak fell into laughter, each offering their own retelling of the scene with Galil, embellishing the humour for each other's amusement. Konan, however, remained as stoic as ever, his expression unreadable as he took a measured sip from his goblet. Like Malament, he had consumed cautiously, his restraint a clear testament of his own unique discipline.

Malament, sitting quietly, let his gaze follow his mother as she guided Galil through the throng of mingling guests. Pride stirred within him—Amelia's intervention had been timely and composed, sparing the maid further humiliation, if only temporarily. His sharp eyes flicked briefly to the brunette maid, her relief palpable as she disappeared into the crowd, though Malament's thoughts lingered on the inevitable. She would not likely escape unscathed tonight, but at least dignity had been preserved for a while longer.

Once his mother vanished from view, Malament's attention shifted, his eyes scanning the room with calculated precision. He surveyed methodically, taking in every detail: the clusters of Nordon and Borlong merchants in animated conversation, their gestures exaggerated under the influence of wine; the soldiers, both northern and southern, some mingling at the edges of the hall, some engaging in camaraderie while others remained watchful.

The atmosphere was markedly different from the first feast in this hall. Where tension had previously dominated, there was now an air of revelry and ease. Groups of men burst into song, their voices rising in unpolished harmony, while others laughed heartily, tankards clinking in jovial toasts. On the periphery, a few figures lingered in quieter conversation, their posture and darting glances betraying whispers of business or intrigue.

Malament's attention sharpened as he observed the Nordon soldiers in particular. Their movements were deliberate, even in leisure. They laughed and drank, but their postures betrayed a discipline that was hard to ignore—the way they shifted their weight evenly, the subtle positioning of their hands near weapons even as they raised their tankards. These were men accustomed to battle, Malament thought, his eyes narrowing slightly. Even in celebration, they are prepared.

He noted the subtle distinctions in their garb—fur-lined cloaks and thicker tunics suited for Nordon's brutal winters, contrasting with the lighter, more decorative attire of Borlong's soldiers. Yet it was not their attire that held his attention, but their camaraderie. While Nordon's men mingled, their conversations often punctuated by glances toward the Borlong men. They observe as much as they indulge, he realized, a quiet respect mingling with his wariness.

Malament leaned back in his chair, his fingers brushing the rim of his goblet. He had not taken a sip in over half an hour, preferring to keep his senses sharp. As the din of the hall grew louder, he let his gaze roam once more, every detail filtering into his mind like pieces of a larger puzzle. The Nordon men were here to feast, yes—but also to watch, to listen, and to measure their hosts. Much like himself.

And so Malament remained still, his expression composed, as his sharp eyes continued to scan the room. Each movement and each word spoken seemed to settle into a larger pattern, one that he could not yet fully decipher. Then, a subtle but nagging realization crept over him—the Nordon contingent seemed more numerous tonight than before. Surely not, he thought, brushing the notion aside as paranoia.

Yet, despite himself, his mind began tallying their numbers. Subconsciously, his attention flitted from group to group, silently counting the soldiers. Thirty-seven... thirty-eight... thirty-nine. His heart sank slightly as he noted the others lingering at the edges of the hall, their presence less obvious but no less certain. The count tipped over forty, and a quiet unease began to stir in him. Am I mistaken? He started again, this time more deliberately, his mind methodical despite his growing concern. The number climbed higher, past forty again, with more silhouettes in the background. Their numbers have swelled. How? And why?

A faint frown marred his otherwise composed expression, the weight of his realization pressing on him. This is not coincidence. His thoughts raced as he considered the implications, but his musings were abruptly interrupted by an icy sensation creeping down his spine. Slowly, he became aware of two heavy dark eyes fixed on him, sharp and unrelenting. He did not need to look to know whose it was.

Konan.

Malament resisted the urge to meet the Nordon warrior's dark brown eyes, but the intensity of the man's stare was impossible to ignore. It was not the casual scrutiny Malament had grown used to from Konan in these settings; this was something different. Menacing. Predatory. Konan looked at him as if prey, a chill running through Malament. His breath caught for a moment, though he quickly steadied it, forcing himself to maintain his outward calm.

When he did finally glance toward Konan, it was as though time slowed. The Nordon warrior's expression was charged with something primal, something Malament could not name but instinctively feared. Konan's broad shoulders seemed impossibly still, his presence an immovable force amid the revelry. His stare carried weight, pressing down on Malament, who suddenly felt far smaller than he had moments before.

Malament's stomach tightened, quickly looking away, refusing to acknowledge the glare with so much as a polite nod. His attention snapped back to the crowd, searching for an anchor, something to break the moment.

Relief washed over him as he spotted Luka's familiar face in the sea of bodies. His friend was gesturing subtly, trying to catch his eye, a faint smile tugging at his lips as if to offer reassurance. Malament seized the opportunity, rising gracefully from his chair. "Excuse me," he said, his tone steady and polite, though his movements were brisk. He avoided looking at Konan again, though he could still feel the warrior's penetrating eyes following him as he stepped away from the table. Only when he reached the relative safety of the crowd did he allow himself a quiet breath of relief. Whatever game Konan was playing tonight, Malament was not ready to be its pawn.

Malament approached Luka with measured steps, his composure firmly in place despite the tension still clinging to him. Luka's face lit up with a welcoming grin, though there was a flicker of something beneath it—an edge of seriousness that did not escape Malament's notice.

"Malament," Luka greeted, clasping his arm in a firm but familiar grip. "I was beginning to wonder if you'd abandoned me to this chaos."

Malament allowed a faint smile, though his sharp eyes studied Luka's expression. "Not at all, Luka. I'm just late to the reprieve." Their handshake lingered, and Malament felt the faintest hesitation in his friend's grip, as though Luka had more on his mind than casual pleasantries.

Luka gestured subtly toward a quieter corner, lowering his voice. "Come. Let's find a place where we can talk... the wine and the gossip can wait."

Malament followed, his shoulders still stiff. The ease he had hoped for in Luka's company was tinged with unease. Whatever Luka had to share; it would not be trivial.

Konan's ruthless glare remained locked on Malament, unwavering and predatory, following his every step like a wolf stalking prey through the snow. Even as Malament strode purposefully away, Konan's dark gaze never faltered, every movement of the young lord carefully measured, scrutinized. He watched intently as Malament exchanged words with his companion, their conversation outwardly light yet betraying a tension in their postures, a secret unspoken. When the pair finally turned and disappeared into the crowded corridors beyond the dining hall, Konan's focus lingered, as if his mind followed them beyond the walls.

For a moment, his attention shifted back to the table, settling on his goblet of wine. His hulking hand wrapped around the delicate stem, the contrast striking, as if the fragile metal might shatter under his grip. He closed his eyes briefly, his mind pulsing with a battle prayer to Shiva, the words resonating silently within him.

*'Durak karesh, Shiva vékar torak.'*

*'Strength to you, Shiva shields the brave.'*

Without hesitation, he drained the goblet in a single motion, the deep red wine vanishing like blood wiped from a wound. The empty goblet clicked softly against the table as he set it down, his hands pushing firmly against the polished surface to raise his towering frame. The weight of his axe shifted against his back, it's reassuring presence a silent promise of what was to come. His fingers flexed briefly, anticipating the weapon's familiar heft. It would be loose soon.

As he stood, Karak's green eyes caught his, sharp and knowing, their unspoken connection bridging the space between them. Her conversation with Malum halted mid-sentence, her words freezing in the air as she regarded her brother. Her expression, poised and regal, betrayed nothing to her host, but her gaze spoke volumes.

She inclined her head slightly and uttered in the language of Nordon, her voice low but firm. "Durak karesh."

Konan's lips curled into a deadly, eager smile; the expression cold. A shadow of anticipation danced across his face; his readiness palpable. The hall around him buzzed with laughter and conversation, yet for Konan, the world had narrowed to a single, inevitable purpose.

"Durak karesh," he echoed.

# BORLONG'S BANQUET CHAPTER FORTY SEVEN

The echoes of laughter and song from the feasting hall faded into a distant murmur as Malament and Luka stepped into the vast reception area. The grand chamber, typically alive with the bustle of courtiers and servants, now seemed cloaked in an unsettling stillness. The tall stone pillars stretched upward into the dark, their intricate carvings catching the dim light and casting distorted, serpentine shadows across the polished floor. The faint rustle of their footfalls was swallowed by the emptiness, leaving only the occasional crackle of a guttering torch to punctuate the silence.

The air here was colder, sharper, carrying the faint metallic tang of stone and a lingering trace of incense that clung to the shadows. Malament's pace slowed, his sharp turquoise eyes narrowing as he surveyed the space. The usual attendants and guards were conspicuously absent. Even the torches lining the walls seemed to waver uncertainly, their flames curling low and sputtering, as though hesitant to defy the oppressive quiet.

Ahead, Luka moved with measured steps, his silhouette taut with unspoken tension. His easy, relaxed demeanour—the one that had drawn so many to trust him—was gone, replaced by a purposeful edge that caught Malament's attention immediately. The subtle stiffness in Luka's shoulders, the precise way his hand hovered near the hilt of his blade, spoke volumes.

Malament's attention lingered on his companion for a moment before breaking the silence. "You don't pull me away from a feast unless there's something wrong," he said, his voice low and steady. Beneath the calm exterior, there was an edge—sharp, deliberate, like the first scrape of steel on a whetstone.

Luka glanced over his shoulder; his expression carefully blank. "You've always been astute," he replied, his voice a muted rasp against the vast emptiness.

They paused behind a towering pillar, its cold surface offering a momentary reprieve from the open expanse of the chamber. Shadows pooled around its carved base, the faint grooves of ancient patterns catching what little light the flickering torches provided. Luka pressed his back against the pillar, his vision darting toward the corridor beyond, scanning for movement before speaking. Noting every darkened corner, every potential threat hidden within the shifting shadows.

"Mal, the day Auron was attacked," Luka began, his voice low, almost a whisper, as if the words themselves carried weight. "You asked me to find out what I could."

Malament stilled, the faint chill of the stone seeping through his tunic. The mention of Auron cut through the haze of his thoughts, a sudden, sharp reminder of unfinished business. He had not forgotten—he never forgot—but the arrival of the Nordon delegation had pushed it further down his ever-growing list of priorities.

Now, the memory surged to the forefront, accompanied by a quickening pulse. His heart thudded once, twice, faster now, as if anticipating what Luka was about to reveal. "What did you find?" Malament asked, his voice steady despite the mounting tension curling in his chest.

Luka hesitated, his lips pressing into a thin line before he glanced at Malament. "What I have to say... you may need to hear it somewhere quieter," his tone clipped, his eyes flicking toward the darkened corridor ahead.

"If you have something to say, Luka, let it be said," Malament demanded, his voice quiet but firm, cutting through the oppressive stillness. His piercing gaze locked onto Luka, unrelenting.

Luka hesitated, his jaw tightening as his eyes flicked toward the corridor. A faint shuffle of footsteps echoed in the distance, drawing closer. Both men fell silent, their breaths shallow as they pressed deeper into the shadows of the pillar.

A maid appeared, her head bowed, carrying a tray of empty goblets toward the feasting hall. She moved with steady efficiency, her steps light and measured, oblivious to the weight of the moment she interrupted.

The pause stretched, the quiet filled only by the faint rustle of her skirts and the soft clink of glass against metal. As she disappeared around the corner, Luka exhaled, his posture relaxing slightly.

"Now," Malament urged, his tone sharper this time. "What is it?"

Luka's expression darkened, his voice low and weighted with meaning. "What I'm about to tell you… you won't like. The words shall not come easy, and you heard it not from me."

Malament held his breath, his chest tightening with a sudden mix of anger and foreboding. The cold stillness of the reception hall seemed to press in around him, amplifying the pounding in his ears. His hands flexed instinctively, fingers twitching as though already anticipating the need for action.

Luka's sharp eyes studied him carefully, noting the faint flush creeping into Malament's face, the tightening of his jaw. "Mal," he said quietly, almost pleading. "This is not easy news to give. Tell me truthfully… have you had much wine tonight?"

Malament's gaze snapped up, ice-hard and seething beneath the surface. His voice came low and strained, like a drawn bowstring on the edge of snapping. "Stop this lingering," he hissed. "I rarely drink—you know that. What difference does it make?"

A tense pause stretched between them, heavy with unspoken meaning. Luka's expression remained unreadable, but his shoulders stiffened, his hand resting near the hilt of his shortsword—not in threat, but in preparation. His voice, when he spoke again, was calm but firm. "What I'm about to say would drive lesser men to rash action. I need to know —" he leaned in, his gaze steady "—that wine isn't what guides your next move."

Malament's breath hitched. His pulse thundered, his anger simmering just beneath his measured exterior. He could see the truth in Luka's words, feel the weight of whatever revelation loomed between them. It was something grave, something Luka clearly dreaded saying—but also something he feared Malament's reaction to. He forced a slow, steady exhale, willing his trembling fingers to still. "I am calm," he lied, his voice strained with barely controlled fury.

Luka studied him for a long moment, the hall stretching silent around them. He knew Malament's words were hollow, but there was no more time for delay. Glancing over his shoulder one last time, ensuring the corridor remained still and empty, he turned back.

"I own an establishment… let's call it… just north of the docks," Luka started, his voice low and measured, each word carefully chosen. "What happens there… well, let's say it doesn't always align with the Lord's law." His eyes flicked up, gauging Malament's reaction before continuing. "It's understood—by those who need to understand. A gold piece here, a favour there... and certain eyes conveniently look away."

Malament's expression remained stony, though his fists tightened at his sides. He already knew this about Luka's shadowed dealings, though hearing it now, framed with such deliberate precision, only deepened his unease. Luka was still circling the truth, delaying—but why?

"It's given me... access," Luka continued, his voice dropping further, almost conspiratorial. "To people, to contacts. If something needs doing—something that doesn't fit the... more conventional path—well..." He let the thought trail off, his meaning clear.

Malament's eyes narrowed, his patience thinning like ice underfoot. His breath hissed through clenched teeth, though he forced himself to remain silent, listening.

"The people who frequent this place..." Luka hesitated, searching for the right words. "Let's say they wouldn't be welcome in our circles—but they have their uses." His brow furrowed as if regretting even acknowledging their existence. "The man who runs it—someone I trust to know things—I asked him what he might have heard."

A pause. Too long. Deliberate.

"And?" Malament prompted, his voice sharp, a blade honed on impatience.

Luka exhaled slowly; his gaze steady but grim. "From several different sources—ones he believes to be reliable—a name kept coming up." His tone hardened. "Dakeard. A local... contractor. A man for hire. He was overheard boasting about a job that would... raise his profile."

Malament's blood ran cold. The edges of his vision seemed to sharpen, focusing on Luka's face, reading every flicker of truth in his features.

"That name is dead now," Luka added quietly, his voice a strained whisper. "Your lad... Auron saw to that."

For a heartbeat, Malament could not breathe, his chest tightening as anger surged through him like a storm threatening to break. His mind wrestled for control, reason clawing against the primal urge to lash out, to act. His pulse thundered in his ears, drowning out the dim crackle of the torches. When he finally spoke, his voice was low and strained, trembling with barely restrained fury. "So, all we have is a name? Dakeard? A hired knife?"

Luka shifted uneasily, his gaze flicking toward the darkened corridor as though expecting shadows to stir. "There's more," he admitted, his voice dropping into a low whisper. "When I asked about the man… one detail came up again and again." He paused, measuring his words. "Dakeard boasted constantly—loudly—that his profile would rise." His lips curled bitterly. "Repeated it so often even the rats came to believe it."

Malament forced his breath to steady, each inhale sharp and deliberate, a fragile tether holding back the tempest within, his eyes narrowing dangerously. "And?" he hissed, his voice low and strained, barely concealing the fury that simmered just beneath the surface.

Luka swallowed hard, his throat bobbing. "One night… someone asked him directly: How? How would his profile rise?" His voice wavered, thick with unease. "His answer…" Luka hesitated, dread tightening his features. "The client," he forced out. "His client was someone powerful. Someone with the means to pay handsomely… and elevate his standing."

The words landed like a dagger between them. For a moment, the hall seemed to constrict, the cold stone walls pressing inward. The faint crackle of a dying torch echoed distantly, swallowed by the mounting silence.

Malament took a single, deliberate step closer, his breath now fast and shallow, every muscle wound tight. "Who?" he demanded, his voice cold and sharp, a blade stripped of all pretence.

Luka lowered his head, unable to meet Malament's searing gaze. His voice trembled with quiet regret. "Malament… I'm sorry."

The words hung in the still air, a death knell tolling deep in Malament's chest.

"It—it was your father." Luka forced the final blow. "Lord Malum hired Dakeard."

Malament's world seemed to tilt, narrowing into a harsh, unyielding focus. The edges of reality fractured like shards of shattered glass, memories driving through his mind—jagged, merciless. His father's cold, calculating indifference… the affair with Cora, the cruel spectacle of the failed flogging, meant as punishment yet ending in defiance and self-mutilation. The blood-stained straw of the stables, the broken boards still vivid in his memory… the broken pitchfork, brutal and deliberate, its fractured remains speaking of more than mere chance… Finally, the lifeless form that Auron bestride had a name, had a purpose. Every thread, every cruel detail, tightening like a noose—all weaving toward one grim, undeniable truth.

His father. It had always been his father.

The air felt thinner, pressing against Malament's chest like iron bands. His breath came sharp and ragged, burning with each inhale. His vision swam, not from confusion, but from clarity—a searing, brutal clarity that left no room for denial. Lord Malum had orchestrated it all.

Auron's life was never spared by luck or fate—it had been targeted. The stables were chosen, secluded and far from prying eyes. The pitchfork —a cruel instrument meant to mimic either an accident, or a staged execution wrapped in deceit.

The realisation struck like a hammer on an anvil—merciless, final. Rage surged through Malament's chest, scorching through reason and restraint, stoking a fire so fierce it consumed his very breath. His hand tightened around the worn leather hilt of his sword, trembling —not from fear—but from a rage so absolute, so perfectly forged, it felt destined. There would be no forgiveness. No redemption. His father would answer.

His blade sang as it cleared its sheath, the sharp ring cutting through the thick, suffocating silence. The cold torchlight kissed the steel, illuminating its edge—keen, relentless, a deadly promise forged in betrayal.

"He is no father of mine," Malament growled, his voice ragged, trembling with fury barely contained. His eyes burned with violent intent. "He will suffer for this."

Luka stepped forward, his face tight with concern, his hands half-raised in a placating gesture. "Malament… be stilled—there is still much we don't know."

"I swear it!" Malament roared, his voice echoing like thunder off the cold stone walls. "I swear it here and now—not to you, but to the gods themselves! Gigas, hear me—he will pay."

He spun toward the feasting hall, determined to end it—to find his father, to end this farce of blood and betrayal—now.

But Luka lunged, seizing his shoulder in a desperate grip.

Instinct took over. Malament twisted with lethal precision, his blade arcing upward in a flash of silver fire, slicing through the narrow space between them—deadly, unforgiving.

The tip of his sword halted—quivering, pulsing with restrained violence —just shy of Luka's chest, poised over his heart like death held by a thread. The steel hovered, trembling with the force of his rage, eager to strike.

"Choose, Luka," Malament hissed, his voice low and venomous. "You stand with me—or against me. There is no middle ground."

Their eyes locked, fury met resolve.

Friendship. Loyalty. Trust.

All suspended on the edge of that steel.

Luka held his ground, breathing steady but tight, his sharp eyes fixed on Malament's blade, still hovering—a single heartbeat from blood. Slowly, he raised his hands in a cautious gesture, palms outward, a fragile plea for reason. Slowly, he retreated a few measured steps, his attention never leaving the twin-edged blade poised before him. His lips twisted into a grimace, not from fear—but regret.

With agonizing reluctance, his hand drifted to his own hilt, fingers brushing the familiar worn leather. The rasp of steel echoed low and menacing as his blade slid free, the sound carving through the cold stillness of the hall.

"Malament," Luka said quietly, forcing steadiness into his voice, though it wavered beneath the weight of what was coming. "You are my friend. I only seek to help you... put down your blade." The words hung between them—a bridge already burning.

Malament did not move. His chest heaved with raw, burning rage, his breath sharp and strained. His knuckles turned white as his grip tightened around his sword's hilt, the edge trembling, aching for release.

"Be still," Luka urged again, stepping cautiously into the storm, his voice edged with desperation but steady. "We are friends... but Malum—he is my Lord... my commander." His expression darkened, eyes hardening with reluctant conviction. "What you seek... is treachery."

The final word fell like a dagger between them—irrevocable.

Malament's breath hitched, his mind fracturing between reason and rage. His father's name—Malum—cut deeper than Luka's blade ever could, igniting a fresh surge of anger that burned away reason, leaving only betrayal and retribution.

In an act of unrelenting rage metal met metal.

Sparks erupted as their blades collided, the harsh clang reverberating through the stillness of the hall. Luka gritted his teeth, barely managing to parry the brutal strike. For a moment, nothing existed but the furious ring of steel, the blaze of their locked eyes—brotherhood shattered.

Malament drove Luka back with a vicious swipe, their swords clashed again. Fury roared in his chest, untamed and relentless, his breath coming in ragged bursts. Luka deflected each blow with tenacious precision, his own face tight with grim resolve—but still, his steps faltered under Malament's unyielding assault.

A tense, seething space opened between them, their blades still trembling from the last furious clash. Malament's chest heaved, every breath burning with rage, his sword raised and ready for the next brutal strike.

Luka steadied his stance, his feet firmly planted despite the ache radiating through his sword arm. His grip firm around his hilt as he braced for the inevitable—the next assault, the next reckoning.

Then—A roar split the heavy silence, primal and consuming, reverberating through the grand stone hall like the howl of an ancient beast. The very air seemed to shudder under its force, rippling through the darkness with a thunderous power that felt almost otherworldly.

"DRENGIR VAKNAR! DØDEN TAR ALT!"

The words rang with brutal finality, a war cry forged in blood and iron.

Both men staggered at the sheer weight of the voice, their blades dipping as the echo surged through the empty hall. The torches guttered under the force of the cry, their flames shrinking into trembling embers.

Footsteps. Measured, deliberate, each one a resounding thud on the polished stone, slow as the toll of a death bell.

From the far shadows, Konan emerged, a towering storm given flesh. His fur-lined cloak billowed faintly, casting dark, jagged shapes along the marble floors. His massive battle axe rested against his shoulder, its blade glinting like a hungry predator under flickering torchlight.

His deep-set eyes gleamed—cold, merciless, and knowing.

Malament tightened his grip on his sword, his knuckles aching from the force of his rage. He did not lower it.

"This is not your fight, Konan," Malament growled through clenched teeth, his breath still ragged with fury.

Konan stepped closer, slow and deliberate, his gaze never leaving Malament's. His mouth curled into something dark—a smile, though there was no warmth in it, only certainty.

"It means..." he said, his voice a deep, menacing growl, "Warriors awaken... Death claims all."

His Kadun was near flawless, save for the guttural undertone of his Nordon accent—a sharp edge that only made the words more final.

The hall seemed to hold its breath.

Steel remained raised, tempers still burning, but for a single, agonizing moment—fate itself paused, poised on the edge of each blade. Malament and Luka instinctively stepped back from one another, their blades still poised but their focus shifting—sharpening—as if some unspoken truth had just been laid bare. The oppressive stillness of the hall seemed to stretch, wrapping around them like a coiled serpent. The real enemy had revealed himself.

Malament's breath steadied, his seething rage tempered—but only for a moment. His sharp eyes locked on Konan's towering figure, searching for meaning behind the calculated malice in his gaze.

"You speak our tongue as if you have done so for years," Malament hissed, suspicion cutting through his anger like ice through flame.

Konan's lips arched into a cruel, predatory smirk. His voice dripped with disdain, cold and unyielding. "I am the Queen's brother, boy. Royal blood." His eyes gleamed with savage amusement. "Of course I speak Kadun... you ignorant cunt." The insult struck, venom-laced and deliberate, hanging in the charged air like the promise of violence yet to come.

Without hesitation, Luka snapped his blade up, the steel gleaming in the dim torchlight as he took an offensive step forward. His expression was locked in hardened defiance, his voice steady as iron. "That is the future Lord of East Kadun." He bared his teeth. "I would have your tongue for that."

Konan's smirk widened, twisting into something far darker, a spark of savage anticipation igniting in his eyes.

He took a slow, menacing step forward, his massive battle axe shifting ever so slightly, its cruel edge catching the dim light—a blade accustomed to splitting skulls.

"You can try."

His voice was low, almost a whisper—but there was no mistaking the deadly promise behind it.

For a heartbeat, the hall stilled—fate suspended on the edge of steel.

With a roar born of defiance and loyalty, Luka drove forward, his blade a blur of tempered steel. His boots scraped across the marble as he closed the distance in a single, fluid motion, aiming directly for Konan's exposed chest—fast, fierce, final.

Konan moved like a beast unleashed. His battle axe swung downward off his shoulder with terrifying precision, intercepting Luka's blade with a deafening clang! Sparks flew, scattering like shattered stars as steel bit steel. Their weapons locked, trembling with the force of the collision.

Malament did not move. His breath hitched—frozen, trapped between fury and disbelief, his hand still clenched around his blade's hilt—but his feet remained rooted to the cold stone floor, stunned by the brutal inevitability unfolding before him.

Luka twisted, driving his weight into the lock, his face morphed with raw determination. He pushed hard, forcing Konan back half a step. For a fleeting moment, it seemed as though he might gain ground.

But Konan was waiting.

With a vicious snarl, he ripped free, spinning with fluid, lethal grace. His axe arced through the dim torchlight—a sweeping, unstoppable crescent of death.

Luka barely managed to see it, narrowly dodging the first swing. His own blade lashed out in counter, cutting toward Konan's exposed side—a perfect strike.

But Konan's gauntlet-covered fist slammed into Luka's face with brutal force, snapping his head back with a sickening crack. Blood sprayed across the stone, vivid and final. Luka staggered, struggling to remain upright as his weapon clattered against the floor, his fingers refusing to hold the hilt.

Konan's axe rose high, its cruel edge gleaming like fate's executioner.

Malament's voice caught in his throat, strangled by shock and fury.

"LUKA—!"

The downward swing came with merciless finality, cleaving through flesh, bone, and soul in a single, unstoppable strike. Blood erupted, spraying across the cold marble in thick, crimson arcs, the brutal force of the blow leaving his torso gaping open, barely held together by sinew, shattered bone and Konan's battle axe.

The Nordon warrior exhaled slowly, his breath steady and cold as he yanked his axe free with a sickening wrench. Blood dripped lazily from its wicked edge, crimson trails gleaming in the uncertain light.

Luka's body collapsed to the ground with a wet, final thud, his head split clean in two, the savage cleave shearing through his skull and deep into his chest. His arms twitched involuntarily, fingers still searching for his fallen sword before going still.

The hall fell deathly silent, broken only by the slow, sickening drip of fresh blood pooling beneath his ruined form, widening rivers in the dark, mingling with the flickering shadows cast by the sputtering torches. Konan stood still for a moment, towering over Luka's disfigured features, the man's face lost forever, the warrior's expression one of absolute indifference.

Malament's breath was ragged, driven by wrath, grief, and the unmistakable pull of fate. His fingers dug painfully into his sword hilt, trembling—not afraid, fuelled with rage so fierce, it threatened to consume him whole.

Konan turned slowly, his dark eyes locking onto Malament with deadly intent. "You should have joined him." His voice was ice, empty of malice, empty of anything but certainty.

Malament took a single, determined step forward, every nerve ignited by the roaring need for vengeance.

"Come then," Konan growled, his voice cold and steady, like the ice-choked rivers of Nordon. He lazily adjusted his axe, its murderous edge catching the torchlight.

With a furious roar, Malament charged, his blade a streak of silver vengeance. His boots thundered towards Konan. His first strike came fast and lethal, a fierce lunge aimed in a downward arc directly for Konan's head—a strike meant to kill, swift and final.

But Konan moved with startling speed, shifting with predatory grace as Malament's sword whistled past his side, missing by inches. His massive axe flicked upward brutally deflecting Malament's second lunge with a harsh clang, sparks exploding where the steel kissed.

Relentless, Malament sent a third deadly backhand slash. Konan twisted at the last instant, his axe intercepting the blade with brutal precision. Sparks exploded as the two weapons screamed against one another, their impact reverberating through the stone walls.

Launching a relentless flurry of strikes, Malament's blade danced left, right, low—his sword, each swing driven by unyielding fury. The metal blurred with sheer speed, fuelled by grief, anger, and an unstoppable need for justice.

But Konan was more than ready. His axe rose and fell with crushing precision, effortlessly deflecting each of Malament's wild attacks. He sidestepped, weaving through the onslaught like a beast untouchable in its element. His expression remained infuriatingly calm.

Growling through gritted teeth, Malament sent his blade slashing in a savage upward stroke aimed at Konan's exposed side. But again, the Nordon warrior twisted effortlessly, letting the blade pass mere inches from his fur-lined cloak.

Before Malament could react, Konan struck—not with his axe, but with his iron-clad fist.

The punch slammed into Malament's jaw, whipping his head to the side. Pain bloomed hot and sharp, his vision flashing white as he stumbled backward, blood spraying from his mouth. He barely kept his footing, instinct driving him into a defensive stance.

Konan just stood, his expression taunting.

Rage overtook reason. With another defiant roar, Malament lunged again, his blade slicing downward with brutal intent. Konan parried the blow effortlessly, spinning with terrifying grace and bringing the haft of his axe crashing into Malament's chest.

Malament staggered back, air driven from his lungs in a choked gasp. But he refused to fall. His eyes burned with savage determination, his chest heaving with laboured breaths. He spat a thick stream of blood onto the cold marble, the crimson splatter stark against the unforgiving stone, a defiant act against the agony searing through his body.

Konan's smirk widened, wicked and knowing.

The son of Borlong charged once more, sword whistling through the air in a vicious arc. Konan ducked low, his axe slashing upward in a ruthless counter meant to cleave Malament's leg—but the younger warrior shifted his weight away at the last instant, narrowly avoiding the killing blow.

Their weapons collided again, shrieking steel against steel, the deafening clash echoing through the hall like the toll of a funeral bell. The floor beneath them was slick with blood and sweat, their boots scraping over the treacherous marble.

Malament pressed the attack, driving Konan back with sheer force and fury. His sword was a blur of relentless strikes—precise, powerful, deadly. He fought like a man possessed, the fire of vengeance propelling him forward.

But Konan never faltered. He blocked, dodged, and twisted with terrifying grace, always staying just out of reach, just beyond the killing edge. His dark eyes narrowed, cold and calculating, he was not merely defending—he was dissecting Malament's every move, studying him with cruel amusement. Every movement measured despite the storm of fury driving Malament's relentless assault. His breath remained calm, steady, a stark contrast to the frenzied rhythm of Malament's wild, desperate strikes.

Steel clashed again, sending harsh, jarring vibrations up both their arms. Malament surged again, muscles straining as he swung his blade in a brutal overhead arc, aiming to cleave Konan in two—a killing blow fuelled by sheer rage.

But Konan moved with lethal grace, sidestepping like a hunting wolf evading a snare, his eyes gleaming with deadly focus.

Before Malament could recover, Konan twisted with terrifying speed, his massive axe spinning in a vicious arc. The flat of the blade slammed into Malament's exposed ribcage with bone-crushing force.

The sickening sound of snapping ribs echoed through the hall, sharp and unforgiving. Malament's world exploded into pain—searing, blinding, all-consuming. His sword slipped from his fingers as he was lifted off his feet by the sheer force of the blow.

He hit the cold marble floor with a sickening thud, sliding across the blood-slick stone until his broken body finally came to rest. Agonizing pain exploded through Malament's chest, ripping through every nerve like wildfire. His ribs buckled under the crushing impact, a strangled breath escaped his lips—a sound caught between agony and defiance—as his shattered ribs fought to expand, every breath a new torment, a ragged, choked gasp.

His teeth clenched in fierce defiance, his lips pulling back into a grimace as he fought through the agony, forcing his body to move. Through blurred vision, he saw Konan advancing, his axe low and steady, Luka's blood still stained its cruel edge, a gruesome reminder of the merciless fate that awaited him.

Desperation surged through Malament, driving him to move, defiant even in agony. He lurched upward; jaw tightened against the blazing pain tearing through his side-but he never made it.

Konan's boot struck with vicious precision, crashing into Malament's face with merciless force. The sickening crack of shattering bone echoed through the hollow corridor, sharp and final.

Blood exploded, hot and blinding, spraying across Malament's face as his head jolted back, colliding with the unyielding marble in a bone-jarring impact, leaving the cold stone stained with fresh crimson.

The impact left his mind reeling, consciousness fraying as fresh red bloomed beneath his skull. His vision blurred, darkness crowding the edges of his sight. A heavy shadow loomed over him, cold and inevitable. Konan. The towering Nordon stared down, his face a mask of calm contempt. His eyes gleamed with something darker—certainty—as if the fight had ended before it had even begun.

"I actually expected more from you, Malament." His voice was low, lethal, like a blade scraping against stone. "I wasn't even meant to kill you."

Malament blinked, his mind swimming, struggling to focus through the daze. Blood dripped steadily from the gash in his scalp, mingling with the spreading crimson stain on the cold floor beneath him.

Konan crouched slightly, his axe now resting casually against his shoulder, its blood-slick edge glinting in the dim torchlight. "But you're pathetic." His voice curdled with disdain.

Malament's fingers twitched toward the hilt of his fallen sword, desperate, defiant. Konan saw and did not care. "Do you want to know the real reason we're here?" he asked, his tone almost… amused.

Malament's breath came ragged, his chest burning, but he met Konan's gaze, defiant even through the haze of pain and blood.

Konan smirked, mocking.

"Vĕktirhald," he said coldly, the word like a death sentence as it hung in the air, echoing with inevitable finality.

Malament's brow furrowed, struggling to comprehend.

Konan's smirk widened. "In Kadun… there isn't really a word for it. Perhaps…" he mused, "seizure by force… or claim of might." His voice darkened; every syllable etched with lethal certainty.

"We are not here to build on old alliances."

A cruel laugh followed, sharp and cutting.

"No, Malament… we are here to measure Borlong's strength—your armouries, your defences, your numbers." He stepped closer, his towering frame casting Malament in shadow.

"We are not impressed."

Malament's breath hitched, his mind reeling, the meaning slamming into him like a killing blow.

Konan's face hardened, his voice turning cold and final:

"Durak karesh, Malament."

His axe rose, gleaming, a merciless arc poised for the killing strike.

# BORLONG'S BANQUET CHAPTER FORTY EIGHT

The feasting hall thundered with life, its soaring beams trembling beneath the weight of boisterous laughter and the rhythmic pounding of tankards on heavy oak tables. The rich scent of roasted venison still clung to the air, mingling with the sharp tang of spilled ale and the faint smokiness from the towering hearths blazing at either end of the hall. Echoes of off-key singing rose above the din, weaving a raucous melody that tangled with the hum of animated conversations, creating a chaotic harmony that banished the chill of the world beyond the thick stone walls.

Near the edge of the bustling hall, where the fire's warmth still reached but the noise softened to a tolerable hum, Egil and Braddos sat side by side at a well-worn wooden table. Between them rested a heavy jug of ale, its frothy contents threatening to spill with every hearty thump of Braddos's fist as he recounted a particularly wild tale. Egil threw his head back with a booming laugh, his eyes gleaming with genuine amusement. Gone were the wary glances and guarded words of old; in their place was an easy camaraderie born of hard-fought duelling and shared respect. They drank deeply, savouring not just the ale, but the rare comfort of trusted company.

The din of the hall ebbed and swelled around them, a comforting backdrop of revelry that seemed distant in their shared corner. Flames crackled in the hearth, casting a warm glow over their weathered faces as the jug of ale between them slowly diminished. Their conversations were often fragmented, stitched together with shared gestures, knowing looks, and the occasional burst of unrestrained laughter.

Braddos jabbed his tankard toward Egil's own, miming a question about the ale. "Good, yes?" he asked slowly, his East Kadun accent thick, the words deliberate.

Egil snorted, understanding enough from Braddos's gesture. He gripped his handle and drank deeply, swallowing with exaggerated approval. "Möttur!" he declared, pounding his chest for emphasis. His voice boomed like distant thunder.

Braddos blinked, clearly puzzled. "What's... Möttur?" He mimicked Egil's chest-thump but received only a hearty laugh in response.

Egil wiped his mouth with the back of his hand and tried again, this time thumping the table with a heavy fist. "Möttur!" He flexed his bicep, the gesture universal enough to bridge the language gap.

Braddos barked a laugh, clapping Egil's arm in shared amusement. “Strong! Möttur!” He flexed his own arm playfully, earning a nod of approval from Egil.

Encouraged, Braddos grabbed the jug of ale and held it aloft. “Drink?” he offered, miming a long, exaggerated swig.

Egil's face split into a wide grin. “Ale!” he echoed, reaching for his own tankard. “Drikka!”

“Drink,” Braddos repeated, pointing between them. “Ale... drikka.”

Their tankards clashed in a resounding thud, frothy ale sloshing over the rims. “Skål!” Egil boomed, raising his drink high.

Braddos hesitated, recognizing the intent if not the word itself. “Skål... drink?” he guessed.

Egil shook his head fiercely. “Skål!” He gestured between them with emphasis, his expression earnest despite the language barrier.

Braddos's smile widened as he repeated, “Skål... friends.” Their tankards met again, this time with a deliberate clang.

As they drank deeply, the tension of the past weeks seemed to dissolve in the shared simplicity of the moment. Though words came slowly and awkwardly, gestures filled the gaps where language failed, each exchanged grin or nod weaving a deeper understanding.

Their shared laughter rippled through the feasting hall, warm and unrestrained, cutting through the din like the crackling of a hearth on a winter's night. Nearby, a group of Borlong's younger soldiers exchanged curious glances—not out of hostility, but something closer to bewildered curiosity. They had grown used to seeing Borlong and Nordon warriors sharing drinks and tales over the past few weeks, old grudges tempered by contests of strength and endless rounds of ale.

But Braddos and Egil were... different.

Since the Nordon company's arrival, the two had been near inseparable, their bond forged through fierce competitions, shared victories, and bruises worn like badges of honour. Where others traded wary politeness, they shared something unmistakably genuine—something stronger than mere alliance.

Their easy laughter and the way Braddos clapped Egil's shoulder with unguarded familiarity stood out in a hall where most friendships were still edged with caution. It was not suspicion that lingered in the younger soldiers' eyes, but a quiet wonder—how two men from opposite worlds, once enemies by fate, could seem like lifelong friends.

Braddos caught their stares, his eyes gleaming with amusement. With deliberate defiance, he lifted his tankard in a mock toast, grinning broadly before turning back to Egil without a second thought.

The Nordon warrior met his smirk with a knowing nod, reading the unspoken tension as easily as a battlefield signal. "Nó líkr," Egil rumbled, gesturing toward the staring soldiers with a dismissive tilt of his chin. "Think... skrangr." He tapped his temple with two thick fingers, frowning in mock disapproval.

Braddos chuckled, shaking his head as if brushing away the stares. "Let them." He jabbed a thumb toward Egil, then himself. "We... strong." He flexed his arm with exaggerated bravado. "Möttur."

Egil's booming laugh echoed through the hall as he slapped the table with approval. "Möttur!" he roared, pounding his chest with pride, his eyes shining with fierce amusement.

Their mismatched words collided like sparring blades—imperfect and unpolished yet cutting straight to meaning. They did not need fluent speech. What bound them went far deeper: not battles fought side by side, but the quiet recognition of shared struggles, shaped by lands that hardened men into survivors.

They respected the strength forged in each other—not just in muscle or steel, but in resilience. Egil was the fierce wind of the Nordon wilds, shaped by harsh winters and endless skies, relentless and untamed. Braddos was Borlong's tempered stone, sharp-edged and enduring, honed by duty and unyielding pride. Different lands, different fates—but beneath it all, the same enduring will to endure, to thrive, to live.

It was more than mere camaraderie. It was understanding. Both had endured the weight of expectations, of proving themselves against a world that cared little for weakness. In each other, they saw not an enemy or rival, but a man shaped by hardship, by country, by fate—and still standing.

They were just men, after all—men who bled, fought, laughed, and drank. Men who found solace in shared strength, trust earned without ceremony. No fragile alliance could forge such a bond—it was built in glances, gestures, and the unspoken understanding that they were cut from the same stubborn, unyielding cloth.

As the ale flowed freely, their conversation unfolded in a patchwork of Nordon, Borlong, and wild gestures—laughing, pointing, and miming their way through stories of near-misses on the training field and stubborn victories claimed through grit alone. Their words came in half-sentences and full-hearted laughter, stitched together by shared experience and an understanding that needed no translation.

The feast surged on around them, a distant storm of voices and music, but their world narrowed to the battered table and the bond being reforged with every story told, every thundering laugh shared.

Egil lifted his tankard, his expression serious now, though warmth gleamed in his storm-grey eyes. "Brad-dos... Bróðr." His deep voice softened; the word heavy with meaning beyond language.

Braddos's brow furrowed as he turned the unfamiliar word over in his mind, searching for meaning in Egil's steady gaze. Realization dawned, slow but certain, and a rare, genuine smile tugged at his lips. He clapped Egil's arm, firm and resolute. "Egil... brother."

Their tankards met in a resounding clang, the echo cutting through the feasting hall like a spoken vow. In that moment, there was no need for more words. Respect, trust, and shared strength hung unspoken between them—something forged not through war or bloodshed, but through the unyielding persistence of two men who recognized the same fire in each other.

Laughter rippled around them, the hall still roaring with life—but for a breath, neither man moved. They did not need to. Their bond had been sealed long before this night—by trials faced, struggles endured, and the stubborn will to stand, no matter the cost.

Egil's expression shifted, turning sombre yet resolute. His thick fingers brushed the heavy ironclads braided into his beard—symbols of honour and warriorhood in Nordon, each earned through battles fought and hardships endured. His dark brown eyes met Braddos's, filled with intensity and purpose.

Without breaking eye contact, Egil gripped one of the ironclads bound tightly into the thick braid nearest his jaw. With a sharp, deliberate pull, he tore it free, strands of red hair snapping with the motion. The braid unravelled slightly, loose and wild now, but Egil paid it no mind. He held the iron clad between thumb and forefinger, turning it slowly in the flickering firelight.

Braddos's breath hitched, his eyes widening. Even without fully understanding the Nordon customs, he sensed the enormity of the gesture. His gaze flicked from the scarred warrior's earnest expression to the iron clasp, realizing this was no casual offering—this was legacy, carried in steel.

Egil extended his hand, the iron clad resting heavy in his calloused palm. His voice rumbled low in the harsh, guttural tones of Nordon:

"Jarnbandr... styrka."

The words were steeped in meaning, spoken with raw sincerity. Braddos struggled for comprehension but felt the weight behind them. Egil slowly tapped the iron clad against his chest, right over his heart, then pressed it firmly into Braddos's hand, closing the younger warrior's fingers around the cold metal.

"Möttur... Braddos," Egil declared with finality. "Bróðir í vopnum."

The room around them faded into a dull hum as Braddos clenched the iron clad in his fist, its rough edges biting into his palm. He could not translate the words perfectly, but he did not need to. He understood. Egil was offering him more than friendship—he was offering a warrior's bond, forged in iron and respect, declaring Braddos as his equal... as his brother in arms.

Swallowing thickly, Braddos drew his short sword from his belt—not in challenge, but in reverence. He placed the blade flat across his palms and held it out between them, a warrior's offering in return. His voice was steady, roughened by emotion.

"Egil... brother."

Egil nodded slowly, a faint, satisfied smile tugging at the corner of his scarred mouth. With deliberate care, he pressed his hand over Braddos's sword, palm down, sealing the vow in shared understanding. No further words were needed.

At that moment, their separate worlds—East Kadun and Nordon, tradition and pride—collided and merged, bound by steel and shared purpose. Whatever battles lay ahead, whatever dangers awaited, they would face them together... brothers in arms.

Braddos nodded with solemn approval, sliding his short sword back into its worn leather sheath with deliberate care, as though marking the moment in steel. His gaze remained steady, fixed on Egil, no longer seeing a foreign warrior but a brother bound by honour.

Without hesitation, Braddos extended his arm. Egil's hand met his in a fierce warrior's grip—fingers locked, forearms pressed tight, the strength of their clasp speaking more than words ever could. It was a gesture older than kings, forged in the traditions of men who lived and died by their word.

Braddos held the grip firm, his voice steady, resonant with newfound understanding. "Durak karesh."

He spoke the words not as a borrowed phrase learned through drunken tutoring, but as something earned—felt. The Nordon words rolled from his tongue with the weight of truth: Strength to you.

For a moment, Egil's eyes widened in surprise, then softened with deep approval. He squeezed Braddos's arm tighter, the faintest spark of pride gleaming in his grey eyes. He did not need to correct Braddos's pronunciation or explain the phrase further—it was perfect, because it was true.

"Durak karesh," Egil repeated, his voice low but resolute, sealing the bond between them with iron-clad certainty. Their hands remained clasped, a silent promise burned into memory, forged in shared purpose and mutual respect.

For them, there was no need for grand declarations, no formal ceremony. The vow had been made, unspoken yet unbreakable, etched into their very being, tempered by hardship, strengthened by trust, and sealed in steel.

The firelight flickered, casting dancing shadows across their clasped arms, as if the world itself recognized the gravity of their bond. For a fleeting moment, there was only stillness—unshaken, absolute.

Then the feasting hall's merriment fractured like brittle ice underfoot.

A sharp commotion erupted near the entrance, piercing the din of laughter and revelry like a dagger through silk. Voices rose, sharp-edged with urgency and tinged with alarm. The familiar harmony of tankards clashing, songs bellowed off-key, and roaring fires faltered, replaced by a harsh undercurrent of tension.

Braddos and Egil's heads spun toward the entrance, their hands instinctively hovering near their weapons. Chairs scraped back with grating finality as nobles stumbled to their feet, their fine robes catching on carved table legs in their haste. Soldiers exchanged wary glances, palms resting on sword hilts as instinct overtook revelry.

Serving maids froze where they stood, clutching empty trays like makeshift shields, faces drained of colour. Tankards tipped, ale spilling unheeded across scarred tables, forgotten in the rising tide of anxious murmurs.

The feasting hall, once so alive with unrestrained joy, now stood on the edge of something darker—uncertainty thick in the air, every breath held in quiet dread.

Braddos's eyes met Egil's in a sharp, wordless exchange. Instinct burned through them both—there was no need for orders, no hesitation. In one fluid motion, they rose from the table, boots scraping against the stone floor. The heavy oak chairs they had occupied groaned in protest before toppling backward with a dull thud, forgotten.

They moved with purpose, strides measured but tense, cutting through the shifting crowd like twin blades through water. The air crackled with unease, thick with the bitter scent of spilled ale and the acrid tang of something far more dangerous, uncertainty.

Half the feasting hall was already emptying, its revellers spilling into the grand reception hall like a tide retreating before a coming storm. Braddos scanned the crowd, eyes narrowing as he spotted familiar figures emerging from the confusion.

Lord Malum loomed near the edge of the hall, his expression carved from stone, mouth set in a grim line that spoke of unwelcome truths. Near him, Queen Karak stood poised, her piercing eyes gleaming with cold, calculating intent. She was not startled—she was ready.

Egil's hand hovered near the worn leather strap securing the great axe across his back, fingers flexing as though itching to draw steel. His body coiled like a hunting wolf, taut with readiness, every sense sharp.

He muttered something low in Nordon, his voice rough as grinding stone —words Braddos could not translate, but their meaning rang clear in the charged stillness. Trouble.

Without another word, the two warriors pressed forward through the dispersing crowd, slipping into the restless tide of nobles, merchants, and soldiers flooding the grand reception hall.

Braddos and Egil surged through the throng like hunting hounds unleashed, their broad shoulders cutting an unyielding path through the disoriented masses spilling from the feasting hall. The vast reception hall stretched before them, lit by flickering sconces whose trembling flames cast fractured shadows across the gleaming marble floor, turning every moving figure into something spectral and uncertain.

The air crackled with tension—sharp, electric, and suffocating. Raised voices barked harsh commands, blending into a chaotic symphony of urgent footfalls, panicked gasps, and the scrape of shifting steel. The towering stone columns loomed like silent sentinels, amplifying every sound into a dissonant echo.

Suddenly, a violent clang of steel meeting steel sliced through the noise—a brutal, ringing impact that reverberated off the stone like a bell tolling doom. A heartbeat later came a guttural roar of defiance, raw and primal, silencing the chaos for one breathless instant.

"Malament!" Braddos hissed, recognition striking like a blade to the gut.

His pulse thundered in his ears, adrenaline searing through his veins. His hand shot instinctively to the hilt of his sword, fingers tightening around the worn leather grip as they closed in on the source of the clash.

Beside him, Egil let out a harsh, guttural Nordon curse, his grey eyes blazing with fierce intent. No orders were needed—only action.

Without another thought, they broke into a full sprint. Boots thundered against the marble floor, scattering startled servants and stunned guards like leaves before a gale. Every step drove them closer to the heart of the unfolding chaos... the Clash of Steel.

They rounded the next towering pillar just in time to see Malament collapse to one knee, his breath ragged and shallow, his sword hanging limply from trembling fingers. Blood darkened his tunic, pooling beneath him like a spreading shadow.

Towering above him, axe raised high, was Konan. The Nordon warlord loomed like a living storm, his eyes blazing with savage purpose. His axe, slick with blood and gleaming cruelly in the flickering torchlight, seemed forged for destruction itself-unstoppable, brutal, deadly. Every inch of him radiated violent inevitability, as merciless as an avalanche crashing down a mountainside.

"NO!" Braddos bellowed, his voice tearing through the hall like a thunderclap.

He hurled himself forward, reckless and unyielding, his sword flashing in a desperate arc. Steel met steel with a deafening CRASH, the impact erupting in a cascade of angry sparks.

The collision drove through Braddos like a battering ram. His teeth clenched against the searing pain as his arms locked under the crushing weight of Konan's brutal strike. The force alone should have broken him, but he stood firm-had to stand firm. His legs buckled but did not yield. His boots skidded across the slick marble floor, leaving scuffed lines carved by sheer will and desperation.

Konan snarled, his grip iron-tight, forcing Braddos lower with relentless power. Every muscle in Braddos's body burned with strained effort, his arms trembling from the impossible weight pressing down. His breath came in harsh gasps, but still, he held.

Not for honour. Not for pride. For Malament.

With a defiant roar, Braddos surged upward, shoving against the descending axe with every ounce of strength left in his body. For one blinding instant, the tide held-balanced between life and death, steel grinding against steel.

The hall erupted in a thunderstorm of drawn steel as Borlong soldiers surged into the fray, swords gleaming like jagged lightning under the flickering torchlight. Boots pounded against marble, forming a defensive line between the fallen Malament and the towering Nordon warlord.

Malament lay crumpled on the blood-slick floor, gasping for air, fingers still weakly clutching his blade as though sheer will alone kept him tethered to the fight. His breath rasped painfully, sharp and shallow.

Braddos did not lower his sword, though his chest heaved with exertion, his muscles screaming from the strain of defying Konan's brutal strike. His voice, raw and edged with unyielding defiance, sliced through the charged air.

"Stand down!"

Konan's dark, storm-tossed eyes burned with fury, wild and unrelenting—a predator denied its kill. His axe remained poised, its blood-streaked edge glinting hungrily in the wavering firelight. For a fleeting, harrowing moment, it seemed he might surge forward, uncaring of the swords now aimed at his chest.

But then his gaze swept over the ranks of Borlong soldiers blocking his path—resolute, unwavering, their swords gleaming like a wall of defiance. His lip curled in disdain, but there was calculation in his stillness, the mind of a warrior weighing the cost of blood.

Braddos held his ground, arms trembling from exhaustion but blade steady, every fibre of his being braced for the next strike. The Borlong soldiers closed ranks tighter around Malament, their faces grim with readiness.

A sudden, heavy thud echoed across the hall as more Nordon warriors stormed in, their own weapons drawn and glinting with cold intent. They flowed like a tidal surge behind Konan, forming an opposing wall of steel and muscle.

And then—Egil.

He moved without hesitation, slipping into formation among his Nordon kin, his axe gripped tight, shoulders squared. His eyes met Braddos's across the brutal divide—porcelain-hard, filled with unspoken desperation.

For an instant, neither of them breathed. No words passed, but the weight of what lay between them—duty, loyalty, and something far deeper—

settled like iron chains. Brotherhood forged in fire now held by the thin, fraying thread of fate.

Konan's gaze lingered on Braddos's blade, then swept over the grim-faced Borlong soldiers forming a defensive line. Slowly, deliberately, the warlord lowered his axe, though his grip remained firm, knuckles bone-white against the worn leather haft. His expression stayed carved from stone, simmering with contempt barely held in check by cold calculation.

With a sharp, guttural command in Nordon, Konan stepped back, his boots grinding against the blood-slick marble with a slow, deliberate scrape. Like a pack of wolves responding to their Alpha's call, the Nordon warriors shifted into formation with deadly precision, blades gleaming like exposed fangs.

There was no drunken brawling swagger now—only the silent, brutal grace of seasoned killers. Their swords, axes and hammers hung low but ready, hands steady, bodies coiled like predators held on a fraying leash. Every breath they took seemed measured; each step calculated for violence. They were men forged in the crucible of war—scarred, relentless, utterly lethal.

Across the marble, Borlong soldiers mirrored their readiness, their weapons held high and unwavering. Their stances radiated defiant determination—willing to die where they stood, if it came to that. Behind them lay their fallen lord, wounded but alive—a living reminder of what they fought to protect.

Braddos kept his sword raised, its blade still trembling faintly from the brutal clash moments before, though his grip remained iron tight. His breath burned in his chest, but he ignored it, his gaze locked on Konan's every calculated move.

Then, his eyes found Egil once more, standing resolute in the front Nordon rank, axe at the ready, his expression fierce yet unreadable.

For an agonizing heartbeat, the hall hung in breathless silence—thick with unspoken threats and promises of blood. The torchlight trembled, shadows writhing like restless spirits awaiting the carnage to come.

Konan's voice rumbled low, steady; each word sharpened to a cruel edge as he spoke in his native Nordon tongue:

"Þú ert dauðr. Ek mun fylgja blóði þínu til enda."

*'You are dead. I will follow your blood to the end.'*

The words hung in the charged air like a death sentence, cold and inescapable. His dark eyes burned with savage promise, unwavering despite the gathering soldiers before him. This was not a threat—it was destiny declared.

Braddos met his gaze without flinching, his blade still raised, steady despite the searing ache in his muscles. He spat to the side, defiance burning in his own glare. "Borlong... Möttur."

The words rang out like a challenge, fierce and undeniable—Borlong Strength. Not just a defiant boast, but a declaration of unyielding will.

For a heartbeat, the hall was still balanced on the knife's edge of violence.

A growl rippled through the Nordon ranks, low and primal, their hands tightening around axe handles and sword hilts. Their blood sang for battle, their eyes flashing with raw, unrestrained fury at Braddos's audacity. They shifted forward, predatory and purposeful, like wolves ready to strike at their leader's unspoken command.

Konan's eyes narrowed, flicking toward his warriors—not to stop them, but to consider. His lips twisted into something between amusement and contempt. The line between restraint and slaughter stretched thinner than a drawn blade.

Steel glinted, hearts pounded, and for a single, breathless instant, the hall seemed to shudder beneath the weight of impending bloodshed.

# BORLONG'S BANQUET
# CHAPTER FORTY NINE

The hurried echo of booted steps ricocheted off the cold stone walls as Lord Malum stormed through the shadowed corridor, his dark cloak billowing behind him like an omen. The distant clash of metal still rang faintly in his ears, sharp and accusing, driving him forward with grim purpose. As he rounded the final corner, the vast expanse of the grand reception hall unfurled before him—and he froze.

Two opposing lines stood locked in a brutal, breathless standoff less than ten paces apart. Blades gleamed like sharpened fangs in the flickering torchlight, held steady in calloused hands primed for slaughter. Tension crackled between them, fierce and alive, as though the air itself braced for the inevitable onslaught.

On the right stood the warriors of Nordon, grim and uncompromising, their faces chiselled from stone and weathered by countless battles. Their forms loomed like an advancing tide held just at bay, muscles taut, weapons gripped with the lethal patience of seasoned killers.

At their forefront towered Konan. His war axe, still slick with blood, rested low but ready—its brutal edge gleaming with cruel purpose in the trembling torchlight. Every line of his scarred, battle-hardened frame radiated lethal calm, violence tempered only by the cold precision of a warlord who killed when he chose, not by impulse.

His storm-dark eyes swept across the Kadun soldiers like a blade drawn slow, filled with simmering disdain. There was no rage there—only calculating certainty. One wrong move, one breach of the fragile, fraying truce—and he would not stop.

To the left stood the soldiers of Kadun, tense but resolute. Their light armour bore faint scuffs of wear—symbols of readiness, not of war. Their polished steel caught the flickering torchlight, glinting with a deceptive sheen of invulnerability, though none among them felt it.

Their swords remained steady, unwavering despite the brutal, battle-hardened warriors glaring back. Each soldier gripped their weapon with white-knuckled determination, knowing full well they faced men who lived for war—killers forged in blood and iron.

At their backs lay Malament. His face streaked with blood, his form crumpled on the polished marble floor, chest rising and falling in shallow, broken gasps. His fingers still curled weakly around his fallen sword, as though even in defeat he clung to its familiar weight-a soldier's last act of defiance. His tunic was soaked with dark crimson, a blood-streaked trail marked the floor where he had been dragged behind the Kadun line. He was wounded... but alive, for now.

Malum's breath hitched, his chest tightening with a cold, suffocating dread. For one shattering moment, he did not see the bloodied, battered commander his son had become-but the boy he had once been. Eager. Headstrong. His. The memory struck like a dagger, sharp and unforgiving.

Fear surged through Malum-not the fear of his own survival, nor the dread of lost power, but the primal, bone-deep terror of a father watching his child teeter on the edge of death. His hands trembled before he clenched them into rigid fists, forcing control over the rising panic threatening to consume him. He could not afford weakness.

Then he noticed just beyond the two hostile lines, just within the torches' wavering reach, lay a motionless corpse-its features shattered and bloodied beyond recognition. Someone's son... someone's father... someone whose life had already been claimed by the violence left unchecked. The next body would be Malament's if this continued.

Malum's mind seized the scene, desperate to master the chaos with sheer force of will. There was still a chance to stop this, to pull Malament back from the abyss, to keep the fragile peace from shattering into irreparable war. But if one blade swung, one spark ignited-whether by rage or misstep-it would unleash war... merciless, absolute.

His throat clenched as his gaze snapped toward Konan. The Nordon warlord stood like a storm barely contained, his bloodstained axe hanging low but ready, its edge gleaming like fate itself. His eyes burned cold with brutal intent, not enraged, but calculating... waiting.

Malum knew men like Konan. He had faced them before, commanders forged by war, ruled by cold logic wrapped in the guise of control. If this escalated, no word, no reason, no plea would stop him. The line between battle and massacre had already blurred. One mistake... and there would be no turning back.

A surge of movement from behind Malum drew his attention, a flood of panicked nobles spilled into the reception hall like water breaching a dam. Some fled toward the estate's main exit, their silk draped forms disappearing into the shadows, driven by primal fear. Others lingered at the edges, faces pale with dread yet alight with morbid fascination, drawn by the lure of violence about to unfold. They pressed against the stone pillars and half concealed alcoves, whispering behind trembling hands, their eyes wide and unblinking.

Before Malum could act, a new rhythmic tap of boots echoed behind him, sharp and measured—unyielding as the inevitability they heralded. He did not need to turn. He felt her arrival—cold, commanding, relentless as a coming storm. Queen Karak.

Malum turned to meet her as she emerged from the dimly lit hall like a shadow given shape. She swept onto the scene with measured grace, her dark gown flowing like liquid night, rippling with each deliberate step. Unarmoured, obstinate, unafraid.

Her piercing emerald eyes, cold and calculating, cut across the tense lines of warriors locked in grim readiness. She assessed everything with detached precision, the trembling nobles, the flickering torches, the inches separating steel from steel.

This was no surprise to her. There was no hesitation, no trace of uncertainty. She was not there to witness; she was there to command.

Malum stepped forward, his voice cracking with urgency despite his effort to steady it. "What is the meaning of this, my Queen? Please..." His breath hitched, raw and pleading. "This is madness."

His words hung in the charged air, swallowed by the heavy stillness between the two-armed lines. Desperation bled through his tone—not the desperation of a lord clinging to authority, but of a father standing on the brink of losing his son... and everything.

His eyes locked onto Queen Karak, searching for reason, for mercy—for anything that might stop the coming carnage. No response came.

She stood still, a dark silhouette framed by the flickering torchlight, her expression carved from ice, distant, unreadable, absolute. Her focus fixed on the line of drawn blades, watching and calculating.

Malum's breath quickened as silence pressed down like an iron shroud.

His gaze darted from her to the deadly line of Nordon warriors, their weapons gleaming with cruel intent, then back to his son, broken and bleeding, clinging to life.

Still, she did not move.

Her dark gown flowed like spilled ink against the marble floor, making her seem more wraith than woman. Malum swallowed hard, his throat dry and tight. Fear dug its claws deeper into his chest, cold and merciless. His voice rose again, more frantic now, edged with desperation he could no longer conceal.

"Please!" he implored, taking another shaky step forward. "You have the power to stop this! Say something..."

Yet still, nothing.

The growing stillness gnawed at his resolve. The longer she stood silent, the more his panic twisted into something worse, certainty.

She was waiting... for something.

Malum spun toward his own men, his voice trembling but resolute, fuelled by sheer desperation. "Do not attack!" he commanded; his tone bereft under the weight of rising panic. "Stand down, men!"

His soldiers hesitated, their knuckles white around sword hilts, eyes darting between their fallen lord and the towering Nordon warriors ready to strike. The line wavered but held, their loyalty clashing against the instinct to defend.

Behind him, Queen Karak's focus never wavered, her expression still cold, still calculating. Without turning her head, she spoke—her voice low, sharp, and commanding in the harsh cadence of the Nordon tongue.

"Halda... en verid reid."

*'Hold... but be ready.'*

Her words sliced through the charged air like tempered steel. Instantly, the Nordon warriors stiffened, adjusting their grips, weapons held just shy of deadly purpose. Their breathing slowed, chests rising and falling in measured rhythm, predators held in check, but just.

Malum's pulse thundered in his ears. The thin barrier of restraint stretched to its breaking point, fragile and fraying. “My Queen...” Malum’s voice strained with desperation, his eyes pleading. “My men—they will not attack. I’ve ordered them to stand down.” His attention darted toward Malament’s crumpled form, then back to Queen Karak.

“Please... stop this.” His words came faster now, raw and urgent. “What is the meaning of this? How have we come to this?” His voice faltered, thick with disbelief and growing panic. “How have we fallen so far?”

His fists clenched at his sides as he fought to keep control, his every instinct demanding action while reason held him frozen. His eyes searched hers, desperate for some shred of recognition, of reason.

Queen Karak studied her desperate counterpart with chilling detachment, her eyes steady and unblinking. She watched every twitch of Malum’s trembling hands, every strained breath, every crack in his fraying composure. He stood before her not as a Lord, not as a father, but as a man on the edge, barely holding back the chaos threatening to consume his world.

She let the silence linger, weaponizing it like a drawn blade—letting him feel the weight of her judgment, letting him know he was being measured, tested... and found wanting. Without shifting her gaze from Malum, her voice rang out—cold, commanding, and sharp as winter’s edge.

"Konan..." Her tone carried no urgency, no anger—only expectation. The name alone was a leash pulled taut, iron-willed and absolute.

"Hver er hinn dauði maðurinn?"

*‘Who is the dead man?’*

Her words were calm, almost dispassionate, spoken not with curiosity but with calculated intent—information demanded, not requested. In that moment, she was not a queen seeking answers—she was judging consequences, already weighing lives like pieces on a war-board.

Konan’s grip tightened on the haft of his war axe, his storm-dark eyes never leaving the Kadun soldiers. His voice rumbled low, harsh, and devoid of emotion as he answered in his native tongue:

"Heimskingi, sem hugsaði sér að sigra mig. Ek veit ekki hver hann er. Hann og sveinninn börðust þegar ek kom."

*'A fool who thought he could best me. I do not know who he is. He and the boy were fighting before I arrived.'*

His tone carried neither remorse nor pride—just fact, cold and infinite, as though the dead man's fate had been inevitable from the moment he had dared to raise a blade.

Queen Karak's lips curved into the faintest, knowing smile—not of amusement, but of strategy. Her eyes gleamed with cold calculation as she turned her attention back to Malum, her expression serene, almost... sympathetic.

Her voice softened, smooth as velvet drawn over steel.

"Konan says... Malament and the dead man were fighting." She let the words linger, letting their weight settle like a blade pressed just shy of flesh. "He stepped in to aid your son... but they turned on him."

Her focus hardened, sharp and cutting. "He only defended himself."

The hall seemed to tighten around her words, silence pressing in like drawn breath before a killing stroke. There was no accusation in her tone —only cold, undeniable truth, carefully crafted to shift her narrative and the balance of guilt.

Malum's brow furrowed, confusion rippling across his strained features. His gaze snapped back toward Malament's crumpled form, still gasping weakly on the blood-slick floor. His mind raced, struggling to piece together the fractured puzzle Karak had laid before him. Aid...?

His eyes drifted toward the dead man, the shattered, unrecognizable corpse sprawled beyond the ranked men, soaked in crimson. If Konan had helped Malament, why was he still so gravely injured? Why had no one called for him sooner? The pieces refused to align, slipping like sand through trembling fingers.

"My son..." Malum's voice trembled, caught between disbelief and dawning dread. "He... he wouldn't..." The story felt wrong, twisted in ways he could not quite grasp. He knew Malament could be reckless, perhaps, but not this. He would not have turned on an ally, not in the heat of battle. His chest tightened further as he tore his focus away from Queen Karak, her calm, unrelenting composure gnawing at the edges of his mind. Facing toward the broken figure lying crumpled on the marble floor. Malament, his son. His breath calmer now, his senses seemingly sharper.

“Son...” He swallowed hard, fighting the knot in his throat. “Is this true? Were you... fighting this man?” The words trembled under the weight of unbearable hope, that Malament could explain, that there was some truth beyond this twisted, blood-soaked nightmare. He needed an answer... needed it to make sense.

Malum searched his son’s battered face, praying for recognition, for something—anything—that would unravel the tangled web of accusations closing in around them.

Their eyes locked for the first time, Malament spat a thick, crimson stream of blood onto the cold marble, the sickening splatter echoing through the tense silence. A string of dark red clung to his split lip before snapping loose. His breath hitched in ragged gasps, but it was not pain that twisted his features, it was disgust.

His bloodshot eyes focused on his father, burning with venomous hatred. His voice, hoarse but seething with defiance, tore through the hall. "Yes, it's the truth... Father." The word dripped with contempt, as though it hurt him to say it.

Horror flashed across Malum's face, twisting his sharp features into something hollow and stricken. His mind reeled, clawing for an explanation that might make sense, something that might fix this before it spiralled further out of control.

"Why, Malament?" His voice addled, raw and pleading. "Why?"

Malament's teeth clenched as he shoved himself upward, forcing his trembling body to obey. His blood-slick fingers tightened around the hilt of his fallen sword, driving its tip into the marble with a sharp scrape as he pushed himself to his feet. He staggered, dizziness clawing at the edges of his mind, but he refused to fall.

A nearby soldier reached out instinctively, steadying him. Malament shoved the man's hand away, planting his feet with stubborn defiance. His chest rose and fell in ragged gasps as he fought to stay upright, every muscle trembling from exhaustion, yet his eyes... His eyes were steady. Blazing with pure, undiluted hatred. Directed at Malum.

"This is your fault," Malament hissed, his voice a low, venomous snarl. "All of it."

He raised his sword, its edge trembling slightly, not from uncertainty but from sheer, exhausted rage. With heavy, laboured steps, he advanced toward his father, his glare locked.

Malum staggered back, heart pounding in a way it had not in years. This was no reckless outburst, this was execution. He could feel it in the lethal intent radiating from his son's every tortured step.

"What is the meaning of this, Malament?" he demanded, his voice rising with both fear and desperate authority. "Still yourself!"

But Malament's advance did not slow. His knuckles wrapped round the hilt of his blade with intent, every breath drawn with painful purpose. His free hand clutched his broken ribs, as though sheer will alone could hold him together. His battered frame sagged to one side, his shoulders hitching with every strained inhale-but still... he came forward. Heavy steps, uneven, yet resolute, each dragging footfall echoing through the silent hall like a death knell. There was no hesitation in his blazing, hate-filled gaze. No plea for reason. No search for mercy. Only judgment. Only reckoning.

From sheer panic, Malum's voice broke as he barked, "Seize him!" Kadun soldiers surged forward but froze just as abruptly when Malament stopped.

He planted his feet, steadying his battered form despite the agony wracking his broken ribs. Blood seeped from his fractured nose, streaking his face with dark red. His blood-slick hands tightened around his sword's hilt, gripping it in both hands-ready. Not as a soldier prepared for battle, but as a man standing at the edge of his final reckoning.

His hate-filled glare burned into Malum, sharp enough to cut through steel, unyielding even as fresh blood trickled from the corner of his mouth. His next words spilled from his lips, raw and venomous, driven by more than rage, by betrayal.

"This is your fault," Malament snarled, his voice fierce. "You had an assassin enter our home... to kill Auron." The accusation struck like a thunderclap with brutal finality.

"You lied! You kept lying-hiding your tracks... pretending it never happened!" His breath hitched, seething through clenched teeth. "He is a boy, Father!" Each word cut deeper than any blade.

The weight of the truth crashed over Malum like a breaking wave, leaving him stricken. His throat clenched, his chest hollowed by a sudden, crushing ache. His mind reeled, scrambling for reason, denial, anything-but nothing came. His lips parted, but no words followed. His voice-his power-deserted him. He could not speak.

A low murmur rippled through the gathered crowd like a brewing storm, sharp whispers weaving through the hall like threads of fire. The nobles heard—all of them. Their wide, calculating eyes gleamed with the thrill of scandal, mouths half-hidden behind trembling hands as they exchanged hurried, breathless words.

An assassin... a boy... treachery within the estate...

The air thickened with tension; every word laced with dangerous potential. The scent of spilled blood no longer dominated the hall—it was the stench of opportunity. And at the heart of it all... her.

Queen Karak's gaze sharpened with quiet triumph, though her expression remained coldly composed. She stood still, her dark gown a flowing shadow against the gleaming marble, her presence as still and inevitable as an oncoming tide. She needed no words, no commands. This moment was already hers. The truth no longer mattered; it was perception that would shape what came next. And now... everyone had heard.

Malum's fortress was crumbling. Her fingers curled ever so slightly at her side, the faintest flicker of satisfaction gleaming in her penetrating green eyes. Let them whisper. Let the flames of doubt and treason spread unchecked. Let him drown in what he could no longer contain.

# BORLONG'S BANQUET
# CHAPTER FIFTY

Auron had never been welcome at the feasts. He told himself it did not matter, he was not meant for such places, but deep down, the sting of exclusion lingered like a thorn he could not quite pull free. The grand dining hall, with its towering archways and glittering chandeliers, seemed like something out of a fireside tale, a world of velvet-clad nobles and jewelled goblets, dazzling yet unreachable. It belonged to them, the lords and ladies who moved with effortless grace through its gilded expanse.

He, however, remained on the edges, an unnoticed shadow skirting the borders of grandeur, forever looking in but never stepping across the threshold.

The first few nights, he had stayed in his new chamber, a modest yet tasteful room within the estate. The walls were smooth stone, softened by woven tapestries depicting distant forests and noble hunts. A sturdy wooden bed with a thick woollen blanket sat beneath a high, arched window framed by heavy drapes. A small writing desk and a polished oak chest rested near the far wall, their craftsmanship plain but refined.

Yet he lay there, listening to the distant hum of revelry drifting through the stone walls. Laughter rang out like cruel mockery, while the haunting notes of unfamiliar songs twisted through the dark, tugging at a hollow place deep inside him. Sleep evaded him, driven away by restless thoughts and the ache of loneliness he could not quite admit, not even to himself. It was not the feast he longed for, but something real, something that made the emptiness retreat.

Drawn by that need, on the fourth night he slipped quietly into the kitchens. At first, he lingered at the edges, unnoticed, his sharp eyes wide with wonder. There was something magical about the kitchens. The air was thick with the rich scents of baking bread and spiced stew, wrapping around him like a protective cloak. The warmth from roaring hearths drove out the chill clinging to his skin and soul alike. Life thrummed with purpose, knives thudded against cutting boards, pots hissed over crackling flames, and hurried voices wove together into a familiar, comforting rhythm.

Before he knew it, he was scrubbing cutlery and stacking plates, working alongside the bustling staff as if he'd always been meant to be there. His hands moved with eagerness, soothed by the familiar repetition. No one shooed him away or questioned his presence, there was too much work to care where help came from.

For that first time Auron felt... useful. Now here, surrounded by noise, heat, and purpose, he was not just a forgotten boy in a nobleman's estate. He was part of something real, something alive.

Tonight was no different. Auron stood at the heavy stone sink, arms plunged into hot, soapy water as he scrubbed dishes until his fingers wrinkled and a dull ache settled in his wrists. The sharp scent of lye stung his nose, mixing with the lingering aromas of roasted venison, fresh-baked bread, and the faint tang of spilled wine. Steam rose in gentle wisps, curling through the dimly lit kitchen, wrapping him in warmth despite the chill that clung stubbornly to the estate's old stone walls.

He worked in steady rhythm, letting the familiar scrape of brush against ceramic and the quiet splash of water lull his restless thoughts. The repetitive motion dulled the ache in his chest, another night spent on the edges, unnoticed and forgotten, far from the grand feasting hall and its distant world of light and laughter.

A heavy hand landed on his shoulder, firm but not harsh. Auron flinched instinctively, heart skipping a beat, before glancing up. It was Quinn. The head cook's thick, calloused arms were crossed over a flour-streaked apron, his face lined and weathered like old leather but softened now by something that almost resembled approval.

"Good work, lad," Quinn rumbled, voice rough but steady, carrying a quiet weight that made Auron straighten just a little taller. "Not many your age know how to pull their weight without bein' told."

Auron squared his shoulders under the rare praise. "Figured you needed the help," he said, wiping his damp hands on his trousers. "Didn't want to sit 'round doin' nothing."

Quinn grunted, half a chuckle, half a growl. "World's full of folks sittin' 'round doin' nothin'. But not you, eh?" He jabbed a finger at a stack of grimy pans. "Finish those off, and maybe I'll see about savin' you a slice of that poached pear, if the lords haven't devoured it yet."

Auron's eyes lit up with something more than hunger. "Thanks, Quinn."

"Don't thank me till you've earned it," the cook shot back, already turning toward the roaring hearth. "And don't dawdle, those pans won't clean themselves."

With renewed purpose, Auron plunged his hands back into the soapy water, scrubbing harder than before, fuelled not just by hunger, but by the strange, warming satisfaction that came from being noticed... from being needed. The ache in his arms faded into the steady rhythm of work, each plate leaving his hands gleaming and spotless. He stacked the freshly cleaned dishes onto the growing pile at his right, their smooth surfaces cool against his damp fingers.

A sudden movement caught his eye. A maid hurried past, balancing a tray with practiced ease, her delicate hands moving with graceful precision. She paused only briefly, scooping up the plates with a murmured, absent "thank you," her attention already fixed on her next task.

Something about her struck Auron, the soft wave of her auburn hair, catching the firelight in coppery glints, and the way she carried herself with quiet purpose, head held high despite the rush around her. For a fleeting moment, she reminded him of Lady Amelia, not in appearance, but in presence. There was the same calm determination, the same quiet strength beneath the surface.

He watched her disappear through the main kitchen entrance, vanishing into the shadows of the corridor beyond. The thought lingered longer than he expected, stirring something bittersweet in his chest, something he could not quite name. For a moment, he strained to hear her fading footsteps, but the relentless clatter of pots and busy kitchen workers quickly drowned them out. With a quiet breath, he shook the feeling away and reached for another stack of plates, letting the rhythm of the work pull him back into the present.

A sudden, violent crash shattered the familiar rhythm of the kitchen, the sound of breaking ceramic splitting the air like a lightning strike. Auron's head snapped up, heart pounding as his hands shot from the soapy water, droplets scattering across the worn stone floor. The crash reverberated through the kitchen, cutting through the clatter of pots and hiss of boiling stew, plunging the space into a stunned, breathless silence.

For a moment, nothing moved, only the lingering echo of destruction. Then footsteps. Not the steady, purposeful strides of a servant but frantic, uneven pounding, growing louder with each desperate step.

The same maid burst through the kitchen entrance; her tray long forgotten. Her face was pale and twisted with panic, breath coming in ragged, shallow gasps. Terror burned in her wide, tear-filled eyes as she stumbled toward the centre of the room, clutching the front of her apron as though it could somehow shield her from whatever horror she had fled.

"They... they're fighting!" she gasped, her voice trembling with desperation, tears streaking her flushed cheeks.

Quinn's face darkened, his brow furrowing deeply. He strode forward, looming over her like a fortress of iron and muscle. "Who?" he demanded, his voice sharp and unyielding, cutting through the chaos like a blade.

"The Nordon men... and Lord Malament!" she sobbed, clutching the front of her apron with trembling hands. "They—there's blood... they'll kill him!"

Quinn swore viciously under his breath, his fists clenching. "Damn fools!" He spun toward the scattering kitchen staff. "Get out! Move, all of you! Use the back entrance!"

Panicked servants scattered like startled birds, chairs scraping and pots crashing as they fled toward the back exits. The air pulsed with urgent shouts and the clatter of overturned cookware. Quinn whirled back to Auron, who stood frozen, fists clenched, his young face pale but rigid with fierce determination. His chest rose and fell in shallow breaths, but he did not move, he would not run.

"Come on, lad!" Quinn barked; his voice rough but edged with concern. "We've no business near that fight—let the guards handle it."

Auron shook his head sharply, defiant. "I'm not leaving him." His voice trembled, but his eyes blazed with something far stronger than fear.

Quinn's mouth tightened, frustration twisting into reluctant respect. "Don't be a fool, you'll get yourself killed."

"Maybe," Auron shot back, already taking a step toward the hall. "But maybe I can help."

Quinn swore under his breath, raking a calloused hand down his face. "You're bloody mad," he growled.

Before he could stop him, Auron spun on his heel and bolted toward the grand hall, vanishing into the darkened corridor without a backward glance. Quinn stood there, breathing hard, watching helplessly as the boy disappeared into the fray.

"Damned if you aren't braver than half the men I've known," he muttered, turning grimly back toward the remaining staff. "Get moving—now!"

Breathing hard, Auron surged toward the main hall, where the maid had fled. His boots crunched over shattered ceramic, the jagged shards of countless plates glittering like broken bones beneath the flickering torchlight. The destruction stretched ahead, a path of chaos etched into the dim corridor, shimmering faintly as if marking the way toward something far more dangerous.

At the corridor's end, wavering torchlight spilled weakly into the vast, open expanse beyond, where the grand reception hall loomed like a dark, yawning abyss. Shadows writhed across the shattered marble floor, dark silhouettes darting between overturned tables, broken furniture, and torn banners hanging limp like defeated standards. The air reeked of spilled wine and something far more bitter, fear.

A sudden crash split the suffocating stillness, a heavy table overturned, goblets and shattered plates scattering like fallen debris from a lost battle. Panicked bodies surged toward him in a frenzied tide, maids clutching their skirts, nobles stumbling past with wide, terrified eyes. The chaos was suffocating, pressing in from all sides. Auron gritted his teeth, planting his feet against the surge. He would not be swept back.

He forced his way through the crush, shouldering past a pair of fleeing servants, breath hitching as dread coiled tighter in his chest. Every instinct screamed for him to turn back, to run, but he pressed on, driven by something stronger than fear. Then he heard it, cutting through the noise like a blade drawn from its sheath, fierce, commanding, unmistakable. Malament's voice.

His breath hitched, resolve hardening into something sharper, stronger. Whatever was happening, he needed to see it. Needed to understand. He broke free of the frantic mass, stepping into the cavernous grand hall and there at the heart of the chaos stood Malament, his eyes blazing with fury. Auron's breath stilled, his pulse hammering in his chest. He might have been young, but he understood enough.

This was not just a fight. It was war.

Without a second thought, Auron sprinted toward Malament, his feet pounding against the slick marble floor. Fear clawed at his chest, but he shoved it down, letting raw determination fuel his every step. He was not a soldier, nor was he strong-but Malament had saved him more than once. Now it was his turn.

# BORLONG'S BANQUET
# CHAPTER FIFTY ONE

Malament stood defiant, his breath ragged but steady, framed by the harsh flicker of torches lining the cavernous hall. His men loomed at the edges, their loyalty tested, fingers twitching round the hilts of their swords. His father's face, pale and twisted with fear, betrayed a lifetime of buried regret surfacing in one agonizing instant.

The Nordon warriors stood like statues carved from ice, their brutal stillness promising death with the faintest movement. Konan's towering frame loomed among them, carved from iron and stone, his massive hands clenched purposefully around the weathered shaft of his axe. Its dark-stained blade still reeked of blood-Luka's blood. The memory tore through Malament's mind, the savage arc of the axe, Luka's lifeless body crumpling to the floor, and Konan's expression cold, merciless, unmoved by the life he had just extinguished. Hatred burned hot and relentless in Malament's chest, searing through his veins like molten iron.

Queen Karak watched on, detached and regal, a faint, knowing smirk curling her lips—predatory, patient, victorious. Her sharp, calculating gaze lingered on the unfolding chaos with the satisfaction of a master strategist admiring the final move of a well-played game. Konan's brutal revelations echoed in Malament's mind, each truth cutting deeper than any blade.

It all started to make sense now. The carefully threaded web of lies, the manipulated fates—every misstep, every betrayal—woven together by cunning far beyond his father's feeble grasp. Malament's hands trembled on the hilt of his sword, his breath coming in harsh, ragged gasps as realisation sank its claws into his chest.

His father... that man. The one who had raised him, commanded him... failed him. A hollow shell draped in the tattered remains of power, blind to the venomous treachery festering under his very roof. The lies. The manipulation. His father's hand, bloody and undeniable, in the attempt on Auron's life.

His breath hitched, raw and sharp. Rage burned through his chest, searing away the last vestiges of hope that the man he had once obeyed, once trusted, had ever been worthy of the title "father." There was no redemption, only betrayal. Malament's mind reeled, the final pieces falling into place with brutal clarity.

The weight of that truth crushed down on Malament's shoulders, filling him with a violent, consuming hatred that roared through his veins like wildfire. His fingers tightened around his sword's hilt, trembling from the force of his grip. He could almost feel his father's throat beneath his hands, fragile and breakable.

The face he had once sought approval from became the face of everything he despised—weakness, cowardice, and unforgivable failure.

His vision blurred with rage, the hall fading into a haze of flickering torchlight and dark shadows. This ends now. He would not be his father's pawn, not anymore. He would tear down the legacy of lies his father had built, even if it left nothing but ashes in its place.

"I'll kill you... if it's the last thing I do," he growled, his words raw with fury, stripped of all pretence. With a feral snarl, he surged forward, every shred of willpower igniting into a reckless, desperate charge-fuelled by hatred, despair, and the hollow promise of vengeance.

Malum stood frozen, a portrait of fear etched in sharp, unforgiving lines —his eyes wide, his lips parted as though gasping for words that would not come. His authority, once dominating, seemed to crumble beneath the weight of inevitability. The men of Kadun hesitated, their loyalty stretched taut between father and son, blades drawn but unmoving, caught in the fatal gravity of blood and betrayal.

The Nordon warriors remained statuesque, cold and unyielding as the weapons they carried. Their expressions betrayed neither curiosity nor concern, they were spectators in a deadly game, bound only to Karak's will, ready to strike or stand at her command.

Malament's knuckles clenched around the hilt of his sword, muscles coiled like a drawn bowstring ready to unleash deadly precision. Every scar, every betrayal, every drop of blood spilled surged through him, narrowing his world to this one inevitable moment—a final reckoning. Sword raised, his fury outweighing his wounds, the distance closed.

But then a sudden, slight movement pierced the haze of rage clouding his mind. A small figure broke through the ring of stunned nobles, slipping through the shifting mass of onlookers with desperate purpose, Auron. Dark hair clung damply to his forehead, his thin chest rising and falling in shallow, panicked breaths. His wide, searching eyes locked onto Malament, freezing at the edge of the bloody chaos.

Malament's breath caught, the all-consuming inferno within him faltering—splintering like shattered stone struck by an unseen blow. His blade wavered, sagging in his trembling grip until its battered tip scraped the cold marble with a hollow, resonant clang—a sharp, lifeless sound swallowed by the cavernous hall.

Pain surged through his battered frame, no longer dulled by adrenaline or fury. His knees buckled, sending him crashing down with a bone-jarring thud. His chest heaved, ragged and uneven, as a flood of emotions broke free—relief that Auron, his charge, his responsibility—still breathing, still here. His fingers loosened their death grip on the sword's worn leather hilt, trembling from exhaustion. His gaze remained locked on the boy, then something fragile, trembling at the edges of his fraying mind. Something dangerously close to hope.

"Auron..." he rasped, the name escaping like a lifeline, grounding him in the one fragile truth left in a world of shattered loyalties and broken promises.

The boy's eyes widened in recognition, his face paling at the sight of Malament's broken, bloodied form. Without hesitation, he started forward to help. But before Auron could close the distance, a roar of fury shattered the fragile stillness.

"YOU!"

The hall trembled beneath Malum's bellow, his voice raw with anguish and desperate blame. His trembling hands clenched into trembling fists, veins bulging in his neck as he stepped toward Auron like a man possessed.

"BY TITAN'S WRATH... THIS IS ALL YOUR DOING!"

Malum's voice thundered through the hall like a divine judgment cast from the gods, vibrating with fury, desperation... and something far darker, guilt. His words echoed off the cold stone walls, leaving a tense, crackling silence in their wake.

Malament knew. There would be no salvation for Auron this time, no desperate rescue from the suffocating depths of the bathhouse, no protective shield against a lash's brutal bite, no thwarted assassin's blade held back by fate or mercy. Those moments had been borrowed victories, stolen from the jaws of inevitability.

But now... now there would be no escape.

His father's fury burned hotter than steel in a forge, blistering and unchecked, fuelled by fear and his own guilt. Malum's world was collapsing, the weight of every past sin crushing down, leaving only reckless, murderous desperation behind. He could not control the unravelling, but he could lash out. He could destroy.

And Malament knew, with an icy certainty settling in his chest, that his father's next act would be his most unforgivable, he would kill Auron. Right here. Right now.

The cold reality crushed what little hope remained. Blood dripped steadily from his trembling fingers, the pain he felt turned into sobering desperation. He had failed. But there was one thing he could still do. One final act. With the last of his failing strength, Malament threw back his head and screamed, his voice raw and desperate, a single word that cut through the roaring chaos like a blade forged from sheer will.

"RUN!"

The hall shook with the force of it, echoing through the towering stone pillars and silencing the stunned, gawking nobles. The command was unmistakable, urgent, unforgiving, final. There could be no mistaking its meaning.

Malament's weight buckled beneath him, his strength spent, his battered frame crumpling to the cold marble floor with a sickening thud. His blood-slicked sword slipped from his grasp, clattering uselessly as his eyes fluttered, still conscious, but fading.

Kadun guards surged forward, their boots pounding against the bloodstained marble. Rough hands seized his failing body, holding him upright as his head lolled forward, breath rasping in shallow, pained bursts.

But Malament's command still echoed through the hall—RUN! And Auron obeyed. His slender frame darted through the tangled mass of startled nobles, slipping between flowing cloaks like a hunted shadow. His feet hammered against the cold stone, driving him deeper into the yawning darkness of the hall, away from the searing hatred that burned behind him.

He did not look back. Behind him, a savage roar erupted, raw and inhuman, fuelled by rage, fear, and vengeance.

"SEIZE THAT BOY!"

Lord Malum's voice tore through the hall like a thunderclap, his face twisted in a mask of unrestrained fury. His outstretched hand trembled with rage as he pointed toward the retreating figure.

"I WANT HIS CORPSE TONIGHT!"

His words slammed into the still-shocked soldiers like a whip-crack, spurring them into action. Swords flashed in the flickering torchlight as armoured boots thundered in pursuit. The Kadun defensive line fractured, breaking apart like splintered glass as soldiers surged after Auron. Their formation crumbled into chaos, driven by their lord's furious command.

Only a dozen remained. They lingered uncertainly near Malum, eyes flicking between their fallen commander, Malament, and the towering wall of Nordon warriors still standing ready. Their breath came sharp and shallow, tension vibrating through their rigid stances—waiting.

Konan had not moved.

He stood silent at the head of the Nordon line, his bloodstained axe hanging loosely in one hand. His expression remained cold and unreadable, but his dark eyes gleamed with calculation. He was waiting, watching, every twitch of muscle, every faltering breath measured and weighed.

Behind him, his warriors remained unshaken, their weapons still raised—not as a threat, but as a promise. The balance of power had shifted. And Queen Karak's smile curved slowly, revealing a singular emotion—not joy, not amusement—but victory, cold and absolute.

The battle… had been won. Without a single drop of Nordon blood spilled.

Her eyes flicked toward Konan, whose hand still rested lazily on the haft of his war axe, though he had not moved a muscle. He gave a faint, almost imperceptible nod—a silent acknowledgment of shared purpose.

With deliberate grace, Queen Karak turned toward Malum, her expression void of mercy, sharp as tempered steel. Her dark gown whispered against the bloodstained marble as she closed the distance between them, each step measured, absolute.

Her voice rang out cold and unyielding, clear enough for everyone to hear. "I made fair terms last moon phase." Her words sliced through the breathless stillness like a blade drawn slow. "You dishonoured me by ignoring them."

She stepped closer, her focus locked menacingly onto Malum's as though weighing his very soul. "Now..." she continued, her tone dropping to something more dangerous, more final. "You will not only honour them... you will double my demand for the same price."

The room tightened with the threat coiling behind her measured voice—a predator speaking with absolute certainty. "There will be no negotiation."

Malum's breath staggered, his chest tightening as though an iron vice had closed around his ribs. The dim torchlight cast harsh, flickering shadows across his ashen face, deepening the lines carved by fear and dawning realization. His gaze shifted, wild and desperate, but there was nowhere left to run, no power left to wield. He was trapped, stripped of authority, a king without a throne... a man without control.

Her next words fell like a death sentence, "you will agree... or you will make an enemy of Nordon." She took one final, deliberate step—close enough for him to feel the icy weight of her promise. "And I swear this, Lord Malum Thalron..." Her voice was a venom-laced whisper now, edged with certainty, power, death. "I will bring a thousand warriors to your gates and burn your rule to ash."

Lord Malum said nothing. The weight of Queen Karak's words pressed down on him like a blade held to his throat—cold, inevitable. His clenched fists trembled at his sides, the nails biting deep into his palms until fresh blood bloomed, but he could not act.

His rage burned hot—furious, helpless, like a caged beast howling against its binds—but even rage had limits. Reality sank in, cold and definite. He was at her mercy. There were no more words, no more bargains, no more moves left to make. The shattered remnants of his power lay scattered around him—his son broken, his men scattered, his control shattered beyond repair.

This was peace... stripped bare, naked, and merciless. Agree... or fall.

Malum lifted his chin, pride still etched into the hard lines of his face, though his eyes betrayed the hollow defeat settling deep within his chest. Slowly, with the weight of a man condemned, he nodded. A silent acceptance.

The Queen's gaze hardened, her eyes burning with fierce intensity. She held Lord Malum in her stare, sharp as tempered steel, her will an immovable force forged in fire and ambition.

Her voice cut through the heavy silence—cold, final, and edged with undeniable authority. "We will take our leave in the morning." She paused just long enough for the weight of her words to settle, each syllable deliberate, precise—measured domination. "Galil and his men will remain for a few days longer to oversee the trade and agreements." Her tone hinted at command, supervision, and control.

Her expression darkened, eyes narrowing as she delivered her final warning, low and venom laced. "You would hope... not to see me again, Lord Malum." Each word dripped with cold certainty—not a threat, but a promise, wrapped in inevitability. She had no need for further posturing; the game had already been played... and won.

With a final, searing glare, Queen Karak turned sharply, her dark gown flowing behind her like a living shadow, disappearing into the dimly lit hall. The heavy weight of her words lingered in the charged air, sharp and suffocating, impossible to shake.

Konan followed in her wake, his blood-stained axe still resting loosely in his massive hand, his dark eyes sweeping the hall one last time. His warriors fell in line without a word—silent, disciplined, and lethal. Wherever she went this night, they would follow—always.

The fading echo of their boots reverberated through the blood-soaked hall, leaving only silence behind, a silence thick with dread, regret, and inevitable consequence.

Lord Malum's fists trembled, veins bulging beneath his pale skin, his jaw clenched so tight it ached. His chest burned with the weight of everything lost... everything shattered. Slowly, his hollow, empty gaze swept across the gathered nobles, still lingering like scavengers over a dying beast, their faces pale but their eyes hungry. He saw the gleaming spark of opportunity, of gossip, of power to seize. Like vultures.

With venom dripping from every word, he spat, "enjoy the show!" His voice lashed out, sharp and vicious. "Go on— do what you always do! Talk. Spread your gossip. Whisper your lies." He took a threatening step toward them, his eyes blazing with cold fury. "Be gone... from my sight."

The nobles flinched, recoiling like startled prey before scattering into the darkened hallways, their whispered murmurs already igniting into rumour and scandal.

Malum stood alone, but for his remaining men and Malament, slumped and broken at his feet. His chest heaved with ragged, shallow breaths, the grand hall stretching before him like an empty battlefield, one he had lost.

His gaze fell upon his son, bloodied, defiant, and unrecognizable. Taking a slow, trembling step forward, his voice low but sharp with accusation. "What have you done?"

Malament lifted his battered face, eyes hollow but clear—the rage that had consumed him burned out, leaving only clarity. "Father..." he rasped, his voice thick with disdain and finality. "You are more a fool than I ever thought possible."

Malum flinched, as though struck but Malament pressed on, his tone growing stronger, sharpened by bitter truth.

"The moment they entered our gates, they were never here for an alliance." He spat blood onto the marble, the crimson smear vivid against the cold stone. "They came to assess. To judge us. We were never a trade partner; we were a rival." His bloodshot eyes burned with defiant conviction as he met his father's stunned gaze. "You look to me, or to Auron, to place the blame but the fault lies at your door."

The silence that followed strangled the air. Malum's fists clenched, trembling with restrained fury, but something else flickered behind his eyes, uncertainty. For the first time... doubt. He stared down at his son, his mind reeling, searching for the reckless boy he had known, but seeing only this stranger, bloodied and unyielding—a man.

His jaw tightened as he forced himself back into control, cold authority wrapping around him like a steel gauntlet. His voice came low, hollow... final, "take him from my sight."

His words fell like a death sentence. "I hear there's a free lodging in the servant quarters..." His tone turned sharp, venomous. "Have him locked there until I decide what to do with him."

Malament's eyes narrowed, but he said nothing—nothing left to say.

Malum fixed his son with one final, searing glare—a look forged from equal parts hatred, betrayal, and the bitter sting of defeat. The traitor. The failure. The one who had shattered the fragile foundation of power he had so carefully built. Malament might have slipped beyond his grasp for now, but there was still one piece left on the board—Auron. He would see the boy's broken body delivered like a cursed gift, the final price Malament would pay for his defiance.

His voice dropped into a low, venomous growl; each word laced with cold, calculated menace.

"You have dishonoured this house... and your country."

The unspoken promise of retribution hung in the air like the edge of a drawn blade, sharp and inevitable.

# BORLONG'S BANQUET CHAPTER FIFTY TWO

Malament's desperate plea reverberated through Auron's mind, a single, searing word, not a warning but a command, carved into his very soul. 'Run.' It was a plea born from love, desperation, and grim inevitability. Auron understood its meaning, not just to escape, but to survive. He would not be broken by this place, would not become another forgotten casualty swallowed by its merciless stone walls.

The guards were in pursuit, their harsh shouts slicing through the dimly lit hall like jagged blades. Their boots hammering against the floor with each stride, the distance close enough to make out their grim expressions.

Auron ran, his memory clawing back to that distant morning on the streets of Borlong, when he had fled like a hunted animal, driven by nothing but desperation. That boy had stumbled, hidden and finally been beaten within an inch of his life.

But he was not that boy anymore. He would not run with blind, aimless terror he once knew. His feet struck the cold stone with steady purpose, each step precise and calculated. Panic did not consume him this time, his thoughts were sharpened into something clear, something useful. His mind assessed every sound, every flicker of torchlight casting dancing shadows along the walls. The faint tang of spilled wine and oil lingered in the air, thick and cloying.

He knew this hall, this estate, from countless stolen adventures, wandering where he shouldn't. Every hidden alcove, every forgotten servant's passage, every blind corner lived in his memory. The estate's winding corridors unfolded in his mind like a well-memorized map.

The guards' heavy boots pounded after him, their clattering greaves betraying their movement but the distance between them was closing. Auron's youthful stamina countered by their longer strides. A pillar loomed in front; its towering frame lurched upwards into the dark. He twisted sharply round it, letting its shadow swallow him whole as he threw his body up against its surface. His breath steadied, quiet, controlled.

The guards were upon him, their breath came heavy and ragged, weighed down by steel and ale. Their swords held tightly, deadly, impending, made for bloody battles, yet became a clunky tool in a chase. Three thundered past, their heavy boots striking the marble with dull, echoing thuds. The pillar shielded Auron from their searching eyes, its cool, worn surface pressing against his back as he held his breath. He waited until their curses turned into confusion as they briefly lost their target before slipping out, every movement silent, deliberate.

Yet there were many more pursuers, a fresh shout rang out sharp and furious from a new group as they spotted his agile silhouette leave the pillar. Auron forgot the lighter footsteps and opened into a sprint toward another pillar, weaving between ancient stone columns like a phantom. Torchlight flickered wildly, shadows stretching and twisting, making it harder for them to track him. His heart pounded, but his mind stayed sharp.

A sudden glint of silver caught his eye, a fallen goblet discarded in the aftermath. Without breaking stride, his hand snapped down, fingers curling around the cold metal. With a powerful flick of his wrist, he hurled the goblet across the hall. It skipped and clattered along the marble floor with a deafening crash, its sharp, echoing sound splitting the darkness.

Several guards spun toward the noise, weapons raised as they charged toward the sound, chasing its misleading echoes. Their snarled shouts tangled with confusion as they surged to the wrong area, oblivious to the watchful presence lingering behind them.

Yet Auron wasted no time. He darted deeper into the shadows, head low, breath steady, legs tinged with exertion. He needed to exit the open space of the hall, lead the guards away if he could and return to reach his chambers on the upper floor. Hidden within his worn chest were parchment-wrapped stores of stolen food, dried fruit, hard bread, cured meats snatched from forgotten platters.

His first precious meals... a lifeline for the days ahead. The streets of Borlong raced to the forefront of his mind, dark and hungry, threatening to reclaim him, but he was no longer the frightened child lost in its twisting alleys. He would not be reduced to scrambling for scraps or hiding from the cruel fists of strangers. This time... he would thrive.

His instincts were sharper, honed by countless trials. He was stronger, faster, far more dangerous than the frightened street boy he had once been. The estate, with all its brutal lessons and silent battles, had done more than shelter him, it had forged him into something unyielding, something resilient. Tempered steel beneath a boy's skin. Whatever came next... he would endure.

Auron pressed himself against another towering pillar, his breath steady despite the thunder of boots echoing through the hall. His sharp eyes tracked a group of guards drawing near, their faces twisted with determination and frustration.

With calculated precision, he stepped into the dim light, ensuring they caught sight of him. Shouts erupted with anger and triumphant tones.

"There he is!"

The guards surged forward like a pack of ravenous wolves, their broad shoulders colliding in their eagerness to seize their elusive quarry.

Auron waited, a single breath stretching into eternity ensuring they committed to the chase.... then moved. With a sharp pivot, he rounded the pillar and shot off into the dark.

The first guard lunged, but his boots skidded on the slick marble, sending him sprawling with a sickening thud. The others collided into him in a tangled heap, limbs thrashing, curses spilling into the air.

Eyes turned to the scene as Auron left in the dark, he kept his pace steady, not reckless, but fast enough to stay beyond reach. His legs yearned for rest, but he pushed through the ache, driven by a fierce, stubborn will.

Yet more guards spotted him from across the hall, bellowing orders as they broke into a ragged sprint. Auron's eyes scanned the dark, up ahead, a wide corridor leading toward the dining hall stretched, its grand archways framed by flickering torchlight. In the distance drunken stragglers still stumbled out, weaving unsteadily with flushed faces and sluggish steps.

Their staggering, unpredictable movements were a perfect hazard no pursuing guard could navigate. Yet for Auron, it was a living labyrinth he could slip through like smoke. Opening his stride into another sprint, he charged toward the drunken crowd, ready to vanish once more into the chaos.

The nobles and merchants were blind to Auron as he glided through their drunken ranks with subtle ease, weaving between staggering bodies with the fluidity of a water slipping through stone. The guards barrelled after him like a charging herd, their numbers growing turning the wide corridor into a bottleneck.

Predictably, chaos erupted. Startled by the sudden assault of sword bearing figures, the drunken nobles cursed and stumbled into one another. Angry shouts turned into heated arguments, and within seconds, the corridor devolved into a mass of flailing limbs and venomous accusations.

Auron did not wait to see how it ended. He had already vanished. Breathing steadily, he followed the winding corridor until it spilled back into the expansive hall. His sharp eyes scanned the vast, familiar space, its polished surface reflecting faint torchlight, distorting it into rippling waves that danced across the walls like restless spirits. Shadows stretched and twisted, clawing at his nerves as muffled shouts echoed distantly, a constant reminder of the hunters prowling nearby. He allowed himself a single breath of relief. He had evaded them... for now.

But the respite was fleeting. He could not afford to linger, the crowd behind him would soon disperse like a breaking wave that would inevitably carry tracking guards in its wake. His vision locked on the staircase fifty paces away, its carved stone frame shrouded in thick shadow. The crimson carpet draped over its steps was barely visible, muted in the dim light. At its base, torchlight pooled and flickered, casting uneven glimmers across the marble floor, a beckoning path that promised escape but whispered danger.

Instinct gripped him like a vice, every nerve on edge, he could run, but running invited eyes... and blades. Cautiously, he began his approach, crouched low, moving with a predator's careful precision. Each step was deliberate, his boots gliding soundlessly across the marbled floor. Auron's pulse thundered in his ears as he slipped closer to the staircase, its frame rising from the gloom like the ribs of some ancient beast.

Suddenly, the silence fractured, a muted clang of steel and the steady, deliberate strike of boots echoed from his right. Auron's pulse surged as dark figures emerged from the gloom, their movements sharp and purposeful. His body tensed instinctively, pressing tightly against the cold stonewall of the hall's edge, letting the shadows consume him, every muscle screaming for stillness. He held his breath, his chest barely rising, as though even the sound of his heartbeat might betray him.

The guards came closer, their swords swaying erratically, the faint glint of steel flashed with each step, casting jagged shadows across the polished floor. The low murmur of their voices, indistinctive yet menacing.

Auron's throat tightened, the stale air catching in his lungs as he fought the urge to exhale. Time stretched unbearably, each footstep a hammer blow to his nerves. He willed himself invisible, a part of the wall, no more significant than the flickering shadows that danced about him.

They passed within meters of him, their forms looming large and imposing as their eyes scanned the space ahead, unaware of how near they brushed against their quarry. As quickly as they had appeared, the guards moved on, their boots fading into the hall's distant depths. Leaving Auron once more cloaked in the heavy veil of shadow.

He dared a shallow breath, his chest heaving silently as his eyes roamed the expanse of the hall. Marble shimmered faintly in the flickering light, the polished floor distorting distant figures like phantoms racing through the haze. Shadows danced erratically on the walls, and the faint murmurs of voices rose and fell like a distant tide.

His vision swept cautiously across the cavernous space, each corner a potential threat, each flicker of movement a new source of dread. He scanned the columns, the alcoves, the staircase, his heart pounding faster with every passing second. And then... he froze. Auron's stomach churned as his breath caught in his throat.

In the dim, flickering light, he saw him. Malament.

Two guards half-dragged, half-supported his battered form, their fists clenched around his arms as if even in defeat, he might still be dangerous. His legs faltered, dragging uselessly, his bloodied head hanging low, strands of damp hair masking his face. His tunic, once regal and precise, hung bloodied, stained, a cruel reminder of his defeat.

Sorrow crashed over Auron like a relentless tide. This was not the Malament he had admired, the man who had taught him strength, pride, and purpose. This was someone broken, stripped of power, dignity, everything. Four more guards flanked grimly around the group, blades drawn, a prison escort, not a rescue. Auron's nails bit into his palms, trembling with helpless frustration. He could not move or act, only watch, every instinct in his body screaming at him to do something.

His breath hitched as they reached the old, weathered door of the servant quarters. The heavy wooden frame creaked open, and without ceremony, they shoved Malament inside, vanishing into the yawning blackness beyond.

The door slammed shut with a resounding finality, the echo reverberating through the hall and then faded into a suffocating silence. Auron stood statuesque though his body trembled, not just from exhaustion, but from the torrent of emotions threatening to break free, fear, anger, and a growing, crushing sense of helplessness. He hadn't just seen Malament taken, he had watched the only person who had ever fought for him, who had given him a glimmer of hope, dragged away like a criminal.

His breath came in uneven shudders, each one feeling like a battle to regain control. His chest tightening with a heavy ache settling there as if his grief were trying to consume him whole. The image of Malament's face, broken in capture, burned behind his eyes. The urge to cry out, to lash out, clawed at him, but he knew it would mean the end.

Swallowing the knot in his throat, Auron knew he had to press on. The shadows clung to him like a second skin, but they offered no true safety. These next crucial steps required stealth, if he could make the stairs without being seen he had a chance. With a final glance around the hall, he pushed off the wall, but fate had other plans.

His boot struck something unseen, another fallen goblet. It skidded across the marble floor, bouncing erratically. The sound was deafening. Each skip and roll echoed through the vast hall like the tolling of a bell, shattering the fragile silence. Auron froze, his body tense, his breath caught in his throat.

The goblet crashed into the nearest pillar halting its progress with a sharp clang. Before it came to rest on the floor beneath its looming presence it spun on its rim, the metallic hum jeering at his stillness, mocking his attempts to remain hidden. It finally stopped, the sound fading into a silence so complete it felt as though the entire hall held its breath.

Auron's heart thundered, his body poised to move, yet unwilling to break the silence first. For a fleeting moment, he thought he might remain unseen. Then hope crumbled.

"Over here!" a shout erupted, sharp and triumphant. Torches swung toward him, their fiery glow illuminating his hunched form. Shadows peeled away as the light engulfed him, leaving him exposed and vulnerable.

Another voice, closer, barked a command. "Get him!"

The air seemed to shift, the oppressive quiet giving way to chaos. Heavy boots pounded against the stone, closing in from every direction. Auron ran, no longer the predator weaving through the darkness, he was the prey under the harsh scrutiny of flickering torches. The guards seemed everywhere, their numbers multiplying with each frantic heartbeat.

The once-vast hall now felt suffocating, the polished marble a stage for his desperate flight. He darted forward, his legs burning with effort, his breath coming in ragged gasps. He was out in the open, the shadows no longer his allies.

The base of the staircase loomed ahead, Auron's only fragile promise of escape. His pulse hammered in his ears as he pushed himself harder, every fibre of his being screaming for him to move faster.

But the guards were too close. As his feet struck the final stretch of the hall, two figures appeared from the side, their silhouettes stark against the flickering light. Auron's eyes widened as one lunged, a burly man with a jagged scar running down his cheek.

The man's hand shot forward, fingers grazing the frayed edge of Auron's tunic. For a sickening moment, it seemed he had him. Auron twisted sharply, his momentum wrenching him free, but the force sent him stumbling. He caught himself on the banister, the cold metal biting into his palm.

"Don't let him get away!" another voice bellowed, rage sharpening every word.

Auron did not look back. Looking back meant slowing down. He spun around the banister and began his ascent, his boots striking the steps in hurried, deliberate strides. His movements were precise, honed by sheer desperation, each step calculated to gain precious seconds.

The scarred guard was on him again, his hand outstretched, mere inches away. Auron's muscles screamed as he lunged upward, skipping steps in fluid motions. His heart thundered in his chest, his breath shallow and ragged, but he did not stop.

The man's fingers clawed at empty air before falling to the carpeted stairs, his frustrated growl blending with the pounding boots behind him.

The staircase was a battleground now. Auron felt the heat of their pursuit, their shouts rising like a storm at his back. Every step seemed heavier, the air growing thinner, the climb endless. The polished banister glimmered faintly, catching the torchlight as he propelled himself upward.

"Cut him off from the top!" a voice yelled below.

Panic stabbed at Auron. He could hear more footsteps echoing above, new threats converging, ready to trap him. His mind raced, calculating his options, his path narrowing with every frantic breath could he jump the banister to the ground level below. It was a high drop now, an error could be fatal, whether that be a bad landing or capture, the risk was too great.

Gritting his teeth up was the only option, he surged forward with renewed determination, his legs burning as he reached the halfway point. The landing above came into view, torchlight spilling over its edge. His sharp eyes caught movement, shadows growing larger, the unmistakable forms of two figures descending the staircase.

Auron's breath caught. Lady Amelia and Galil.

Their laughter drifted down like a cruel reminder of normalcy, entirely unaware of the chaos below. Auron's steps faltered, his body torn between relief and urgency. He could not afford to stop, could not afford to explain, yet he was running straight into them.

Behind him, the guards closed in, their voices a cacophony of threats, the pounding of boots louder than ever. His escape route was crumbling, the fragile promise of the staircase now fraught with dangers. He pushed forward, survival demanded everything of him, even when the odds seemed insurmountable.

Amelia's eyes met Auron's, and for a brief moment, a flicker of genuine happiness softened her features. But then her focus shifted, locking onto the approaching guards in relentless pursuit. Her expression changed, tightening with urgency as her eyes darted back to Auron. No words passed between them, yet everything was said in that fleeting exchange. Auron needed her, desperately. She did not know why, did not know what danger pursued him, but she understood instantly that she had to act. Her choice was made in a heartbeat.

Galil, standing beside her, followed her line of sight, noticing the boy. His expression betrayed nothing but mild annoyance as Amelia's attention drifted from him.

"Galil, stop those men," Amelia said, her voice sharp with urgency, the plea spilling out instinctively.

His brow arched in disinterest, his lips curling in a faint smirk. "Why? They're your soldiers," he replied lazily, as though the situation was beneath his notice.

Auron was no more than four steps away now, his face etched with dread. The guards were not after mere punishment they meant far worse; Amelia could see it in their frantic pursuit. She had no time to explain, no time to argue, and certainly no time for Galil's hesitation. Auron was good, she knew it. Whatever he had done, it did not matter. He deserved better than whatever fate these men intended.

"Galil," she said, her voice dropping to something more desperate, yet dangerously compelling. "Stop those men and meet me in my chambers later. Do that, and your desires will not go unanswered."

Her words laced the air like a forbidden promise, the kind of bait that Galil's drunken mind could not resist. His smirk deepened, shifting from casual disinterest to a glint of calculated hunger. His gaze lingered on Amelia for the briefest moment, the torchlight catching in her golden hair like strands of fire, her poised figure radiating an elegance that only heightened the allure of her offer.

The air between them crackled with the unspoken exchange. In her unwavering expression, he saw not just urgency but sincerity, a silent vow that her offer wasn't a bluff. Galil weighed his options in a heartbeat, his reluctance melting away as a decision formed. With a subtle nod, he turned, his steps heavier now with intent.

Auron surged past them in that fleeting moment, his breath quick, his body trembling with exertion. A twisted smile flickered across Galil's face, equal parts amusement and anticipation. The boy was not his problem, not yet, but the guards barrelling toward them were. Galil faced the oncoming soldiers, his stance widening, his body swaying slightly under the weight of wine and resolve.

As the gap between them narrowed, he took a steadying breath, every muscle coiling in preparation. The torches behind the guards cast their shadows forward, tall and menacing, as though the darkness itself chased Auron. Their eyes locked on the fleeing boy, blind to the obstacle now in their path.

At the last moment, with reckless abandon, Galil launched himself forward. The impact was brutal, a collision of steel and flesh as he threw his weight into the charging men. The lead guard barely had time to raise an arm before Galil slammed into him, their bodies crashing together like a boulder hitting a rushing stream. The second guard stumbled in shock; their footing lost as Galil's momentum carried them all into chaos.

The staircase became a tangle of limbs and curses, their fall a cacophony of clanging swords and muffled grunts. One guard's head struck the banister with a sickening thud, his head snapping back as he collapsed in a daze. Another tried to catch himself on the carpeted steps, but his gauntlet slipped, dragging him into the pile. By the time they reached the bottom, at least ten men were a tangled heap, groaning and disoriented, their weapons scattered across the floor creating a temporary human barrier.

Amelia exhaled sharply, her breath trembling as she steadied herself. Galil had certainly played his part well enough, though the consequences of her promise lingered in the back of her mind. She hoped he would not disturb her slumber tonight, but if he did, perhaps she'd sink another bottle of Borlong Red to dull her senses and her regrets. For now, there were far more pressing matters to attend to. She turned sharply, her gaze snapping back to the staircase, where she spotted Auron reaching its summit.

Without hesitation, she sprinted after him, her dress swishing with each hurried step. Her voice rang out, sharp yet laden with concern. "Auron!"

At the sound of her call, Auron froze mid-stride and spun around to face her, his expression caught between relief and urgency. He could not delay, he knew every second mattered, but he also could not bring himself to ignore her. "Amelia," he said, his voice almost trembling, barely above a whisper. "I... I must go. I must leave this place now."

Amelia reached the top of the stairs, her breathing steady despite the rush. She stopped directly opposite him, her eyes locking onto his. There was no judgment in her eyes, only understanding and something close to desperation. "I understand," she said softly, her tone firm yet gentle. "Come with me, Auron."

Auron hesitated, his eyes darting over her shoulder, searching for any sign of pursuit. He shifted his weight, his instincts screaming at him to keep running, but something in Amelia's tone stilled him. She was not just offering refuge; she was offering trust. "Why?" he managed, his voice strained. "You don't even know what's happened."

Amelia stepped closer, her voice low but steady. "I don't need to know.

What I do know is that you don't deserve whatever fate those men intend for you. Trust me, Auron. Let me help."

The sincerity in her words cut through his panic, but the weight of his predicament was still heavy on his mind. "If they catch me," he said, his voice wavering, "it won't matter. You'll be punished too."

Her lips curved into a faint, almost defiant smile. "Then we'd better make sure they don't catch you." She extended her hand, her gesture unwavering. "Come with me, Auron. I'll get you out of here."

For a moment, Auron stared at her, torn between his instinct to run and the flicker of hope she offered. Her hand, steady and unwavering, felt like an anchor in a storm. With a sharp nod, he made his choice and grasped it tightly, the warmth of her touch grounding him in a way he had not expected.

# BORLONG'S BANQUET CHAPTER FIFTY THREE

Amelia charged through her door without hesitation, ushering Auron inside, but closed it softly behind them, leaning against the solid wood for a moment to catch her breath. Her room was bathed in the gentle glow of candlelight, their warm flickers softened by the cool summer night breeze drifting through the open balcony doors. The air smelled faintly of lavender and the distant pine forest beyond Borlong's walls.

Though the room was shrouded in a dim light, Auron could see enough to marvel at its luxury. The four-poster oak bed, carved with intricate designs was imposing and stately, its canopy of deep green fabric draped elegantly. It was much wider and taller than anything on which he had ever slept. A vast fur-lined rug stretched across the polished wooden floor, softening the space, while a grand hearth, now dormant, seemed to promise comfort and warmth when lit.

Amelia's eyes swept her familiar surroundings, her mind racing. There was no safe place here for him, no obvious hiding spot for someone who would be hunted relentlessly. Her gaze landed on a long-cushioned bench at the foot of her bed, its sturdy oak legs slightly elevated above the floor. "There, under that," she instructed, her voice low but firm.

Auron did not hesitate. He dropped to his knees and slid under the bench, his frame just managing to fit in the narrow space. The gap was small, not even a foot off the floor and his shoulders pressed against the wooden frame to make room. His breath was shallow, his pulse loud in his ears, but he was hidden.

Amelia darted to a large chest at the corner of the room, flipping open the heavy lid in a swift motion. Her hands frantically searched its contents until she pulled out a thick goatskin fur, its dark colour blending with the bench's upholstery. With hurried precision, she draped it over the bench, letting it fall naturally to obscure most of the gap. It did not cover everything, but it did not need to, it looked like it belonged there, just another element of her well-appointed room.

She stepped back, inspecting her work. The fur hung slightly askew, but in the dim candlelight and with the room's opulence as a distraction, it was unlikely anyone would notice. Auron's breathing was steady beneath the bench, his body still as a shadow. Amelia exhaled slowly, her heart still racing.

She crossed to the balcony doors, the cool night air brushing against her skin as she eased them closed. The latch clicked softly, a deliberate choice to leave them unlocked, a silent admission that Auron might yet need an escape. The room fell still, the gentle rustle of the curtains subsiding as the breeze was shut out. Yet the quiet did nothing to ease her nerves. Instead, it pressed against her, heavy and suffocating, filling the space with an oppressive stillness.

Amelia's eyes drifted toward the cushioned bench where Auron lay hidden, his small frame concealed beneath. For a moment, she envied his stillness, the way he seemed untouched by the chaos threatening to burst through the walls. But she knew better. The boy's stillness was not peace, it was a fragile illusion, one that could shatter at any moment.

Unable to stay rooted, she began to pace the room in measured strides, the soft soles of her sandals brushing against the polished wood. Her gaze flicked between the sturdy wooden door and Auron's hiding place, her mind caught in an endless loop of anxiety. Each step carried the weight of her spiralling thoughts churning with possibilities, each more troubling than the last

The distant echoes of commotion seeped through the walls, faint but persistent. Voices carried up the corridor, muddled and indistinct, like a tide rising with each passing moment. The sounds gnawed at her composure, each one a phantom threat creeping closer.

Then came the knock.

It was sharp and deliberate, breaking the fragile quiet like a stone through glass. Amelia froze mid-step, her breath catching in her throat. For a fleeting moment, her mind blanked, her instincts torn between answering and fleeing herself. The knock came again, firmer this time, carrying with it a weight that demanded acknowledgment.

Auron tensed beneath the bench, holding his breath as Amelia straightened, her composure snapping into place. She smoothed her dress, crossed to the door, and opened it just enough to see who was there.

"Galil," she said, her tone measured, though the flicker of relief she felt was short-lived. He leaned against the doorframe, his posture casual but his expression smug, tinged with irritation. His dark eyes lingered on her, tracing the line of her neckline before meeting her gaze.

"You owe me more than a promise," Galil said, his voice low, with a drawl that made his meaning unmistakable. "I've a bruised arm, a torn sleeve, and my pride's in tatters, all thanks to your little game." He shifted slightly, his hand brushing the edge of the door as if testing her willingness to let him in.

Amelia raised an eyebrow, her voice cool and dismissive, masking the unease simmering beneath. "You performed admirably, Galil. Rest assured; I always honour my word."

He tilted his head, a slow, deliberate smirk creeping across his face. "Oh, I don't doubt that" he said, his gaze dropping again, lingering far longer than was appropriate. "But I'd prefer we settle this sooner rather than later. Why wait until later, when I'm already here?" He leaned in slightly, his lips curved into a faint smirk, but before he could add further suggestion, the sound of boots echoed down the corridor. Both turned as a pair of guards rounded the corner, their expressions grim.

"Galil," one of the guards barked curtly. "All Nordon residents are to leave the estate immediately. Orders of the Lord."

Galil's frown deepened, his irritation quickly morphing into genuine confusion. "On what grounds?" he asked, his tone laced with indignation. He glanced between the guards, clearly not accustomed to being treated with such brusqueness.

A second guard stepped forward, Braddos, his expression hard and unyielding. "It's not up for debate," his voice clipped and authoritative. "You'll be escorted out of the gates immediately. Gather what you need if it's in your chambers, but you'll leave tonight."

A second pair of guards rounded the corner with hurried steps, their swords glinting faintly in the torchlight. Their presence swelled the small group to four, each man armed and alert, their expressions hardened by the chase.

Galil glanced at Amelia, his confusion giving way to a flash of irritation, though he quickly masked it with a familiar smirk. "A shame," he said, the words dripping with mock regret. "It seems I'll have to delay claiming my... reward." His eyes lingered on Amelia with unmistakable insinuation, his tone dropping lower. "But don't worry, I'll hold you to your promise, no matter how long it takes."

Amelia's stomach tightened at his words, but she kept her expression neutral, her lips pressed into a thin, resolute line. "Safe travels, Galil," she said coolly, her voice steady despite the tension simmering beneath the surface.

The guards stepped closer, flanking Galil with a presence that left no room for argument. For a moment, he hesitated, his smirk faltering as he seemed to weigh his options. But then he straightened, brushing off his robe with exaggerated nonchalance. "Until then," he said with a mock bow, his smirk returning, though it did not quite reach his eyes.

Amelia inclined her head just slightly, giving nothing away, and watched as the two new guards turned him toward the hall. The sound of their boots thudding against the carpet as they disappeared from view. She waited, her hand still on the door, until the fading of footsteps melted into silence, the tension in the air lingering after they were gone. Only then did she turn to close it, her mind racing with the events of the evening. But as her fingers brushed the latch, a voice cut through the stillness.

"My Lady," Braddos spoke from her left, his tone polite but firm. He stood with the first guard, his stance rigid. "Apologies, but you were seen with the boy, Auron. We have orders to search your quarters."

Amelia's heart jolted, her composure slipping for the briefest moment before she forced it back into place. How had she not noticed them? Her focus had been entirely on Galil. Steeling herself, she turned to face them, her expression one of cold indignation.

"My quarters?" Her voice was measured, but an undercurrent of fury seeped through. "Not even my son or Lord Malum enters here without invitation. Who dares to give such orders?"

Braddos had no such orders, but from his position of safety, he had watched the chaotic collision of guards and bodies tumbling down the staircase, a tangled mess of limbs and curses. Amidst the commotion, his sharp eyes had drifted upward, catching a fleeting but telling moment on the upper landing. There she was, Lady Amelia, her movements swift and purposeful as she whisked the boy away into the shadows with a grace that belied the urgency of her actions.

The sight had been brief, but it was enough. Braddos prided himself on his sharp instincts, he was not about to ignore what he had seen. He was not a fool. The boy was either long gone by now, spirited away through one of the estate's hidden passages, or he was still here, tucked away in the sanctuary of Amelia's chambers. The latter seemed far more likely, given the way she had shielded him with such determination.

Braddos's lips pressed into a thin line as he considered his next move. He was not about to let this slip through his fingers, not when the stakes were this high. The Lady's reputation for defiance was well-known, but tonight, her noble rank would not protect her from his persistence.

"Your lord husband," he replied evenly, his eyes never leaving hers. "He gave the command, my Lady. I promise not to disturb your belongings. I'll be as quick as I can."

The lie slid off his tongue with the polished politeness Lady Amelia was accustomed too, but he knew the risk it carried. If Amelia called his bluff, there would be no recovery from it. He paused, watching for any crack in her armour, any sign that his words might land.

Amelia's eyes narrowed, her mind whirring as suspicion flared. Of course this had Malum's fingerprints all over it, his cruel machinations, his insidious need to control and harm. Her anger surged, her cheeks flushing a deep red as her grip on the door tightened. What possible reason could her husband have to target Auron once again, to make him a pawn in his relentless games?

Yet even as her outrage built, she felt the weight of the situation pressing down. Refusing the guards outright would only raise further suspicion. Her breath caught in her throat, frustration and fury mingling with a growing sense of helplessness. She shook her head slowly, a reluctant gesture of defeat, though her eyes burned with defiance.

"Move out of the way wench," the second guard slurred, his drunkenness stripping him of caution as he spoke. For a moment, Amelia stood frozen, her eyes narrowing in disbelief. No guard had ever dared address her in such a manner. The audacity of the words left a chill in the air, the silence stretching taut like a bowstring.

Braddos reacted before she could. In a blur of movement, he spun on his heel, his hand shooting out with deadly precision. His fingers clamped around the guard's throat, the suddenness of the grip causing the man to stagger backward, his eyes wide with shock. The guard's hands flew up, gripping Braddos's wrist in a futile attempt to break free. Braddos's hold was unrelenting, a vice of tested strength from his earlier clash with Konan.

The drunken man gasped, his face flushing as Braddos's iron grip compressed his windpipe. Braddos leaned in, his free hand dropping deliberately to his sword hilt. The faint creak of leather and steel was no accident; it was a message, a calculated display of dominance that left no room for misinterpretation.

"That," Braddos growled, his voice low and venomous, "is Lady Amelia of Kadun. You owe her your allegiance and will watch your tongue or feel my wrath. Do you understand?"

The guard gurgled, his fingers clawing at Braddos's wrist in a desperate but futile bid for release. His breath came in ragged gasps, his knees trembling as his strength waned.

"I said," Braddos hissed, his grip tightening like a noose, "do you understand?"

The trapped man's lips parted in a strangled attempt at speech, but no words came. Finally, his head jerked in a frantic nod of submission, his wide eyes pleading for mercy.

With a sharp, deliberate motion, Braddos released his grip, stepping back as the guard collapsed against the wall, clutching his throat and gulping down air in noisy, ragged breaths. His humiliation was palpable, his face flushed with pain and defeat.

Braddos's cold gaze lingered on him, a predator ensuring his prey understood the consequences of defiance. "Take your position," he commanded, his voice a blade slicing through the man's shame. "Stand in the corridor and watch for the boy. Do not speak unless spoken to."

The guard hesitated only for a moment before stumbling to his feet. He shot Braddos a wary glance, his body tense with fear, before retreating several paces down the corridor. There, he pressed his back against the wall, his gaze cast downward in quiet submission.

Satisfied, Braddos turned back to Amelia. His demeanour shifted, the fire in his eyes cooling to something more composed. He inclined his head slightly, a gesture of respect. "Please forgive the unpleasantness, my Lady," he said smoothly, his voice now calm and measured. "I shall be swift, so as not to disturb you any longer."

Amelia regarded him with a mixture of anger and begrudging acknowledgment. Though she resented the intrusion, Braddos's swift defence of her honour had not gone unnoticed. For a brief moment, their eyes met, and she wondered if the man before her was entirely loyal to her husband or if there was more to his actions than mere duty.

After a moment she nodded helplessly, she had to hope Auron's makeshift reprieve would suffice. She flicked a smile and stood to the side allowing the soldier in. Braddos gave a small nod, his expression unreadable as his boots moved from the carpet onto the varnished wooden beamed floor of her chamber.

His sharp eyes swept over the space, noting the meticulous order that seemed to define Lady Amelia's quarters. Every object appeared purposefully placed, from the neatly arranged books on the side table to the perfectly aligned cushions on the fainting couch. There were few places to hide in such a space, no convenient shadows to slip into, no disorder to mask a presence. Though his years of experience made it second nature to take in every detail. The way the curtains hung undisturbed, the faint indentations on the plush rug that hinted at recent movement, the arrangement of furniture so precise it bordered on obsessiveness.

Then his gaze landed on the chest. At first glance, it seemed inconspicuous, tucked neatly along the wall like any other piece of furniture. But as his eyes lingered, the details revealed themselves. A blanket hung unevenly out of its closed lid, partially caught in the seal, an odd imperfection in an otherwise immaculate room. Around its base lay a few scattered garments, their haphazard placement clashing with the careful order of the rest of the chamber. It was subtle, almost dismissible, but to a soldier accustomed to noticing the slightest inconsistencies on a battlefield, it stood out like a beacon.

Braddos exhaled slowly, his chest rising and falling with the weight of conflicting thoughts. Did he truly want to find the boy? His hand hovered over the hilt of his blade, not in preparation to draw it, but as if to anchor himself, to remind him of his duty.

He thought he did, but Auron's face flashed in his mind, not the face of a fugitive, but of a boy. A boy whose enthusiasm had shone brightly in fleeting moments, a passing glance in the stables, shadowing Malament with quiet determination, or practicing with wooden swords as if the fate of nations rested in his hands. Braddos recalled the duel with Konan, a victory for Auron in defeat that had carried a rare promise, a spark of something unpolished yet extraordinary, perhaps destined for something greater.

And yet, here he was, reduced to prey, hunted through the night like a common criminal. Braddos could not shake the question gnawing at the edges of his mind, what could the boy have possibly done to deserve this? The orders he had received were clear, but the reasoning behind them was not. Auron was not some threat to the estate or its lord. No, this was personal, driven by forces Braddos was not privy to, it unsettled him. He was not serving justice by carrying out these orders, but merely indulging Malum's whims.

He stepped closer to the chest, his shadow falling across its surface. The faint scent of lavender hung in the air, masking the sharp tang of tension that seemed to radiate from the room itself. Braddos hesitated as his hand reached out toward the lid, the conflict in his heart as palpable as his fingers curled around its edge expecting Auron's eyes to be peering back up at him.

The lid creaked open at his command, revealing only a pile of clothes and blankets. Braddos's hand snaked inside, his fingers probing the soft layers with methodical precision, searching for any hidden depths that might conceal the boy. But his fingertips met only the unyielding surface of the wooden bottom.

With practiced efficiency, he gathered the blanket that hung halfway out of the chest, folding it neatly before placing it back inside. The lid closed with a soft thud; the small task executed with an unsettling calm. He straightened, his sharp eyes scanning the room once more, their calculating focus seeking out potential hiding spots.

His gaze landed on the bench at the foot of the bed, its base concealed by a draped goatskin. The narrow gap between the floor and the bench's frame was just wide enough for a child to fit. Suspicion flared, and his attention flicked to Amelia.

"Step back, please," he said, his tone firm but eerily calm.

Amelia's face betrayed her, a fleeting shift in her expression that revealed far more than words could. In that single moment, Braddos knew exactly what he would find.

Without hesitation, he drew his sword, the scrape of steel against its scabbard filling the room with a cold finality. His boots struck the polished wood with measured purpose, each step resonating like a judge's gavel. As he approached the bench, the floor transitioned into the soft rug that beneath him absorbed his steps, but the tension in the air was deafening.

He spun back to Amelia, ensuring the distance between them was unthreatened, his eyes briefly scanning hers for any indication she might interfere. Then he turned back, lowering himself to the floor, one hand braced against the rug, followed by his knees sinking softly into its fibres.

Another glance at Amelia. Her wide, pleading eyes met his unspoken words hanging heavy in the air. She remained still, her silence more telling than any protest. Braddos dipped his head, his sharp gaze disappearing beneath the bench, and there he saw him.

Auron was curled against the wooden base, his torso pressed tightly between the bench and the floor. His dark hair hung messily over his face, but it could not hide those piercing turquoise eyes. They stared back into Braddos's own, a striking mixture of defiance and sorrow. It was the look of someone who knew the race had been run, that defeat was inevitable, and yet there was no fear, only reluctant acceptance of whatever came next.

Braddos's first instinct was to reach in, grab the boy, and drag him clear. To deliver him to Lord Malum and fulfil his duty as expected. But he paused, his hand hovering in the space between them as his thoughts spiralled.

The night unravelled in his mind, the bond forged with Egil, their shared resolve amidst a sea of uncertainty; Malament's courageous defiance against Konan, standing for Kadun with unwavering strength. Then the arc of the Nordon's warriors' axe, at that moment Braddos had thrown everything he had to block that final, killing blow. And the tense standoff between the two lines of warriors, ready to slaughter each other at the whim of a Queen or the failings of a Lord.

All of that for what? To save Malament so that he, Braddos, could now betray the man's last act of will? That final, desperate command to Auron to run? If he undid that act, if he snatched the boy from his sanctuary, then every choice he had made tonight would be for nothing. He may as well have let Konan's axe fall.

His thoughts turned bitterly to Lord Malum. A man who cowered beneath his own roof, conceding to the Queen's every will without resistance, his plea's a stark contrast to Malament's defiant stand. The son who even in defeat had risen above his father's failures, cursing his weakness with his last shred of strength. And now Braddos found himself holding the thread of fate that tied father, son, and boy together.

Any other guard would pull Auron free, but it was him. Braddos had been the one to find him. There was something in this night, something in this boy, which felt orchestrated by forces far beyond his understanding. As if the Gods themselves had brought him to this moment, and it whispered its answer in his ear.

If the boy were to be caught, it would not be through Braddos's hand.

He made his choice. Slowly, deliberately, he lifted a single finger to his lips, the universal gesture of silence, locking eyes with Auron. The boy's defiance flickered, replaced by a glimmer of cautious hope.

Braddos pushed his palms against the rug, lifting himself to his feet with the same practiced composure as always. His sword remained in his hand, its weight grounding him, though his steps betrayed none of the conflict raging within.

He moved away from the bench; his expression unreadable as he methodically inspected the balcony. The cool night air whispered through the slightly ajar doors, but nothing betrayed the presence of the boy. He crossed to Amelia's wardrobe next, its ornate doors opening to reveal neatly hung garments and polished boots, nothing out of place. Finally, he knelt to peer behind the freestanding mirror, the flickering candlelight casting warped reflections against its surface.

Satisfied or at least pretending to be, Braddos straightened, brushing the dust from his knees before turning back to Amelia. His features softened into a courteous, almost apologetic mask, though the tension in his eyes remained. "I'm sorry we troubled you, my Lady," he said evenly, inclining his head. "There has been… much unpleasantness tonight. I suggest you remain in your room until morning for your safety. Should you happen upon the boy, Auron, please inform one of us guards immediately."

He paused, his gaze lingering just long enough to emphasize his words, then added, "Again, my apologies for the disturbance."

Amelia's heart pounded in her chest, but she schooled her features into a mask of calm. Stunned, she managed only a faint nod in return, her voice caught in her throat. She watched as Braddos turned and strode to the door, his heavy boots carrying him away with deliberate precision. The door clicked softly shut behind him, leaving the room in fragile silence.

For a moment, Amelia stood frozen, she exhaled slowly, the tightness in her chest loosening just enough for her to breathe. Her nerves felt frayed, her composure thin as paper, but she forced herself to stay steady. She listened intently, waiting for the sound of Braddos's boots to recede down the corridor. Finally, the faint echoes faded into the distance, leaving her alone in the stillness.

Turning her focus back to the room, her gaze immediately fell on the bench where Auron remained hidden. The flickering candlelight cast soft, wavering shadows across the fur-draped seat, wrapping the moment in an eerie calm. She hesitated, her mind replaying the confrontation, the tension in Braddos's eyes, and the way he had ultimately chosen not to act.

With slow, deliberate steps, she crossed the room, each movement carefully measured as though she feared the silence might shatter. Her voice, when it came, was barely above a whisper. "They're gone," she said, the words slipping from her lips like a sigh. "For now."

Hours passed. The estate grew still, the earlier commotion replaced by the muffled calm of the night. Amelia sat by the balcony, staring out at the stars as the cool breeze brushed against her skin. Finally, she turned to the bench and lifted the edge of the fur. "Auron," she whispered, kneeling beside the bench, "it's time."

Auron slid out carefully, his movements stiff and awkward after being confined for so long. He stretched briefly, rolling his shoulders to ease the tension. His turquoise eyes darted toward the door, then back to Amelia, his face a mix of exhaustion and apprehension.

"I don't know how to thank you," he said softly, his voice trembling with a mixture of gratitude and uncertainty.

Amelia stood, extending a hand to guide him toward the open balcony doors. The cool night air poured in, sharper now, carrying the faint scent of pine and damp earth. "There's no need," she said, her tone steady but gentle. "Right now, the only thanks I want is for you to get out of here safely."

She stopped at the threshold of the balcony, gripping the edge of the door frame as she turned to him. "You need to leave before dawn. Keep to the shadows and move quickly. Avoid the main paths, the guards will still be patrolling for a while."

Auron hesitated, his hand resting on the cold stone of the railing. "You didn't have to do this," he said, his voice barely above a whisper. "You're risking so much for me."

Amelia stepped closer, her green eyes steady and resolute. "Auron, I couldn't stand by and do nothing," she said firmly. "You've done more for me than you realize. I'll make sure you're not forgotten, not abandoned." She paused, her voice softening. "When it's safe, watch the estate from a distance. Saanvi will leave regularly, and I'll ensure she has food and coin for you. She's kind, and she'll help you if you approach her. And give me time, Auron, I'll find a way to secure work for you, somewhere safe. You may be gone from this house, but you're not gone from me."

Her words hung in the air, heavy with meaning. Auron swallowed hard, his throat tightening as he nodded. "I'll wait," he said, his voice steadier now. "And I'll do as you say."

Amelia reached out, resting a hand lightly on his shoulder. "Good," she said softly. "But no matter what, you must survive. Promise me that."

"I promise," he replied, his gaze unwavering.

With a final, lingering look, Amelia stepped closer, her expression softening as the weight of the moment settled between them. She leaned in, her touch gentle as she placed a hand on Auron's shoulder, steadying him. Her lips brushed his forehead, warm and fleeting, a gesture filled with unspoken care and hope.

"Good luck, young sir," she murmured, her voice barely above a whisper, the words carrying the weight of both a farewell and a prayer.

With one last look at her, he climbed onto the balcony railing, his movements careful yet swift. Balancing on the edge, he turned back, his eyes locking with hers. "I won't forget this," he said, his voice filled with quiet determination.

"Go," she whispered, stepping back into the shadows of the room. She watched as he slipped into the night, his silhouette fading into the darkness until he was gone.

The wind stirred the dense brush encircling the estate, its whisper weaving through the shadows like a quiet warning. It mingled with the heavy silence of the household beyond, a stillness that felt almost unnatural, as though the estate itself held its breath. Amelia remained at the balcony; her own silhouette framed by the pale glow of moonlight. Her arms were crossed tightly over her chest, a protective gesture against the chill in the air and the heavier weight pressing on her heart.

Worry clung to her like a shadow, every rustle in the dark drawing her gaze toward the garden hedges where Auron had vanished. Yet beneath the fear, like a candle flickering in the wind, there burned a spark of hope, fragile, but steady. It was not much, but in that moment, it was enough.

# BORLONG'S BANQUET
# CHAPTER FIFTY FOUR

The feast was done, the tense standoff over. Lord Malum sat in his study, where he had remained the last few hours. The air heavy with the scent of parchment and the sharp tang of Borlong Red. The walls, once a comfort with their dark walnut panels and rows of orderly shelves, now seemed to close in around him. The first pale streaks of dawn filtered through the narrow windows, throwing thin, amber light across the polished floor. It illuminated the clutter on his desk, maps, ledgers, scattered papers, a battlefield of failed strategy. His glass rested in his hand, its contents swirling as he tilted it absently, the deep red liquid catching the faint light like blood in water.

*'Let's stay up until dawn,'* he had said earlier, his voice full of jest and self-assurance. A toast meant to signify triumph, camaraderie, strength. Now, the words mocked him. He had meant it as a celebration of control, of mastery over the evening's challenges. Instead, dawn had found him alone, the weight of ruin pressing against his chest.

The alliance with Nordon was in tatters. Queen Karak had seen to that, her blade-like words cutting through his authority and leaving him grasping at shreds of power. The trade agreements she had forced upon him were a humiliation. Timber and grain, the lifeblood of Borlong's economy, promised away for a fraction of their worth. It had been a surrender, his city, his country, reduced to a pawn in her game of dominance.

He took a slow sip of the wine, the warmth of it doing little to ease the cold knot in his stomach. He swirled the glass again, watching the ripples fade before setting it down with a deliberate clink. His gaze fell to the tapestry of East Kadun's crest behind his desk, its faded threads catching the weak dawn light. It was a symbol of stability, of power. Now, it felt like a relic of a dying age.

Malament's betrayal loomed largest of all, casting its shadow over every thought. His son, his heir, had stood against him, not in private, but in the full view of their nobles. He had questioned Malum's leadership, accused him of blindness. The memory was a fresh wound, one that bled with every passing moment. And yet, beneath the anger was something deeper, more painful, the bitter sting of truth in Malament's accusations.

*'The moment they entered our gates, they were never here for an alliance. They came to assess. To judge us. We were never a trade partner; we were a rival.'*

The words echoed in Malum's mind, sharp and cutting. Was the Queen really only here to test him, to assess Borlong's worth or its weakness?

He leaned back in his chair, his gaze fixed on the ceiling as if searching for answers in the intricate carvings of vine motifs. His jaw tightened as he replayed the events of the night. The Queen's knowing smirk, Konan's cold brutality, the nobles' horrified whispers. Malament's face, bloodied and defiant, flashed in his mind, and Malum's fingers curled into fists. His son's insurgence had not just fractured their family, it had shattered his authority. Every noble in that hall had witnessed it, they had seen him undermined and worse, humiliated.

And then there was Auron.

The boy had fled amidst the chaos, slipping through the cracks like water through cupped hands. Malum had ordered his capture in the heat of the moment, his rage finding a convenient target. Yet now, with the quiet clarity of the early morning, he found himself... relieved. The boy had been a victim, caught in the web of Malum's failings. It was not truly his fault. But he had needed to direct his anger somewhere, and it could not be his son. Not in that moment, not with so many eyes watching.

He sighed heavily, his shoulders sagging under the weight of exhaustion. Auron's escape was a small mercy, one less burden for him to carry. But it was a fleeting relief, swallowed quickly by the storm of his thoughts.

The dawn's light grew stronger, casting harsh lines across his face and deepening the shadows in the room. He turned to the window, pulling back the curtain to let more light in. The city beyond was beginning to stir, the faint hum of life rising from its streets. It was a reminder that the world would not stop, no matter how broken he felt.

But broken he was. His son's betrayal, the Queen's manipulation, the nobles' judgment, and the boy's escape—all of it weighed on him, a mountain pressing down on his chest. He had fought to build a legacy, to protect Borlong's place in the world. Now, he wondered if there was anything left to protect.

His hand tightened around the glass, the cool surface grounding him as his mind spiralled. He would have to act, to salvage what he could from the wreckage of the night. But for now, as the first full light of dawn spilled into his study, he allowed himself this moment of stillness. Malum closed his eyes, the weight of his failures pressing down like a physical force.

A sharp knock at the door pierced the heavy silence, startling Lord Malum out of his depressive thoughts. His grip faltered around the glass; the rich red liquid sloshing dangerously close to the rim. He set it down with a deliberate, steadying motion, the faint clink against the wood sharp in the stillness. Straightening his shoulders, he willed his composure to return.

"Enter," he called, though the word was more a low murmur than a command. The door creaked open before the sound had fully left his lips.

Two guards stepped inside, their boots striking the floor in careful, measured steps. Amudi, his own man and a towering presence in the estate, held the door open, his broad frame blocking the faint stirrings of the restless household beyond. The pair carried an unmistakable hesitance, their movements rigid, stopping just short of their Lord's drained figure.

Malum turned slowly to fully face them, his movements deliberate, measured, and yet lacking their usual force. His sharp gaze swept over them, probing, calculating, though the exhaustion shadowing his eyes dulled its usual intensity. The rays of dawn cast flickering patterns across his face, softening the hard lines carved by the night's trials.

The taller guard, visibly unsettled under Malum's scrutiny, cleared his throat. The sound was tentative, almost reluctant, as though afraid to disturb the fragile tension in the room. "My Lord," he began, his tone even but carefully respectful, "the nurse sends word. Malament's concussion has passed... and you may see him."

Malum remained still, his expression an impassive mask. His piercing gaze locked onto the guard, dissecting every word with unnerving precision. For a moment, the room felt heavier, the faint sounds of the estate fading into irrelevance. Then, just for an instant, the faintest twitch of his jaw betrayed him a crack in the veneer of his control, a subtle ripple of emotion too fleeting to name.

He exhaled softly; the sound barely audible but weighted with something unresolved. His hand hovered near the desk, fingers brushing the edge as though seeking purchase against the tide of thoughts now rushing to the surface. When he finally spoke, his voice was low and deliberate, his tone as carefully measured as the guard's.

"Very well," he said. The words were simple, but the tension in his frame lingered. The guards stood silent waiting for further instruction, but Malum allowed the moment of silence, giving his mind time to still.

For a time, Malum himself did not know how to react. Earlier in the night, his rage had been a storm with no centre, untethered and destructive. In that moment, he had not known his limits, nor cared to find them. Punishment had seemed inevitable and necessary even. His son had defied him, humiliated him in front of the court, and shattered the fragile foundation of his authority. But now, as the clarity of dawn set in, so too did the weight of realisation.

Malament was his son. Regardless of the betrayal, the defiance, or the wounds inflicted upon his pride, he was still his. And he had been nearly killed under Malum's own roof, under Malum's supposed protection, by a foreign man wielding power that Malum had invited into his halls. The decision to imprison him after the chaos now felt hollow, like a poor substitute for action born of indecision and anger rather than justice.

The thought gnawed at him, the weight of it pressing down on his chest until it felt as though the air in the room had grown thinner. His arm, still resting on the edge of the desk, trembled under his own weight. For a fleeting moment, his body threatened to betray him; his knees weakened, and it felt as though the ground might rush up to meet him.

The taller guard stepped forward immediately, his broad hand steadying Malum with a firm yet careful grip beneath his arm.

"My Lord," the guard said, his voice low with concern, though his posture remained stiff and respectful. "Are you well?"

Malum's first instinct was to recoil from the touch, to snap at the man for daring to acknowledge his momentary faltering. But the words stuck in his throat, and instead, he forced his grimace into something resembling a strained smile. Yet the anger remained, not at the man, not even at Malament, but at himself. The self-pity that clung to him like a shroud felt intolerable, and the shame of it etched deep lines across his face.

Straightening, Malum placed a steadying hand on the table, his movements deliberate as he willed strength back into his frame. "The toll of leadership," he said finally, his voice heavy with resignation.

The guards exchanged a brief glance, their surprise evident despite their disciplined stances. For their Lord was usually a figure of unshakable authority, whose commands were carried out without question, to speak so candidly, so openly, was unheard of. They stood uncertain; their training ill-prepared for such a moment of vulnerability from the man they served.

Malum caught the flicker of their hesitation but chose to ignore it. There was no time for pride, not now. His son waited, and whatever conversation lay ahead would require more strength than he currently possessed.

"I will see my son," he said, his voice firmer now, though it carried the weight of a decision made reluctantly.

The guard nodded, releasing his Lord's arm with a measured step backward. He bowed deeply, and the second guard followed suit, their movements synchronized in a display of respect. Rising in unison, they pivoted with practiced precision and began their march toward the door, their heavy footfalls echoing faintly in the quiet study.

Malum hesitated, his gaze lingering on the room around him as if searching for something, answers, solace, perhaps even the man he had once been before the night had stripped him bare. But there was nothing here for him now.

He followed the guards without a word, his steps measured and deliberate, though the turmoil within him churned with relentless force. Each stride felt heavier than the last, burdened by the weight of his failures and the uncertain path that lay ahead.

Approaching the door, his steps slowed, the weight of his thoughts dragging at his heels. His eyes met Amudi's, a moment of unspoken understanding passing between the long-serving master and his loyal servant. For the briefest of moments, a faint smile tugged at the corners of Malum's lips. It was a ghost of the man he had been, a man with confidence, control, and purpose.

Amudi returned the smile, subtle but genuine, a rare glimpse of warmth from the towering guard. It was not just duty that bound him to Malum; it was trust, earned and weathered over time. The moment lingered, fragile yet profound, a quiet acknowledgment of the burden they both carried in their own ways.

"My Lord," Amudi said, his heavy accent lending weight to the words, though his tone was uncharacteristically soft. There was a steadiness to it, a trace of encouragement woven through the formality, as if his voice alone could bear some of the burden Malum carried.

Malum paused, a faint nod followed, his composure sliding back into place like a well-worn mask, though cracks still lingered at the edges. "Thank you, Amudi," he said, his voice quieter than usual, its depth speaking volumes that needed no further elaboration.

Amudi inclined his head in silent acknowledgment, his expression as stoic as ever, though his dark eyes betrayed a flicker of something deeper, concern perhaps, or respect forged through years of unwavering service.

Malum stepped through the door without another word, his stride measured but heavy. The connection between them began to fade as the gravity of duty reclaimed its hold, yet Amudi's presence remained tangible, his giant footsteps falling in rhythm behind his lord.

Though fleeting, the exchange lingered in the air like the final note of a melody, a quiet testament to the unspoken bond between them, a bond that endured, even in the shadow of collapse.

The guards led the small procession along the upper landing, their boots absorbing into the crimson carpet. The grand stairwell loomed ahead; its sweeping steps illuminated by the muted glow of dawn filtering through the high windows. Each step seemed heavier for Malum, the weight of the night's chaos echoing through the silence.

The scene of such commotion earlier now bore an air of muted industry. The hall below buzzed with subdued activity as maids and guards worked to clear the remnants of the night's destruction. Torn banners, shattered furniture, and shards of fine ceramics lay scattered across the floor, stark reminders of the discord that had raged mere hours ago. The faint scent of spilled wine and burnt candles lingered in the air, mingling with the metallic tang of blood.

As they descended the grand stairs, Malum's gaze flicked toward the far-right corner of the hall, the site of the confrontation between East Kadun and Nordon. It was there that Luka had fallen, his lifeblood staining the marble in a gruesome testament to the night's events.

But now, there was nothing.

No blood, no debris, no evidence of the violent standoff that had unravelled his authority and shattered fragile alliances. The area had been meticulously cleaned; every trace of the confrontation erased as if to deny its occurrence. The banners hung undisturbed; the marble floor polished to a sheen that belied the horror it had so recently borne.

Malum's jaw tightened as he reached the base of the stairs, his gaze lingering on the pristine floor where Luka's body had lain. It was as though the hall itself had conspired to forget, to wipe away the stains of his failure. But he could not forget.

His focus shifted forward, the destination clear, the servant quarters, where his son awaited. The guards led the way, their movements efficient but subdued, as if aware of the gravity that hung over the journey. Amudi lingered behind, his towering presence a quiet reassurance. As Malum stepped through the narrow wooden door leading into the lower level, the sharp scent of damp hit him immediately, mingled with the faint musk of wood and stone.

The stairs were narrow, their dark surface uneven with age, and Malum's hand brushed the rough wall for balance. The faint sound of muffled voices and clattering echoed from above, where the estate's maids and guards continued their efforts to erase the chaos of the night. But here, in the damp quiet of the servant quarters, the air was thick with silence.

The narrow staircase turned into an equally constricted corridor, dimly lit by lanterns hanging from rusted supports. They passed door after door, the wooden planks warped and stained by years of use. Malum's sharp eyes took in every detail, his lips tightening in distaste. How long had it been since he had last ventured into this part of the estate? He knew the answer too well. The sight of the corridors now filled him with a sour mix of shame and anger.

The guards came to a halt before a door Malum recognized immediately. It had once been Auron's quarters, a small, dark space he had seen only fleetingly during the boy's brief tenure here. The realisation struck him with an unexpected pang, a cruel twist of fate that his son now occupies this same space.

He shook his head, displeasure flashing across his features. The irony was bitter, and the thought of his bloodline reduced to this, to the damp, narrow confines of the servants' world gnawed at his pride.

The first guard rapped his knuckles against the wooden door, the sound sharp and hollow in the silence. The door opened abruptly, swinging inward to reveal the cramped room beyond. The guards stepped aside, their posture stiff, allowing Malum to enter.

He hesitated for a moment, his hand brushing the rough edge of the door frame as if seeking reassurance from the solid wood beneath his fingers. The pause was brief but telling, a rare flicker of uncertainty that passed through him like a shadow. The smell of damp and faint blood seemed to intensify, clawing at his composure as he finally stepped forward, forcing himself into the small, oppressive space.

Amudi, ever watchful, remained stationed by the door, his towering presence a silent sentinel. The guard's gaze followed his lord, his expression impassive, though there was an unmistakable tension in the way he stood. A readiness to intervene if needed, yet an understanding that this moment was not his to intrude upon.

Malum took in the room at a glance. It was little more than a cell. The walls were bare, a single narrow bed dominated the space, its linens worn and thin, the mattress sagging in the centre. Beside it, perched on a small, rickety chair, sat Saanvi. Her sleeves were rolled to her elbows, her fingers deftly rinsing a bloodstained cloth into a bucket at her feet. Her expression was calm but focused, her presence a steadying force in the oppressive atmosphere.

On the bed, propped against the wall, was Malament. His head was wrapped in thick bandages that obscured much of his hairline; a faint streak of dried blood visible where the cloth met his temple. His arm cradled his ribcage protectively, his posture stiff with pain. He turned his head slowly, his piercing eyes finding his fathers with a mix of defiance and exhaustion.

Malum's gaze swept the room again, his lips pressing into a thin line as he assessed his son's state. The bruises, the bandages, the air of vulnerability that clung to him, this was not the son he had raised. The sight stirred a storm of emotions within him, anger and guilt wrestling for dominance. He had come to confront, to question, to demand answers. But now, faced with the reality of Malament's injuries, his resolve wavered.

The room felt smaller than it was, the weight of unspoken words filling every corner. Malum's chest tightened, but his face betrayed nothing. Slowly, he stepped further into the room, his voice low and steady, though tinged with an edge he could not quite suppress.

"How is he?" he asked, directing the question to Saanvi though his eyes never left his son.

Saanvi wrung out the cloth and placed it neatly on the edge of the bucket. For a moment, her hands rested in her lap, her steady composure a stark contrast to the tension in the air. Her voice, when it came, was even but carried the quiet authority of someone who had tended to worse injuries. "A nasty gash on the back of his head. I've stitched it. His nose was broken but we've reset it, and several cracked ribs will need a few moon passes to fully heal. But he's stable, my Lord."

Malum nodded, though his expression remained guarded, his gaze shifting briefly to the bandages encasing his son's head. The sight of Malament, bruised and battered, did little to soften the hardened lines of his face. If anything, it seemed to deepen them.

Across the narrow room, Malament's eyes locked onto his father's. They burned with something fierce and unspoken, a simmering anger or perhaps a challenge. It was impossible to tell. Yet he said nothing, his silence cutting sharper than any words might have. He sat stiffly against the wall, his arm cradling his ribs, but his posture betrayed no weakness. If he was in pain, he refused to show it.

For a moment, the room felt suspended in that silence, the weight of the night pressing down like an invisible force.

"Leave us," Malum ordered, his voice breaking the stillness with an edge of finality.

Saanvi rose from her chair, smoothing her apron with a faint flick of her hands. Her gaze lingered on Malament for a brief moment, and she offered him the smallest flicker of a smile, a gesture of reassurance, or perhaps quiet solidarity. Without a word, she stepped past Malum, her measured footsteps fading as she disappeared into the corridor.

The solitary guard hesitated briefly by the door, his sharp focus sweeping the room before inclining his head. With one last glance toward Malum, he turned and followed Saanvi out. The door closed behind him leaving the room cloaked in an uneasy quiet.

Now, there was no one left but father and son, the unspoken words between them heavier than the silence.

Malum took a hesitant step closer, his gaze fixed on his son. For a moment, the sight of Malament, battered and bandaged, broke through the layers of anger and humiliation that had clouded his mind. His voice, when it came, was softer than Malament expected, almost gentle, tinged with concern.

"You shouldn't be like this," Malum said, his eyes searching his son's bruised face for some trace of the boy he had raised. "You're my son. My heir. This... this is not who you were meant to be."

Malament's lips curled into a bitter smirk, his expression as unyielding as the stone walls surrounding them. He leaned back further against the stone wall bed frame, every movement deliberate, designed to show his disdain. "And what was I meant to be, Father?" he asked, his voice sharp, biting. "Another man bowing to a queen who spat on our house and our people? Another pawn in your endless, futile game of power?"

Malum flinched as though struck. He opened his mouth to respond but faltered, his jaw tightening.

"You knelt to her every whim," Malament continued, his voice rising with a mix of anger and incredulity. "You begged her for mercy—begged! And when she demanded everything, you gave it. You gave her Borlong's future, our future, for nothing but scraps." He spat the last word with venom, his eyes blazing with the same defiance that had burned in the hall the night before.

"I did what I had to," Malum snapped, the softness vanishing from his tone, replaced by the sharp edge of defensiveness. "For Borlong. For East Kadun. For you. Do you think I wanted to bow to her? Do you think I had a choice?"

"You had a choice!" Malament's voice cracked, raw with fury. "You could have stood your ground. You could have shown strength. But you didn't. You showed her the same cowardice you've shown me all my life."

The words struck Malum harder than any blade could have. His fists clenched at his sides; his breathing uneven. "Mind your tongue," he growled, his voice low and dangerous. "You forget who you speak to."

Malament let out a bitter laugh, the sound harsh and hollow. "No, Father. You forget who you are. You're not the man who raised me. The man who taught me that East Kadun was stronger than Nordon, that our people would never bow. That man is gone. And what's left...?" He gestured weakly toward Malum; his expression filled with cold contempt. "What's left is a coward."

Malum's composure snapped. He took a step forward, his face contorted with fury. "If you weren't my son," he hissed, his voice trembling with restrained rage, "you'd be hanging from the gallows for what you've done."

Malament did not flinch, didn't so much as blink. He held his father's gaze with an unwavering stare, his voice cold and final. "And if you weren't my father, no one would have stopped me from killing you."

The silence that followed was suffocating, the weight of their words hanging in the air like an executioner's blade.

Malum's chest heaved with shallow, uneven breaths, his knuckles white as he gripped the back of the chair Saanvi had vacated. He looked at his son—bloodied, broken, yet still defiant—and saw no path forward, no bridge unburned between them.

"I hope you like this little room," Malum snarled, his voice a venomous growl as he swept his gaze around the cramped quarters. "Because it's yours now. You'll stay here like the servant you've made yourself. And once you're fit and able you're gone from this estate." He stepped closer, his presence towering, his tone escalating into a roar of fury. "I'm sending you to Cordon. Let's see if the savages can make a man of you since I clearly failed!"

His words slammed into the room like a thunderclap, reverberating off the walls with unrestrained force. His chest heaved as the heat of his anger consumed him, veins visible in his clenched fists.

Malament, slumped on the narrow bed, lifted his head slowly. The bandages over his temple accentuated the gaunt hollowness of his face, but his gaze burned with unwavering defiance. A bitter, humourless laugh escaped his cracked lips, cutting through the thick tension like a blade.

"Still the coward," he said, his voice low but sharpened with contempt. "You'd send me to the edge of the world, to the Drylands, so you wouldn't have to deal with the problem. Is that your solution, Father? Run me off like a dog, just as you bow your head to every threat you face."

Malum's face twisted in rage, his voice trembling with fury as he stepped closer. "You will not speak to me that way!" he thundered, the words exploding from his mouth. "You think you know what it means to lead, to bear the weight of this estate, this country? You know nothing!"

Malament's lips curled into a sneer, his gaze cutting through Malum's fury like frost on fire. "I know enough to see a broken man when he's standing in front of me. You're a shadow of what you should have been. You gave Nordon everything, you gave Karak everything, and in return, she took what little was left of your pride. If she'd owned a cock you would have been on your knees."

Malum lunged forward with the fury of a tempest, his fist connecting with Malament's jaw in a sickening crack, snapping his son's head back into the cold stone wall. The impact reverberated through the room, fresh blood splattering against the unyielding surface in vivid streaks.

Malament slumped for a moment, his head resting against the wall as if absorbing the blow. His chest rose and fell, his breathing laboured but deliberate. Slowly, agonizingly, he turned to face his father, his movements deliberate, defiance burning in his eyes.

Blood pooled in his mouth; the metallic tang sharp against his tongue. He worked his jaw briefly, chewing on the pain as though testing its limits, before dipping his head and spitting the thick crimson mixture at his father's feet.

The blood landed with a grotesque splatter, stark against the cold stone, and Malament's gaze rose to meet Malum's with a searing, unrelenting intensity. A bitter, taunting smile tugged at the corners of his swollen lips; his words low but sharp enough to cut.

"Is that all you've got... Father?"

The room froze, the silence punctuated only by Malament's ragged breaths and the faint drip of blood onto the floor. Malum stood rigid, his fist still trembling from the strike, his knuckles reddened and raw. For an instant, the mask of authority slipped from his face, replaced by something darker-rage, guilt, and the gnawing sting of humiliation.

This moment was more than a clash of wills. It was the shattering of what little remained between them, the final act in the destruction of their bond.

"Fine," Malum said at last, his voice brittle, the fury in it now tempered by something colder, something final. "Cordon it is. Pray you survive the savages, boy, because if you return, it will be in a box."

Malum turned sharply, his boots striking the stone floor with deliberate force as he strode to the door, his breath ragged with barely contained rage. His hand gripped the handle, ready to leave the suffocating room behind. But something darker stirred within him, a venomous need to lash out one final time.

He paused, his fingers tightening on the doorframe, and wickedly turned back to face Malament. A cruel smirk tugged at his lips, his words slow and deliberate, each syllable dripping with malice.

“By the way,” Malum sneered, his tone as sharp as the blade he intended his words to be, “if you were wondering... Auron? He didn’t get away. He’s dead.” He exaggerated the final word, letting it hang in the air like a noose tightening around his son’s hope.

The room seemed to darken in the silence that followed, Malum’s satisfaction short-lived. Malament’s eyes, bruised and bloodied burned with a feral, untamed fury, locked onto his own. The intensity of his son’s glare struck him like a physical blow, primal and unrelenting.

It was the stare not that of a beaten man, but something far more dangerous. A predator poised to strike. In that instant, Malum wished he had not turned back, wished he had left the room without a word. He felt as if prey beneath a plunging hawk's talons, small, exposed, doomed.

“We both know that’s a lie, Father. But lies won’t protect you when the truth finds you.” Malament growled, his voice low and guttural, like the warning rumble of a beast that could no longer be contained.

# THE REACH CHAPTER FIFTY FIVE

The Reach loomed ahead like an ancient sentinel, its twin towers standing in perfect symmetry, each a testament to the indomitable will of two nations once united but now irrevocably divided. Queen Karak walked at the forefront of her company, her crimson mantle trailing behind her like a banner of fire against the muted grey of the fortress ruins. She felt the chill of the wind cut through the air, carrying with it the scent of old stone and the faint bitterness of ash. The structure was a marvel, but its solemn presence pressed down on her shoulders, heavier with every step. She had faced the ice goddess Shiva, betrayed allies and her king, crowned herself queen, yet something about this place unsettled her most. The weight of its history whispered to her, reminding her of the blood it had swallowed.

Her boots crunched against the broken stone of the path as her soldiers moved behind her, their steps careful, deliberate, and reverent. They carried themselves with rigid discipline, their faces grim as their eyes darted over the skeletal remains of the eastern fortress. The remnants of the once-proud fortifications rose on either side, their jagged edges like broken teeth silhouetted against the pale sky.

The gateway of the fortress loomed before them, its massive stone arch framing the ruins beyond. Time and war had stripped it bare; the oak gates, once mighty and reinforced with bands of iron, had long since been burned to nothing. Charred fragments of wood still clung to the blackened hinges, a testament to the flames that had consumed them decades ago. Now, the gateway yawned open, exposing the crumbling courtyard beyond, where moss and creeping vines claimed dominion over the past.

Karak paused beneath the archway, her gaze sweeping over the ruin. The air grew cooler here, the shadows of the fortress walls pressing in around her. Above, the ravens cawed and flitted from perch to perch, their cries echoing like the mournful voices of the dead. The courtyard stretched out before them, littered with rubble and overgrown with weeds that poked through the cracks in the stone. Faint scorch marks still marred the walls, scars from the siege weapons that had brought the fortress to its knees.

Her soldier's formation tightening as they passed under the arch and into the heart of the ruins. Even Konan, towering and broad-shouldered, seemed subdued as he walked in her shadow, his axe resting lightly on his back. His voice broke the silence, low and gruff. "The wars left nothing untouched." His vision swept over the remains, his expression unreadable.

Karak slowed her pace, her eyes lingering on the remnants of a once-grand tower to her left, its top sheared clean off as though struck by a giant's blade. She could almost hear the echoes of battle, shouts of commands, the clash of steel and the screams of the dying. It had been twenty years since the Divided Wars ended, yet the weight of those years lingered here, woven into the stones and the soil.

"No," she said finally, her voice steady but cold. "It wasn't just war that stripped this fortress bare. It was the broker of peace."

Konan turned his head toward her, a faint flicker of curiosity breaking through his stoic demeanour.

"Once Lord Malum came to power," Karak continued, her gaze fixed on the blackened edges of the gateway ahead, "he sought peace. The cost was this fortress, razed to the ground by his own decree to appease the West." She gestured to the ruins around them, her tone sharpening like a blade. "Along with other great houses and families."

The words hung in the air, a sad bitter truth. Konan's expression darkened as he took in the ruins with fresh eyes. "Peace bought with blood," he said, his voice low. "A fragile bargain."

Karak's lips curved into a faint, mirthless smile. "Fragile? No, Konan. It was deliberate. A calculated show of submission, meant to pacify the West and secure his position. He thought he could trade strength for stability." She paused, her gaze hardening. "But this—this was no peace. It was surrender, dressed up in treaties and handshakes."

Konan grunted in agreement, his hand instinctively brushing the haft of his axe. "And now? What remains of his 'peace'?"

"Nothing but ghosts," Karak said, stepping forward once more. Her voice was quieter now, almost as though she were speaking to herself. "This place is a grave, Konan. Not just for the dead but for all things the East once stood for." The wind howled through the broken archways as they walked on, the weight of her words trailing behind them like shadows.

The path narrowed, funnelling them through a corridor of towering walls that cast long shadows over their company. The scars of war and its peace everywhere, cracks running like veins through the stone, chunks of masonry missing as though torn away by some great force. Here and there, fragments of rusted weapons lay half-buried in the dirt, a broken spear, the hilt of a sword, the edge of a shield warped by fire. Each was a relic of a time when this place had been alive with the chaos of war.

They emerged from the corridor into another open expanse, and the bridge itself finally came into view. It spanned the yawning gorge ahead, its massive stone arches rising from the ravine like the outstretched fingers of the God Titan, gripping the cliffs on either side. The structure seemed both timeless and formidable, defying the ravages of wind and rain that had shaped the jagged canyon below.

The intact towers of the western fortress rose imposingly, their outlines etched sharply against the afternoon sky some three hundred feet away. They cast long, imposing shadows over the bustling town clustered at its rear, where smoke curled lazily from chimneys and faint echoes of life reached across the void. Here, on the eastern side, there was no such vitality, only silence and decay, a stark reminder of East Kadun's concessions and scars.

They passed beneath the remnants of the eastern battlements, the jagged stones above threatening to crumble with the slightest provocation. Dust drifted down in fine clouds as their footsteps reverberated through the cracked stone passage, the sound swallowed almost immediately by the oppressive stillness. The air grew colder as they moved under the broken arch, the faint scent of moss and mildew clinging to the ancient stones.

Karak hesitated as her boots left the uneven earth of the fortress and met the polished surface of the bridge. It felt different, colder, harder, as if the stone beneath her feet carried the memory of every soul who had crossed before her. Her hand instinctively brushed the hilt of her sword, seeking the reassurance of its weight. She exhaled slowly; her gaze drawn downward despite herself.

The drop into the gorge below was dizzying, a sheer plunge of over four hundred feet. The cliffs on either side were jagged and unforgiving, their weathered faces streaked with lines of white where rivulets of water had carved their paths. Far below, the river glistened like a silver thread, winding through the canyon with an almost tranquil elegance that belied the violence of its current. She knew better than to linger on the sight, it was the kind of view that lured the mind into dangerous places, where even the firmest resolve might waver.

Karak clenched her jaw and forced herself forward, her boots striking a steady rhythm against the ancient stones. Each step echoed faintly, a hollow sound that seemed to mock the silence of the ruins behind her. The bridge was nearly forty feet wide, enough space for an army to march shoulder to shoulder, yet it felt impossibly narrow with the abyss yawning on either side. The low stone walls that lined its edges bore the scars of time and war, pitted with cracks, their surfaces weathered smooth by the ceaseless assault of the wind.

Here and there, faint scorch marks marred the stone facade, their fractured patterns whispering of fire's fury. Among them, the faint discoloration of old bloodstains was etched into the surface, muted by the passage of time but never truly erased. The stones beneath her feet bore silent witness to countless horrors. Duels fought to the death, and the slow, desperate final moments of the fallen. Thousands had perished here, their blood seeping into the very foundation upon which she now strode.

The air itself seemed heavy with their memory, thick with an unseen presence that pressed against her chest. The ghosts of those who had perished lingered in the air, their cries faint but distinct, carried on the wailing wind that howled through the arches. It was a mournful sound, a dirge sung by the bridge itself, echoing with the sorrow and rage of lives lost to ambition and war.

This place was not a bridge; it was a scar, a reminder of the folly of unity and the inevitable pull of division. For all her victories and machinations, for all her careful planning and ruthless execution, she could not help but feel small here, dwarfed by the scale of The Reach and the weight of what it represented.

The soldiers kept pace behind her, their footsteps a steady drumbeat on the ancient stones. Every echo carried the weight of her presence, her authority, and her resolve. She would not falter here, not under the shadow of The Reach, nor under the judgment of its ghosts. Her red mantle swept behind her like a banner, defiant against the wind that threatened to steal it away.

She was the Queen of Stormhold, and no gorge, no ruin, no relic of war would make her tremble.

Suddenly, Konan broke the silence, his voice bellowing with sharp authority, cutting through the whistling wind like a blade. "Hold!" The command was laced with urgency, a thunderous warning that sent a ripple of unease through the ranks. The sound of forty-four armed Nordon warriors grinding to a halt echoed ominously against the stone. The rhythmic stomp of boots ceased, replaced by the whistling wind and the distant murmur of the gorge below. The company stood frozen; the tension pressing. Their hands hovering over undrawn weapons, tension coiling in their muscles.

Karak turned sharply to her brother, confusion flickering in her emerald eyes. His outstretched arm pointed toward the western battlements. Her gaze followed, and her breath caught.

The battlements, moments ago lifeless and shadowed, were now bristling with movement. Figures emerged like spectres from the gloom, too many to count. Each bore a bow, their arrows nocked and held with calm precision. The archers stood in grim silence, their postures rigid and alert, the weight of their focus palpable even across the expanse of the bridge. The arrows pointed low, not a threat yet, but unmistakably warning, one that carried the promise of swift violence should the line be crossed.

Then, from the fortress gate, a larger force spilled forth. Their movement was deliberate and disciplined, like a tide of steel and leather surging onto the bridge. The dull clatter of armoured boots against stone reverberated, a drumbeat of disciplined power. Karak's eyes narrowed as they fell into formation—twenty men across the full width of the bridge, their broad shields locking together in an impenetrable wall. Behind them, four more columns extended deep, their ranks dense and precise. The shields, polished to a mirror-like gleam, caught the dim light and reflected it in distorted rays of sun that danced against the stone.

The sheer unity of their movement, the weight of their formation, sent a cold knot twisting in her stomach. There was no hesitation, no flaw in their lines—only the quiet, unyielding confidence of men prepared for war.

Her mouth turned dry, and for a moment, she could not find her breath. The bridge beneath her seemed to shift, as though alive with the echoes of the battles it had borne witness to. The Divided Wars felt as though they were unfolding again, but now she played a key role. This time, it was her army defending the eastern side, vulnerable and outnumbered.

Konan spun on his heel, his eyes blazing with the instinct of a seasoned warrior. "To arms!" he barked, his voice like thunder, shattering the stillness.

The Nordon soldiers obeyed without hesitation. Their swords, axes, and hammers sang as they were drawn from their sheaths. In a single motion, they fell into formation, three lines deep stretching the width of the bridge. The sound of steel on stone reverberated through the air as they braced themselves for whatever came next.

Konan unsheathed his massive battleaxe, the blade gleaming wickedly in the light. The sound of its release was sharp and deliberate, a prelude to violence. He stepped forward, his boots striking the stone with weight and purpose as he approached Karak.

"We're being tested," he said, his voice low and steady, but his grip on the axe was white knuckled. "Stay behind the line."

Karak did not respond immediately. Her heart hammered against her ribs; her eyes fixed on the western force. She fought to steady her breathing, the weight of her mantle and crown heavier than ever. She clenched her jaw and forced her voice into calm command. "I will when I must, we will not retreat."

Konan's lips curled into a grim smile, "no we will not."

The wind howled between the battlements, carrying with it the promise of confrontation, its icy breath slicing through the stillness. Karak stood tall, her chin lifted in defiance, though every muscle in her body was taut with tension, her fingers twitching near the hilt of her sword, once more seeking reassurance in its weight. The air crackled with unspoken threats, a silent stalemate that held the world in suspension.

The moments dragged on, stretching endlessly, the weight of the standoff pressing heavily upon them like an unseen hand. The murmur of the gorge below, once a faint and distant sound, grew louder in the oppressive silence, the river's relentless flow a cruel reminder of the abyss waiting to claim anyone who faltered. The sun, high and commanding just hours earlier, began its slow descent, its light growing feeble. Shadows lengthened and twisted across the bridge, creeping like spectres over the ancient stones and cloaking the ruins of the eastern fortress in a shroud of sombre twilight.

The golden light faded, replaced by the first hints of a cold, blue dusk. Karak's soldiers held their line, their breaths forming faint clouds in the cooling air. The faint clink of armour and the occasional shuffle of boots were the only sounds from her company, their discipline unwavering despite the mounting pressure.

Karak's focus flickered between the opposing force and her own men. Every passing moment stretched her nerves tighter, every shift of an enemy's foot or flex of an archer's bowstring gnawed at her resolve. She could see it in their eyes, both sides were waiting for the other to move first, each calculating the cost of action and the price of hesitation.

Konan stood beside her, his axe resting heavily in his grip, his expression carved from stone, save for the faint tightening of his jaw. "They're probing our patience," he muttered, his voice a low growl edged with frustration. "Waiting to see if we crack before they make their move."

"They'll be disappointed," Karak replied, her voice steady though her throat felt dry. Her gaze remained fixed on the opposing shield wall, the flickering torchlight from their ranks casting distorted shadows across the stone. "We hold."

Konan grunted in approval but said nothing more. Behind them, the Nordon soldiers stood ready, their weapons gleaming in the dimming light, their faces set in grim determination. The bridge, once a silent monument to a bloody past, now felt alive with tension, as though the ghosts of the Divided Wars had risen to witness the next chapter of its story unfold.

The light continued to fade, and the wind picked up, howling through the gorge like a mourning wail. Karak's crimson cloak billowed behind her, snapping sharply in the gusts like a banner of defiance. Every muscle in her body ached from the strain of standing firm, yet she refused to yield a solitary pillar of resolve amidst the growing uncertainty. The weight of leadership pressed heavily upon her, as unrelenting as the crown upon her head.

Finally, a stir of movement rippled through the opposing ranks, breaking the fragile stillness of the standoff, the silence shattering. From behind the wall of armoured soldiers, a man on horseback emerged, his presence radiating authority. The opposing army parted like the low tide receding from the shore, revealing a path carved through the sea of shields and steel. The rhythmic clatter of hooves echoed across the bridge as the rider approached, his white-armoured horse trotting with a deliberate and regal grace.

The horse bore a full tabard emblazoned with the unmistakable emblem of West Kadun, three white towers, standing tall and proud as a symbol of resilience and dominion. Every detail gleamed in the dimming light, the polished plate armour of the horse and rider reflecting the dying sun's faint glow. The man's burgonet bore long white plumes that danced with the wind, and his matching cuirass was adorned with intricate engravings that caught the flicker of the torches lining the battlements behind him. A shield was strapped to his shoulder, the emblem of the white towers displayed boldly on its face, and at his side hung a longsword, its scabbard gilded with fine detailing.

Karak's sharp eyes tracked his every movement as he advanced, her vision narrowing on the calculated precision in his posture, this was no ordinary soldier. The effortless control he wielded over his mount was undeniable, every hoof-fall of the white-armoured horse measured and deliberate, as if orchestrating each step to command attention. His poise, unwavering, spoke of high rank and a purpose that extended far beyond the battlefield.

He advanced to within twenty feet of the Nordon column, and with a sharp tug on the reins, his horse reared abruptly, hooves cutting through the air before slamming down heavily onto the stone. The impact shattered the stillness, the resounding thud echoing like a drumbeat of authority, sending ripples through the tense silence. Sitting tall in the saddle, the man surveyed the Nordon warriors as though appraising each one individually, his visor hiding his face beneath. His posture was a study in composure and control, radiating an unspoken command that demanded attention.

For a moment, the bridge fell silent again, the tension coiled so tightly it seemed the air itself might shatter under its weight. Karak's heart thrummed in her chest, but she forced herself to stand taller. Her chin lifted high as she locked eyes with the distant gaze that pierced through the narrow slit of his helm, the armoured figure exuding an air of quiet menace and authority. Whoever this man was, he was no herald of peace, his very presence felt like the prelude to a storm.

Konan shifted beside her, his axe resting heavily in his bear-like hands, the muscles in his grip flexing as he studied the rider with a glint of suspicion. "Well," he muttered, his voice a low rumble meant only for Karak. "It seems the West has sent their champion."

Karak did not respond immediately. Her hand brushed the hilt of her sword as she watched the rider, her mind racing. Whoever this man was, he had made his intent clear, the West Kadun force had not come to parley, they had come to send a message.

The horse moved left to right, its hooves striking the stone with deliberate precision as it snorted and tossed its head. The rider's gaze swept over Karak's forces, his every movement measured, his demeanour calm but calculating. The weight of his scrutiny was palpable as he took in every detail, the Nordon soldiers' stances, their formation, the armour they wore, and the Queen who stood before them.

"You are Queen Karak Thørn?" he finally said, his voice clear and authoritative, carrying effortlessly over the wind and the echoing expanse of the bridge.

Karak held her ground, her emerald eyes locking onto his. She nodded once, her expression unwavering.

"You speak Kadun?" he asked, tilting his head slightly, his tone less a question and more an expectation.

Again, the Queen nodded, her chin lifted slightly. She said nothing, allowing her silence to convey the dignity of her station.

"Good," the man continued, his voice steady and formal, each word deliberate. "I am Prince Tylun Whitehart of White Towers. By my father's decree, King Ruben Whitehart of White Towers, I extend his welcome to you."

He paused, his sharp gaze sweeping over the foreign force one final time, his expression hidden. "Welcome to The Reach, Queen Karak Thørn," he said, the words carrying an edge of restrained authority, as though the welcome was a formality weighed down by unspoken judgment.

Before Karak could respond, he pulled the reins of his horse with practiced ease. The animal turned sharply, its hooves scraping against the stone as it pivoted.

Without further acknowledgment, Prince Tylun began to ride back toward the fortress. His white plumes trailed behind him like a streak of pale fire, the emblem of the three towers on his shield catching the last rays of the sun. The sound of his horse's hooves echoed across the bridge, growing fainter with each step.

As he departed, the archers melted away from the ramparts, vanishing into the shadows as swiftly and silently as they had appeared. The force on the bridge began to retreat in unison, their shields still raised as they backed away toward the western gate. Within moments, the bridge was clear once more, the presence of West Kadun's army reduced to a lingering tension that hung in the air like the final notes of a song.

Karak's soldiers held their ground, their weapons still at the ready, their breaths measured but heavy. Konan muttered something under his breath, his knuckles white on the haft of his axe.

Karak exhaled slowly, her grip on her sword loosening, though her posture remained rigid. The Reach had told another story, one without bloodshed this time, but the message was unmistakable. This was no mere welcome; it was a calculated display, a declaration that the West would meet any challenge with unwavering force and precision.

These were not the pliable Eastern neighbours she had so easily manipulated with whispers and schemes. Here, they were in the lion's den, where every step must be measured with patience and calculation. There could be no reckless show of strength between soldiers, no suggestive or overly aggressive manoeuvres at the negotiating table. Their hosts would offer no ground, no leniency, and certainly no mercy. The walls of the western fortress seemed to echo that reality, a silent reminder of who held the advantage.

"We move," she commanded, her voice slicing through the tension with sharp finality. Her soldiers obeyed immediately, their formation tightening as the company began its march forward once more. With a nod to Konan, Karak took the lead, her steps steady and purposeful. The sound of boots on stone reverberated through the silence, a stark contrast to the earlier clamour of the standoff.

The shadow of the western fortress grew larger with every step, its towers rising like sentinels against the dimming sky. It loomed, vast and unyielding, a reflection of the kingdom she now faced. Yet, with every stride, Karak's resolve burned brighter. She would not falter. She could not.

Her plans, her ambition, like the bridge beneath her feet would carry her forward, no matter the danger.

# THE SHAMAN
# CHAPTER FIFTY SIX

The young mother's anguished wails pierced the stifling air of the cramped birthing tent, her cries muffled only by her gritted teeth. Sweat drenched her brow, and thick black hair, matted and slick, clung to her face like rags soaked in a storm. Her trembling hands clenched the midwives with bone-crushing intensity, a desperate anchor as she strained and pushed with all her failing strength. Between her legs, an elderly witch doctor knelt, her gnarled hands working tirelessly to massage the mother's inner thighs, murmuring chants to coax the stubborn newborn into the world. But still, the child would not come.

Necruss Khan stood just four paces away, his aged form shrouded in shadow, his expression a mask of disinterest. Arms crossed, he watched the scene with cold detachment, his presence as still and timeless as the desert itself. The screams, the desperate pleas, and the fervent invocations of witch doctors and healers were nothing new to him. He had witnessed it all countless times across countless generations. To him, it was a tired ritual, predictable in its futility. Sometimes the process was accompanied by elaborate rites, chants, dances, and ceremonies meant to ease the labour. Other times, there was nothing but the raw, primal agony of childbirth.

He had seen animals slaughtered in the name of producing a son, their blood spilled as an offering to the sun God Solar. He had watched hearts of beasts consumed by expectant fathers; rituals intended to imbue strength to unborn children. Yet the results were always the same, the sex, the health, the survival of the child remained as uncertain as ever.

He recalled a moon-long ceremony performed for a chieftain's wife, the tribe's finest shaman presiding over every detail. The result? A stillborn child. He remembered a warrior woman from the Shadelands, fierce and powerful, succumbing to death mere hours after delivering her child. Even on the rare occasion when both mother and babe survived, Necruss felt no triumph. What he sought was never there, never the one, never the child of prophecy.

It foretold that the descendant of Mitsurugi Khan would come, born with white skin and blood-red eyes, destined to unite the Drylands and its fractured tribes. Yet, every infant born under his watch had failed to fulfil the omen. The mother's shriek shattered his thoughts, a raw, visceral sound that reverberated through the oppressive confines of the tent.

Near the entrance, a large man, the father no doubt, peered in through the narrow slit of the tent flap. His broad shoulders blocked what little light filtered in, his face etched with worry. The witch doctor turned on him with a hiss, her voice sharp and commanding. "Away! You only worsen the anguish!" The flap fell shut, leaving the tent steeped in dim firelight and the suffocating weight of expectation.

Necruss Khan felt the dryness clawing at his throat, a parched ache that mirrored the desolation of the midday sun overhead. Its searing heat bore down on the cracked, unforgiving earth of the Drylands, turning the tent into an oven of stifling air and suffocating expectation. His scrawny, veined hand reached for his worn leather water satchel, the weathered lid creaking as he unfastened it. Tilting it to his lips, he drank deeply, the tepid water doing little more than dulling the rawness of his throat. Even the ageless, he mused with faint bitterness, could grow parched.

The ageless. The sightseer. The whispers of those who both revered and feared him echoed faintly in his mind. Necruss Khan, the eternal. The one who bore the curse or the blessing of unyielding life, of visions that pierced the veil of time itself. His eyes, sharp and unrelenting, could peer into the fragments of the past or the shifting shadows of futures yet to be. And yet, despite all his gifts, he found himself here again.

A nomad's tent, thick with the acrid scent of sweat, blood, and burning incense. Another labouring woman, a distant descendant of the great Mitsurugi Khan. Another round of screams and blood and waiting. Always waiting. His bony fingers tightened briefly around the satchel before letting it fall back to his side. The years had rendered him indifferent to the spectacle of birth, yet not to its purpose. He waited now, as he had countless times before, for the first glimpse, a crown of hair, a wriggling limb. But most of all, he waited for the sign he craved above all else, the pale skin of an albino child.

The sun crawled across the sky, dragging the day into its descent. Necruss Khan waited still, his patience worn thin by the hours of strained cries and muted hopes. Finally, as the golden light of early evening spilled into the tent and a cooler breeze crept in, a newborn's wail pierced the stagnant air. The mother's anguished struggle was over, replaced by tears of joy and exhaustion streaming down her face. The sound, so familiar yet laced with fresh potential, jolted Necruss into motion. He strained to see past the midwife and the hunched witch doctor, his eyes hungry for the sight he had craved for centuries.

Yet his hope crumbled like sand through fingers. The commotion cleared, and it was undeniable the prophecy had failed him once more. No albino. Instead, a baby girl emerged, her skin tinged with a pale reddish hue, her dark, slanted eyes reflecting the northern lineage of this Drylands clan.

The goat skinned Necruss Khan let out a low growl of disdain, hacking up a wad of bile and phlegm, he spat in the general direction of the mother and child, the glob landing just short of its intended targets. He muttered a curse under his breath, dismissing the mother's suffering. Though the mother paid him no heed. She cradled her child tightly, oblivious to the seer's derision. Her love for the infant was as immediate and fierce as the heat of the sun itself, untainted by the weight of prophecies or unfulfilled destinies.

Necruss turned sharply, his furs swirling around his gaunt frame. He needed no further confirmation. Another failure. Another waste of his time. His crooked walking stick struck the ground with force as he moved to leave, only to find his path blocked by the hulking form of the father, now framed in the tent's entrance. The man's eager eyes sought his daughter, his pride radiating like the sun's final rays. Necruss tried to shove him aside with the base of his staff, but the father paid him no mind, stepping aside of his own accord. The seer was nothing to him. His only thought was for the child and her mother, and he brushed past without a word, eager to meet his newborn daughter.

As Necruss stepped out, the sharp evening sunlight stung his eyes, momentarily blinding him. He squinted, palming the tent flap aside as his vision adjusted. Around him, the nomadic clan moved with purpose. Fires crackled to life in small circles, casting shadows that danced across the dry, cracked earth. Herds of cattle were corralled into makeshift pens for the night, their lowing blending with the murmur of voices and the clang of cookware. Women stooped over cauldrons, preparing evening meals, their laughter and chatter a grating reminder of the simple, unaffected lives they led.

The vitality of it all, the bustle, the laughter, the persistence of life only deepened the bitterness curdling in Necruss's chest. He could not stand to be in their midst a moment longer. Pivoting sharply, he set off, his walking stick stamping the hard ground with every step. Tent after tent blurred past him, his mind already elsewhere, plotting his next search. Always another tent. Another birth. Another failure. His shadow stretched long and thin behind him as the sun dipped lower, leaving the tent of hope and disappointment far behind.

He reached the edge of the camp without so much as a glance back. He had endured five long nights among the nomads, a tiresome and fruitless stay. During his time there, he had read the palms of every clansman, not once but twice, and found nothing of value in any of them. Their fates were as barren as the land they called home. Age, disease, and the relentless weight of family responsibilities drained most of their vitality. One young hunter's fate offered a brief spark of interest, he would die from a beast's horn, a fate Necruss had delivered to the youth with thinly veiled satisfaction. Another woman had wept as he foretold her barrenness, a prophecy that shattered her hopes of motherhood.

It was not cruelty that fuelled his words, nor was it any sense of sadistic pleasure. It was boredom. The centuries stretched before him like an endless plain, and delivering grim tidings was merely a distraction from the monotony. Necruss had spent lifetimes seeking the prophesied albino descendant and reading the trivial fates of ordinary tribesmen had become a dull routine.

The elders of the tribes spoke of time accelerating with age, how the moons seemed to pass quicker with each turning year. Yet for Necruss, time had long since lost meaning. He had witnessed the birth and death of so many that their lives blurred into a foggy, indistinct haze in his mind. They were fleeting impressions, like shadows cast on the sand before the wind erased them.

He allowed his thoughts to drift as he walked, the camp shrinking behind him until it became little more than a dark smudge against the horizon, eventually vanishing entirely. The last light of evening bled away, leaving behind the cool embrace of night. The God Lunar climbed high, its pale light silvering the cracked earth, and the stars pricked the vast darkness like grains of salt scattered across an endless void.

Hours passed, and Necruss continued his journey, his mind dull and unfocused. His pace was steady but lethargic, his movements as silent as the grave save for the rhythmic tap of his walking aid striking the dry ground. Occasionally, the distant cries of feral creatures echoed across the plains, a faint reminder of life stirring in the shadows. But they barely registered in Necruss's consciousness.

The vast emptiness of the Drylands stretched before him, a mirror to the void within. His steps carried him forward, but toward what, even he no longer knew. Only the moon and the stars bore witness to his solitary march, their cold light illuminating a man trapped between the echoes of eternity and the ceaseless pull of an unfulfilled destiny.

Dawn crept closer, painting the horizon with faint strokes of light. Necruss Khan finally stopped, his weary legs forcing him to pause. The sky above him had softened from black to a deep blue, while behind him, the haze of the rising sun spilled golden threads across the vast expanse. Ahead, the jagged silhouette of the Gigas Mountain range began to take shape, dark and foreboding. He knew the path he had been following would soon funnel into the throat of the mountain, a narrow passage that led to one place, Cordon.

Once a proud fortress, Cordon stood as a sentinel against the southern clans, barring them from invading the so-called civilized world. Its towering walls and battlements still loomed over the land, manned by soldiers clad in armour. But a fortress it was no longer. Over the years, it had decayed into a haven for smugglers, a breeding ground for gangs, and the heart of the southern slave trade. The men stationed there, soldiers in name only, made more coin selling southern prisoners than their meagre wages ever afforded.

Behind the fortress, an ever-expanding shantytown sprawled, a chaos of patched tents, wooden hovels, and filth. The gangs ruled there, their influence unchecked, their power growing like a cancer. The soldiers, too comfortable in their corruption, turned blind eyes to the debauchery in exchange for coin, women, or the promise of fleeting pleasures. What had once been a bastion of order and defence was now a festering wound on the borderlands.

Necruss frowned, his grip tightening on his staff. The thought was not new, but it still gnawed at him, it would take little more than several united tribes, a few thousand warriors wielding strong arms and sharp blades to bring Cordon to its knees. From there, the floodgates to the north would open, unleashing the chaos of the south into the so-called civilized lands. And yet, even this grim vision seemed impossibly far away. The southern tribes were as fractured as the parched earth beneath his feet, bound by blood feuds and territorial grudges that ran deeper than their shared disdain for the people beyond Cordon.

Only the prophecy could ever change that. Only the albino child, born with blood-red eyes, could unite the clans under one banner, forge them into a force capable of shattering the northern walls and forging a new destiny. But even that dream was beginning to fade. What had once been a promise whispered in the halls of the ancients now lingered on the lips of old women as little more than a wistful tale. A story to lull restless children to sleep.

Even if the child were born, Necruss thought grimly, it would take years of bloodshed to unite the clans. Decades of pain and sacrifice. And that was assuming the prophecy could overcome the hatred and distrust woven into the fabric of their culture.

He turned his gaze to the mountains again, their imposing shadows like silent guardians looking down on the Earth. Staring into the receding darkness, he searched the horizon for the Fortress of Cordon. But there was nothing, just the endless dry flats stretching into the void.

Time slipped by, as it always did, unnoticed and indifferent. The first light of dawn began to paint the barren landscape in muted hues, chasing away the shadows and revealing the desolation beneath. As the gloom lifted, something stirred in the distance, catching Necruss's eye, a solitary figure, faint and wavering like a mirage on the horizon.

He narrowed his focus, transfixed as the shape hobbled closer. It moved slowly, unevenly, as if every step required immense effort. The silhouette resolved itself with each agonizing stride until, no more than twenty paces away, the figure emerged from the early morning haze.

A girl, almost a young woman, staggered toward him. She was draped in tattered rags that barely clung to her frail, bruised frame. Her gaunt hands cradled a swollen belly, and her eyes, hollow and sunken, seemed to pierce through Necruss with a haunted intensity. For a fleeting moment, the seer felt something stir within him, a rare pang of empathy, as he took in the pitiful sight. Her face was mottled with fresh bruises from a beating, her lips cracked and dry. Streaks of dried blood marred her soiled clothing, and her bare feet, blistered and raw, left a faint trail of crimson droplets on the cracked earth behind her, like breadcrumbs leading to her suffering.

For a fleeting moment, her hollow eyes flickered with something, a spark of recognition as if they had caught sight of something just beyond the veil of the visible world. Her gaze traced an invisible path, following a movement no one else could perceive, until it came to an abrupt halt before her. Slowly, her gaunt arm lifted, trembling with effort, her skeletal fingers stretching outward, reaching for something unseen, intangible.

The moment passed, her eyes glazed over and her trembling legs struggled to hold her upright. Her knees buckled, and she swayed unsteadily before collapsing to the ground with a sickening thud. Dust rose in a lazy plume around her, but she made no sound, no cry of pain.

She simply lay there, still and silent.

Necruss sighed, an old weariness tightening his chest. Every instinct urged him to continue on, to leave her where she had fallen and spare himself the pointless inconvenience. But curiosity, as always, tethered him to the moment. With deliberate steps, his walking stick tapping against the dry ground, he approached the motionless girl.

Her eyes fluttered open as he loomed over her, their dullness now replaced by a flicker of desperate life. Blood oozed freely from a deep wound at her temple, pooling into the dust beneath her. The crimson stain spread slowly, greedily absorbed by the thirsty earth. Her gaze locked onto his, filled with an unspoken plea, a silent understanding of her fate. She knew, as did he, that her time was short.

Necruss followed her gaze as it shifted downward. Her dirt-streaked hand rested on her swollen belly, the gesture painfully deliberate. She was with child. A wave of recognition passed over him, his eyes narrowing as the pieces fell into place.

Before he could react, her head lolled back, her eyes rolling lifelessly into their sockets. She exhaled a final, shallow breath, and the fragile spark within her was extinguished. Necruss crouched beside her still form, his bony fingers brushing the dirt from her face. He lingered there for a moment, staring at the lifeless body and the swollen womb that remained her only legacy.

The dry wind tugged at his goatskin cloak, its touch a reminder of the weight pressing down on his crooked shoulders, the unrelenting burden of eternity. Another failure, perhaps, or another thread in the tapestry of fate. Necruss straightened, his expression as impassive as stone, though his thoughts churned beneath the surface. A question flickering at the edge of his mind, had fate brought him to this moment?

His skeletal fingers closed around her cold hand, the touch devoid of warmth or life. The ritual was one he had performed countless times, but never on the dead. The act carried a strange gravity, a pull that stirred something long dormant within him.

Closing his eyes, Necruss whispered an incantation, the words flowing like water from a deep, ancient well inside him. The air around him thickened, heavy with an otherworldly energy. His mind plunged into the spirit world, a realm of shimmering light and shadow where souls lingered before crossing to the eternal plains. He saw her essence, a faint glow of holy energy rising slowly from her body, fragile and unsteady. It drifted upward, untethered, seeking the afterlife's embrace.

But Necruss raced toward it, his own spirit reaching out, halting its ascent. The light pulsed faintly, resisting his intrusion, but he pushed through, forcing his energy to intertwine with hers. The connection was brief but powerful, a collision of lives and memories that surged through him like a flood.

Her past unfolded in flashes, each moment bleeding into the next. He saw her life as a servant in Lord of Borlong's estate, her hands raw from scrubbing stone floors, her face twisted in quiet anguish as the Lord used her for his pleasure. She had carried his bastard, a burden she bore with no hope of reprieve. Necruss brushed past these scenes, uncaring. He pressed further, delving deeper into the river of her ancestry.

Her mother, a woman of Kadun descent, appeared in his mind's eye, a fleeting image of her final moments, succumbing to the agony of childbirth. Her death and heritage held no significance to him, a detail as irrelevant as a grain of sand in the vast desert. Then her father emerged, a man of the Drylands, his rugged frame trembling with terror as the bloodthirsty crowd roared their approval, cheering his death in the brutal chaos of the arena.

Necruss pressed on, uninterested in their tragedies, his focus fixed on the deeper currents of ancestry. He pushed past these recent lives, tracing the girl's lineage further back. Generations flickered before him like shadows cast against a roaring fire, faces collapsing into one another, their stories fleeting and indistinct. The images quickened, a cascade of births and deaths spiralling into the past, until suddenly, the torrent slowed. The vision sharpened, crystallizing into a single, vivid figure.

Mitsurugi Khan.

The great conqueror stood before him, a figure of unyielding power and undeniable presence. The sight sent a tremor through Necruss, not of fear, but of recognition. The girl was a descendant.

The realisation seared itself into his mind as he released her spirit. The faint glow drifted upward once more, free to ascend into the abyss. Necruss's connection severed, and with a jolt, he snapped back to the present. His breath came shallow and ragged, his hand trembling as it let go of hers.

For the first time in decades, something close to excitement stirred within him. The Drylands' future teetered on the edge of possibility.

Callously, Necruss pushed the girl's lifeless hand from her belly, the weight of it hitting the dusty ground with a hollow thud. He replaced it with his own, pressing his palm against the swollen bump. The skin beneath his touch was still faintly warm, but no movement stirred within. He felt nothing, not remorse, not pity only the cold resolve of purpose.

Ruthlessly he reached beneath his robes and drew a curved blade from an unseen sheath. Its cruel edge gleamed faintly in the dim morning light. Necruss pressed the blade into the soft flesh just above the girl's hip, the sharp steel parting her skin with an ease that belied the brutality of the act. Blood, thick and dark, welled from the gash and spilled onto the dry earth in viscous rivulets.

Without hesitation, Necruss plunged his hand into the wound, his fingers delving into the slick warmth. The grotesque squelch of flesh and fluid filled the air as he searched blindly, his fingers finally closing around the fragile form of the unborn child. He pulled with a sharp, deliberate motion, dragging the infant free from its mother's lifeless womb.

For a moment, the flats were deathly silent, the world holding its breath. Then, a piercing wail split the air, raw and primal. Necruss's breath caught as he stared down at the blood-soaked infant in his trembling hands. Two eyes, impossibly red, stared back at him from the pale face of an albino boy. The prophecy. The child of legend.

# ACKNOWLEDGEMENT

To You, the Reader—

Thank you for walking the bloodied halls and fractured nations of Rise of Tyrants. In a world of prophecy, shifting loyalties, and rising monarchs, your presence in these pages has meant more than you know.

Stories like this are forged in solitude—but they come alive only when shared. If the tale stirred something in you—rage, wonder, hope, or dread—I would be honoured if you left a review, or passed the book on to another soul brave enough to face the Whispers of War.

And this is only the beginning.

To speak with me directly, hear whispers of what comes next, or follow the journey behind the words:

Email: callummbrooks@outlook.com
Instagram: @callummbrooks
TikTok: @brooka_44

Until next we meet in Tides of an Avalanche,
Callum M Brooks

Printed in Dunstable, United Kingdom

64971204R00323